UNDENIABLE VENGEANCE

RULES OF VENGEANCE, BOOK II

GIACOMO GIAMMATTEO

INFERNO PUBLISHING COMPANY

FORLANDIA SOUTH

$\mathcal{M}$ap of the southern world

INTRODUCTION

When Sethia doth rise again the world will drown in gore

And once the Dreaded One is loose, the world will be no more

Both man and beast will take up arms and fight both friend and foe

For in these days of blood and death, how is a man to know.

Blood shall reign and blood shall flow till rivers all turn red

And mothers' breasts shall wither up as babies go unfed.

But more than babes will wipe their face with tears from more than eyes

As all of man swears fealty, yet no one hears their cries.

— SETHIAN PROPHECY

Saying found on a stone tablet near the Sethian Desert in the Empty Lands

EYES OF THE ANCIENTS

In the void, where time is irrelevant, where centuries pass like days, it serves no purpose to record the passing of time. But this is a time not far removed from the present, as close as can be judged.

She watched from her prison through eyes that were not eyes, held captive by walls that were not walls. No walls could hold her, yet she could not escape. It would not be for long though, only a fleeting moment. She knew that the one who would free her was coming; she had witnessed his birth.

The memory carved a smile, and the vaporous form shivered with unbridled excitement. Seldom did a new life beget a smile; she drew her strength from death. But this birth was different—a shadow of the world's new order, a harbinger of death to come. And with each death, new life would spring within her soul. New energy to fill the void of aeons. New power to destroy the gods of old.

Time grew close, but she could be patient. After waiting so many centuries, the lifetime of a mortal would be like tomorrow, like the blink of an ancient eye.

She fought to restrain the racing of her heart, for already the omens had begun: bitter cold lay waste to the sacred lands, and searing heat burned bright in the flames of the Sethian desert. Soon the battles would start. Soon the blood would flow. For soon, she knew, the Awakening would come.

The thought stirred old memories—images from before the birth of this world and beyond—back to times before the Creation, before the heavens blistered with the fires of new life.

Her memory was long and, once free, she would remember those who had worshiped her—and those who had not. The pain of eternity dwelled in her bosom and coursed her veins, and the wailing of countless dying warriors sang in her ears and wept in her soul. But they too, would soon be awakened. Through her, their power would be restored. Through her, they would live to die again.

THREE PAIRS of eyes watched from a grave that was not a grave, through eyes that were not eyes. They desperately sought the one who could win their freedom. For so long all the world had beckoned them with festive tunes and rousing dances. Now the onset of the great suffering was near, and their people cried out from shallow memories beckoning gods they no longer knew.

They listened in earnest to the prayers of salvation, but any action would have to await his arrival. All hope rested with him. But if he turned, if he faltered, if he failed to see the truth—then she would be set free. And if that fate befell the world even the stars would shiver, for they were old enough to remember. They had seen moons collide and worlds shaken apart, and they had seen the last spark of light extinguished from the brightest among them. They knew that their existence was no more than a thought to her. If she were Awakened, nothing would be safe again.

"The time is right. We are in agreement on the champion. We must send the message."

"So be it."

"The message is sent."

THE BREACH in the shield struck with the suddenness of a *forcebolt*. As the thought oozed through the mystic barriers that formed her prison wall, her heart grew anxious.

There is only one reason for a communique. They have chosen!

She prayed they had not decided on him, then prepared to receive the message, reluctant, almost afraid to hear the announcement.

Finally, a champion worthy of the task! But have I waited too long?

A terrible shudder precipitated her collapse. She struggled to compose herself. Madness! She felt it more frequently of late, and each time it proved more difficult to seize control. The bouts came suddenly, like the storms that churned the roiling seas on Gorshan, and the attacks, if less enduring, were no less violent.

Who wouldn't be mad—millennia spent alone, imprisoned, and faced with the prospect of suffering through all eternity. Countless centuries waiting for a puny mortal whose life was but a flicker in the darkness. She had seen the lives of many millions come and go, insignificant lives for the most part. But now—now was different. For the first time, there was more than one possibility, and an eternity of isolation and imprisonment awaited the wrong decision.

Until now she had held the message in abeyance, but she could wait no longer. "We have chosen," they said.

She heard their selection. It had seemed an eternity awaiting the name —and now it was done.

A smile preceded the cackle, which itself heralded the cascade of laughter. *How could they not have seen? How did they not know?*

Almost, she could taste the spice of freedom, the sweetness of battle, and the euphoria of destruction. After thousands of years, it would be all the more precious.

She could hear the voices of her people rising once again in adoration, and she could see them lying prostrate at her feet. A giddiness swept over her, though she brought it to heel quickly. Protocol demanded that she form a response and, though she could wait until the next turn of the sun, she knew a swift reply would confuse and worry them.

They will have eternity to ponder their decision. All eternity to wonder where they went astray.

She formulated the thought and dispatched it. "I, too, have chosen." She let a touch of laughter linger at the end of the message and then revealed her champion.

"The Awakening will soon be here."

IMMORTALS DO DIE

Sethia

Iazzo's body lay twisted among the rocks in the Sethian desert, gases from rotting flesh and baked blood forming a miasma. Balls of maggots squirmed in empty eye sockets, and the flesh on Iazzo's face bubbled where they tunneled toward his nose. Two red-beaks feasted at his stomach, flapping large black wings as they squabbled over entrails and other choice morsels.

Pack Leader Drogg led the Wolfen through the blistering sands at Sethia's outer border. His pointed ears stood tall, high above the coarse-gray fur bristling in the wretched heat. A three-fingered hand, long since evolved from a paw, brushed sand from the sheath that housed his long knife.

Drogg cursed Sethia, and its heat, and its sand. How he longed for the cold mountain air and the snows that his ancestors had romped in when packs swelled with pride, and the Pack Lord led the Winter Hunt.

He stopped, head raised, and bared ivory-white teeth as he caught hold of a particular smell. His sleek snout twitched to identify the scent. "This way," he said, and headed west. His hand stayed loose, ready to reach for the leather-wrapped hilt of his long knife, or the curved sword draped across his shoulder. A silver wolf's head adorned that blade. He stopped again, sniffing. "Keep searching, Pack. Something is dead, and it's not far."

The Wolfen spread out, padded feet leaving few marks on the desert floor. "Pack Leader, I saw two vultures land behind the rocks ahead."

Drogg snarled, and a guttural growl emerged. Red-beaks! "Don't let them feast, no matter what is dead."

Meetcha nodded and rushed to investigate. "Over here," he called, a moment later.

Large boulders guarded a narrow pass leading up the mountain. As Drogg made his way through the pass, four vultures flew away.

vulture

Red-beaks have no honor.

Drogg's ears pricked to attention as he stooped to examine the body, scouring the remains with his amber eyes. "It's Iazzo. We must tell the Master at once." He stood, scanning his pack. "Meetcha, you and Karff bring what is left of him."

For two days they carried Iazzo through the barren sands, reaching the city as the sun began to rest. "Open the gates," Drogg called to the guards. "I carry Iazzo with me."

The pack leader marched to a remote spot in the courtyard before stopping. "Set him down, Meetcha, and guard him well. I will tell the Master."

Drogg's fur bristled as he stared at the palace—the Throne of the Sun. It stood several stories tall and was faced with black granite on the right side and white granite on the left side. Arches and domes dominated the architecture, and broad sweeping steps rose to an entry that looked as if it might take Drogg to another world. His stomach tightened, and his throat constricted. "Stand tall, Pack. The Master is watching."

Drogg breached the entrance and shivered at the greeting from cold, damp air. *How was the air inside so cold?*

His eyes wandered, anything to take his mind from the mission he must complete. Plush Farizi carpets sat atop marble floors, and tables carved from emerald and blackthorn held Pomandan crystal and Khataran pottery. For all of the beauty and elegance, sofas and chairs sat empty; Drogg didn't even see guards.

He focused as he trod along the corridor to Lukaan's chambers, soft padded feet making less sound than his racing heart. When he turned the final corner, the doors swung open, and the coldness of the chamber leaped out and swatted him. A shiver raced from shoulders to feet, when only moments ago his fur had burned. He wondered again how the air was kept cold when it was so hot outside.

corridor leading to Lukaan's chamber

Drogg stopped, arms pressed against his sides.

"Enter."

The command—heard only by Drogg—reverberated in his head, rumbled as if it were thunder.

Inside the chamber, mist swirled and writhed. It climbed the walls and crept through the air. Drogg walked along a clear path, but fear slowed his steps. A dark beacon shone through white mist atop steps lined with floating globes of light. He saw a form ensconced on the throne. It was a dark, forbidding form, surrounded by a darkness that drank the light.

Drogg turned quickly, afraid he might be drawn in himself.

"Where is the body?"

Drogg trembled. He fell to his knees, head pressed against the marble floor. *How did he know?* Fear, not courage, found words for Drogg to speak. "In the courtyard, Great Lord. We—"

"Where did you find it?"

"Hidden in a small enclave of rocks along the path to Mount Riesle"

"You may leave, Pack Leader Drogg. You have done well."

The Wolfen rose, bowing as he exited the chamber. He wasted no time in rejoining his pack. Despite a successful outcome, he had no desire to linger or to ever visit again.

Lukaan sent a message to the Banished Ones. *Examine Iazzo's body, then report to me.*

Lukaan sat on his throne, immersed in thought. He remembered a time when he had ruled, when he was worshiped—

Melissara arrived first, interrupting his contemplations. She fiddled with her hair—wrapping long blonde tresses into a bun tied at the back of her head—while waiting for the others. Within heartbeats, Tirzinitzia and Sendra appeared, then Zorn. Last was Ghruehne, who came with fire in his eyes, shaking a fist still red with flames and his body full with power.

"I want Mikkellana for myself. Did you see what she did to Iazzo?"

"Control yourself, Ghruehne. Else I will give you a scar to match the one Antar put on your cheek, the one that ruined your pretty face."

Ghruehne's face turned as red as his hair, but he quickly doused the flames and rid himself of power. To incur Lukaan's wrath would be suicide—worse. He had seen him level cities. Shake worlds. "Forgive me, Great Lord, I—"

"Enough. Let Melissara speak."

"Mikkellana didn't kill him. She would never have left his body for us to find. My sister—"

"You du Savarras sicken me," Ghruehne said. "Even after what she did to you, you protect her."

"I protect no one, least of all Mikkellana, but I know my sister. She would hide Iazzo's body, leave us to wonder if he was dead, or if he had betrayed us." Melissara stroked her sapphire necklace, one she had chosen to complement her eyes. "And it wasn't Xanthes or Mesan. Mikkellana would never let them off the leash. It had to be Aentarra."

Ghruehne scoffed. "Aentarra is not strong enough. She—"

Melissara stepped forward. "Did you see any marks on him? Any Lightning? Fire? Was he sliced in two by a shield?" Melissara shook her head as she turned her back on Ghruehne. "No, there are no marks because Iazzo fought on the Planes of Mind, and my little sister is wily enough to have beaten him there."

"Even Aentarra would not dare that. She would—"

Lukaan leaned forward. *"Never deign to think you know what Aentarra might do. She is more like Antar than anyone cares to admit."*

"The madness that claimed Antar's mind has found a new home with Aentarra. The same madness that drove him to launch the assault." Lukaan adjusted his position on the throne.

"And do not forget the boy. He is strong."

"He's just a boy," Ghruehne said. "I'm not worried about him."

"That's your problem, Ghruehne—you don't worry when you should, and you worry when you shouldn't." Lukaan returned to his position of recline. *"You may all leave. I must think."*

~

Tirzinitzia sat in a hard-backed chair while Melissara paced the tiled floor in her desert home. It was sparsely decorated—much like the environs—and what furniture there was had been carved from desert sycamores and hackberries.

"There is something Lukaan knows that we don't. Why would be even mention the boy?" Melissara tapped on her necklace as if it would stir thoughts. "What does he know, Tirzinitzia?"

A long silence ensued—Melissara pacing and fidgeting, while Tirzinitzia sipped te.

Lines of worry creased Melissara's brow. "He knows it was Aentarra, yet he mentions the boy. 'And do not forget the boy', he said."

"He also said, 'He is strong'," Tirzinitzia added. "He said the boy was strong."

"Yes, he did. But—" Melissara's pacing came to an abrupt halt. She stopped fidgeting, and her glare fell on Tirzinitzia. "Do *you* know something that you're not telling me?"

Tirzinitzia could withstand almost anything. Melissara had been there when Lukaan burned the red suns into her cheeks, like two rubies set in a ring of flesh. She had withstood that torture without so much as a whimper, so Melissara knew she would never pry information out of her if she didn't want to give it. "You must trust me. We must trust each other."

More silence. Melissara turned, pacing again.

Tirzinitzia wrapped slender fingers around her cup of te. She took a long, slow sip, then set it down. "One of the boys has Coldfire."

Melissara spun around like a wolf to the bleat of a lamb. "What! Why didn't you tell me?" She raced over and shook Tirzinitzia. "How do you know?"

"There are things I can detect. Things that others can't."

Melissara chewed on a fingernail, a habit she had abandoned long ago. "My father and Lukaan were the only ones ever strong enough to wield Coldfire. That means..."

"Yes," Tirzinitzia said. "Which one?"

Melissara nodded. "Which one indeed?"

REVELATIONS

Sunnara, Entiria

Rahg's gaze swept the battlefield as he registered the horrors of a maddening day. Pockets of smoke—like fallen clouds—hovered above mounds of bodies, and the air reeked of boiled blood and charred flesh.

He dragged his foot, tripping over the body of a Victa. Green blood brushed his boot as it oozed from the lizard's limbs. A shiver raced through his body. It wasn't caused by the blood. His clothes and boots were caked in blood, but the Victa leader had almost killed him, the blade digging to the bone. His hand ran across the ridge of a slight scar where a short while ago he thought he might lose the arm, if not his life. Mikkellana had healed it well—that wound and a few others— but the memory of battle would not fade overnight.

Once again he scanned the carnage. Dead and half-dead were strewn about like corn after the crows had feasted, their bodies bearing the marks of sword and ax, shovel and pick. Other bodies, many others, bore scars from weapons and powers far too unnatural for this world.

Fire, Lightning, and Shields that formed spinning discs and sliced bodies into halves.

To his left lay an Entirian with half a torso, a Victa's ax had worked him well. All battles were fierce and bloody, but this somehow seemed worse, worse even than Twin Forks, where his father and most of his childhood friends had been killed.

Some of the wounded still crawled or reached out with battered limbs to beg for healing or a merciful end. Rhaven had ordered a quick death for any of the enemies that lived. "It does no good to be cruel," he said. Rahg didn't agree with him on that, but he had no wish to argue with anyone right now, let alone Rhaven.

He looked back to see Darstan hobbling along, the Victa blood smearing his olive skin. His shirt and pants were torn, both stained with his blood. Camissa supported him each step of the way. The festering wound on Darstan's leg had darkened. If he didn't care for it soon, the blackish-green death would set in.

"Hold onto me," Rahg said, and reached to help support him. "You should let Mikkellana heal you."

"My leg will heal by itself." He held up his arm to reveal the stump where his hand had been. "This won't."

"From what I heard she's not to blame. She only—"

Darstan's iron jaw locked in place, and a scowl formed on his face before Rahg finished. "She ordered Takar to cut it off. As far as I'm concerned, she's responsible."

Hatred burned in Darstan's dark eyes, and Rahg decided not to pursue it. *She must have had a reason.*

"Don't worry, Darstan, we'll figure out what to do when we get to Sunnara. We'll—"

Rahg's smile turned down, and his advance halted. He stared ahead, eyes agape. Aentarra stood on the path in front of him, long dark hair flowing in the breeze. *She just left a short while ago. What could bring her back so soon?*

AENTARRA STEPPED over the corpse of a Victa and walked a path that took her among the wounded and dead, walnut eyes scouring each of the bloody remains.

Rhaven and Mikkellana rushed to catch up. Danger must have pricked at her mind when Aentarra arrived. Ragged brown hair dragged across her shoulders, and her plain face exaggerated the few wrinkles that had begun to show. Mikkellana had been up all night, tending to the wounded, and she looked as if she hadn't slept in days.

"What is it, sister? What have you forgotten?"

Aentarra shuffled through bodies, blood staining her haggard clothes. She let silence hang in the air, then she stopped the search and let her penetrating gaze fall on each member of the party surrounding Mikkellana. She stared at Rhaven, then the others until her glare settled on Rahg.

"I asked if you had forgotten something." Mikkellana's tone brought Aentarra's attention to her.

"No, I thought that I had, but it is of no consequence. Besides, sister, it concerns matters you would not understand."

Rahg had felt the glare burn through him, and try as he might to suppress it, the memory refused to fade. His hands balled into fists, trying to control the fear.

She knows I have it. She must know.

Angst filled him as he recalled the image of Marro's body, returned to haunt him so soon. His skull had split like a melon and, amidst the blood and brains, lay something aglow—a crystal ablaze. Rahg could almost feel the warm sensation when he picked it up and the shiver that coursed his veins as he tucked it inside the fold of his cloak. He had never seen its like before, but he knew it to be dangerous and powerful.

He pulled his cloak tighter, afraid others might see the light. Rahg found the courage to lift his eyes, just as Aentarra moved toward Mikkellana.

Rhaven drew a sai and a sword, then stepped to block her path. A face chiseled from stone framed steel-blue eyes, and they fixed on Aentarra.

Aentarra cast a sidelong glance toward Rhaven, then back to her sister. "Have you taken to hiding behind a man's sword, Mikkellana?"

Mikkellana stood at Rhaven's side, her lip curled. A half dozen soldiers moved to support her.

"Does it surprise you that no one stands with you, Aentarra? You have never had trouble drawing *men* to your bed, but friends were never to be counted among them."

As Aentarra scanned the group who stood with Mikkellana, Darstan withdrew. "I'll not stand with her, Rahg."

Rahg nodded. Once Darstan set his mind, changing it would be like moving a mountain. His head was as hard as a blacksmith's anvil.

Aentarra's smile brushed across Darstan, then settled on Rahg, standing halfway between the sisters. "I saved your life on the ship, boy, and here, on this field of game."

Confusion overtook Rahg's thoughts. She *had* saved him twice now.

She must have noticed him swaying. "Do you think you are safer with her?" Thin lips gave way to a snicker. "She's a clever one, I'll grant you that. But do not turn your back, or close your eyes at night. Not while she's around."

Camissa stood beside Rahg, but she stared at Aentarra, focusing on her alone. Camissa's face turned as gray as old bones.

"You killed him!" Camissa grabbed Rahg's arm. "She killed Shera Kevon."

Aentarra spun toward Camissa with her teeth bared and the look of a mad dog in her eyes. "Lessons come hard to you, girl. I thought your experience on the ship would have tamed your curiosity." A raging fire burned no hotter than Aentarra's glare. "*Never* touch my thoughts again."

"Did you?" Rahg stared at Aentarra. "Did you kill him?"

Aentarra let silence bore into Rahg's mind. "Ask the sun if any died of thirst today or the sea if any fishermen drowned."

"You *did* kill him."

"And if I did? Have you not killed before?"

"Not anyone who didn't deserve it."

"And who is to be the judge of that? The insect that you swat off your neck is closer to you than that insignificant priest was to me. Do not place yourself too high, boy. The fall might prove dangerous."

Rhaven's sword–hand twitched, but Mikkellana swiftly restrained him.

Aentarra turned, lightning-fast. "You were gracious to stay his hand, sister. You must favor the warrior."

"Heed your advice. Do not place yourself too high."

"Him? I worry more about a tree falling on me than I do any mortal taking my life."

"Trees have been known to fall," Rhaven said.

Rahg moved closer. "Why did you kill the shera?"

Mikkellana shrugged. "That's the way Aentarra is. Sooner ask the wind why it blows or the sun why it shines. Life means no more to her than that."

"And you profess to be better, sister?" Aentarra looked again to Rahg. "Ask her about Romel. I told you about him, the one she left gasping for air, his last breath a plea for help. Not that I could blame her, there were important issues at stake—titles, lands, issues of first rights."

Aentarra's chest heaved. "I wanted to heal him, but that talent never favored me."

"Who is Romel?" Rahg asked.

"Ask Mikkellana. The secret is not mine to reveal, though it doesn't surprise me that she hasn't shared it with you."

"Enough of this, Aentarra. Begone. Leave before I wrap you in a shield and put you in Sethia. I should have done it long ago. You are not fit to be loose amongst the sane."

"I will go, sister. But tell them of Aentarra. Tell them I will remember where they stood today." Aentarra disappeared, and, when she had gone, Rahg wondered how close he had stood to Mikkellana, and what Aentarra would think of it.

Mikkellana avoided Darstan while she thanked the others for supporting her. "I offer gratitude for your support. It would not have been wise for me to test her strength just then; the Healing left me weakened." Mikkellana touched Rhaven's arm lightly. "Stay with him, warrior. He will need your help." She stared at his sword, then back to his face. "I crafted that sword to fit your hand, but I had no idea you would need it so soon."

"It is a great gift, My Lady, one with no equal."

A frown replaced the smile that had come to Mikkellana's face. "Only one other of its kind ever existed, but that was long ago, and it is now gone."

"Then the wrong man must have held it. A warrior who holds a sword such as this should never lose it."

The lines on her cheeks creased deeper, and her lips turned down.

"No, the one who held that sword was meant for battle. When the gods made him, they had a sword in mind. It was fortunate for all that they granted him no powers or the worlds would have never known peace. Every breath he took was for battle."

Rhaven bowed as he spoke. "I will do my best to keep a firm grip on your gift, My Lady. And I shall keep my head attached."

"That pleases me," Mikkellana said, then turned to address Rahg. "Be steady in your journey, Rahg, you have a long way to go."

"Tell me about Romel. Is what Aentarra said true?"

Mikkellana's face lost its warmth. "Believe what you will, but do not think to put me to the fire of questioning. I was through with that before the first of your blood breathed life." Rahg took a step back. "And remember, you are oath-sworn to me."

Rahg's stomach tightened. Mikkellana had mentioned this twice in as many days.

"Yes, oath-sworn. And I may call in that oath soon. Very soon." As she turned to leave Mikkellana's gaze fell on Darstan. "You, too, have a destiny, Darstan. Do not let bitterness destroy you."

Camissa tugged on his shirt, holding him back, but he shrugged her off and moved toward Mikkellana, lifting his arm as he advanced. "Put back my hand, Mikkellana. Replace my hand, and I'll dance you a jig. Until you can do that, don't chide me for bitterness. I see no limbs of yours missing."

"Believe what you will," she said.

"My Lady." Rahg's call seemed a plea.

"What is it?"

"It's just... well, I wanted to ask about Aentarra, about what she said."

Mikkellana stared at Rahg then called him aside. "Do you have what she sought?" She analyzed him. "Yes, you have it. I can see that now.

Well, it's too late to worry over, but keep a tight grip on it. Aentarra would peel your skin for that little sliver of crystal." She started to turn away, then stopped. "And by the way, it's called a Slicer."

Rahg let his hand slip toward the inside of his cloak. "What is it? What does it do?"

Mikkellana paused before responding. "It is a weapon of considerable magnitude. That's all I can say."

Before he could clear his mind of questions, Mikkellana disappeared.

Rahg's hand found the Slicer, and he shook with fright.

THE SHULAN'S WORDS

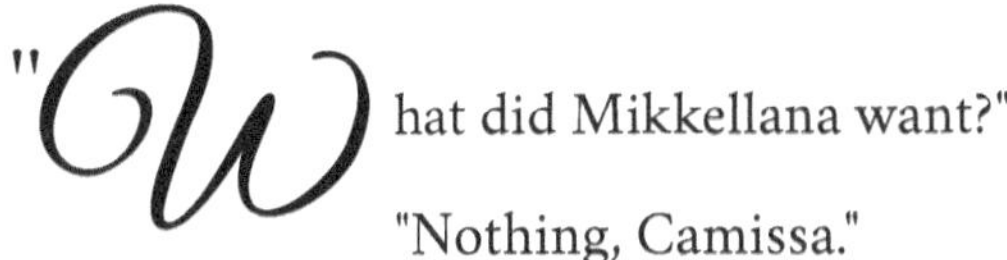

"What did Mikkellana want?"

"Nothing, Camissa."

Rahg rejoined Rhaven and Tobias, busy arguing with some Entirians because Tobias had suggested burning the bodies of the dead.

"Bodies cannot be burned." The Entirian in command seemed appalled by the thought.

Tobias shook his head and rubbed the white stubble on his chin. "I meant burn the Victas and Wolfen. Sethians too. No sense in wastin' hard sweat over them. You can bury the Sethians if you want, though I don't know why you would."

"They must all have a place in the ground. We will dig the graves. It is our honor."

"Your honor?"

"The tall Entirian bowed low. "It is the shame of the victors that they must bury the dead. In this way, it is hoped that the next battle will not be engaged so quickly."

Tobias mumbled as he walked toward Sunnara. "C'mon, lads. Let's get back to the city. I'm not diggin' graves for lizards."

Sunnara came into view over the next knoll, where a throng of people parted to show the way into the "City of the Sun." Rahg felt tired, exhausted, even depressed, but the reception stirred his emotions—victory proved exhilarating. He smiled as the crowd's cheers grew to a deafening roar. He liked the feeling of victory; it made him feel good.

Aenaila tapped Darstan on the shoulder. "They are screaming for you, too, Darstan." Almost an afterthought, she turned to Wisp. "You too, Kender Darnell. You are as much the hero as the rest of them."

"I don't need to be a hero." Wisp's pace quickened, and his gaze shifted, searching every face in the crowd.

"Who are you searching for?" Darstan asked, "that little thief?"

"Don't say it with such disgust. You make me feel guilty."

Darstan finally put a smile on his face. "I think Wisp has grown attached to that little beggar, Aenaila. He can't get his mind off him."

"I don't care one way or the other for the beggar," Wisp said. "I just want to make sure he didn't get into too much trouble while we were gone. I won't shoulder the blame for his mischief."

The noise of the crowd came in waves as they neared the city. Tobias scooted up to take a position between Rahg and Darstan. "Magmar would have been proud of you lads. He always said you would be something special. Probably clawin' to get out of his grave right now at the thought of you havin' powers. But aside from that, he'd be proud."

Rahg smiled. "He used to come storming onto the porch when he was angry, hollering because some chore wasn't done. And he used to yell at those pigs..."

Darstan's voice drooped with sorrow. "I wish he could be here, Tobias. It sure would be nice to have him with us."

A skinny black-haired boy bolted from the grasp of an Entirian priest dressed in a white robe. He ran straight to Wisp.

"Master Kender! You are alive. Are you hurt? I prayed for your safety, Master Kender. You see, I am good luck for you. The gods have blessed you now that you have me."

Wisp disentangled his arms from the little beggar. "He grabbed him by the wrist. "I see you still have all your fingers. They must not be so strict here. I'm surprised."

The white-robed priest was close by Adju, and, as he came near, Adju ducked behind Wisp and clung to his garments even though blood coated them. "Do not let them near me, Master Kender. And do not believe what they say. They are full of lies, all of them. Their tongues do not recognize the truth."

Darstan roared. "I've never see anyone better suited to be a son of yours; his tongue is as quick as your knives. He even accuses a priest of lying. Are you certain you weren't in Khatara ten or twelve years ago?"

The priest stared at Wisp, frustration showing in his eyes. "I do not wish to be the bearer of bad news, especially as you are a guest in our land, but the young one has caused much trouble."

The priest heaved a sigh. "We watched him as you asked, but before the day grew warm, he escaped to try to join you on the battlefield. We captured him only to have him make good on two more escapes. Then when we locked him in the temple for safety, we discovered he had stolen from the sacred altar." The priest wore a look of disgust on his face. "He was brought before the shulan for punishment, but when we left the hall, we found that he had stolen the ring from the shulan's finger."

"Adju!"

The little thief let go of Wisp's cloak and stepped out from behind him to face the wrath of the priest. "I will take my punishment with them, Master Kender. You do not have to scold me. If they take a finger, I will have then learned." Adju heaved a heavy sigh. "Maru llam sarag."

"Speak up, you little thief. What does that nonsense mean?"

Camissa looked at Adju with sympathetic eyes. "Whatever the gods will," she said, then her eyes found Wisp. "It is an ancient Khataran saying. When someone faces an uncertain fate, they repeat this prayer hoping for mercy from the gods. I'm surprised that one so young is familiar with it; he must have had a hard life."

"Don't let him fool you with sad tales and sadder eyes, Camissa. He has practiced lies and stories so much he could compete with Tobias." Darstan's smile had almost returned to normal. "If he admits to being a liar, a beggar, and a thief, *that* you can believe. The first time we met, he stole my purse, then he tried again after we had already caught him. And when he finally knew he was captured, he lied about having to feed a sick mother, and sisters so hungry that death was knocking on their door."

Darstan had not laughed so much since his hand was lost. "And I believed him. If it hadn't been for Wisp, the little thief would have gotten away."

Camissa's eyes hardened under the truth. She held no place for thieves, even though her friend was one of the most notorious.

Adju burst into mock laughter. "Master Darstan enjoys telling tales, fine lady, but do not believe him. I will..."

Wisp grabbed Adju by the hair and yanked him back to his side. The priest had waited patiently for an answer. "I will see to his punishment. And rest assured, it will be nothing like what you had in mind."

"Make way for the shulan, High Lord of Entiria. Make way."

The noise of the crowd subsided, an angry wave to a ripple in a pond. The throng of people parted to let the shulan pass through. He wore a white robe and carried a walking staff in his right hand. The ring on his finger shone like the sun.

"We of Entiria offer our gratitude." He bowed respectfully to each of them, then settled a hardened gaze on Rahg. Rest well tonight, young warrior, we must speak in the morning."

"Speak of what? We're finished. The battle's done."

No smile lit the shulan's face. "This battle was won, it is true. But the war has not yet begun, Rahgnar Fal-Thera. It has not even begun."

RAHG STARED out the window at the dismal gray sky. Seldom did the sun stay hidden in Sunnara, but this morning he was glad it had—a gray sky suited the day. It would not seem appropriate to have a sunny sky while so many lay dead on the hillside.

Rahg looked at Darstan, sitting on the side of the bed. "What did Mikkellana have to do with you losing your hand? I didn't hear the whole story."

"There's not much more to tell," Darstan said, his head hung low.

"Not much more to tell? I remember when you could spend half a day telling me about a fish you *almost* caught."

Darstan laughed. "I guess you're right, Ragh." After a short pause, he continued. "Wisp told you about Gregor, how we tried to save him from the Wolfen. While we chased them, Mikkellana appeared and ordered us to stop. I kept going after Gregor, and Takar grabbed me. That's when I found out I was stuck."

Darstan stared at the wall. "I panicked, Rahg. My hand went through the shield, but it wouldn't come out. Hundreds of Gnakas were coming, so Mikkellana ordered Takar to cut it off. I screamed when it happened. And then the Fire came. I don't remember much after that, but Wisp told me I killed them all." Darstan's gaze fell to the floor then back up again to Rahg. "What's wrong with us? How do we have powers? Why?"

"I don't know how or why, Darstan, but I think Aentarra and Mikkellana knew about it before we did."

"They know more than they tell. I'm certain of that." Darstan stood and stretched. "I could see your shield during the battle. It struck me as odd because I couldn't see the one in Sethia."

"Camissa said she couldn't see the Shield. I wonder why you could."

"I don't know, Rahg." They sat in silence for a moment, Darstan staring at nothing and Rahg pacing. "What are we going to do? Everything is so different now."

"The shera wants to see me this morning," Rahg said. "I'm sure everyone has a thousand plans for me, but I don't intend on letting him put a bit in my mouth and tug me around by the reins." Rahg plopped down in a chair next to the door. "They want me to kill the Messenger, whoever that might be. Just go kill somebody I don't even know."

"I'll help you, Rahg. And don't worry so much, we can do it. Besides, I'm sure Rhaven and Tobias will come. Perhaps Wisp." Darstan walked to the window and opened it, breathing fresh air. "I've come to like that thief. He has honor."

A pang of jealousy crept into Rahg's heart. He had seen how close Darstan and Wisp had grown, and it hurt a little.

A knock at the door interrupted them. "Come in," Rahg said.

Camissa opened the door and entered. "You look better, Rahg."

"I bathed."

"Yes, so did I."

Rahg smelled the scented oils in her honey hair, and saw the freshness in her face. Another stab of jealousy hit; a man had bathed her.

"They sent me to get you," Camissa said.

"I'll tell Aenaila," Darstan said, as he closed the door.

As soon as Rahg and Camissa were alone, she threw her arms around him. "I was so frightened. Afraid you would die." Tears ran from soft blue eyes.

Rahg nestled his head against her neck. "You worried me, too. When you went off into... whatever that place was. I didn't know what to do." Rahg won the fight with tears, but his eyes had reddened. "I'm just glad you're back." He stared into her eyes as he unfolded her arms, then he stopped, his lips moving toward hers. Just as they touched, Tobias burst through the door.

"Time to be getting'—" Tobias flushed and turned his head. "Sorry, lad." He rushed the apology and closed the door as he left.

Rahg and Camissa both laughed, then she grabbed him and finished the kiss they had started. "I think you had more than a kiss in mind, Rahg, but that will have to wait. It's time for us to go."

"I don't want to talk with those priests, Camissa."

"Come, Rahg, the shera is waiting." Camissa grabbed his arm.

He yanked his hand away. "Tell the shera to come here if he wants to talk with me."

"They are only trying to help."

"What they're trying to do, Camissa, is have me find and kill the Messenger because they believe he will free the evil one." Fear had secured a hold on Rahg.

"But the prophecies say—"

"The prophecies say many things. Who can decipher them? For all I know they could be telling me to kill someone who's good."

Camissa tried calming him, but he shook her off again.

"How do I even know if I can kill him? He's probably got powers." Rahg resumed his pacing. "Perhaps I won't. Maybe he'll kill me."

Tobias poked his head into the room. "What's takin' so long, lad?"

"He's worried, Tobias. Afraid—"

"I'm not afraid!" Rahg's face turned red and he glared at Camissa. "I never said—"

"Nothin' wrong with bein' afraid, lad. We were all scared at Twin Forks, and in Pomanda, and on that voyage here. I've been more afraid these past ten moons than I have all my life."

Tobias reached over and patted Rahg on the back. "Don't worry though. I'll help you. And so will Rhaven and the others. We'll all be there, lad. We'll win, or we'll die, but we'll do it together."

The prospect of winning or dying should not have calmed Rahg, but it did. "All right, Tobias, we'll go." Rahg smiled as he took Camissa's arm and headed for the door. "Sorry, Camissa."

AENAILA BOWED LOW TO MIKKELLANA, hoping to mend the damage Darstan might have done when he shunned her. "My Lady." Her voice was soft as fresh snow.

"Hello, pretty one."

The pink in Aenaila's cheeks grew darker. "My Lady is too gracious. It is you who holds the beauty."

Mikkellana's tone hid none of her irritation. "A lie dipped in honey is still a lie. I know what I am, and beautiful does not describe it. I could be, if I wished, but then it would not be me. Do not fret though, I hold no grudge against you, nor do I covet your beauty; it is as much a curse as a blessing. But I do want to know why you hold such interest in the prophecy. And I would like to know how you managed to Shift to Entiria. You could not have been here before."

"Kender had seen the boat at the dock in Genda. I used that image to bring us to the boat."

Mikkellana's eyebrows raised high into her brow. "His recall is so good?"

Aenaila smiled. "His mind is perhaps even more nimble than his hands. And he—"

"The prophecy, Aenaila, we were discussing your attraction to it."

"The prophecy is of interest to all, My Lady. If any of us are to survive we must do our part to see the Evil One kept in Sethia."

Mikkellana's gaze could burn through stone. "And what is your part? Where are you from, and what do you want from Darstan?"

Aenaila's coloring reddened even more. "I hail from Khatara, My Lady, and I only wish to help Darstan. He has won my sympathy."

"Pretty words and a pretty face do not make a thing true. Your charm might work on the men who dote on you, but it has no effect on me."

"But I speak the truth, My Lady. Many in Khatara can attest to my story."

"Yes, I'm confident that if I investigated, I could find those who have known you long, but I doubt that any will have known you for as many seasons as you have lived. And even that, I suspect, is far past the number you lead people to believe."

Aenaila narrowed her eyes and a scowl formed on her face.

"Your pretenses are wasted on me, Aenaila. Your powers could not be so great, nor your mind that rich in so few summer droughts."

Aenaila felt like the rat caught in the alley that Wisp always mentioned. She was fabricating a response when Darstan opened the door.

He glanced at Aenaila then stared at Mikkellana. "Is everything all right, Aenaila?"

"Fine, Darstan. We were just talking of Khatara. She grabbed his arm. "I'm glad you came to get me."

"We shall finish our discussion of ... Khatara, some other time, Aenaila." Mikkellana would not take the hook from her mouth so soon.

"Yes, My Lady, another time," Aenaila said, and stepped into the corridor.

❦

"Hurry, Darstan. I don't want to be late."

"What difference does it make? Those priests will probably question Rahg long into the night. And besides, he'll tell us if we miss anything important."

Words alone would not deter Aenaila. "He does not know what is important. Not yet."

Aenaila was burrowing in an empty hole, Darstan thought, but he could tell her mind was fixed, and he was not one to argue over nothing. "No sense pickin' over bones," Magmar always said. "If we're going, let's go," he said, and quickened his pace.

"I want Kender to join us, Darstan. He sometimes hears things others might not."

Darstan smiled at her observation. "You have gotten to know him well in such a short time."

Aenaila's chuckle made her blush. "I think that even Kender Darnell does not know Kender Darnell; however, some things are easy enough to ascertain. He can tell a mare from a nag when it comes to people."

"If Kender comes he'll bring Adju." Darstan knew Aenaila didn't care for the little thief.

She sighed. "I know. That pup has yet to be weaned, but it's just as well. If left alone, he would steal the hat from the beggar's hand."

Darstan smiled.

"You should choose to smile more often, Darstan."

ADJU SAT CROSSLEGGED on the cold stone. A chair sat empty nearby, but he preferred the floor. He looked up at Wisp, pacing in front of him. "I offered apologies, Master Kender, what else is there?"

"Why did you steal from them, Adju? You were a guest in their house." Wisp stopped pacing and stared down at him, finger wagging like a schoolmarm scolding a student. "Guests do not steal."

Adju had the eyes of a lost puppy, and when they swelled with tears, he proved difficult to resist. "I did not think, Master Kender. How could I know if you were even coming back? I was stuck in this strange land and had to get as much as I could."

Wisp let the silence judge Adju; the pause only lasting a moment. "Also, Master Kender, they do not punish thieves here, so I did not think it was wrong."

"What do you mean they don't punish thieves?"

"They do not." Adju's voice raised. "If a thief is caught he is put in the house of the person he stole from to work for a while. But, Master Kender, all that time he is fed, and he has a bed to sleep on—a real bed, one with feathers. And they give the thief food." Adju looked at Kender and whispered, "And no one loses a finger."

Wisp tried explaining that things were done differently in other lands, but he could not help but wonder about the riches he could take in just a few nights in Sunnara. He stared at a blank spot on the wall.

"What is wrong, Master Kender?"'

Wisp shook his head, clearing the dangerous thoughts. "Nothing, Adju, I was just thinking about something, but it wouldn't be fun anyway."

"Tell me about the battle, Master Kender. Are you a hero? I heard people call you a hero."

"I'm no hero. Just a fool who nearly got killed." Wisp reached his hand out for Adju to grab. "Come, little beggar, we're meeting Darstan and Rahg." Wisp pulled him up from the floor. "The next time you ignore my rules, Aenaila will issue the punishment."

Wisp saw the look in Adju's eyes; the little thief knew Aenaila would be stricter than him. *That might keep him good for a while.*

Adju opened the door and bowed to let Wisp exit before him. "Was your bath relaxing, Master Kender? I saw the one who bathed you. Her face looked like a Qorami."

Wisp could not contain his laughter. "And what would you know of Qorami, little one? In fact, what would you know of women at all?"

Adju never seemed to get embarrassed. "I have heard about Qorami. They are beautiful, with silk for skin, and roses in their cheeks. They have—"

Wisp's laughter would not stop, but Adju kept up his chatter.

"...and I know much of girls. I know a man, Mufed, who has a daughter named Khalina. You know Khalina, Master Kender, remember, we stayed there, and—"

Footsteps from the next corridor interrupted Adju. "Good morning, Mistress Aenaila. Your face shines like the emperor's sun."

Aenaila smiled despite the source of the compliment. "Stop it, Adju. You are beginning to sound like Kender Darnell. I'll not have two of you badgering me."

When Aenaila turned her head, Adju tugged on Wisp's sleeve. "I think she likes you."

Wisp returned the whisper. "And I think she doesn't like you."

Adju brushed his hand in the air, as if Wisp's comment was so much nonsense. "Why are we meeting Master Rahg?"

WIDE SWEEPING STEPS graced the entrance of the temple. Twenty-one times Rahg lifted each leg to climb the polished gray and blue stone; he had been here once before when he first met with the shera and the other two priests. That was before the battle with Iazzo.

Camissa had a firm grip on his arm and a smile on her face, but Rahg knew she worried as much as he did about the prophecy.

Rhaven and Tobias stood behind one of dozens of pillars on the landing at the top step. Tobias had a lit pipe in his mouth, smoke billowing out like a small forest fire. His back had been leaning against the columns, but he came erect when Rahg and Camissa neared the top. "I thought you'd be late, lad. Don't want to keep the shulan waiting."

Tobias arrived everywhere far too early. "We're not late, Tobias, besides, Darstan and Aenaila are supposed to be here. I think Wisp is coming too."

"Let them come when they can," Tobias said. "We better be gettin' inside. I saw the priests enter before I lit my pipe."

"All right, Tobias, I'll go, but you wait for Darstan.

The large bronze doors had carvings of things Rahg had never seen.

They opened on their own accord. A second set of doors led to the sacred temple and stood just ahead. Rahg breathed deeply before he entered. The chamber was as big as he remembered. The three priests were there, as before, standing in the circular designs of inlaid stone but the shulan was also present.

The shera wore a black robe; the other two priests wore red. The shulan's robe was white with a purple sash adorned with jewels. His rings sparkled with rubies and diamonds and other gems, and he gripped a staff carved from what appeared to be blackthorn, though Rahg knew the trees didn't grow in Entiria. The shera spoke first.

"It has begun, Rahgnar Fal-Thera. Our last conversation is yet fresh in my mind and the struggle has already begun."

Rahg didn't like the manner of the shera; the way he spoke, everything was already lost, no hope. Rahg wanted to wait for Darstan to arrive, but he wanted this over with even more. "What is it you want from me, Shera? I have already given my blood."

"It is not what I want, Rahgnar Fal-Thera. It is not a question of what anyone wants. You are tied to the fate of the world. What is written in the prophecies cannot be undone."

"Anything can be undone, Shera." Mikkellana had entered unseen and though her presence unnerved Rahg, he smiled because her presence bothered the shera more.

"I have not yet learned my lady's name," the shera said, his bow courteous, nothing more.

Camissa bowed. "My Lady, it is good to see you again." Camissa completed the bow and faced the priests and the shulan. "This is Mikkellana."

This time the shera's bow swept the floor. "My apologies for not understanding, Lady. Forgive the ignorance of a lowly priest."

"No forgiveness is required. I came to listen to the prophecies, to help, if I could."

Heels slapping on the marble floor announced Darstan's arrival. He took up a position next to Rahg, Aenaila at his side. Wisp and Adju stood next to Rhaven.

Aenaila leaned to whisper in Camissa's ear. "What have I missed?"

"Nothing. Mikkellana just arrived."

The shera began speaking again. "You must kill the Messenger, Rahg. And to do that you must go to Arangar."

Camissa whispered to Rahg. "I sensed anger from Aenaila when he mentioned Arangar. But why?"

Rahg nodded. "You have told me about going to Arangar, Shera. How do I find the Messenger? And then what do I do?"

"It is not so easy as that."

Rahg's head darted to the right; it was the shulan who had spoken. "What do you mean?"

"You must enter the Paaren, and you must seek the knowledge of the Ancient Ones."

"What is the Paaren?"

"We do not know what it is, Rahg, but the only way to enter is through the Portals of Darkness."

Mikkellana cringed. "How will he know what to do, Shulan, and how will he find the Portals?" She stepped forward, her presence intimidating. "What do you know of the Portals?"

"This will lead him to the place of knowledge." His outstretched hand held a necklace with a heart-shaped amulet bearing a crystal as black as the deepest cave. It reminded Rahg of the obelisk.

"What is this?"

"It has been passed down to each shulan since before our memories can know. It came from the Ancient Ones, and legend claims it will lead you to the place of knowledge."

"What is this place of knowledge?"

"We know nothing more."

"What will I find there?" A wave of fear roiled in Rahg's stomach.

"We do not know. But we can provide one more bit of help. The Paaren is a place of mystery—a place where every footstep is lost once taken. It is told that no one has ever survived the Paaren, but perhaps that is because they have never had a Pathfinder."

Rahg's confusion and fear built to boiling frustration. "I've had enough of this, Shulan. You can't tell me anything about this place and then tell me nobody has ever survived, but you expect me to go anyway. Well, you'll not catch me running off to find some portal and end my life. I'll wait for Lukaan to come get me."

Rahg had begun his turn to depart the temple only to discover Mikkellana blocking his way, her eyes glowing with menace.

"I have seen more centuries than you have moons, boy, and I'll not forfeit my life to Lukaan because you refuse to accept your fate. You will complete this journey; you will find this knowledge. And you will slay this Messenger. Then you can help me defeat Lukaan." Mikkellana fought to control a temper held too long in abeyance. "You will do these things, or I will squeeze the breath from you myself—now, as we stand here."

Darstan stepped between her and Rahg.

Her glare drilled into Darstan. "Don't you *dare* challenge me, boy. If I sense one bit of of fire burning in you, I'll cut off your good arm and your legs, too."

Rahg grabbed Darstan's shoulder. "No, Dar. Let me handle this." Rahg forced fear and pride back down his throat. The mention of her squeezing the breath out reminded him of what Aentarra had said about Ronell. And Mikkellana had nearly choked Rahg to death that day just for asking about it. Perspiration beaded on Rahg's forehead and rolled down his cheeks. He turned back to the shulan. "I'm sorry, Shulan. Accept my apology for being rash. What can you tell me to make the journey more successful?"

"There is little we can tell you. You must go to the lands of Arangar and in the Maze of the Mist, you will find a Pathfinder. You then must find the Portals of Darkness, and, once inside the Paaren, the amulet will lead you to the place of knowledge."

Rahg tried to maintain his composure, though the shulan's way of speaking in riddles frustrated him. "What does a Pathfinder have to do with this and why would it help me?"

"The Pathfinders are an ancient race that roamed the lands long before man. Legend states that a favorite pet of the gods wandered far from home one day and became hopelessly lost until a Pathfinder brought it home. As a reward, the gods blessed the Pathfinders with a special ability—no matter where they went, even in the Paaren, they could always find their way back. It is especially important because in the Paaren something happens, and people cannot find their way back out. This is what the legends say, and since no one has ever returned..."

The shulan's somber expression worried Rahg, but the prospect of Mikkellana strangling him proved to be the more immediate threat; Arangar was a far-off land, Mikkellana stood only a few paces away. "How will we get to Arangar?"

"I have a ship being prepared even now, Rahg, and the captain is an experienced seaman who has ridden the waves since he was a child."

"How will Rahg find the portal, Shulan. Do any of your scrolls or legends mention that?"

The shulan looked to the shera for advice. "He will find it as he finds it, My Lady. We know nothing more. Perhaps the Pathfinders have more knowledge."

Mikkellana nodded. "You have the map for your journey. All that remains is to take your departure."

"We have time before we go running off to some distant land."

"You have no time. You must leave before Aentarra returns and discovers your destination. She must not be allowed to follow you." Mikkellana's tone implied danger.

"Why can't she just go there?"

"Because she has never been. Now go and prepare. Every moment is precious."

Rahg fingered the amulet hanging from his neck, and he thought about the upcoming journey. His life had changed so much since Twin Forks and that was just last winter.

Rhaven offered a suggestion, one just short of a command. "We should meet and discuss our plans for departure."

"I suggest you follow the warrior's advice," Mikkellana said. "Now you must leave. Be brave on your journey, Rahg; it will be rife with peril."

MIKKELLANA STAYED, wandering through the chamber until everyone except the shera had gone.

"Does My Lady require anything else?"

The shera seemed uncomfortable in her presence. Mikkellana met him at the center of the hall, her gaze riveting him. "Yes, Shera, there are many puzzles that I need answers to. Tell me of this structure, this obelisk which you call home. Who built it and when? What kind of stone is this? I have never seen its like."

"As to who built it, we do not know, My Lady. Our people came to Entiria more than five thousand years ago, and according to our records, it was here when we arrived. There were no people on the island, nor any evidence other than this obelisk and the structures surrounding it." The shera paused. "I have a particular interest in old buildings, My Lady, and I have searched this island from shore to shore. There is no trace of the stone that was used. Not even a pebble."

Mikkellana nodded as if the shera had told her something new. "You may leave now, Shera. I thank you for your help."

The shera bowed, then departed the temple. Mikkellana probed the chamber floor and walls, even the air itself. There was power here, great power. She raced to possible conclusions but none of them made sense. None of her kind had ever been to Entiria, so it could have nothing to do with any of them—and if not them, then who? Once again her mind drifted to Vallah and the mystery of who had built such a magnificent city. Even more important was why had they abandoned it? So many questions and nowhere to get answers.

Perhaps this land of Arangar will provide clues, she thought. *Perhaps it will.*

PREPARATIONS

*C*amissa stood next to Rahg in the center of the room. It bristled with fear and anxiety. Wisp sharpened his knives while Rahg paced the floor. "I'll go it alone," he said. Insanity had taken the place of fear. "I don't want anyone else to die because of me."

Camissa was the first to voice her opposition. "I'll not sit by and let you bungle this, Rahgnar Fal-Thera; too much is at stake. I'm going with you to make sure you do it properly."

Tobias fumed as much as his pipe. "Lad, I watched you be raised and taught you how to do more things than you still know. You can't tell me I'm stayin' here. Wouldn't know what to do if I wasn't scared half to cryin' like I have been these last ten moons."

Rhaven stepped forward. "Mikkellana swore me to help you. It will prove a difficult journey—no doubt—but I feel you will come to appreciate our company. The matter is settled. I'm going with you and so it seems are Tobias and Camissa."

Rhaven looked to Darstan standing with Aenaila and Wisp. "And you, Darstan? We could use someone with your talents. That goes for you too, thief, though I shall miss the bickering between you and the bounty-man. It is a pity fate found him so soon." Rhaven turned to Aenaila. "And you, fine lady, you would be welcome."

"I can't go." Darstan stared at Rahg. "I'm sorry, but I promised Aenaila that when this was over, I'd go back to Khatara with her. I promised, Rahg."

Rahg stared at Darstan, feelings slighted.

"I gave my word," Darstan offered in response to Rahg's unspoken sign. "If you need me, wait until I finish this business with Aenaila, then I'll come."

Rhaven interrupted. "Is this business of yours so important, Aenaila? Can't it wait for our return?"

"No, Rhaven. Darstan gave his word, and I'll not have him compromise it on my account." Rahg smiled at Darstan. "We'll be fine, brother. It was enough that you offered, and while I'd like you to come, I'm afraid that wouldn't be possible. As you heard Mikkellana say, we must leave at once."

Camissa tugged on Rahg's sleeve, whispering. "Ask her what's so important. I sense bad feelings about this."

"Leave it be, Camissa."

Rhaven stared at Darstan. "How did you lose the hand?"

"There's nothing to talk about. The hand is gone, and it won't grow back."

"I've seen men lose hands, Darstan. Better a hand than a foot; better an arm than a leg."

"Those words come easy for a person with all their limbs."

Camissa used her senses every chance she could. A dozen vows had fallen this day already, but she had abandoned the fight with her conscience long ago. Despite her vows to respect the privacy of her friends, she had to know whether her powers still worked properly. A dangerous journey lay ahead, and she might have need of every advantage she could muster, so she poked and probed and reached out to touch everyone's mind.

Rahg's demeanor offered little surprise—dread and fear prickled under a thin layer of bravado, a very thin layer. Darstan had lost some of his bitterness, only brought to the surface when someone raised the issue of how he lost his hand. Aenaila proved to be a fortress of stone; Camissa could extract nothing from her. Camissa ignored Wisp. He had been her friend for many years and through much strife; that was one vow she could afford to keep a while longer; besides, Wisp held no secrets she cared about.

Camissa had purposefully avoided Rhaven all day; she had probed his mind on the way to see Shera Kevon, and the experience proved unsettling. She finally relented and convinced herself to try again. Her mind touched his, and she immediately sensed the tenseness and strong emotions.

Rhaven got up and approached Aenaila, his voice hesitant. "I would ask a favor, Aenaila."

Aenaila's green eyes stared at Rhaven. "What is it? If I can help you, I will."

"Argus was left behind in Genda. I need to check on him. I'm told you can travel like the immortals." Rhaven paused before adding, "And if you can bring him back, I will pay generously in gold."

Adju's eyes ran up and down Rhaven's body as if he were looking for the gold.

Aenaila hesitated. "If Kender knows the place well enough, I can take you, but as to bringing back the horse, I dare not risk it. There are dangers involved with Shifting."

Camissa saw the sorrow in Rhaven's eyes. No probing was necessary.

"You are most kind, Aenaila. If you just take me to him, I'll arrange for his safekeeping until I can return."

"I will take you, warrior." The voice that came from the corridor had everyone turn at once.

Mikkellana's form seemed to fill the doorway, yet it didn't. Rhaven's smile broadened his face. "My thanks, lady. I will be in your debt."

"You are already in my debt. Now the purse you owe will be fatter." Mikkellana's smile lit her eyes. "Prepare to leave."

"Will we be able to bring him back?" Rhaven's voice shook with anticipation.

Her soft gaze fell on Rhaven. "Yes, we can. Now grab my hand." She turned to the others, "Prepare for departure in the morning."

"We have barely rested from the battle," Rahg said.

"The voyage at sea will afford plenty of time to rest. More time than you would care for. I told you earlier I wanted you gone before Aentarra returned. Once you leave, she won't be able to find you." Mikkellana took a firm hold on Rhaven's hand. "We shall return shortly."

IN A BACK ALLEY off a side street in Genda, the air cracked and shimmered. Mikkellana and Rhaven stepped through a rift onto broken pieces of old, worn cobblestone. Rhaven appeared truly stunned. For a brief moment he said nothing, and when he did, it was a single question. "Can Rahg do this?"

"In time he will learn."

Rhaven thought of all the marvelous possibilities it presented in battle. "A man with this power would have many advantages over the enemy."

"A woman too," Mikkellana said.

Rhaven laughed. "Yes, a woman too."

"Where is the horse being kept?"

"A friend of Sennar's is keeping him. It's only a few streets away."

Rhaven increased his pace to almost a run by the time he reached the stable, his heart bursting with anticipation. "I didn't know how much I missed him."

"In my experience, animals make better friends than people," Mikkellana said.

A LARGE, brawny man met them at the front of the barn. "I see no mounts to stable."

"I've come to get mine," Rhaven said. "A black stallion. Argus is his name."

Panic showed in the man's eyes.

"Where is the horse, stableman?" Mikkellana demanded.

"Where is the horse?" Rhaven yelled. The man backed up at Rhaven's advance.

"He wouldn't even let me feed 'im; he was a wild one. Scared all the others so much I couldn't take in more business. Had to do somethin'. Can't blame a man for that, can ya'?"

Rhaven's hand trembled, squeezing the hilt of his sai. "Where?"

"Sold 'im at fair market on the docks—"

"Who?"

A sai pressed against the man's gut. He had already backed against the wall; there was nowhere else to go.

"Who bought him?" Rhaven asked.

"I don't know. He had gold, that's all I know. Good gold."

Rhaven's fist dropped him to the floor, and his boot struck hard at the man's stomach. Between gasps of spitting blood, the man pleaded for his life. "I'll find 'im. I'll get your gold."

Rhaven prepared to strike.

"No!." Mikkellana's command halted him, a wild dog on a tether.

Rhaven stopped to look at her, his arm shaking with fury.

"Leave him," she said. "I'll find Argus."

"How? You said we have little time."

"I do not ask how you wield a sword, warrior."

Rhaven nodded. He had regained some of his composure. "Lead on."

Mikkellana soon located the new owner of Argus. He was living on a large estate outside of Genda. A rap on the door brought a servant to open it.

"I have come for the horse," Rhaven said, without any introductions.

Mikkellana laughed. "I feel quite certain he has more than one horse. Perhaps you should let me speak."

Rhaven fought the desire to handle things his way, but he placed his trust in Mikkellana. The servant stared at him like he had lost use of his senses, but he listened well when Mikkellana spoke and went to get his master. Rhaven felt he had chosen well to let her speak.

The man listened to the Mikkellana's story, asking no questions until she had finished with the tale. "It is a fine story, my friends. A fine story. But how do I know if it's true? The horse is a wild one; if it recognizes you as the owner, we can then negotiate. I have no wish to sell him, but I'll not keep another man's horse." The man stood and motioned for them to follow. "Come, he is in the barn."

Argus's neigh pierced the night air as soon as he caught Rhaven's scent. He reared and kicked wildly. Mikkellana sent a message to Argus, then walked up to him as if they were old friends.

"You have a way with animals, my lady," Rhaven said. "Argus lets no one come so close."

"Yes," she said.

The man nodded. "I have no option but to acknowledge the horse belongs to you; none of my horse trainers have been able to get so close. "The horse is yours," he said. "All we need do is discuss the price."

"I'm not one to bicker on price," Rhaven admitted. "Name a fair price, and it is yours. I have gold."

Mikkellana saw the greed glowing in the man's eyes. "I think a fair price would be what you paid for the horse; what you fed the horse; plus three silver dirnars for your troubles."

The words seemed to come with difficulty, but he soon found himself uttering them nonetheless. "I accept your generous offer."

Rhaven found the coin quickly and paid the man; then he led Argus out onto the road to Genda. "It has been a long time, Argus, but I came back." Once again, Rhaven found himself in Mikkellana's debt. "You seem to have a way with people as well as animals."

"Only some of them, my friend, only some of them."

Aentarra appeared at the docks alone. She needed only a moment, just enough time to commit the scene to memory. She had no intentions of participating in the voyage itself; all she needed to do was Shift aboard once they were close to the destination. The journey would take about a month the Entirians had said, which provided ample time to conduct more studies in the library. *There is much to learn before I get to Arangar.*

She heard the footsteps long before they arrived and realized it was no one she knew. The captain of the ship and several of his men came aboard, crates laden with cargo were stacked high but not quite blocking the view of Aentarra. It was the first mate that saw her first, his stop so abrupt the captain bumped into him. They had seen her at the battle and knew who she was.

"May the Ancient Ones smile on you, Lady. I bid you good morn." They all moved aside to give her wide berth.

THE CAPTAIN BOWED LOW, holding his position longer than normal, longer even than he would to address the Shulan, leader of all Entiria. There was no future in risking an offense to this one. Too many whispers had crept along the halls of the temple regarding her. "I'm making preparations for departure, My Lady." The captain had somehow managed the words without his voice faltering. "If I could but know when you are through so that I do not disturb you."

The captain, standing erect, looked to her for a response, and though taller than her by a head, his eyes avoided meeting her dark, penetrating gaze. He paid special attention to keeping his hands far away from weapons, not wishing to give any reason for her to think he meant harm. A cautious glance found an unexpectedly warm smile on Aentarra's face. Once again he was caught off guard. H brought all his willpower to focus on concentrating, trying not to leer or overstep his bounds. He had a tenuous understanding at best of what they were anyway.

Her voice could have melted the ice on top of Mount Sharmand. He barely managed to restrain his own racing heart.

"You have my leave, Captain. And don't worry, I won't linger to frighten your men."

She glanced toward the stern where the men huddled as if conversing, though they looked to be straining to hear every spoken word.

Aentarra's voice touched his heart again. "You carry cargo that holds my interest, captain. I need to know if you anticipate trouble, and I need to know how long this voyage will last."

The captain cleared his throat, full of nerves and close to being full of bile. "The winds should be favorable and the seas calm. We should be there just before their spring. That would be about thirty days from now."

The length of the voyage didn't surprise Aentarra.

"Is anything wrong, My Lady?"

"It is no matter, captain... what was your name again?"

The captain shook visibly. "My name is Katsu."

"Katsu. I shall remember. And as for you, Captain Katsu, remember that we will meet again, and unless you want it to be unpleasant, you will make certain that no one knows of my visit today."

Captain Katsu trembled under the threat. "Yes, My Lady. You can rest assured." Katsu thought that Aentarra was leaving, but then he saw her turn to him again. "I would see your cabin, Captain. Show it to me."

Katsu opened the door to his cabin and stepped aside to let her enter. He'd not be the one to enter before her. Aentarra walked slowly around the room, staring at all the walls, then the bed and desk. She nodded her head a few times, then abruptly turned to depart. "That will do, Captain. But remember, tell no one of my visit."

Katsu bowed lower than ever, this was the second time she had reminded him of that, so it must be important. "Yes, My Lady, no one."

"And your men, Captain, make certain that they understand as well. Inform them of my interest."

Katsu bowed to let her know he understood, but when he raised his head to address her, she was gone. He tried to stop the bile from rising in his throat, tried to stop his limbs from shaking, but he couldn't. "Meet again…" echoed in his mind like the clang of steel after a battle. It was not a memory he'd cherish. A heavy sigh helped start the clearing of his head; there was much to do.

He hurried topside. "Come, men. We sail before the dawn." The men came warily, each one scouring the ship—probably for signs of the sea witch.

FAMINE

Chun village, Arangar

Korg 'en Terdra sat alone atop the rocky outcropping, lines of worry creasing the weathered skin of his brow. Despite the biting cold of the wind, the hood of his cloak lay resting upon his shoulders.

For the first time in memory, no Harvest Festival had blessed the lands of Arangar. Drought had drained the life from the Shuthvin Valley, and the most severe winter ever battered the Norkaan Mountains. The snow touched virgin marks on the trees, and rivers that were thought to be ever–flowing had seen the summer pass with cracked beds. The snow promised hope for the following year, but hope did not feed the hungry.

mountains covered with snow

Grief creased deeper lines in Korg's face as he stared at the women gathered in the square below, their garments hanging loosely from frail frames—the wives of Chun warriors reduced to scavenging for roots and nuts and anything else that might serve as nourishment. Only the rats and red-beaks owned less pride.

Korg worried for their survival; the drought was in the second season, and even though snow had fallen twice, the storm seers predicted little abatement.

Marta hobbled on one leg, a basket of roots dangling from a shaking, bony hand. She once carried her husband halfway up the mountain after he had suffered an attack from a shadow cat. The icy wind froze a tear on his cheek. Marta would never carry anyone again, her right foot lost last Prayer Day to the bite of the frost.

Korg rose from the rock and made his way up the trail toward the hut he shared with his wife and children. Long, forceful strides pushed him quickly while the wind whipped the cloak about his frame. Several villagers stepped out of Korg's way, perhaps noticing the set of his eyes.

SAMA GREW anxious about Korg's return and peered through the tiny crack in the shutters, boarded up to stifle the cold. Worry weighed heavy on her heart for Korg had departed early and in such foul humor. Finally, she saw him. "Kavi, stoke the fire. Your father will be cold. Reyna, prepare soup. Cold fills a warrior with hunger."

"There is little soup left, mother. Not even enough for supper."

Sama's hard-eyed glare found Reyna. "Say nothing, daughter."

Korg's son grabbed an iron poker and stirred the coals to flame, then placed two pieces of wood on top to fuel the fire. "I ate enough this morning to last all day, Mother."

Sama gazed out the window. "Warriors must eat. Now hush. Korg comes."

KORG PUSHED through the door and stepped briskly to the hearth, rubbing life back into his nearly brittle hands. "Prepare for a journey, Kavi. We must find food."

Kavi's look darted to his mother. Shock marked her face.

"Where will you go, husband? There is no food to be found. Even the animals have abandoned us. Our only hope lies in prayer." Sama's soft-brown eyes teared. "We have offended the Ancient Ones. Their punishment is harsh."

Korg traded his cloak for the heavy fur of his warmest coat. "Take an extra quiver of arrows." He tied a sword belt to his waist, checked the blade, then slid it into the sheath. "And take two knives."

"I always wear two knives, father."

Sama reached out and took hold of Korg's sleeve. The set of his eyes had been hard, but they softened for her. "You can pray, Sama. Pray until your throat is parched if you want, but I must find food, or we will starve, and the Forest Men will claim our lands."

Korg cupped Sama's face in his hands and he looked into her heart. "If you must pray, wife of mine, pray for a deer to cross our path, or a lamb—even a nest of serpents."

Korg laughed at Sama's shocked expression. "I would eat the eyes of a worm, wife—if I could find one. I would even eat a red-beak, but they have disappeared as well with no carcasses for them to pick."

Sama nodded, keeping her head bowed low. "Go, husband. Pack your things. I will help Kavi."

Sama finished tying the chord on a leather sack stuffed with bread, seeds, and a handful of nuts. She buried her head into the heavy fur of Kavi's coat and squeezed him tightly, tucking the sack into the fold inside.

Kavi looked down at her with an innocence that fifteen harsh seasons had not stolen from him. "What is this, Mother?"

A mother's fear filled Sama's heart. "Say nothing, Kavi."

In the corner across the room, Korg remained watchful; the innocence of Kavi's eyes had not sprung from Korg. His old, seasoned gaze had seen most everything, and as he checked the last few arrows, he called to his wife, knowing what she had planned. "We will not take your bread, woman. Empty the sack." His words were as cold as the winter wind.

Sama had managed to restrain her tears until then. "What of Kavi? How will he eat? How will he live? If you care nothing for yourself, think of our son." Tears traced her cheeks.

The ice had not melted in Korg's voice. "We will take none of your food. I have seen enough women with bones showing through skin."

Korg slung the second quiver of arrows over his back. "Come, Kavi. We must go."

Sama's eyes glazed over. She ran to the wall and grabbed a knife, plunging it toward her own heart. Korg seized her hand and held it secure. The coldness left his eyes, and his gentle words carried to her on a breath of warm air. "Sama, woman of my heart, why do this?"

Sama didn't let her own gaze fall, and if her voice cracked, her words rang true. "If I am gone you will take the bread. I will not see you and Kavi die because of me."

The muscles of Korg's arm bulged with the strain of holding her, but his face displayed no sign of pressure. "I will take half the bread with me."

"And all of the nuts," Sama said. "I have no need for nuts." She smiled at Korg, but continued pressure on the blade.

Korg held her gaze for only a short moment. Finally, his hardened face cracked, and he smiled. "What good is it to be a war chief, if I cannot win even one argument?"

"You win all arguments," Sama said, "just not with me." She smiled as she took the sack from Kavi's hands and divided the contents. "Husband, how will you find food? Where will you look that we have not already worn the paths smooth from searching?" An exasperated sigh escaped Sama's lips. "Perhaps we should go, too. Go where the sun is kinder, and the gods are not so sparing with the gift of rain."

"We will find food, so don't move my hut while I'm away."

Sama pushed the largest portion of bread into Kavi's sack, then retied the chord, securing the pouch. As she handed it to Kavi, it must have struck her why Korg was so confident of finding food.

"No!" she screamed. "You cannot go! You cannot take Kavi!" Sama threw herself at her husband's feet and wept. "Please, Korg? No one returns from there." She clutched his coat with both hands and begged. "Do not take my son. Please? He's my only son."

Sama's distress disturbed Kavi, but he didn't let it show. "We will return," he said. "And with food." He laughed. "No two warriors such as this have ever gone to the Paaren. We will come back."

Sama knew her son's courage to be an act but played her part well. Summoning all her strength, she stopped the tears and forced a smile but all the while fought to control sobs. "I will keep the fire warm until your return." Sama squeezed Kavi as hard as she could and placed a warm kiss on his forehead. Then she turned to Korg and kissed him for a long time.

"That should warm me for days," Korg said, and held her tightly. Tighter than he ever had before.

Sama cried, but she would not let the tears show. "Go, my husband. I expect meat on my table by the next seventh day."

Korg laughed lightly, but his smile was genuine and warm. "Sama, when you go to face the Ancient Ones, and they ask who you will have as Eternal Mate, I only pray the name that springs from your lips will be Korg."

Sama smiled again, and this time she didn't have to force it. "Husband, I can give my answer now. When the Ancient Ones ask, I will say that I choose Korg 'en Terdra, War Chief of Chun, greatest hunter in the Norkaan Mountains and fiercest warrior in Arangar."

Korg's eyes lightened and moistened; then he kissed Sama again before leaving the hut. Kavi was close behind. As the door shut tightly, Sama released her tears; they flowed rapidly and freely. She wept and sobbed and heaved her shoulders, for she knew she would never again see Korg or Kavi. Not until the Day of Naming when she faced the Ancient Ones.

But that won't be long. We will all die soon. Soon we will all see the Ancient Ones.

KORG AND KAVI walked in near silence for five days, the bitter cold making it easier to remain quiet; it was an effort to breathe, let alone talk. They had forsaken all the traveled trails—the ones that led to the old hunting grounds—opting instead for a trail that rose upward toward the crest of the peak.

Korg pointed toward a large evergreen with long-reaching boughs spreading from its trunk. "We should rest here and get warm."

Kavi ducked under the branches and tucked himself against the trunk where it offered the most protection. He pulled the fur-covered hood from his head and looked to his father. "What is it? You look worried."

"You knew we were going into the Paaren?"

Kavi lowered his eyes and nodded. "All the legends speak of game in abundance in the Paaren, and since we have searched everywhere else, I assumed the rest."

"The legends also speak of demons and death. They speak of no one ever returning. Did you know that as well?" Korg slapped his son's leg lightly, a reassuring gesture. "I won't be unhappy if you choose to stay. No one would question your honor, and—"

"I know, father, it would save mother many tears also. But I intend to return, not die."

They were both silent, lost in the moment. "If no one has ever returned," Kavi said. "How do we know the game is abundant? If none have ever come back, how do we know that demons and death await us? I say they are stories meant to frighten people." Kavi looked into his father's eyes. "Besides, without food, hunger will take us. Does it matter how we die?"

Korg beamed with pride. "You will make a great war chief, my son. The greatest Chun war chief that Arangar has ever seen."

The cold got worse as they climbed higher along a path that continued to narrow until they could only advance by turning sideways and creeping along the sheer cliffs behind them. Kavi looked down. Far below, he could see the tops of trees that earlier in the day he had strained to look up to. He shivered.

"Kavi," Korg called out loudly, his voice straining to be heard over the roar of the wind. "Kavi, hold onto the wall. Take your gloves off to get a better grip. The wind will blow us off if we don't hold fast. Be strong. We only have a short distance to go."

Kavi knew the legends, all in the Chun villages knew the legends of the Paaren. Its entrance was said to lie at the top of the peak, but what they should look for or where no one knew. Kavi looked ahead. Anything was better than staring down. There were large trees where the narrow ledge opened to a plateau. Solid footing was only a few steps away.

Korg removed his gloves, then took two steps. Kavi carefully removed his gloves and crept onward, each step taken with care. He slid his hand along the wall to find a crack, then slid his feet along afterward. The wind blew hard, threatening to tear them from the ledge, but Korg and Kavi pressed their backs against the wall, holding on for their lives.

Kavi noted where Korg placed his hands and feet so that he could duplicate the moves. Suddenly, his father's eyes went wide in disbelief. Then Korg fell backward *into* the rock wall of the cliff.

Korg clutched at the crevice with his hand, desperately trying to stop his fall. Kavi grabbed Korg's arm. Miraculously, he was able to maintain balance but only briefly. Korg's momentum was too much, and Kavi followed him into the sheer cliff, both of them screaming as they tumbled through darkness.

A NEW PATH

*R*ahg stepped lightly along the marble floor of the corridor trying his best not to disturb anyone's sleep. *I'll not be the rooster this day,* he thought, recalling the lashing he had received from Camissa for making too much noise the last time. He sneaked past Aenaila's room, then Tobias's, and then a room containing some of the temple's treasures. It suddenly struck him that there were no guards. *Guards weren't needed in Twin Forks either,* he thought, and sad memories flooded his mind as he dreamt of better days and better nights.

A spark of envy itched under his skin, but more than envy lit the fire —Rahg was afraid. Afraid of what he must do, and of what awaited him. It seemed as if so much time had passed, and yet, only last winter he had celebrated Wish Day in Twin Forks with Darstan and Magmar.

Thoughts of his father haunted him when he wasn't worrying over assassins or immortals. How he wished he could see him just one more time. Hear his voice—even if it was to yell. But that part of his life was gone, and on this Wish Day he'd have no one to celebrate with. Not even Darstan.

The sound of his boots clicked noisily on the marble floor, just when he thought he had sneaked safely past everyone's room, and as he hurried to make the turn a door cracked open.

"It's early for a stroll. Anything wrong?" Wisp stepped silently into the hall and closed the door behind him. The whisper of his voice seemed to carry only as far as Rahg's ears. Wisp had a knack for that, along with his other talents.

"Nothing wrong. Just thought I'd get some air." As Rahg wondered how Wisp had heard him, he felt a presence behind him and spun to see Rhaven.

"It's difficult to sleep with someone stomping through the corridors."

Rahg ignored the remark. He had the feeling that no matter how quiet he'd been the two of them would have heard. "I couldn't sleep so I thought I'd take a walk by the sea. I want to see the ship before we sail."

"I'd rather ride than sail a ship again," Rhaven said. "I feel ill at ease on the sea, like being caught without a weapon."

Rahg was surprised; he had never heard Rhaven mention being uncomfortable. "It can't be as bad as it was coming here. Sennar said that was the worst he's ever seen, and even Malakai thought we'd die." Rahg paused for thought. "I imagine it has to be better than that."

Rhaven nodded. "I brought Marchall back from Genda. They took good care of him."

The smile brightened Rahg's face from ear to ear. "You brought Marchall? Where is he? I can't wait to see him."

"He'll wait until we get through."

"Will we be able to take him on the ship?"

"The captain will accommodate us," Rhaven said with certainty. "I already informed Shulan J'en Kar. I'll not be sailing without Argus."

Rahg smiled. He'd have given a silver crown to have heard that conversation. "I'll be glad to see Marchall again. It won't feel so strange in this new land if I'm riding him." Rahg's thoughts started to drift. It never took much to cause his mind to roam. "I wonder what the people are like in Arangar?"

"The people will be like the land," Rhaven said. "Once you know the land, you'll know the people. It's the land that makes the person."

Rahg nodded but wondered what fiery inferno sired Rhaven. *Sethia itself couldn't produce men as hard as him.* "It will be interesting to see," Rahg said, and departed for the dock. "Kender, I'll see you before we leave. I want to make sure you and Aenaila keep Darstan out of trouble."

"It's you we had to come rescue," Wisp said. "I had only begun to see what Khatara had to offer when Darstan insisted we come find you." Wisp smiled. "But Khatara will always have rich merchants waiting for me."

"Then I'll see you tonight," Rahg said, and continued his walk toward the dock.

The streets of Entiria were wide, and clean, and organized. Perhaps too organized. All streets emanated from the temple, branching off in all directions, then spreading out again in a methodical fashion.

Rahg thought he would grow tired of it after a while. A nice, curvy street that seemed to go nowhere, like some in Pomanda, or a narrow dead-end alley like so many in Sykor, would have made him feel more comfortable. Or perhaps it was just that his stay here was going to be so short, when he wished it could last longer. Perhaps that was at the root of it. *Gods, but I hope this ends soon,* he thought, and turned onto the street that led to the ship.

The ship was big, bigger than the Sea Skate, with more masts and sails than any Rahg had seen in Genda. If nothing else, he'd feel more comfortable on a larger ship. Feel safer.

Men were already at work loading cargo aboard and checking planks and sails. They all seemed professional enough, though anyone who'd sailed twice could have fooled Rahg with what little he knew. Although it would take a lot from a captain to make him forget Sennar. Much as he'd disliked Sennar at first, he liked him as much now. The voyage to Entiria had been one of constant danger, and if it hadn't been for the gnarly old captain, they would have never made it.

"Check your numbers, seaman. It won't do to be halfway to Arangar and run short of food."

All sea captains must yell like that, Rahg assumed, and smiled at the man standing on the dock issuing orders. The man seemed young to be a captain, but then, most would seem that way after sailing with Sennar.

"Good morning, sir," Rahg said, and extended his hand to greet the man. "I'm Rahgnar Fal-Thera. I wanted to see the ship before we sailed."

Rahg studied the ship from fore to aft. The name of the ship was "Destiny;" he had seen it carved from the wood, and wondered if the name had been chosen before or after they knew of him. Or had it been waiting here all along? Things like that seemed to happen a lot lately. "It's a big ship, Captain. Have you sailed it much?"

The captain hadn't stopped except for a cursory glance since Rahg arrived. At first, Rahg took it for him being busy, but now his manners bordered on being rude.

"I know who you are, lad, but I'm tending my ship right now. And unless you want to go hungry at sea you'd be wise to let me finish. I'm not a man that's good with numbers, so I must be careful." The captain returned to his duties, checking everything that went on board and crossing it off as it did. "Don't know why they picked me to go," he muttered, shaking his head side to side. "Half a dozen men better suited."

"I want to go aboard, Captain. Is that all right?" The man was doing nothing to instill confidence.

"No. It's not all right, lad. Nobody boards my ship until we're ready to sail. I can't be disturbed."

Captain Katsu shook his head vigorously. "You'll have plenty of time to see the ship. More than enough time." He looked up from his work, meeting Rahg's gaze with his own. "You might be somebody special to the folks at the temple but to me you're just a passenger. And you're the reason my son won't be seeing me for many moons."

Captain Katsu's gaze became a glare. "Don't expect anything from me. I'll do my duty; do as I'm told, but I'll not do more." The man stared at the chart of goods again. "How many barrels of cheese, Ned?"

The captain scribbled a number next to a line on his chart. "I don't mean to be harsh, lad, but it's something easy to be bitter about, so you best be off now. As I said, I don't keep good track of things when I'm distracted."

Rahg nodded. He thought about saying good bye but simply turned to leave, wishing it was Sennar who commanded the ship.

From the corner of his eye, Captain Katsu saw the dejected look on Rahg's face, and a pang of guilt pricked at his heart. "Halt, men! Enjoy the sun or a mug of khaffe."

Katsu hollered to catch Rahg's attention. "Lad, my words weren't meant to be harsh. It's just that I can get that way at times. I had no mind to send you off with the bitters. And don't fret over this journey. It's one I could make in my sleep. It's not the journey that worries me —it's what you've got to do."

Rahg turned to face the captain. "I was hoping to find some comfort here, Captain. I don't like to say it, but I'm afraid."

Katsu shook his head in sympathy. "I know you are, lad. Fear's sunk a hook or two in me as well."

Rahg noted the somber expression. It was not the response he had hoped for. He hated the thought of putting to sea again at all, let alone with a captain who was afraid. Old Sennar might have been half crazed but at least he wasn't afraid, or if he was, he never let on. Rahg had hoped to be somehow relieved after seeing the vessel that would carry them, now he found himself more upset than when he came, and he just wanted to get out of there. "How long is the trip, Captain?"

Katsu tugged on a beard that wasn't there.

He must have had whiskers once, Rahg thought.

Katsu recalled another conversation he had recently and had to force himself from trembling. It wouldn't do to disappoint that one. Not her.

"If the winds are favorable—and they should be—we'll reach land before Ranalla comes full turn." The worried look remained on Katsu's face. "After that, lad, it's up to you. I'm a seaman. It's my duty to get you to Arangar, but then you'll have to rely on your wits or those who travel with you."

Rahg nodded, but he wasn't paying attention.

"Don't blame you for being afraid, lad. It doesn't sit well with me either. But you'll have my prayers. You'll have at least that. I don't know your beliefs, and I'm not the kind to meddle in another's affairs, but it couldn't hurt to talk to the shera no matter what beliefs you hold. He's a man that's listened to a lot of woes and has helped more than he's hurt. Go see him. He's taken the fright from my mind a time or two."

The captain's words hit a note with Rahg, and he brightened a little. "I think I will, Captain Katsu. The last time we met, I left many questions unanswered."

Katsu's raised voice stopped Rahg even as he hurried off in the direction of the temple. "Say a word to those you worship. They won't mind if it's in a different temple. Don't forget, lad, 'cause I have a feeling that your words might mean more than others, and you'll likely have need of all the blessings you can get before this journey's over."

THE STEPS LEADING to the temple had suffered no damage from Iazzo's Lightning. Rahg stared at the shattered buildings surrounding the temple, and he wondered anew why the obelisk showed no scars; he had seen the Lightning hit it.

Perhaps their gods protect it. Something sure did.

The wide, sweeping steps fell quickly to Rahg's energetic climb. He was anxious about another discussion with the shera, but he wouldn't leave with his mind so cluttered and worried, and he was supposed to leave tomorrow. The heartbeats came closer together as he approached the massive doors guarding the entrance, and the echoes of his footsteps against the marble floors accelerated as well.

The shera sat on the floor in the center of the circle just as he had the first time Rahg met with him. The hem of the black robe was ringed with dust, just as it had been then. *Was he expecting me?*

Rahg quickly discounted the notion. No one knew he was going there. He hadn't known himself until Captain Katsu suggested it. "Good morning, Shera." Rahg's voice boomed in the vast chamber. He wished he hadn't talked so loud. Somehow, it didn't seem right.

The shera raised his head, then bowed. "It is a fine day, Rahgnar Fal-Thera. I am pleased you have decided to visit." His hands spread in a gesture inviting Rahg to sit and join him.

Rahg worried over how to deal with the shera and elected to be honest and direct. "I need answers, Shera. There is much on my mind that I think you could help me with, but I don't want you to spit out riddles and prophecies to every question I ask."

Rahg already rued his temper, but wouldn't draw it back now. "I don't wish to appear ungrateful, but I don't have much time. We're leaving tomorrow, and there are things I need to know."

"There is much we all need to know. And as to your concern about time, it is a worry we all share. The Awakening is near."

Rahg cursed and kicked his foot at the marble floor. "There you go again with the riddles." Anger raised his voice. "I know nothing of this Awakening, and I don't care. I know nothing about the Messenger, or the Fate Sealer, or anything else you can quote me from these legends of yours."

He struggled to control himself. "I just want to know what I have to do and why. Then I'll leave your land and never return."

Rahg looked like a boy who had lost his way. "Are you certain, Shera? Are you sure there couldn't be some mistake?"

The shera's face could not have grown any more somber. "We have made no error. I wish I could tell you differently, but I cannot. I am not one to paint a dark sky blue. All of the signs are here, and now you have come. You must go to Arangar, and you must enter the Paaren. The Amulet will lead you to where you must go. Learn to trust it."

Rahg remembered the time when he was only five years old, and Magmar had taken him to the big pond south of town. They rowed to the deepest part, and Magmar told him to jump in and swim back to shore. The memory still frightened him but not nearly as much as this did. "How can I fight this Messenger? Who is the Fate Sealer, and what is the Awakening?" Rahg screamed at the shera in frustration.

The shera's face revealed no hint of a smile or even a congenial expression. "I know that these things are strange to you now, but you will become intimately familiar with them. Before your journey is finished, you will know each name like a brother."

"Suppose this Messenger has powers? Suppose he has Fire? What will I do then?"

"You fought Iazzo."

"Yes, I fought Iazzo, but I didn't win. He would have killed us all if not for Aentarra." Rahg's voice grew dark. "Your precious city would be in flames right now if not for her. I have no doubt of that."

Rahg's look changed to confusion. "But I can't rely on Aentarra or Mikkellana to be there the next time. I don't even know if I want them there."

The shera's look conveyed sympathy. "There are many ways to fight fire, Rahg. You do not need fire to do it. A bundle of straw will stop an arrow shot from the strongest bow."

Rahg nodded, but he wasn't listening. "All I can do is make a shield, and not even a strong one. Iazzo could have broken mine anytime he wanted." He cursed as he spun to leave. "Don't blame me if he gets out. I asked for help. I hope Lukaan takes you to the grave before I die. Then you'll wish you had helped me when you could."

THE SHERA SAT and watched as Rahg stormed out of the chamber. He watched until the doors closed behind him and then he prayed. "If he is the one, God, then protect him from harm. Drape your Light around him and hide him from the evil. But if he is not the one we have waited for, if he is indeed the Messenger, then please be gentle when you kill him. He is but an innocent lamb cast out among the wolves.

DEPARTURE

*D*arstan slapped his hand against the closed door. "What is so important, Aenaila? Tell me why I must go with you. Or even tell me what it is you want me to do."

Darstan paused, struggling to come to grips with the decision. He wanted to go with Rahg, but he had given his word to Aenaila, and he didn't give his word lightly.

"Are you in danger? Is someone after you?" Frustration began to show. "Give me one reason why I shouldn't go with Rahg. He's my brother, and he's in trouble." Darstan cursed and hit the door with his closed fist. "The whole world is in trouble, Aenaila. That's why you need to give me a reason. You must!"

Shadows darkened Aenaila's emerald green eyes as she held Darstan's gaze, and the silence built tension. "Your word, Darstan; that is reason enough. Or do you place so little value on your word?"

Darstan fought to control his temper. "Aenaila, this is not about my word. This is about Rahg, and prophecies, and the Messenger—"

"The world does not revolve around Rahgnar Fal–Thera." Aenaila's response seemed cold.

Hot blood percolated in Darstan's veins, and restraint almost eluded him. "I have given my word, so I'll go but just tell me why." His patience couldn't wait through the silence. "You don't have to answer, but I would like you to. I'll go with you either way so just tell me."

WISP HAD BEEN KEENLY OBSERVING their reactions and, for a moment, he thought Aenaila might respond. Her lips started to form a word, but then she stopped.

She straightened her clothes and looked into Darstan's eyes. "As you were so kind to mention, I owe you no response. I have your word, and I trust you will honor it. And now I plan to retire for the evening as we leave at first light."

After Aenaila had gone safely from earshot, Adju said, "She is a good lady, Master Darstan. Everyone in Khatara knows her as good."

"I know that, Adju, but it doesn't explain why we have to go with her now. Whatever favor she wants, I could do after helping Rahg."

Wisp had an answer for everything. "If not for Aenaila we would never have made it here; in fact, we might even be rotting in a dungeon in Jattan-Kir waiting for the emperor to devise a fitting torture."

"Or staked to the sands of the Kurabi so the laughing wolves could eat us. The Emperor likes to do that to people, Master Kender. Sometimes he even watches." Adju was quick to add his opinion to any conversation.

laughing wolf

Wisp laughed. "Those tales are meant to frighten little thieves, Adju. But the dungeons are enough to deter me, and I have no doubt that some of us, or even all of us, would be there now if not for Aenaila."

Adju frowned. "I have heard them, Master Kender. One night I stole a merchant's purse, and his guards came after me. I ran all through the city but could not get away from them. Soon they had many men looking for me, so I hid in the desert. All night I hid under the brush near the Samukett. It is a place of worship, and no one is allowed there after dark, so I thought I would be safe. During the middle of the night, I heard the laughing wolves."

Adju's face twisted as he retold the story. "They came closer and closer. There were many of them. It sounded like they were laughing because they were going to eat me." Adju looked from Wisp to Darstan as he repeated the experience. "I got so frightened I ran back to Khatara. I did not care if the guards caught me, Master Kender. I thought it would be better to lose a finger than to have the laughing wolves take me."

DARSTAN DIDN'T laugh at Adju's story even though he wanted to. The little thief obviously believed it. But they both had it right, if not for Aenaila he would never have reached Entiria; he would still be in Khatara, or in a dungeon, or staked to the Kurabi waiting for the laughing wolves. Darstan let the chuckle stay hidden. "All right, I'll not ask her any more questions, and I won't argue. We'll leave at first light."

"Can't we go some other way, Master Kender? I don't like that thing she does. It scares me."

"There's no other way to get back. Besides, if you think the laughing wolves are bad, you should see what the sea hides at night. There are things much worse."

Adju took Wisp's hand. The mention of more deadly things in the sea seemed to have eliminated his thoughts about other means of transport. "Let's go to bed, Master Kender. I will just have to keep my eyes closed when she does it. Perhaps then it won't be so bad."

DARSTAN AWOKE EARLY and went to Rahg's room. He found Rahg in the hall speaking with Rhaven, Tobias, and Wisp.

Rahg greeted Darstan with a big hug. "Dar, it's good to see you smiling. Are you ready to leave? Kender said you'll be going to Genda."

Darstan's smile remained, but he almost teared. "I wish I could go with you. I don't want you facing this alone."

"Alone!" Rahg laughed. "I've got enough people going with me to stop an army." Rahg sighed. "But I will miss you, Dar. Don't worry though; we'll get this over with soon enough."

Darstan gave Rahg another hug. He squeezed hard and kept the tears from coming. "You do that, Rahg. And take care of Tobias; he seems to be losing more hair."

Tobias laughed as he embraced Darstan. "Don't let Kender turn you into a thief, lad. I feel like I half raised you, and I don't want to have to call you a thief."

Wisp had followed Darstan. He reached over to shake everyone's hand. "Tobias I could no more make him a thief than you could grow hair."

Tobias nearly choked on the smoke from his pipe. "All right, lad. All right. Just take good care of him."

Darstan grasped Rhaven's hand and smiled. "Thanks for everything. You not only saved my life a few times, but you've taught me a lot as well. I'm honored to call you a friend."

Rhaven nodded. "You have become a warrior on your own, Darstan. Warriors are born. I only helped bring out the talent that was there. Have no worry though, we will meet again. All of us."

"Say hello to Takar, thief." Rhaven called to Wisp, who was already making his way down the hall.

"I will," Wisp said. "I imagine when we finish this business with Aenaila, we'll have to come to your rescue again."

They all laughed as Darstan and Wisp departed.

"ARE YOU READY, Aenaila? We should be going."

"I'm near ready. Be patient."

"Are you rested enough?" Wisp asked.

"I could use more rest, but I prefer we leave before Adju gets into any more trouble. Where will be going in Genda?"

"There is a place by some warehouses, and since it will be night in Genda, we should go unnoticed."

Aenaila gathered a few belongings in a sack and announced she was ready. "Adju, are you prepared?"

"Yes, Mistress Aenaila."

"Good, and don't worry, nothing will harm you." She held her hands out to join with the others. "Kender Darnell, form the image."

THE STREET alongside the warehouse was deserted and dark. No one saw them arrive. Darstan grabbed Aenaila's arm to support her as she nearly collapsed.

alley

"Are you all right?" Wisp asked.

"Yes," she gasped, "just tired. But I don't understand why. This isn't nearly as far as Khatara, and I had Kella and Evin with us when we Shifted from there to Entiria."

"Then it's a good thing we didn't try Khatara again," Wisp said, trying to make light of it. "Don't worry, Aenaila; we will get a room so you can rest."

"Gods," Darstan cursed. "I have no money for a room. Do you?"

Wisp tossed a pouch to Darstan, who emptied the contents into his hand and gasped. "Gods Blood! Where did you get all this gold?"

Wisp laughed. "I relieved a finely dressed, rather plump gentleman who was on his way to the temple in Sunnara. Most likely he intended to give it to his gods, but I determined our need to be greater."

Darstan laughed again. "And you berated poor Adju for doing the same thing."

Adju looked indignant. "Master Kender, I thought you said not to steal from the people in Entiria."

"This was an emergency. Now help Aenaila. Darstan, give me the gold, and I'll secure us some comfortable rooms in a nice quiet inn."

CAMISSA WANTED to make the rounds and show her appreciation. "The Entirians have lost many lives, Rahg. Many women have lost children or husbands, and many children have lost fathers. It's only right that we thank them."

Rahg nodded. The Entirians had suffered much. "Even though they professed to be people of peace, they fought bravely. No soldier could have done better."

"I want to see Sennar again too. Despite his gruff demeanor, I grew to like the gnarly old goat. The voyage to Arangar won't be the same without him. I only hope the new captain proves to be as adept."

She found Sennar in the courtyard with some of his men. The old tar had worn a smile since Mikkellana healed him and fixed his face. "Good morrow, Captain Sennar. It's another fine day."

"Everyday's a fine one, lass. The sun is always shinin' somewhere." Sennar laughed. "Though this fine place seems to have a healthy climate for a man like me. I might stay awhile."

Camissa kissed his cheek. "What of your men, Captain? Don't they want to go back to Genda?"

"Some do," Sennar said. "But I might raise a new crew and come back. Don't be surprised if you return here to find Ol' Crazy sittin' in the sun, eatin' fresh fruit, and drinkin' good wine."

Camissa laughed. "You'd no sooner quit the sea than the sea would dry up. You were born a seaman, and you'll likely die a seaman.".

She stared at his face and marveled at the healing Mikkellana had done. His face was no longer a bunched up mass of scarred flesh, and his hand had become useful again. It gave her something to look forward to—not that she could ever achieve that level of proficiency, the wonders of an immortal—but she could improve on what she did know, and that might let her heal minor burns or mend a broken bone. Already she could sense a strong growth in her powers of sensing and probing, and the more she used them, the stronger they grew.

When she lived in Sykor she had shied away from using powers, but since they had gone on the road, she had trained herself to be more alert, more aware of what was going on around them, and as a result, her powers had grown.

Each new moon brought hidden talents or abilities she had not known were there, subtle little things like increased sensitivity to peoples' thoughts, or a new way of looking at things. One of the most important discoveries was what she now called "Suggestion." She discovered if she formed a thought, then sent that thought out much like she would a probe, that she could touch the mind of someone with that thought and influence their decision.

Perhaps only on little things, things that the person was undecided on, but in the future she might be able to change someone's mind entirely.

That would be a power to reckon with. I must practice.

Camissa said farewell to Sennar and his men and wished them good fortune in their endeavors.

"Don't waste a thought on us, lass. Ol' Crazy will be fine. It's you and yours I'm worried about. I'd come with ya', if I didn't have to take the crew back to Genda. But the good Lady Mikkellana said there'd be things I could do, so I'll wait for her command." Sennar squeezed her tightly. "You keep safe, lass, and take care of Rahg. I do believe he'll need you to help him."

Camissa smiled. "Don't worry, I'll keep a rein on him," she said, then bade Sennar a good trip and made her way toward the temple to find the shera. During her earlier meeting, she had gotten "itches," small feelings of uncomfortableness from the shera. It was nothing drastic, but every time Rahg's name was mentioned the shera reacted slightly, and she intended to discover why. She found the shera in the temple at his prayers. He readily agreed to see her.

"What is it, my dear?"

"That is precisely my question, Shera. What is it? In our earlier conversation I noticed that every time we mentioned Rahgnar's name or the journey, you had an uncomfortable look about you. What caused it?"

The look on the shera's face was one of shock, more than uncomfortableness. His eyes narrowed, and he focused intently on Camissa. "I do not claim to be without fault and do not claim to know all, but I have lived to see the snow fall on Mount Sharmand for more than fifty winters, and I have felt the summer heat for as many. I have told countless mothers that their children were born still and have comforted brothers, sisters, and wives when the Ancient Ones called their loved ones to the next world. And I have done this without so much as a shift of the eye. How is it that you can tell a prickle under my skin?"

Camissa smiled warmly. It is not so difficult, Shera, not when I can sense other minds."

The shera relaxed. "Now I see why the Ancient Ones have blessed Rahg with you for a companion; you will prove to be invaluable on this journey."

Camissa nodded her acceptance of his compliment. "My question, Shera, is why are you uncomfortable." The shera hesitated too long.

"There is something about him, Camissa, something about the mission. I cannot find words to explain my feelings, but it is there."

Then I will take special care to watch out, Shera and you may be assured that we will watch out for him."

The shera bowed again. "Does the warrior possess powers?"

Camissa's lips didn't move for a long time. "I would be in haste if I said no. He doesn't have powers in the way you are thinking, not like myself or Rahg, but his abilities are so far beyond the ordinary man that I would say his powers are genuine. He is more than a warrior. Much more."

A NEW MISSION

Sethia

Ghruehne stormed through the narrow streets of Sethia, boots pounding paving stones ground smooth from centuries of wear. Ancient houses rose to three or four levels, their once proud coat of stucco splintered from dry winters and parched summers. Coined corners stood stout, embracing windows that graced the outside walls. Roof tiles baked under the midday sun, and, from the streets below, they looked like the upturned leaves of the yanta plant, pleading for a drop of moisture.

A bead of sweat rolled down Ghruehne's cheek, halting as it edged against the ridge on his face. He rubbed the moisture into his cheek as if it would help smooth the scar—a scar older than these ancient houses. The blemish stretched from ear to eye along a path that resembled a crooked road, and though it had once cut to the bone, it was not nearly as deep as the gouge left on his mind. It was a gift from Antar during the Wars of Light—a gift Ghruehne intended to repay, even if it had to be to Antar's daughters.

He turned the corner into a plaza that once bustled with merchants and craftsmen from countries as far away as Khatara. He imagined the voices of the women as they shopped for daily needs and chatted with friends, and he pictured the children laughing as they splashed in fountains gushing with fresh water. Now the fountains were dry, and Ghruehne's footsteps echoed through an empty square. He once had seven worlds to roam; now all he had was Sethia.

One more reason to kill Antar's daughters.

He focused on the mission. "Bring me the village boys" Lukaan had said. "Preferably alive."

I'll bring them all right. But they'll be dead, both of them.

Ghruehne pushed open the door to a temple long since abandoned. Half the roof was gone, and the back walls had fallen to one of Lukaan's rages, but it still served a holy purpose. Ligarns gathered here to practice their skills and, if rumors were to be believed, to chant prayers to long-forgotten gods. They came every day to wait for a mission like priests seeking salvation.

The Ligarns stood silent, holding swords, knives, and other weapons which they sheathed when Ghruehne entered, but none of them showed fear. It irked Ghruehne that they showed no fear. All mortals should fear him.

"Summon Jen Pal at once."

One of the Ligarns nodded and went to the rear of the building.

Jen Pal returned, stepping into the room on soft leather boots tucked under brown pants. Cherry-black eyes sat deep in his face surrounded by skin as dark as chocolate.

Silent as a snake, he made his way toward Ghruehne across a floor strewn with rubble and traps, never once taking his eyes from the Banished One. He took the final step, then bowed, though it was merely a nod in disguise.

The lack of respect irked Ghruehne all the more. *How I would love to kill them all. Insolent dogs.*

Blood dripped from a long gash that raced across Jen Pal's gut from rib to rib. "I see practice has been harsh, Jen Pal."

"Shatir."

Ghruehne nodded. "I think she may be joining you."

"If you had told us you were coming, we would have made preparations to make you comfortable."

There it was again. Jen Pal's voice dripped with arrogance, and there was the insolence of no honorific. His confidence stuck in Ghruehne's side like a thorn, but there was little Ghruehne could do about it; the Ligarns were Lukaan's favorites. In all these years, they had never failed Lukaan. And the gods had never made better assassins.

A thin smile cracked Jen Pal's face. "I presume you have a mission for us... My Lord."

Ghruehne fumed, fists balled together, teeth ground tightly. "An important one."

All the Ligarns twitched in anticipation, their gazes riveted on Ghruehne, their ears pricked to catch his next words.

"There is a boy from the mountain village of Kamnor. His name is Rahgnar Fal-Thera."

They nodded.

"He and his brother are to be brought here. If they are dead, the Master will be pleased. If they are alive, he will be more pleased."

The last statement seemed to dishearten them. Frowns replaced smiles on several of their faces.

"Do not be lulled to sleep by this assignment. The village boys travel with a small band of warriors. Bold, dangerous warriors. And never forget that the Master will be watching. Do not fail. Do not dare fail." Ghruehne paused to let them contemplate. Some smiled. Some licked their uniformly thin lips.

"We are honored by this chance to be raised before the Master," Jen Pal said and bowed low. No mockery showed in his actions. "May we know the history of our prey, My Lord, so that we can honor them when the mission is over?"

"Only the Master knows that."

Jen Pal bowed even lower. "I shall select a karn at once."

"No, I'll select the ones to go. This mission is my responsibility. If it fails..."

Jen Pal did not smile, and Ghruehne knew why. "Have no concern, Jen Pal. You will be one of them. I will select the others."

JEN PAL SIGNALED for the others to join him, then he stepped back, observing.

Ghruehne's cold-eyed stare swept the room before settling on Messa, his gaze lingering too long. Messa met him look for look until the sweat forming on the Ligarn's head forced him to cede.

Ligarns seldom collapsed under pressure, but Ghruehne was a Banished One, and his quick and unpredictable temper was legendary. Stories told of him killing people for so little as a suspicious glance or a failure to bow in respect.

Shame splashed across Messa's face as he dropped his eyes, eliciting a cruel smile from Ghruehne. "Messa will not be joining us, Jen Pal."

Jen Pal felt the sorrow of his friend. They had trained together since childhood and had remained close through the endless summers of Sethia. When Ghruehne turned his head, Jen Pal cast a quick, consoling glance to Messa; he knew what shame would force him to do.

Die well, my friend, and wait for me at the Gates of the Sun. May the Ancient Ones guard your soul.

Ghruehne's discerning gaze scanned the Ligarns again. He possessed an unusual talent for detecting doubt or fear. If Ghruehne had ever known mercy, he forgot it long ago. Soon he narrowed the decision to six, from which he must select three.

"There are twenty captives," Ghruehne said. "Four are Sykoran guards, and the others are also accomplished fighters. To offer a challenge, it will be one Ligarn against three or four of the warriors." He searched for signs of weakness or expressions of fear.

"We will do with less if My Lord wishes," Jen Pal said.

Ghruehne shook his head. "I will decide based on how the kills are conducted." The Banished One started to leave then spun around to face them again. "One final thought. There is one who travels with the village boy and provides him protection. He is said to be dangerous."

All of the Ligarns smiled. Some laughed.

"The frail ones call him Rhaven."

Jen Pal did not recognize the name.

Ghruehne leaned toward them and whispered. "You know him as Black Death."

The laughter vanished. The room fell quiet. The smiles disappeared. Ghruehne dangled the name in front of them like fresh meat. "Black Death," he said louder. "Black Death is the boy's protector."

The name rolled around the room on anxious whispers, dancing from one set of lips to the next. Drool dripped from Jen Pal's mouth. "Black Death," he whispered. *Black Death.*

A LONG VOYAGE

Captain Katsu directed the final loading of the Destiny from dockside. Dawn had just broken in a new day, and from the looks of it, it would be another fine one.

Rahg stood to the side with Rhaven, Tobias, and Camissa. Argus and Marchall seemed even more impatient than Rahg, though it had eased his mind when Kella showed up on their way to the ship. She would not only be a comfort but a formidable ally when trouble started, and he had no doubt that they would encounter their share of trouble. "I'm glad Kella came even though I'd have preferred to have Darstan."

"Darstan wanted to come, I could tell, but don't let it bother you. It was nice to see two brothers who are so close." Rhaven's spirits had lifted since Kella came.

Camissa stood between Rahg and Rhaven and watched as they fawned over Kella. She stooped to hug the vargel. "I sure hope you appreciate this attention, Kella. Perhaps I should disappear once in a while. Someone might pay me some mind if I did."

Tobias coughed out a billow of smoke. "I do believe that remark was directed at you, lad."

Rahg's face reddened. "I'm going to see if we can board yet."

THEY HAD ONLY BEEN out to sea for half the morning, and the tension on deck was already tight. Captain Katsu's scornful look aimed at Rhaven, though he quickly turned when Rhaven's gaze fell his way. It wouldn't do to have that one turned against him at the beginning of a voyage. Katsu hadn't wanted to bring the horses on board, but Rhaven had talked to the Shulan and convinced him that they needed to come. Katsu thought Rhaven's horse would kill half his men when they tried to get him below deck, then the black-cloaked demon calmed him down.

The voyage promised to be bad enough by itself, let alone having those two aboard. And that lad, with powers... The visit he'd had from Aentarra came to mind, and Katsu shivered. He looked around warily, afraid she might yet be lurking about. You could never tell what one with powers might be able to do. She might even be able to read his mind. The thought of that stifled further speculation.

He had not wanted this journey. Had not even wanted the prophecy to come true. Now he was leading it and carting these people off to Arangar and lands where nobody had any business going, trying to find things that shouldn't be talked about. He cast another glance at Rhaven, not a scornful one, but his gaze held some animosity. "It'll be you that'll have to feed that beast. I'll not be givin' orders for my men to go near it."

Rhaven held his gaze until the captain turned away. He never liked sea captains; in fact, he cared less for them than he did captains in the guard or force commanders. And he liked ships even less. The sea was no place for a man to be.

Camissa approached from behind. "Has Argus ever been on a ship before?" She thought she had surprised Rhaven, but she couldn't tell from his expression.

"Once."

"Was it a long voyage?"

"All voyages on ships are long. The sooner my feet touch ground, the better I'll be."

"Have you noticed that Tobias seems jittery?" Camissa asked. "Unusual for someone born in Genda."

Rhaven showed the first signs of interest since Camissa addressed him. "Have you sensed something?"

She hesitated. Pangs of guilt tugged at her conscience whenever she probed a friend's mind. She had sworn early in life not to do that, but lately she found herself doing it almost daily, and always in the name of duty. It had to be done. But duty didn't stop the guilt or ease the discomfort.

"There's fear there. Fear where there shouldn't be, not for a man raised in Genda. I haven't felt fear at any other time on our journey except when we left for Entiria. Why would he be afraid of ships and sailing? I purposefully checked before the battle with Iazzo. He was afraid, but not like this. What could make him fear the sea more than he does a Banished One?"

Rhaven thought for a while. "I don't know, but I intend to find out."

Panic struck her. "No! He mustn't know what I've done. He can't know I've read his mind." Camissa's face took on the same desperation as her words. "I... I don't even feel good about doing this myself. I don't want to do it, but I must. And you are the only one I trust with this knowledge. Please, Rhaven, don't tell him." She didn't need to probe to see the tension ripping at Rhaven's insides.

"So be it. He'll not hear it from me." Rhaven's voice turned colder. "But tell me if you sense anything else. If the fear takes a turn for the worse, or if you sense anything unusual in anyone else." Rhaven paused. "And above all, keep a sharp sense on Rahg. If anything at all comes about, let me know. Remember what the Shera said. He has powers, and he's dangerous. I know you have feelings for him, but this goes far beyond a friend's trust—or even love."

~

KATSU STOOD with several members of the crew, and though they had work to keep them busy, he focused on Rhaven or Rahg continually. "Pay heed to your work, men. It's my duty to worry about our guests."

"Guests!" the man fixing a sail spat disgustedly. "My work's gettin' done, Captain, but I'm not at ease with that one around. None of us are. We saw the way he wielded that sword during the battle."

"He doesn't have powers," another said. "It's the one with powers that bothers me. He's strong. I couldn't see the shield they say he makes, but I saw the effect. He held off the attack of half a hundred men. Weren't even men—Victas and Wolfen."

The first man smirked. "Oxen are strong, too, but a wolf scares me more. That one with the sword is crazed."

Katsu scoffed. "Just keep to the duties, men. I'll do the worryin'." He moved to his quarters to finish some charts, and as the door to his cabin shut tight, he sighed and turned to get his instruments.

"So busy already, Captain?"

He froze at the sound of her voice, sweat beading quickly on his forehead, and his body trembling.

"Have faith, Captain. I'm not here to harm you. If I were, you would even now be pleading for your life. But I can see that you are not a man who can guard his emotions well. Perhaps I'll give you something to help you along. It would not do for that little girl to be poking around inside your head only to discover my plans. I have no doubt that on such a lengthy sea voyage she would take advantage of it on numerous occasions. Her curiosity knows no bounds, and she lacks all sense of morals."

Aentarra opened a pouch at her side, and for the briefest part of a moment, Katsu saw a glow emanate from it. What he didn't see, however, was the tiny crystal shard hurtling through the air toward his head.

He screamed when it punctured his head just above the ear. Aentarra chuckled at the frightful look on Katsu's face as he examined the blood staining his hands. He was in agony now, but in less than a moment, all that would remain would be a dangerous association between Aentarra and pain.

She sneered. "I would have thought a sea captain to have more control over his emotions. You disappoint me. But keep this in mind. Remember the pain. I will allow you to remember the pain so that you might judge your actions in the future. If you disappoint me again, you will look back to this pain as the joy of a bridal night in the bedchambers compared to what I will do to you should you fail me." Katsu clutched his head and cried, but Aentarra had already departed.

TWO WEEKS PASSED UNEVENTFULLY, but Rahg had not wasted time. The warnings from Mikkellana and Aentarra stayed with him, and he used his spare time practicing with the Shield. Aentarra had given him good advice, which at first he thought little of. She told him to practice with the natural elements—that they would present the greatest challenges.

Originally Rahg ignored the advice, opting instead to be challenged by people with swords, bows, staffs, and the like. But once, when he was alone, he tried weaving shields to deflect the wind. It was then that he discovered the true meaning of Aentarra's words—the wind proved to be a more difficult challenge than anyone with a weapon. Since that time, he designed many new shields including ones to protect him from the heat of fire, ones to keep him dry and warm when the wind blew waves at him—and most difficult of all—shields to harness the power of the waves. But in this short time, he felt his power grow. Now he understood what Mikkellana meant when she said that the number and kinds of shields he could design would prove to be endless—each weave unique.

"Good morrow, Rahg." Camissa's voice carried to him, sweet as ever. "What are you working on today?"

"New shields. I've made a shield like a net, and I'm going to try to catch fish with it. I've asked some of Captain Katsu's men to help me try it out."

Camissa beamed at Rahg's growing confidence, though she knew that underneath he harbored grave concerns. She watched as the crew instructed Rahg on where to cast his net. "If this works I'm going to need plenty of help hauling it in."

Skepticism embraced the crew, but soon the sight of their bulging eyes gave away the truth. Camissa looked over the side and saw them using the hoists to haul up a load of fish, but the eerie thing was that, with only the shield, it looked as if the fish were rising from the sea on their own. Fear clung to the crew like cold on a wet winter night.

"Camissa, did you see that? Did you see the shield?" Joy overcame him. "This is the first good net I've been able to weave."

"I saw. The fish looked like they were leaping out of the sea. Was it difficult to make?"

"I tried several times before I figured it out, but once I did, it was easy." Rahg paused to reflect for a moment.

"Aentarra told me that planar shields were the simplest, just flat ones, then blocks and bars, then webs and nets. Soon I might be able to make weapons."

"I'm happy for you. It will help us for you to grow stronger."

~

NEAR THE FRONT of the ship, Aentarra watched from a Cloaked state. *Yes, my little one, practice. Before long you will need that strength. Before too long another Banished One might be loose, and this one you might have to fight yourself.*

Aentarra thought about the shields she had learned and by exhaustive practice and experimentation what else she had learned. Most experienced weavers could make shields that blocked the sun or cold, but none of the fools had discovered that it was only a few short steps from there to learning the secrets of Fire. Even that fool, Mikkellana, who obviously had extensive powers, even she was ignorant of the possibilities.

Or perhaps she just doesn't think like me.

But to her credit, she had designed the famous Sethian Shield, a miraculous design that even Aentarra couldn't decipher. Aentarra held suspicions that Mikkellana had, in fact, intertwined some Cloaking into her weave, perhaps a latent talent that she didn't suspect she possessed. No one without the abilities to shield could see the weave and even those skilled in Shielding could not see the intricate weaves. Mikkellana had also woven false webs into her design with pitfalls to prevent anyone from experimenting with it. She stared at the mark on her hand; it served as a reminder that the pitfalls were no mere slap of the wrist. She vowed to get even for that as well.

It seemed like the three of them—all the daughters of Antar—were gifted with many talents, many more than most. Aentarra herself was gifted with more powers than anyone, commanding Shielding, Storm, Fire, Quaking, Healing, Lightning, Shifting, and Stealth. The only powers she lacked were Bonding and Persuasion, and of course, Cold-Fire. But she had time yet to figure them out—if it were still possible. To her knowledge, no one could Bond anymore, but that was a dangerous way to think, for the others thought that no one could Cloak anymore.

Aentarra wondered how long it would be before Melissara discovered she could Shield, if she hadn't already. Though she doubted it would be of any benefit. Being able to Shield and being capable of unraveling Mikkellana's design were two different things. ColdFire came to her mind again, her only real regret. In the past, there were legends of powers that went beyond ColdFire to other degrees, but she didn't know of them or what they did.

If she had not seen Lukaan use ColdFire in the Paaren and during the Wars of Light, she would not have believed it still existed. Only her father and Lukaan had ever been able to use it. It irked her that she had not figured out how to use it. She had seen the destruction it had caused on the dreaded ones in the Paaren.

Her thoughts, as always took her back to Antar, the image of her father. The Light of Lights, The Seventh One, The High Seat, He Who Drank the Darkness. Antar du Savarra the greatest ever known in Nelstar—greatest warrior, greatest mind, greatest thinker, greatest leader, and military strategist. The lists went on and on. Antar du Savarra. He had been it all. And he had commanded every one of all the powers and every degree of every one.

At times she cursed him, but even then she felt love for him. She cursed him most though when she felt the pain, and she wondered, again, what had driven him mad. She wondered, too, if it was happening to her. There were times when she could feel an unquenchable desire to laugh, then a depthless wish to kill. Kill anyone or anything.

And how she loved the pain of others. To see them weep and cry. To hold them in her grasp. How she loved to control their lives. Like holding an insect by its wings and watching it struggle to go away.

Would you like your freedom my little sweet? Perhaps if you please me, I will let you live.

There were times when she wondered why she liked that, why she did what she did. Often she gave deep thought to it, but at other times, too many other times, she cared not at all. The only thing that was constant with Aentarra was her love for the birds. She loved the way they flew and fluttered and fought. She loved to hear them sing and quarrel and cry. There was one other thing that remained constant too, one thing that had stayed with her for a long, long time—the undying vengeance in her heart. The vengeance she would reap on the Lights. The vengeance she would visit on the entire world if they dared to oppose her.

RAHG STROKED Marchall's neck lightly, rubbing his hands through the horse's mane. "Tired of this ship, boy? It won't be long before we get you some nice green grass and let you stretch your legs."

"I've got some carrots for him, lad." Tobias came up behind Rahg without him even knowing it. "Good horse you got, lad. A good strong horse. Young too. He'll last you many a season that one will. Had a horse myself that lasted more than thirty years. I've seen some go longer, but not many, not if you work 'em. If you work 'em on a farm or just ride 'em, most'll give out before then. And if they last that long they've done their duty. Next to a good family and a fine blade, a good horse is the most important thing a man can own."

A sigh escaped Tobias's lips. "The one I had I called Whisper. Named him after a friend that died in the Swamp Wars. Whisper did everything with me, lad."

A look of sorrow filled Tobias's eyes. "Haven't been able to care much since he died. And Shia. They both died about the same time."

Rahg was shocked by Tobias's outpouring of emotions. It was the first time Rahg had ever heard him speak of Shia, his wife. She had died a long time ago, and Tobias had always remained silent about her.

"What's the matter, Tobias? You seem to be worried."

"Worried? Lot to be worried about, lad. There are lots of folks that like to see a blue sky all the time. As for me, I like to see a storm comin'. I've traveled over all these lands and seen and done so many things and now we're going to a place I've only heard talked about by men who had drained too many mugs of ale, or when bards thought to enthrall a room. Don't know what to think anymore, lad, but it seems bad."

"It will get better."

Tobias puffed on his pipe. "Hope so, lad. I sure do."

SHIFTING

The stay in Genda had been short but fruitful. Wisp found a small house to rent and negotiated a fair agreement with the owner. They had also made friends with a few of the neighbors, explaining to them that they might be away for extended periods of time. Aenaila rested for the better part of two days and was eager to be off to Pomanda.

"Where are you thinking about, Wisp?" Darstan spent most of his time in Pomanda with Wisp, so Wisp knew most of the spots Darstan might choose.

"We could go to that alley I showed you, the one where I was trained. I don't think anyone would see us, but if a drunk or two were stumbling around no one would believe their tale anyway." Wisp thought a moment longer. "The Inn of the Turtle is an option. You would like to see Mara again, wouldn't you?"

Darstan took a long time to respond. "No, I don't think I would. I made a bit of a fool of myself the first time, drinking too much and talking like I'd drank even more. Besides, Mara is a nice girl. She doesn't need my troubles."

Wisp was quiet. "And I don't want to meet her by chance on the street either. Maybe I've been around you too long, Wisp, but I now view coincidences as something more than I once did."

"Perhaps you have been in my company too long. There's another inn we could go to. It's only a few blocks north of the alley," Wisp said, then seemed to get lost in thought. "Darstan, we've become good friends. So there is something I need to discuss with you."

Darstan sat upright. "What is it?"

Wisp stalled before he started. "I never thought I'd be having a discussion like this, so I find myself treading uncomfortable ground."

"Is it about Aenaila?"

A smile cracked Wisp's serious expression. "I see now that we have indeed been in each other's company too long. Yes, it's Aenaila." Wisp sighed. "I don't want anyone, even someone as lovely as her to get in the way of our friendship. And I don't even know that we have any reason to be talking about this. She might not give a rat's tail for either one of us; however, I suspect she favors your charming smile."

Wisp hesitated only slightly. "But given a thief's good chance, I'll try to win her away from that opinion as long as I don't have to battle you to do it. I don't mind having to fight her feelings, but I won't fight you as well."

Darstan stared at the floor, then looked into Kender's cunning eyes. "I don't know that I've ever seen a more beautiful woman. Her hair is smooth as silk, her skin even softer, and her eyes sparkle like nothing I've ever seen on a person.

"Given that, I don't know why I'm going to say this, but I have no desire for Aenaila. I've tried to fight my thoughts about it, but it didn't do any good. Something is just not there. As to your guess that she might have eyes for me... I don't think so. I don't feel anything. I think she likes you."

Darstan shifted in his seat. "But you might have the right of it as well; she might be using both of us for her own purpose, whatever that may be. I know one thing, Wisp. I think stealing into her heart will be the most difficult challenge you'll ever face. And I think you'd be safer trying to get into the Sethian Palace and steal jewels from Lukaan himself."

Wisp breathed a sigh of relief. "A challenge doesn't frighten me. And it certainly won't keep me away. But I have to agree with all that you've said. She is strange and dangerous. But by the goddess's blood, she is gorgeous."

"Who is this goddess you are always swearing by?"

A snicker formed on Wisp's lips. "Why the Goddess of Death herself. All thieves swear to her when admitted to the guild."

Aenaila walked into the room. "What are the two of you talking about —ale or women? I've rarely seen two or more men get together without discussing one or both."

"Aenaila, you betray your limited knowledge of men with a statement like that. It is obvious you have never sat in on a discussion with thieves or bounty–men."

"Nor would I wish to, Kender Darnell. Have you decided on where to Shift to in Pomanda?"

"I think so. There is an alley near the center of the city that will afford us a good chance of privacy, especially if we wait until dark."

Aenaila shook her head. "I should have presumed that somehow we would be in an alley. Do you have images of any decent places in your head?"

Adju tried to save the conversation; besides, Shifting frightened him. "It is almost dark now, Mistress Aenaila. Can we just get this over with?"

Aenaila smiled warmly. "All right. I will gather my things and be back in a moment."

~

THEY REAPPEARED in the alley where Wisp had trained. Fortunately, no one saw them, and they made their way the few blocks north to the inn Wisp had spoken of. He secured two rooms for them, then they sat and ate a late supper before retiring. Aenaila was tired, but not exhausted, not nearly as bad as she had been going from Entiria to Genda. "I think I can sleep all night," Aenaila said, "but I should rise early. I want us to get an early start."

"I know that you are in a hurry to get back to Khatara. We'll finish our business in Pomanda as soon as possible. It shouldn't take more than a day or two."

"I should hope so, Darstan. And Wisp, you get Adju to bed. He needs his sleep."

Aenaila retired, leaving them at the table. "Where are you going tomorrow, Darstan?"

"I'm going to try to find Nirida. I'd like to see her again."

Wisp nodded. "It might be difficult to find her in such a large city, but then again, she might have a nice business going. Rhaven gave her quite a bit of gold to help her get started again. I'll ask around when I'm out. I need to see Sengua about getting us a room or a small house here. After that, when we get a place in Sykor, we could have a tremendous business going."

"Who will I be with, Master Kender?"

"You will be with me. Just keep your hands out of other peoples' pockets and purses. They don't treat thieves here like they do in Entiria."

Darstan paid the tab. "Let's go to bed. I plan on getting an early start."

Wɪsᴘ ʟᴀʏ on a cot wide awake. He couldn't sleep at this time of night, so he decided to go out and find Sengua.

Adju lay on a mattress on the floor, and Darstan had the bed against the wall. "Where are you going, Wisp?" Darstan whispered.

"Out. My only alternative is to lie here awake half the night."

"Want me to go with you?"

"I'll be back before too long. But you can think about how you will help me win Aenaila. Your smile works wonders on a woman."

"That's between you and her."

From the mattress on the floor, where Wisp thought him to be asleep, Adju popped up like a cobra. "I'll help you, Master Kender. Mistress Aenaila loves me. I will speak to her and say kind words about you. She will do anything for me."

Wisp sighed. "Just go to bed. I'll take care of Aenaila myself."

Aᴇɴᴀɪʟᴀ ʟᴀʏ ɪɴ ʙᴇᴅ, unable to sleep. Her body was tired, but she could not force her mind to relax.

It must be him. It must be him it refers to. He's the only one I've found so far who fits the pieces. He possesses a Cergalan Sword, The Cergalan Sword. And he has powers—strong powers.

The only thing that bothered her was that if the Prophecy stated so much, why did it not mention the one hand. There was no mention of a one-handed man. She thought that would have certainly been important enough to mention. How could a prophecy tell so much and yet tell so little?

It made her question everything about prophecies and legends. How could they be right? Perhaps it was like the old woman in Cilia said. She said prophecies were made by gods to confuse people and give them things to think about. Some are true, and some are lies, just like life. Or, maybe they all could be true at any given time, depending upon which path a person takes. Depending on what a person does or doesn't do.

Aenaila shook her head to dispense with the nonsense. She had come to these lands to get a man with powers—a man who wore a Cergalan sword, and Darstan was the only one she'd seen who fit, so she had full intentions of taking him back with her. That Wisp would come along at this point... well, perhaps it would be an added benefit, perhaps not.

Depends upon how his friendship affected Darstan or how Darstan's affected him. She knew shortly after meeting them it was Darstan she was after, not Wisp. She had concluded that early on, but at the same time she had come to like the thief and had grown fonder of him since. Besides the fact that it might be easier to take Darstan back with Wisp along, or did she only convince herself of that fact because of her feelings toward Wisp. Perhaps it was she all along who wanted Wisp to accompany her.

Darstan was true to his word, that she could tell. He held strong convictions and lived with them. Even when he wanted to bend them, if forced to live with them, he would. That was important for her to know. It might be needed later. And the thief also, he was an honorable man in his own right. He looked after that beggar like his son, and he held to his word like a noble of legend. The thief hid his affection and honor behind a mask of bravado, but it was there to be seen, enough for her anyway.

Darstan's other friends were a different matter. She hadn't liked Rahg much, something about him caused her neck to itch, and whenever that had happened in the past, her intuition had proved correct. And there was Camissa, Even though she had not liked her at first, she was a nice enough person, one with a measure of courage. Tobias was a likable enough old man. Aenaila couldn't think of anyone who wouldn't like Tobias. He seemed to like everybody and everything, even if he did growl at times. It reminded her of her aged grandfather.

A long pause followed. Rhaven—the black-cloaked warrior. Aenaila could probably have twisted his guts and turned his head inside out with her powers—if she had been quick enough. If she could issue a thought before he struck with that demonic sword of his. She had witnessed his killing, and he seemed to enjoy the killing too much for her liking. Far too much.

While Aenaila thought of Entiria, she couldn't help but recall the immortals she had met. Try as she might, their memories would not leave her mind. Mikkellana and Aentarra. Aenaila didn't trust either one of them, but if there were one she'd have to give her life's debt to, it would have to be Mikkellana. Aentarra seemed not to care if a person lived or died so long as she had her way, and if there was a person she cared about, Aenaila hadn't seen them.

Mikkellana, too, though, seemed to have an agenda, and Aenaila wasn't privy to what that was, and until she knew she was not going to reveal her secrets and plans to anybody, certainly not any one of them.

AENAILA FOUND Wisp and Adju drinking khaffe when she came to the table. "I slept later than I intended. Must have needed sleep more than I thought." Aenaila sipped her khaffe. "Where did you go last night, Kender?"

"Why do you think I went anywhere?"

"If I were to leave a lamb chop on the table, I know the dog would eat it, and just as I know that, I know you couldn't let a night slip by without going out to revel in the dark."

"Mistress Aenaila, you make me laugh. Master Kender thinks he can fool everyone, but you know him too well."

"Where did you go, Kender?"

"I find it difficult to sleep. It might have come from a lifetime of late nights but no matter the cause, I feel as if I must prowl the streets at night."

"In all of your talking, you have yet to tell me where you went."

"Many of the people I wished to see can be found easier after dark. Sengua, an acquaintance from my earlier visit to Pomanda, was one of those people. I secured his help in getting a room and other assistance for future purposes."

"Did Darstan go with you? Where is he?"

"Darstan stayed with me, Mistress Aenaila. Then he left very early this morning. He went to look for a lady he knows."

Aenaila's face turned red with anger. "Why did you let him go out by himself? Especially to go traipsing after some "girl."

Wisp's mood dampened. Is that jealousy I detect? Perhaps Darstan was wrong. Perhaps she does have feelings for him. "Darstan can take care of himself. He doesn't need me to watch him."

Aenaila sighed. "Of course. Perhaps you should join Darstan and help him. Adju and I will keep company while we explore Pomanda."

"Master Kender promised me I could go with him today."

Another sigh escaped her lips. "All right, but you better watch him, Kender."

ADJU FOLLOWED Wisp as he made his way through the city. It was as if he had lived there all of his life. Wisp had already spoken to two people who remembered seeing Darstan and he had an idea of where he might be headed. Nirida had been a woman of the night in Genda, and from the few places Darstan had been looking, it appeared as if he thought she might still be associated with that life. Sengua had mentioned a new "Ladies House" that recently opened, a house that served the needs of wealthy merchants and nobles, and with all the gold Rhaven had given her, she could have used that as a base to build a business like that. He'd find out soon enough.

DARSTAN HAD SPENT the entire morning searching, but finally, he had tracked her down. Supposedly, he would find her at this "Ladies House." He was sorry to see that she still practiced her trade, but he would not hold that against her.

A young woman greeted him at the door, blonde hair, soft skin, beautiful—perfect for the part.

"May I help you, sir?" Her voice didn't disappoint him; it was as warm as her looks.

"I'm looking for Nirida. She's a friend of mine."

"Lady Nirida?"

Darstan thought it odd to call her a lady. Perhaps they call them ladies. "Yes, I suppose it is Lady Nirida. Tell her that Darstan is here. We met in Genda."

"Sir, I doubt that—"

"Just tell her."

She opened the door to usher him in. "Please wait here. I will find Lady Nirida."

Darstan barely had time to look around before he heard the sound of hurried footsteps on the stairs. "Darstan!"

The smile lit his face like sunshine. "Nirida!" Darstan opened his arms to greet her, and they embraced warmly.

"Darstan, I can't believe you're here. I never thought to see you alive again. What happened? And what—" The sight of his missing hand stopped her. "Oh, Darstan Did they do this to you?"

The smile disappeared from his face. "No. This wasn't them. But forget about me, Nirida. I came to see you. How are you? You look wonderful."

Nirida led Darstan to a separate room. "The night I met you was both the best and worst night of my life." She paused, almost in tears. "I didn't think I would make it past that night, but somehow I got up the next day. That's when your friends came to see me. Camissa helped me through the worst of it, and then Rhaven... that kind man gave me a small fortune. I didn't even realize how much it was until they were long gone." Her eyes sparkled. "But my life wasn't fixed again until today. I'm so happy to see you."

Darstan couldn't help smiling. He wanted to tell her everything, about his hand, his powers, the Banished Ones, but he felt he better not say so much—not even to Nirida. "One reason I wanted to find you, Nirida, was to tell you."

"Tell me what?"

"They're all dead, the ones who did that to you. All the others, too. Bartel, Cain, Wehr, even Evin, the young one. That's what their names were, but they're dead now. They'll not hurt anyone again."

"Oh, Darstan!" Nirida cried, her head pressed against his shoulder. "What you must have gone through!" They hugged and then she gathered her composure. "Darstan, half of this is yours. I have always sworn that if you lived, this would be half yours."

"Half of what?" Darstan asked.

"All of this. This business."

Darstan looked confused. "You mean you own this business?"

"Every bit of it, thanks to Rhaven. And it is a very profitable business." Nirida blushed. "I no longer work. I haven't worked since I met you, if that makes any difference. Not that I expect anything from you... it's just that..."

Darstan sat in the chair by the door. "It makes a lot of difference. I'm happy for you more than you know, but..."

Nirida knelt in front of him, her hands on his lap and her gaze locked on his, pleading. "But what? I know this is crazy, and I can't even believe I'm saying it, but, I love you. I love you, Darstan, and not just from that one night. I have thought about you every night since then, the things we talked about, dreamed about."

His face softened. "It has nothing to do with you, but there are many things I must do. Things that will take me away from here for a long time. I don't know how long."

"What do you have to do? Can I help?"

Darstan let a smile slip. "No, you can't help. The truth is I don't know if anyone can." Darstan pulled her up as he stood again. "There's so much I would like to say to you, Nirida, but it wouldn't be fair. But there is something you could do to help."

"Anything, just tell me."

"I don't know where our journeys will take us, but we might need to return to Pomanda sometime. If we do, I would like to count on your help."

"You will always have my help," she said, and kissed him firmly.

"Darstan, do you want—"

Darstan blushed. "No, as it is I don't have much time. I have to leave for Sykor." He saw the hurt in her eyes. "We will meet again, Nirida. I'll be back." Darstan kissed her again before he forced himself to leave.

He knew if he stayed any longer he might not find the will power to leave at all.

"Goodbye, Darstan." Her eyes teared.

"Goodbye, Nirida. I love you."

∼

WISP NOTICED a familiar walk a short distance away, and then he noticed how the man kept his left arm tucked inward.

"Darstan!" he shouted, then whistled.

Darstan recognized the voice. Wisp had tracked him down. He waited for him and Adju to catch up. "Did you find Sengua?"

"Last night, and we have everything arranged. Did you find Nirida?" Wisp assumed by the somber look on Darstan's face that he had.

"I just came from there. She's doing well. Very well. And she sent her thanks. She's one we can count on for help if we ever need it."

Wisp didn't know what kind of help she could provide but nodded politely. "Well, if you have no other business to take care of, I know a good place to eat."

"Lead the way," Darstan said.

They had not traveled very far when Darstan spotted the Fountain of the Ancients. "Let's go see that, Wisp."

"I thought you saw that the last time we were here."

"I did, but there's something I want to look at."

When they reached the fountain, Darstan looked puzzled.

"What is it?"

"The last time I was here, there was a shadow from the goddess in the water. I don't see it now. In fact, I don't see any shadow from her."

Fountain of the Ancients

Wisp laughed, even a few strangers laughed.

"It must have been the ale and summer heat that got to you, lad. That fountain has been here for a thousand years or more and never once has it cast a shadow."

Darstan appeared confused, then concerned. Soon another person spoke. "That's the goddess of death. She never casts a shadow."

He continued staring into the fountain as if it would change. He knelt, reached his hand toward the water, almost afraid to touch it, but then stuck his hand deep into the water. It felt cool, soothing, like water from a fountain should feel. Darstan sat, stared at the statue, then back again into the water.

Wisp tugged on his sleeve. "I'm getting hungry. Let's go. I've still got a few more people to see.

Adju clung to Wisp's sleeve. "I want to leave, Master Kender. I do not like this goddess statue."

Aenaila had explored Pomanda, visiting sights that she had often heard about from traders and merchants in Khatara. How she wished life could be so simple. Her thoughts drifted to her obligations, and a somber mood overcame her.

"A beautiful woman shouldn't look so lonely."

Aenaila started at the sound of the stranger's voice, and her thoughts were jerked back to the present. She looked to see who addressed her. The man was short, with a wiry build, but he had smooth skin and blue eyes that sparkled. A handsome crop of dark hair faded into stubble on his cheeks, and when he smiled, bright white teeth shone against his tanned skin.

"Loneliness has nothing to do with beauty," Aenaila replied. Her eyes sparkled with false pleasantry.

"But a pretty lady should never have to worry about company." The man persisted.

"Loneliness has nothing to do with company either, my friend, but if you have such concern for lonely people I'm sure you'll find many others at tables in other taverns. I, for one, wish to be left alone."

The man chuckled, a taunting little laugh that grated on Aenaila and did nothing to improve her opinion of him. "What's a pretty lass like you do on long cold nights? I'm sure you need company."

She maintained her composure, though her patience was fraying. "I have strikers, good sir. They light a strong fire. And I find the flame from a good hot log will keep me warm much better than any man might." She maintained her smile, and that proved to be a stronger deterrent than a dozen guards with blades drawn. The man appeared to be losing his resolve, but when he started to leave, he returned and pulled up a chair.

HE HAD no sooner sat down than his head began to throb. He brushed it off at first; he could put up with a little pain especially in the company of such a lady. But then the agony increased, and, soon he could no longer ignore the pain. The throbbing got worse and worse until he had to stop and put his hands on his head. He squeezed like he had to hold it together, like his insides were about to burst, and he begged for the pain to go away.

"What's the matter, little man? Does your head hurt?" The pain showed on his face. He twisted and contorted, and his skin—taut as it was—pulled tighter yet. Aenaila never let the smile touch her lips, but it was in her eyes, if someone had looked they would have seen it.

Everyone in the tavern seemed to be staring and gawking at the little man, now writhing with his head held between his legs. His pleas for mercy had become cries of anguish, and those cries drew one of his friends from an upstairs room. "Stop it! Stop it," he begged. "By all that's good and holy, stop it."

She let go her hold of him just as the others rushed to see what was wrong. There was no sense in creating a ruckus over him. Besides, he had learned his lesson.

"What's the matter, Benton, you got a problem?"

Aenaila looked at the man's friend. He wasn't quite as handsome as... Benton, and he didn't smell quite as good, but they had shared the same bed with too many women—of that she felt certain.

As the new man helped Benton to his feet, supporting him as he carted him away, Aenaila bid him a farewell. "The pain should leave you shortly," she said. "I have seen this happen to others."

Aenaila enjoyed a long respite during which she had two cups of wine and a smattering of bread and cheese. She was about to go to her room and retire when she saw Darstan, Wisp, and Adju walk through the door. Adju scanned the room even quicker than Wisp, and Aenaila could tell when he found her; he tugged on Wisp's cloak.

"There she is, Master Kender."

Wisp slid two chairs from a vacant table for him and Darstan while Adju took the one Benton had left behind. Wisp pulled his chair alongside hers. "Is the city of Pomanda so dull that none deserve your company, my dear?"

Aenaila's smile was genuine. "Why only now, Master Kender, four of Pomanda's most handsome guards left my table, but they promised to call on me later." Adju laughed, and Aenaila couldn't help but laugh along with him. He had an infectious laugh. It seemed that no matter how she tried not to, she was growing to like him, too.

What is it with thieves and me?

The tavern was small and as the room wasn't crowded. The innkeeper himself was taking orders. The bottom of his apron was soiled from where he continually wiped his hands, and food had stained the better part of the upper portion of the apron. Aenaila could tell by the mark of his voice that his long beard had dipped too often into a mug of ale.

"Well?" Aenaila asked. "Did you find her, Darstan?"

"I did."

Aenaila could tell he had no desire to discuss it. "And you, Adju, did you have a good day with Master Kender?"

"Yes, thank you for allowing me to go. I saw the city and even saw the fountain of the goddess, though that scared me."

Aenaila grew concerned. "Statue of the goddess? Who would erect a statue to her and why?"

"There are many people who swear to the goddess to grant them fortune in their lives. All thieves do," Wisp said.

"Swear to her!" Aenaila almost shouted. "Do you people not know what she will do? Do you not understand the consequences? People who worship her are no better than—"

Wisp interrupted. "I don't worship anyone. And as to the answer to the rest of your questions, the goddess only asks for her payment after you are dead; the others take their due all during your life. They suck it out of you every day that you live. I'd rather live every day as full as I can. I'll pay my dues at the end."

Aenaila tried her best to remain calm. "There are some who believe in an eternity of life after death, Wisp. If that is so, you would be sacrificing everything that comes after for so little now."

Wisp looked as serious as he had ever been. "I plan to have enough for a lifetime while I'm alive, right here on this world. That way if there isn't eternity afterward, I'm already far ahead of the game."

"And if there is?"

"If there is, then I figure that I'll break even."

Much as it seemed as if the gods of fortune might strike them down at any moment, Darstan was forced to laugh again.

Aenaila set her glass on the table and stood. "Good night, gentlemen. I'm going to bed."

"Wisp grabbed her arm. "Before you go, tell us what you want. We're not going away, and I cannot imagine that whatever it is you want could be worse than fighting a Banished One."

Words began to form on her lips, then she paused. "That was not part of the bargain, Kender Darnell. When you gave your word, it was to do my bidding. No mention was made of me revealing the details beforehand."

Wisp nodded. "I remember things well, Aenaila, and you are correct. You don't have to tell us, and I'll not ask again, but if kindness should visit your heart anytime between now and when we arrive at your mysterious destination, please remember that an inquisitive man would like to know his destiny."

Adju perked up at the sound of travel. "Where are we going? Am I going, too? I can work to pay for food."

Aenaila laughed again. Wisp and Adju together were almost charming enough to make her tell them everything. Instead, she again bade them a good night. "I had better retire before you convince me to do something I'd surely regret." She paused only a step from the table. "I would like to leave early, gentlemen, so be prepared. It would be nice to be in and out of Sykor before the day is done tomorrow."

Wisp stood and gave an exaggerated bow. "Until the morning, fair lady. I pray no tears stain your pillows tonight in worry over me."

Wisp ordered more ale, and he even got a mug for Adju.

"Thank you," Adju said, then after a pause, "Master Kender, if you are going to try to win Mistress Aenaila's hand, you must do better than you did tonight. I will start teaching you tomorrow. I know what she likes."

DARSTAN AWOKE in the middle of a night of restless sleep, his eyes drawn to a candlelight in the corner. Wisp sat propped against the wall, cleaning his nails with one of his many knives. It didn't surprise Darstan that Wisp was awake, he always seemed to be; in fact, Darstan rarely saw him sleep. "Have you thought much about where Aenaila might be taking us, or what she wants us to do?"

"No, but I didn't expect her to tell us anything. Her lips are sealed tighter than a jeweler's safe." Wisp saw that Darstan wore a worried look. "Still thinking about Nirida?"

"I guess so. It would have been nice to have spent some time with her, to see if I still felt the same as I did in Genda." A long pause lingered. "And to see if she felt the same way about me."

Wisp suspected that the real reason he sought Nirida was to see her reaction to his missing hand. The wound was too fresh, and Darstan felt the pain like it just happened. "I think you would be surprised, Darstan. Things like that don't mean as much to a woman. Not a good woman like her."

Darstan didn't know how Wisp always knew what he was thinking, but he seemed to get it right. He forced a smile, a thin one. "I hope you're right," he said. He sat on the edge of the bed, wiping sleep from his tired eyes. "I see the little one is sleeping."

"No need to whisper, Darstan. He's like a puppy—running full of energy all day, but at night he sleeps soundly." Wisp continued picking at his fingernails as he talked. He had an obsession with keeping his hands clean, especially his nails.

"I don't know why she won't tell us," Darstan said. "I thought for a moment she would, but then I guess she thought better about it. What could she want? Do you have any idea?"

"I don't know, but there's something strange about her. I've been trying not to think about it, probably because I like her, but it itches at me like fleas on an alley-dog."

Darstan waited for him to continue.

"Back in Entiria, when she mentioned the place of the dead, she called it Nargond. I have never heard anyone call it that."

Darstan brushed the comment aside. "That doesn't sound like something to worry you; besides, how many names have you heard for the place of the dead?"

"Plenty." Wisp shook his head. "I have known men from all the lands. Among thieves, the realm of the dead is spoken of often, but in all the conversations I've had with men, from every land I know, I've never once heard it referred to by that name."

Wisp leaned forward, speaking softly as if she could hear him through the walls. "And when I questioned her, she hesitated, as if she had to make a lie. I should have found out right then. I should have made her tell me."

Darstan grabbed the corner of the blanket and pulled it over himself. "Good night, Wisp. Don't worry, I'm sure we'll find out soon enough, but I can't let her intentions, no matter what they are, worry me out of a good night's sleep."

"No, you can't do that," Wisp said. "You need sleep to keep your strength. Whatever she has in mind for us, I'm certain it will be rife with trouble. I don't want you weak when I need you to defend me, so I'll be here to ensure you get your proper sleep."

"That's odd coming from you," Darstan said. "I seldom see you get enough sleep."

"I might not sleep as long as others, Darstan, but when I sleep, I sleep well. I go to bed each night with my mind free of worries, and my soul free of guilt. And that, my friend, proves refreshing."

Darstan chuckled as he closed his eyes. "How could your soul be free of guilt?"

Wisp tucked his blade back into the sheath strapped to the upper part of his arm, then laughed a little himself. "Because I've done no wrong." Another slight chuckle escaped his lips. "Perhaps it's just thieves that sleep soundly. Look at how comfortably Adju rests. You might consider giving that some thought, perhaps change your occupation."

"I have no occupation."

Wisp laughed a little louder. "That may be even better than a thief. Think on that as you toss and turn tonight."

Darstan smiled, but it was a false one. Inside he grew worried, very worried, but not over Aenaila's mysterious mission, or even her strange name for the place of the dead. What worried Darstan, worried him greatly, was this talk about the goddess, and he shivered at the thought of what that touch of her shadow had meant.

A NEW LAND

Katsu paced the deck, feet stomping hard on the old planking. "Full sails, men. I want every bit of wind I can get."

Tobias stood to the side, careful not to get in the captain's way, but his orders puzzled Tobias. As Katsu paused to address him, Tobias took the opportunity to ask his questions. "Sails full bloom, 'eh captain? I've always been one to catch the wind when it was offered, but we're running smack into a storm."

Katsu nodded. "Trying to make up a little time, that's all."

Tobias let the smoke from his pipe seep out the sides of his mouth, the wind sweeping it away. "Didn't know we had such a schedule. Have we got ladies waiting?"

Katsu glared, ignoring Tobias. "Keep 'em up, men. I want all the wind."

The first mate, a man who had sailed on more than a few voyages with the captain grimaced. "Captain, we could slow it down and let the storm pass ahead of us. Might even miss it if we slow enough."

"I'll have the hide of the first man who brings a sail down," Katsu shouted, then he stormed past Tobias on a furious pace toward his cabin. The day had been rough and was sure to get rougher. He hoped for a little rest before the storm called him to duty.

Fear gripped him before the door had opened halfway. He smelled her first, then saw her on the bed. Katsu froze, unsure whether to enter or leave, but her voice resolved his dilemma.

"How good to see you again, Captain Katsu. Close the door and come in."

The command of Aentarra's voice was like the rumbling of a field general's, although she had barely whispered. He mechanically pushed the door shut, then turned to face her, a sweeping bow performed as gracefully as a sea captain could. Katsu forced himself to move inside. "Good day, My Lady."

"How has your voyage been, Captain?"

"Fine, My Lady. We have been blessed by the ... we have had no trouble."

Aentarra stifled a laugh at the man's reluctance to speak of the gods. When will you arrive at your destination?"

"If the winds are favorable it shouldn't be too much longer. Five or six days will put us safely there." His eyes would not stay on her face while he spoke.

Aentarra rose slowly from the bed, and his head was jerked to stare into her eyes. He was riveted in place and couldn't move as if his chin were drawn out with a rope.

"My dear Captain." Her voice was so cold he shivered. "You say five or six days, and yet only this morning I heard some of your men speaking of reaching land late tomorrow, perhaps the day following, but certainly no longer than that." Aentarra walked around him, and his head followed unwillingly.

He thought it was going to rip from his neck, but mercifully she released whatever hold she had on him, and his neck snapped around again to face forward, just as she returned to stare into his eyes. He was on his knees, shaking.

"By chance, dear Captain, do you not wish me to accompany you on this journey? You would not try to mislead me for purpose would you?"

The captain could only shake his head. His words would not come. When her chuckle came, he recognized its dishonest nature.

"No, I thought not, Captain Katsu, for you look like a man who relishes life and would not suffer well under pain of torture, but then, no man suffers my torture well. I will have to show you sometime. I think you would find it interesting."

Aentarra let him shake for a moment before she started again. "And just so that we have a clear understanding. When I ask a question, answer directly, with no attempts to mislead me in any fashion. If I suspect even once that you do, you will find your life forfeit, but not before I have a wonderful time with it. Trust me, Captain, I'm creative in my means to make men weep; in fact, I rather enjoy myself, so do not give me reason to come for you."

The captain's head shook vigorously until he could find the words to make his tongue work. "Your will, My Lady, your will."

"Good. That is how I like my men. Obedient." She chuckled as she reached for her shoes, still lying on the bed. "Farewell for now, and remember, I shall meet with you again."

"Prepare to land!" the captain hollered. "Lower sails and man the oars."

Tobias rolled sleepless eyes around the place where they would land. The harbor looked safe enough, even if the terrain behind it appeared a bit rugged. No matter, he'd rather face some rugged terrain than a village full of hostile people. There were no signs of inhabitants anywhere. Strange, he thought, to have a good, safe harbor and no settlement nearby. There were no buildings, no houses, and no ground that had felt the blade of a farmer's plough. There was no sign that a ship had ever docked against these shores.

Rahg came alongside Tobias and Katsu. "Why don't we sail until we find a city or a village with a dock. Surely one cannot be too far from here."

The captain's head bobbed up and down during Rahg's talk. "Right you be on that, lad. There's a fishermen's town not too far from here, but I haven't seen the waters of that place in four years, and I'll not risk everything we've come so far to do counting on them being hospitable. I told ya once already—these people like war. A battle is never far from their mind."

The captain stared after the lad, but when Rahg said nothing he elaborated. "Remember, lad. This is no warship. This is a trading ship. And there are not many fishing ports that I know of likely to look kindly on a strange ship sailing into its port, let alone these people. We're not geared for battle."

Tobias had his hands resting on the rail while he scoured the shoreline. "Lad, I'll agree with Captain Katsu. There are ports and villages even in our land that a ship hesitates to sail into unannounced. I'm not one for relying on the goodwill of people we don't know. I say, let's land here and make our way to a city. The land looks like it could use some rain, but I'm sure we can find food and water."

KATSU ISSUED the final orders to his crew as they anchored in the harbor. They lowered the boats to take them ashore and packed supplies necessary for several weeks of travel. Rahg said farewell to the crew, but Captain Katsu surprised him with his response. "We're coming with you, lad. There'll be no getting rid of us so soon."

"Who's coming?"

"All of us. We signed on to come with you. Keep you safe and help protect you. I know you've got your friends, but from the tales I've heard of Arangar, you may need all of us and more.

Rhaven looked at the crew, then back to the captain. "And the crew?"

The captain sighed. "We're all of the same oath, if not the same mind. We've said our peace at the temple. There's nothing can be done to us now."

The shore proved to be barren with no signs of frequent use. Katsu ordered a few of the men to return the boats to the ship. "Sail safe and strong, men. We'll make it back when we can."

Rhaven saddled Argus while Rahg, Camissa, and Tobias prepared their horses. The Shulan had sent horses for Tobias and Camissa. Katsu's men huddled on the beach in discussion until Rhaven's voice interrupted them. His voice could chill a man, no matter the weather. "Too many men will slow us down, and I have no intention of prolonging this journey. You'll need horses to keep up with us."

Captain Katsu nodded. "The Shulan thought as much, which is why he gave your mounts passage. He also gave me enough gold to buy horses for all my men."

The captain was a determined man and a dedicated one. Even if he wanted no part of this journey, he had given his word. "You'll wish differently about having us along if thirty or forty bandits decide to take that pretty horse from you." He realized as soon as he said it that he probably had said the wrong thing. The look in Rhaven's eyes and the transformation on his face told Katsu that no bandits would ever take that horse.

"Argus would kill the first man to sit upon him," Rhaven said without any sense of humor. "He's done it before. He's killed more Victas than most soldiers, but he's not shy about who he kills." The big black stallion snorted hot air and pawed the ground with his hooves.

The captain cast a worried glance to Rhaven and then to Argus. He had a feeling the man was right. He'd certainly not sit upon that beast; in fact, there were times when he thought the horse should have worn a sword instead of a saddle. "We're going with you. We'll keep up as we can, or we'll catch up when we can, but we're going with you. I've got a son who begged me not to go. Asked me why I had to go. Just like you're askin' now, and the only answer I could give him was the truth. The people of Entiria have been waiting a thousand years for a prophecy that they've held to be true. Each person at birth swears to do their part in helping that prophecy come to be."

The captain cocked his head to one side, and his face grew defiant. "Well, I'll not be the one to break an oath. We've enjoyed wonderful winters with the sun shining most days, and we've had fruit growing on nearly every tree on the island, but now it will turn dark, and not just for a day or two. The blackness is coming just like the legends tell. Somebody has to help the lad do his part. I've had my time. Been fortunate enough to marry a good wife and raise a good family. I'll not be the one to deny the lad. If somebody doesn't help him, my son won't grow to live as long as me. I know that. I feel it in my heart."

The determination in the captain's face had hardened. "I might be dying here, or I might die somewhere else, but I know this, I'll be helping that lad to find whatever it is he needs to find and to do what he needs to do. I know I can't go home and tell my son I failed—that I doomed him and all the others. I can't tell him that the world will turn black and rain fire just because I couldn't do what I had to."

The captain didn't know what part of what he said had struck a chord, but something did. He saw the change in Rhaven's eyes, and he saw him nod, slowly. "Try your best to keep up. I set a fast pace. We'll get horses at the first town we come to. There are bound to be towns soon." Rhaven stared at the group lined on the beach. "If you are to travel with me I'll know each man, and what his talents are"

Over the next day or two, Rhaven proceeded to ask each one who could handle a bow and arrow; who could handle swords and knives. Most of them couldn't do much of anything. They missed the mark with the bows and arrows, and he could tell by the way they held their swords that they hadn't done much, if any, of swordplay, but they were men who had been roughened by one of the harshest taskmasters—the sea—and if they couldn't handle a sword, they could a knife or an ax. The men had spirit and a roughened soul. They would do fine.

RAHG ENJOYED SEEING new lands and, as they traveled, he took in the sights. For two more days the terrain remained flat to slightly rolling, wide open and semi-arid with a few trees and scrub brush scattered among the rocks. The group was relaxed. They could see as far as the eye would allow and there was no terrain that would harbor bandits lying in ambush.

They still hadn't seen a river or even a good flowing creek, but they had enough water for several more days at least. On the third day, Rhaven spotted vultures soaring, perhaps only a half league away. They made quick time getting there and found that the terrain was changing. The hills grew steeper, and copses of trees grew taller and stood bunched together, even if their branches seemed bare from lack of moisture. After a brief respite, barely enough time to swallow some cured meat and water, Rhaven signaled the continuance of their journey.

As brief as the respite was, Rahg gave thanks because he had the feeling that if it had been only Rhaven's decision there would have been no rest at all. He and Argus seemed to be able to go forever without stopping.

As Rahg reached for the horn on Marchall's saddle, Rhaven put a halt to him. "You walk, lad and let one of the other men ride." Rahg seemed stunned at first, but then he felt ashamed that he hadn't offered to share the mount to begin with. But his shame was quickly washed away by Rhaven's next words.

"We will soon be in territory where there will likely be people, perhaps bandits. With the hills and trees to offer cover, an ambush could await. No group of bandits would likely attack a group as large as ours, but considering we have only four horses bandits might attack us with arrows in an attempt to get our mounts. If they do that they'll shoot for those of us mounted first. They won't waste an arrow on a young lad walking in the middle of a crowd."

Rhaven looked to the captain. "Captain, you said you knew what you were getting into when you came. Now is the time to start proving that. Select a man to take Rahg's mount."

The captain moved with haste. "I'll sit the horse. I've never been one to ask something of my men that I'd not do myself."

Rhaven nodded, seeming neither surprised nor grateful.

As they progressed, Rahg practiced with his shields. He formed protective barriers on each flank and focused on maintaining a balance of power to each. They proved easy to weave, but it required stamina and strength to maintain them for an extended period. He wasn't strong enough to shield the entire group, not without exhausting himself. Two more days sped by uneventful, with the exception of finding a couple of small watering holes, actually small depressions in dry creek beds.

Rhaven dismounted, then stooped to examine the water. "They haven't had rain in a long time. Do you see where the normal line of this creek is?"

Tobias stood beside Rhaven, nodding. "With a drought this bad we might have a difficult time finding game. Fill your sacks with all the water you can carry and take a belly full before we leave. Don't know when the next water will be."

Three more days brought nothing new. Kella had been out every night but had come back with nothing, then, one night, she came back barking a tone that Rhaven interpreted to mean they should follow her. He suggested the others continue while he followed her, only to return a short while later. "Saw a farmer and a young lad. We should see about getting some supplies."

Rhaven took Tobias, Rahg, Camissa, Katsu, and three of his men with him. The farmer ran toward the house when they approached. As they drew closer, Rhaven had Katsu and his men stand back while the rest of them walked toward the farmhouse. Tobias stayed in front, hands raised with palms up, signifying peace.

The farmer came out of the house and walked toward them, but slowly. "What is it you want?"

Hearing the language shocked Tobias. There were accents in his land he found more difficult to understand. He looked all about as the man drew close. Two arrows pointed at them from cracks in the shutters on front of the house.

That'd be his children, Tobias assumed, or his wife and child.

The farmer carried an ax, the one he had been splitting wood with when Rhaven first saw him, and he had a firm grip on it.

"We mean no harm," Tobias said. "We'd like to buy some food. And horses if you have any."

Even as he spoke Tobias looked all around for animals. There were pens for chickens, and the fencing put up for keeping pigs, but he didn't see any about. Even stranger, he couldn't smell any sign of them having been here recently.

The man seemed to go on edge as soon as he heard Tobias speak. The accent was noticeably different. He studied them top to bottom, and if he stared a little longer at Rhaven, that was understood. "Where are you from? I don't see men often on this end of the land. Seldom see anyone, which is why we chose here."

Tobias struggled to find an answer he deemed suitable. "We're traders who got lost at sea. Nearly lost our lives as well. So now we're lookin' for some food. Also, need mounts for the rest of my men, and if you're kind enough, directions to a nearby village."

The farmer scanned him like he could hear the lies in each word. "Traders from where?"

Tobias chuckled like he'd been caught in a mistake. "From far off. So far off we don't even know where we are. Where is this place anyway?"

The farmer spit tobacco juice he'd been chewing and looked them over once again. He looked to the captain and his men standing behind Tobias by about twenty paces, and then the gaze lingered on Rhaven. His head nodded slowly. "There's some back there that might be traders," he said to Tobias, "but you don't look to be one." Then his head turned slowly as he nodded at Rhaven. "and that one hasn't traded goods in his life."

"Every trading ship needs guards, friend; you should know that."

"What do you trade? I see no goods."

"As I said, we got lost, and the ship went down. We had to leave the goods behind, or we'd have all gone down with it."

The farmer spit more tobacco, then sniffed the air, a dog seeking a scent. Finally, his eyes fastened to the pouch containing the dried meat, and next found the water sack hanging on their back. "I've not seen a trader yet who had enough sense and not enough greed to leave valuable goods and take only water and meat." The farmer gazed at the pouch that held the dried meat.

Tobias chuckled, and let the laughter linger a while. "Right you are about that. There aren't many of 'em that are like that, but our ship went down rather slow and when we saw how far we were to shore we had time to think properly before we acted. The men saw it as a chance to take the best of the goods, but it was my good friend here, the warrior, who convinced us otherwise. He's a worldly man and doesn't take much to trade or goods or wealth. He's the one who told us what we'd carry, and to a man, no one had a mind to argue the point."

For the first time, the farmer acted like he believed what Tobias said. He chanced a quick shot at Rhaven and then back to Tobias. "If you mean no harm, what is it you need? I see you have water. If you need them filled, I've got enough to spare but not much more. As for food, got barely enough to feed my family. It's been two harsh years, but I'm not complaining. We've been lucky. Luckier than most from what I've heard of other parts of the land." The farmer stared hard at them before he continued. "Though it doesn't look as if you suffer from starving where you're from."

Tobias remembered the pens for chickens and pigs and noticed the fencing for sheep, but none were around.

"If you're looking you know," the farmer said. "There's no food for the taking. We're down to our last as it is."

The sound of a horse neighing from behind the barn drew Tobias's gaze.

"I've kept them until last," he explained. "Raised them all since they were colts stumbling at their mothers' teats. But time's coming soon where I'll have to make a decision, much as I don't want to."

Tobias stepped forward, slowly. He didn't worry about frightening the farmer so much as whoever held those arrows, but even his slightest movement gave the man pause, and he gripped the ax tighter. It made Tobias worry about the ones in the house. "There might be a means to feed you and let your horses live."

The farmer looked at him curiously. "Go on, man. I'll listen to the chirps of a bird if it'll save my horses."

"We'll give you four days food and pay a fair enough price in silver for each horse you sell us."

The farmer's eyes lost the glimmer of hope that Tobias's words had sparked. "I told you, trader, we're hungry. My family can't eat silver. We need food."

Rhaven's words were never soft, but this time they held no threat either. "I know hunger when I see it. We will give you enough food for four days, as Tobias said, enough for you and your family. And on top of that, we'll pay enough in silver to allow you to buy a cow and a sheep for each horse that proves to be a good mount. That should keep you fed until the drought lessens." Rhaven watched the man's eyes.

"And I can offer my word that your horses won't fall to a supper plate. I'll kill the first man who tries."

The farmer stood silent for a long time. Tobias took a quick glance to the house and noted that the arrow still focused on him.

The old farmer spat and laughed sarcastically. "Stranger, I've got four good horses. Four that I'd gladly sell before I ate them, but I can't believe you've got enough silver. Not now. Cows and sheep are protected like the king's daughters. And they charge more for a chicken than the ladies in the houses of Chingua.

Tobias nodded as if he understood, and he felt fairly certain that the man must refer to "bawdy ladies," and from the sounds of it, they must be expensive.

The farmer shook his head, but it was more in frustration than anything else. He had hoped for a cure to his woes. "No, friend, the only cows and sheep left are under such guard that it would take more men than what you've got to even think of stealing one." He scoffed. "And it would take more than silver to buy four cows and four sheep right now. It'd take five gold crowns to buy that much. Maybe more."

"Five gold crowns!" Tobias nearly jumped out of his skin. "Why that's a—"

Rhaven's hand barely moved, but it was enough to silence Tobias. "How much does your gold crown weigh, farmer?"

"A gold crown's a gold crown," the farmer bit back, looking to Rhaven as if he were crazed.

"Then I shall amend my offer. I will give you enough food for four days for you and your family, and, I will give you six gold crowns, in case five isn't enough. Also, we'll go with you to the village, and we will act as if the purchase is for us. It might put an end to any notions the sellers might have of attacking after the sale."

The light returned to the farmer's eyes, and at the same time, Rhaven looked to the captain still standing behind them. "Katsu, come here. Bring the gold."

Rhaven told him what was needed and the captain dug into his pouch and counted six gold crowns then handed them to the farmer.

The farmer stared in solid disbelief. He picked one piece of the six and examined it like it might be poisoned. He rolled it over in his hands several times, then let his tongue taste the mineral. Tobias thought for a moment that tears might come to his eyes he looked so stricken with joy.

"I'd have not believed it when you arrived. I still don't believe it except that I'm seeing the gold and feeling it. I don't know where these crowns come from. They're not from here, I know. Not with a picture of this obelisk. But they're gold; I can see that, and they feel the right weight." The farmer shook his head in disbelief. "I don't know if you're all crazy with the fever or if the gods themselves have sent you. I've been praying enough that they should have heard me. Well, none of that now, I've given my word, and you've given yours. The horses are in the barn. You can take the saddles with you. I don't want to be reminded that I sold 'em off. Treat 'em good. And if you do get to the point where your belly's screaming for more than you got, be gentle on 'em. That's all I ask, be gentle on 'em."

Rhaven nodded his head so slowly that the farmer must have thought he was bowing in reverence. "Know this, farmer. I would never harm an animal. Not for any cause. I value Argus's life above most men. They will be treated well. You can sleep knowing this."

The old man didn't know what to believe after a morning like he'd had, but of it all, he believed what this warrior told him. And it made him feel all the better for it. He shook his head and hollered into the house, and the arrows dropped from the shutters.

ON THEIR WAY to the village, the farmer spent a good amount of time educating them on the surrounding areas. "There's been a drought like we haven't seen before. Still find some water here and there, and the deeper wells are working, but food is short. Lot of men would kill you for the sack of dried meat on your side. And for these horses, they'd risk almost anything.

Rhaven wanted as much information as possible. "What of the guards? Don't they patrol these lands?"

The farmer grunted. "Guards! It's a bad time here, my friend. The guards commit as much crime as the bandits."

Rhaven nodded. Corrupt guards were not news to him. "I thank you for your worries, my friend. We will keep a sharp eye. You just take care of yourself and your family."

THE PURCHASE of the livestock took a lot of negotiating, but that was a chore Tobias relished. He managed to strike the deal for only five of the gold crowns, even though he had met resistance at first, along with many questions about where these crowns came from. Rhaven noted, too, that as they walked through the city, hungry eyes followed them and the guards owned more than a few pair of those eyes.

Rhaven steered them east, away from the farmer's house. "Where are we going? My farm lies west of here."

"Too many people showed an interest in our purchase. We'll let them believe it's for us and head east. Once we're safely away from here, I'll send a few men with you for protection. Kella will accompany you as well. With her along it would take a sizable force to overpower you. She is a great warrior."

The farmer looked at Kella and nodded. He wouldn't wish to be against her. Soon they reached a point where he said he could take leave. "This road goes north of town along the hills. I can reach my farm without trouble."

Katsu sent two of his men with the farmer, and Rhaven gave each of them a horse to use. As the farmer took his leave, he turned and faced Tobias and Rhaven. "It's not any of my business, but seeing how you treated me fair, I feel the need to warn you. If your lands are truly in the south—if that's really where you're from, I wouldn't be telling anybody about it. Because if anyone gets wind that you have food there, there'll be hordes of hungry people coming down to steal your herds and raid your crops. I imagine an army could keep them out, but they'd have to kill them. Hungry men will do about anything for food, though I reckon you already know that. Anyway, that's all I have to say. Good luck to you, friends."

As THEY MADE their way east, Rhaven ordered the captain to select the men who would ride and suggested that they take turns so no one would get too tired. He also ordered Camissa to ride on the inside of him to afford her more protection. He expected to find a dour look on Rahg's face when he heard the order for him to remain walking, but the lad never showed it if he felt anything. Rhaven's opinion of him grew a little more. The lad was growing fast, too fast for most, but he seemed to be handling it well. Besides, Rhaven knew him to be strong; he could take the strain of walking better than the seamen.

Tobias dismounted and offered his horse to one of the crew, but Rhaven halted him. "Old man, we need you as much as myself." Tobias grunted at the statement, but Rhaven took no heed. "You can track, and if an arrow takes me, they'll need your experience to keep them alive."

Tobias nodded while he lit his pipe. "Don't know if I'm all that good, but that argument is good enough to convince me to keep my back-side on this horse."

RAHG LAY ON HIS BACK, no clouds to block the view of the stars, a whole sky full of stars. For the first time since leaving Entiria, he felt some degree of comfort. They had not encountered any trouble in Arangar, not yet. But even as he thought that his stomach soured, and his heart raced. He could not fool himself for long; it was only a matter of time before trouble sought them out. And from what his experience had been this past year, it was sure to be bad.

How long? How long before the killing starts again?

PREPARATIONS FOR JOURNEY

A fire provided warmth, but the food was neither sufficient nor tasty. The landscape had remained barren, perhaps even deteriorated as the party moved farther east. Food was again running short, prompting Rhaven to issue restrictions on both food and drink.

"We've got enough food for five or six days," Tobias said. "Water's the problem."

"A town is hidden somewhere in these hills, Tobias. We should send scouts farther out each day."

"Trouble is, we need people who can pick up tracks. There's not a tracker one in that group of seamen. I could go—"

"No! I told you already. We need you here, even if we need to make trackers out of these seamen. It can't be too difficult to teach them to track horse or wagon trails."

Rahg perked up. "I've learned a little of tracking. I could take Kella with me."

Tobias finished his supper then lit his pipe. "You stay here, lad. Don't need you going off to get killed. What would we all do then?" Tobias chuckled. "We can train some of these sea salts. All they need to do is find a track and follow it to a town. Can't be any easier than that."

WITHIN TWO DAYS, Jarrell, one of Katsu's men, had located a town, and not more than a league north of where they were. "Not a big town, but it looks as if they have food and an inn."

"I've wanted a warm bed ever since we left Sunnara," Tobias said. "I hope they grow tobacco in these lands, 'cause I'm scraping the bottom of my last pouch."

Camissa laughed. "It will do you good to lose a day or so of that pipe. You worry over tobacco more than food."

"Lass, this pipe's been with me longer than any woman since my Shia, and longer than any horse other than Whisper. And it's given me more pleasure than any but those two. I've got a new one that the Lorns gave me, but this one's still has a place. With that being the case, I like to take care of it, clean it, stuff it full with good tobacco."

Camissa laughed all the harder at Tobias's rantings. "I wish someone cared for me as much as you do that pipe."

THE SUN HAD SETTLED below the hills by the time they entered the town, and as they moved down the main street, the size of the group drew more than a few stares. With eight on horse and as many more afoot, they presented a force larger than most guard patrols. Fortunately, Kella had remained in the forest, avoiding a town like a fire.

They entered the inn and found enough tables for almost all of them. A few of Katsu's men stood at the bar as there were no more chairs available. The townsfolk appeared apprehensive at first, not so much at the size of the group as the fact that they wore no uniforms. The guards often traveled in large patrols, but they were easily identified.

The innkeeper busied himself serving the guests, a warm smile on his face. "We seldom see a band so large as this. Are you guarding travelers or merchants?"

"We've put together a hunting party," Tobias said.

Disbelief crossed the innkeeper's face. "Hunting party? There's not that much game within a hundred leagues."

An urge to be truthful struck Rahg. He saw no harm in being honest with these people. "We're here to find the Pathfinders," he said. "Any information you have on them would be worth a price."

Tobias coughed on smoke he swallowed, but Rhaven showed no change. The innkeeper, though, laughed heartily. "The Pathfinders!" He turned to some townsfolk at the tables nearby and announced their intentions. "Another band of hunters hoping to find the little demons."

A man seated by himself near the door offered his advice. He came to the table and extended his hand in friendship. "You'd be better off to go back home. People have been searching for the last of them for a long time. My father died trying to find them, and they nearly took me."

"They're dangerous, then?" Rhaven asked.

A choke sprayed a little ale. "Don't know, stranger. Never seen one. Nobody has. I believe they're all dead. Nobody has seen one since the last big drought, and that was forty winters past." The last swig of ale wet his throat. "But if you still have a mind to search for them, well there's lots of gold to be had. If you find them that is. But that's just where the danger comes in. In trying to find them. If they're still alive they live in the mire, a land they say is as big as half of Arangar, and no matter what you think, you can't track them. The mire is protected on three sides by mountains so steep the big horns can't climb them.

The only way in is through the river. It empties out into swamps so big and so dense that the river twists and turns through there like a serpent through a forest. Before you've gone half a day, you're lost. It nearly cost me my life trying to get out of there; it did cost my son his."

"Is there food and water?" Rhaven asked.

"There's water; that you'll have too much of. Problem is findin' any that's fit to drink. Can't drink the swamp water. Only way I ever survived was catching rain in a pail. Food's another matter. I went in with three others. On the first day, Josh got real hungry for some fruit he saw hanging over the channel we were in. If I hadn't been on the oars, I'd have taken some, 'cause the way he described how delicious it was made my mouth water. Pete did take a bite, and before we had gotten a quarter league away, they both began moaning. They lasted until late that night before they died. From then on the two of us left agreed there'd be no eatin' anything. We had enough food we figured to keep us for a while, especially now that Josh and Pete were gone. And it rained nearly every day. Even if it was only a little, it was enough to drink."

The man had shaken hands with Rhaven when he first came to the table; now he offered his hand to Tobias. "Tomkins is my name, just Tomkins." He shook Tobias's hand and nodded to Rahg and Camissa, then he ordered more ale, pulling a recently vacated chair from a nearby table to sit on. "Lips are gettin' dry," he said.

"After ten days we ran out of food and still hadn't found a way out. Those swamps seemed to get bigger and bigger, and the river had more legs than a spider's got webs. We were lost for sure. Eben panicked, complained about being hungry. I told him not to eat anything. The other fruit looked good, too, I reminded him, but it killed Josh and Pete. He held out for two more days, both of us just drinkin', not eatin' anything at all, but then he broke and swore he'd just as soon die from the poison.

"We ain't gettin' outta' here," he moaned. "You know it, pa.'"

"Wasn't much arguing I could do; fact is, I almost followed him to the grave. Hunger'll make a man do lots of things. I held out though, and I can't tell you how much it hurt me when Eben got sick. Sad thing was he thought he'd found a good batch. Loaded up the boat with it, and talked and talked about how good it tasted, just like Josh had said. The memory of that helped me keep control. When Eben realized it was bad, after the pain started, he begged me to kill him. Begged me."

Tomkins mechanically lifted the mug of ale to his lips and gulped a large swig, a process he must have repeated a thousand times before. The mug landed hard on the table. "I didn't know what to do. Suppose it's only the cramps, Eben, suppose you're just sick? I surely didn't want to kill him, but he kept beggin' me, said it was just like Josh.

"I don't want to go like them," he said. "No sense in waiting that long."

Tomkins looked as if he might cry. Tears welled in his eyes. "Well, I did it. I bled his neck just like he asked me to. Blood all over my hands and arm. I had to rinse it out a dozen times in the swamp." He wrung his hands all over again as he retold the tale. "I left his body in the boat long as I could stand it, then finally dumped him over. By now I'd given up and decided to go myself. I tried to use the knife, but six times I held it to my throat, and each time I couldn't find the courage to do it. Finally, I decided to go the way they did, just felt bad that I'd have no one to help me like Eben asked me to help him. I picked three of the fruits, figuring it might make things go quicker."

Tomkins smiled a little, but then it vanished. "By the good gods, they were sweet. Sweeter than I could have believed, though it might have been because I was waiting for the ride to Chugarra that they tasted so sweet. I kept rowing, don't know why I did, just for something to do, I guess. Took my mind off the poison. Wasn't long before the pains started, ripping and tearing at my gut like a dull blade. I kept on rowing not knowing what else to do, but each time I moved it tore at me something fierce."

"How long did it last?" Tobias asked.

"It was nighttime before I realized I wasn't dead, and I was still rowing upstream. The pain had lessened, nearly gone. I realized it had been a while, quite a while and I still wasn't dead. Soon, I felt no pain at all. I ate three more of the fruit. This'll do it, I thought. But come morning I still had the oars in my hands, and the boat was still heading up river, against the current."

"I'm guessing it didn't make you feel too good," Tobias said.

Tomkins shook his head. "Next thing I knew I was thinking differently again; now, I wanted to live, find my way outta' there. I had a few of the fruits left and I made sure to save one to compare so I could pick ones exactly like it to keep feedin' myself. Took me nine more days, but I finally made it out of there and staggered back to town. That was two winters back, friends, and I still can't stop thinkin' about it."

Tears flowed freely. "I used to be a good man; now I'm not a man at all. Things will do that to ya though. Was my only boy I cut back in those swamps. Eben was my son." Big gnarly hands cupped tearful eyes.

Rahg grimaced. He had never seen a man cry in a public place. He looked about, embarrassed, but thankful that no one else seemed to be paying them any mind.

"He begged me," Tomkins offered as excuse. "He begged me. I couldn't let him suffer."

Rhaven nodded. He had seen it happen to men before; a good man go sour over a death he felt responsible for. Sometimes there was only one cure. "Your company would be welcome on our voyage, Tomkins. Your knowledge of the fruits and the waterways would help."

Tomkins looked at Rhaven like he had just asked him to swim the Endless Sea. "You asking me to go back there?" he said, a look in his eyes that said he thought Rhaven was mad.

"I ask no one to do what they have no wish to do. I simply said your company would be welcome."

Tomkins stared at Rhaven for a long time, and in a strange way, as if he saw for the first time the weathered face, the warrior's hands, and the eyes of the eagle. "We'll all likely die," he said matter-of-factly.

Rhaven said nothing.

Tomkins turned to stare at Rahg and Camissa and Tobias. "You all agree? Did you hear nothing of what I said to you? You'll die in there. You'll die, and you won't even see a Pathfinder." His voice had risen to a shout.

Camissa could sense Rahg's fear of the unknown, but it had been tempered with his unquenchable passion for the adventure of exploring someplace new. She could sense trepidation in Tobias. And in Rhaven, nothing.

Tomkins stood and looked straight to Rhaven. "I'll go then. By the Blood of the Holy Ones. I'll go. I never gave Eben a proper burial; never even said the words over his body. He needs them said if he's to climb the Chugarran Path. All this time I've been afraid of going back to give him his rights, and he's been in there rotting away in those swamps waitin' for me, probably cursin' me. Well won't be long now, Eben, I'm comin' to send you home."

Rhaven showed no reaction, like he knew all along that Tomkins would join them. "I have gold to pay your wage."

Tomkins' eyes grew fiery bright. "I'll not accept gold or even a copper. It wouldn't be right to confuse the reason why I'm going. I'm going to say the words over Eben's grave, and that's all. I don't want the gods to misunderstand my motives. And I don't want my boy to misunderstand either. After that's done, I'll do what I can to help you. We'll likely all die anyway, and you seem as good a bunch as any to die with."

Tomkins stood to leave. "Let me have until the morning after next to get ready. I need to make some preparations; settle a few debts. Don't have much, but I'll not go out owin'."

"What will we need for provisions?" Rhaven asked.

"I've got one boat," the man said. "We'll need to get another one or two. Enough to carry whoever's going. How many do you figure?"

Rhaven answered immediately as if his mind had already been made before the man asked the question. "Seven," he said. "Though there could be an eighth."

Camissa suspected he was thinking of Kella, and she smiled at his concern. Rhaven had an odd sort of affection for that beast, and it seemed to be returned in kind; the vargel stayed by him like a loyal hunting dog, even if Rahg claimed to have named her, and Rhaven was the first to say she belongs to Rahg, Camissa knew better. The vargel was Rhaven's if she was anyone's.

"Even with seven of you we'll need three more boats. We can't haul more'n three in a boat." Tomkins paused in thought. "Might not be bad to get an extra boat anyway; could haul extra provisions and give us hope if something goes wrong with one of the others."

"Where will we meet you?" Rhaven asked.

"What about the horses?" Rahg asked. "What about Marchall?"

"Katsu's men will protect them," Rhaven said.

The captain perked up at the opportunity to contribute. "They'll protect them with their lives," he said. "I can assure you."

A hideously dark mood seemed to cover Rhaven. "They will, or they will answer to me."

Rhaven instructed the captain to gather provisions for the journey. "Get enough food for a month," he said, "and get empty wine jugs to use for water."

Tobias shuddered at the thought of the captain overpaying for everything and offered to go along with him. "I'll do the bartering. I know the Shulan gave you a lot of gold, but there's no sense in wastin' it. This will be a long journey, and I'm certain we'll need plenty of gold." He mumbled to himself.

That man throws gold around like a farmer sowing seeds.

"What we need is that little skimp of a thief," Tobias said. "Then we wouldn't have to pay any gold."

Camissa, as always, rose to defend Wisp. "He would never steal food from hungry people."

Tobias laughed a little. "Perhaps he would and perhaps he wouldn't, but that little beggar he picked up in Khatara certainly would, and from what I saw of him in Entiria, he could steal the egg from the hen before it got laid."

Rhaven finished his ale and set the mug on the table. "Rahg, you and Camissa come with me. We need to make arrangements for a ship."

"Boat," the captain smiled, and he almost laughed. If it had been anyone but Rhaven, he would have.

"A boat then." Rhaven corrected himself, then turned toward Tomkins. "Where shall we meet?" he asked again. "We'll be ready as soon as we gather the provisions."

"I figure that'll take you the best part of two days, so I'll be ready myself by then." Tomkins turned to his left and pointed with his finger. "If you take the south trail for about half a league you'll come to my farm. You'll see the oak fencing with a small cottage down a narrow path. There's a big stone marker out front by the road with my name carved in it."

The man wiped a tear that hadn't yet formed. "My boy did that. A smart one, he was. Learned his letters young and carved my name in that stone to surprise me." A tear did form now. "Well, that's where I'll be waiting. And don't worry, you won't be going none out of your way, from there we just keep on the south trail until we get to the mountains."

~

TWO DAYS later they set off on the first leg of the journey to find the Pathfinders. Rhaven had roused them at dawn, setting a brisk pace even though the road they traveled was anything but a good one. The extended drought had left the trail hard as rock.

Rhaven constantly scanned the landscape.

"Do you expect trouble?" Rahg began to worry himself.

"I always expect trouble, but I'm looking for Kella. I hoped she would join us."

"Do you think she'll come?"

Rhaven sniffed the air as if some scent would provide him information. "For some reason, I do."

Soon, they reached the marker that Tomkins had told them about and saw the narrow path leading toward his house. Lining the walkway were trees that once embraced the trail and formed a shaded canopy to protect from summer's heat, but now the aged giants were near death themselves. A tree needed water and water had not visited these lands in a long time. The grasses had been burnt brown, and where cattle and sheep once grazed nothing remained to feed them, if, he had any to graze. The cottage was small but tidy and looked as if it had been tended by the hands of a meticulous woman.

Tomkins came out to greet them even before they had a chance to dismount. He carried a bow, a sword, and two knives fastened to his waist belt. He also had a sack packed with provisions, and his quiver was filled with arrows.

~

THEY TRAVELED ALL DAY, the going slow with having to haul the canoes and only some of the men having horses, although everyone had taken turns riding when they did mount the horses. At other times they let the horses rest. Only Argus carried a single rider. They would have let Camissa ride all the way, but she insisted she take turns with the rest of them. Rhaven walked as often as he rode and when he walked his pace was so strong that the men complained.

It was near dusk when they set the camp for the night. Rahg and some of the other men had gathered wood for the fire; there was no shortage of dead wood in Arangar, and while they built four fires, Tomkins helped Tobias and Camissa with the brewing of te and khaffe. Rhaven had gone into the woods to scout for signs of game and bandits, and Tobias was busy telling stories to Camissa when from the corner of his eye, he spotted Tomkins drawing back his bow. It was aimed toward the forest.

"Don't know what it is," Tomkins whispered, "but it'll sure feed a lot of men."

Tobias heard his whisper and shot a glance to where the bow was pointed. "Kella!" he screamed, as loud as an old man can, and instantly, he drew his knife and leaped toward Tomkins, slicing the bowstring with one slash, but the arrow had already released.

Rahg heard Tobias's yell, and he saw the arrow leave the bow, then he saw Kella. His voice joined Tobias's in warning the vargel, but simultaneously, instinctively, he wove a shield and threw it at Kella, only hoping to be in time. The arrow stopped dead and fell to the ground just short of Kella by a hand. Kella had begun to move, and her growl shook Tomkins to the bones, not to mention the seamen, who had never seen her angry.

"What kind of beast is that?" Tomkins hollered, all the time wondering why they seemed so undisturbed.

Rhaven had rushed with his sword drawn, no doubt to slay Tomkins if Kella had been hurt. It would not have mattered to him if Tomkins was the one to guide them; he'd have killed him before Kella's blood had spilled to the ground. Rahg knew that as sure as he knew the sun would rise tomorrow. Rhaven loved that vargel only slightly less than Argus, and Argus he placed well above any man.

Rhaven inspected Kella, ignoring her fierce growls and the frozen stare she cast at Tomkins. "You're fine, girl. I don't know how this happened, but nothing touched you."

"I threw up a shield," Rahg said.

Rhaven looked up to him and smiled. "You should be proud. Now you reap the rewards of diligent practice."

Rahg could not have smiled any wider unless he split his cheeks. A compliment from Rhaven was a hard-earned reward.

THE PAAREN

Korg woke first, a painful howl emerging from his wind-burnt lips as he attempted to stand on a badly sprained, or broken, leg. He collapsed and looked to his right. He had tumbled into darkness, and Kavi had been with him. That sparked a frantic search in a night so black he could see nothing. "Kavi! Kavi, where are you?"

A moan followed by grunts caught Korg's attention. He struggled, reaching for the sound that he hoped was coming from his son. "Is that you?"

Kavi shook his head as he gained consciousness, and panic claimed his voice. "Father, are you all right?"

"Hurt my leg. I think it's only sprained, but it will be a while before I can walk normally."

Korg felt his way toward Kavi's voice, not daring to stand and walk while he couldn't see; there was no sense in risking another fall. "Stay where you are, Kavi. I'm fine."

It only took a moment for Korg to reach Kavi, where the conversation quickly led to their predicament. But no sooner had they begun, then the sky became bright as a midday sun.

Korg recovered his wits first, rubbing his eyes, which were still sensitive from the dramatic shift of night to day. Once his vision cleared, he cast his gaze in all directions. "The snow in the mountains is gone!"

The shock in his father's voice made Kavi blink twice and gape. His tone held wonderment and fear. "Where are we?"

Korg's eyes rose above him and then behind him searching far into the distance, and still, he had not answered the question.

Korg continued scanning their surroundings, though he focused on the more immediate area. Only twenty paces away a brook ran swiftly to join a brother in a nearby glade. Green trees lined its banks, and a meadow beyond looked as fertile as the Shuthvin Valley had once been—long ago. The sun burned hot through moist air, promising relief from the bitter winter they had known until now.

Korg stretched to shed his heavy coat unless the weather proved to be as erratic as the daylight, he would not need the coat today. "Where is the cliff we fell from, Kavi? I remember falling, and my leg is proof."

Kavi's eyes grew wide. "We were on the ledge. On the cliff! You fell into the rocks. I remember too, but it's all gone."

"I don't know for certain where we are, but we're no longer in Arangar. This must be the Paaren."

Kavi nodded. "This isn't the Chugarran Path, so it must be the Paaren."

Fresh rays of sun warmed their skin, and birds from a nearby tree sang a melodious tune. Korg looked at the fruit dripping from the branches, and he nodded his agreement. "The legends were right about one thing, Kavi; there's plenty of food."

Kavi stood, stretching a hand toward his father. "I'm going to get us food. I'll help you to those rocks. You'll be safe until I return."

The Chun leader grabbed his son's arm and rose. "I will have my feet in a few days. Bring me some fruit to eat while you hunt. I'll be fine."

Kavi was soon off in search of game, comfortable that his father was safely tucked into an enclave of rocks. His bow could stop any predator, and the brook was close enough for him to get water if needed.

"Come back before dark, even if you have no game," Korg warned him. "Until we get to know this place we should treat it like it's the Chugarran Path."

The laughter felt good. It had been a long time since a Chun warrior had something to laugh about. Kavi started his journey at a brisk pace, following the brook through the lush valley toward a small rise shortly ahead. He could almost imagine the herds of wild game waiting to be taken. The next hill led to a sun-dappled meadow, its gently rolling hills shaded by green-leafed trees, and the air vibrant with the sweetness of blossoms carried on a soft afternoon breeze. He devoured the images, afraid he might wake from a cruel dream that teased with the temptation of food and pastureland—a dream worse than any nightmare.

He stooped to sip from the cool waters of the creek and thought of the barren branches of the trees at home. Even the Shuthvin Valley, with all its growing fields, could not compete with the richness of this soil.

cool creek

Kavi slowed to a fast walk, while his mind mixed feelings of envy and hope. At the crest of the next mound, he stopped, mouth agape. The hill he stood atop descended steeply through a forest of short trees that led into a canyon where a herd of deer grazed lazily—twenty of the most delicious looking deer he had ever seen, and even though he knew his state of near starvation might have made them appear better, they were fine specimens just waiting to be taken. All that remained was for him to pick the fattest one, then... Kavi's mouth watered at the picture of a roasting fire, he and Korg feasting on a hind portion.

This is the Paaren, he reasoned, and all the legends are true.

Chun training had taught Kavi well. In silence he crept through the trees, avoiding detection and careful to stay downwind. The wind would bring the deer no news of him. Thick brush spread wildly at the edge of the forest where it met the canyon floor, and with his brown and green garb, he was all but invisible.

Kavi's pace slowed, like a serpent stalking mice. He could afford to be patient, but he could not lose the meal. Hunger churned his stomach, producing a growl that sounded loud enough for them to hear. Suddenly, something caught his eye. Chun elders had trained him to always observe the prey, and, while approaching, he noticed the mature buck go stiff. Kavi recognized the posture of the male deer and spread his gaze to search for signs of the buck's distress.

Fear of losing the herd quieted his nervous, empty stomach. He froze, measured breaths calming him as he watched the big buck send the danger signal, alerting the herd. The least indication of trouble, sight, or sound would be the spark that sent them scurrying into the woods. Kavi dare not move, and as he puzzled over what triggered the alert— something ran past him at breathtaking speed.

It charged the herd, sending them scattering in all directions, though almost half of them bunched together as one. Whatever chased them had two legs, and only two. That cannot be, he thought, nothing on two legs can outrun a deer. But he had to believe his eyes as he saw the creature gain on the herd. He squinted to block the sun so he could focus on the chase. The predator passed swiftly by a small doe, keeping to her left, but whenever the doe tried to break for the woods, the creature pushed her back in.

It's herding them into the canyon.

The herd broke and headed in the direction of a grove of trees on the opposite side, but just as they reached the tree line, several more creatures emerged and engaged in the pursuit. They steered the deer straight toward him. Kavi instinctively checked his cover and dug further into the brush. For a brief moment, he considered moving, leaving, and finding other fields to hunt, but the next moment proved his decision to be a wise one.

As the herd entered the grove where he lay hidden, several creatures dropped from trees at the bottom to surround them. A loud thud startled him, and he looked quickly to the right.

It stood less than four lengths away, and though the brush was thick, he could still see the creature. It stood on thick, broad paws that resembled a wolf's, though twice as big, and they were covered with coarse gray fur. Kavi let his gaze rise along legs rippling with muscles, where he noted the fur was colored darker, almost black. He stared at the creature's chest when a young doe broke loose, making its way almost to the brush where Kavi lay. The beast that was close to him lunged forward, and it was then that Kavi saw the claws. With a long sweep of its paw, it seized the doe. Claws like the talons of a giant eagle dug deep into tender flesh. The doe screamed, a pitiful wail that cried for mercy, though it only served to excite the predator who fed on her fear.

Blood gushed from the deer, and the creature reveled in the kill. Kavi's throat tightened, and he wanted desperately to close his eyes. He prayed that they could not sense his terror. The creature lifted the doe in the air and sunk curved teeth, like blades on a Nafton sword, into the soft fur of her neck. In all of his hunts, he had never felt sorry for the animals pursued, until today, and he offered a silent prayer to the Ancient Ones to let the next ones die with less suffering.

Blood splattered on the ground only a length in front of him—more had joined the slaughter. The deer ran wildly through the grove but with no hope of escape. The beasts killed them mercilessly and fed on the frenzied killing. Kavi had always considered himself brave, but now he wondered, as terror coursed his veins.

He pressed his face firmly into soft dirt and tried to hide. All he could hope for was that they could not hear the rattling of his body or the rapid beating of his heart, pounding like a war drum.

He cringed as a hawk-like shriek penetrated his ears, but before he recovered a long guttural growl issued a warning. He opened his eyes to see two of them engaged in a ferocious dispute over the head of a large buck. The ensuing battle was the worst he had ever seen, and if his stomach had been full, he would have puked. He had once seen two dogs fight to the death, ripping and tearing at each other until one opened a deep gash in the other's throat, sealing its fate and putting an end to it. This was worse by far.

Kavi stared, mesmerized. The growling one, "Growler," he had named it, appeared to be stronger than "Shrieker," but they both moved with agility that Kavi thought possible only with smaller animals. They danced and leaped, dashing in, then dodging, and continually swiping at each other with talon-like claws. They seemed to be an odd mixture of several animals, and the best of them, too. They hunted and herded like wolves and, at least from what he had seen today, possessed a pack's ability to coordinate the hunt for maximum efficiency. They owned the stealth of a mountain cat and the claws of an eagle.

It didn't take long for Growler to claim victory, emitting a howl that chilled Kavi to the bone. He closed his eyes and begged the gods to kill him before they let the beasts take him.

Kavi stayed hidden all night. By the next morning, he felt certain they would not return, and he moved slowly from the cover of the brush, muscles twitching nervously and eyes seeking signs of their presence. At first, he started at each sound he heard, but his fear soon dissipated along with the morning dew, and his concern for Korg drove him to increase the pace. He ran most of the way back, but once he saw that his father was all right, he mustered the courage to relate his tale.

"Their fur was gray like a wolf, with long dark patches streaking their legs. They had paws like hands at the end of their arms with wisps of white fur, but the claws were like talons of the largest eagle." Kavi paused to breathe, still winded from the long run. "And their faces were—"

"Like that?" Korg asked, and Kavi looked past him to a spot behind his back.

Terror spun him faster than he could have himself. Not ten paces ahead stood three of them. "It's Growler!" Kavi said. He could not keep the fear from his voice. He tried to nock an arrow, but his legs failed him, sending him to the ground. Only the presence of Korg forestalled him weeping.

Korg sat still as a rock, then moved slick as a weasel as he nocked an arrow, but all the while his gaze stayed fastened to the creatures. Korg's composure instilled confidence in Kavi, and he, too, was able to nock an arrow. "Wait until they are closer," Korg said. "Wait until you are certain you can't miss. We'll get only one shot."

The three creatures advanced slowly with Growler taking the middle position. Straight at me, Kavi thought, and could not keep the images of the bloody fight between Growler and Shrieker from his mind. Kavi drew back slowly, very slowly, on the bow string.

If I can shoot before he charges, I'll have him.

But even as he prepared the bow, he continued staring at Growler's face.

Something changed. He could not believe it, but fear shone in Growler's eyes, and he stopped his advance. Kavi looked at the other two beasts, retreating slowly, warily. "Father, what's happening? Are they afraid of us?"

"Not us, son. Look behind you. Turn slowly."

Exercising caution, he turned to look. On the rise behind him stood a warrior. He wielded a sword that seemed to glow, and, on his forearm, he wore a buckler that shimmered like the sun off a calm lake on a summer afternoon. Talons of the creatures decorated his gray–fur loincloth and black-leather boots. And around his neck hung a necklace that appeared to be carved from the teeth of the beasts. The man had long, flowing, blond hair that blew in the breeze as if it rode the wind.

"Kavi!"

His father's warning alerted him, and he spun to see Growler charging. Korg's arrow took one of the creatures in the shoulder; it had turned with lightning speed to avert what would have been a deadly strike, then continued charging Korg. The Chun warrior drew his blade and, though he could not stand, prepared to fight.

Kavi missed with his shot, and as Growler closed in on him, the bronze-skinned warrior leaped over Kavi and struck the beast with his shining blade, cutting its leg off at the knee.

Without stopping, the warrior sped toward Korg, and with one measured strike, lopped off the creature's head. He let his momentum spin him in a circle until he faced the last of the creatures, who fled swiftly.

Kavi had nocked another arrow and was about to shoot Growler when the man returned. A thrust from the blade to the nape of the beast's neck finished it.

Kavi looked to see if Korg was all right, then to the carnage before him. The warrior uttered something in a language Kavi didn't recognize, and Kavi lifted his gaze to meet the man's eyes. He flinched at their touch; they seemed to stare right through him, to pierce his soul. His instinct was to turn away, but instead, he reached for his sword. It was then he saw the shining blade of the warrior's sword, and he felt the impact of blunt steel against the side of his head.

SYKOR AGAIN

*A*enaila took care to close the door lightly; it was early, and she didn't want to wake anyone. The planked corridor groaned as she walked toward the steps. She had not slept well last night and looked forward to the morning khaffe.

"Good morning, fair lady."

Aenaila jumped, startled by Wisp's unexpected greeting. He stood in the doorway, arms crossed and leaning against the side. He apparently harbored no reservations about waking people.

First a frown, then a smile came to her face. "Good morning, Kender Darnell. I hope you slept well."

"I always do." he said, and before he could get another word out Adju pushed by him and stepped into the hall.

Adju made a sweeping bow with his arm tucked into his chest. Had his hair been a painter's brush he would have marked the floor. "Good morning, Mistress Aenaila, seeing you makes the day seem brighter."

Aenaila couldn't help but smile even as she shook her head. It was difficult to tell the boy he was lying as he flattered her in his most sincere manner. "I'm hungry, Kender Darnell, and I'll not wait on you or Darstan. Join me when you can."

As she started off down the hall. Adju rushed after her. "May I join you? I am hungry, too. Master Kender barely fed me last night."

Kender started to protest the lie, but he knew that Aenaila wouldn't believe the little beggar. "You'll go nowhere with those feet still bare. Where are the boots I bought you?"

"My feet burn in them."

"Put them on or go hungry. I'll wait."

Aenaila's voice had barely reached the lad before he rushed through the door in search of his boots.

Kender dodged him and watched as he sat on the bed and reached to pull them over his bare feet. "Put on the stockings first," Wisp called from the doorway.

"But, Master Kender—"

"Put them on," Wisp said, and the tone must have been harsh enough, for Adju dropped the boot and reached under the bed for a sack he carried. He pulled the stockings out of it.

"All right, Master Kender, there's no need to watch me."

"If you plan to do as I say there's no reason why you should mind my watching."

Adju pulled the stockings over his feet. "Master Darstan," he called. "Get up. It is time to eat."

"Leave Darstan alone and go with Aenaila."

Adju finished dressing and walked awkwardly into the hall, still not accustomed to the boots. They clopped noisily with each disjointed movement.

~

WHEN WISP and Darstan joined them at the table, Aenaila questioned them. "Where are we going now?" She liked to know beforehand exactly what kind of situation they would be Shifting to.

"We are going where you won't be able to call me Wisp—to Sykor."

"I will finally see your home, Kender Darnell." Aenaila chuckled. "It seems odd, calling you Kender Darnell when I have just begun to call you Wisp."

"It will seem funnier yet if you call me Wisp and they hang me from the roof of the nearest tavern."

"Should we even be going there?" The question had been eating at Darstan ever since Wisp had told him they'd be going to Sykor."

"Maybe we shouldn't go there—not yet." Aenaila knew what had happened in Sykor and that both of them were hunted by the guard.

"What is the matter with Sykor, Master Kender?" Adju's curiosity knew no bounds.

"I know Sykor well enough, Aenaila. I know where we can and cannot go, and who will help and who will sell our souls."

Darstan nodded. "He knows the city. None could deny that. There's not a street or alley or crack in the wall that he hasn't memorized. If he says we'll be safe, I'll go along with it."

Aenaila was not yet convinced. "If there is a chance of danger we should wait."

"The only people who will know we're there are the ones I let know."

"When I was a small girl the wolves raided our flocks twice every month. Then, one night—"

"Mistress Aenaila, there are no wolves in Khatara. Only laughing wolves."

"I was not always from Khatara, Adju, and besides, wolves roam freely in the mountains of Jattan-Kir, though I'd not expect one from the Hajaran to know that."

Darstan thought that Aenaila's reaction was unusually harsh; Adju's statement was innocent enough.

I wonder why she did that, he thought, but then cast the worry aside. "Where will you go, Wisp, to the inn?"

Wisp had already decided it should not be the inn. He would move as cautiously as his furtive mind could conceive. "Cynamar's house, the one we stayed in while waiting to leave the city."

Aenaila's disposition grew more dour after hearing the news of their destination. "Is this the famous Princess Cynamar, the one Wisp is so fond of?"

Darstan ignored the question; he'd let Wisp manage his affairs.

Adju was wise beyond his age; he knew when a situation needed interruption. "Master Kender, I'm hungry. When will the food come?"

"I'm famished myself, Adju."

Aenaila looked like the boy who was winning when the fight stopped, and she had not finished with Wisp. "Have a pleasant breakfast, Kender Darnell," she said, her voice weighted heavily with sarcasm.

A good meal brought clear minds and fresh views to everyone. Wisp had given more thought to the situation in Sykor and had decided it would be wiser to arrive concealed. Adju didn't know of his powers, but he would be told soon. And he would experience the feeling of disappearing so that he didn't panic when it happened.

Being cautious never killed anyone, Wisp reminded himself.

They repeated the shift three times, from Aenaila's room to the one shared by Darstan, Wisp, and Adju, and all three times, Adju nearly screamed from shock. On the last attempt, he emitted only a gasp, but still enough noise to get them killed in the wrong situation.

"You must learn to be quiet. We can't afford a mistake. Pretend you are in the chambers of merchant Bulta, a necklace of gems in the palm of your hand and you hear a door open." Wisp let the thought sink in. "That, is how quiet I want you to be."

Adju nodded vigorously. He was trying his best, but the thought of his body disappearing unnerved him. "I will try, Master Kender. But every time it happens I think of going to the realm of the dead, and I get afraid."

Aenaila laughed. "Only people like Wisp go there. Nice little thieves like yourself do not. If you stay good in this life, you climb to the top of the Chugarran Path."

There she goes again with that Chugarran Path, Wisp thought, but then dismissed it.

After several more tries, they finally got it right. Aenaila grabbed Adju's hand. "Get ready, and remember, Adju, don't let go of my hand until Wisp says it's all right."

Adju nodded, he was holding his breath and thinking of the merchant's chambers so that he might remain silent.

THE AIR SHIMMERED AND CRACKED, and Aenaila brought them through the rift to a dark room under the streets of the city. Wisp had almost forsaken the cautionary measures he had taken previously of concealing everyone with his powers when they Shifted in the event that unexpected visitors would be at the other end. But he had been so sure that this house would be safe, and now, he thanked the goddess who looked after him that he had decided to Shift to a room near the tunnels below the house, and this only on the highly unlikely chance that Cynamar herself might be there.

Wisp dropped the Concealment, but immediately sensed danger. "Sh. Something's wrong!"

"What is it?" Aenaila asked though she had the forethought to whisper the question.

"Someone's upstairs," Wisp said, "and it surely isn't Cynamar." The noise he heard sounded like the heavy footsteps of guards. "Quiet! I can't conceal us again this soon, at least not for more than a moment or two." Wisp's voice was barely a whisper.

Adju squeezed Darstan's hand and stayed silent as a rock.

"Who do you think it could be?" Aenaila whispered back.

"They make noise like guards," Wisp said, "but Cynamar rarely lets guards in her house, not unless something is wrong." Even as he said that he heard footsteps approaching the door to their back from the tunnel. Wisp didn't know how long his concealment could last. He felt weak, and for some reason, the Shifting took more from him than ordinary even though he had nothing to do with the power of that. "More guards coming from the tunnel," Wisp said. "We're trapped."

"What can we do?"

"Can you Shift again?"

"Not now."

"How long?"

"A lot longer than it will take for those guards to get here." The sense of urgency kept her voice at less than a whisper.

Darstan drew the sword from his sheath. "We'll have to fight."

"I don't intend to do any fighting. You'll likely kill half the guard and have the city in flames before we escape."

Aenaila leaned over and whispered to him. "I could hide us with Illusion. Make a wall appear to be here instead of us."

Wisp disagreed immediately. "They're sure to be carrying candles, if not lamps, and if they've been here before and see a wall not meant to be here the first thing they'll do is poke it with their swords. Guards poke everything with their swords. I don't intend to be a cushion for a guardsman's curiosity."

"It's our only option," Aenaila said. "They grow closer."

"Let me try first. If I can't hide us, it's up to you. Grab hold now. I'll do it when the door cracks."

The guards' footsteps grew louder, and then he heard the key in the door just before it creaked open. Wisp concentrated his powers on concealment.

Please work, he prayed, or we'll be trapped like rats with their bellies full of cheese.

A NEW FRIEND

isp didn't like the feeling of standing so close to angry guards with swords ready to shed blood, and no matter how many times he'd done it, the odd feeling of being unseen and yet being able to see everything better than normal still gave him an odd sensation. He could feel Adju shaking as he used both hands to hold onto Wisp's arm. Aenaila was calm and still as a rock, though he expected no less. The one who surprised him was Darstan. He felt the slightest hint of movement, though not from fear, it felt like anger and hinted at an urge to strike.

I'll have to keep him close to me.

He counted six guards, and luckily, they moved swiftly to the bottom floor to the steps. He made sure to watch as they ascended, and counted again as they disappeared through the door to the upstairs. Only then did he feel comfortable enough to release the power and let them become visible.

Amidst the noise of reports being given and other conversations above, Aenaila was more interested in how to get out of there. "I still can't shift for quite some time. We need to find a safe place to hide. Is there any way out of here? Do you know these tunnels?"

"I know them well. We can find a haven." Now that he had dropped the power of concealment he could not see as well in the dark, but it was just as well, for he thought certain that Aenaila's face had fury painted all over it.

"Not with her!" She said it as a command, not a question.

Wisp was certain she meant the princess. How women could get riled like this, he'd never know, but he'd seen it enough to know what to do. "No, not with her. It wouldn't be safe to go there in light of the guards being in her home. I don't know what this is about, and I would like to stay and listen, but I feel it's better to just get out of here."

"Where to?" Darstan asked.

"Don't worry. Just stay alert."

~

THEY ENCOUNTERED guards two more times in the tunnels before turning down one Wisp said would be the last. The first time they were able to duck down a side passage before being seen. And the second time they were trapped in the middle of a corridor. Aenaila had recovered enough powers to use Illusion to disguise them and make it seem as if the path were narrower than it was, forcing the guards to one side. Fortunately, the passage was wide enough to let the guards pass without them brushing together. Both Aenaila and Wisp were now dangerously short on power, and if any more guards came, they would be forced to fight.

"Only a few more steps," Wisp said, then turned to the right down another tunnel that was thin and dark.

"How can you see?" Adju asked.

Even though he wasn't using his power, he could still see better than most at night, and he knew these tunnels like he knew most of the merchant's homes. He could tell how many steps it was from the jeweler's house to the merchant who sold spices from Khatara, and how many from there to the chandler's shop, to the tannery and back as well. They were important because they were sympathizers to the thieves guild. That Carmine paid them a handsome every month contributed to their beliefs, Wisp was sure.

Wisp lit a small candle, revealing a large bronze door with two sets of locks. It appeared impenetrable even in the dim light provided by the candle.

"How will we get past?" Aenaila asked. She knew Wisp was a thief, but she didn't relish the thought of waiting for him to open the locks with the prospect of more guards to come at any moment. While her thoughts were still forming, she heard the door open, a screech of metal upon metal that denied recent use. "Did you have a key?" Surprise carried in her voice.

Wisp allowed himself a chuckle. "I own keys to every lock."

Adju's eyes opened in disbelief. "Can you teach me that, Master Kender?"

"We are under the River's Edge district," Wisp said. "It's a poor section, not as bad as the Dongrel, but poor. A person can find a meal and drink without much notice here, although I feel we'll be testing the fates to even walk on the street.'

"Why don't we just stay here, Master Kender?"

"We can't risk another encounter with the guards. We'll be safer on the streets even with the attention we'll draw. Besides, there's a tavern only a few blocks west of here. It's a small one, and the food isn't good enough to attract a crowd, so we'll likely go unnoticed."

Aenaila nodded. "How far is it to Khatara? Is it farther than from Pomanda to Sykor?"

Wisp thought for a moment before answering. "A little, perhaps, but not by much. That depends, too, on how you judge distance doing what you do. If you mean as the crow flies, it may be closer to the same."

"Then by midday, I should be ready. If we wait a little longer, I certainly will be."

Darstan frowned. "You worry too much, Wisp. Who's going to notice us out of all the people on the streets?"

Wisp shook his head in exasperation. "I try to teach you, Darstan. Did you forget you're wanted by the guard? You embarrassed Ludar. Do you think he'll be satisfied with anything less than your death?"

He paused for a moment. "There are a few guards who know your face, and more than a few know mine. But that isn't what worries me. In case you forgot, you killed Sykoran guards in Khatara, and the ones who survived will have reported back to Ludar by now, and they will have told of a one-handed man—a one-handed man with powers."

Wisp saw the recognition in Darstan's eyes, even though he knew the mention brought pain with it. He didn't want to cause Darstan discomfort, but he had to make his point; hurt feelings healed faster than gashes with the sword.

"Nobody will recognize us. I've never even been to this part of Sykor, and we won't be here for long."

Wisp looked at him with disbelief. "Darstan, your looks alone draw the stares of women and men, but when you add the fact that you only have one hand to that, everyone who passes will first stare at your hand, then to your face to see if they know you. And enough people will have heard of the one-handed demon with fire by now to identify you. Remember, the guards killed the old man's son that Camissa knew just before we left for Pomanda?"

Wisp held up a hand signaling them to stop while he listened at another door. "Where does that lead, Kender?"

"It's the door to the street. It comes out in a narrow alley near the river. The tunnels were abandoned long ago and outlawed by the king more than twenty years ago. All the entrances were either closed up with dirt or rock, or they built doors around them, and only guards have keys. It was meant as a means for the guards to move quickly through the city when necessary, but they never use it."

Wisp paused for a moment like he had just remembered something. "Not until now, that is."

Wisp worked on the lock for only a few seconds. "I watched you this time, Kender. I didn't see anything. It looked as if you simply waved your hands over the lock, and it opened."

"That's how it's supposed to look, Aenaila." Wisp smiled.

"When we go out, Darstan, walk with Aenaila on your left and let her pretend to hold your hand. If Adju and I cover you from the front and rear, perhaps no one will notice."

Wisp cracked the door to ensure no one was nearby to see them exit. "Once we get to the inn keep your hand under the table and keep your good looks away from the door. The same goes for you, Aenaila. There aren't many women as beautiful as you, which will help us, I hope."

"How do you mean?" Darstan asked.

"I mean we can hope to draw the stares of most men to Aenaila instead of you and your hand. With them gawking at her, I doubt they'll have time to look at you."

"I would have never thought you to notice, Kender Darnell."

"I notice everything. Remember?"

The grin on Adju's face stretched from ear to ear. He tugged on Aenaila's sleeve, and when she bent down to look at him, he just winked at her. The little imp drew a smile from Aenaila equal to his own.

Wisp pushed the door open and stepped out slowly, eyes checking all the spots he could not see from inside. When he discerned it to be safe, he waved them forward. "And don't call Darstan or me by our names. The guards are bound to know those, too."

They crossed the street to the River's Edge Tavern and walked through the door. As Wisp had surmised, there were tables aplenty. He spotted a vacant table toward the back and hurried them to the seats, reminding Darstan to sit with his back facing the door and to let Aenaila sit at his left to cover the hand.

"Keep it under the table," he said to Darstan, then pulled a chair from the next table, and he and Adju took seats facing the door. "Order slowly, and eat slower," Wisp said. "The longer we can pass the time away here, the better it will be. I don't want us out on the streets."

The afternoon rolled on monotonously. Small talk comes with difficulty when it is forced, and it drags on even slower when false names are used. The inn had filled to nearly halfway shortly past mealtime, many of the patrons having come from begging or working at other establishments.

"It looks to be a callous group, my friend." Aenaila had done her best to keep the comment a whisper, but a lady at a nearby table heard.

The woman who rose stood nearly as tall as Darstan and she was a stone heavier than Wisp, if not more. Strands of tangled gray hair fought to hide what had appeared to have been blonde many summers earlier, and perhaps many children ago. She was bony, but not frail—like a mongrel left on the streets too long—and her hands could wrap a jug of wine or cheap ale, and looked as if they had on many occasion. Her mouth was full of big teeth that launched words louder than a man wrestling bears—words that jumped off a jaw that jutted out halfway to the person in front of her.

"I don't mean to say I know what that word is, fancy lady, but I don't think ya meant to say nothin' nice 'bout us." The big woman had stepped all the way to the table, and she hovered over Aenaila like a wolf over a crippled lamb.

Aenaila clutched Darstan's sleeve tighter; she knew he would be tense, and as she grabbed him, she felt the sleeve tug as he tried to pull away. She smiled sweetly and stared straight into the woman's eyes—pale blue, and beautiful. The only beautiful thing on a woman who had lived a tragic life. Aenaila's smile grew genuinely warmer until she realized she had been silent too long. "Pardon me for staring, but your eyes... they are so beautiful."

She gently patted Darstan's arm then let go his sleeve so she could stand. She rose to face the woman, and though not nearly as tall, and not nearly so big, she presented herself with a force of its own. "I beg your forgiveness if I offended you. I meant no harm by what I said." Aenaila waited for a reply, but none came.

The woman just stood, staring, her lips locked like a vise. It had been many a day since anyone had called her beautiful—man or woman. She was silent a long time, so Aenaila continued.

"Perhaps I was wrong in speaking, but truly, I meant no harm. I admire a hard person, one who works for a day's food."

"Don't look like you've done no work."

Aenaila thought she could detect the hint of giving in the tone. "No, I fear you're right. I have done less than I should have, but I have been fortunate. More fortunate than most in many ways."

The woman had not expected such a display from Aenaila. If she had been a coward and tried to bluff her way out of this with haughtiness, or if she had been coy and tried to hide behind her men, then she would have known how to handle her, but this... well, the woman didn't act like she was supposed to. "Well, don't guess any word can hurt me." The woman tried her best to quit without losing face. "Guess I'll go now."

Once the woman had reclaimed her seat, Aenaila walked quietly to her side and tapped her arm lightly. "Excuse me, but you didn't tell me your name. Mine is Aenaila."

The woman was surprised again by Aenaila's behavior. She could have gone on with her fancy friends and just been done with it. Why'd she want her name? She looked again to Aenaila and this time saw not a fancy lady but a gentle one.

"Mine's Grell," she said, quietly, embarrassed, but held her hand out to grasp, like men do.

Aenaila took her hand and gently closed it between her hands; it was almost as big as both of hers. "Grell, when I said I was sorry, I meant it. I feel ashamed."

Grell blushed, but Aenaila continued. "And when I said your eyes were beautiful, I meant that too."

Grell looked astonished, and for a moment Aenaila thought she was going to speak again, but her smile said everything, and Aenaila took her leave.

When Aenaila returned to her seat her face was still flushed red with embarrassment.

Adju was the first one to speak. "I know you did not mean it, Mistress Aenaila. You were always kind to everyone in Khatara." Adju looked to Wisp and then Darstan, his soft, brown eyes holding their attention. "In the harjana where I come from, Mistress Aenaila is known by all. She is known as the kind healer, the healer who does not take payment."

"My apologies to you," Aenaila said.

"No harm has been done," Wisp said. "Now, if you feel ready, I suggest we leave."

Aenaila finished the last sips of her te then rose to signal she was ready. A cautionary look from Wisp reminded her to grab Darstan's sleeve while they departed the tavern.

When they opened the door to step outside, the sight that greeted them sent shivers up Wisp's spine. Three guards were beating a man, not twenty paces from the steps of the River's Edge Tavern. One guard wielded a club, one used the hilt of his sword, and the other kicked the man every time he went down, but the man continued to resist and fend blows with his arms and back, stumbling and crying out at the same time.

Wisp grabbed hold of Darstan's good arm, and with only a breath of time to spare, for Wisp could already see that Darstan had pulled free of Aenaila and was moving in that direction.

"Let it be." Wisp whispered his advice in Darstan's ear. "We can't put ourselves in the middle of every squabble in Sykor. The man is likely a criminal. Perhaps he deserves the punishment."

Darstan teeth ground together, and his eyes burned with fury. "Nobody deserves that."

Wisp could see that Darstan would be difficult to persuade, so he elected for another option. Besides, he had to agree with Darstan, no matter what the man had done it didn't call for that kind of beating. Wisp exhaled loudly, the sigh all but confirming his decision. "I'll take care of it. Stay with Aenaila and Adju. Make your way back to the tunnel, and I'll rejoin you shortly."

Darstan stopped moving, but he made no motion to leave. "Go on, Darstan. This won't take long." Wisp walked over until he stood less than three paces away from the guards, still beating the man mercilessly. He raised his voice so he could be heard, even over the screams from the man in the street.

"Do you need help, mighty Sykoran guards? Stop and let me beat him for a while. You appear to be tiring. Let a fresh hand strike the man. Yield your club, soldier, and let me have a whack or two on him. I'll show you how to punish a man."

The guards stopped to analyze the man approaching them, confusion set in their eyes.

Wisp aimed to keep them off balance while he drew closer. "Or, if you prefer," he said, "just hold him, and I'll finish the job. Let me carve him with the blade. Peel some skin? Would you like him dead or simply maimed?" Wisp drew a fiendish smile on his face, a smile he knew would further confuse them. Even guards didn't smile when they inflicted punishment.

The guards' attention was fully riveted to the crazed man who addressed them. They didn't know how to react to such as this. But as they deliberated, two more people emerged from the tavern, the noise from the street perhaps having rumbled inside when Wisp and his party had opened the door to leave.

Wisp wanted no problem with the guards, but he needed to put a stop to this, not only for the sake of the man bleeding in the street but even more so to keep Darstan out of the ruckus. If he got involved the flames would travel a lot further than the River's Edge. He'd have all the guards in Sykor after them.

Two men stood on the steps leading to the tavern, and he saw the look in their eyes. They had no love for the guard; no one in River's Edge did. The biggest one had his fist clenched and ready. The other appeared to be a man who was always ready to brawl. They would be the key to stopping this.

"Come, good friends, come and help me control this man who has almost worn these three Sykoran guards to a frizzle.

The men on the steps, wearing scratchy beards and brawny shoulders, moved slowly toward Wisp. Their lips found a chuckle for Wisp's statement, but their eyes—focused only on the guards—held no love and contained no laughter. The smaller one, the one who appeared to have known many brawls, let his right hand creep toward the back side of his britches. A knife lay there, Wisp was sure, and the man likely knew how to use it. His movements were poised, alert.

Wisp turned to see that the guard with the club had tightened his grip, the whiteness showing in his knuckles. The other two looked less certain, more apprehensive. Wisp knew the guards well—they wanted no part of a fight where the odds were close to even.

Just then a woman and her son rounded the corner. She let out a gasp when she saw the scene, but hurried the young lad past, shielding his eyes with her shawl. Two more people came out of the tavern, one of them the big woman, Grell.

The growing crowd proved too much for the guard, and the one who had been kicking the man on the street grabbed the guard with the club and pulled him back. "Let's go," he said, loud enough for Wisp to hear.

"What about him?" the other guard asked.

"Leave him. Let's go." The three of them turned and started walking, each one looking back every five or ten paces to see that no one followed.

The one big man from the tavern, the one with the balled fist, came alongside Wisp. "That's a brave thing you did, lad. Those guards might just as likely turned to strike you."

Wisp looked at him, thinking it odd that the man would call him lad. He was well beyond the age for someone to call him lad, and even worse, this one looked to be only four or five years older.

"It was a foolish thing I did," Wisp said. "But I'd not see the man be beaten to death, no matter what he did. I might be setting loose a man who committed murder, but I suspect less."

The man on the ground moaned. Breath came in gasps, and he struggled with each one. Wisp rushed to his side arriving just as Aenaila did. Four times the man tried to get up only to fall back down. Blood ran freely from his head and nose, and his right arm appeared to be broken, from the way he held it.

Aenaila examined him closely, taking care first to look after the head wounds. She pried his eyes open and noted the hazy, glazed look. The man was in bad shape.

The big woman, Grell, knelt beside Aenaila, looking like a giant next to the petite woman. She placed her big arms under the man's head to lift him up.

"Don't move him, Grell," Aenaila ordered. "He is injured badly."

Grell opened the man's eyes and looked into them, nodding as she saw the problems. She ripped a piece from her blouse, a dirty patch of cloth that held as much grit as the street the man lay upon. She used it to apply pressure to the wound on his head.

Aenaila gently touched Grell's arm. "Do you know this man?"

"He lives only a few doors from me. He's a good man. I know his wife. And my child plays with his two boys." Grell seemed upset. "He's a hard worker. His wife will be lost without him. I know that."

"Please, Grell. I know something of these things. I have... helped others before."

The pause had been evident, and Grell looked into Aenaila's eyes for the truth. "You say you're a healer? Never seen a healer so young. And you without herbs or potions. How are you gonna heal him? Besides, I think he's past the healing."

Spittles of blood gurgled from the man's mouth even as they spoke, and he rambled on senselessly like someone caught with the fever. During it all, Aenaila heard Wisp almost hissing from beside her, his cautionary warning.

She stood to see what bothered him, a flash of impatience in her emerald-green eyes. "What is it? I need to tend to this man."

"You shouldn't do anything. If someone reports you as a healer, the guard will throw you in prison—if you are lucky. In Sykor it is not unheard of to kill people with powers."

Aenaila acted as if she had not heard any of his argument. "Would you have me leave him to die?"

Wisp was silent, and during the silence, Aenaila took his hands in hers, the smoothness of her skin placed a smile on his face. When her eyes found his, she held him fixed. "If you can tell me that you would do the same if you were me, then we will leave. If you can, with all honor, say that you would let the man die, when you knew you could help, then I will give you no more argument." She saw the frustration and the indecision building within him.

"All right," he said, "but hurry, and don't let anyone see you."

Aenaila nodded. "Do your part, Kender Darnell. Keep everyone away from me while I work, and I will do my best to finish with haste." Three quick steps found Aenaila back beside the man on the ground. He was barely breathing now.

"There's nothing to do for him," Grell said.

"I can try. Hold his head tightly. Don't let him slip." Aenaila looked into the woman's eyes. "Grell, no matter what you feel, don't allow his head to fall."

Grell looked at her like she was crazy. "I can hear ya, woman. Do ya think I'd let the man go?" Grell mumbled under her breath while Aenaila prepared for the healing.

This one was near gone and would require great power. Aenaila focused, let her mind go blank while she reached deep within her body. Deep, to let her mind find the power within her until she could see the power. And then, she could feel the power.

Her mind took over. She could feel the flow as she commanded it up from the hollows of her stomach. She felt it flow through the channels in her chest and into each shoulder, then down each arm and into each hand. Finally, the power rested where she needed it, and she let it ooze out from her fingertips. She guided it into the man's head, and when the first surge flowed into him, Grell jumped back.

"What was that?" she asked.

"Sh. Please?" Aenaila whispered. "Please, Grell. I'm trying to help. Just hold his head or, if you must, let go, but nothing will harm you. On that, you have my word."

Grell stared at her like she was a mountain cat let loose in the city, then she stared back at the man she knew lying on the ground. "I'll hold him. I won't be movin' no more."

Aenaila once again focused on the powers and on channeling them into the man whose life depended on it. She could feel them surging, could feel them spreading through his body.

Grell shuddered. She must have felt the vibrations again, but this time, she didn't pull away. She squeezed her eyes tightly together and whispered prayers to her gods that everything would be all right like the healer woman said. And when the power surged up her arm almost to her elbows, all the muscles in her body tensed. She prayed more.

Aenaila focused on the worst of the gashes, and then she imagined the power entering the other one's mind, searching, searching until it found the problems. Once she saw the damage, she began to weave protective shields to seal off any problems. Soon she was finished, and with a few quick movements of her deft hands, she healed the remainder of the major cuts. The only thing left was the broken arm. Aenaila let her hands run up and down the man's bone between the elbow and hand. She could feel the break and needed to get inside. Sometimes a break could be healed from the outside, but one as bad as this required different measures.

She used the power to create the tiniest of holes in the man's arm, then, she went inside. Aenaila used the power of the shield again, first to straighten the bone, drawing a wail from the man that looked as if it scared Grell half to death, and then, once the arm was straightened again, she wove a protective armor around it to keep it stiff and allow it to mend itself. Finally, Aenaila was done. She placed her hands on her lap, and her head sunk low. She appeared as if she might collapse.

Grell opened her eyes when the man screamed, and this time she kept them open.

The bleeding had stopped from the horrible gash on his forehead; in fact, it looked like little more than a scratch now. The other cuts had healed also. And when she saw his eyes cleared and alert, and heard him mumble words in a coherent voice, her mouth dropped open. Grell almost dropped his head, but then felt him rising.

Aenaila sensed Grell's gaze on her and looked at the woman. There was almost a sadness in her eyes, combined with fear.

Grell held Aenaila's gaze for only a brief moment before bowing her head low. Her words were as soft as butter left in the sun. "Forgive me, My Lady. I didn't know."

"No, Grell, don't. There's nothing to forgive. I made the mistake at the inn, and I owed you an apology."

"But, My Lady, what you have done—"

"Sh. Please, Grell, if you would like to thank me, then tell no one of this. Let no one know what happened here, and tell no one that I helped him. That would be my reward."

"You have my word, My Lady. None shall hear it from my lips."

Wisp had kept more than busy trying to keep the curious crowd away, so he had enlisted the aid of the two men who had been going to help him against the guards. With them, plus Darstan, they were able to keep everyone far enough away so that no one saw what Aenaila had done. His explanations to let the women do their work had sufficed until they heard the man talking and some saw him nearly rise to his feet.

"He's all right," one said, and pushed through to go see himself.

Seeing that the healing must be over, Wisp let them go and rushed to Aenaila's side to see if she needed help. She had told him before that healing took a lot from her.

Grell took command of the situation quickly, and with authority. "Bock, Tomas, get him home. His wife will tend to him."

As a crowd gathered closer, she stood. "Get on home or back to the tavern. There's nothin' but trouble waitin' here. Those guards will be back before long, and they'll have more than just a few with them."

Wisp supported Aenaila, letting her use his shoulder to aid her in walking while she was weak. Darstan and Adju had come over also, but she refused their aid.

"I'll be fine in a moment. It doesn't take long for me to recover, at least, enough to walk."

"But you'll need rest," Darstan said. "You'll need a lot of rest before you can take us to Khatara."

Aenaila nodded, but said no more as Grell had come to join their group.

"If it's rest you're needin', My Lady, you can rest at my house. It's not much, but it's clean, and I'll swat the young one outside, so it'll be quiet for you."

Wisp stood ready to object, but he quickly recognized the advantage of staying in someone's home as opposed to an inn. He offered no objections, ceding the decision to Aenaila.

Aenaila smiled. "That would be nice, Grell. I would be honored to accept your hospitality."

Grell's face beamed with pride as she led the way down a side street, her long stride slowed for Aenaila's comfort.

They stayed the remainder of the day and all through the night at Grell's, listening to horror stories of how the guard had been treating the citizens of River's Edge and the Dongrel.

"My mother brought us here when we were little," Grell said, telling them some of her background. "But if I could, I'd go back. Back to the country on a little farm and never come here again. It'd be hard work. Hard enough for a man and woman together, but I got no husband. Just me and the little one." She stopped to sigh, and perhaps to think. "But I'd do it," she swore.

"There are farms in Pomanda that can be bought for small amounts," Wisp said. "But you have to agree to share the food with any of the lords who might be passing through. Not much, and none to take away, just offer them a meal, and something wet to quench a parched throat."

Grell sighed again. "Pomanda's a might far piece away, friend. And I got no horse and wagon to take us, and no gold to buy a farm." Grell laughed, a good-natured attempt to make fun of herself. "Truth is I got nothin' but a dream. But I'll not let that die. It might be that someday I can save enough for my boy to buy himself a farm. And if that happens, then it'll be grand enough for me."

Grell stood up from the chair she sat in and gave Aenaila a big hug. "I need sleep, My Lady, but you are all welcome to sit up and chat so long as the noise is not so much to wake me. I need to leave early in the morn, but you can stay the day."

Aenaila thanked her but said they too would be leaving early. They had a long journey ahead of them and must be off. "Thank you again, Grell, for your friendship. And thank you for the room."

Grell blushed and waved her off. "It's nothin' any good person wouldn't do. Now, ya had better get a good night of sleep if you'll be travelin' all day." She turned to Wisp and Darstan. "And you men take care of this lady, do ya hear?" She stooped to tousle Adju's hair. "And take care of this one too. He'll have a face to break a lot of hearts when he's old enough, so mind him." Then she smiled and bade them all a good night.

～

Wisp woke them long before dawn had arrived, and despite the protests from Darstan and Adju, they all agreed that they must be going. "If we leave now," Wisp said, "We can Shift from here and never have to leave the house."

Everyone agreed, and they prepared to leave, but Aenaila excused herself to go downstairs. "Where are you going?" Wisp asked.

Aenaila stepped back a step and whispered lightly. "I want to leave some coin for Grell. At least enough for the food we ate and for her trouble." Wisp seemed upset, but she had no idea why.

"I already left something," Wisp said. "Now, can we go?" He appeared anxious.

"I'll only be a moment. Tend to your affairs and let me be to mine. I won't leave without saying a proper farewell."

There was a determined look in her eye. "Go on, then, but hurry."

Aenaila mumbled to herself as she stepped softly on the steps, careful not to make much noise. Grell had insisted on sleeping in her sitting room with her son, allowing them to sleep upstairs in the bedroom. Aenaila crept through the kitchen and tapped gently on the door to the sitting room.

Grell opened it almost immediately. "I heard the floors upstairs."

"I wanted to see you before we took leave." Aenaila reached to hug the big woman, and as they prepared to depart, Aenaila held out her hand, offering two silver coins to Grell, but she took one look at it and shook her head furiously.

"No, My Lady, I'll not take coin from you. You keep it, or give it to others as you see fit. Me and mine won't go hungry."

"All right," Aenaila said, "But thank you, Grell. You will always be counted a friend."

The woman closed the door before tears caught her eyes, and Aenaila stepped away. As she passed back through the kitchen, something on the table caught her eye. She peeked behind her to see if Grell was looking, then stepped over to the table.

On the table sat a small purse tied at the top, and scribbled onto a piece of paper was a crude picture of a farmhouse, complete with animals. Aenaila opened the purse and let the contents slip into her hand. Fourteen gold crowns! It was enough to buy a small farm outright, and stock it, too. She quietly slipped the coin back into the pouch and tied the top.

The thief has more honor than I imagined, Aenaila thought and wiped the tears from her eyes.

Wisp seemed nervous when she reached the top of the stairs. "Are you ready, Aenaila?"

Aenaila smiled, but she'd not show him she knew his secret. If he had wanted her to know he would have said so. Besides, the real measure of a man's heart lay in the doing, not the gathering of praises for the deed. "Yes, Kender Darnell, I'm ready."

"Where to, Aenaila? Your home?" Darstan asked.

"I think not, Darstan. I know a friend's house that we can use. I would prefer to go there, in the event something is wrong." Aenaila held out her hands for them to grab, and after concentrating, she Shifted.

THE WARRIOR

The bronze-skinned warrior picked through the remains of the creatures he had slaughtered: a severed head found a resting spot attached to a belt-hook; fresh teeth joined others on a necklace draped from a bull-thick neck; and talons adorned the rim of his leather boots.

Korg paid keen attention to everything the man did. He had heard of tribes that marked themselves with the bones and flesh of enemies—a taunt to the honor of slain foes. Korg tried to stand but collapsed.

The warrior motioned for Korg's hand, then helped him up and threw him over his shoulder as if he were a sack of grain. He lay across the man's back, awaiting his next move. The hunting knife in his front belt pressed hard against bone and reminded him that he yet had that as an option.

Kavi sighed when the warrior plucked him off the ground to drape his other shoulder, and his father winced at the sight of so much blood on his son's face, but he also found cause for joy; at least his son lived. He used the sleeve of his coat to wipe the blood from Kavi's face and forehead. The wounds weren't serious—even minor head wounds produced a lot of blood.

Within a few moments, Kavi came alert. "Father, are you all right?"

Korg's smile answered before his words. "We're fine for now, though we have yet to see what he has planned for us. I don't think he wants us dead or he wouldn't have saved us from those beasts."

Just then Kavi caught sight of the severed head dangling from the warrior's belt-hook. It startled him, and he reared up.

"Chugarra's Gate! Does this man claim trophies?"

"He took the teeth and talons, but only the one head," Korg said.

"That's Growler's head. At least that's the name I called him." Kavi seemed to be recovering his senses quickly. "I wonder where he's taking us?"

"Do you still have your knife?" Korg asked.

"Both of them, though I think this one could kill us both before we cleared the sheath."

Korg swallowed a lifetime of pride. He was accustomed to his son regarding him as the ultimate warrior, though he suspected that pride would be the least of his worries. "Focus on the terrain. Note any new markers. This is new land, and we need to learn it quickly."

Kavi had instinctively marked the trail: a steep incline with markings on it that looked like an ancient waterfall had carved its mark on one precipice; a tree that resembled an old oak, but the knots of roots that protruded from its base declared it a different breed of tree; and the sharp bend in the creek as it coursed around a huge boulder, round as it was tall. He marked the distance before they came to another swift-flowing stream and the lush field that looked as if it spread for a league from the bank on the far side. With meticulous detail, he committed their path to memory while the sun rose to full height in the sky. During this time, the warrior had not stopped. "Does he never tire?"

The lump of pride in Korg's throat swelled, but he knew his son meant no harm. "We could use some warriors like him to fight for us. What would our enemies think of that?"

Kavi laughed.

At the sound of laughter, the warrior stopped and let Kavi slide from his back. He motioned Kavi to walk, and when the warrior saw that he had no problem, he continued, Korg still on his shoulder. Kavi forced a fast pace to keep up, but at least this allowed him a better view of the terrain.

After navigating another steep incline and a heavily wooded plain, a large grassy meadow crashed into a sheer cliff rising to several spans. A narrow path cut into the rock forming a steep and tortuous trail. It was barely wide enough to accommodate one man. Heads and limbs of the beasts decorated the rock walls, sitting in pockets cut from the stone itself. The trail led to the top of the cliff where a gate carved of stone blocked further progress. More heads crowned the stone, and even more body parts decorated the walls, with stains underneath where the blood had dripped onto the rock. Teeth and talons littered the floor.

The warrior set Korg down, then with his hands placed in an awkward position, he pushed, and the giant slab turned to open a gateway for them. The warrior held the slab and motioned for Kavi to bring Korg inside.

Tall, spindly trees blocked the path ahead, obscuring the view, but through one dense copse, an entrance to a cave showed.

hidden entrance

They made their way through the trees and entered into a huge cave, but with light coming in from slits deep to the rear. In addition, a set of stairs had been carved into the rock leading up, but to where, Kavi couldn't see.

The warrior led them deeper into the cave, passing by numerous beds made from strange leathers and cushioned with straw, leaves or feathers. Several large cisterns lay filled with water, and weapons of various types hung on walls or were positioned in stands.

They stopped beside a bed with large clay pots at its head. The warrior grabbed Korg from Kavi's back and lowered him to the bed. Before long he had stripped Korg of his trousers and mended the injured leg. Kavi helped make a splint, and afterward, the warrior brought a tree limb for Korg to use as a walking stick.

"Thank you," Kavi said.

The warrior nodded his head.

Kavi stayed beside his father as he slept, and then, after he awoke, they shared some meat by a small fire. Smoke curled its way up the walls, then out through vents in the upper reaches of the cavern, natural chimneys that afforded him the luxury of fires for cooking and warmth.

"He brought this meat earlier," Kavi said, as he took another bite. "I don't recognize it, but it tastes good."

Korg grabbed another piece of meat and devoured it in two voracious bites. "It could be a red-beak for all I care. It's been a long time since I've had anything this good." Laughter expressed their relief.

THE BRONZE-SKINNED WARRIOR sat on his haunches and observed them talk. Perhaps these two would be the ones to lead him out of this land—lead him to a civilized world once again. Pieces of memory sprayed vivid images of a time long ago, a time and a place when he had lived in a different world. He had lived in splendor. He remembered some of that, but mostly he recalled scenes of battle—dark, hazy battlefields splattered with the blood of thousands.

inside cavern

A movement by the young one caught his attention, and the warrior focused once again on observing their speech. Very little escaped his keen eyes: he noted how they formed their lips; how their tongues touched the roof of their mouth on certain words; the set of their eyes; and the expressions on their faces. He had heard this speech before and was confident of his ability to learn this language. He had even learned the language of the krengs—the animal warriors that dwelled here, the hunters of this land.

It had been so long ago, so many seasons had passed since he first came here—wherever "here" was. Try as he might he could not recall how he came to be in this place or what had happened to his memory. One of the only things he remembered was how to fight, and how to survive—that he could do well.

At night, when all was quiet, and he was comfortably within the caves, he recalled images from the past, from before he came here: scenes of battle, vague recollections of warriors' screams and the echoes of blades clashing against steel. And the smell! The smell of blood on a field of battle. And of flesh, charred and burnt, its unique putridity permeating the air and causing fear to run rampant through the weaker ones.

Even now he could smell a kreng lurking outside his lair. It was probably a brave young female just reaching her age—they became bold at that age, and since the females ruled in the kreng packs, they were the ones who sought glory. She, no doubt, wished to reach for immortality by killing him—their persecutor. Before he came, they ruled these lands. Just thinking of them made him want to kill again.

The warrior shifted his stance and caught another scent. Yes, she has come of age, he thought. But he knew she would leave soon. The krengs could not get into his impenetrable fortress, and even if they were able, they would not because their customs forbade them to dishonor their dead that adorned his walls.

The warrior thought about how his sense of smell had improved since coming to this place. He could track the krengs by smell alone. Vivid memories flooded his mind. He recalled how they had stalked him at first, had marked him for prey. They had surely imagined him as their feast that first night, but they had grievously erred. Had they sent all of the warriors at once he would not be sitting here now, but they had underestimated him and sent only a few. Not nearly enough.

He relished the remembrance of their horrified screams as he sliced them to bits. His blade had claimed many lives that night. It had fed well.

He had escaped and evaded their pursuit. Before long he had learned their ways, their plans, and strategies, and their preferences: where they liked to sleep, to feast, even where and when they performed their ritual acts of mating. Cleverly, he had turned the tables on the krengs. When they sat down to a feast, he would attack from afar using a bow and arrow, slaying four or five before ceasing. If one strayed from the pack, he would stalk it and take it silently with a knife. And while they slept he crept into their lairs and cut throats or severed limbs.

He shivered with delight as he recalled the occasions when he had caught them mating, and how he would slay the male and leave the female. At times, he would listen to her scream until her breath was short and her voice hoarse, and then he would slay her too. At other times he allowed the female to live to spread his tale of terror to others. If there was one thing he knew, it was how to cause fear.

The warrior smiled. Before he came, the krengs had feared nothing, but he had learned their tongue and had listened to them speak of him. At first, he was reviled, though respected. As the seasons passed, they spoke of him with awe, and by the time the first of them had sired children, his name was mentioned with fear. Within a few generations, he had become a legend, a story to be told to the young at night, a shadow to be wary of.

He smiled. Now, after only the gods knew how long had passed, after the original krengs he battled had been dead for centuries, now he knew, the fear of him was inherent in their race. Each new kreng was born with a fear of the bronze-skinned warrior, or, as they now knew him—Death With A Long Claw.

Kavi's raised voice captured the warrior's attention once more. He focused on their words. Soon, his lips parted slightly, and he pushed the breath out. A sound escaped that was not a grunt or a growl, but a real word. "Ka...vi," he said.

Korg and Kavi shot startled looks in his direction. He smiled, and they smiled in return. Then he stared at them with his piercing eyes. Tongue and lips once again made the connection. "Korg," he said this time. He was learning quickly.

MEMORIES

*D*inner wasn't much; Rhaven had ordered everyone to cut the food by almost half once he realized the land they traveled had been in a drought. He cut water consumption as well, even though Tomkins had insisted there would be fresh water in the swamps. Rhaven was not a man to risk anything based on information a man might have had from two winter's past, or whenever it was he had been there.

A gnarled, old cedar tree bore the brunt of Rahg's weight as he leaned heavily against it, slowly chewing a piece of dried meat, sucking out all the flavor before he swallowed. It would provide nourishment, but the flavor disappeared after the first few chews. The bread was stale, but the cheese was tasty, and he saved that until last.

Rahg reached behind him and pulled the blade out of the sheath he kept tucked in his pants. He drew his knees up close and began whittling on a branch he had broken off just before he sat down.

With each layer of skin, the aroma of the cedar wafted into the night air and touched his senses. The smell of cedar reminded him of home, of the chest where Magmar had kept his mother's belongings. A smile lit his face as he pictured his father opening the chest, touching her treasures, restoring old memories. There was a sweater she had knitted him for Feast Day and some socks to match. Magmar never wore them, afraid the memories would fade with the wearing of the garment. There was a ring, Rahg remembered, and a silver cup for te, though he felt certain it had never been used, not even when his mother had been alive. At the bottom of the chest was the dress she had worn the day they wed, and Rahg recalled him taking it out when he felt especially lonely. The smell of the cedar made him think of the magnolia trees also, and how he used to crush the berries, their scent so sweet.

The sound of Tobias' voice brought Rahg back to the present with another smile. Tomkins was still shaken up from the events before supper when Kella had come out of the woods, and Tomkins' thought that the demons themselves had come after him. When he drew his bow to protect himself, Tobias jumped at him and cut his string, hollering like he was shooting the Queen of Sykor. The man had probably thought he traveled with a band of lunatics, at best.

A rustling of leaves above drew Rahg's attention to the high branches where he saw a squirrel running on a limb. It had frozen when he looked up, but he could still make out the bushy tail. I should tell them, Rahg thought, but he wanted no part of squirrel for food.

We're not starving. This one can live.

Rahg went back to his carving, thinking on the journey they were about to undertake. He looked forward to the trip, hoping it proved to be an adventure, one without so much danger, at least compared to what had come their way of late. He always liked canoes, and though these were half again as large as a canoe, they were similar, and the waterways they would be traveling would be rivers and swamps—not the sea. Somehow that made it seem safer. Tomkins had made it out to be a horrible journey, but then, he had lost his son; considering that, anything would be horrible.

Besides, Rahg thought, even the Entirians had thought this part of their trip would prove easy when compared to the rest. They had heard no legends speak ill of the Pathfinders; nothing evil had ever been associated with their people, if that's what they were. Suddenly, Rahg realized that he didn't know what the Pathfinders were, people or animals, not that it mattered, but it would make it easier if he knew what one looked like.

Did Tomkins say at the tavern? I'll have to ask him if he knows. With Rhaven and Tobias and Kella, he didn't think he had too much to worry about. It was the part after that that worried him, the part after he found the Pathfinder, when he would have to go into the Paaren. That's what scared him the most.

Rahg carved a notch from the branch and stared at Rhaven seated twenty paces away, Kella lounging close to him, sprawled on the ground with her head propped on his bedroll. Even though he couldn't see Rhaven's lips moving, he knew that he was talking to the vargel again. He talked more to her and Argus than he did to any of them, and as Rahg thought on it, he realized that oddly enough, the animals seemed to listen to him.

As Rhaven talked, Argus cocked his ears, brushing his tail now and then in response. And at times, his neigh and scratching of hooves on the ground proved enough to convince even the biggest doubter. And Kella stared intently at Rhaven while he talked to her, a silent listener to his words.

It wasn't long before Camissa began moving toward Rahg. Rhaven had been her companion for most of this journey. At first, he was almost glad, it gave him time to think and wonder. But after a while, he began to feel almost jealous, though he knew there was no justification for it. And besides, he had given her no indication that he felt any more for her than just a friend, so why should she stay with him. The past few days, however, when she started spending more time with him again, Rahg was happy.

She talked a lot about her earlier childhood days, and the fun things she remembered. She also seemed to miss Wisp, though Rahg didn't find that unusual. Camissa had known him a long time, a lot longer than Rahg had, and he already missed the company and wit of the thief. He always found some way to brighten everyone's mood.

A chuckle slipped from his lips as Camissa came toward him. She had taken to wearing the clothes of men when she was outside the cities—britches and a shirt too big for her, and boots made for a man. If her hair had been cut, no one would have guessed her to be a woman, unless they got close enough to see her skin, how soft and pretty she was.... "Agh," Rahg shook his head. He had to stop thinking like this, especially when they were alone in the wilderness. It would do him no good to torture himself every night. And with her being able to read thoughts, he quickly reminded himself and tried to block his mind at once.

TOBIAS HOLLERED something from where he stood talking to Tomkins. Camissa laughed, glad that Tobias had provided her the opportunity, she didn't want Rahg to know she had been listening. She didn't feel guilty over this, though, it was not something she did on purpose. Since she had been in Arangar, she had not tried to probe into others' minds, but the thoughts came unsolicited. Mostly they came from those she knew the best: Rahg, Rhaven, and Tobias, but also, an occasional thought from Captain Katsu popped into her head, although his thoughts were so garbled she could not make heads or tails of them.

She remembered a new sensation, though, when they were in the village to purchase the cows and sheep for the farmer. She had begun to sense strange feelings from the entire town. It was an overall sense of fear, and hopelessness, and hunger. Pictures of food and starving people raced in and out of her head, and for a while, she thought she might go mad, then, finally, she found a way to block them and returned to normal. She had not discovered what it was she did to block them and didn't know if she could duplicate the feat, but they were gone, and for now that was enough. She only prayed that it never happened again.

Camissa placed herself right next to Rahg, close. Too close. Her body was touching him.

Rahg stirred, restless. The feelings rose in him, and he moved slightly aside. "Are you worried about the journey, Rahg?"

"You know I am." He chuckled, a humorless laugh that bit with sarcasm. "Not as worried as I was about fighting Iazzo. Not as worried as I was about many things, but yes, I am worried. You heard what Tomkins said." He let the same laugh slip out again. "I suspect we'll face worse if our luck continues to hold as bad as it has."

Camissa started to speak, but Rahg forestalled her. "Who's going to taste the poison fruit? Rhaven will probably take some men from the ship along to try it out on them, but it will give me no relief knowing that more men will die for me. For a cause, I have no belief in. No heart for."

"If it has to be done—"

Rahg grimaced as the knife dug too deeply into the cedar stick he had been carving. "Nothing has to be done. Who said so?"

"The prophecies say so. And you know why. Lukaan and the Banished Ones will escape."

Rahg shuddered at the sound of his name. Camissa noticed his reaction but kept right on. "Yes, Rahg—Lukaan. I will say it again if you wish—Lukaan. If that frightens you, think of what his being free will do."

Rahg threw the stick away. It was ruined anyway. He slid his left leg down and rested his chin on the other. "The prophecy is just words. Somebody wrote those words, even if it was long ago. We could make a prophecy right now. Let's think up some words and things to talk about and write them down. Somebody in the future will read them and say this is a prophecy. And then I'll have ruined someone else's life."

"They have predicted too much, and you know it. Look at Shera Kevon."

"Yes, look at Shera Kevon. He thought I was the Messenger." Rahg leaned forward to stare into her eyes. "He had it wrong. That's my whole point. There could be a thousand people like me who fit the description."

"There can be no other, Rahg."

Rahg let his hands fall as he stared up at Rhaven, startled by his sudden appearance. He lost some of the tension from his tone, though a little harshness remained. "Why do you say that? What makes you any more sure than the shera? We've seen a lot of prophecies and heard many legends, and they all say different things."

"It is none of those things."

Rhaven's eyes had never been any colder. Now Rahg seemed frustrated. It was difficult to argue with Rhaven, he said so little, and yet, his expressions told so much. "Then what? What convinced you?"

"It is myself that has convinced me. The gods have not kept me alive through so many battles where I should have died just to waste me on a false prophet. I have thought about this often. There were many times when I wondered whether it could have been you, or perhaps Darstan, or even the thief. So I let everything go as it did, trusting fate to force the decision. And here I am with you. Darstan and Wisp aren't with us. That's good enough for me. It's an answer I will live by. Or die by."

"I didn't know you had such faith in the gods, Rhaven. I've never seen you bowed in prayer."

"Because I don't beg the gods for my bread every day doesn't mean I don't believe in them. I believe little of what the priests chant about, but I do believe in the mountains, the rivers, the moons, and the Endless Sea. And since we already know they weren't made by people such as Mikkellana and her kind, then I'll cede it to the gods."

"Suppose it's Lukaan and the Banished Ones. Suppose they're the gods."

"Then we shall have a fight on our hands. The fight I have longed for all my life. The one I live for." Rhaven turned quickly on his heels and departed, like a snake sneaking through the brush.

Rahg was glad he left. He didn't need more tension. If the man was willing to stand there and say he'd fight the Evil One, there was nothing else Rahg could say. He turned toward Camissa and saw the smirk on her face. He wanted to lash out at her but he couldn't.

"Hard to argue with him, isn't it?"

"Few are so stubborn as to try."

The frown remained on Rahg's face. "I deserved that. I'll not give you an argument either. No better arguing with you than it is with Rhaven."

Camissa let him sulk for a moment in silence. "Then brace yourself for the inevitable, Rahg. You and I are riding with Rhaven. With no one to argue with or arguments you can't win, this will be a long journey."

Rahg finally laughed at his predicament. "I'm sorry. Sometimes I talk when I shouldn't."

"We all do."

"Did Rhaven say who else was going?"

"Tomkins will be with Tobias, and the other two boats will be Captain Katsu, Jarrell, and two of the other seamen."

"What about Kella?"

"I asked Rhaven. He said he'd rather take Kella than Katsu's men, but he doubted she would go. He said it would be her choice."

A sigh tumbled from Rahg's lips. "I doubt she'll come."

Camissa stretched and yawned. "The morning will tell. No sense in losing sleep over it. As for me, I'm tired."

"Wait, Camissa. Don't go."

Camissa had already started to leave but turned at his request. "What is it?"

"I just wanted to... just wanted to know if you have... sensed anything with this Tomkins fellow."

"He seems no different than he appears—a man who has lost all hope. He has prepared himself for the Gates of Death and whichever path that might lead him to."

Rahg shook his head slowly, back and forth. "I don't know that I want to travel with someone like that."

"What do you think he would feel if he knew who he traveled with: a woman who could read his thoughts; a half-crazed warrior who wants to battle the Evil One; and you, a man with powers who the Evil One and all the Banished Ones are after. Tomkins is the one who should be worrying about his traveling companions."

Rahg nodded. "You have the right of it, Camissa. I guess I'll get some sleep. Morning will come soon enough."

"It will be no earlier or later than usual, Rahg, but as you say, that is soon enough. Good night."

Rahg curled up in the bedroll and tried to force sleep to visit him. For a long time, he just lay there thinking of how the expedition might turn out. The conversation between Tobias and Tomkins was like a noise in the background, like the chirping of birds on a morning in spring.

Tomkins didn't do much of the talking. For every two words he spoke, Tobias spoke a hundred, and that seemed a generous allowance for Tobias. Several times Rahg heard him clear enough to know he was spinning tales about the swamps back home and stories about the sea. It made no difference to Tobias that Tomkins had no idea where these places were; he didn't even know what lands Tobias spoke of, but it made no difference, he just kept the stories going.

He could tell stories to someone speaking a different language, Rahg thought, and even that wouldn't deter him.

Tomkins was almost the perfect listener for Tobias, he just nodded his head now and then and stared off into the distance. Every so often he'd ask a few questions, but he never tried to compete with Tobias for the opportunity to talk.

Perhaps Camissa is right. Maybe he's just a man set on crossing through the Gates of Death. Well, he'll likely find it sooner than later, traveling with us, Rahg thought, and he realized how many people had died around him since leaving Twin Forks.

Images of Magmar flashed through his mind, but he quickly dispelled them; he could not afford to drag his mind down with thoughts of his dead father. It happened often enough as it was, but he would need to be alert on this voyage, or he'd find himself joining Tomkins at the Gates of Death.

The dismal gray sky teased the land with hints of rain, but there was no moisture in the air, no real promise just a false hope. It was cold but dry—dry as a Sethian summer. Rahg shivered as he woke, then hurried to the fire Tobias had started. He rubbed stiff fingers together and bent to let them touch a taste of the flames dancing off the sides of Tobias's pot, near to boiling with hot khaffe.

The aroma of the khaffe and biscuits stirred Rahg to excitement, and he licked his lips. There were people at the last village who might have killed for biscuits or any food. Tomkins sat on a rock next to Tobias, who was still filling him with tales of adventure. "Have you been telling stories all night, Tobias? Give Tomkins' ears a rest."

Tomkins looked up at Rahg for a moment but then focused back on Tobias as if Rahg had not spoken at all.

"Pay no mind to that lad, Tomkins. He never has learned manners, though not for lack of a good teacher. His father taught him right from wrong, but he never listened. I've tried my hand at him since last year and haven't made a difference either. Guess it comes with age."

Rahg lifted the lid off the pan that held Tobias's biscuits, reaching to snatch one, but Tobias's stick proved faster, and he delivered a whack to his knuckles.

"Get out of there, lad," Tobias yelled. "This is just what I'm talking about, Tomkins. He gets up in the morning crying like a colt just dropped from between his mother's legs, and lookin' for a teat to suckle. Doesn't much care whether anyone else has eaten or not, or even if these biscuits were for him."

Tomkins began talking, but his voice was so low it seemed as if he were addressing himself. "Was a time around here," he said, "when food was given freely to friend and stranger alike. If a man came walkin' up to a campfire or a stranger's house, he would be greeted with offers of food and drink. Have him for supper, invite him to share the night and the conversation and break fast with him in the morning. The next day he'd be sent off with food in his pack to last the day, even the night." Tomkins sighed, poking the fire with a stick. "But then the drought started, and soon, strangers weren't offered meals. As it got worse, friends weren't invited over, and if they fell on hard times not so many came with baskets of aid. Last year it got worse yet.

If a man comes walkin' up to a campfire now, he'd be lucky not to get an arrow in his chest 'fore he reaches the light of the fire." Tomkins spit to the side. "Nope, things have changed," he said, "and none for the better." He emitted a long sigh. "Just as well that I'll be goin' down there. Perhaps I'll be seein' my boy soon. I sure do miss the lad."

Tobias made some crazy noises, then flipped the lid off the biscuits. "Don't be talkin' about walking through the Gates of Death so soon, Tomkins." He nodded to Rahg to take a biscuit, which he did, then reached for another.

"I'm taking one to Camissa," he said, before Tobias's stick caught him. He held out two mugs of khaffe in the other hand as proof.

"Be sure that she gets it, lad. And don't think I won't check on it. I'll be askin' her later today if she got it."

Rahg laughed as he walked toward Camissa. He knew Tobias would check with her; he guarded those biscuits like other men did gold. Camissa was sitting against the tree when Rahg got there. He plopped down next to her, his extended hand offering her the biscuit, then let her take the mug of khaffe with the other. "If you don't want this, give it back to me."

"I'll eat it. I'm sure you've had your share, if not more."

"Tomkins sure is a gloomy man," Rahg said.

"He has a right to be. He lost his son in those swamps, and he blames himself for it. Not many lose a child and are able to bear it well."

Rahg nodded solemnly. "I suppose it's like losing a parent."

"Most say it's worse."

Camissa spoke with an air of authority when it came to matters of emotions. Rahg had noted that before.

Thoughts of Magmar once again prickled at his mind. He shook his head, as if to rid himself of the troubles, and sought to change the subject. "How far to the river? Did Rhaven say?"

"He said we would be there before midday, which would give us a good half day before dark."

"I've never been in the swamps. Not real ones. But, from what Darstan told me, if they're anything like the Cypress Swamps, it won't be fun."

Camissa pulled her cloak tightly about herself and fastened it, hoping to forestall a shiver. "It must not be as hot as the Cypress Swamps, not if it is only a half a day's walk from here." Camissa bit her biscuit and took a sip of khaffe. "Have you been practicing with your Shield?"

Rahg's face lit up. "Every day, and I feel it getting stronger. Every few days I can actually feel the increase in strength, though it does make me tired at nights. Last night I went to sleep early, and I still feel as if I need more."

Camissa nodded her head. "What type of practice?"

"Mostly making shields to protect the people traveling with us, just in case something happens." Rahg smiled. "You haven't noticed, then?"

"What?" Camissa's tone betrayed her curiosity.

"The past two days I've had a shield around you while we traveled."

"Around me?" Camissa asked, trying to curb her excitement.

"Just in case," Rahg said and blushed. "I mean, if anyone attacked us, I didn't want you hurt."

"What else have you done?"

"I've been trying to make shields similar to mail to protect myself, but they're too stiff. I can't move with them on." He saw Camissa was thinking on what he said. "Then, last night, I tried what Aentarra had told me. When I finally got tired of listening to Tobias telling stories, I placed a Shield around myself to stop the sound."

Camissa perked her ears. "Did it stay all night? Were you able to keep it around you while you slept?"

Rahg sighed. "I don't think so. I know it wasn't there when I woke, but I don't know how long it lasted after I fell asleep. I suspect that as soon as I dozed, the Shield dropped. It seems like I have to concentrate hard to get anything to work. Every time I lose concentration, my shields drift apart."

Rahg thought a moment more about what he said. "But it must have worked for a while because I went to sleep without hearing Tobias. I just don't know how long after."

Laughter hid behind Rahg's face.

"What are you laughing about? What else did you do?"

"Nothing," he said, but the chuckle wouldn't let him lie.

"You can tell me."

He looked about as if someone else might be listening. "Remember two days ago when Tobias was cursing and kicking because his biscuits wouldn't cook right?" Rahg smiled. "I covered the bottom of his pan with Shield so it wouldn't heat like it should. I was just testing myself to see how the Shield worked against fire." Rahg's eyes lit. "I'll tell you, Camissa, the Shield works easiest against fire. Blocking the fire was easier than anything else."

"I wish we had someone to teach you."

A frown re-appeared quickly on Rahg's face. "I haven't seen anyone yet that I would want to be taught by. I don't trust Mikkellana, not yet. And certainly not Aentarra."

Camissa's eyes burned with anger. "No, not Aentarra. "Not her." They sat in silence for a moment, neither saying a word.

"What about Aenaila? Darstan said she's strong."

Camissa remained silent for a moment more. "She's strong, but I have no clue what she's capable of. Darstan said she can Shift, and if she Shifted from Khatara all the way to Entiria she must be very strong."

Camissa thought for a moment more about the fire being the easiest for Rahg to control and puzzled as to why. "I'll help you, Rahg. We can think of new things to try. And you can help me as well."

"How can I help you?"

"I want to experiment with some new things, but first I want to make sure that I have all the powers I once had, after that ... experience."

Rahg fought for the right words. "You mean that place you went with Aenaila when we were fighting the battle with Iazzo?"

"It is called the Planes of the Mind. And yes, that's exactly what I mean."

Rahg couldn't bridle his enthusiasm. "Will you teach me to go there?"

"No!" It was a shout of finality. "I will never go in there again."

"But—"

"Never!" Aentarra almost killed me in there. If Mikkellana had not been around to save me, I would be dead right now. I never knew about it. I thought it was a place to play. I had heard legends about it, legends my mother had repeated to me, but I ignored them. I always thought it was a place to build, to build dream things that I couldn't have in this world. Never did I imagine what it was meant for."

Rahg fought the urge to ask again, but he knew when Camissa had her mind made up it was next to impossible to change it. He could see the agony in her expression. "Fine. I understand. But I'll help you with anything else. We can help each other grow stronger. I'm sure we'll need it."

Camissa nodded. "Of that, I too, am certain."

Rahg felt sorry that he had brought up the subject of the Planes of the Mind. Camissa's mood seemed to be ruined now. "I'm sorry if I upset you. It's just that—"

"No, that's all right. You didn't know, but you're right about helping each other. There is no question that we have to grow stronger." Camissa sighed. "But for now we have to find the Pathfinders, according to the shera and the shulan, and it is about time we were leaving. I'll help Tobias pack things up so we can leave. Rhaven will be growing impatient."

THEY SET A FASTER-THAN-AVERAGE pace all morning, with Rhaven at the forefront, occasionally scouting ahead to forestall any potential trouble. He had also ordered two of Katsu's men to keep a close guard on each flank.

Towering mountains dominated the landscape, their barren slopes painting a scene as bleak as the rest of Arangar. Trees clung precariously to crevices, some battered and broken from rock slides far above.

Rahg wondered how they would ever get over the mountains, especially if they were to reach the river today, as Tomkins had said. It was then he saw Rhaven riding back with Kella at his side.

"The river is just ahead, though it will be a tough descent." A shrill whistle brought Katsu's men from the flanks, and before long they stood at the foot of the mountains looking down into a small gorge at the river.

"It was once a raging monster," Tomkins said. "Used to come down out of the mountains in the springtime carrying entire trees with it. Was like the gods themselves were pushing it. Cut a path right through these old mountains."

Rahg looked to where the river went, flowing gently through the mountains like a trench in a farmer's field. "Doesn't look so wild right now."

river through mountains

"No, lad. Not now. But after two years of drought, there's not much water to go around. Wouldn't be surprised if there's not enough to hold us afloat in some spots, but the further we go south, the more the other rivers will join us. Then we'll have plenty of water. Plenty. You'll see. More water than you'll ever care to think about."

Rhaven halted, reining Argus in and dismounting. "Here is where we split," he said, and led Argus toward Katsu's men. Rahg took Marchall, while Camissa and Tobias tugged on the reins of their mounts.

Katsu barked an order, commanding his men to take good care of the horses. "Don't let anything happen to them," he hollered, and though his tone carried no threat, the men gave stout assurances.

Rhaven stepped onto a rock to raise himself above them. He stared at every one of them. "If anything happens to Argus, I will kill every one of you." He stepped down and moved toward the river. Rhaven turned to the captain before he left. "Provide enough gold to care for their food and the horses as well. I won't have starvation offered as an excuse."

Rahg smiled as he handed Marchall's reins to one of Katsu's men. He didn't linger. He would have to hurry to catch Rhaven as it was.

When they reached the edge of the cliff, Rahg stopped and stared. "How do we get down there?"

"Walk, lad," Tomkins said. "There's a trail shortly ahead. Not a bad trail. Be easy enough goin'."

"Lead on then, Tomkins," Rhaven said. "The sooner we put these boats in water the better."

Rahg shook his head. Rhaven always seemed to be in a hurry, even when he didn't have anywhere to go.

The trail down to the river proved as easy as Tomkins said it would be, much to Rahg's surprise. The men from the ship had carried the boats down, and no one had objected. The boats were big, about twice the size of a normal canoe, like the kind he and Darstan had used as children in Twin Forks, and they were wider by half again. Three men could sit comfortably in them and still leave enough room for a few provisions.

The water wasn't deep, and though it flowed at a reasonably strong rate, it was nothing that could be mistaken for danger. Tobias and Tomkins took the lead boat. Jarrell and Katsu each had another seaman with them, and Rahg and Camissa took the last boat with Rhaven. They had oars but would have no need of them now, not as long as the current stayed as strong as it did.

"Most likely won't need them oars until we come back," Tomkins said. "If we come back."

"Keep your bow handy," Rhaven said.

Rahg wondered why he said it, but realized Rhaven was one to be prepared. Rahg waved to Kella, standing on the cliff overhead. He was disappointed she hadn't joined them, but he had expected it.

The early part of the ride proved fairly easy, except for the cold. The wind raced down the small gorge, and it bit into bared skin as it skimmed off the water. As they dug deeper into the mountain, the walls of rock on the sides of them grew to be sheer cliffs of enormous height. Rahg couldn't even see the tops. Somewhere around supper time, Rhaven spotted a place where floods from ages ago had carved out a part of the canyon wall, leaving a recess large enough to hold twenty or thirty men.

Tomkins pulled over, signaling the others to follow. "Be a good place to stop for the day. Can eat here and make first night's camp. Won't be nothin' else for a good while."

"How long before we come to another?" Rhaven asked.

"Not before it's too dark to see. Quite a ways after that, in fact."

"All right," Rhaven said, and when the boat touched land, he hopped out like the boat would bite him. Rhaven didn't much care for ships or boats.

There was no wood to build a fire, and nothing to keep the wind from biting at them. They dragged the boats from the water, turning them over on the side to use as shelter. That offered some help.

As they dug in on the leeward side of the boats, the wind was a mere nuisance, a howling in the distance like when it used to howl through the chimney at home.

Rhaven scoured every part of land, and the walls of the mountains on each side. Rahg knew he was looking for danger; he always was, though Rahg thought he might have been looking for some way that Kella might have joined them too. She had followed them for a while during the day. He had seen her from the ridge looking down at them, but long before now he had lost sight of her.

"What will tomorrow bring us?" Rhaven asked of Tomkins.

"More of the same," Tomkins said. "Though we'll get out of the mountains by supper, and the river will flatten out. After that, don't know much what it will bring. Depends on how much the drought has affected things."

"There are sure to be plenty of places to stop," Rhaven said.

"Not the stoppin' I'm worried about," Tomkins said.

Rahg and Camissa talked among themselves for quite some time, casually listening while Tobias entertained everyone with stories. Finally, when the night was half over, Rhaven stood and walked to the boat closest to the river.

"I'll stand first watch," he said. "The rest of you better get some sleep."

First watch? Rahg thought. What is he going to watch for out here?

As if to answer Rahg's question, Rhaven turned toward the group and spoke. "If anyone has been following us, or watching us, this is a good place to attack. They might not think we will be prepared."

No sane man would, Rahg thought, but tucked himself into the bedroll. "Wake me for second watch, Rhaven."

Jarrell hollered for third watch, and Rhaven nodded. "So be it then. Rahg, wake Jarrell for third."

Several of the men were still talking, telling tales of Entiria and the sea, and Tobias was asking Tomkins a lot of questions about the swamps and Arangar in general, while trying not to let him know where they were from.

Camissa sidled up close to Rahg. "Use your shield to cover us, so we don't hear anything."

Rahg smiled warmly. "Get in a little closer. I'll be able to shield us both."

∽

By the third day of traveling they had gotten out of the mountains, and the river had already been joined by two other rivers, one almost as large as the one they traveled, and the other a mere stream, though, from the way its banks were carved, Rahg could tell that floods visited it often. The river had widened considerably, also, and it had gotten deeper. Rahg tried on several occasions to test the depth with the oars but couldn't reach the bottom.

"About two men deep," he heard Tomkins yell. "But when I came here, those trees on the side were near covered with water. Was a lot higher then."

Rahg looked to the sides and couldn't imagine the river being that high, but Tomkins had been here, and though the man seemed odd in a lot of ways, Rahg had yet to hear him stretch the truth, leastwise from what he knew.

The current picked up, and they made good time throughout the day, never once having to resort to the oars. It was at camp that night that Tomkins spoke of the river.

"So far we been lucky," he said, "but if it starts to get deeper, that's when we'll be in trouble. Right now the river is plain to see, clearly marked by the current and the banks, though they're disappearing fast." He took a moment to chew on some dried meat.

"After the next range of mountains, it'll get bad. They'll dump a lot of water into the river and the banks will disappear and the islands will too. And that's when we'll see little streams that go nowhere, and we'll see tangles of brush and vines that grab hold of the boat and won't let go. Kind of like they have a mind to keep ya here." Tomkins smiled, it was chilling for its lack of purpose. "Course, that's if we don't run out of food first and have to start eatin' each other."

For four more days they followed the river, and, true to Tomkins' word, it grew deeper and harder to stay on course. At times, the currents pulled them into side channels and into thick copses of swamp trees and tangles of vines that held the boats like a spider's web.

Rhaven urged them to pay attention to the signs of the river and to feel its flow, but it was more difficult than he realized, and soon they were at the mercy of the muddy mess. It wasn't just the rains that had been raising the level of the river, the mountains to the west had been making streams from rivulets and turning creeks to rivers, and all of them merged with the river they traveled on. There would soon be too much water to handle. The river would be unsafe at best.

By the middle of the tenth day— though the cold had eased some—the rain had been coming down in torrents, and the effect of the wind and rain was chilling. For the remainder of the afternoon, the rain pelted them and stung them, leaving nothing dry in the boats save for the goods and clothes Rhaven had the sense to keep stored in oil cloths to keep dry. Rahg had tried several times to Shield them, but he grew tired too quickly.

There was nothing to lift their spirits except the knowledge that soon the rains must stop. It couldn't rain forever. The river had almost become a sea, with thousands upon thousands of islands tied to one another by strings of vines and roots clutching and grabbing each other like children in a game. They sometimes gave the illusion of land when none was there.

For the next two nights they slept in the boats, not being able to find any solid ground and afraid that they would be swept off to a lost channel if they didn't secure a place for both themselves and the boats for the night. Twice, they had pulled into a swift-flowing current to the side of what they thought must still be the main body of the river and found trees to fasten their boats so as not to be washed away, but come morning they had to row fiercely to fight their way back to the primary channel.

The next day brought more of the same, but worse, the food was nearly gone, and if they had plenty of water, that was a curse, not a blessing. "How much farther?" Rhaven asked Tomkins.

"Can't say that I rightly know. It was about ten days in when we got lost." He looked around like he expected to recognize something. "Don't think we ever got this far ourselves, though it's hard to tell. All looks the same."

"Where do the legends place these creatures? Do they live in the swamps?"

Tomkins laughed, that crazy kind of laugh that irritated Rahg. It made him sound like he was mad, and Rahg hated the thought of traveling with a madman. He had his fill of that with Sennar.

"They don't live in the swamps, not that I've heard. If I remember my tales, they tell of the Pathfinders living in the lands on the other side of the mire, but no one I know of, or even heard of, has ever been there."

"When was the last time someone saw a Pathfinder?" Rhaven asked. He remembered what the man had said in the village the first night they met, but Rhaven had supposed he might have let the drink talk some then.

Tomkins spoke soberly now, if not sullenly. "Told you when I first saw you, nobody's ever seen no Pathfinder. Don't even know if they exist."

Rahg grew afraid, and anger made him shout. "Then why did you come? Why did you go before if you didn't think they existed?"

The boats were close; Rhaven had insisted on tying them together so they couldn't get separated. Tomkins' skin wrinkled as he stared into Rahg's eyes. "Told you, lad. Told you why I come. I left my boy in this swamp. Left him here without words said over him. Came to say the words over my boy's grave."

Rahg felt guilt over questioning the man. He had been nothing if not true to his word the entire voyage. If they had chosen not to heed his warnings, it was not a fault to place on Tomkins. "I'm sorry, sir, just a little discouraged, that's all."

"Can't blame ya, lad. Lost a little of my humor too. This place'll do it to ya."

They ate little for supper that night, Rhaven had ordered them to cut their intake even more, the third time since the journey began that he had done so. They were down to eating less than a man uses in a day, and the effects were beginning to show on everyone.

They still had plenty of water, Rhaven had them fill their sacks each day with fresh rain water, so they had just as much as they started with. It was only a matter of time before they would have to try some of the fruit that hung from the trees all. Some of Katsu's men had already been eyeing the fruit with a look of almost lust, and Rahg suspected it was their fear of Rhaven more than the warnings of death from Tomkins that kept them from sampling it.

Morning brought nothing new; they rowed back to the main channel of the river and soon floated downstream, southward bound again. The familiar honk of geese drew all eyes skyward. Rhaven reached for his bow but, after seeing how high they flew, put it down. As he placed it in the boat, Rahg released his arrow. It took the lead goose in the belly, dropping it. Rhaven looked to Rahg with a glint in his eye.

"That was the shot of an archer. I knew you had a good eye from watching you teach Camissa, but shooting at still targets and live ones are two different things. That's a shot only the best archers could make." Rhaven stared at Rahg. "Who taught you, your father?"

The blush on Rahg's face betrayed his excitement, and he stalled before answering, afraid he would stammer his words. "My father taught us some. But we learned most of it from a friend's father, Kor Trasken."

"Kor Trasken!" Rhaven said, "I know him."

Tobias chimed in from the other boat. He always seemed to be listening to everyone's conversations, no matter how many were going on. "He was the strike force archer under Takar in the swamps."

Rhaven nodded. "A brave soldier. I remember him. Did he live in Twin Forks?"

"Died there, too," Tobias said. "Wasn't but a few moments before you came that Kor caught a Victa's blade."

Rhaven nodded. "So many of the old ones gone."

Tobias kept up the talking. "Lot of Sykoran guards settled in Twin Forks—there, and other parts of Kamnor. Kip Trune settled in Herschwig, and Barret ... Barret..." Tobias laughed a little, "By the gods, but I can't remember that man's name. Anyway, he married a woman from Treschwig and ended up havin' nine children." Tobias shook his head and pulled his pipe out to light it, then he laughed.

Rahg laughed too, but not at his story; he was laughing at Tobias. Once he got this far in a story, it didn't really matter if anyone was listening. When he got started, he'd finish a story even if he had to tell it to himself.

"Funniest part of it was, all nine of 'em was girls. And to beat all, they ended up all bein' like their mother. And that woman was a shrew if I ever saw one."

Rhaven let him finish the story before he spoke again. He paid a lot of respect to Tobias. "You were fortunate, Rahg, that you grew up with so many fine teachers. Continue to practice, and I promise not many will be your equal."

Rahg made a gesture to brush the compliment away, but Rhaven stopped him. "Don't be foolishly humble. I doubt that I could have made that shot, which is why I didn't take it when I had the chance. Kor Trasken will be smiling from his grave for that shot."

Rhaven's compliment kept Rahg smiling for the rest of the day, and nothing that the river dished out would sway his mood. The waters had turned murkier, so dark that he couldn't see half a hand into it, and he just realized that after all this time, that they had seen no fish during the entire journey. Odd, he thought but pushed that worry aside as well. Dinner would bring some meat, and all because of him, and his shot.

Rhaven continued to question Tomkins about the river and what he might know about it, but at some point—and how he determined it Rahg never would know—Rhaven deemed he knew no more. He was not one to peck at a man once he determined he knew nothing else, but how he made that determination was beyond explaining. Sometimes he would continue to question a person who even thought themselves that they had told all, and before they knew it, they were telling more. Him staring with those eyes were worse than the pain of torture, and he always got what he wanted out of people. He seemed to reach in and grab words that a person didn't even know were there.

"Keep watch," Rhaven called. "Keep the bows and arrows handy. If there are geese, we must be near other things."

Rahg smiled. Rhaven's words brought attention to his feat earlier in the day, but he also knew Rhaven well enough to know he thought of more than geese when he ordered them to keep the bows handy. And the thought of whatever might be out there opened his eyes wide.

It was close to evening. The sun had quit early and had begun the slow descent below the treetops. Rahg had been keeping his eyes peeled for trouble and thought he saw something up ahead in the bushes. It looked like a small island, and on the edge of it, he saw something moving. Something big. "Up there," he called. "Look."

Rhaven followed his pointing, but it was Tobias, from the other boat who yelled it first.

"It's Kella!" His shout was like new breath for Rahg. "By the bones, it's that vargel. How she came down here, I don't know, but I'd like to hear that beast speak sometime. There would be a tale or two I'd like to tell."

Rahg was the one who hollered the loudest, after Tobias had named her. "It is Kella! Camissa, it's Kella!"

Rhaven's face lit up with a smile nearly as broad as Rahg's, and it spread all the way to his eyes.

"WHAT A WARRIOR." Camissa heard his whisper, or perhaps it was just a thought that she read. She couldn't be sure anymore. The past few days on the boat, the thoughts of Rhaven and Rahg had come to her and, at times, they sounded like spoken words. She had even responded to them twice, only to be met by dumbfounded stares. She would have to learn to recognize the differences better in the future and be careful. She didn't want them knowing how much she could do.

They steered toward the patch of land where Kella was, and sure enough it was a fairly large island, big enough to make camp on. Everyone was excited, even Katsu and his men seemed enthused to see her—as if Kella had brought good fortune. Camissa smiled. It seemed as if all seamen were a superstitious lot.

They dragged the boats onto the shore and secured them with vines to the larger trees. Tobias had Katsu and his men gather wood, the driest they could find, while he went in search of anything to use as food. They had about two days left in their provisions, and then they would be gone.

After emotional greetings with Kella, Rhaven studied the land. "Come with me," he said and set out with the vargel.

The piece of ground was a good hundred paces wide and Rahg and

Rhaven had already scouted several hundred paces deep before they noticed it narrowing to little more than a trail leading to another island. Kella had prowled ahead of them and had taken the path to the other land. "This way," Rhaven said.

Tomkins ran to catch up to them and arrived just in time to hear Rhaven's comment. "It could be the way to find them."

They followed Kella over three more islands, with her searching each one as if she looked for something. By now it had grown dark; only Ranalla shone that night, and the clouds hid the light most of the time.

"Dark as a wolf's mouth," Rahg said.

Rhaven laughed at the old saying. Darkness and wolves seemed to go together, even though a wolf's mouth was anything but dark. And people knew it but said it all the same. "Kella can see her way. We'll follow her."

"I can't even see her," Rahg said.

"Then follow me," Rhaven said.

"All right," Rahg said, not wanting to tell Rhaven that he couldn't see him either. They followed Kella over several pieces of land, and then down another small path that led to a connecting island. After roaming that one for a while, Rahg realized it was much bigger than the others.

Maybe we're finally on dry ground.

It was long past dark, and Rahg could see nothing. Rhaven's hand touch his chest, a signal to stop, and almost simultaneously there was a rustling in the brush ahead and to the right. Before he could think his next thought, Kella bounded in that direction. There was ferocious growling and the guttural roar of her war cry. A squeal pierced his ears and shattered the night air, and the sound of it led him to believe it must be wild boar.

"Stay here," Rhaven ordered, and headed in the direction Kella had gone. Rhaven sliced through the brambles and even small saplings that blocked his way. His sword cut through them like they weren't there. The squealing had been bitter and loud, but it had not lasted long. Soon the heavy padding of Kella's feet alerted Rahg. As a cloud drifted away from Ranalla, the moon shed a little light, enough to make out the form of a wild pig in her mouth. They would eat well tonight.

Rhaven tried to take the pig from Kella, but she wouldn't let it go. Rahg thought that she might claim it all herself, but she was the one who led the way back to camp. When Katsu's men saw what Kella brought, they greeted her like a friend thought lost at sea. Even Tomkins, who had been terrified of Kella, held no reservations about sharing the meat she had captured.

It took them a while to cook the boar, but it proved to be well worth the wait. Tomkins, in particular, dove into the meat like he hadn't had any since last winter. And perhaps it had been that long.

"Eat hardy while you can," Rhaven said. "Eat well. We have enough for two days, and then who knows how long till the next. Let none go to waste."

Kella had taken a leg and back haunch off to the side, and it didn't take her long to finish it. She was licking bones clean when Rhaven walked to her with a piece of meat in hand. He offered it to Kella, but she would have no more. It was then that Rahg saw a look in her eyes like she knew everything he said.

Rhaven tried to give it to her twice, but when she refused it the second time, he went back to eating it himself, though he plopped next to Kella, apparently preferring her company to that of the others.

Rhaven stroked the back of her head, and while Kella gnawed on bones, he talked. "Once again, you have come to our aid, warrior, and though I would rather have you standing guard with Argus, I can't deny your company gives me reason to smile. Besides, Argus can take care of himself."

Rhaven picked some burrs from her thick black fur. "You've traveled far. From the great lands in the north, and now, so far south. I'd wager none of your kind could boast so much."

Rhaven finished eating and laid his bones alongside of her to lick clean, and then he took his sword out to inspect. "And look at this sword, warrior. I never thought I'd retire my other blade, but this is one like no man has ever seen. I've never even dreamed of a blade like this. Look how it shimmers. I've cut through brambles and vines and hardwoods, and have even struck rock with it, and yet it bears no marks. None. Every night I inspect it, and it never needs the touch of a whetstone. I long for a nick in the blade so that I might see the steel beneath. It would give me something to do at night. Something besides dwell on memories. Now my sai and knives are the only ones that require the touch of stone."

Kella stopped chewing and looked up to Rhaven, her eyes intense. "I wish you could talk." Rhaven sheathed the sword and lay down with his head resting on her shoulder. She rolled to give him the soft side of her belly, and he nestled into the thick fur. "Let someone else stand watch tonight," Rhaven said.

RAHG AND CAMISSA talked long into the night, with Tobias, Tomkins and Katsu and his men. It was the first opportunity that any of them had to show joy since the journey began. The first sign of optimism. The vargel had somehow found a way to them, which spoke of a land path, and she had found game. And the boar was not so thin. The boar had been eating well. The prospects of finding more game filled their hearts with hope. Tobias had given Rahg leave to rest the night too, so he and Camissa had spent the later part of the night together, talking and practicing with the Shield.

It didn't take Rahg long to fall to sleep, and Camissa smiled as she read his dreams. He was dreaming of Twin Forks. It was a pretty little village. She saw Darstan, and what must have been his father, and she even recognized the pretty young girl, Kanella, the one Rahg had been smitten with. Camissa no longer felt any jealousy toward her. There was no reason. Rahg was grown and had a farm of his own. He had sheep and chickens and pigs, and a little house tucked into the end of a valley. He seemed as content as a man could be.

Camissa smiled at the growth of her powers. She didn't know what had brought this on, perhaps it was just being away from Sykor, and the fear of having someone discover that she had powers. Perhaps that is what allowed her to grow. Camissa longed to try new and different things, ideas she had thought of and wished to experiment with. But for now, she would try and perfect the ones she had, and the new ones she had discovered, and at that thought, she shifted her attention back to Rahg.

Let's see, what should I make him dream of now?

A LAND PATH

After breaking fast early in the morning, Rahg had expected Kella to be on her way, but to his surprise, she not only stayed with them during the meal but continued to linger as they packed and got things ready to put in the boats. Rahg helped Rhaven untie the boats from the trees, but as he pushed a boat off into the water, Kella tried to step inside it.

Rhaven laughed. "I think the vargel wants to join us."

Camissa climbed into the boat with Kella, laughing herself at the spectacle of the big beast in a such a small boat. "She chose her seat as well," Camissa said, almost hysterical at the sight of Kella sitting upright in the middle of the boat. "I think Kella will be manning the oars."

Rahg smiled at the sight of the vargel, sitting proudly like she belonged there. "Will she be all right?"

"Not much more than an extra hand," Tomkins said. "That is, if you stay out, lad. With Rhaven, Camissa, and the beast, it'd only be like hauling four men. That boat'll do that." Tomkins grunted. "It'll do that and more."

Tobias's head bobbed in agreement with Tomkins's assessment. "Might rock a little if she moves too much, but other than that it will be no trouble." Tobias looked around to find Rahg. "Lad, you come with us."

Rhaven gave the final shove to send the boat into the river, then jumped in as it took off. "If we need to do any rowing, you'll have to do it," he said to Camissa.

"I can keep up."

Rhaven knew that she meant it. She showed the spirit of a hunting dog, never gave up. At first, he had cautioned her against coming, and he had been as hard on her as any other. He offered no breaks because she was a woman, but she kept true to her word.

Camissa smiled, and though it never touched her lips, she couldn't keep it from her eyes. Rhaven's thoughts had found their way to her mind; pride infused her. It was easier to get gold from a jeweler than a compliment from Rhaven, even if it was only in his mind.

TOMKINS AND TOBIAS were already in the boat, so Rahg shoved it off by himself then hopped in. The day passed with no incidents of note, leaving everyone in much better spirits. Rahg thought it had a lot to do with getting fresh meat when they all worried about food. He also thought it had something to do with Kella. Despite the fact that no danger had presented itself, it made everyone feel better with her along.

Having Kella is like having another ten blades.

They picked sparingly at the remainder of the pig during the day and had enough left for supper that evening, though the bones had been stripped like a lamb in a wolf's den. Kella had gone out again, hunting, Rahg presumed, and though he heard no squeal of pigs or other game she returned with three rabbits hanging from her massive jaws. It wouldn't have been enough for supper by itself, but it proved to be a nice supplement to the meal.

"Just as well eat 'em now," Tobias said. "I don't like to keep rabbits. I've seen 'em spoil fast."

"Keep better than a pig," one of Katsu's men said.

Tobias laughed. "Whether it does or doesn't, we've already taken care of that."

In the morning they finished the last of the khaffe, and though Rahg knew Tobias would miss it the most, he had grown accustomed to it as well and looked forward to having a mug to help rouse him in the morning. Nothing else happened for the rest of the day, and the day after brought more of the same. Rahg picked on the few bits of cheese he had left from the original provisions, but there was little else to eat.

"Drink only when you have to," Rhaven said. "Supplies are running low."

Everyone knew by now that if Rhaven said only when you have to, he meant just before you die of thirst. By the time they had stopped for the evening most of the men were worried about starving.

"What are we going to do for food," Jarrell asked.

Rhaven had his bow slung over one shoulder with a quiver of arrows on the other. "Come with me, Rahg, and bring your bow. Tonight we'll hunt with Kella."

When they were out of earshot, Rahg repeated Jarrell's question. "What are we going to do? Suppose we don't find anything tonight." No sooner had he asked the question than he wished he hadn't.

Rhaven's glare reprimanded him like words never could. "If we go back to camp with no food then you can ask me."

Kella slowed her pace, allowing them to keep up with her. She frequently darted off the trail into the brush with tangled vines, often bulling her way through. She soon came back with a rabbit, but Rhaven insisted she eat it. Soon after, she flushed out a small covey of quail. Rahg missed his shot, though Rhaven managed to get one. It wasn't much to bring back, but it was something, and more than anything it was a sign that there was more game to be had. They stayed out until almost midnight, but success didn't visit them again, so they traipsed back to camp with only the bird. It wasn't enough to encourage the men.

The next morning no one ate, saving what little remained for the meal at midday, or supper. Hunger tested them, and tension grew. They put into shore early that evening, with Rhaven and Rahg immediately setting out to hunt, Kella in the lead.

"There seems to be more land here," Rahg said, noticing how the land seemed to resemble more of a peninsula than an island. "Why don't we follow the trails inland? Wouldn't that be better than the river?"

"We follow the vargel."

They had walked almost half a league when Kella disappeared into some thick brush leading into the forest. Before long, her barking alerted them, and soon enough Kella came, driving a herd of four deer. Rahg and Rhaven nocked their arrows, drew them, and released almost simultaneously. They both hit their mark; unfortunately, it was the same mark. A medium-sized doe had dropped with two arrows in her chest, but the other deer disappeared before they could take another shot.

"Good shooting. Though next time we'll have to take separate targets."

Rahg beamed at the compliment and let loose a laugh. "I'm just glad we got this one. I can almost taste it now."

Tobias's voice reached them long before they reached the camp. "Told you we could count on that beast. That beast and Rhaven. Look at that, carrying back a deer. That is a deer you're carrying, isn't it?"

Rahg laughed. "It is, Tobias."

"It is," Rhaven said, "but you can thank the lad for it. I believe his arrow got there before mine did."

Rahg smiled. "If one had gotten to the deer before the other, heartbeats would have been too slow to time it, but he appreciated the remark. He smiled even more as he heard Tobias continue, shifting his tale with the change in news.

"I told you the lad was an archer. He was taught by one of the best, perhaps the best—Kor Trasken." Tobias let the smoke from his pipe rise slowly. "Good man, Kor was. Lost him last winter in a battle with the Victas. He'd have been proud of the lad. At least his teachings will live on." Tobias took a few puffs from his pipe. "And Rahg's got a brother who is as good, if not better. Darstan's his name..."

Rahg let a friendly frown cover his face when he heard that part. Though he hated to admit it, Tobias did have the right of it. Darstan always edged him in their contests—always took his coin.

Though I haven't tried him in a while, Rahg thought. Perhaps I will when we meet again.

The thought of Darstan without his hand rushed to his memory, and his frown became real. There would be no more contests between brothers, not with arrows anyway.

Rahg ripped a piece of meat from the tender side of the loin and chewed it slowly, savoring each bite.

I forgot how much I liked venison.

The memories brought back images of Twin Forks—of home and Magmar. Rahg forced the images from his mind. It seemed like every time he thought of home, bad things happened.

Around midday, Kella began barking furiously. The sound was not quite a bark and not quite a growl, but some combination. Rhaven responded almost immediately, talking to her and looking about to try to determine what caused her concern. Soon Kella stood up, facing the shore to their left. There was a large piece of dry land, but it appeared to be no different than any other place on the river.

"Looks like she wants to stop," Tobias hollered to Rhaven.

No sooner had Tobias spoken than Rhaven and Camissa steered the boat toward shore. "Pull over," Rhaven hollered to them. "I want to see what the vargel is upset about."

By the time their boat reached shore, Rhaven was issuing orders. "Tie the boats. Prepare as if we are spending the night. Jarrell, get some wood and build a fire. Post two guards. Rahg, come with me."

"Where?"

"Wherever Kella takes us," Rhaven said, and turned to follow the impatient vargel.

Those two make a good pair, Rahg thought. That vargel's got no more patience than him or Argus.

They trailed Kella for about half of the rest of daylight. If they turned back now, they would barely reach the camp before dark, but it was clear she was not on a hunting expedition. She didn't wander off the trails or look for anything in the brush. In fact, several times, Rahg had heard some rustling in the brush that he thought to be small game, but she ignored it. Rahg found it difficult to keep up.

"She leads us somewhere, Rahg."

"Shouldn't we go back and get the others?"

"Not yet, but the next time you hear game, take a shot at it. We could use the food. I believe the vargel will wait on us."

It was close to dark when Rahg noticed that the flat ground started to rise, giving way to rolling hills. At the crest of the next hill they entered a forest, and though it was dark now that dusk had settled, he could see enough to know that they had left the swamplands. Rhaven stared into the night. "Now you can go back, lad. Do you think you can find the way?"

No sooner had Rhaven spoken than Kella started the growl of hers that sounded like a bear. Rhaven and Rahg both started, Rhaven having already drawn his blade, and Rahg reached for his, but it was soon apparent to both of them that there was no danger. Immediately, she began heading back toward camp. "I guess she's going herself," Rhaven said. Rahg didn't need to look to know that a smile covered Rhaven's face like a proud father.

If Rahg thought he was going to get any rest while waiting for Kella to return with the rest of the men, he should have known better. Rhaven never let anyone rest, and he offered little in the way of conversation. The vargel had barely disappeared over the ridge when Rhaven drew his sword and started to practice. "Come on, lad, draw the blade. Can you maintain a shield?" Rahg had barely nodded, when Rhaven responded. "Then keep a good one; my blade won't be slow."

Rahg stared into Rhaven's eyes, pools of icy blue giving no indication of his intentions. The Sword of Mikkellana was back in its sheath. It was strapped to his back, and peeked up over his right shoulder where he could draw it with lightning speed.

Rahg had seen it many times in battle already; Rhaven could reach up and draw the blade and have it crashing down on the enemy's head before their blades had even cleared leather. Everything about his stance, his posture, said he would strike with the sword, and it made sense, most everyone did. But Rahg had also seen him strike with the sai, and with Rhaven the sai were devastating weapons. Not just defensive weapons, but ones to kill.

Rhaven had taught him enough by now for him to look and observe things. Rhaven shifted weight to his right leg, indicating the sai to be his weapon of choice. Rhaven's gaze never left Rahg's either. Tobias had always taught him that the enemy's eyes told when the attack would come. "Just watch their eyes" Tobias had said. Rahg often wondered who had figured that out to begin with, but he trusted the advice.

"Give the word," Rhaven said.

Rahg waited. He wanted to be fair, but he needed some advantage, and knowing when the word would come was a slight edge, but with Rhaven it was only a slight one.

"Now," Rahg shouted, and whipped his sword into a position to block Rhaven's sai. As Rahg had presumed, Rhaven did go for the sai, clearing the sheath with a speed that seemed impossible. Rahg almost panicked as he saw the point aiming for his gut, the long prong in the middle shooting toward him like an arrow, but his sword was in position, and he grasped it firmly in anticipation of the ferocious strike. The sai clanged loudly against the steel of the sword. Rahg smiled as if he claimed victory and stopped to relish his fortune. But then he saw that Rhaven already made adjustments to his attack and, too late, Rahg realized that the sai was twisting the blade from his hand. He felt the jerk but could not recover fast enough to keep a hold. He was now disarmed, and Rhaven showed no mercy. The sai raced back toward him on his right, and while he acted to dodge the attack, he noticed that Rhaven had drawn his sword, and it was now coming in from the left.

Rahg concentrated to ensure his shield was in place. He tried to strengthen it before the blow caught him, but he didn't have the time. Rhaven's blade struck his side before he could do anything. "Gods!" Rahg yelled, jumping aside. "That hurt."

"Good. Pain makes for long memories and quick reactions. As long as you keep your blood, you'll be all right. Draw your blade. Be prepared."

Rahg focused. He could almost feel the energy in the shield that protected him. A power that felt good. Rhaven and Rahg sparred several more times before stopping. Rhaven delivered numerous welts to Rahg's side, and his ribs were bruised and aching badly. The upper parts of his arms felt as if they had been beaten with a hammer, and his legs only worked with a limp.

Each time that they fought though, Rahg resisted the urge to let his anger control him. He held back the emotions, fighting like Rhaven and Tobias had taught him. But each time that Rhaven exposed a weakness and Rahg made adjustments to cover that, he quickly explored other weaknesses that Rahg had not been aware of. Finally, exhausted and out of breath, Rahg begged to stay his misery until another night. "That's it, Rhaven. You've beaten me as much as my body can take tonight. I feel like a log in a woodcutter's pile."

Rhaven sheathed the sai and sword, smiling at Rahg. "You did well, lad. You resisted the urge to lose your temper. I've seen men with much more experience lose their control under such circumstances. You must learn the control, because in real fights the temptation to lose control is worse, and as I've told you before, nothing is more dangerous. At times, I've seen men go into a rage, and it served them well, providing the ferocity to allow them to win a few more battles than their skill warranted, but in the end, they succumbed as soon as they faced a true master. And on our journey, I'm afraid we will be facing many who are more master than student. You must keep your wits about you at all times if you're to survive." Rhaven slapped Rahg on the shoulder as he sat down against a large tree trunk.

"You've got a good start on it. A good start. Not many soldiers have seen the battles you have. You have proved to be of sound stock."

Rhaven let Rahg rest while he gathered wood for a fire and cleared an area for them to spend the night. The wind was quiet, so the night didn't spur shivers as it did on the river, but still, the flames felt good. Kella soon led all the companions into the camp, Tobias complaining loudly about having to move through the woods so late.

The next day found them heading deeper into a forest, not unlike the ones in the northern part of Sykor or Kamnor, larger trees, thickly wooded, but with little underbrush to hamper their way. The leaves displayed their colors now, and some had already begun to fall, a sign that winter was making its way to this part of Arangar. Sometime around midday, Rhaven shot a boar, enough to provide food for a couple of days. It was a stray boar, wandering alone, but shortly after that, they saw a small group of swine. When Jarrell raised his bow to shoot, Rhaven stopped him. "We have enough for a few days. We'll find something tomorrow or the next day."

Camissa smiled at Rhaven's remarks; he had a tender side to him, though it usually only surfaced when dealing with animals. At times she thought he would sooner kill people than animals, and from his actions thus far it would be difficult to convince someone otherwise.

Some of Katsu's men grumbled among themselves about his interference, but none of them raised their voices to Rhaven.

"Never heard tell of anyone finding a forest down here," Tomkins said. "Might be that we've come further than anyone else, or, if not further, found places that no one else knew of."

"Could be that others have been here and never got back," Tobias said.

"Could be," Tomkins mumbled. "Could be."

ON THE SIXTH night in the forest, the dream came again—the same one, the one dream that he hated more than any other, the one that had haunted him since last winter, or longer. It seemed so long ago that it was difficult to tell now. No sooner had he closed his eyes than he had fallen asleep and no sooner had he succumbed to the slumber than the dream began.

The maelstrom came first, the huge swirling vortex that swallowed him up and nearly drowned him. Then, washing up on the rocky shore, battered by howling winds and monstrous waves. Then the top of the cliff, the blood, the heat, and the top of the mountain above the omnipresent cave. He knew the dragon waited. Rahg had passed the dragon before, twice now, but he wondered if at some time the thing might try to stop him. Perhaps this time. Something drew him forward. He knew he must reach the top.

The top! That's it!

He realized that was his destination. That's where the amulet would take him. And even as he thought it, he felt the stone almost burning in his chest. It shook him from his sleep, awakened him with a fright. He looked down and cautiously felt the stone. It was hot, hotter than it should have been.

Drops of perspiration dripped from Rahg as he sat up, panting from the horrible nightmare. He must have screamed or made some noise because Camissa was awake, staring at him as if he were a madman.

"What's the matter?"

"The dream again."

"The same one?"

"The same one," Rahg said. A long pause developed. "Only this time I know what it means, or at least part of it. I know where we have to go now. We have to go to the top of the mountain I told you about, the one guarded by the dragon."

Camissa had heard the dream before. She had made Rahg tell it to her numerous times during their travels to try to get any information she could from it. Her mother had always said there was a lot that could be learned from dreams. She remembered his voyage up to the cave but didn't think that was important. She remembered the dragon, anytime someone dreamed of a dragon it had to be important, especially a black dragon. And she remembered the black tunnels in the cavern, the depthless ones that seemed to lead nowhere. That bore importance too. She thought they might represent paths that they could take, options along the way.

"Do you know where the mountain is?"

"No place I've seen before, but if I ever see it, I'll know. Believe me, if I ever see any of that terrain, I'll know it instantly. And I'll run from it as quickly as I can."

"That's your destination." Camissa slid closer to him and wrapped her arm around his shoulder. "No matter what happens I will be with you. We will get to the top of that mountain together. You and I, Rhaven, Tobias, and whoever else might join us. Kella, I suppose." Camissa rubbed his back and held his hand. "But we will get there, Rahg. And we will help you."

Rahg hadn't noticed Rhaven standing like a shadow in the night.

"Other people's conversations are not mine to interfere with, Rahg, but I couldn't help this time. When you screamed, I came, though I chose not to interrupt while you spoke with Camissa. Voices travel easily on a cold night."

Rhaven continued after a moment of silence. "Camissa has the right of it. It's not something we can run away from, any of us. We came all this way to find your destiny, and find it we will. We'll do whatever these prophecies have predicted you will do, or we'll die trying."

Rahg nodded his gratitude, though he found no comfort in Rhaven's promise that they'd die together.

MISSION REVEALED

The Shift brought them to a small room furnished with nothing but an old chair and a small table. No windows gave light, and the only door was closed. "Where are we?" Wisp asked.

Aenaila raised a finger to silence him. "Wait until I let him know we are here," she said. "We are not expected."

Wisp tensed at the mention of "him," and his mind immediately filled with scenarios of what this person meant to her. Aenaila had grown to mean a lot to him. Perhaps too much.

"Jago, I'm here."

Her voice was as sweet as ever, Wisp thought, but he noted it bore an almost commanding tone. Before he completed the thought, the door opened to reveal a man of medium height with hair as dark as night. He wore a smile that need not be painted, and sparkles shined from deep-blue eyes. Wisp felt certain that he would hug Aenaila at any moment and braced himself for the emotions he knew to be coming, but to his amazement, the man stopped short of her and bowed.

"My Lady."

His tone was respectful, not the softness of a lover, and that gave Wisp reason to smile.

Aenaila's face brightened, like seeing old family. She smiled warmly as she turned. "Jago, these are my friends, Kender Darnell, Adju, and..." She paused and cocked her head toward Darstan's sword as she introduced him. "And this is Darstan Fal-Thera."

Jago stole a glance at the sword, recognition lighting his eyes when he did.

What's going on here, Wisp wondered.

"My Lady, I'm afraid I must offer bad news. Your home is ruined."

"My home!"

"Yes, My Lady, and there is more. I'm afraid that the one you healed and left in my care is gone. The guards have him. I tried to secure his release—first, with bribes through agents, but when that failed I hired men to attack the prison; however, he was guarded too well. And now, My Lady, I have learned that they have taken him to Sykor."

Darstan nearly hit the man. "How could you let them do that to Takar?"

Aenaila's hand shot out to restrain Darstan. "It was not his place to keep the sergeant under locked doors. I asked Jago to care for him until our return. If you let him speak, I believe you will have your story."

Wisp reevaluated his original impression of the man. When Darstan bolted for him, Jago never flinched. Not a muscle quivered. If he knew fear, he hid it well, and yet, he had seemed so apologetic to Aenaila, almost as if he were afraid of her. Jago met Darstan's gaze without blinking.

"I told him what he should do, but your sergeant was stubborn. He insisted on going out by himself. On the third day, when he didn't return by dark, I went looking for him. If my information is correct, they took him to Sykor three days ago."

"We could still catch them," Darstan said.

Jago remained the calm one. "He had an escort of more than fifty guards to take him to the border, and I am told more than that from Sykor awaited him."

"Fifty!" Darstan's mind raced, but he was not thinking clearly. "We could get him out, Wisp. We have to!"

Jago began to speak again, but Aenaila's hand stayed him. "I know you want to help your friend, Darstan, but there is nothing to do for now. Perhaps later—"

"No! I have to help him. He got me out of prison, and now I have to help him. If it weren't for me, he would still be in the guard." Darstan's emotions exploded. "Even Vlad is dead because of me. And Gregor." Darstan raised his hand to his head and slumped against the wall, sliding to the floor in a heap.

Aenaila looked to Jago, who left the room with no more than a glance, then she turned to Wisp and Adju. "Let me be with him for a moment," she said, her voice as warm as a mother's heart. Wisp nodded and walked out behind Jago, Adju on his heels.

"What are we going to do now, Master Kender? How will we save the big sergeant?"

"We'll find someway. Even if we have to kill Ludar to do it."

Aenaila sat on the floor next to Darstan. For quite some time she said nothing, just listened to him as he rued the fates and the troubles he had caused so many others. He fought tears on several occasions, especially when he talked about his father, or at least the one who had raised him, Magmar. He had been killed when the Victas attacked their village.

"It would have been better if I died there too," Darstan said. "At least not so many others would have been hurt."

For the first time since she sat with him, Aenaila spoke, her voice a bright dose of comfort. "You could not have died there, Darstan. It was not in the fates for you. Your destiny has been told for as long as men have written words..." Aenaila paused for a moment as if trying to recall something. "Perhaps, even longer."

Darstan nodded as if he agreed. "First Vlad got killed, then Wehr and Gregor. They didn't deserve to die." Aenaila let him talk. She knew he only wanted to say the words and hear them himself. "Then I killed the guards in Khatara. They weren't all bad. They just followed Ludar's orders, like Evin and Wehr when they captured me."

Another pause filled the space between him and Aenaila. "And then I let Evin come to Entiria—only to die. He'd only been out of Sykor once or twice, and I took him halfway around the world to get killed." Darstan pounded his fist on the floor. "Now Takar is captured. Might as well be dead, once Ludar gets hold of him. Probably be better off to be dead."

Aenaila felt Darstan's sorrow. She wished there was something she could do, something she could offer to console him, but the truth of it was, things were only bound to get worse. Especially for someone foretold in prophecies older than the oldest trees and the ageless rock. If he rued his life to date, she could only weep for the rest of it, the part he had yet to experience. For Darstan, the troubles were only just beginning, and whether she liked it or not, Aenaila was the one who had to lead him down this path. She found some softness and thought of a small comfort she could offer.

"Darstan, when we finish with our journey I will take you back to Sykor. Between the three of us, I feel certain we can free your friend,

Takar. And if I ask him to, Jago will accompany us. He is a good man to have when danger threatens."

Darstan's solemn expression darkened more. "I forgot about our promise to you, but don't worry. I'll go as I said. And Wisp will too. He would never break his word."

Aenaila almost smiled, but held it in abeyance for Darstan's sake. She too, was beginning to know Wisp, and she liked much of what she saw. Very much.

"How long will we be?" Darstan asked.

Aenaila came close to a frown on this question, and she hesitated before answering. She didn't want to give him false impressions, but she knew she dare not reveal it all. Not yet.

"In truth, Darstan, there is not much to do. Once we arrive, there will be a small bit of work to do, and a few things that you must help me with." Aenaila forced a smile. "After that, I would be free to bring you back if you wish. Either here or Sykor."

Darstan seemed to grow suspicious again. "The way you avoid answers makes me suspicious, Aenaila. Exactly where are we going? And what is it we have to do? Are you in some trouble?"

Aenaila thought about how to respond without breaking the truth. "If I told you our destination you still would not know. Even if I told you exactly how we would get there." Aenaila's lips tightened. "And as to your question of trouble—yes, Darstan, I am in trouble, but then again, at some time or another we all encounter trouble, don't we? But enough of my troubles. What you have to do is help me. I have a mission that must be completed and, though I'm not able to provide you with all the details, it is you who must help me. You alone."

Darstan shook his head. "That was a good way of saying nothing, Aenaila. But I'm tired of these games. And it doesn't matter. You have my word, so let's get it over with. I'm ready if you are."

Aenaila stood and offered her hand to Darstan. "Good. Then we will make plans for the journey. It will take several days for Jago to arrange everything. If you tell me what you need, I will see that it's taken care of. I presume you will want some new clothes, and we will all need supplies for the trip. Unfortunately, you will not be able to leave the house. I'm afraid that Wisp was right about that part. They will be searching for you, and a one-handed man is too easy to identify."

Darstan grabbed Aenaila's hand and pulled himself up from the floor. "Adju will be delighted you trusted him with duties. He adores you."

Aenaila thought of how much the beggar boy liked Wisp. It took a good man to win the heart of someone like Adju. "Let's join the others. We have kept them waiting long enough, and I know Jago will have other news for me. If we expect to leave in even two days we must take advantage of every moment."

Jago brought a jug of wine to the table with three mugs. Aenaila looked at Wisp and scoffed. "I should have known not to leave you for too long," she said. "Already you have that lad gulping wine when he should be learning to sip te, or at worst, khaffe."

"Would you have me wait until he grows to a man? On his first night's outing, he would be too drunk to walk and likely fall prey to a cutpurse."

"Or a thief," Aenaila said.

"Thieves don't rob poor people; they steal from merchants or nobles."

"I'm sure there is a difference somewhere, Wisp, but I fail to see it. No matter though, we have important work to do the next few days, so I suggest we get our rest." Aenaila picked a piece of fruit from Jago's table and took a bite. "Jago, I will need you to arrange transportation for our journey. You know what we need."

Jago nodded his head, then bowed slightly, the gesture re-igniting Wisp's curiosity about both of them.

"What transportation do we need? Perhaps I could help."

There was no hesitation when she answered. "Not with this. Jago is quite capable, I assure you. But there is much to do, so your talents won't be wasted." Aenaila finished her fruit, yawned, then excused herself. "Jago, I will take your room and leave you to my friends."

Jago bowed even lower than he normally did. "Of course, My Lady."

Mother of Rats! I intend to find out who he is, and, who she is before this journey is over.

AENAILA STEPPED INTO THE ROOM, already dressed and ready for the day's activities. Jago leaped up from what appeared to be a dead sleep as soon as he heard her footsteps. "Would my lady like to break her fast?"

"I can get my meals. Tend to your duties and report to me as soon as you can." Aenaila snatched some fruit from the bowl as she passed. "Adju, did you sleep in those clothes again?" Her tone carried a coating of anger, unusual for Aenaila; she normally woke to a cheerful mood.

"Not all of them, Mistress Aenaila."

"If you think to fool me with the lies that Master Kender taught you, think again." Aenaila stopped and stared at Adju, holding him pinned with her glare. "Which clothes, exactly, did you not sleep in?"

Adju gulped and lowered his head to avoid the contact with her eyes. "My boots."

Aenaila almost laughed in spite of herself. "Your boots! As I thought. Now, put those boots on and eat something, then prepare to leave. I have important errands for you to do."

Adju's eyes opened as wide as a sangra's mouth. He rushed to slip his boots on, his mouth working the entire time. "You will be proud of me, Mistress Aenaila. I will get anything you want. You will see. Anything."

Jago offered to show Adju where to go to get the items Aenaila needed, but the little beggar insisted he knew.

"I know everything about Khatara," he said.

"Just remember to make sure no one follows you back here. If anyone does—"

"Master Kender, you make good jokes. No one can follow Adju; you know that. I once—"

"I know," Wisp said, "You once outran all the emperor's guards. But make sure that no one follows anyway."

Soon after Jago and Adju left, curiosity got the better of Wisp. He knew he'd never pry information from Aenaila, but he thought he might be able to follow Jago, see where he went and what he was instructed to do. "I think I might go wandering the city myself. I need some clothes for the journey, so does Darstan."

Aenaila's gaze caught hold of Wisp. He felt as if she knew his plan. "You might be recognized."

Wisp fought the advice. "I was only here for two days. Few, if any, would remember me."

Aenaila laughed. "Yes, the two of you are so difficult to remember. A tall, thin man with a long crooked nose and the eyes of a weasel. And another with a face girls would cry over and a smile to melt their mothers' hearts. Not to mention that he is missing one hand."

Darstan, at first, took offense, but realized she meant no harm; in fact, she had the right of it. "You win. We'll wait until night."

"I like the night better anyway," Wisp said.

"Thieves usually do," Aenaila added. "Which reminds me. Your little apprentice needs to be taught manners and a proper trade. I refuse to let you bring him up as a thief."

"When do you expect him back?"

"Before midday," she said.

"If he's back before dark it will surprise me," Wisp added. "He'll likely visit old friends, and he most certainly will stop at Mufed's to tell lies to Khalina, though I warned him I'd cut out his tongue if he breathed one word of where we were."

"And does one thief listen to another?" Aenaila asked.

"I know when to open my lips, Aenaila, and I—"

"It is a pity you do not know when to close them." Aenaila's rebuke proved sharp.

Wisp let out an exaggerated sigh. "This might prove to be a long journey, Darstan. A very long journey."

Aenaila suspected that Wisp wanted to follow Jago, or at the least that he sought to gain information that would help him determine their destination. She dared not risk anyone else discovering her plans, and yet, she felt apprehensive about revealing her plans to them.

Darstan must have noted the change in her. "Aenaila, why don't you just tell us where we're going? We gave our word."

Aenaila stared at each of them in turn, her emerald-green eyes burning deep into their souls. "All right," she said. "If I have your word—"

"You already have our word," Wisp said sharply.

Aenaila nodded but remained silent for a long time. "I will tell you where we go, nothing else. And you must promise not to question why." Aenaila awaited their response, which they gave at once.

"The destination will suffice," Darstan said.

"Will it?" Aenaila said, and knew it would not. She walked across the room and stood by the door leading outside. "We go to Cergala."

Darstan and Wisp, neither one, showed any sense of shock or surprise, though Aenaila had suspected it would not register so quickly. Finally, she noticed the spark in Darstan's eyes.

"Cergala!" He looked instinctively to the sword at his side. "My sword! It's called a Cergalan sword."

Aenaila only nodded her head.

"What does it have to do with any of this? Or does it? And where is Cergala?" Darstan peppered her with questions.

"I've never heard of Cergala," Wisp said, "and I have heard of most everything."

Aenaila did smile, now. "In the lands that I come from, Wisp, there are birds that live their entire lives in one grove of trees, and yet I'm sure they think they know the world."

"I have been many places, Aenaila, but I never heard of Cergala."

"That is my point. There is so much you have never heard of. But rather than confuse you with riddles, I will tell you what you want to know." Aenaila paused. "Cergala is my homeland. It lies across the Endless Sea."

"That's impossible! Nothing is across the Endless Sea."

Aenaila never lost her composure. "Then I am nothing, Darstan, for I come from there; in fact, there are more people in my land alone than in Sykor, Khatara, and Pomanda together." She waited for the impact of her statement to hit them. "And Cergala is but one of many lands. Some are even larger."

Darstan looked dumbfounded. "That can't be," he said, but knew even as he did that it was foolish to say so. He wouldn't have believed Entiria existed six months ago, but he had fought a battle there and had seen people die, many people. Now he grew nervous. "What do we have to do?"

"That was not in the agreement. I said I would tell you our destination, and I have done that."

"How will we get there?" Wisp asked.

"Jago is arranging that. I sent him to hire a ship and crew to take us."

"Mother of rats! I despise ships. Why can't you take us by Shifting?"

"It's too far, Wisp. Too far even for me."

"Mother of rats!"

"Why are we going?" Darstan asked again.

Aenaila sighed. She had known before she told them that they would not be satisfied with only knowing the destination. But at least she had warned them.

"Very well, Darstan, if it is punishment you wish, I'll tell you, but you will regret you asked." Her back straightened and she planted her feet squarely on the floor. "You have been foretold, Darstan. I was sent to bring you back for a test—a test that will determine if you are the One. But of that, there is little doubt. The prophecies tell of a man with powers of fire. Of a man from across the Endless Sea who will wield a Cergalan sword."

Darstan looked as if he'd fall over. "There must be a mistake. Many people have powers, and the gods only know how many carry a Cergalan sword." Darstan laughed. "I found this one at the bottom of a box full of swords in Sykor. No one else even wanted it, that's why it was there. Even Ludar tried to convince me to take another."

Aenaila nodded to every statement, as if in full agreement. "Did you ever wonder why you chose that particular sword when so many others looked better?" Darstan started to answer, but Aenaila waved him off.

"But enough of that, I will concede that others have powers. I will even grant that more than a few might wield a Cergalan sword—but none, Darstan, none carry a sword such as yours. I knew the moment I saw you. The sword you carry bears the mark of its maker on the hilt." Aenaila walked to him, gently lifted the sword from its sheath, and laid it across her outstretched palms. "Look at it.

Darstan interrupted. "How do you know this?"

"I know this, Darstan, because every child in my land learns this from the time they are born. There is only one sword like yours. And you wear it."

Darstan lowered his head into cupped hands. "Blasted luck! First, they tell Rahg he's in some Prophecy. Now you tell me I am. I just want to get this over with."

So do I, Aenaila thought. So do I.

A VICIOUS ATTACK

For two days they traipsed through the forest, the trees growing steadily larger the deeper they moved into it. The terrain changed considerably too, reminding Rahg much more of Kamnor, with rolling hills and valleys lush with green grass and small bushes. The game proved to be plentiful enough, and while not abundant, it was a stark contrast to the barren, drought-plagued lands they recently left. Each day they managed to get deer or rabbit or boar, and twice they claimed a wild turkey. Rhaven had taken one and Rahg the other. It was a kill he had taken pride in; turkeys were no easy mark.

Rahg and Camissa continued to experiment with his Shielding power. The tests they conducted to determine whether or not he was able to hold the Shield after he went to sleep at night proved false. The Shield fell as he succumbed to slumber. "I know it can be done, Camissa. Remember on the way to Entiria when Aentarra fell unconscious? She kept her Shield. She kept it for two days when she was unconscious."

"That was Aentarra, Rahg. She's a lot stronger. But keep trying. Try to think of things differently. Something will happen. But if we do see Aentarra again, or even Mikkellana, ask them how they do it. It would be good to know."

"I won't ask them," Rahg said.

"You are a fool if you don't. They are there to learn from. Are you going to let this Messenger destroy you without a fight? As weak as your powers are now, whoever this Messenger is, will surely be stronger. You better learn all that you can, while you can, or we might as well stop now."

Rahg was taken back by the anger in her voice. He seldom saw Camissa get angry. "There's no reason to be so upset."

"There is every reason to be so upset. We have little time, and if you are so childish as to think that the morning sun will increase your powers tenfold some day, then I feel that we have already been defeated."

Rahg shrunk back from the lashing. The sharpness of her tongue stung more than her words, but even so, she had the right of it; he knew that. If a Banished One found him now, he would be like a mouse trying to escape the hawk.

But even if she's right she has no right speaking to me like that.

"Good night, Camissa." Rahg's voice held no anger, but no warmth either.

Camissa allowed herself a slight smile as Rahg tucked himself in a bedroll.

He might be angry at me now but he will forgive me when his powers save his life. He needs a little hardening, and he needs someone to push him to it. "

Good night, Rahg." Camissa kept her tone even-keeled as if nothing had happened. She lay in her bedroll, her back facing his. She thought about what they would do once they found the Pathfinders, and she thought of all that had happened since last spring when she first met Rahg, relishing the memories of how he had fixed her te, always taking care to make it just right so that she would enjoy it. The thoughts warmed her heart.

I wish just once that Tobias would make te in the morning instead of khaffe. I like khaffe, but I miss the te sometimes. Before long Camissa found herself drifting off with the pleasant memories and soon after remembered waking.

She started to rise, then tucked herself back in the blankets; the morning was cold. Soon, however, the smell of food cooking over the fire wafted her way, providing the impetus to rise. "Good morning, Tobias. That smells good." Camissa stretched her hands over the coals to warm them.

"Why thank you, lass. I made it just for you. Thought I'd make it special for you after all this time; wasn't very polite of me to not think of you sooner."

Camissa furrowed her brow and looked at him with a puzzled expression on her face.

"Te," Tobias said. "I made you te. I thought that's what you meant when you said it smelled so good."

Tobias must have thought he had done something wrong when he saw the look on her face. "Are you all right, lass? You look like you've seen a Banished One."

"Huh? What? Yes. Yes, I'm all right, Tobias. It's just that... nothing." It must be a coincidence, she thought, as she brought her emotions under control. It has to be a coincidence.

Camissa sat by herself to break her fast, still troubled somewhat by the odd coincidence of Tobias making te. He hasn't made te since we were in Pomanda, she thought and wondered again how it could have happened, but at the same time still tried to convince herself that she had nothing to do with it.

"You wish to share those troubles, lass?"

Rhaven startled Camissa. I should have known it was him. He can sneak up on a snake. "Nothing, Rhaven. I was just thinking of things. Of home, and things that used to be."

"Nothing is ever the same as it used to be." Rhaven waited for her to respond, but when she didn't answer, he went on. "I want you to continue to work with your powers. I need you to see what kind of sense you can make of these Pathfinders when we find them. We have no idea if they will present themselves as friend or foe."

"Do you expect trouble?"

"I expect nothing, but I try to be prepared, so at the first sign of them, I want you to find out all that you can. Is everything else the same, what we had talked about before."

"No change. Tobias seems to be in a much better mood since we landed in Arangar. Rahg has shown no change either."

THE FOREST REMAINED dense while the terrain grew rougher. Kella continued as if she had a map of the land. Twice during the morning, Rhaven thought he saw something, but whatever it was disappeared before he could be certain. He found a few tracks also, but they were unlike any he had ever seen. "Be alert," he warned. "Something has been watching us these past few days, and whatever it is has been exceptionally good."

Rhaven posted a two-man guard and Katsu's men drew the first watch. While they spoke of past voyages and Entirian summer nights, a beast prowled the nearby woods waiting for the right opportunity. During a moment of soft laughter, the beast struck. The first seaman fell instantly to the claws and bites to the neck. The other man panicked, opting to run, but he only made it a few steps before the beast seized a hamstring and severed it with one ferocious bite. The jaws then clamped to the back of the neck and ripped through flesh and veins, bringing almost instant death. As the beast finished off its victim, Kella arrived with teeth bared. Despite her formidable posture, the beast didn't flee.

Blood-stained lips lifted from the man's body and feral eyes stared into Kella's. It leaped at the vargel before she could even move. Long curved claws, like talons from an eagle, sunk into her fur at the neck and its teeth bit through to find flesh. Only Kella's thick mane stopped the initial bite from reaching her veins.

Kella roared, rearing up to fling the beast off, but it clung to her, clawing and biting in a frenzied fashion, drawing more blood with each strike. Kella rolled onto her back, eliciting a cry of pain from the beast, but when the vargel righted herself she found that the beast still maintained a fierce grip on her. Again she rolled, but this time she remained on her back, pressing hard into the ground to crush the beast.

Rhaven arrived just as she rolled for the second time. He ripped the beast from her back, throwing it to the ground. The creature had only been stunned, but before it could recover Rhaven's sai found its heart. The wail of death told its brothers in the forest that it had died. Everyone in the camp had been alerted by now, and Rahg hurriedly erected a shield to forestall further attacks.

"Do you think they're the Pathfinders?"

Rhaven cleaned the blood from his sai as he spoke. "If they are, then we have an interesting mission ahead of us. It's unusual for any beast to attack so many, especially with fires in the camp. And Kella."

Rhaven paused for a moment. "Very odd that it struck at the vargel. Even an animal with the sickness knows not to attack the stronger ones."

Rhaven's words did nothing to alleviate Rahg's fears; in fact, he had stoked the embers of a new fear.

Suppose these are the Pathfinders.

The next two days brought nothing save a few false starts; the men were on edge after the attack the other night, and the least movement created an alarm.

I knew some of them would die on this journey. I wish they hadn't come.

By the middle of the third day, they reached a brook bubbling with fresh water. "We'll make a camp here. Time to rest and eat," Rhaven said. "Fill your flasks with water, but stay alert. Katsu, you and Jarrell stand guard while the others eat. We won't be caught unaware again."

Midway through the meal, Kella stirred from her resting place and walked slowly toward the edge of camp. Rhaven noticed the tenseness in her and drew his sword. "In the bushes behind us," he said very softly. "Several of them. Make no sudden movements, but be prepared to act. Rahg, make your way toward your bow, but do it slowly."

Rahg stood and carefully made his way to the brook, stooping as if to drink from it, but he came up with the bow in his hand and an arrow already nocked. At the edge of the camp, the hair on the back of Kella's neck bristled with a warning of danger. Her lips curled in anger, and her eyes scanned the forest.

"Be prepared to shoot, Rahg." Rhaven moved to a spot ten paces from the edge of the clearing, and he now held both a sai and the sword.

Pity the fool that attacks him, Rahg thought but kept a firm grip on his bow. Tobias, he noted, had also nocked an arrow, as had Tomkins.

"Camissa," Rhaven called, but barely above a whisper. "Get up slowly and walk this way. Move to the center of the camp. You'll be safer there."

Tobias moved to stand between her and the forest. "Go on, lass, I'll not let anything get you." Tobias guarded her, bow strung and arrow nocked. "Rhaven, there's more to our left. Can't make out what they are, but I saw something stirring. And there was more than one of them."

"Stand farther apart," Rhaven ordered. "Give enough room to swing a blade." Rhaven kept his eyes focused on the perimeter of the clearing. His hands shook, probably with the anticipation of battle. "Rahg, can you cover us with a shield?"

"It's already done," Rahg said. "I've got it around all of us."

"Well thought, lad," Tobias said. "You sure you can hold 'em off?" Tobias seemed nervous. "I saw what happened to Katsu's men and how that one attacked Kella."

"I can hold it, Tobias, but for how long I don't know. Certainly for a while; I did it against Iazzo, and I wasn't as strong back—"

The first one attacked, crashing against the shield behind him. He was startled by the noise, a terrifying scream that agitated the fear inside him. The creature hit the shield with a ferocious force, its claws digging and scratching in an attempt to get at them. Katsu had been the target, and he jumped back toward the center of camp.

"Rahg's got the shield around us. Don't do anything foolish," Katsu yelled.

Rahg heard another bone-shivering screech and turned to see two more had struck the shield from the other side. As he thought about their method of attack, a fourth one lunged from the bushes where Kella stood, but his shield held it at bay. Another of the beasts flew across the creek, clawing wildly at the shield to get at Rhaven's back. Their claws looked as long as a man's finger. They seemed to be smart, too, not staying long in any one spot. As soon as they saw that they couldn't get through the shield, they moved to another area to try. The beasts checked out every part of the shield, then instead of wasting energy as most might do, they simply stepped back into the bushes and waited.

There was a collective sigh of relief from all, even Rhaven, as the demons moved back to the woods, though none were so gullible as to think they had seen the last of them. "Relax the shield, Rahg. As long as you can put it up fast enough to prevent their next attack. They can't see it, so there's no sense in holding it until it is needed. Katsu, check behind us and to the left. Tobias, you and Camissa watch the right. Rahg and I will watch the front. Tomkins, keep a roving eye all over; you might spot something others would miss."

Rahg felt comfortable with Rhaven's precautions but stayed on edge. He feared another attack at any moment. Kella remained inside the shield, standing close to Rahg and Rhaven, her teeth still slightly bared, and her eyes alert. Rahg thought she looked bent on revenge, and though he questioned whether or not a vargel could harbor such feelings, he wouldn't want to be the first of those beasts to meet her.

They were trapped in the camp throughout the rest of the day and had to make the most of it. Rhaven ordered a small fire to be built for cooking supper, but also to see how the beasts reacted to it. No one had not seen any of the creatures since shortly after the attack, but Tobias and Katsu reported hearing them rustling in the bushes at the edge of the forest. There was little wood for the fire, not enough to last the night, though an ample supply lay nearby, at the other side of the creek.

"We can't stay here much longer," Tobias said. "The lad won't be able to hold the shield while he sleeps, and he's gonna need sleep to stay strong."

Rhaven nodded, then turned to Rahg. "You'll have to do without sleep tonight. We can't risk an attack, and they might be waiting for darkness."

Rhaven's assessment proved to be right, twice that night they attacked. The first time there had been plenty of warning from Tobias, and Rahg raised the shield quickly, but the second time one of them got through.

Rahg felt the pressure at the last moment, just as the shield was closing. It was like trying to close a door with someone's foot between the door and the jamb.

"Watch out!" Rahg yelled the warning but had no time to protect himself. The beast landed on the ground and sprung back toward Rahg, teeth, and claws prepared to strike, but before it could take another step, Kella pounced on it, seizing it by the neck and shaking it like a farm dog does a rat. She continued even when it was evident no life remained in the beast, and it was then that Rahg thought he must have been right in his earlier presumption about vargels and their sense of vengeance.

Rhaven stood over the dead animal but there was no reason to check for life, Kella had torn it in two. "We'll have to make a break early in the morning," Rhaven said. "If we can lose them before nightfall tomorrow then Rahg can get some sleep. If not, we'll find a place to make a stand."

Earlier, Rahg had been tired, but the attack had roused him to a state of alertness, and for the remainder of the night he talked to Camissa and Tobias, and occasionally Rhaven, though he mostly roamed the camp watching for the beasts.

As it neared morning, Camissa proposed a plan. "Rahg, I have been thinking," she said. "If we stay close together, and if everyone walks slowly and keeps a good watch, we could still use your shield. You could stay in the middle of the group, and as soon as anyone sees one, you can use your shield."

Tobias puffed on his pipe as he considered the suggestion. "That would be slow progress," he said. "The shield would block us as well. And it might be hard for the lad to do." Tobias looked at Rahg. "Would it, lad? Could you keep a shield around us while we walked?"

"I can try," Rahg said. "But it'll be slow if I can do it at all."

"Slow or not, at least we could move," Camissa said. "It would give us a chance to get to someplace safe or, at the least, a better spot to defend ourselves."

"She's right," Rhaven said. "We have to leave here, and I can't think of another means as safe. At least wait until we find a clearing."

Tomkins had been quiet most of the morning even though Katsu's men had told him something about Rahg and the power he had.

Tomkins acted as if he didn't believe it until he saw it work. "Lad, can you do things like... well, can you control this shield you have?"

"I can control some things, Tomkins. What did you have in mind?"

"Could you just let the shield down a little bit, or, for just the blink of an eye—long enough to let one of them get inside so that we can trap it and kill it."

Tobias coughed out a big cloud of smoke. "Be sorta' like lettin' the weasel in the hen house, wouldn't it, Tomkins? You saw what they did to the others. I'm not of a mind to let one of them in here."

Rahg looked to Rhaven and saw that he was considering Tomkins's suggestion. Rahg was surprised that Rhaven hadn't marched into the woods after them.

"I think that your plan has merit, Tomkins, and I like the idea, but Tobias is right. There's too much risk in letting one inside; besides, Rahg might not be able to let just one in, and if two were to get in someone would surely get killed."

They had not gone twenty paces from the camp when the creatures attacked again, five of them. They clawed and scratched and almost climbed up over the shield. One of them leaped high in the air and landed on top of the shield.

Rahg had set the upper limits just barely above the tallest of the

Entirians, and when the beast landed atop his shield, it shocked him. He almost lost concentration. Sometime during the assault, though there was nothing to do but stand in horror and watch them, and pray that the shield held. Escape wasn't possible, as Rahg found it difficult to hold the shield and move while the beasts were attacking.

Camissa received a pounding in her head. She held both hands cupped over her ears and shook her head as if trying to rid herself of something.

"What's the matter, Camissa?" Rhaven asked.

She shook her head violently several times. "I don't know!" Her voice filled with panic. "I keep getting this strange feeling. There's a strange buzzing noise in my head. It won't go away, and t's getting louder."

Stop it! She heard.

"Stop what?"

Stop it. Stop! Stop the attack.

Camissa was still frantic, but the pain and overwhelming sense of confusion had gone from her mind. Now there were only voices. She looked around to determine where the voices came from, but it was no voice she recognized. In fact, it was unlike anything she had ever experienced with her powers. When she sensed things before, she could mostly sense feelings and emotions and, with those closest to her, the essence of their words, but this was almost like someone in her head was shouting.

"Are you all right?" Rhaven asked.

Camissa cleared her mind so that she could speak. "Yes, thank you, I'm all right." Camissa paused while she looked around. "Look, Rhaven, they're moving back. They've stopped the attack."

"For now," Rhaven said. "What happened?"

"I heard voices."

"What kind of voices? I heard no one."

"There were voices hollering to stop the attack."

Tobias looked all about, and so did Rahg, but the rest of them focused on the retreating beasts. Suddenly a voice called from a spot near where the beasts had entered the forest. "We didn't know that your kind could hear us like that."

All attention was drawn to the mysterious voice. "Stay your arms. We mean no harm."

To everyone's astonishment, a small creature on two legs walked from between two bushes near the perimeter of the woods and slowly made its way toward them. It was only as tall as a Lorn, perhaps shorter, and was covered with a thick coat of fur from top to bottom—silver fur. Rahg almost fell over backward, for when he looked closely, the face was that of a man even though the fur covered it like a wolf or a bear.

"You speak our language?" Tobias asked.

"I see you are observant."

The creature's attitude irritated Tobias, but he bit hard on the stem of his pipe and checked his anger. "We mean no harm to anyone; we came in peace. It was those creatures who attacked us." Tobias' face wrinkled into a growl.

"You came in peace?" The one with silver fur asked, its tone mocking and obvious.

Tobias clenched his teeth around the stem, afraid he might break it. "As I said, we've come in peace. We're lookin' for—"

"The three deer that you have eaten since entering our territory would differ with your statement about peace, as would the hares and the boars."

Tobias looked shocked, and he didn't need to look to know everyone else was shocked as well.

"Yes," the little creature said, "I know all that you have taken from our lands. I've heard the cries of each one as your arrows pierced their skin. The welgars attacked in retaliation."

When the creature noted the dumbfounded expression, it explained, spreading short, fur-covered paws toward the brush. "The "beasts," as you call them, are called welgars. They are the guardians of these lands."

"Who are you to be challenging us?" Rhaven didn't hesitate to interrupt.

"I am a Mordi," he said.

Pathfinder! Camissa thought, and as she did the Mordi turned toward her, his gray–brown eyebrows raised in surprise.

"Yes, you are right. We are the Pathfinders, though I have not heard that name used in many long winters."

Rahg was the one who almost fell. They had come so far to find them, and now here he was facing one of the legendary creatures. It was much different than what he had expected, even though he had no idea what to expect.

The Mordi continued staring at Camissa. "How is it that you know of us, and why does the race of man come to the lands of the Mordi and the welgar?"

"The race of man?" Tobias' ire was up now. "Well, who by the gods do you think you are? You talk like a man, and you look like one even though you are a little furry."

"We chose to leave the race of man long ago," the Mordi said.

Rahg stepped to the front of the line and looked down into the Mordi's eyes. "The gods sent us," he said. "We are to go into the Paaren, and they said a Pathfinder could lead us out." Dead silence followed Rahg's announcement, even though they all had known the destination all along, it wasn't a thing that anyone talked about or that anyone cared to.

The Mordi stared at Rahg for a long time. He looked like a man who had just learned of the death of his mother. "So, the time has come," he droned.

"What do you mean by that?" Tobias asked.

The Mordi didn't lift his eyes to speak. "The gods said that someday they would ask a favor of us. Now that day has come."

"How do you know that this is it?" Tobias asked. He seemed bent on an argument, and it didn't matter much which side he took.

"The stories of our people tell that the favor will come in a request of men from the northern lands."

Tomkins jumped into the conversation with what he thought was proof of denial. "These men aren't from northern lands; they're from the south of Arangar."

The Mordi looked at him in shocked disbelief. "My foolish friend, these men are from no part of Arangar, nor ever have been. I would venture to say that it might be the first time they have set foot upon this land."

Rhaven did nothing to calm Tomkins down. "Enough of this," he said. "We have no time to be wasting. Tell us what we need to do, Pathfinder. Will one of your people come with us?"

The Mordi looked at Rhaven with compassion, almost pity. "We have no need of leaders, only teachers."

"Then who leads your people?" Rahg asked. "Who enforces the laws?"

"No one leads us," the Mordi said. "And we have no laws."

Tobias spit on the ground, a scowl on his face. "What do you do with the thieves and murderers?"

The Mordi laughed. "When there is nothing to steal there is no place for thieves. And when there are no rules there is no need for war."

"Well, what about—" Tobias intended to keep arguing no matter what answers he got, but the Mordi interrupted.

"We will talk more as we make our way to the village."

"What about those creatures?" Tomkins asked.

"They won't bother anyone now—as long as no one shows hostility."

"Why did they attack us?" Tobias asked.

"I told you why," the Mordi said. "They are the protectors of these lands and of the Mordi in particular." As the Mordi started off, a welgar emerged from the woods and came down the hill to walk by his side.

welgar

Everyone stepped aside, giving it a measure of respect worthy of such a ferocious creature. Rhaven's hand rested on the hilt of his sai, and Katsu and Jarrell dropped back toward the rear. Kella rushed in alongside Rahg and Camissa and kept a wary eye on the beast.

Despite the assurances from the Pathfinder or Mordi, as they liked to be called, Rhaven had suggested to Rahg that he put a shield between the welgars and them, just to be safe. It was good practice for Rahg, so he didn't mind; anything he could do that was different to keep up practice would help him develop his powers faster.

They walked the remainder of the day before coming to a large clearing in the forest. It was about four or five spans across with trails leading in all directions. Rahg could see houses through the trees at the perimeter, and down several trails were smaller clearings with houses lining them. Other houses were built high atop hills, where the forest thinned.

"Is this where you live?" Rahg asked the Mordi, his tone only partially hiding his disappointment at the primitive state of their dwellings, but the Mordi needed no tone to tell him Rahg's thoughts.

"Pretty buildings are not necessary for comfort."

Astonished, Rahg looked at the Mordi and before his words could be uttered, the Mordi responded. "We know your thoughts before they become words, Rahg, so be careful how you think."

Embarrassment showed on Rahg's painted face. "Well, what I meant was, why would you choose to live this way instead of building nice homes to keep you warm and comfortable?"

The Mordi smiled and bowed his head. "We are warm enough, even without our homes, and on the bitterest of nights, the homes keep us plenty warm. During the summer they shade us from the sun and keep the rain off our backs."

"But what about a bed to sleep in and a place to eat?"

"We have beds made of the finest straw, and others woven from the hair of vines. We string them from poles in our huts. It makes for a comfortable night's rest. We choose to eat in the forest next to our friends. If it is raining, we find large trees to shelter us, or we eat in our huts."

Rahg seemed flustered. "What about wild animals? You don't even have a door."

"If we wish privacy with our mates, we hang a blanket, and as to the animals they are always welcome, though why would they come into our huts when they have the world as theirs."

Rahg insisted on finding problems with the Mordi's method of living. "How do you determine who gets what ground? Isn't there any fighting over land?"

The Mordi laughed, the first time it had done so, and it caused Rahg to think about how much these creatures seemed to be like them. The laugh was identical.

"For all that is good about any one piece of land, there is something bad as well. The land is no different than any creature on this world; it has good and bad."

The Mordi must have noticed Rahg's puzzled look and continued to explain. "The one who lives atop the hill has to bring water a long way, and he has to walk up and down a steep hill to gather food. The soil is not as good for growing which means he must trade more to eat."

Rahg nodded his head as the Mordi spoke; it all seemed logical. "Why doesn't everyone want the land in the low regions then or by that lake over there." The clear waters of a large lake were just now coming into view through a thickly forested section of the woods. Houses rimmed the shore of it.

"Those lands also carry burdens that are unique. The lands by the water attract more of the animals, and they eat much of the food. Another factor is that by living close to the water a person draws many visits from neighbors; at times it is too many visitors."

Some houses were tucked neatly into small, cleared fields sprinkled with large oaks and other hardwoods. "What about these homes? Doesn't look like anything wrong with them," Tobias asked.

"Yes," the Mordi said, "that is where the old people live. The ones who are wise enough to know the troubles of all the other spots. But we all started out on the hill, or by the lake. It is only with time does the true nature of peace come to even the Mordi."

Further questions were stalled by the sight of Mordi crowding the clearing from the huts nearby. They continued coming until over one hundred were present.

And almost as many welgars, Rahg thought, scanning the gathering and shuddering at the sight of so many of them lurking about. "Stay close to me, Camissa," Rahg said. "I have a shield around us in case they attack."

"You will have no need of the shield," Camissa said.

Rahg hated it when she did that, told him things with such confidence. And he hated it all the more because she was almost always right. With a grunt of disapproval, he let the shield go.

One of the older Mordi approached, sensed the apprehension. "I can assure you there is no need to worry about the welgar. They have sworn not to harm you."

"And how do you know that?" Rhaven asked.

"We can converse with all the animals," the Mordi replied.

Rhaven stared at the Mordi for a long time, while Rahg wondered if it was a male or female. The one who had led them to the village was male, but with this one it was difficult to tell, though he felt it was male.

"Then tell me something about the vargel," Rhaven said, nodding toward Kella. "Tell me something only she would know."

The Mordi looked at the vargel, and its eyes went wide with disbelief. "I cannot."

"As I suspected," Rhaven said.

"No, it—"

As the Mordi prepared to speak, Kella's thoughts pushed into his head. I will allow this one time, and no more. Tell him you cannot break my trust. Tell the warrior that I was there when Lyssic fought his battles. I was there when Mikkellana gave me my name. And I was there long before that. Tell him this and nothing more.

The Mordi related what the vargel had said. The response must have satisfied Rhaven, for he made no further accusations, but he didn't acknowledge anything either.

The Mordi questioned them all through the night on about every issue Rahg could think of. Each one of them took turns asking questions of different members of the party.

"I've already told you," Rahg said. "I don't know what we are supposed to do. I know nothing more than what I've said."

Rahg sighed. Frustration had been building for a long time now. "I don't know. I don't know! By the gods, for people who are supposed to communicate so well with everyone you don't seem to understand what I'm saying. I don't know. All I know is that I'm to go into the Paaren where I will be led to a special place by the amulet. The only thing I know for sure is that I'm supposed to kill this Messenger."

"But you do not know who this Messenger is?" one of the older Mordi said.

Rahg shook his head from side to side. "No, I don't know." He brushed tears from his eyes as the smoke from Tobias' pipe irritated him. He had heard Tobias in the background all night long; he had been as busy as the Mordi, questioning them about everything and filling them full of tales about his adventures. He hadn't put the pipe down since they sat by the fire, and once he got puffing on his pipe, the tales seemed to rise like the smoke.

Tobias put his hands on his knees and stood abruptly. "Looks like you tired the lad out tonight with your questions. He's not much for conversation. Likes to ask questions, but he's not nearly as fond of answering them. Anyway, I think you've learned about as much as you can from all of us. Now, who is it that's gonna take us into this Paaren place?"

Several of the older Mordi looked at each other, consternation marking their fur-covered faces. "We shall take a show of hands to see who goes." Their expressions were dour and the voice more so.

"You don't have to make it sound so horrible," Tobias said.

"How would you sound?" the Mordi asked, "if asked to place a noose around one of your peoples' necks."

"Put a noose around their neck? We're not askin' ya' to kill them. We're askin' them to go with us."

"You are asking us to have someone take you into the Paaren." The elder hung his head low. "A noose, perhaps would be better. It would be more merciful at least."

"That's no way to be speaking. No reason to be scaring this lad half to death with your tales."

The Mordi turned slowly toward Rahg and stared, as if evaluating him, then turned back to Tobias. "He does not look like a lad to me. He looks a man. And he has taken on the responsibility of more than a man. It would not do us well, nor the one we send, nor you or himself, if we were to tell him any less than what it is."

"I want to hear," Rahg said. "I want to know everything you can tell me of the Paaren. Have you ever been there?"

"Long ago, some of our people went there. They thought to hide in the Paaren, to live a new world where the others would not bother us, but..." the silence stayed with the pause.

"But what?" Rahg said. "What happened?"

"They left just before planting season. The weather fine and their spirits high. They had taken enough food and supplies to keep them for many moons, certain that they would find lands to settle and begin a new life. But before the next winter, they came back. Two of them did."

"Two of them?" Tobias asked. "How many went?"

The silence was longer this time, until finally the oldest Mordi breathed deeply and sighed. And with his eyes almost closed, he began. "More than a thousand," he said.

Rahg had no desire to pry further. He felt bad enough as it was. Even Tobias refrained from asking more questions, but Rhaven didn't.

"The two who were there, are they still alive? Can they tell us anything about it, anything to help us?"

The old man turned slowly to Rhaven. "I was one of them," he said. "And I can tell you this. It is not fit for anyone."

Rhaven nodded his head. "Select your person, then. I would like to leave in the morning."

As they started to leave, Rhaven grabbed hold of the one who had led them to the village. "When you spoke to the vargel, did she say nothing else?"

A question mark lit the Mordi's face. "She said nothing else," he said. "Why, I wonder, do you ask?"

"No reason," Rhaven said.

"We will choose tonight and inform you of our decision tomorrow morning. Sleep well."

Sleep well! Rahg laughed to himself. How can I sleep well knowing I must go into the Paaren?

ALLIANCE

The bronze-skinned warrior watched the carnage from a vantage point offering safety as well as a view of the destruction. Krengs were born warriors, but dorgans were born to kill. Thirteen krengs had already gone through the Gates of Death today, or wherever it was that krengs went when they died, and only one dorgan to claim for so many lives. Dorgans died hard. Four krengs remained to battle one dorgan—the krengs would die.

He smiled at the sight of so much kreng blood, but it didn't please him as it should. Something was wrong; something nagged and picked at him, burned the pleasant thoughts away. Memory had eluded capture for so many winters that the occasional flash of recall or an intermittent glimpse of the past served little purpose; he could not put the pieces together. He had not even succeeded in bringing a name to his lips, but something about the dorgans pricked at his mind and would not let go, holding on like a leech to virgin flesh.

Hatred bubbled in the cauldron that was his stomach, churning and roiling as it mixed with fear. He rejected the emotion as foreign, not meant for him, but try as he might to abolish it, it remained, and as it brewed in his body it mixed with the hatred, and the warrior erupted.

His scream stopped the battle, drawing all eyes to the enclave of rocks where he stood.

The dorgan waited, unmoving, perhaps to see what his presence would bring to the battle.

The warrior and krengs were known enemies, for centuries he had slain their kind.

The kreng leader gave silent commands to her pack, "the battle grows more dangerous. Death With Long Claw has come."

The four remaining krengs made new plans for battle; strategies must be changed. Retreat was never an option—not for a kreng.

The steep hillside fell to the bounding strides of the warrior, his sword drawn, glistening in the late afternoon sun like a hundred crystal shards.

Somehow the kreng leader knew and issued new orders to attack the dorgan. "Only the dorgan," she said. "Draw no blood from the furless one."

The first sweep of the blinding blade carved a piece from the dorgan's arm, one of four that had ripped limbs from many foes in its aged life. The horrifying shriek pierced ears and shook the ground where it stood. Three appendages searched for a grip on the warrior, but he dodged the tentacles with preternatural skill, the agility honed from battles with too many foes.

The crystal blade bit a chunk from the dorgan's face, bit and dug and flicked a hunk of red and blue flesh dripping blood—a white, milky substance like the round brown fruit that hung from the trees in the summer lands.

The warrior's slowed reaction earned him a gash that cut through flesh and struck bone. No anguished scream or screech of pain; he funneled the furor into a brutal chop from the sword. It severed a claw from one of the three remaining useful limbs. The krengs attacked the dorgan's blinded side while the warrior held it occupied. They set upon it with a fervor to almost match the warrior's.

Kreng claws, sharpened bone to equal a steel blade, dug at the eyes of the dorgan, costing him vision from one of them. The youngest didn't leap fast enough, dorgan teeth severed its head, and it fell to the ground amidst shrieks of anguish, a mother losing a child.

The dorgan's life was failing from too many strikes by kreng and warrior—the alliance proving too much for a wounded dorgan. It swung to wrench a kreng's neck, leaving an opening for the blade to strike. The underside of a dorgan's neck was vulnerable; blood spurted profusely, then it fell, a heap of horrible flesh massed on rock and dirt and blood.

The warrior breathed heavily; it had been a hard–won battle, costing much in blood, and much in life. His sword-hand twitched, his thirst not yet sated, the milky white blood not enough. Only three krengs remained, all badly injured, all but one unable to stand—a limb missing, a leg gashed too deep to heal—both might die.

The pack leader knelt to examine her young, her blood dripping to mix with theirs as she hoisted both up in her arms. Wary eyes warned the warrior she could, and would, still fight to protect her own.

The sword went back into the sheath. He approached the kreng unarmed. After so many thousands of battles, enemies learn to communicate; he had learned their language and knew how to address them. "The dorgans die hard." He pointed to the monstrous, bloody heap on the ground.

The kreng's eyes held fast. She dared not blink. The warrior had slain her brother two winters past, and only last season, when the summer heat peaked, her soulmate had fallen to his blade. Her lip quavered, the fur wrinkled and teeth like daggers bared ivory white.

"Stay back." Her words may not be understood, but there would be no mistaking the intent.

The warrior stood still. "I have killed many krengs."

Claws grated together, an eerie sound. "You have not fought me, furless."

He understood her well and continued delivering his message. "It is time to stop the killing. I offer myself in peace, as ally against the dorgans."

She had not blinked yet, and her claws had not retracted.

"I can help heal the young. My cave is close, closer than yours."

DEATH CAME IN MANY FACES, and his had been seen too frequently by kreng warriors, yet he did offer help for her young, and he had fought the dorgan—enemy to all. "Walk to your home. I will follow."

The warrior's strides covered ground like the krengs—swift, long and silent. Her arms had grown tired when they reached the cave. She snarled at the sight—kreng claws hung like beads from the cave's entrance—a message to their kind, a warning. The trophies sickened her and served to stir suspicion not fully gone. Trepidation slowed her pace and shortened her stride.

inside Arton's cave

The warrior stared out from a darkened cave, but inside light shone, and it looked roomy. He didn't smile; she would not have trusted him if he had. One who has slain so many could not smile and be true. She saw the Leaves of Healing he gripped in one hand, their powers known to all in the summer lands. Gathering them took seven sunsets, and they only lasted one full moon. A potion filled the other hand. It was not one she knew, but trust, or death, would have to come soon. She entered boldly and set her young on a bed of branches and straw. The time had come to trust—or die.

"Kavi," he yelled, and a boy came from deeper in the cave.

The kreng's fur bristled, teeth bared.

"He will help take care of your young ones," Death With Long Claw said, then he knelt alongside her and offered the leaves of life, only four remained.

She took them without a thought. One capped a severed foot of her youngest, the youngest left alive, and the second lay on a chest wound too close to the heart. The third saved the leg of her oldest. She stared at the hungry yellow leaf, eager to taste blood and save a life.

She stood, relieved to have saved them, and eager to stop the gushing wound in her side; dorgan claws dug deep pits. Before the leaf touched the wound, however, the warrior's arm caught her attention. Krengs could see well at night, and she saw that the warrior's arm almost dangled from the elbow; he needed the leaf. She offered it to him purely. He had saved her young. "Take it."

The warrior shook his head. "No. You can run faster, and your caves are closer than the gathering place. Besides, neither of us could wait the seven days it takes to harvest them. Use the leaf then bring me more."

Could she leave them under his protection? They would be well in one day; the leaves worked their magic fast. But he would be worse by then, perhaps dead. Her eyes searched the walls of the warrior's home. It was sparse, much like a kreng home: reeds and vines; herbs; dried meat; jugs of water; and weapons, many weapons. The pelt of a jelnik faded with her passing glance, as did hides and claws from many other animals she recognized.

A snarl grew into bared teeth when she saw kreng talons, but then her gaze caught those hanging next to it—two men, but only their heads. There seemed to be no pattern to his hatred, no escape from his sword. She returned to the jelnik, plucking several of the longest strands of hair. "Bring your arm." Her eyes had softened since the battle.

The warrior held the wound closed while she sewed it shut, her expertise told of experience in many battles healing many wounds. Krengs learned how to mend wounds early in life. When she had finished with the warrior she applied the leaf to her side, the healing began instantly, though it would take a day and a night to recover fully, perhaps longer since she would not be resting. She could make the run quickly, a day to the cave, a day back. The warrior should last that long, but she had to ensure protection for her young. If nothing else the warrior was noble—he had proved that before, and she knew he had courage, every kreng born could attest to that.

She bowed low to him. "I am Kyra. I give you my name. All that is mine is now yours to protect."

There, it had been done. Krengs could give out their name only twice before death. Her soulmate had taken her first name, and now, she had given her other name to the one who had slain him. Kyra grew anxious; the warrior had not responded. Her eyes probed for him to speak.

"I know of your customs, kreng." The warrior bowed low in return, as low as the floor leaving his neck open to attack. It was the beginning of the response. "While I live, your young will live. If they die, then I shall die."

He had repeated the customary phrase perfectly; it pleased Kyra. How did he know the words, she wondered. Kyra stood still; a stone moved more. He had not yet completed the ceremony. Teeth bared on the kreng's face as he rose and stared at her.

"I will offer my name when I know my name." His eyes didn't move.

Kyra stared into them to seek the truth. She saw the truth and nodded. The leaves of life must be gathered quickly. "I take my leave, Nameless One. May your eyes be sharp, and your claws be sharper." Her paws padded softly out into the night.

"My eyes will not close, Kyra. Not until you return."

NEW COMPANIONS

Rahg awoke to a throbbing head. He recalled having many dreams the previous night, none of them good, at least none that he remembered. The worries of this voyage to the Paaren weighed heavily on his mind.

He saw Camissa helping the Mordi prepare food for breaking fast. The aromas tempted him with promises of good food even though the cook pots were devoid of meat. He discerned from the conversations last night that Pathfinders abstained from meat, a concept he couldn't imagine.

A smile crossed Rahg's face as he saw Tobias sitting by a fire with his pan of biscuits, jabbering away at several Mordi.

Probably telling them what a good cook he is, thought Rahg. At least I'll have the biscuits, in case the Mordi food isn't good.

The food turned out to be more agreeable than Rahg had anticipated. The Mordi mixed potatoes with several kinds of vegetables and cooked them in a pan with onions. When eaten with Tobias' biscuits and some milk and cheese taken from goats, it was more than a satisfying meal. About halfway through the meal one of the elders arrived accompanied by a younger Mordi.

"This is Mulka," the elder said. "He will be your guide."

Katsu and Rahg had their eyes fastened on the welgar, not Mulka. "And that is Garnock," the elder said. "Garnock is Mulka's protector."

Rahg studied the younger Mordi and the welgar by his side, like a dog with its master.

Tobias swallowed a gulp of hot khaffe and stared straight at the welgar and then at the elder. "We appreciate the beast for protection, but we won't be needing it. We've got our means."

"I am afraid you misunderstand," the elder said. "Garnock will accompany Mulka anywhere he goes. Garnock is his life protector."

"What do you mean by that?" Tobias asked.

"Ages ago the welgar swore a blood oath as our protectors. There was a time when all feared the welgar, and they had none to call friend. One day a young welgar got lost and wandered into a camp of hunters. The men were about to kill it when a Mordi saved it and took it home. The gods favored the welgars, and as a reward they blessed the Mordi with two gifts: the first gift was that of direction; we can go anywhere and never be lost, ever able to find our way home; and the second, which is by far the best gift, is the ability to communicate with any animal.

"The welgar didn't forget our kindness to them. They pass down the life history of their race with each newborn, and it was told how the Mordi saved the son of their queen. But we didn't truly know the extent of their gratitude until the race of man tried to destroy our kind. It was a summer day like so many others, hot and sticky, and our village was alive with little ones playing after chores were finished." The elder sighed, tears welling in his eyes.

"The first arrows came as a complete surprise, taking two of the youngest Mordi and several of our elders who watched them play. By the time the alarm went out, more than a hundred men had converged on the village, shooting arrows at anyone who moved. When they ran out of arrows, they began using knives. Only a handful of Mordi remained, mostly young ones and women huddled into corners of huts. Soon the welgars came from the brush and the trees and the rocks. They swarmed the men and destroyed them. It didn't take long; welgars are fierce warriors, and they are at their best when killing."

Mulka sat close to Rahg, a full plate of food with him, and the welgar by his side.

"Does the welgar always go with you?" Rahg asked.

"Wherever I go, Garnock goes, but don't worry, he vowed not to cause you any harm, though he has stopped short of saying he would protect you."

"Why were your people upset about the deer and rabbits we killed? The welgars eat meat."

Mulka looked confused. "The welgars only take the weak and sick; they never take the pride of the animals, leaving them to breed new healthy young. They only take the ones that the bitter winters or dry summers would claim if they had not."

Rahg nodded as if he understood, but he didn't. These are strange new companions. Very strange.

NOT LONG AFTER BREAKING FAST, Mulka started them off down a trail that appeared to lead east.

"We came in from the west," Rhaven said.

Mulka never bothered to turn. "There is more than one door to the forest. There is no need to go back by way of the river."

"How else are we going to get back? We left our horses and the other men on the river, and we—"

Tobias was interrupted by Mulka, who stopped and turned. Garnock did too. "I know where your horses are. We knew of your arrival before you set foot in the boat, and we watched your journey as it progressed each day."

"And you never offered to help us!" Rahg was upset.

"Should we have offered aid to those who have tried to kill us for so many seasons? We knew nothing of your mission; you were only another band of hunters seeking Mordi pelts, a trophy for their wall."

"How will we get through the mountains?" Tomkins remained suspicious. "I never heard of a pass through the mountains."

"There are many things people have not heard of, but that does not make them any less true."

The rest of the day consisted of walking east, then north, climbing all the time. Soon they stopped for the night. Mulka sat by himself with only the welgar for company. When Mulka laughed, Rahg went to speak with him.

"What are you laughing about by yourself?"

Mulka looked up at Rahg as if he were reprimanding a child. "I am not by myself; I was sharing laughter with Garnock."

Rahg was stupefied. "You talk to him all the time?"

"He is a friend," Mulka said.

"What does he say?"

"He says many things."

"What did he say that made you laugh?" Rahg's curiosity drove the questions.

Mulka looked Rahg in the eyes. "Some things that Garnock says are not meant for your ears. You might not like to hear it."

Rahg drew back, offended. "I can take anything he says."

Mulka looked at Rahg for a long time, then said, "He said that you carry the scent of man, and at the next river you should bathe." Mulka laughed again. "Garnock said it was no wonder you had to use weapons to hunt because you stink so bad you couldn't sneak up on any game. Not even the weak or sick."

At first, Rahg was offended, but then he laughed along with Mulka—he was right, they did stink. All of them except Camissa.

For two more days, they traveled and had not a single piece of meat to show for all the hunting they had done. Rahg suspected it had something to do with Mulka.

He must be warning them, Rahg thought.

And yet, each night Garnock came back with a hare or foul, or voles, but something. The Mordi had given them provision to last half a month, but Rahg preferred meat. On the fourth night Kella brought back a small boar, and from the surprised look on Mulka's face Rahg could tell that the Mordi had not expected her to be successful. Kella came into camp with the boar hanging from her jaws, walked to Rhaven and dropped it in front of him.

Rhaven smiled, patting her head. "Thank you for the gift, My Lady."

Tobias laughed so hard that he soon had everyone's attention. "Rhaven, it's gettin' to be that we've been away too long when you start calling that beast "my lady." We need to find a town and get you fixed up with a real lady of some sort. Pardon my manners, Camissa, but I believe it to be true." Tobias laughed until his side started cramping.

Camissa, not the least offended, was laughing along with the rest of them. It brought a well-deserved sense of relief to the camp. Even Mulka laughed. The rest of the night passed quickly, and with meat in his stomach, Rahg slept better than he had in days.

Mulka set a blistering pace the following day, and by the middle of the afternoon, they were climbing a trail that looked as if it dead-ended into the face of a huge mountain. The trail proved to be tortuous and more than a little dangerous. A misstep would send a person plummeting to certain death. The wind had also increased, at times the gusts proved strong enough to knock someone from the cliff. The higher they got, the colder it became as well. There were snow-covered peaks above them.

"I never heard of a pass through these mountains," Tomkins hollered, doubt evident in a voice that made no attempt to hide suspicions.

Mulka never turned at Tomkins' accusations. If he heard it he paid it no mind. Garnock led the party, followed closely by Mulka, then Rhaven and Katsu.

"Darkness will soon set," Rhaven hollered to Mulka. "How much longer before we find a place to stop?"

Rahg had not given it any thought, but Rhaven had posed the right question. On a trail as narrow as this there would be no place to stop before dark, and they certainly couldn't stand up and sleep. "

The reason for our quick pace was to reach a place where we could stay the night in safety, and shelter. There is a cave not too far ahead that will offer comfort for us—shelter from the wind and cold, and a dry place to sleep." The news about the cave excited Rahg and he passed the information to those behind him.

The entrance to the cavern was well hidden. Rahg never saw it until they passed a bend and Mulka continued to wrap around the rocks into a concealed opening. Rahg had to duck to get into it, but once inside it turned out to be very large. Almost the size of the one by Twin Forks.

cave entrance

There were rents in the cave walls above with enough light forcing through to make it as bright as a dimly lit room. If nothing else the respite from the cold made it seem more comfortable than it was.

"We shall spend the night here," Mulka said, "and then be off tomorrow."

"Where does the cave lead?" Tobias asked.

"It will take us through the mountains," Mulka said.

Rahg almost laughed at Tomkins. The way he shook his head and mumbled reminded Rahg of Tobias and his mannerisms.

The next day they stumbled their way through the caverns, using their hands to feel their way along. Garnock led the way, with Mulka close behind him.

"Why can't we light torches?" Rahg asked. He hated traveling through the darkness.

"We will only light torches where we need to," Mulka said. "The smoke would be too bad if we kept them lit all the time."

For most of the morning they seemed to be traveling down, but at times they took a trail that led up again, and all the trails, no matter which way they went were narrow and twisting.

"You sure you know where this goes?" Tobias asked.

Rahg heard Mulka's laugh. "I have been through here many times, Tobias. Pretty soon we will be able to stop at a clearing and eat. It is almost time for supper."

Although it was impossible to tell night from day or to discern time while in the cavern, Rahg felt like he had already been walking two days, yet Mulka said it was only time for supper. Rahg plodded along. His hands ached from scraping the walls, and his knees ached from fumbles and missteps. "How long before we get out of here, Mulka?

"Soon we will stop for the night. Tomorrow we will reach the other side of the mountain."

"How far then until we reach the point on the river where we camped?" Tobias asked.

"Another day," Mulka said.

"Another day?" Tomkins's suspicions lay just beneath the surface, ever ready to erupt. "That can't be. Took us fifteen days to get to your village."

"As I said," Mulka explained, "there is more than one door to the land of the Mordi."

As Mulka had predicted, early the second day they reached the exit, though he bade them to stay inside while Garnock scouted the area.

As Garnock left the cave, Kella moved up to follow, and though the welgar offered a ferocious growl, that proved to be the extent of the resistance. Kella seemed determined to go.

"We should eat while we wait," Mulka said. "It will be a while before Garnock returns."

Even before Tobias lit the torch, the aroma of his pipe permeated the air. The familiar odor relaxed Rahg, reminding him of home.

Garnock and Kella returned shortly after supper reporting that all was well. The cave exited to a small plateau, where all that remained was a short hike down to level ground again.

Rahg gasped when he saw the forest, compared to the lands of the Pathfinders, this looked naked, stripped by winter's angry bite.

drought

"There is a spot not far from here that will offer protection and a good campsite."

It felt good to be back on this side of the mountains again, though Rahg couldn't explain why he felt this way. They quickly settled in and ate supper, not much was different, but that night he curled deeper into his bedroll.

THE WOODS WERE silent save the occasional breeze that rustled a few leaves, and their feet churning the duff of the forest floor. Kella was scouting a short distance ahead of them, and Rhaven was just ahead and to the north side, away from the mountains. The screech of a hawk caught everyone's attention, and Mulka tilted his head back and his eyes skyward.

Come to me winged friend. It is I, Mulka of the Mordi. We claim friendship with Soarkin and Sandros, two who traveled the skies south of the Green Mountains.

What do you want with me Mulka, of the Mordi? I have little time to spare. Hunting is sparse, and I have missed the last three meals.

I need your eyes to scout ahead and information you might provide. For your aid, I will give you food when we reach the camp.

I am listening, the hawk said.

It was only a screech to Rahg, and everyone else, but Mulka heard the words.

But if your camp is across the river in the short woods then I am afraid you have come far for nothing.

Instinctively Mulka looked to Rhaven and Rahg, but then he kept his conversation with the hawk. What do you mean, winged brother, tell me.

When the last moon was full, many men came with shooting sticks and killed them while they slept.

Mulka stopped. They kill even their kind—still. I would have thought they would have learned by now.

Camissa had been about ten paces ahead of Mulka. She stopped and whirled around.

"Who?" she asked. Who got killed?" She turned to Rhaven. "Something's the matter. I think you better come."

"What's the matter, Mulka?" Rahg asked.

The pathfinder didn't respond, but spoke instead to his friend in the sky. All of them, my friend? Are they all dead?

The screech was soft and low, but it carried through the forest. All of them. And if they were your friends I am sorry. Some of my kind, even myself have used them for food. Not something I am proud of, but when hungry even the taste of man will do.

All are eventually food for something, Mulka said. I would not deny you any more than the ants or worms or the red beaks.

The screech this time was loud and carried throughout the forest. Then it is true; the Mordi are wise. My name is Klor. If there is anything else I can help you with, Mulka of the Mordi, you will let me know. I shall be near.

By now, Rhaven had reached Camissa's side, and she told him what she had sensed.

"What is it, Mulka?" Rhaven asked. "Camissa said that someone had been killed."

Mulka looked again with admiration at Camissa, then back to Rhaven. Mulka's features, though hidden by fur, expressed his solemness. "Not someone, all of them. The entire camp was slaughtered."

"Argus!" Rhaven yelled. "Was Argus hurt? How do you know?"

"I have found out from the hawk flying above us. He said it happened on the last moon. Many men attacked and killed them."

"Argus!" Rhaven screamed again, his hands seizing the fur of the Mordi. He had to restrain himself from physically shaking him. "My horse," Rhaven hollered. "Find out if my horse is dead."

The commotion had brought everyone back, and only Kella's timely appearance between Rhaven and Garnock stopped the welgar from attacking Rhaven when he laid his hands on Mulka.

"It is all right, Garnock," Mulka said to the welgar. "He means me no harm."

Garnack growled ferociously, and he stared through Kella to Rhaven, but the bared teeth of the vargel was assurance that the welgar would never get through her.

"I will contact him again," Mulka said. Klor, Klor.

The screech made everyone look up. What is it you wish so soon, Mulka?

There were horses with the men at camp. Did they also get killed?

I ate the flesh of one, Klor said, but I saw no others. If there were others, they must have gotten away. The dead one was a mare, a white mare.

Mulka looked to Rhaven. "Was your horse a white mare?"

"No," Rhaven said with a sigh.

"Then your horse was not killed. there was only one dead horse, and it was a white mare."

Tomkins shook his head side to side. "She was a good horse. Must have been a big patrol or else several got together and got em. Can't imagine how they let the horses get away though."

"Argus must have sensed them," Rhaven said. "He is ever alert at camp. But I don't know why they didn't listen to him. He would have raised the alert."

Mulka looked back up at Klor, still circling close by. I know you are hungry Klor and we have no meat to share, but should we get some we will offer you a share of it. If you could do anything to help us find their horses or tell us where they went.

The screech was almost laughter. I can find the voles scurrying through the brush. An animal as big as a horse cannot hide from me. I will tell you soon.

Rhaven looked as if his nerves were frayed. Camissa walked cautiously to his side. "I'm sure that Argus is fine. He must have escaped or else he would be dead like the other horse. You know he would not let them take him alive."

"On that, you are right, Camissa. He would never let them take him alive." Then Rhaven laughed. "Not Argus. You must have it right. He must be alive. And that means Marchall is with him, Rahg."

"How many men were in the camp?" Mulka asked.

"Seven," Rhaven said.

"So many? It must have been a large force of bandits to have taken them. How could they have taken them by surprise?"

Katsu is the one who spoke this time. "They were seamen; knew little enough about the woods; fact is, didn't know much about anything except the sea."

Rhaven paced. "I'm going to the camp. Everyone else can stay here."

Mulka worried. "It must have been a very large force to have killed so many. I could send Garnock to see if anyone lives."

Mulka felt his mind touched by Kella. I will go, she said. I knew all the men, and I can track the horses. Kella's communication surprised him, but he agreed.

"Rhaven, let Kella go. Garnock will remain here. We might need his awareness. No one will get close with Garnock to guard."

Rhaven reluctantly agreed. "Hurry, Kella. Find Argus."

As they prepared for sleep, Rhaven paced. "Rahg, keep a shield around Camissa and Mulka, at least until you fall asleep."

KELLA ARRIVED at the camp late that night, careful to make no noise. When she discerned no one was there, she inspected the site thoroughly. All the seamen lay dead, most slain in their sleep. Their bodies showed signs of ravaging by scavengers. Kella saw Tomkins's mare and wished she could have gotten away. After meticulous checking, she discovered Argus's tracks, and Marchall's. They appeared to have gotten away, headed in the opposite direction from the attackers. She wasted no time in following them.

KLOR'S SCREECH found Mulka asleep, though he quickly woke. I have found those you wished. They are not two leagues from here and heading this way.

Is there a large, bear-like dog with them?

Yes.

What is it? I have never seen its kind.

Never mind, Klor. Follow us, and I will have your meat in a day or so.

Mulka decided not to wake Rhaven; Kella would have them here before long.

RAHG SHIVERED under the cover of his bedroll. It was not from the cold; the bedroll kept him warm, it was the thought of the Paaren that proved the catalyst for these shivers. Rahg had not let worries overwhelm him while the Paaren stood as a place that could not be found, but now, with the Pathfinders claiming knowledge of its whereabouts it loomed as a real danger, one he had to worry about. Rahg wanted to run; he wanted to hide, to cry. What he didn't want was the Paaren. Dark dreams started to come again; sometimes they came while he lay awake. He feared the dreams and dared not sleep, and yet, he feared the Paaren, and dared not wake.

By all the gods, what will I do?

SHATIR—A NARROW PASS

Shatir tucked herself deep into the crevice, wedged in among thorns and jagged-edged rocks, not moving, barely breathing. She heard them coming up the narrow pass, their whispers carried by dry winds. There were four of them—two Sykoran guards and two caravan mercenaries—all experienced fighters.

She let the first two pass, taking slow, measured breaths to fill her lungs, calm her body. Each hand clutched the hilt of a slender blade, almost as long as the Wolfen long-knife, the steel sharpened on both sides, narrowing to a fine, stabbing point. The making of the steel was a secret, folded a thousand times from the finest metal and hammered to perfection by artists trained since childhood.

All Ligarn weapons were custom fitted to the one who would wield it, and during the crafting a drop of blood was added to the process, bonding the warrior to the weapon. Shatir had chosen the knife as her bed partner, and there were none, with the possible exception of Jen Pal, who could wield it with such deadly grace. The most important decision in a Ligarn's life was when they chose which weapon they would wed and which would be second.

Shatir liked the feel of cold steel as she lay in her bedroll, the blade hugging her flesh. She had taken the bow as her second choice, an appropriate balance. The knife for close-in fighting, the bow for distance. With a bow none could equal her; she won every competition, spurring rumors and comparisons with legends of ages past. The Ligarn children bragged that she could shoot the beak off a crow as it flew, and others swore they had seen her shave a rattle from a wagger's tail at fifty paces.

The men she faced were big, armed, and afraid. It was their fear that provided her the edge. The knife would be fine. She could have taken them with the bow from afar, could have gotten two or three of them before they even ducked for cover, but the rules called for her to use hand weapons only; if she had chosen the bow, she would have gotten no arrows. Shatir preferred the knife. The steel felt good as it pierced the skin, felt powerful.

Just as the third one—a caravan guard—approached the crevice, she lunged, the blade in her left hand taking him across the throat, blood spilling sharply across the hardened steel and down his chest. A thin stream gushed onto her, but she paid it no mind.

Shatir fluidly stepped forward and with her right hand, plunged the other knife into the back of the leg of the Sykoran Guard in front of her, severing the hamstring. He wailed as he collapsed, effectively blocking the path from the guard in front. With the first mercenary dead, and one of the Sykorans wounded and blocking the path, she spun to face the last in line.

The man in the rear lifted his sword to strike, eyes glazed over, but Shatir's left hand had not stopped moving, and she brought it back toward his unprotected left side. As he reached for it, she aimed the blade for his palm, penetrating the skin like the leafy sac on a sentry plant.

The mercenary was knocked off balance by her strike. Shatir was fast, and she had followed through with her right hand letting it cut across the neck and up into the chin, continuing over the lips and nose. His scream echoed in the canyon below, but she didn't wait to savor the victory—there were more men to deal with.

The man in front had managed to climb over his fallen comrade, moving quickly toward her. Shatir spun, threw the bloody knife with her right hand to a mark she had eyed in his chest. It missed the heart but was close enough to stop him. He gasped as he clutched his chest, but all the while struggled to get her with his sword.

The second man, too, attempted to stage a resistance. His hamstring prevented him from standing, but he had managed to free his sword and held it out and up in defense, just barely behind his companion, now straining to pull Shatir's blade from his chest. She deftly avoided a barbarous strike from the sword and dropped to a squat, her right leg shooting out to sweep him. He roared as he tumbled from the ledge. Only one remained, the one with the hamstring injury. She could wait him out, but it would not bode well with the small god, and only three were to be chosen for the karn. She had to make her best show.

He waved the sword in front of him like a wounded deer fending off a pack of wolves. The outcome was no longer in doubt, just the timing, and Shatir wanted it done quickly. She waited for the right moment, just when he committed his sword from right to left; it was always more difficult to bring it back again.

As the sword passed by her, she threw the remaining knife. It stuck just below his eye. As he screamed, she grabbed his sword-hand and wrestled his blade free then dealt him a swift, honorable death.

Shatir checked the other one to ensure he was dead, then climbed down to retrieve her blade from the guard's chest. Shortly after, she arrived at the spot where Ghruehne and Jen Pal had observed

Ghruehne's lascivious gaze scoured her body; lean and muscular, a perfect specimen. She had already cleaned the blood from the blades, and they rested comfortably in soft leather sheaths.

"They were talking among themselves before battle, Shatir, and they all felt fortunate to have won a woman as a foe."

Shatir only nodded; it was Jen Pal who spoke. "If anyone thought a woman was weak, they have never faced Shatir." Jen Pal's thin smile would have been unnerving to anyone but a Banished One. "They would have fared better against a pack of Wolfen or a Brood of Victas. Shatir's mercy is a swift death."

Ghruehne nodded. "You have been chosen."

She allowed herself a smile, while she bowed slightly to Ghruehne, then to Jen Pal. "I am honored."

STREETS OF KHATARA

*J*ago returned from his second attempt to hire a ship, but again with no luck. "No one will dare send a ship out. There has been trouble with pirates."

"There must be ships going out," Wisp said. "Khatara's trade surely hasn't stopped."

Jago shook his head. "No, trade has not stopped, but most merchants now ship goods along the caravan route, not by sea."

Aenaila stood from the table where she sat. "We must have a ship, Jago. If we cannot hire one, we will have to buy one."

"My Lady—"

"We have no option."

Jago bowed, but Wisp interrupted. "Aenaila, even if you can buy a ship, you will still need to hire a crew to sail it, and if the threat of pirates is so strong, that might prove to be the more difficult of the two."

When Aenaila opened her mouth to respond, Wisp again spoke up. "I'm going out. I'll see what we're facing."

Aenaila paused only for a moment. "All right, Kender Darnell. Just be careful."

Wisp gave a sweeping bow to Aenaila, then grabbed hold of Adju's shirt. "Come. It's time you showed me the wonders of Khatara."

Adju's face lit like Wish Day Morning. "Yes, Master Kender. I know everything about Khatara. I can take you..." Wisp dragged him out the door just as Aenaila's words assaulted them.

"Kender Darnell, you cannot take that boy with you."

Darstan smiled despite his mood. Even Jago hid a chuckle. Aenaila slammed the door after them.

"Do you want me to follow them, My Lady?" Jago asked.

Aenaila shook her head. "You couldn't follow them around the corner. Let the thieves go about business their way."

"MASTER KENDER, where do you want to go? Most seamen go to the Red Sand or the Island Kettle."

"Where do the merchants gather?"

"That is easy, Master Kender. The rich ones go to the Tracks in the Sand, but only the very rich. The Wing and Talon is where small merchants go."

"Lead me to the Wing and Talon. We'll learn what we can there."

Adju held his head high as he led Wisp through the streets of Khatara. He pointed out every building he knew and greeted every person he had ever seen. "It is not far now, Master Kender. Only two more streets, then we go about fifty paces toward the market."

The Wing and Talon was about the same size as the Trader's Inn, though it didn't seem as boisterous, at least the crowd tonight didn't.

They took seats at a table near the center of the room, but toward the front. Conversations from half a dozen tables drifted past the seats. "Two ales," Wisp told the serving girl.

"Ale for such a young one?" she asked.

"This one has lived twice his years. He's earned an ale tonight."

"Two ales, then. Will you be taking food?"

"Perhaps we will, but our thirst must be quenched first." Wisp leaned toward Adju. "Listen well, but don't let anyone suspect."

Adju nodded, but Wisp didn't care for the grin he wore.

They drank ale and talked, but mostly they listened to the conversations at the tables surrounding them. From the little he heard already, Wisp could tell the merchants were worried, and, angry. It had been half a year since the pirate attacks started and every merchant in Khatara felt the effects it had on trade. They complained bitterly about the loss of business and the increased costs involved in transporting goods over the caravan route, the only sure method since the shipping lanes had been all but closed.

Adju slipped off the seat and moved close to the table next to them. He stood, silent and patient, until one of the men recognized his presence.

"What is it, boy?"

Adju bowed. "A thousand pardons, Master, but I heard you talking, and—"

"Well, what is it?"

Adju pointed to Wisp, now wearing a scowl of disapproval on his face. "My brother must take me to Genda, and we wanted to travel by sea. But... but I heard you speak of pirates." Adju paused, a pleading look in his eyes.

The men at the table straightened, and the man who Adju had

addressed turned in his chair. "There's not a lie in what we told, young one. Not a single lie. I lost two loads of goods myself. Now I have so little left I could only fill two carts on the caravan." His head snapped back as he downed the last of the ale. "Every merchant in the city has suffered. Even Bulta, though he still sends out ships. The only one who can afford to risk it."

The man caught Wisp's full attention with the mention of Bulta. The Bultas were notorious thieves posing as merchants, but they were not honest thieves. The Bultas stole and cheated the common people.

Somehow, the Bultas are behind this.

Wisp joined the men at the table. "How is it that this merchant, Bulta, can get his ships through?"

The merchant shifted in his chair to face Wisp. "So the elder brother speaks. Bulta has lost goods; though not as many as others. Harun Bulta is the wealthiest merchant in Khatara. A few losses won't sink him."

Wisp and Adju drank another mug of ale, gathering information all the while.

They had managed, mostly through Adju's introduction, to draw three more tables of merchants into the conversation. People seemed to open up more to each other when tragedy and losses were involved, each telling tales of woe. Wisp finally leaned to Adju and whispered. "Time for us to go."

It was late when they left the Wing and Talon, but Wisp still wanted to go to the Tracks in the Sand.

"Do not worry, Master Kender, I will take you. I am not sleepy."

"I wasn't worried about that. But in this inn, we will have to do things differently. The wealthy merchants are not as willing to speak openly."

～

ADJU'S MOUTH fell open when they stepped through the door. All of his life he had wanted to enter the Tracks in the Sand, and now he was here. Smooth hardwood planks covered the floor, and the tables and chairs had all been carved from the dark, ripe wood of the Bija trees that grow in the Kir-Fan mountains. Adju was still examining the wonders of the inn when Wisp tugged on his arm. "This way."

They sat at a table made for nobles, and when the serving girl brought them ale, Adju marveled at the fine mugs.

"Stay here while I speak to some of these gentlemen," Wisp said. He moved to a table where he had heard snippets of conversation dealing with shipping. "Good sirs, I find myself in an awkward situation. I am in need of transportation to Genda, and I must arrive long before the next caravan could carry me there."

The three merchants examined him like a jeweler buying a gem. "You will do better to arrive late," the merchant closest to Wisp said.

"Better than not at all," another put in.

"I'm grateful for your concern, friends, but is there no one who might get me to Genda?"

The one merchant who had not spoken stared at Wisp. "If you are in dire need you could go to Harun Bulta. He is the only one still shipping goods, but his price will be steeper than the peaks in the Kir-Fan range."

Wisp nodded. "I thank you for your information, gentlemen. I hope my purse is as deep as my need. I bid you a good night," he said and rejoined Adju.

DARSTAN HAD WAITED up for them to return. "Well, Adju, did you keep Master Kender out of trouble?"

"I did, Master Darstan, though several times I worried over him."

Wisp looked about the house nervously.

"She's in bed, Wisp. She was tired." Darstan smiled. "Jago is in the room next to hers."

Wisp sat next to Darstan. "I think we can get a ship, but to do it we'll have to deal with Harun Bulta. And that will be expensive, possibly even dangerous. And if we get a ship it will have to be under the pretense of going to Genda. No one would let a ship out for an unknown destination."

"I'll leave that to you. Besides, I seem to be restricted to the house."

"Then I shall wish you a good night, Darstan, as I will be getting an early start."

AENAILA WAS eager to be on the way, but without a ship, she could do nothing. The bottom of the khaffe mug was just showing when Wisp awoke. "Good morning, Aenaila."

"And to you, Kender Darnell. Did you find us a ship?"

"Not yet, but I believe there is one to be had with enough gold. I'll find out today. How much is too much, Aenaila? I need to know what to negotiate for."

He thought he saw a mischievous smile under her calm exterior, but if it was there, it vanished as quickly as it came.

"Negotiate the best price you can. Whatever terms you come to will be acceptable."

"No matter the cost?"

Aenaila finished the khaffe with a final gulp. "No matter the cost. And now, I believe you should go. Time is important."

Wisp wondered where these people he traveled with got their gold. Rhaven always had a sackful handy, the people in Entiria had more gold than all of Sykor, and though she didn't display it, Aenaila seemed to have more than her fair share. As he prepared to leave, Adju popped up from his bedroll in the corner of the room.

"Wait for me, Master Kender."

"Hurry. Aenaila has no patience."

"He should stay here, Kender."

Wisp took Aenaila by the hand and whispered. "He'll be fine with me. Adju helped last night; perhaps he can be of assistance today as well."

The smile remained on Adju's face long after they left the house. "Thank you for your kind words."

They walked in silence for a moment, Wisp and Adju both melting into the rhythm of the city. "Where do we go today?"

"The market first. From there we'll likely go see Harun Bulta."

"Merchant Bulta! But Master Kender, you cannot see him. No one sees Merchant Bulta. Master Kender, the market is not yet open. We have time... could we... I would like to see Khalina."

Wisp could almost see the tears. How can I tell him no? "Adju, you know we can't go to Mufed's. He knows who we are. They—"

Adju tugged fiercely on Wisp's sleeve. "Please, Master Kender? You met Mufed. He would never do anything to hurt you. And besides, those guards from Sykor are gone. You heard Master Jago say so."

Wisp stopped walking and stared down at Adju. "How much time before the market opens?"

"Enough time for khaffe and a meal at Mufed's. It is not far from here."

Mufed placed mugs of khaffe on the table for some travelers from Jattan-Kir. "Our khaffe is very good. I am certain you will enjoy it."

"Master Mufed!" Adju screamed his name as he entered the inn, running to greet him. "Master Mufed, it is Adju. Remember me?"

Mufed wiped his hands on the front of his apron, then, with both hands free, he embraced Adju. "Little Adju, how we have missed you."

Tears welled in Adju's eyes. "And I, Master Mufed. How I have missed you. And Khalina." Adju relished the embrace.

"Where have you been, Adju? We thought after what happened—" Mufed released Adju to greet Kender, his hand extended. "Forgive me, good sir. Your face is familiar from your last visit, but your name, I am afraid, left with you."

"Kender Darnell."

"Ah, yes. How could I have forgotten? Please forgive an old man his poor memory."

"I would wager that your memory is as sharp as your cheese, Master Mufed, and I remember the bite of your cheese."

"Ah, little Adju always brings such noble patrons. Come, come and enjoy a meal and some khaffe."

Mufed led them to a remote table and quickly brought three mugs of khaffe, taking a seat himself to join them. He looked around, suspiciously, Wisp thought and wondered what was wrong.

Mufed did not make him wait long; he leaned close and spoke in hushed tones. "The emperor still looks for those you traveled with," Mufed explained. "One of the men hurt by the fire was a cousin of the emperor, a merchant. There is even a reward."

Wisp sensed it in those last words, the chance for Mufed to grow wealthy. Now, what to do? The only way to be certain was to kill him, but... Mother of rats! The little beggar would never forgive me if I killed Khalina's father. "How much is the reward?"

Mufed brushed it off with a laugh and a pass of the hands. "It is nothing, my friend. What is any amount of gold when compared to friendship?"

Wisp saw through the protestations, and Mufed had let him know that gold was involved, not silver.

"I would not think to buy your friendship, but tell me, what value does the emperor place on my friend's life?"

Mufed cleared his throat and seemed to be in thought. As if he has not counted that gold a hundred times in his head. I would wager my last breath he began counting the moment he saw us enter.

"I believe that he offers eight gold crowns, my friend. Eight!" Mufed's eyes turned green with greed. "Your friend should stay well-hidden." His eyes darted about the room again, suspicion in every glance. His next breaths were whispers. "I do not want to know his whereabouts, but you should find the best place possible. A place where no one would look."

Mufed straightened in his chair, though his voice remained a whisper. "I know a few such places, but... no, no, forgive me. I speak too soon. I do not wish to know, so please ignore me."

Wisp decided to do just that, but he didn't want Mufed to think he suspected him, nor did he want the innkeeper running to the first guard he saw to collect a reward. "I will have my friend take your advice. If I convince him, perhaps you would be kind enough to show us where we could hide."

Wisp let it sink in for just a moment. "Of course, I would not expect you to do this without a favor, and to show my goodwill I ask you to keep this silver Sykoran Crown until I return. You will be well-rewarded for your efforts." Wisp saw the smile hidden behind Mufed's worried expression. He wouldn't turn them in yet, not until he got their money too.

"Yes, my prayers for your friend's safety," he said. "I will not speak a word to anyone." Mufed stood, clasping Wisp's hand between the two of his. "Tell no one, my friend. No one."

Wisp bowed to Mufed. "No one," he repeated, but now I must drag Adju from here. We have work to do."

"But you have not yet had a meal. It is being prepared now. Please—"

"We cannot, Mufed. Already I have lingered too long, but remember, I will be back with my friend."

Mufed tried to hide his smile, but he was not quick enough. "May the gods go with you," he said, waving as they left.

"Master Kender, why did we leave so early? The market does not open until—"

"Later, Adju. For now, lead the way to the market. I will make sure we are not followed."

"Who would follow us, Master Kender? No one knows we are here except Mufed, and he..." Adju stopped suddenly. "Master Kender, Mufed would not tell anyone."

Wisp nodded. "I prefer to be safe, Adju. I trust no one."

"It will be all right, just follow me," Adju said.

"I MUST SEE THE COMMANDER."

"I can take your message; the commander is occupied."

"I must see him. This is a message of some importance."

The guard remained in place.

"The emperor himself will wish to hear my news. It concerns the one with powers."

"Come with me, citizen. What is your name?"

"Mufed. My name is Mufed."

DREAMS AGAIN

The dreams came again just when Rahg thought he was rid of them; this time though, they began differently. All of the original scenes from before flashed by quickly, very quickly, and yet he vividly pictured every scene, each one etched in his memory now, a part of his life. And here he was, standing before the dragon once more, smelling its fetid breath and seared by flaming eyes. It was both disruptive and inviting. This couldn't be real—he knew that, and yet how could it be anything but real. He had been injured before, though he had told no one except Camissa. Who else could he tell, they would surely have thought him mad.

The dragon lowered its massive head, red eyes glowing with flames and a cavernous mouth leaking smoke from an internal kiln.

"What do you want?" Ragh asked, agitation painted by fear drove his voice.

What do you want? the dragon asked. You are the one who comes to me, disrupts my slumber, invades my lands.

"It's not me!" Rahg shouted. "I don't bother your dreams. I never asked for this."

The dragon's laughter shook the cave. *There are many ways to ask for things, young one, and though you might be unaware of your actions, you have indeed been asking.*

"What is this all about?" Rahg demanded to know.

A heavy sigh escaped the dragon's mouth and hit Rahg with the force of a gale wind. *The young always want answers before they are ready. Be patient. You will know too soon as it is. Yours is not a fate one should wish to rush.*

"What fate? What are you talking about? Why don't you just tell me?"

Many paths are yet undecided. You have yet to choose a tunnel.

"I won't do it," Rahg said, his mind planted as firmly as a ten-year green emerald. "I'll not pick a tunnel, and I won't come back here. Not until you tell me what I need to know."

Rahg felt heat from the dragon's eyes, and he shrunk from its glare. He had thought it looked feral before this, but the change in its face made him realize it might have been a smile before.

You will come back. You will return again and again until you decide on a path or you die. The option is not yours.

Rahg felt the air being sucked from around him, almost sucked from his lungs, and he realized the dragon was drawing breath—air to turn into fire. "No!" he screamed, and ran toward the opening of the cavern, a wave of flames in heavy pursuit.

I⊤ WAS STILL DARK when Rahg woke, soaked like the fever had held him for days, but he knew the reason he remembered these dreams. He mopped the sweat from his forehead and face, crawled from under his blanket and made his way to the fire. The flames chased the cold from his hands, and soon enough from his neck and back as well.

Rhaven stared at him from his bedroll, and once again Rahg wondered if the man ever slept. He never went to bed until after everyone else; he was up before anyone, and the whisper of a snake would wake him.

Gods, but I wish I could do that

"What woke you, lad?"

Rahg nearly jumped, blinking twice. Rhaven had somehow managed to slither over to him without Rahg even noticing. "Nothing, Rhaven. Just woke up cold and wanted to get warm."

Rhaven stooped to warm his hands. "I saw you stirring in your sleep, and I see your hair is wet. Dreams again?"

His directness gave Rahg pause, but he couldn't lie to Rhaven, the man always seemed to know. "Same ones, Rhaven. Same every time." A sigh escaped Rahg's lips. "I'd do anything to stop them."

Rhaven poked the coals with a fresh stick and placed a few small logs on the fire. "I don't know much about dreams, but I've heard too many tales of people who dreamed things that were real. I think at the first chance we should find someone who knows something about them, perhaps even Mikkellana."

"No!" Rahg nearly shouted, but managed to keep it in whisper form. "I don't want her poking around in my head. I know she healed me, but I still don't trust her. I don't want anyone with powers creeping through my mind."

Rhaven sat on his haunches while he continued to stir the coals. "There are others who interpret dreams in Khatara, and I would wager we could find some even in a land like this."

Rahg scowled. "Who's to say they don't have powers, too. Before I left Twin Forks, I didn't believe anyone had powers, thought all those stories were children's tales. Now it seems it's not so uncommon—Camissa, Wisp, Aenaila, even Darstan and me. And that's not to mention the Banished Ones or the other immortals." Rahg shook his head as if in denial. "By the gods, Rhaven, what have we gotten into?"

"I leave conjecture to philosophers. I simply follow the path that fate has marked for me."

The crackling of the fire was the only sound until Rahg spoke again. "Part of the dream is a vision of a dragon, and it tells me that someone close to me will betray me." Rahg moved closer to the fire. "I can't believe that anyone I know would do that, and yet there is something about the dragon's voice that makes me believe it."

Rhaven thought about how he swore to kill Rahg if they discovered he was the Messenger. "You shouldn't have told me. Tell no one else." Rhaven remembered his conversation with Rhalan Teldren about what he would do if Rahg proved to be evil, but he shook the thought away. His pale eyes went icy. "You never know who you can trust. I had a brother who betrayed me."

The stick snapped in Rhaven's hand, and the noise startled Rahg almost as much as Rhaven's words had scared him. Rahg remembered the fight Rhaven had with his brother, Damon Pirrhar, the leader of the Black Rose assassins.

"What about Camissa?" he asked.

"No one!" Rhaven said. "Trust no one."

Rahg remained by the fire even after Rhaven had gone. He seemed to need the warmth more than ever, now.

I sure wish Darstan was here.

A COLD WIND

*I*n the five days it had taken them to get out of the Green Mountains, the weather had gone from spring back to winter. Biting winds and bitter cold drove them to shelter early each night and set Rhaven on a quest for warm beds and food.

Garnock reported back early the following afternoon that an inn lay half a day journey east of where they were. Rhaven set a fast pace, determined to make the inn by dark, but the sun had set a while ago, and they still had not reached their destination.

"It's not far from here," Mulka said.

As they moved through the next clearing, the lights of the inn came into view, though it was still far away. Rahg reached to fasten his cloak, the wool hugging him but rippling from the wind.

Rhaven turned, facing them. "Stay here until I get back," he said and disappeared into the darkness.

"I don't know how he does it," Rahg shouted over the wind, teeth chattering from the cold.

"It's all in the mind, lad. That much I know, I just wish I knew where in the mind to find it." Tobias tucked his hands under his arms. "It's colder than beaver teeth."

Rahg laughed to himself—"colder than beaver teeth." The mirth struck a splinter of warmth. Tobias had more sayings than any six men, and half the time his sayings made no sense.

LOOSE CLAPBOARDS SHOUTED at the wind, but it wouldn't stop, slapping them hard against the tavern's frame. Rhaven's cloak whipped as wildly, but he fought off the cold as he made his way toward the inn. The windblown trees painted shadows on the ground that danced in the moon's glow. Rhaven seemed to be one of only many.

"A bitter night to be out alone, stranger."

Rhaven whipped about. Three men had sneaked up on him with the wind at their backs. He eyed them suspiciously, admonished himself. How could he have been so careless? "You are half right; it is a bitter night."

The men looked about. "I don't see any companions," the tallest one said, and each of them slowly reached for their weapons. "They want a silver for each bed in there, but that's because a bed comes with a meal. A heavy price they're askin'. And me and mine, well, we can't seem to find our coin. Thought you might loan us a few silver."

Rhaven moved quickly, and before the men had drawn full steel, they faced two sai. Rhaven flipped one sai back against his left arm as he raised it to ward off a blow. He stepped into the man as he raised his left arm, a move meant to throw the man off guard. He caught the tall one's sword with the sai in his right hand. A hard, jerking twist ripped it from the man's grip, then the point of the sai found the soft flesh of the belly.

The wind drowned the scream, but it couldn't hide the blood, giving the others pause. The last man stood frozen with fear, so Rhaven focused on the first one. His opponent had withdrawn the blow when it met the sai instead of flesh, and now he reared back for a second attempt, a slice toward the left side.

Rhaven flipped the sai back to its original position and stabbed downward, into the right part of the chest. When the man wailed, the right sai punctured the left lung. In only moments the lung would be suffused with blood. The night had another victim. The third man started to run, but Rhaven's command forestalled any notion of escape. "Hold!"

He stopped at Rhaven's command.

Rhaven stared at him for a long time. "If it was food you wanted, you should have asked. I would have shared what we had."

The stranger swallowed a lump of pride. "I'm sorry for what we done, for the way we acted. I got a wife and child to feed. That's why I joined up with the other two."

Rhaven assessed the man, trying to determine if he was telling the truth or fabricating a story now that he was caught. "What kind of place is this inn?"

The stranger shivered from the cold. "It's old but clean. One of the few inns that might have any food, though soldiers guard it night and day."

Rhaven sighed. "We could use a bed and a good meal."

The stranger snickered. "You better have a lot of coin. He charges a silver for each bed, and it only comes with one meal. If you want extra food, it's almost as much for that." He stared at Rhaven. "That's why we needed the money. Haven't eaten in two days."

"What else lies ahead?" Rhaven asked. "Any towns?"

The man looked as if he would weep. "There's a town all right, but it's one cursed by the gods. Even the soldiers steer clear of it."

Rhaven reached into his pouch and drew two silver coins. "Take this for your family."

The man fell to his knees and tried to kiss Rhaven's hand, but Rhaven brushed him off. "Just go."

THERE WERE soldiers all over the inn and at least a dozen at the tables. The innkeeper hired them to keep the peace and to collect money. The man had not lied about how much they wanted for food. They could have bought meals for a week in Sykor or Pomanda for what they paid for supper and a bed here. He thought about the hot food and the warm bed, then he thought about the Mordi, and how he had to stay outside. At least he had Kella and the welgar to keep watch for him. There would be no one sneaking into camp with them around.

"Where do we go after this, Rhaven?" Rahg always had questions, but Rhaven's glare silenced him.

"The guards listen to everything we say."

Rahg nodded. Nothing seemed normal anymore. He had to be careful about everything he did or said. He had never felt so alone.

AFTER A LONG, satisfying supper, they sat near the fireplace keeping warm. There were a half dozen other men at the tables, and ten of the guards remained but sat across the room. Rhaven was speaking to Tobias when he heard a voice in his head. He turned quickly to Camissa. It was her voice, but she wasn't speaking. When his eyes met hers, the voice continued.

It's Camissa, Rhaven. It's me speaking to you through your mind. Do you hear me?

"Yes, I do, but—"

Tobias looked confused. "What did you say, Rhaven?"

Do not speak aloud, Rhaven.

The voice came to his head again. I can hear you if you just think; there is no need to speak.

Camissa almost laughed. It was the first time she had seen Rhaven completely surprised.

How are you doing this? Rhaven thought in his mind.

I have been practicing and have made progress. Camissa smiled at him, then turned to the fire. Don't look at me. People will wonder why we stare and don't speak. You can focus anywhere you want, just listen.

She waited until Rhaven turned his head to face Tobias before continuing. Tobias was talking, but it was his usual banter, and she felt sure that Rhaven could listen to him and still concentrate on her thoughts.

I have been spying on the guards while we ate and several of them, if not all, are curious as to where we got so much gold, and how much we have left. They are even discussing a plot to kill us and take it all. Only moments ago they sent a rider to fetch more guards.

Tobias was trying to talk to Rhaven, but found him staring blankly at the fire. Finally, Rhaven responded. "Not now, Tobias. I'm thinking."

Tobias puffed hard on his pipe a few times but wasted no time in turning to Tomkins to talk.

Rhaven thought about what to do. They couldn't leave now, or the guards would stop them, and even if he thought they could outfight them, someone would get injured or killed. If they waited to leave, they might run into the new guards. He took two long swigs of ale and thought some more until clarity came to his head. He hoped Camissa was still listening.

Camissa, are you able to speak to Mulka?

He's far away, but I can try.

Good, then listen.

MULKA STIRRED from under the brush cover he had made. Someone was trying to communicate with him. There was a whisper in his mind, like the itch of a flea that wouldn't go away.

Mulka, Mulka, I need to speak with you.

Camissa? He felt certain it was her, but if so, she was growing stronger, as this was a long way to communicate. Camissa, is this you?

It is, Mulka, and we need help.

She quickly explained their situation and Rhaven's plan.

I will take care of it. Stay safe, and warm.

Camissa collapsed when she broke off contact with Mulka. It was only Rahg's quick reaction that saved her from hitting her head.

"Camissa! What's the matter? Are you all right?" Rahg panicked, but Tobias soon took charge.

"Carry her upstairs, lad, and put her on a bed. Tomkins, get some hot water from the innkeeper and come up with it quickly." Meanwhile, Rhaven kept keen eyes on the guards as Tobias and Rahg made their way up the stairs with Camissa. Katsu and Jarrel stayed with him.

GARNOCK CREPT EVER-CLOSER toward the hare, almost tasting its succulent flesh. He was only a few paces away when the urgent call from Mulka came. He listened, looked hungrily at the hare one last time, then sped off in the direction of the inn. He had a mission—track the soldier who left the inn. Garnock would have to go to the inn to pick up the scent, but once he got that, the rest would be easy. Even with the long lead the soldier had, Garnock would catch him. When it came to rough terrain and mountains, nothing could move better or faster than a welgar.

A large rut where a creek once ran retained enough moisture to carry a thin sheet of ice where one of the last pools stood, but it barely groaned as Garnock's quick paws touched on it then sprang forward. The wind whipped fiercely, carrying the welgar with it, and he never slowed until the inn was in sight, and only then to check for humans and to catch the scent. Only one man had recently come from the inn and gone to the stables; only one mount had departed this night and gone east. The welgar followed the trail, gaining ground continually. He cut through passes where a horse would be forced around, and he navigated the forest as if he had been raised there.

Garnock caught the soldier less than three leagues from the inn, and long before he had any opportunity to deliver a message. The horse was resting; the man huddled in a cluster of trees for warmth. He didn't plan to stay long, else he would have built a fire. Garnock crept closer, watching as the man rubbed cold hands together. The welgar struck without the soldier ever knowing. His claws cut through the cape and raked his neck to the bone, and his teeth ripped the artery clean. Blood rolled over Garnock's tongue and oozed down his throat. He tried to stop it, not that he wanted to, but he had sworn oaths to the Mordi, and he would not break his honor for this man.

The welgar coughed, as if a bone were stuck, and spat out the trickle of human blood. Garnock's red eyes turned to the horse, and it screamed in terror; welgars were known for killing horses, but this one was hobbled and could not escape. Garnock padded to the horse and clipped his tethers with razor-sharp teeth. The horse stared at the welgar with huge wild eyes, but Garnock only growled before departing.

Live for tonight, my friend; I will not kill one chained to the ground. Garnock hunts his own food.

The horse neighed loudly and ran off, opposite from the welgar.

Before he reached the inn, Garnock had communicated with Mulka and told him what happened.

Stay to protect them, Garnock. They might need help.

I will only help if I can kill others of the man race.

You might have to do just that, Garnock, but only the soldiers, and only if necessary. You have spilled enough blood for the night.

Inside the inn, Camissa heard the voice of the Mordi, clear, though distant.

The soldier's message will not be delivered.

ROADS OF ARANGAR

It was a windless night with a sky as bleak as the countryside. The withered leaves of the shuka trees stood still as stone, and the lack of light from stars and moons dampened what few dreams lingered in children's minds—dreams of rain and food and happiness.

"Any idea where we are, Tomkins?" Tobias always wanted to know where they were, even though he'd have no frame of reference in this strange land.

Rahg thought about this often. Back home he did the same thing to Tobias, even though he had never been to any of the places he asked about, but that was different because at least he had heard their names and heard stories told about them. That somehow made it different.

Even the names sounded strange in Arangar. Harsh names like their land. But then again, that's what Malakai's wife had said about him, that he had too harsh a name for such a lad. Thinking back on it made Rahg wonder about Malakai and how they were doing. Perhaps he had the right of it, hiding out on those beautiful islands.

It sure seemed peaceful. I doubt if Lukaan could find me there.

"Iazzo found you on Entiria."

Rahg spun to see Camissa smiling at him, his face painted red from embarrassment. She startled him every time she read his thoughts, and he wondered if he'd ever get used to such an intrusion. "Stop it, Camissa."

"Why, does it bother you so much? I remember a time when you begged me to perform tricks for you, like a bard at a village fair."

Camissa had a way of twisting Rahg's emotions, no matter what he was feeling. Joy turned to tears, and anger brought laughter. He had been indignant at her intrusion, and now she had him nearing an apology for something he did so long ago. "Don't try working your guile on me. I'm starting to learn your little games. It's not me who's the guilty one here. I was only—"

"Oh, Rahg, you do get carried away so." She laughed as she slid her arm through his and moved him along a path by the woods. "It's a pretty night, don't you think?"

"It sure is," Rahg said, holding her hand tightly. "It sure is."

"Do you think much of home?"

"On nights like this, I do. Reminds me of winters in Kamnor. Most people like clear nights with the moon and stars shining. I kind of like it like this."

"I do, too," Camissa said. "You have to make your own dreams on nights like these."

"I wonder where Darstan is. Khatara, I guess." Rahg turned to look at Camissa. "Did Aenaila ever tell you why Darstan needed to go with her?"

Camissa rolled her eyes. "She never told me anything. I don't trust her. Something wasn't right about that whole affair and the way she kept it all so secretive."

Rahg sighed. "We'll get together again soon. Wisp, too."

"I hope so," she said and wrapped her arm tighter around Rahg's.

TOBIAS SAT on a rock by the fire, whittling on a piece of shuka that he found in the woods. "Not a bad wood," he muttered. "Not as good as maple, mind ya, but then not much is in my opinion. This wood's a little too hard." Tobias often talked to himself, but thankfully he expected no replies.

Rhaven nodded, his whetstone gliding over the steel of a knife. He missed the times at night when he had sharpened his sword blade, gentle caresses that coaxed nicks and wounds to a fine edge, but ever since he got the Sword of Mikkellana he had no use for the whetstone. The blade never dulled, never took a nick or even a mark.

Rhaven slid the sword from the scabbard. It was silent, as always, though he didn't know why, and that formed a puzzle that bothered him. Whetstone in one hand, he turned the blade slowly, inspecting every detail.

"Still sharp as a woman's tongue, ain't it?"

Rhaven laughed at Tobias's colorful sayings. He seemed to have one for every occasion. "If I didn't know it to be impossible, I would say the edge has grown sharper."

"Carve on this wood for a while. It'll dull a good blade."

"Tobias, what do you remember about the story Shera Kevon told us? Did he mention anything about the blade?"

"The only thing I remember is him saying that Mikkellana made it, and he'd been waitin' around since Lysic's time to give it to someone— if you can believe that. Course, I can believe just about anything after what we've been through."

"She said there's another."

"What's that?"

"Mikkellana said she had made another one, a long time ago."

"Where is it? Who's got it?"

"I don't know, though I believe the one who held it is dead. I still wonder where the sword is. And I wonder who he was." Rhaven sat silent for a moment. "Have you ever heard of tales of a warrior with a sword like this?"

Tobias continued carving with his knife. The wood was beginning to take shape, the hint of a large bird just peeking out. "Can't say that I have." He stopped carving and put the figure down beside him. "And now that you've brought it up, it does seem strange. Seems like we would have heard some tales about a warrior with a sword like that. They've already got tales about you, and that's without the sword."

"Perhaps it was so long ago that people have forgotten."

"Folks don't forget heroes. Villains neither. Look at Lukaan and the tales from Sethia. And that was as long ago as anybody remembers."

"Then perhaps it was before then."

Tomkins popped up out of his bedroll. "Don't know what you two are talkin' about, but I never heard of any of them people. Not Lukaan or that other lady either. And the only sword I ever heard tell of is that one the barbarians are always looking for."

"Which sword is that?" Rhaven asked. "And who are the barbarians?"

Tomkins scratched his head. "Who are the barbarians! The ones on the other side of the mountains. The ones we've been fighting since the good gods put us here. Who'd you think I meant?" He stared at them, then shook his head.

"I know you're not from around here, but just where are you people from anyway?" His brow furrowed in suspicion. "Being from anywhere in Arangar you should know."

"Where we're from people don't hear much of nothin', Tomkins. We're far enough out that the business of Arangar doesn't concern people much. They're more interested in eating and having enough water for crops."

Rhaven stopped and stared at Tomkins. "What do you know of this legend?"

"The legend's as old as the hills. Says that someday a man will come to them with an ancient sword—a sword of legend, and that man will lead them out of the valleys and over the mountains into Arangar. "… and the Gates of Paradise shall fall…" That's what the legend says. I remember that part, the one about the Gates of Paradise."

"Sounds like the same tales I've heard from a hundred lands. Seems like every village and people have dreams of a savior." Tobias kept whittling on a piece of wood.

Tomkins looked straight ahead. "What makes this one so different is how much they believe in it. Every mother teaches each child from the day they're born. They're told about the legend at their first blessing and at every occasion of note they are reminded." Tomkins' smile vanished. "The difference is, that true or not, every man, woman, and child in Cergala will follow whoever they choose to the death. And that kind of fervor is hard to defeat."

Rhaven nodded. "Have you ever been to Cergala?"

"Nobody from Arangar goes to Cergala. Not if they want to live. Besides, the Chun warriors guard the mountain paths, and I believe they're as bad as the Cergalans. They don't take kindly to strangers or to anybody from the cities." Tomkins scratched his beard while he talked. "Though the Chun might not be guarding much. They say they've been hit worst by the drought. Who knows, maybe Cergala got hit bad too."

"It may be that we'll have to go to Cergala. We don't yet know our final destination. Only Mulka knows that, and he isn't telling much."

Tomkins snorted disapproval. "Not that you'd care much about a tired old man like me, but if you're going to Cergala, I'll be leaving you. I didn't care if I died when I agreed to come with you, but now I've said my words over my boy's resting place, and suddenly I've got a new feel for living. Guess I care more than I thought."

Tobias laughed aloud and reached for his pipe. "Can't say I blame you too much. Even people old as us got somethin' to live for. If I hadn't sworn to help this lad, I'd likely go with you."

"What's the lad got to do with anything?"

The lad's got everything to do with it. You already know about his powers, the way he can make shields."

Tomkins nodded. "I saw. I was afraid to ask too much, though. Never heard of people who could do those kind of things."

Tobias tapped his pipe on a rock next to him, then packed it full with more tobacco. He seemed to be mulling over thoughts of how much to say as he performed the ritual of packing his pipe. Once the tobacco began burning again, he continued with the conversation. "There's been a lot of change in this world, Tomkins. The past year or so has seen a lot of things turn upside down." The smoke billowed from his pipe now. "Trouble is, things are bound to get worse."

Tomkins appeared to be listening, but his confused expression told he did not understand it all, or even a large part of it. "What's getting worse? What does Rahg have to do?" Tomkins stopped, but picked it up quickly, not waiting for Tobias's response. "By the good gods, Tobias, the lad's got magic—powers as you say. Who could be after him, the goddess herself?"

Tobias ignored Tomkins' remarks and his questions. He should never have said so much. "Let's just say that he's got a lot to do, and we have committed to help him. If you don't want to come—"

Tomkins quickly interrupted. "I've never shied from a fight, fair or not. I said I'd come with you, and until I say different, you can count on me being there with my sword."

Tobias leaned back a little, resting comfortably against a large rock. "That's good, Tomkins. We need men to help us on this journey. Especially men with swords."

RHAVEN HAD PUT the sword away, and the sai, and now he coaxed a tiny nick from one of his knives, just near the tip. He thought about what Tomkins had said about Cergala and Arangar, but what stuck in his mind was what he said about the sword. Darstan carries a Cergalan sword. Like the thief, Rhaven was suspicious of coincidence.

PIRATES IN THE SAND

"It is very near, Master Kender. Only a few more moments."

When they turned the corner Wisp saw the market spreading for two to three hundred paces east to west. Tents towered above houses, and the merchants flew banners over each tent to denote the goods displayed inside. Bolts of silk and other fine fabrics lay boldly exposed for prospective buyers to feel the quality of the goods. Other merchants flaunted the finest gowns for those wives or mistresses who could not bear to be without unique designs. And at each table, the merchants boasted of their offerings being the best. Price was never discussed until a selection was made.

Shopkeepers walked about touting their wine and cheeses as the best and even offering samples to for people to taste. Wisp was lured to a table from across the tent by the aroma of khaffe that slowly danced its way throughout the congregation until the temptation was too much.

He passed by tents offering food rich with the scent of rare spices, but there were no samples of these unless a purchase appeared imminent. The jewels are what intrigued Wisp the most. Row after row of tables displaying a tremendous variety of gems and diamonds, all with a full complement of mercenaries to guard them.

"They are the best mercenaries," Adju said, pointing to a row of guards standing rigidly before a tent draped in blue silk. All were armed with the famous Khataran curved sword and a dagger which they kept tucked in their belt.

With a few quick questions to the proper people, Wisp soon found his way to the tent of one of the largest merchants in Khatara. "I was told you could provide passage to Genda, Merchant Carfa."

Carfa's laugh was larger than he was, but his voice was thin as a rib. "The only way I can get you to Genda is on a horse. I no longer ship my goods." Carfa looked about carefully. "Harun Bulta's ships seem to have the blessing of the gods, though why they would favor him no one knows."

Wisp was careful with his words. "Would a person feel safe traveling so far under his protection?"

Carfa thought for a long time, his hands busy arranging some goods on his table. "Harun Bulta gives all passengers his assurance of safety."

It was now Wisp's turn to think. "Merchant Carfa, I must ask you to give serious thought to my question. If you wanted to move your family to Genda, would you purchase passage with Harun Bulta?"

Carfa needed no time to formulate a response. "I would hope that my journey would not require such haste. I prefer the slower pace of the caravan route."

Wisp bowed. "Merchant Carfa, you have convinced me that we might also enjoy the sights along the caravan route. Your wisdom is appreciated."

When they were far enough away, Adju began the questioning. "Master Kender, why did you tell the merchant we would take the caravan? Will we go see Merchant Bulta now?"

"Yes, Adju. We will."

HARUN BULTA HAD four tents to display his goods: silks, jewelry, spices, khaffe, te, and other rarities from the farthest reaches of Jattan–Kir. Inside of his main pavilion women of the Qorami entertained prospective customers, but only those whose purses were counted among the fattest.

The Qorami were known throughout the lands as the most alluring women in the world. They were bought from their parents when they were young—no older than twelve—and then trained in the arts of love.

A special breed of mountain goat produced the finest milk, and the Qorami bathed daily in it. Each night their skin was rubbed with olive oil, and their long hair was brushed several hundred times by servants dedicated to waiting on them. If they were not deemed of the proper quality by the time they reached 16 years old, then they were sold to someone else as prostitutes—or sold as slaves. It was debatable which fate was worse.

Adju tugged on Wisp's sleeve. "There they are, Master Kender. They are Qorami."

Wisp could not help but stare, though he quickly forced his thoughts to the business at hand. "I see them, Adju. A man could lose himself in that beauty. The problem is that most men forget who they are when faced with such a woman."

"You would not, Master Kender. I know you."

Wisp kept walking, but inside he wondered if anyone could truly resist. He shook his head to clear such thoughts, then saw the mercenary guarding the entrance to an inner chamber cordoned off from the rest. As expected, the guard blocked entry.

"Only those invited by Merchant Bulta."

"I have a business proposition for him."

"Are you a jeweler or a shipper?"

"I would be discussing shipment of goods, enough to fill an entire ship."

"Master Seaman Batu oversees shipping. You can find him at the docks."

"Adju, are you taking us to the docks? I smell no seawater."

"Master Kender, you always make me laugh. You know I cannot get lost in Khatara." Adju turned a corner onto a major street. "The docks are far from Mistress Aenaila's house, but we will be there soon."

True to Adju's estimate they arrived at the docks in short order, though Wisp was amazed at the lack of activity.

Dockhands were busy loading one ship, but that was the only one. It proved easy enough to locate Bulta's man, as everyone working there was in his employ.

Master Seaman Batu reminded Wisp of Tobias, and if he was not as old, Wisp could picture him resembling Tobias more in the years to come. Short stubbles made up a scraggly gray beard, and the gray continued to pepper his dark hair on the sides and the thinning top.

Tough, weathered skin showed that the sea took a toll on men as well as ships. His wiry build was not dissimilar to Tobias's own, and Wisp thought if he pulled out a pipe he would swear him to be kin of some kind to the Marek family.

"A good day to you, Master Batu. I would beg some of your time to discuss business."

Batu clasped hands with Wisp then reached down and rubbed the top of Adju's head. "And a great day to you, lad. If you were here alone, I'd strap you to the rigging and give you a proper education." The seaman's laugh rattled in the small room. "I would say you haven't seen twelve summers yet; my papa had me on a ship at nine."

Wisp let the mirth build inside him. Batu could challenge Tobias for conversation also. *I better stop him before the tales stretch too far.* "Master Batu, perhaps he will see his education yet. We need passage on a ship. Five of us."

The hint of a frown touched Batu's face at the interruption, but he didn't let it linger. "Well, lad, you won't get a true education if you're going along willingly, but..." He brushed Adju's head again, then focused on Wisp. "Your name slipped by me, sir, or it slipped through the holes in my head. At times I can't distinguish the two."

"Kender Darnell, and the little one is Adju."

"Adju. Good name, lad. But I've not heard your name before. Kender, you say? What kind of name is Kender? Sounds like a name from across the plains." Batu opened the door and stepped outside without waiting for an answer to his query. "Join me, gentlemen. It's a fine day and business is best discussed with the smell of the sea in the air." Batu lifted his head high, then tilted it back and sniffed several deep breaths.

"We'll need a ship and provisions for two months. I can provide a crew—"

Batu spun around as if a demon addressed him. "Your own crew! Not with my ship. No one sails one of my ships unless it's with my crew."

The seaman lifted his chin and scratched. "Two months? Where would you be going to take so long? Genda's not so far, and no one sails to the capital from here. Even if you wanted to sail the river to Sykor and then on to Genda, it wouldn't take that long."

"Perhaps I should speak to Merchant Bulta directly."

"You've put a bug on me, sir. I don't mind saying so. If I had a tail, I'd be itching it." Batu shook his head after his conclusions failed. "Tell me where you folks are bound. The worst I can do is say no."

"Master Seaman, I wish that things were different, but I can't disclose our destination as yet." Wisp thought for a moment. "Perhaps I should just see Merchant Bulta. That may be best."

Batu shook his head again. "Ruin such a fine day. That's what you did. Got my mind agitated, wondering where you could be going, and now you'll leave. Well, you'll need my mark to get in to see him. Come back inside, and I'll get it for you."

BEFORE THE MIDDAY MEAL, they stood before the mercenary guards in front of Bulta's office. Wisp held out the mark of Batu, which the guard dutifully scrutinized. He led them through the door where two more guards met them to provide escort.

The office was not as plush as Wisp had expected; in fact, he had seen several shops in Sykor that were as nice as this and a few others that were superior. Wisp caught sight of decorations in odd places and paintings in awkward positions.

Likely spots for spying, he thought.

Further examinations were precluded by the brisk pace the guards set, and the subsequent appearance of Merchant Bulta.

Bulta's frame could have supported a bear, and if he had been covered in fur instead of swarthy skin and silk robes, he would have looked the part as well. For any hair that might have graced his body, the top of his head had not seen it in quite some time; it was smooth as a creek stone, and many Khataran merchants would attest that his head was indeed harder than those same stones.

Large, rounded eyes sat comfortably above a nose that a bloodhound would envy, and that hung over a mouth like the opening to a large cavern. Adju nearly stumbled when Bulta's laugh rumbled out of him like echoes in a canyon.

"Have merchants gotten so small? Or are you to be captain on one of my ships?" Bulta let that bellowing laugh out again.

Wisp deduced him to be the type that liked to laugh at their own wit, strange as it might be. "We spoke to Master Seaman Batu this morning and are here at his suggestion." Wisp wanted to keep this meeting brief.

Bulta's eyes fixed on him. "Yes. Yes. I know all about your visit to Batu. Did you think I would not?" Huge thick hands reached out to seize the one Wisp had extended, a vigorous shake ensuing. Adju shied away from his expected greeting. He had never met a man so large.

Wisp watched him keenly. The man was not the jolly merchant his demeanor portrayed him as. "Should we begin, Merchant Bulta? We have much to discuss."

"My friends, how could you suggest such a thing? Let us break bread together. We will eat and sip wine, and after we have quieted the noise from our stomachs, then we can discuss the tedious details of business." Bulta put an arm around each of them and ushered them into a separate room for dining.

Servants had set the table and were even now filling the wine glasses, three of them.

Bulta lowered himself into an oversized chair puffed high with cushions to support his bulk. Wisp and Adju settled comfortably into cane and wicker chairs with seats covered in a fine velvet fabric. Adju reached for the cheese before the servant's hand had left the tray.

Adju's eyes lit up at the first bite. "This is delicious!" he said.

He next plucked some grapes from a wooden bowl and a handful of dates from a stack that lay neatly across a silver platter.

Bulta had not been idle, so he emptied his mouth before speaking. "Little Merchant, if you continue eating like that, you will be as large as me before you wed. And unless you are as wealthy also, it could make it difficult to find a bride."

Adju's laugh was loud and natural. "Master Bulta, I am thin as a stick and have always been. Even your good food could not fatten these bones."

A servant returned to the table with more wine to refill Merchant Bulta's glass. Wisp looked, but could not determine how the servant knew when to come in, but his cursory inspection of the room did reveal a spot where a safe may be hidden. He had his glass refilled but stopped Adju at the one glass. Aenaila would have his hide if Adju reeked of wine in the middle of the day.

When the servant exited, Wisp felt it appropriate to begin. "Merchant Bulta, as I told Master Batu, we need a ship and provisions for two full cycles. There will be very little to load other than personal items, and the return will differ only slightly."

Bulta had eaten almost a dozen dates and a generous amount of cheese and grapes. He swallowed the last bite of a fruit Wisp didn't recognize, then replied. "You have me at a disadvantage, Kender Darnell, I..." He stopped in mid sentence. "Did I say your name properly?" he asked, and at Kender's nod, he continued. "I believe a man's name is of utmost importance. But enough of that. As I said, you have won an advantage already by initiating these negotiations before I have finished my meal." He let a thin chuckle escape, a very thin one, but it was as natural as if he meant it.

"But since you are not from Khatara—I know this from your name—then you would not be familiar with our customs." Bulta set his wine glass down, wiped his hands, then sighed. "So, let us begin, my friend. What price did you have in mind for this very long voyage?"

Wisp sighed as well, but with relief to be started, and not a little bit for the thrill of negotiations. Khatarans were notorious negotiators. They would buy nothing without first negotiating, and they would never pay the full price asked. It was known throughout the lands that to deal with a merchant from Khatara one must include the "Khataran discount" before the negotiations began. It had become such a part of the race that some said merchants were born with the need to negotiate.

"We only require one of your smallest vessels, Merchant Bulta. There are only five passengers, and the voyage is not very long."

Bulta leaned back in his chair. "Only five passengers, yes, but food and provisions for an entire crew, and there is yet the crew to speak of. A good captain costs much."

"I will supply my own crew," Wisp said. "Or at the very least, my own captain."

Bulta sat upright so fast he appeared to be projected forward. "No! No, good friend. I cannot allow that. My ships sail under my crews." A false smile crossed his face. "But do not worry so much on the cost. Since you are a new friend and, I pray, a new customer, I will assure you a good crew at a fair price."

"And tell me, Merchant Bulta, what is a fair price?"

"There are things I must know. If your journey takes you through treacherous waters, like the straits east of Jattan–Kir, then—"

"If the weather does not raise the seas there will be no hazards. I believe your smallest ship will suffice."

Bulta leaned back into the chair once again. "If you are not destined for Genda or its isles, and you are not going through the straits, then you must be sailing south into the Endless Sea."

Bulta's eyes narrowed to a hawk's predatory gaze. "What have you found, my friend? A secret isle perhaps? A land rich in gems?"

Bultas's stare jumped from Wisp to Adju and back. "Ah, I see the both of you are good, closed-mouth men. I like that. I have always said that a secret cannot be kept by more than one man. And I have yet to meet the woman whose lips can stay sealed for more than a fortnight."

Wisp finished his wine and settled back into his chair. "Merchant Bulta, I am bound by honor, so I cannot reveal my destination; however, I understand your concern and your curiosity."

Wisp paused while he thought how to phrase what he wanted to say. "I can assure you of the safety of the crew and the ship from anything in my power, but of storms and pirates I wield no command."

"My captains fear no storms, but you are correct about the pirates. It seems as if danger rides the crest of every wave." Bulta's smile thinned. "There are ways to ensure no trouble with the pirates, though. They are, after all, businessmen."

Wisp met the merchant's smile. "And what will that cost?"

Bulta must have had the numbers in mind before they entered. "The cost of provisions and the wages of the crew will be your burden. Food and supplies at my cost plus an additional tenth. Plus you must pay for any damages incurred on the voyage. For this plus the use of the ship... twenty Khataran gold crowns."

Wisp nodded, no expression on his face, but from the periphery, he saw that Adju had nearly fallen from the chair. "You take full advantage of the newest rash of piracy, Merchant Bulta. I would wager that when competition returns this same fare might well be half that, even less."

Bulta should have been an actor in a troupe, Wisp thought. He contorted his face to change expressions at will.

"My friend, I wish the seas were safe. I long for the days when Khataran sails were spotted in every port and rode in with each tide. High prices are a merchant's worst foe, but I must charge so to remain a profitable business."

"Have you lost so much to the pirates?"

"The gods have smiled on me," Bulta said and patted his chest three times with both hands open. "Two of my ships have gone down, both with full loads, but my loss has been small compared to some others."

"Who is doing this? Do you know?"

Revenge filled his eyes now, a difficult expression to mimic. "It is Malakai. None other than the Sword of the Sea, himself. How is a poor merchant to best him?"

Wisp nodded again. "I suspected as much when I heard of the piracy. I never did believe him dead as so many claimed. With this news, Merchant Bulta, I am grateful to have found you to safeguard us. Shall we take seals to parchment at the sum of ten crowns?"

Bulta leaned forward and slammed his hand on the table so suddenly that Adju jumped back, cursing.

"By the Hand of the Lady!" he shouted.

He drew a glare from Wisp, but an even more curious and probing look from Bulta.

"An odd saying for such a young one to have waiting on his tongue," Bulta said.

Adju's face colored. "An apology, Master Bulta. It is a saying I learned near the market."

Bulta's false smile returned. "My ears have heard worse than that, young one. It is no wonder you have learned such things at the market; the air is rife with curses, though I suspect it is not something you learned at the market. That curse is only issued by thieves, for who else would call on the blessings of the Lady."

Bulta eyed the two of them suspiciously. "And those words slipped from your tongue with ease. It gives me pause."

Bulta popped another fig into his mouth and said, "Ten gold crown! I am afraid you have misunderstood my position, friend. Twenty gold is not negotiable."

Bulta saw no sign on Kender's face. What is his game?

"I understand your position, Merchant Bulta, but ten gold is what I can afford at this time. Perhaps we could make other arrangements?"

"Very well," Bulta said. "Ten Khataran gold crowns to get you to your destination, and ten more when you return." Bulta's laugh shook his bulky frame.

"Very well," Wisp said, and extended his hand to seal the agreement. "I accept your proposal."

Bulta's laugh stopped so suddenly it shocked Wisp. This man had control over himself. "But I only jested," he said. "The price is—"

"Ten Khataran gold crowns," Wisp said. "You do not strike me as a man who jests about his business. You have proposed an arrangement, and I have accepted it. I know you offered it in good faith, as the merchant's guild—"

"Yes, I am aware of the laws of the guild, as a presiding judge must be, but somehow I feel certain that this information is not new to you." The merchant's face reddened despite his dark complexion. Harun Bulta was not a man to be taken advantage of. "I pray that my good faith will not fall into a forgotten realm."

Wisp stood to leave, signaling Adju to do likewise. "I will certainly not forget you, Merchant Bulta, and I feel we will do business again." Wisp took one of Bulta's massive hands between his. "When will they be ready to set sail?"

Wisp's long slender fingers looked as if they had not done an honest day's work. It must have given Bulta more pause. "The ship will be ready in five days. See Master Batu by tomorrow. He will tell you how much the provisions will be and instruct you further." Bulta slid his hand away from Wisp's grasp. "And now, I must go," he said. "May fortune smile on your journey."

Wisp and Adju both bowed as they left. "And you, Merchant Bulta. May fortune smile on your household."

WISP TURNED the corner with Adju close on his heels. "Master Kender, did I do it right?"

Wisp tousled the hair on Adju's head. "Perfect, Adju. Did you see the look on his face when you swore by the Hand of the Lady?"

"I was too nervous, Master Kender. I did not see him."

"Well, it was perfect. Now, let's get home to Aenaila."

NO SOONER HAD Wisp and Adju departed than Bulta had several guards in his office, along with the captain of one of his vessels. "Borzu, I want charts kept of this journey. Every bit of it. The most accurate charts you've ever kept. We may want to return to this place."

"Where will we be headed, Master Bulta?"

Bulta's smile was no longer needed, and as such, a scowl painted his face. "They must have discovered something in the Endless Sea. Fools! Do they think to keep it a secret from me?" Bulta gestured to the guards. "Both of you will board as crew. And, Borzu, see to it that they are believable crewmen. Take along a few extra men as well, and when you arrive, find out what our passengers have discovered. When they are no longer needed, kill them."

The captain nodded. "As you will, Master Bulta."

"But not until you have what they seek!" Bulta shouted as a reminder.

CHINGUA

Three more weeks of bone-weary travel had them all on edge. Food was running out, and game grew more and more scarce as they approached the city. "We should keep off the road," Rhaven said. "The forest will provide the cover we need; besides, the road is growing crowded."

"What about food?" We need to get some soon, and the city is probably our best chance."

"We're all hungry, but we must be careful. These are dangerous times in Arangar."

"What's your plan, Rhaven?" Tobias had been silent for so long Rahg had almost forgotten he was with them.

"I thought that you, and perhaps Tomkins, would go to the city with me. We'll see about getting food and fresh horses if we can."

"I'd rather go to the city than stay here," Rahg said. "Besides, if you run into any trouble, I can help."

"Rhaven can take care of himself, lad. He's just taking Tomkins and me so we can stop him from killing so many people." Tobias pulled out his pipe to light. "Every time we go into a town Rhaven kills someone. Just can't seem to stay away from trouble, so me and Tomkins will be there to help."

Rhaven smiled. "Tobias is more right than he thinks. I don't want to draw attention, so he and Tomkins can handle the negotiations and make the arrangements for getting the food."

Mulka stepped forward. "I will send Garnock east and south scouting for game; Kella can go north. Between the two of them, they should find enough to fill a few plates. Some of the others can help me. I am certain we can find some roots and other morsels."

Rahg grimaced. Just what I need when I'm hungry, more of Mulka's roots.

Rhaven nodded. "Post a heavy guard, especially if you're sending Kella and the welgar out." It wasn't long before Garnock returned carrying a fowl of some sort.

"Looks like you'll have something to nibble on," Tobias said. "That should keep ya till we get back."

welgar with food

RHAVEN MOUNTED Argus and spurred him forward. "Let's go. We're wasting time."

After a few hours, the city came into view.

"Big enough city," Tobias said at the sight of Chingua. "About the biggest I've ever seen and then some."

"Biggest I know of," Tomkins said. "Was a time when a million people lived here. That was back before the drought and before the wars got worse. Now they say only half that many are left."

"Still more than any I've seen," Tobias said.

Rhaven stopped and stared at the gates to the city, slowly patting Argus's neck. "Have you ever been here, Tomkins?"

"Not here, not inside. But I've heard plenty about it." Tomkins chewed on his tobacco. "Once we get inside we should go to all the taverns and markets. With enough money, we can buy food and anything else we want. That's one thing about a big city; you can get anything you want if you have the money."

The first two vendors had so little to sell that Rhaven passed on buying anything. They had, at least, recommended someone they could go to, a man who had meat but at high prices.

Tomkins led the way down two side streets, then into a small shop at the corner. The sign in the window offered books and linens for sale, but the dust had grown a thick coat on most all the books. There were a few old cloths, but nothing that could be called linen, and nowhere was there a hint of food. "We came to look for some books," Rhaven said. "Some with a history of the city and perhaps maps of the mountains."

The man behind the counter stood no higher than Camissa, and if he weighed more, it was not by half a stone. His hair was thick though, and he wore a beard that would take a year or two to replace. His eyes shifted from one to the other before he responded.

"Books, yes. I have many books on Chingua, and even a few on the Norkaan Mountains but none, I fear, that would offer any maps."

He stepped from behind the counter and shuffled to a stack leaning against the outside wall. "Ah, here is the one I was thinking of. 'The Chingua Glory.' This is a good telling of the city from the Founding all the way to King Norander's reign. It truly—"

"How much for the book?" Rhaven interrupted him. Tobias frowned but said nothing.

The shopkeeper straightened himself and appeared to collect his patience. "It truly is a great story, as I was about to say, good sir. Now, as to price, I would need a copper crown and two marks. I simply could not—"

Again Rhaven interrupted. "Done," he said. "Tomkins, pay the man."

The shopkeep bristled at the rude treatment, but a smile hid beneath the slight.

"Since we've paid your highest price for the book," Tobias said, "We need to negotiate the price of the meat."

THE MAN PROVED to be a keen negotiator, as his face never registered surprise at the statement. Or maybe it was just that in these times everyone wanted food. "There is a chance I could find some food for a few hungry gentlemen like yourselves, but there are many shops who could offer you better."

Tobias let him finish, and before Rhaven could speak, Tobias laid a hand on his arm. "We could use enough meat and supplies for about ten men and at least two to three weeks."

The shopkeep nodded his head slowly as he carried the book back to the counter. "So much?" he asked. "That could prove difficult at best. And expensive. But I believe we could arrange something." He nodded his head again. "Yes, perhaps we should wait until after dark, though. If you were to be seen with so much food in the streets, it would stir a riot. I will also need time to get to my supplies, as I have them hidden."

The man leaned toward them and whispered, though no one else was in the shop. "There is a warehouse not four streets north of here with the name of Caulvin on the doors. Meet me there just after dark, and bring a wagon."

"How many pounds do you have, and what price are you asking for it?"

"I could sell as much as five stone of meat, two barrels of flour for biscuits, six stone of cheese, and two barrels of wine—not good wine, but wine all the same."

Tobias gnawed on his pipe for a moment. "And the price?"

The shopkeep tapped his hands on the counter and did some calculations. "I could do that for twenty gold crowns."

Tobias yanked the pipe from his mouth and choked on his smoke, a ploy he often used when negotiating. "Twenty gold crowns! You might as well hold a knife to our throats and take our money now."

"As it is I risk my life selling so much to you." The king forbids it, and his guards are ever keeping a watchful eye. If I were to be caught, it would mean a painful death."

"I'll give you eight gold crowns, but you have to get us a horse and wagon to haul this with."

"You present a strong case, my friend. I will agree to the horse and wagon, but for fifteen gold crowns."

Another round of coughing and Tobias spat out "Twelve crowns. If that isn't good, we'll take our business elsewhere."

Tobias didn't like the hidden smile on his face, but the man extended his hand to seal the deal. Before they sealed the pact, however, Tobias negotiated one last time.

"Twelve crowns it will be, but if we go that far, I need some good fresh tobacco and three sacks of khaffe to help keep us warm." The man hesitated so long that Tobias thought for a moment he wouldn't do the deal. "Pretty soon you'll be the richest merchant in Chingua, with the prices you're getting from us."

Finally, the man smiled and shook hands. As they were walking out the door, Rhaven turned to go back in. "I forgot my book."

The shopkeep's smile covered his face and only narrowed slightly when he saw Rhaven returning. "I forgot my book," Rhaven said. When the man handed him the book, Rhaven seized his arm and pinned it to the counter, then a knife appeared as if from nowhere, and he pressed it to the man's throat.

"If we show up tonight and discover a trap, or if we happen to be robbed this day before we go, or if the king's guards should happen to check our wagon and discover our food—then know this one thing, little man. Before anything else happens, I will kill you."

The man's face glistened with sweat and his eyes no longer smiled. He swallowed his fear and nodded. "There will be no trap."

"Good, I would rather not kill you." Rhaven let him loose and walked out the door.

Tobias's pipe was puffing furiously. "Last moment negotiations?"

"I had to arrange for security."

Tobias and Tomkins both laughed.

THERE WERE no signs of a trap at the warehouse, none that Rhaven could see, and he had made it a point to get there long before dark so that he could see people coming or going. *Perhaps I scared him enough.*

"What do you think?" Tomkins asked.

"It looks all right to me," Tobias said. "And here he comes now, alone too."

Before the merchant reached the doors, Rhaven slipped across the street and waited to meet him. "Remember my words, shopkeep."

The man gulped but kept his composure. "I remember. There's no one else here, and the food is inside. I inspected it myself." He opened the doors, and before long they had concluded the deal, with the wagon loaded.

"Stay to the side streets," the shopkeep said. "The road from my shop takes you to within two streets of the northern gate. That way you will avoid the guard."

Rhaven scanned the street ahead and the side alleys as they moved away from the warehouse. After only a few streets he stopped them. "I want to scout ahead of us before we go. I still don't trust that merchant."

"We'll keep a close watch. We can handle whatever comes, leastwise till you get back."

Rhaven dismounted and handed Tobias the reins to Argus. He patted the horse's neck as he left. "Keep alert, boy."

Within twenty paces Rhaven seemed to disappear into the shadows. "By the great gods, but that's a scary man. I was watching him with both eyes and the next moment he was gone. Just gone."

Tobias nodded. "That man can hide from a bear in its own cave. Walks like a spirit in a graveyard too. I tried tracking him a few times, but he left no marks I could find."

Tomkins and Tobias chatted idly, but all the while kept a sharp eye in each direction. Moments later, Rhaven returned. "There are guards waiting, but not only on this street, the ones surrounding it as well. He must have tipped them."

Tobias smacked his hand against the wagon. "Blasted coward! Not even man enough to take up with thieves—got to get the guards involved."

"They'll likely have our description and a complete list of our goods." Rhaven stood, thinking.

"How many?" Tomkins asked.

"Too many for us," Rhaven said. "A full patrol on this street and no less than two half patrols spread between here and the main street."

Tobias gnawed on the end of his pipe even though it wasn't lit. "We could turn around and try to make our way out of one of the other gates."

Rhaven shook his head. "They'll be searching if we don't show soon. We could, though, make it too costly for them in lives. They'll think twice if I take five or six out before any confrontation begins."

Tomkins had been silent. "I'm not afraid to wield a sword, and if the fighting starts I'll hold up my end of it, but I think there's just too many of them. No sense in us getting killed and losing the food too."

"What do you propose?" Rhaven seemed attentive.

"I think there might be a way to get out without any trouble and keep most of the food too. Even all of it."

"Go on," Tobias said. He itched to light his pipe but didn't want to draw attention.

"This city's got a lot of hungry people. People who would do most anything for food. I say we find twenty or so and offer them a few coppers each to go with us out the gate, maybe a spell further. With that many people, the guard won't bother us."

Rhaven took no time to decide. "Good idea. You and Tobias gather the men. We'll offer a copper crown each to get us out the gate and another for each once the wagon is safely away. I'll meet with you shortly."

Tomkins seemed to relish the praise from Rhaven, no one immune to his rare compliments.

"Where are you going?" Tobias asked.

"To keep a promise."

Tomkins had no problem finding enough men, and it had taken only half as long as he thought it would. "I hope Rhaven gets back soon with those coppers. These men need some proof, and soon."

"He'll be back," Tobias said. "Won't be long."

RHAVEN STALKED the warehouse as if it were a hunting ground. He saw the light from the candles in the front and heard the rustling and shuffling of papers. Each shadow held its own angles, color, and depth. Some concealed better than others, and some even seemed to move with a force of their own. Rhaven knew how to use the shadows, how to dance to their unique rhythms.

Nerves had frayed on this merchant long ago, a rapid deterioration that paralleled his depravity. Nervous men are suspicious men, and suspicious men are jittery, always alert, and yet he never heard Rhaven until he felt the steel against his neck. A gasp rushed from his lips and recognition forced bile to rise in his throat.

"What... what can I do for you, my friend?"

Rhaven smiled. "I know you to be a smart man; it takes a learned man to do accounts of books and run a business. I never learned much of books, but I'm grateful that my teachers instilled a strong sense of honor and a respect for the truth. I was taught that a man's word is his life."

The merchant broke into tears. "Please show mercy, my friend. I have a good wife. I have children."

"A pity you could not keep your word," Rhaven said. He slid the knife along the merchant's neck. Sharp steel opened his veins, spilled his blood.

"ABOUT TIME YOU GOT HERE," Tobias said. "This group is getting mighty anxious, and I just saw two guards down that side street, off to report about us, I imagine."

The crowd parted quickly as Argus pranced his way through them, a ploy by Rhaven to distract them and keep them afraid. He held out a hand with several copper crowns and a few silver coins. "You know the arrangement. I have a copper crown for each of you to get us outside the gate. There will be another once the wagon is safely away."

"What's in the wagon?"

"The first man who needs to know can leave. The first one to touch the wagon, I'll kill."

"I'll take my crown now, mister." The demand rose from a man near Argus's right flank. Rhaven moved his knees a few times, and Argus spun quickly, then kicked the fellow, knocking him flat.

The man screamed. "I think my ribs are broke."

Rhaven ignored him. "Anyone who needs the money now can leave. The rest of you will get yours at the gate."

"What of the guards?" someone asked.

"If the guards try to stop us we'll fight. I don't expect you to take up arms against the guards, but for any who do, the pay will be extra." A few murmurs arose. "And if anyone is killed I'll see that his family gets a gold crown."

"Won't do me no good if I'm dead," one man yelled.

"No, it won't," Rhaven said. "No amount of gold will help you when you're dead, but it will take care of your family." Most of the men seemed to be with him. Only a few walked away. A quick count showed sixteen still with him. Enough, he thought.

A FULL PATROL awaited them at the gate, a barricade of guards with swords drawn. "Stop and be searched," the patrol leader ordered.

Tobias had a bow next to him in the wagon, arrow at the ready. Tomkins held a sword in his lap. The men gathered close to the cart but none, as yet, had drawn weapons. Argus moved to the front, snorting wildly. Several of the guards took a step back, and when they examined Rhaven closely, they took another step back.

"Do you have a charge against us, soldier?"

"I have orders to search all wagons."

"All wagons, or just those coming from a certain merchant?" Rhaven let his icy glare catch each guard, lingering longest on those most afraid. Fear could take a man out of a fight entirely, and if it got to that, he wanted to have as few to fight as possible.

"I take no orders from merchants. We inspect all wagons."

Rhaven leaned toward the patrol leader, and Argus stepped even closer. The guard held his ground, but not without reservations. "You won't search this wagon, soldier." Rhaven kept his voice to a whisper, but to the guard it was like the whisper of a wolf. "I'll kill you first if you try. You know I can kill you. Is it worth it? Do you have a family?"

The patrol leader's brow grew sweaty. Rhaven noted his fear and knew his dilemma. This time, he spoke loud enough for all to hear. "Don't die for a wrong cause. We have no wish to kill you."

The patrol leader struggled with his decision. Finally, he shook his head. "I'll not die for his greed," he said. "Let them pass."

Tobias breathed a sigh of relief. They were leaving the city without having killed anyone, though he strongly suspected that the merchant had passed away.

THE VOYAGE BEGINS

Darstan peered through the crack in the curtains at the darkened street. He had not seen anyone pass since supper. "What do we need to take with us, Aenaila? How long will we be gone?" He had grown anxious being cooped up in Jago's house all this time.

"Be patient, Darstan. We have a few days yet before we depart. And you will need nothing special, just your clothes and personal items."

He paced and fidgeted. "This is worse than a voyage. I think I'll go with Wisp today."

Wisp sat slouched against the wall, his knife scraping dirt from under his nails. "Aenaila's right, Darstan. I dare not say it, but I find myself aligned with her again."

He slipped the knife back into the sheath at the top of his boot before he stood. "Besides, I told you about my visit with Mufed. The emperor is still searching for you."

Adju rushed to defend his friend. "Mufed would not do that, Master Darstan. He is my friend."

Darstan pulled Adju close and hugged him. "I believe you. If he is half the man you are, he'll not betray us. But Wisp has the right of it; I better stay here to be safe."

Adju held the hug for a long time. "Master Darstan, I am not afraid of you anymore," he said, then squeezed him tighter.

Darstan stooped down, face to face with Adju. "What do you mean? Why would you be afraid of me?" There was hurt in Darstan's eyes.

The sleeve of Darstan's good arm wiped tears from Adju's face. "What's the matter? Tell me."

A few sniffles and sobs later, Adju let his eyes touch Darstan's. "Ever since the fire, when you hurt Takar. When I... when I saw you shoot fire, I was afraid, and ever since then, I—"

Darstan pulled him close again, hiding tears of his own. "Oh gods, Adju. I would never hurt you. No matter what happens. You should know that."

"I do now, Master Darstan. It just took me a while. You understand. When I heard stories about people with powers, they were always bad people."

"Don't worry. We'll soon get this over with, and when we do Wisp and I will take you to visit Sykor. Really visit, not just a day or two."

Adju wiped his eyes again. "Thank you, Master Darstan. I will never be afraid again."

Wisp laughed. "I'm glad you can say that because I don't know if I can. Darstan scared me enough when I first saw him with powers." The mood in the room lightened at his remark. "Now it's time for me to take your leave."

"Where are you going, Master Kender?"

"Stay here, tonight. I must act alone on this."

Aenaila stopped and shot him a rigid glare. "What demands your attention so late at night?"

"There are certain matters that I must attend to. Matters that are better dealt with after the sun settles."

Aenaila put thread and needle away, then moved to his side, close enough for a whisper. "What is it? Whatever you go to do, I can help. If you need something, anything..."

Wisp took her hands in his, and the warmth raced through his blood. It was difficult to stare into her eyes—emerald gems, they reminded him of. Priceless emeralds. "I promise, Aenaila. No harm will visit me tonight. This is just a matter that needs tending to."

"Then I shall—"

"No." Wisp squeezed her hands. He felt weak. "You can't go with me." He let go her hands, opened the door and slipped into the night.

"Where did he go, Mistress Aenaila?"

"He refused to say. Though I fear Master Kender is like that at times. As close−mouthed as a Chun."

Darstan laughed. "What's a Chun? Is this another one of your secret words?"

A laugh forced its way out despite her mood. "I suppose I have let a few words slip out. It is just—"

Darstan hugged her. "I know, Aenaila. I worry about him too. But I swear, outside of Rhaven, I've never seen a man more capable than Wisp." Darstan rubbed his hand through her hair, that wonderful honey hair. Whenever he got close to her, the attraction grew. How could it not? She was as gorgeous as the morning in spring. "Do you want me to go look for him?"

Aenaila laughed loudly. "That's all I need. If anyone cocks their gaze at you the wrong way, you would set the city afire, and Wisp would steal all the jewels before the houses burnt to the ground." She snatched her thread and needle from a table and returned to sewing."

"He will be fine, Mistress Aenaila."

"I hope so, Adju."

WISP'S rapid pace carried him swiftly to the merchant district. He kept close to the buildings, careful to walk in the shadows. A few people still roamed the streets, but not many and, of those, more than a fair share were guards.

Harun Bulta's office sat on a small rise at the end of two main arteries leading to the market area. Wisp had checked the area when he and Adju visited. A light cast a glow from the back room, next to where they had met with Bulta. There was a recess between two buildings that provided the perfect spot to wait. He ducked into the darkness and bided his time. Aenaila kept popping into his head, but he brushed the images away. This was not the time to be distracted by her. Before long, he saw the light extinguish. It was almost time.

Harun Bulta locked–up and exited through the front door, his bulky frame almost filling the entrance. A nod to the guard, and he was on his way, walking briskly down the street.

Wisp hugged the building, cheek pressed flat against the damp stucco wall and eyes narrowed to slits. Eyes were the easiest to spot at night, eyes and teeth. He waited until Bulta turned the corner then slinked along the wall and across the street. One guard stood at the front, and one in the rear, but they never checked the grounds or the windows. After all, who would steal from Harun Bulta.

The window on the side was locked, but a few quick twists with his tools and it cracked open without a squeak.

Good servants, thought Wisp.

A lean body followed lanky legs through the crack, which he promptly closed again. His steps made no sound; Wisp could walk on broken glass and not get hurt; on dried leaves and make no sound. Ever-watchful, he checked every doorway and every corner. Someone could be lurking anywhere.

He had known jewelers in Sykor that kept inside guards. At length, he made his way to the room where they had met; the room where he felt sure the safe lay. Another careful examination revealed no one in the surrounding rooms, so he went to work. He ran his fingers lightly behind the edges of the picture, checking for trip wires, but found none. Very carefully, he removed the picture. Ah, as I thought.

The safe proved to be a built-in wooden box with a locking door. Wisp reached inside his cloak and grasped the thin wire he kept inside a specially sewn pocket. The lock was a good one, better than most he had seen in Sykor, but it presented no real challenge. Tobias could not have lit his pipe in the time it took Wisp to open the lock.

Two small sacks lay on the bottom. Wisp lifted them carefully. Coins, he guessed and set them back down. He was not here for coins. He could see better than anyone at night, but even his vision could not help him distinguish what else this safe contained. He would have to Cloak himself; once Cloaked, he could see as if the sun shone. Wisp focused his thoughts, willing everything else to the periphery of his mind. Soon there was only himself in all the world. At precisely that point, he disappeared, and simultaneously, everything in the room and the safe, became clear to him.

Near the back of the safe, on the second shelf, lay a velvet pouch. He emptied the pouch into his hand and stared at a bracelet of unparalleled beauty. Wisp realized its worth at once.

This will do, he thought, and slipped it into another inside pocket.

He stopped just before exiting to review his checklist: safe locked, picture rehung, doors closed. He thought about how to lock the window behind him but dismissed the idea. Bulta will have enough to worry about as it is. He left through the same window and soon was walking the streets toward Jago's house, whistling a merry tune. It was night, past midnight, the time Wisp liked best.

HARUN BULTA NODDED recognition to the guard, then let himself into the office. There was no need to call for khaffe, the servants knew to have it prepared for him as soon as he entered. They posted watch at the front window and began the process the instant he could be seen making the long climb up the street. Bulta sipped the hot brew then sat alone in his sitting room. The day must be planned in solitude.

Before he had finished a second cup, two of his jewelers arrived. They spoke briefly of the day's upcoming business, then Bulta lifted himself from the chair and went to the room where he hid the safe. The key dangled from a chain on his neck, which he pulled out to open the door.

The jewelers stood some distance behind him; they knew of the safe, but they had been more than fifteen years in Merchant Bulta's service. Bulta lifted the two sacks of coins, handing one to each man, then dug further back in the safe. "Take that coin for purchases. I also want to display some more finery. I hear there are several wealthy cousins of the emperor here to visit. They may wish to please their wives."

The royal family of Jattan–Kir was widely known to covet fine jewelry and expense was rarely an issue. "I cannot find it!" Bulta said.

"What is it, Master Bulta?"

An anxiousness crept into Bulta's voice, and he shoved his arm into the safe like a bear grasping for honey. "It is not here! The bracelet is gone!" Even as he said this, he began extracting items one by one until the safe lay empty.

"Where is it?" He shouted so loud that he frightened his jewelers, and the noise brought the guards running.

"Where is what, Master Bulta?"

"I have been robbed! Someone has robbed me."

One jeweler slipped silently toward the door, while the other backed himself against a wall. "Master Bulta, how could that be? No one has a key but you."

Bulta peered down at the key with a malevolent glare. If he could have accused it, he would have, but he knew better than anyone that the key had remained with him at all times, even at night, even when he and Sulima... at all times. "Guards! Who came into the office after I left?"

Both guards bowed; the tall one spoke. "Master Bulta, you must have forgotten, but we are the morning watch. The night guards left shortly before you arrived."

"Find them!" he bellowed, but even as the guards scurried out the door, he knew that the night watch would tell him nothing new.

It was the thief! he thought, and knew he was right.

THE MORNING they were to depart, Wisp, Aenaila, Darstan, Adju, and Jago arrived at the docks just as the sun sparkled above the horizon. Batu showed surprise at seeing them, but if he thought anything suspicious he didn't voice his fears. Wisp had settled affairs for provisions four days past, and in a pouch that hung at his side, he had ten gold crowns that Aenaila had given him.

"I'll be needing that coin before you set sail," Batu said.

Wisp jangled the pouch. "It is here, Master Seaman. Though I believe Merchant Bulta will be here to see us off."

Batu nodded. He knew that to be true, though he didn't know why the lad had not run for his life if he knew that much. "Come with me to meet your captain. And remember, on this journey, it will be him that's giving orders."

"I follow orders well," Wisp said.

Batu gave him a look as if he had said sharks don't bite. "You might do a lot of things well, lad, but I doubt following orders is one of them."

A snicker crossed Darstan's face. "Master Seaman, we would like to see our cabins before departing. And we have some bags to stow."

"Follow me," he said.

As they boarded the ship, the captain met them each with a friendly hand and a warm good morning. "My mother blessed me with the name of Borzu," he said.

"I'm Darstan. This is Adju, Kender, Jago, and Aenaila."

"You are all welcome to my ship," he said and stepped aside with a graceful bow. "Han, show our guests to their quarters."

As they crossed the deck, Adju and Wisp observed everything. Wisp had spent much time training him to be observant, and the little thief proved to be a good student.

A tug on his sleeve brought Wisp down to Adju's level. "Master Kender, those two men by the barrels, they are the guards from Merchant Bulta's house."

Wisp risked a quick glance, but one he was sure would not be seen. "Why would two guards pose as seamen?" Wisp pulled Adju closer yet. "Don't tell Mistress Aenaila; in fact, don't tell anyone yet." Wisp began to straighten, then added. "You learn quickly, Adju. I hadn't noticed them."

Adju nodded and straightened his back. He felt as tall as Wisp right now.

There were only three barrels left to load when Bulta came storming down the street surrounded by a patrol of his private guard.

Wisp could almost feel the fury emanating from the man. He turned to Aenaila. "Stay here. This won't take long."

Aenaila knew better than to ask by now, so she remained silent. The presence of so many armed men and the hurried look they wore bothered her, and though she dare not risk a confrontation, she alerted Darstan to be at the ready.

Wisp greeted Bulta with a smile and a cheerful voice. "Good morning, Merchant Bulta. It is early to be up and about so."

Bulta panted from his haste in getting there, and his jowled cheeks were red and puffed. "Do not play words with me, Kender Darnell. I am missing a bracelet, a very valuable one, and I want it back."

Wisp lost his smile with a sigh. "I heard that you suffered a loss. I'm deeply sorry. I did wonder, though, why this thief stole only the bracelet; there must have been other items of value."

Bulta gritted his teeth, and for a moment Wisp wondered if he chewed on stones. "Since you seem to be well–informed perhaps you could explain this mystery."

"I knew of a similar case in Sykor. It seems a petty thief had entered into an agreement with a man whose reputation didn't inspire trust, so as protection the thief stole a valuable ring and held it hostage as surety of his safe return."

Harun towered over Wisp, and as he drew nearer, he grew more angry. "I want my bracelet now, thief. I will not await anyone's return."

Wisp's eyes darted to the guards surrounding him. "Set them back, Merchant Bulta, so that we might speak in private."

Bulta motioned his men away, yet they remained within quick striking distance. Wisp moved closer, the stare in his eyes borrowed from a wolf. "Listen well, Bulta. I know of your plans and your false pirates. I know what you would do with us once we reach our destination, but I trust in the greed of your soul. You will ensure our safety in return for the bracelet."

Bulta's temper steadily rose. "I will torture it out of you, then kill you. All your friends too. No one holds my goods hostage!"

Wisp let his natural smile return. "There is one error in your judgment, Bulta. Your threats are only effective with someone who fears death. As for me, I challenge the Lady every day. It is a game between us." A tinge of fear crept into Bulta's eyes. Gossip had named him a superstitious man, especially regarding the Lady.

Wisp sighed. "I know in the end that she will win—when my skills lose their edge—but for now she allows me to best her and, I believe, she is amused by it. In fact, Merchant Bulta, she may not look favorably upon the person to put an untimely end to her amusement."

Harun shivered at this. Anyone who bandied her name about so frivolously must be half mad at best. And had not his actions proved that to be true?

"I will await your return, Kender Darnell. But my bracelet had better be with you, or no one will save you." Bulta cast a glance toward the ship where Adju peered over the rail. "As for your little apprentice, I will cut off a finger a day until he has none. We shall see if he can earn his bread as an honest man does."

Wisp thought about killing him here and now. A dagger to the throat would be quick and sure; he might even escape in the confusion. His hand twitched with anticipation. How he would like to rid the city of this blight. But no, he had Adju to worry about, and Aenaila. Darstan could care for himself.

I'll wait, Bulta. But it won't be long.

Wisp bowed his head, keeping his eyes on Bulta all the while. He knew that as soon as he returned the bracelet, Bulta would have him killed.

Try to have me killed, Wisp thought. But I'll deal with that when the time comes.

"Good day, Merchant Bulta. It was a pleasure to do business with you."

TRIALA—DESERT BLOOMS

en Pal stood in front of the Ligarns who were participating, a test to determine who would join the karn. "Triala." Jen Pal called the name, and a tall, lean body stepped forward. All Ligarns had similar features: darkened skin; tall, lean bodies; and cherry-black eyes. "You shall have the Nyaurans."

Triala's eyes glittered, and a smile flitted on her face. The Nyaurans were fierce warriors, experts with the bow and arrow. They would be granted two arrows each, along with a supply of water that should last them three days. Her allocation would be half the amount of one of them, water for a day and a half.

In the weapons room she quickly selected the bow, but even as she grasped it, Jen Pal issued the warning. "If you select the bow, no arrows will be allowed."

She nodded. She knew the rules of the karn, and a Ligarn seeking permission to join a hunt was expected to compete on their own merits as a fighter, or with short-range weapons. No spears were allowed, or slings, or chain whips, and bows only with the stipulation that no arrows were taken.

Despite the harshness of the rules, she proceeded with the bow; she had chosen it as her bedmate long ago, and even if she couldn't get any arrows, she always had the knife. All she had to do was get close enough.

Jen Pal brought Triala to face the three Nyaurans. She bowed, honoring them. "May the Gates of the Sun be open for you."

The shortest of the Nyaurans bowed. "And for you."

Triala smiled. This one was bold. Perhaps covering his fear. "Tell me which tribe you claim, and I will send your bodies home with your horses. They will not be harmed."

The Nyaurans treasured their horses above everything except family, and some didn't even make that distinction. All three of them bowed this time, hands steepled. It was the short one who spoke. "We are from the Elk Tribe in the far north. It will be an honor to face you."

Jen Pal instructed them on what needed to be done, then sent them on their way. They would have a strong start on Triala. After a while, Jen Pal signaled to Triala that it was time to depart, and she took her leave. She knew the Nyaurans had a strong lead, but no matter their lead, she would find them.

The Nyaurans only had to stay alive for five days; if Triala had not caught them by then, they would be set free. They must have known that hope was slim, that they could never cover their tracks from a Ligarn, but even a bit of hope could spark a dangerous fire in their hearts, enough to provide them courage.

Triala's trial

Triala arrived at the desert and began a brisk walk toward a spot that lay across several ranges of hills and small mountains. The watering hole, a rarity in the Sethian desert, was a day and a half walk even for a person who knew the ways of the desert. There were signs that others might follow, and if the Nyauran horsemen knew anything of tracking, they would soon be given clues. The challa birds from the far north made daily trips to this watering hole where they filled their bellies, then bathed in the waters to soak their feathers so that they might carry nourishment back to fledglings. A keen observer could spot their path and mark their destination.

More experienced observers could see the occasional damaged scrub bush from predators making their way to drink. The wildlife was more abundant the nearer to the hole, and it was, if not obvious, significant enough for an experienced observer to note.

The Nyaurans might miss some of the less obvious signs, like the different way a wagger slithers the closer it gets to water, or the way the strides of the scavenger dogs grew longer with their anticipated quenching of thirst, but they would not miss the other signs, and since their water would last only two days—three, if they had the sense to be frugal, they would quickly seek out the water hole.

oasis

The sand burned her feet. Only when the karn had been chosen could she allow herself the luxury of leather to cover her feet. She willed her mind to ignore the pain. Before her first naming day, her father had taken her to the desert sands, naked, and set her down. Her father had stood two spans away, and Triala was forced to crawl over scorching, sun-baked rocks and fiery crystals.

She recalled crying because it was the only time a Ligarn was permitted the shedding of tears. By tradition, a Ligarn could not receive their name until the test of the sands, and then, on their first naming day, they celebrated with the given name. After that day, if a tear stained a Ligarns cheek, the warrior would be banished from the clan. No excuses were made, not even for the death of loved ones.

Her bronze skin absorbed the sun, and her hair, the color of a crow's wing, sparkled under the biting rays. A piece of leather from a mountain goat's hide, tanned and cured to perfection by hands taught from father to son and mother to daughter for a hundred generations, covered her loin area.

The suppleness prevented chafing—that, and a powder made from crushing the leaves of a plant that grew only in the great chasm to the south. The leaves were picked by the children, another sort of test for the Ligarn young, who had to descend precipitous cliffs to get to the plants growing in crevices and along ridges where shade hid them from the burning sun. The leaves were left to dry for a full cycle, then they were crushed and pounded into a powder and applied to the sensitive parts of the skin. Her breasts swung freely—no covering while on the hunt.

The bow hung on her back like the mane on a wild stallion, seemingly a part of her. Fastened at the shoulders and hips, it moved with her but didn't chafe the skin. The knife, Triala's second bedmate, hung from a leather sheath crafted with as much care as her loincloth, and the hilt, looking old and ancient, had been carved from the branch of a fabled tree on the eastern border with Khatara.

The Nyaurans would not be easy prey. They were known to be brave warriors, and their skill with the bow was widely known. Triala could never hope to surprise them, not enough to take all three of them, not without taking a shot herself. The Nyaurans would not separate, but they also would not bunch so close together that they could be taken as one.

Triala would be hard-pressed to keep her skin, let alone emerge with few enough injuries to still be able to join the karn. To achieve victory was not enough, she must take their lives while sustaining no injuries, or, minor ones.

Triala stooped to lick a drop of moisture from a sentry plant, small cousin to the sentry trees that guarded the borders to the east. It was still early morning, and moisture remained on a few of the desert plants. Ligarns learned early how to find water in the desert—and food, and shelter. And not just the desert either, they were taken to the mountains, and swamps and great forests to train while young. Lessons learned in training remained burned in memory.

Triala had lost a brother while learning the swamps—a nesting sangra charged, and Suto had been too slow to react. Triala had judged swiftly that she had no chance to save him, so she escaped. If she had erred that day, and left too soon, by decree, she would have been forced to kill the sangra for honor or to die trying. Of all the things she had faced, only the swamps held fear for Triala, and she prayed that if chosen for the karn their journey would not lead them there. Fear was only spoken of when referring to the frail ones, so Triala dare not mention her feelings to another. This was something she would have to conquer herself.

The sun felt hot on her naked breasts. She rubbed the special powder on them again for protection, while her tongue tasted the salt of sweat. It forced her to form a picture of the waterhole, and once again, she examined the terrain.

A small pool of water sparkled with the glare of the rising sun, and a mist lay dormant over the area like a fever-vision. A handful of fruit trees, burgeoning with dates, leaned from the banks and shaded the rim of the pool, and a cluster of desert palms danced in the light breeze to the rear. Reeds poked through a sunlit gap and hid from sight the fallen trunks of trees whose memory reached back to the times of many grandfathers past, and knee-high grasses waved in evening breezes.

Triala knew she must strip them of at least two arrows, at least two. Then, it wouldn't matter if they arrived before her or not. But if she could not get their arrows and the Nyaurans arrived at the watering hole before her, they could simply wait her out for three days, and they would be free. She could not hope to charge them in a defensible position with no weapon but a knife. The easy part would be dispatching them after she got the arrows.

But how to get them? she thought, and her pace increased even as the sands grew hotter.

Memories formed of when her father had taken her to the land called the White Mountains, their peaks covered in snow. They had gone in winter when the winds howled, and storms raged. The frail ones said nothing could live there in the winter. She had heard it mentioned almost everywhere they had gone, and yet her father told her she was a Ligarn, and Ligarns could survive anywhere.

The mountains were so cold she thought her limbs might never work again. Even her mind seemed to slow. Then her father had told her to think of the summer afternoons in the Sethian sun, of the sun-parched earth and mounds of thirsty sand, and as she did, she grew warmer.

She smiled to her father—and she smiled once again as she brought back memories of the cold. She pictured the snow and remembered the cold aches and let it sink slowly toward her burning feet. The sands lost their fire, and Triala's pace increased in defiance of Sethia's sun.

Triala knelt to examine the folded leaf of a naja plant. The naja held water longest of all the desert plants, but it already showed signs of withering. She tried to gently make it take form again, but the sun had stayed too long on the bent leaves.

Fools! thought Triala.

The leaves of the naja must be sipped free of moisture, coaxed, like a kiss on Maiden's Day. But the Nyaurans could not have known that. They knew nothing of the desert.

She stared at the mountain facing her. It was not high, but its precipitous incline proved forbidding to those unaccustomed to such adventures in the desert, and so, Triala knew the Nyaurans could opt to go the longer route around it.

She could have scaled the mount and reached the waterhole ahead of them, but without the arrows, it would be useless. She ignored the tracks that led up the mountain—knowing it to be a false trail. They wasted time in a futile attempt to mislead her, but that was fine by Triala. She would catch them all the sooner for that, and then all she need do was draw their attention and force them into wasting arrows as well.

It was mid afternoon when she caught scent of them. They had never bathed since being captured, even though Triala knew it would have been offered; Ligarns were not barbarians. The Nyaurans should have taken the opportunity, for the smell of their horses clung to them and marked their path like a full moon on a desert night.

Their pace had quickened; they grew anxious about her approach. She examined the tracks, saw the slight twist of the right foot on two of them, an unconscious thing that frail ones did when turning to look behind them, checking to see if anyone followed. The third one had twists toward the left foot. It wasn't always a true indicator, but more often than not it meant that person was left handed. If so, a valuable piece of information to learn before battle.

The terrain ahead lay dotted with small scrub brush no higher than a man's waist and no thicker than a leg. Rocks lay scattered about as if in ages past they had fallen from the sky like rain. And under it all lay the burning sands and earth of Sethia.

Their scent grew stronger, but she didn't seek cover. Two of them were crouched behind a large cactus about one hundred paces ahead, their bows perched to fire. Triala smiled. Nyaurans were not stupid, just not as smart as Ligarns. They thought things out better than most, but they stopped before they should have. The Nyaurans would have known she would see them huddled behind the cactus, so they must have hidden the third one closer in, waiting for her to approach so he could get a clear shot with the bow. Triala would play their game for now.

She ducked quickly behind a small rock, only five hands high, but enough to provide cover. To her right stood a thick copse of small brush interspersed with numerous rocks, and though none were so big as the one she lay behind, the cluster and mix of trees and rock would provide ample protection and, more importantly, shield her actions.

Triala waited a hundred breaths then crept to the cover of the trees to her right, making sure to be seen, but only slightly. Once safely hidden, she lay still until the sun burned brightest and hottest, then she backed out of the cover. She had waited long enough and gotten all the information she needed; the third Nyauran lay behind a boulder only fifty paces ahead to her left. He had finally revealed himself while trying to steal a look at her.

Triala lay flat on her stomach, ignoring the screaming of her body as the brush scratched and fiery rocks burnt and scraped at her bared skin, and the sands, so hot and grating, stuck to her sweat. Her movements were slow—slower than a Victa on cold winter morns, and she was as silent as the flap of a bee's wing.

She moved back, then back more—well beyond the range that the Nyaurans might expect even a Ligarn to do. Then, when Triala felt comfortable that they would never expect it, she began her advance to the left. She would creep behind the hill of rocks to the side, then down to where the Nyaruans were. None would see her. They would all be waiting for her to emerge from the brush.

rocks in desert

Triala kept an eye on the ground in front of them. As the day wore on, they might attempt to advance on her position, knowing she had no arrows or long-range weapons. The sun still blazed, but it was slowly sliding down and would soon let the cool desert night reign.

Triala edged ever-closer to the Nyauran crouched behind the rock ahead. She was only about thirty paces away and approaching from his blind side. He could not see her without poking his head above the rock or turning around to the far side of the rock, and Triala felt certain he would not risk either of those moves at this time. The Nyaurans still presumed her to be in the cluster of shrub brush where they first saw her.

She stretched her arms forward, digging fingers deep into the sand to gain leverage then pulled her body forward in a slow, steady rhythm. Thirsty sand gobbled trickles of blood that seeped from her breasts and burned her bared skin. She could not think about the pain, to do so would muddle her senses, and she needed to be more alert than ever.

Sometimes a wagger would move only a few muscles at a time—of the many hundreds it had—making its movement almost imperceptible. Triala mimicked this as she moved forward, gaining more ground on the unsuspecting Nyauran. The rocks and brush scratched and clawed at her, tearing flesh from open wounds, but it was nothing to sacrifice if it gained her the victory.

She would sacrifice more than a little blood for a chance to join the karn. Much more.

Now only twenty paces away, Triala shifted her glances from the Nyauran in front of her, then back to the two that hid behind the bushes. The day faded quickly as the moon stole more light from the sun, and the wind began to tease the sands with its nightly song as loose pieces of brush rolled and danced across the barren lands. The fading light tempted her to move faster, but Triala knew that patience was the key to victory, and her pace, if anything, slowed.

The other two Nyaurans would soon advance. Nyaurans were not without hunting skills; they would use the night to cover their approach. At this time of day tricks of light made it even more difficult to see than at night. In the time between night and day, the eyes do not fully adjust, and things do not always appear as they are. She would do well to attack before dark.

Only ten paces separated them now. The first step to victory was close. So close. But Triala must get within five paces, and preferably as close as three. If she got that near, the Nyauran would die.

A bramble bush rolled by, and a fierce gust of wind hurled sand in her eye. Almost, she made noise, but her father's teachings held her lips tight and her body still. No hand moved to soothe her eye.

She waited until she had pulled herself up close again, no faster, the same speed must be maintained. She must move with the desert. Finally, near enough, she opened her eye and let fluid carry grains of sand down her cheeks. But still, the scratching had blurred her vision and stung her eye. She opted to keep it closed, but even while making that decision knew that it could affect her perception if she had to shoot arrows—if she could get some.

Triala tensed as the Nyauran shifted his position. It was the third time in as many moments.

Perhaps he is cramping, she thought. Frail ones cramp easily.

She cast her eye back to the others and saw that they had begun their move. They crouched low and advanced toward a bush near a rock about five paces in front of where they had been. She would soon be spotted, as they would continually cast their gaze to their companion, and she was now within their range to see.

Her hand crept toward the knife and rolled ever-so-slightly to free the blade. The familiar feel of the hilt in her hand sent a rush through her veins. She pulled herself forward one more time; she was still five paces from him, but she could wait no longer. Triala slid her leg forward, to a position cocked like a frog preparing to leap, and she lay her left hand on the ground, a brace to push her upward. Her right hand shook with excitement, clutched around the blade and with her knuckles pressed firmly to the ground, her left foot dug toes in to spring forward. A moment passed, then two, and when the next gust of wind raced across her back, she leaped forward like a lizard's tongue.

She took only three strides before the Nyauran saw her. He spun in a frantic effort to position his bow. Triala leaped the remaining distance, judging it to be reachable and wanting the momentum of her weight to slam against him. He had drawn back the string almost halfway when she struck, her left hand grabbing the half-nocked arrow, while her right drove the steel of her knife into his left side.

He moaned as he fought to get his knife, but Triala had jammed her knee tight against him, and he found it difficult to move.

After a bitter struggle, he lost possession of the arrow. Triala spun it around and quickly lodged it in his throat. The Nyauran sagged, his hand released, and he fell to the sands. Triala trailed the blade across his neck, ensuring death was quick, then hurriedly seized his other arrow, and leaped over the rock, diving to the ground. She didn't need to look to know the other two were either advancing quickly or already shooting.

An arrow slapped against the front side of the rock that guarded her, but when she heard no other, she knew they must have split.

The other one is coming, she thought.

The bow was off her back and strung, with an arrow in her hand at the ready. Another lay on the ground in front of her.

He will come with the wind.

As the thought cleared her head, Triala twisted on the ground and rolled backward several times, stopping with the bow at her front, ready to shoot. He would need to get close. With only two arrows each, and one of them already gone, he would not risk another failure.

Triala waited for the wind to pick up again then shielded her eyes to see. The Nyauran took the opportunity afforded by the wind and raced toward her, bow at the ready. But he apparently had not seen her roll away, and she knew the other hadn't either. Recalculating distances in this light and with this wind would be difficult, so she moved.

Triala waited for him to get within ten paces, the near blinding dust and sand made seeing a task, and then she stood. As he came into clear view, his bow nocked and drawn, she let loose the arrow and took him through the neck. Diving almost instantly to the ground, she ran, crab style with blade in hand and ensured the kill was complete.

Triala pulled her arrow out and took his as well. She now had three arrows, and the last Nyauran had only two. The one that had hit the boulder claimed by no one. She thought of going ahead to the water-hole and waiting him out. He would have to go there or die of thirst. But she chased the thought away. Her victory needed to be a bright one to earn a spot in the karn. She would take him now.

Triala leaped into the air, making a sound like the screech of the red-tailed hawk. The wind carried it across the empty land on wings of speed.

The last Nyauran must have shivered with fear. He would now know the others were dead, and he would know he was too. Like the goose before Wish Day, it was only a matter of time; a Ligarn could not be taken in the desert that was their home. The desert belonged to the Ligarns, and so, the Nyauran chose to flee.

As he ran past the next rock, Triala jumped up and took him, her knife slashing his throat, and a second blade claiming his heart.

Triala made the long walk back to town with a lively step. She had every reason to believe she would be one of the chosen. The kills had been made swiftly and honorably, and only one had been killed with an arrow shot from a bow.

Yes, she thought, I shall be in the karn, but I wonder who else will share the glory. Soon, four of us will hunt the village boy—and Black Death.

She heaved a sigh of joy at the thought. I wonder what the village boy has done to deserve the sentence of death. Triala wondered, but only for a moment. Right now, the thought of the hunt held her captivated.

A THIEF'S TRAINING

The captain had them past the breakers before most people in the city had finished breaking fast. Borzu quickly came to them for coordinates, which only Jago knew, so he spent more time with Borzu than he did with Aenaila, though that pleased Wisp as much as anything. He could not picture those two as lovers, yet there was something strange about the relationship.

"I like sailing, Master Kender. From what you told me, I thought it would be terrible."

"It is not even midday, Adju. By tomorrow you will likely beg to be set down in the desert with the laughing wolves."

"Have you been on many ships, Master Kender?"

A rare frown found Wisp's face. "I don't need to be a sailor to know I don't like ships. There are no streets or alleys to walk, no buildings to climb, and no rooftops to tread."

Adju's small nose wrinkled into a smile. "Master Kender, you make me laugh."

Wisp leaned back against the rail alongside Adju, both staring at the vast emptiness. "Now I know why they call it the Endless Sea."

"This is like the Kurabi, Master Kender. Only this is water, and the Kurabi is sand."

They shared a few silent moments before Adju spoke again. "Will you teach me? I want to learn to be like you."

"I don't think I should. You could do much better. You would make a great merchant. Besides, Aenaila might have something to say about you becoming a thief. I think she has other plans."

"Master Kender, if I could be like you, it would be all I have dreamed of. You are already my best friend."

Wisp turned his head. He had no intention of getting teary–eyed. "Go see Jago. Ask him if he'll teach you something of measuring a ship's location."

"But—"

"Go. And when you're done with him, come back to see me." Wisp watched Adju dart across the deck. "You better not let Aenaila see you without shoes again."

Adju waved in response.

Jago proved to be a patient man, enduring a barrage of questions from Adju, and taking great pains to explain the basics to him. "There is much you must understand before you can plot a course for a ship, but if you dedicate yourself to learning, I will teach you."

"Yes, Master Jago. I will study." Adju soon discovered that he had not embraced an easy challenge. He had no schooling, and Jago had to begin at the beginning. Before he realized it, the afternoon had slipped by.

"Time to eat," Jago said. "We will continue tomorrow."

Adju jumped up from the table. "And not too soon, I am hungry."

They ate supper in Aenaila's room, the only one with enough space to seat them as the four men shared a room. "I am learning to chart courses," Adju announced as he put more meat on his plate. "Master Jago said if I keep studying I could be a captain someday."

Aenaila smacked Adju's hand as he reached for a third biscuit. "Since you are learning, you need to do sums. Ten biscuits sit on that plate, and there are five of us."

Aenaila's reprimand stung. Adju slowly put the biscuit down. "Sorry."

Wisp cleared his throat. "You could earn that biscuit."

"How?" Light sparkled in his brown eyes.

"Just tell me what Jago wore when you met him this morning."

Adju's eyes darted to the left. Jago had changed his clothes. "He wore his boots with brown breeches," Adju proudly stated.

"What else?"

"I do not know, Master Kender." Suddenly his expression came to life. "But I do know what those two guards wore, Master Kender."

Aenaila's look told Wisp he would have explanations due shortly. "Adju, I'm glad you know what the guards wore; in fact, it's more important to focus on those you know are your enemies, but you forgot something important."

"What, Master Kender?"

Wisp leaned over the table, but he didn't whisper. "You forgot that we were going to keep that a secret from Aenaila."

Adju's eyes widened in embarrassment, but the rest of them laughed, even Aenaila.

"All right, now tell me what the guards wore."

Adju smiled. "Brown breeches on the tall one, with brown boots, and a dark blue shirt. The other one had no boots, and his breeches were rolled up almost to his knees. He wore no shirt either." Adju was already reaching for the biscuit.

"Is that all?" Wisp asked, seizing his hand that was clutching the prize.

"That is all, Master Kender."

Wisp let go his hand. "You can have the biscuit. You'll need some extra fat to keep the knives those two guards carried from cutting you to the bone."

Adju's smile disappeared. "I did not see any knives."

"The short one had a sheath with a dagger in the back of his breeches, and the other had a boot knife on the inside of his left boot. It was pressing against his breeches."

"I am sorry, Master Kender. I—"

"Earlier today you asked me to teach you. This is how I learned."

"Tell me how you were raised, Master Kender. I want to know."

"No. It's not—"

Darstan interrupted. "Camissa told us about it. Rahg asked her one night, and she told him about how you were beaten."

Wisp let anger take a foothold on him. "She had no business telling anyone. Those weren't memories for her to share; they were ones she stole while I slept." He banged the table. "She calls me a thief, but I steal no one's thoughts."

Aenaila tried to restore calm. "It can be a tale for some other time, perhaps. We need not begin an argument."

Wisp shook his head. "No. It's started now, so I'll finish. It's nothing I hide in my dreams, though Camissa must think so. I believe it bothers her more than me."

Wisp looked straight at Adju. "I was raised a beggar, like you. Like many. I never knew my mother or father, but I was taken in by a man who felt sorry enough to feed me. He was a beggar too, and when I became old enough, he broke my nose to make me a better beggar. People would feel sorrier for me, he said."

"I would have killed him," Darstan swore.

Wisp slowly shook his head as the memories returned. "I bear him no grudge. The man did what he knew how to do. That broken, crooked nose brought us many extra loaves of bread."

He stared at Darstan. "I was a child no one wanted, but I found no Magmar to take me in as you did. A starving dog will take a kick with each bite of food you give. It's only when it gets meat on its bones that it will consider biting back."

"What a horrible way to live," Aenaila said.

"For some," Wisp said. "For others, life is horrible being a nobleman's heir. As I said, I hold no regrets."

"What did you do after that, Master Kender? How did you learn?"

Wisp sighed. "Perhaps Aenaila is right, Adju. We'll save this tale for another night."

Aenaila looked at ease for the first time since the conversation began. "Please make it a night when I am absent?" she asked, then turned to Jago. "Has Borzu given you any trouble?"

Jago bowed his head slightly.

Even at the table? thought Wisp and new questions about Jago and Aenaila raced through his mind.

"He has been cooperative; however, he does record all chart markings in two books."

"Little good that will do," Aenaila said. "Kender Darnell, what was it Adju mentioned about the guards? Have you already courted trouble?"

"It's Harun Bulta's doing. In my travels through the city, I determined that he was the one behind the piracy that plagues Khataran merchants. I'm sure that he steals their goods, perhaps sells them elsewhere to a fellow conspirator." Wisp took another drink of ale. "Since we have no goods, he would have taken our gold or worse."

"Would have?" Aenaila asked.

"I have an assurance of our safe arrival from Bulta himself."

"With what did you purchase this assurance?"

Wisp squirmed in his seat. "I have in my possession a bracelet that Bulta greatly desires. I told him that when I returned, we would strike a deal that would put the bracelet in his hands."

Aenaila's glare froze him. "Where did it come from? Who does it belong to?"

Adju smiled. His eyes were lit, cheeks curled and hands fidgety. Wisp had not told him about the bracelet, but he must have suspected. "The bracelet once belonged to Harun Bulta. Now it is mine."

"I knew it, Master Kender. I knew you would go back there. Where was it?"

Wisp avoided looking at Aenaila at all costs. "In his safe, behind the picture."

Darstan smiled, and to Wisp's surprise, Jago did too. The only one who had not joined the festivities was Aenaila. Wisp finally met her emerald gaze with soft brown eyes. "I felt it would be better this way than to have to fight his crew when we arrive. One of us could have been hurt, even killed. And Darstan would have surely burnt the ship to ashes."

The tension eased, melting under Wisp's sad looks.

Darstan beamed. "He's right, Aenaila. He's right, and you know it. Better for us to deal with Bulta when we get back. We can do that on our terms."

Her nod lightened Wisp's heart, but he thought he better switch topics of discussion. "Jago, how long until we reach this island?"

"Perhaps a month, less if we find favorable winds."

"And from there, how long to Cergala?"

"From the island, we will Shift," Aenaila said. "I can make that Shift. I didn't want anyone finding their way to Cergala, which is why we are only going part of the way."

"Wonderful," Wisp said. "Now we have only a month of sailing to enjoy."

"For someone who sneaks through windows and jumps across roofs, the sea should hold no fear." Aenaila seldom missed the opportunity to taunt him.

"I'm afraid of a lot of things, Aenaila. And not having my feet on solid ground ranks among the highest. Look around you when you go on deck tomorrow. There's nothing but sea, the Endless Sea."

WISP PACED THE DECK NERVOUSLY. He had counted swells, looked for fish and played games in his head with the clouds, but the boredom ate at him.

I'd rather walk the Kurabi, he thought.

Adju came running toward him, fresh from his lessons with Jago. "I am ready, Master Kender. Test me."

"Not now. It's no good to test you when you've had time to prepare."

"But—"

"We'll do it another time. Have you seen Darstan?"

"Not since I went to visit Master Jago. He was talking to some of the crew."

The crew? That surprised Wisp. Darstan had not been very sociable since he lost his hand. He maintained a friendly demeanor around those he knew but seemed uncomfortable with strangers. "See if you can find him. I'd like to speak with him."

Adju tore off, his boundless energy propelling him across the deck. "Master Darstan! Where are you?"

He returned quickly, Darstan following. "What is it? Something wrong?"

"Nothing. I just needed an excuse to test this little beggar." Adju's face drooped like the line drying clothes. "Tell me what the men talking with Darstan wore."

"I... I did not see, Master Kender."

"That's fine, but tonight you get no biscuits."

"No biscuits! Master Kender, I—"

"No biscuits. You said you wanted to learn. When I failed I got the rough end of a stick."

"Yes, Master Kender," he said, but with little enthusiasm.

After the tenth day, Adju had only eaten biscuits once. Every time he thought he had what Kender wanted, Kender surprised him by asking something else.

"Good morning, Master Kender. It is another sunny day."

"Another day of life on the sea," Wisp said. "But at least there will be something different for supper tonight. Look, Adju, Borzu's men have brought up the net. Just look at the fish."

"I love fish, Master Kender. I never did before, but I do now."

"And I," Wisp said. "I feel hunger pains in my stomach now." He remained silent for a moment. "Go ask the crew what kind of fish they caught."

⌒

ON HIS WAY to the crew, Adju watched everything: what sails were up, which of the crew was on deck, what everyone wore, how many barrels looked empty—everything. He would get biscuits tonight.

Wisp wore a smile before Adju got to him, but he was ready. "I know what we will be eating tonight, Master Kender."

"I have no interest in that, Adju. What I want to know—"

"The tall guard has black boots, a knife on the outside right. His gray breeches are tucked inside the boots. No shirt. A bandana on his head, a red one. He chews tobacco and—"

"I find that I have no interest in what he wears either."

Nothing would deter Adju today. "Just tell me what you want. I have the answer."

"How many fish were in the net?"

Adju's huge round eyes grew larger with disappointment. He did not even present an argument. "You know I cannot answer that, Master Kender."

"Why not? You were there. You saw the fish in the net."

"I cannot count so high." Tears streamed down his face and tinged his voice. "Master Jago is trying to teach me, but I am too stupid to learn."

Wisp knelt to hold the little beggar, grasping him by the shoulders. "Then you'll have to learn," he said. "You should have told me sooner. If you're going to be a successful thief you better know how to count large numbers."

Adju laughed between sobs. "You are not shamed of me? I was afraid you would not want me around if you knew."

Wisp fought the tears desperately. He hated to cry. Hated it. He had cried enough as a boy.

And now I have made Adju cry.

He looked straight into his face. "Adju, listen to me. I want you around all the time. Always."

Adju threw his arms around Wisp's neck and hugged him. "I love you, Master Kender."

Now Wisp did cry. It was the first time in his life anyone had ever told him that. "I love you too, Adju."

Jago and Wisp kept Adju kept busy the rest of the journey, teaching him numbers and charts. Adju and Wisp had grown closer since their talk, but Wisp didn't relent on his method of teaching. Adju seldom got a biscuit, but he surprisingly, he didn't complain as much. It was only later that Wisp discovered Darstan sneaking him biscuits at night.

Wisp approached Jago. "How much longer?"

"Two or three more days," Jago said. "What should we do when we anchor? They'll see immediately that it's little more than a string of rocks forming an island chain."

"Why not just Shift from the cabin?"

A blank look passed over Jago's face while he thought. "That may be the best solution, Wisp." Jago hesitated, embarrassed. "I didn't mean to address you so informally. I should have—"

"Nonsense! You've lived in Khatara too long. I prefer to be called Wisp."

Jago bowed slightly, which sparked a question. "Jago, what is your... relationship with Aenaila? I mean..."

Jago reddened considerably at the question, and Wisp now wished he hadn't asked.

"If you are asking, are we lovers—no. Absolutely no." Jago laughed aloud. "Apologies again, Wisp, but you do not know what is so funny."

"Tell me."

"No, it is for Aenaila to tell when the time comes." Jago started to leave, but Wisp grabbed his arm.

"Thank you, Jago."

The Cergalan nodded. "You deserve to know that," he said. He stopped halfway across the deck, paused, then came back to Wisp.

"I have decided to tell you, but you must swear on whatever strange oaths you hold dear that you won't tell Aenaila."

"You have my word."

"I love Aenaila, and I have loved her for many moons, but not as you think. She is my sister."

"What!" Wisp nearly screamed. "Your sister! Mother of Rats, you don't know how happy that makes me."

"I believe I do know," Jago said.

But what will happen when he learns that she must be wed to Darstan? What will happen to these two good friends then?

*J*ago sat with Borzu, checking that the final leg of the journey concluded safely. There were only two spots he needed to worry over, two shallow areas at the final approach to the island.

Borzu looked again through his eyeglass. "I see it, Jago, but it looks like not much more than a mountain or two of rock with a few trees clinging to them. Do people live there?"

Jago disliked a lie, so he chose his words carefully. "I left more than a few friends there myself, Captain. Many more than a few," Jago said.

"We should be safely anchored before the sun sets," Borzu said.

Jago knew what Aenaila wanted to do, so he set the stage. "I believe it best if we take supper and this night aboard ship, Captain. Tomorrow will be soon enough to go ashore."

Borzu looked at Jago from the corner of his eye. "I have my orders, you know. Merchant Bulta owns this ship. I'm not to let your friend out of our protection."

A nod from Jago must have settled Borzu's nerves. "We will keep to our cabins until morn," Jago said.

No sooner had Jago seen them safely anchored than Borzu ordered a watch on the landing boats as well as the cabins of the passengers. "If they give you trouble, do as you will with the rest, just leave Kender alive. Merchant Bulta wants him unharmed."

AENAILA WAS eager to be finally going home. They had barely finished eating when she pushed to begin.

"There is no sense waiting any longer."

"I'd just as soon sleep here and go in the morning," Darstan said.

"It won't go away with another night's dreams, Darstan. Cergala, and your destiny await us. Besides, we will be Shifting to a house that will offer a warm greeting and a soft bed."

"Is this your father's house?"

Aenaila paused. "Yes, though he no longer lives there. It is now mine."

"Tell me what is expected of me, Aenaila. What do your people think I can do to help?" Darstan seemed to grow impatient. Jago remained unflinching.

"Our people have been at war for more than five hundred years. Not a war with battles every day, but a continual, inevitable war. We pray that you will be the one to end these wars, to stop the killing and bring peace to our lands."

"A tall order for a man with one hand."

"When a wolf loses a tooth, its wisdom does not go with it," she said.

"I'm no wolf, Aenaila. I'm just me—Darstan."

"Your sword names you differently," she said, and repeated a line from the Prophecy.

"Rivers flowed with mothers' tears

from centuries of strife and blood

Who is there to soothe the fears?

Who can wade through red–soaked mud?

Endless scores of hungry swords

Dipped in hunger's glow

There is yet time to rally hordes

BlackWolf will make blood flow."

A curse greeted her at the end of the recital. "Blast you and your Prophecies. All they ever talk about is blood."

Darstan swept his hand across the table, knocking his plate and glass to the floor. "I said I'd go with you, and I'll keep my word. But your people better start thinking of someone else to save them from their war. I'm no blasted black wolf."

"You would deny an entire nation a chance for peace?"

Adju placed the plate and glass back on the table. "Master Darstan, perhaps you could just talk to them. Perhaps they will listen to you."

Darstan plopped onto the floor, pushing a sigh out as he landed. "I shouldn't have lost my temper, Adju. Thank you for picking that up." He looked at Aenaila, whose face had not cracked. "You know how I feel. If I can help you, I will. But I'll not go to war and kill people for you. Not—"

"Not like you did for Rahg," she said, her voice as cool as an autumn breeze.

"That was different, and you know it. That was a Banished One trying to kill Rahg. I had to help!"

She nodded.

Darstan popped to his feet. "All right, let's just do it. Come on. Let's go. I give up."

"Fine, Darstan. We will go now. Wisp, Jago, gather your things. You too, Adju."

When everyone had their belongings, she stretched out her hands. "Wisp, you and Adju on my right. Jago, you, and Darstan on the left." Aenaila focused on the image in her mind. It had been a long time, but the memory was there waiting. The stone house atop the hill, a wide wooden door, the plank floors.

Ah, there is the spot, she thought and Shifted.

The air shivered at the rift, allowing them to step into the old house. Aenaila collapsed into Jago's arms the moment she let go of the power.

"My Lady," he yelled, and carried her to the bed.

Adju was the last to open his eyes. He rushed to help. "Mistress Aenaila, are you all right? Can I get you something?"

"I will get some water," Jago said, and grabbed a jug from a closet door.

Wisp knelt beside her, running his hand over her head. "Are you just tired? Or is it something else?"

Her smile warmed him. "No. Just tired. This was a very long journey and with so many... but... I had not thought it as long as the Shift from Khatara to Entiria, and I am far more exhausted."

"Jago went to get water," Darstan said.

"Yes, Jago knows to care for me. He will gather some fruit later, and we can all eat something. You may not be hungry yet, but I need to replenish myself after such a strain," she said, then closed her eyes.

Jago returned shortly with the water, wiping her brow to waken her, then let her sip the cool water for a while. "Get some sleep," he said. "I will get food for tonight and the morning." He stood, then suggested that they all get some rest. "It will be a long day tomorrow. We will need to be fresh."

"Where are we going tomorrow?" Darstan asked.

"That is for Aenaila to say." Jago motioned to a door near the back of the house. "There is one other bed, Darstan, if you would like to rest more comfortably. I will get blankets for Kender and Adju."

"Where are you sleeping?" Wisp asked.

"Outside the door," he said, then led Darstan toward the other bedroom.

Borzu's shouts rung out over the ship, only to be swallowed by the crashing waves. "How did five people get off my ship without you seeing them?" Blood pumped furiously through his veins, bulging the one across his forehead. "And one of them a woman at that. No boats are missing. Did you let them climb down the ropes and swim ashore?" Borzu shook a heavy fist. "By the grace of the winds," he swore. "Get the boats. We're going in after them. They can't have gone far on this island."

For three days they searched, using every means he knew of to track them down. Borzu himself was not a tracker, but one of the two guards was, and he found nothing.

"They left the island," he told Borzu. "That is if they ever landed. I see no tracks or signs that they've ever been here. They must have had a small boat hidden in a cove, then sneaked in after dark and left. The tide would have washed any tracks away."

Borzu shook his head. "Merchant Bulta is likely to have us all flogged for this," he said. Maybe worse.

~

TRUE TO HIS WORD, Jago provided fresh fruits for breaking fast, and even Darstan had to admit they were good. "Are you rested enough yet?" Jago asked.

"Weak still, but enough to begin. The sooner I get to Cartena, the better I will feel."

Jago packed an ample supply of water, but no food. "It is only a one-day journey," he said. "We will find food along the trails."

They stepped from the house through a clearing, then into a forest, thick with heavy green foliage. Vision was limited to fifty or sixty paces, and the sounds of the morning birds surrounded them. "A good forest," Darstan said. "There must be a lot of game."

Jago seemed a different man since arriving in Cergala. He spoke more than he did in a day before this. "Our land is thick with forests, Darstan. We have been blessed with all of the richness in life: plentiful forests, rich soil, many rivers, and sunshine to feed our crops."

"All we lack is peace," Aenaila said. "Peace and the fulfillment of the Prophecy."

Darstan ground his teeth and clenched a fist. Won't she ever let up? He increased his pace to join Jago at the front.

They walked downhill most of the morning, and as the trail narrowed, the forest encroached more and more. Jago's hand stayed close to his sword, yet on several occasions when an animal noise had startled Darstan, Jago had not even moved. Darstan's hand was poised for a quick release of his blade.

Before reaching the bottom, they came to a large clearing in the forest where the sunlight shone through and a small creek lazily ran by. It looked as if it would be a good place to rest.

forest

A sound to the right side drew Jago and Darstan off the path with swords drawn. Adju rushed to Aenaila's side, while Wisp moved to her left. From behind a bush leaped a warrior with staff spinning for a strike. Darstan raised the sword to ward off the blow, but the warrior spun around again and swept Darstan's feet out from under him. No sooner had he hit the ground than he felt the end of the staff at his throat.

"A fine day to die, stranger."

Darstan heard the voice but couldn't believe it. A woman!

"No!" Jago screamed and seized the staff with his free hand. "He is a friend."

"A friend?" she asked, but then took a closer look at Jago. "I didn't recognize you, Jago. You should have announced yourself." She quickly looked around.

"Are you wondering where I am?" Aenaila's soft voice carried to them, causing the woman to spin. Her face went blank. "My—"

"Never mind the formalities. Help my friend to his feet."

Her scowl was fierce, and Darstan thought he heard a growl, too. He reached to grab a hand, and she pulled him up with little effort.

Pretty, and strong. They breed a different woman in Cergala.

"These two are so weak neither one would make a good manservant. Why did you bring them, Jago?"

"It is for Aenaila to say." Jago brushed the dirt from Darstan's back. "I respect your restraint, Darstan. She thought you the enemy, and we are too near to take chances."

"Too near what?"

"The king," Jago said, then turned to the warrior woman, who still held a grip on Darstan. "Mirana, let him be. I already told you he was a friend."

Mirana scoffed when she released Darstan. "The wash woman could stop him."

Darstan accepted the insult without so much as a blink. It was like a summer rain, cold at first, but the shock soon wore off. "What do you eat to make your tongue so strong?" He flashed his charming smile, hoping it had the same effect on girls from Cergala as it did back home. "An old friend of mine used to say that it was hard to catch a fish with an ugly worm."

Mirana never cracked a smile, and her eyes remained cold. "I have never liked fish, pretty one, and when I find worms, I eat them."

Wisp laughed. "Darstan, I'm afraid your charm has been wasted on our new friend."

Darstan's smile disappeared, shiny teeth folding under closed lips. "Perhaps I should let my sword speak for me. You look as if you need taming."

"I urge caution, One-Hand. I see you have not fared well in battle, and you now face a warrior. I would not like to harm you, but—"

Aenaila intervened. "Enough!" She stepped between Darstan and Mirana, but she directed her anger at Mirana. "I share the shame you brought upon yourself by speaking so to a guest. Apologize."

She flashed a look of daggers at Aenaila. It was obvious that apologies were not an ordinary occurrence with her.

No sense in letting things begin like this, Wisp thought and bowed to Mirana.

"Customs are different in other lands. We meant no offense to you, so I offer my words of forgiveness first and hope you will accept them with honor. Perhaps they will light a path for your words to follow."

Darstan fumed. "Don't apologize to her. She's the one who insulted us."

"Apologies don't cut. I've never seen a man bleed to death from offering gratitude or forgiveness. In fact, a few choice words have extricated me from precarious positions in the past. And you know how I despise violence."

Mirana spit. "I knew it. Men with the hearts of sheep."

Darstan grimaced inside but was able to keep his smile. Wisp always lightened his mood. Soon Darstan's lips betrayed the hint of a smile, and he sheathed his sword. "I retract any words that offended you, My Lady." His apology rang with sincerity and a low, graceful bow added to the effect.

Aenaila kicked Mirana lightly behind the leg, but she stood still as a stone, her hand clamped onto the staff and her stance poised for a strike. Aenaila kicked harder, buckling Mirana's leg. She frowned at the prodding but said nothing to assuage Darstan's pride.

Suddenly, Aenaila barked out an order. "Mirana!"

Mirana's face softened and a smile formed, though her eyes remained cold as hard steel. "I have captured my words and slain them, friend of my queen. They will never offend again."

Darstan thought the words strange, but he understood the gesture. He was more interested in what she had said about Aenaila. "What's this, Aenaila? Why did she call you queen?"

Wisp's thoughts must have run wild, and he looked to Aenaila for an answer. "Queen?"

Aenaila cast a sidelong glance, a disapproving one, at Mirana, then stepped forward with an explanation. With her head held high, and her hair bouncing off her shoulders, she focused her emerald eyes on Wisp. "My name is Aenaila de Faloro, First Daughter to Marro and Genea de Faloro, and Heir to the Realms of Cergala."

"I always knew you were special, Mistress Aenaila," Adju said. "Or should I call you Queen Aenaila?"

Aenaila blushed. "Just call me Aenaila. I am the same person I was a moment ago." She looked nervously to Wisp.

He pushed aside whatever other thoughts he may have held, and smiled. "Well, My Queen, you should have told us sooner. We would have treated you more royally." He tried, but could not keep the bite out of his remark.

Aenaila ignored him. "This is Mirana. She was chosen to be my Blood Protector, the Queen's One. It is the highest honor a warrior can achieve."

"My queen does me great honor," Mirana said, and bowed, but only slightly, as before. Cergalan tradition held that a warrior's eyes must ever be alert, and never lowered to the ground unless it is to slay an enemy.

AENAILA SMILED, but Wisp's somber mood worried her. His mood was usually so bright that the slightest hint of unhappiness seemed a deep depression. "Does this news upset you, Kender Darnell?" Her tone aired her concern, and she moved toward him, hands outstretched.

Wisp broadened his false smile and laughed aloud, but the mirth didn't come from the heart. "Bother me? Upset me? Why should that be? I'm surprised but elated."

He cloaked his retort in barbed words meant to bite her, but even as he spoke, he seemed to soften. His feelings for Aenaila wouldn't allow him to hurt her, and as his face softened more his smile grew warmer, lighting his cheeks. Wisp reached for her hands. "Truly, Aenaila, you are a queen. And that could never surprise me."

The emotion shocked Darstan, as it did Mirana. She had not seen her queen in a long time, and now she stood before her embracing such a weak and puny man.

Aenaila held his hands warmly and stepped back. "I am not a queen yet, Kender. I am only the heir. If my father should die, or if the prophecies of lore come to pass, then I will be crowned queen. Either way, it matters not."

She held his gaze a while longer then sought to divert the conversation to someone else. "Darstan, Adju, Kender. I know that Mirana has not met you with her best smile, and she does smile at times, but I beg you to look past today and see her with a different set of eyes."

Darstan looked, but Mirana still displayed no smile. "It would take a stonemason to chisel a smile on her face," Darstan said.

Aenaila hugged Adju, who had come to offer his affection. "Come, let us all go to greet my mother and father. My heart aches to see them after so long."

Aenaila began walking, but Mirana leaped to the trail in front of her.

"You are home now, My Queen. Your First will serve you and clear the path of danger."

Her voice dripped with honey when she spoke to Aenaila, but then she spun to Darstan and Wisp, yelling. "Guard the rear well, dogs. If any harm befalls my queen, I will cook you over a fire."

Jago shrugged his shoulders and took a position on the right. Adju walked alongside Aenaila. "Wisp, you take the left. This dog will guard the rear."

ANOTHER PROPHECY

Mirana stopped so Aenaila could rest, but she paced the site like a hungry wolf. Darstan leaned against a stolid oak while watching her. Strange as it seemed, there was something about her he liked. She stared at Darstan as she passed him, her hand firmly planted on the staff. "Stay alert, One-Hand. There could still be danger, even this close to Cartena."

Darstan's smile came naturally. "Mirana. That's a pretty name. What's your last name?"

Darstan didn't see her hand until it slapped his face, the sting of a whip only worse by a little. Instinct forced his fist into her side, but he regained composure before his kick struck her. Darstan reached out to her, appalled at his behavior, confused by her's. "I'm sorry, Mirana. I..."

The staff lay across her hands as if it would reach out and strike on its own. Only Aenaila's glare stayed her actions. Darstan awaited her reply, but she was as mute as the tree stump behind her. "Mirana, why did you hit me?"

His face still bore the redness of her mark. Darstan looked at her rabid glare, his eyes as piercing as her own. Long ago his smile disappeared, replaced by a grim demeanor. "

Aenaila's hand touched his arm. "Blame me. I should have told you more of our customs. I should have warned you."

Darstan turned to her, questions on his face. "I only asked her name. What could be wrong with that?"

Aenaila patted his arm. "A warrior only reveals their name to someone when they have proven themselves worthy. It is a grievous insult to ask someone their name, as it implies that the deed had been done and that the other person was not honorable enough to recognize it."

Darstan shook his head in confusion. "Blasted stupid reason to hit someone. She's fortunate to be alive. I might have hurt her."

Mirana jumped forward. "You couldn't hurt me, One-hand!"

Aenaila pulled Darstan's attention back to her. "There is more, Darstan. Once a warrior gives their name the person who accepts it assumes responsibility for protecting that person as a friend and companion."

"Then thank whatever gods she prays to that I didn't get her name."

"What happens if the name is refused?" Wisp asked.

Aenaila looked grim. "They would fight—to the death."

Darstan turned back to Mirana. "Again I apologize, Mirana. I didn't understand your customs. There was no insult meant." He tried his smile one more time.

She stared solemnly, but Darstan thought he noticed a crack in her smile. "If you fought as well as you smiled, you might make a warrior."

Aenaila must have seen the expression too. "He has an infectious smile, Mirana. I challenge you to deny that."

Mirana moved down the path. "I believe you are rested, My Queen. Let us make for Cartena."

DARSTAN'S first glimpse of Cartena came through the trees where the foliage thinned. The large cities he had seen before seemed cramped: Khatara, Sykor, Pomanda, all showed houses jammed together on hills, in valleys, anywhere they fit. Not here. Cartena broke the mold of the big cities. Order ruled in Cartena. And there was space. Although the city seemed crowded atop the hill, plenty of open space surrounded it.

Cartena

The forest ended abruptly, granting free rein to the grassy expanse spread at the city's feet where a rolling hill led up to the center. A river wider than the Sykoran rolled down from hills to the north, cutting a twisting swath through the city's north side before turning course and heading east. Houses built from field stone and wood were planted across the valley like corn on a Sykoran farm.

"It's a big city, Aenaila. I guess I wasn't expecting that."

"It is larger than Khatara."

"I don't see the palace," Darstan said. "Where does your father live?"

Aenaila laughed. "Cergalans are not so concerned with such things. The house of my father is not so different from any other. Perhaps a little larger."

The information relieved Wisp a little. Perhaps queens here were not so reserved. "Favian's palace would cover that whole hill," he said.

By the time they reached the edge of the city, people had spread the word, "Aenaila has returned." A handful of men approached, apparently too close.

"Stay back!" Mirana warned, and with a flip of the wrist, the staff twirled. "The queen has been gone for years. She will believe you all mad."

Aenaila smiled at the gathering crowd. "I would never think such as that. Come, follow us to the house of my father."

MORE THAN A FEW hundred waited in the street by King Marro's house, he and his wife Genea among them. Darstan found it almost beyond belief that the king and queen lived so frugally, but then he remembered the Lorns and how Rhalan Teldren lived among his people as just another neighbor. There was no palace in Genda either, now that he thought about it.

Perhaps it's not so different after all.

Darstan saw two people approaching from the crowd, eyes as bright as the sun.

Aenaila raced past Mirana into an embrace. "Father! Mother! Oh, but I have missed you."

"Welcome home, My Daughter. Welcome home."

Aenaila slipped from the arms of her parents to allow Jago his reunion. "Father, Mother. It is good to be home," he said, then he hurried to a waiting wife and child. Darstan's mouth fell open, and he stared at Wisp. He had not known Jago was her brother.

Wisp nodded. "He told me on the ship."

Darstan thought for a moment. "If Jago is her brother then why wouldn't he become king instead of her queen?"

"Perhaps it's like in Khatara, Master Darstan. Whoever is born first is the heir, no matter if it is a man or woman."

Darstan was surprised again. He had not known that either.

"It's true." Wisp said. "In fact, that policy has brought about many murders in the royal family."

"So how is it done here? She doesn't look older than Jago," Darstan said.

"You talk like old women with sagging skin." Mirana's glare silenced them. "The Prophecy determines who rules in Cergala, and that is Aenaila—as soon as she brings him home."

"Who is she bringing home?" Wisp asked.

"The One," she said. "The one foretold in the Prophecy."

Darstan's heart sank with his spirits.

What does this blasted Prophecy say? And who does it say I must kill?

Aenaila took hold of Darstan's hand and led him to her parents. Wisp and Adju trailed behind him. "Father, this is Darstan Fal-Thera from the land of Kamnor." She cast a surreptitious glance toward Darstan's sword.

~

THE KING'S eyes focused on the blade, then stayed glued to it. Marro walked close to Darstan. "I am Marro de Faloro, Darstan. Welcome to Cartena."

Darstan fell silent but managed a smile.

Marro caught his gaze again. "May I look at your sword?"

Darstan nodded, but the fear had already set in. He slowly released the sword from its sheath and offered it, hilt first, to the king.

Marro let it lay across his hands. He examined the blade as a jeweler would a diamond necklace. It was a double-edged, thrusting blade—most Cergalan swords were, but fine craftsmanship decorated this weapon, too fine for any normal blade. Mountains covered with forests had been carved into the ivory handle, and a pack of wolves hid in the forests, white wolves, and one with a green stained neck. The pommel bore the face of a giant black wolf baring teeth stained with blood.

"For hundreds of years, we have guarded the secrets of the book of Prophecy. When the signs first appeared, I sent my only daughter to search for the One." Marro's face darkened, and he began to recite.

When battles rage, when steel doth clash

our foes will win the day.

But when blood stains the white wolf's mane

the enemy we'll slay.

'Round its neck will wrap a tree– green blood

no red will mark this wreath.

But hark! Look at BlackWolf's face.

Red blood drips from his teeth.

Cergalan Prophecy

Marro let the silence linger as he passed the sword to Darstan. He bowed low, as a subject to a king. "Welcome to Cergala, BlackWolf."

Darstan nearly dropped the sword. "Blackwolf! I don't know who you have write these prophecies, but I'm no wolf. I'm just here as a friend to Aenaila."

Aenaila smiled and held Darstan's hand.

Marro nodded. "Fate is seldom kind to any of us, but you should be proud. The Prophecy calls few to its cause." He noted Darstan's rejection of the news, of the Prophecy itself. "There is no denying it. You are BlackWolf."

Mirana's shock was nearly a match for Darstan's. "My King, perhaps we have made a mistake. Perhaps—"

The lines on Marro's face had been chiseled, not worn by weather or age. "No, Mirana. Let your tongue say what your heart feels. You do not want him to be BlackWolf, so you wish it were not so. But wishing will not make crops grow in a drought; wishing will not bring warmth during the moons of hunger; and wishing will not make BlackWolf someone else."

Mirana hung her head low.

"He has power, Mirana. Even he does not know how much." Marro put up a hand to silence everyone, then spoke loud enough for all to hear. "I must spend time with my daughter and son. There will be news to share when we have finished." Marro turned to Darstan and Wisp. "We would be honored to have you join us," he said, then he knelt to be close to Adju. "You have traveled far, little one. Will you come sit at my table?"

Adju smiled, but his fear showed through. "I go with Master Kender," he said. "Or Master Darstan."

"They will be with you."

Adju nodded. "What do I call you?"

"You may call me king, or Master Marro. Whichever you prefer."

Darstan and Wisp had already begun to walk to the house with Aenaila. "King Marro, I do not like what you said about Master Darstan. He is no wolf. He is a good man, a kind man."

"I pray you are right, my little friend. Since the first day I learned of the Prophecy I have prayed every night for the One to be a good man. If he is not, then we all will die."

Adju took hold of the king's hand and walked with him toward his house. As they walked Adju squeezed Marro's hand a little tighter. "He is a good man, King Marro."

"Aenaila, there is much you have to tell us," Marro said, "but first I would hear from your friends."

Darstan had no qualms about speaking his mind. He stood, pacing as he addressed Aenaila's father. "King Marro, I didn't want to say anything in front of your people, but I'm only here because I promised Aenaila I would come."

Darstan composed himself, stopping to face Marro. "I came, as I said, but I'm not the person in your prophecies. I'm not BlackWolf. If my sword is similar to a description you have, it's by chance." Darstan took time to emphasize his next point. "I found this at the bottom of a box of swords in Sykor. It was covered with rust! How in god's name can this be a sword of prophecy?"

The king smiled knowingly. "Perhaps you are right, Darstan. After all, we have only just met. I would not mark a man's fate with so little knowledge."

Suspicion whispered in Darstan's ear, but the king had spoken the words he wanted to hear. "Thank you."

Marro grasped his hand and patted his shoulder. He was as tall as Darstan, if slightly heavier, and he yet wore a full head of hair, and though none could call the man unsightly, it was plain that Aenaila had inherited her mother's beauty. "Stay a while, Darstan. Share our food and our joy. Aenaila will return you to your home soon."

Mirana wore a wicked smile, while Aenaila's face held shock.

"Father, we—"

Marro cut her short with a gesture. "Daughter, I have spoken, and Darstan has spoken his mind. We must have erred."

Wisp's silence must have been evident to Aenaila, and she knew him enough to know his ears had not remained as closed as his mouth. He was ever the observant one. "I believe the king has been blessed with wisdom. Darstan does not look the wolf to me."

Mirana's muttered chuckle didn't go unnoticed. Wisp thought he heard her mumble "sheep," but he couldn't be certain. Aenaila's mood had changed though. She didn't appreciate being corrected, even by the king.

Wisp decided to risk an opinion. "Aenaila, if the Prophecy has truly chosen Darstan, it will call him. I believe in fate, and it doesn't let anyone slip from its grasp." He knew what he had to say might hurt Darstan, but it needed saying. "Darstan, if you are the one they speak of, let it come into the light. You cannot deny your destiny."

"You too, Wisp! Blasted prophecies have turned my friends against me." Darstan fumed. "I just want to get back to Khatara. Aenaila, when can you take me?"

"Seven days at the earliest, perhaps ten or more."

"Seven days! Why so long?"

"Because first, we must send a ship to the isle where we shifted from. Then, when we have allowed enough time for it to get there, we can shift and sail close enough to Khatara for me to shift you to my home."

Darstan slid down a wall to the floor, resting his head on his hand.

Queen Genea made her way toward Darstan, picking up a chair to move beside him. Wisp quickly grabbed the chair and moved it for her. "Please, Queen Genea, let me do that for you."

She smiled, and when she did her eyes lit her face.

Genea's hair was golden, not honey, but the luster yet lingered on every strand, and the shine on her face had managed to stay, somehow fending off the wrinkles that come with age. But even without that, there was still the eyes. Her eyes burned emerald green and with the same mystery as Aenaila's. "My name is Kender Darnell, Queen Genea. I can see that Aenaila has been blessed with your beauty."

She smiled again. A lifetime of compliments had made her immune to such flattery, but she managed a smile every time. "Thank you, Kender Darnell. I need these reminders, as my daughter sometimes forgets that I had anything to do with bringing her into this world. She believes that Marro mixed mud with leaves and baked her in the sun."

"Mother! Our guests do not need privilege to our quarrels."

Genea laughed then seated herself in the chair next to Darstan. She took his hand in hers. "Forgive my husband and his headstrong daughter. At times they forget that people have lives other than the Prophecy. They forget people have feelings."

Darstan lifted his head. "Do you believe me?"

"I have lived outside this Prophecy for many years, Darstan. I understand how difficult it can be to fight the battles you face. Aenaila is her father's child. People say she resembles me in my youth, but she has ever been Marro's daughter."

"I don't want any part of this prophecy, Queen Genea."

"And I do not blame you, my son." She patted Darstan's head in genuine concern. "I must take my husband away for now. He has matters that need attending." She stood and glared at Aenaila. "Perhaps Mirana will show you the things we've changed since you have been gone, daughter."

After they left, Darstan got up and began pacing the floor, counting the tiles. Every fourth tile had a diamond at the corner, and four tiles equaled about one good pace. Nine, ten, eleven... "Rats blood! This is a big room." He turned, staring back the way he'd come then looked at the width.

Wisp sat on the floor carving a figure with his knife. "It's six paces across in case you're wondering."

"And about twelve long," Darstan said. "That's half as big as our whole house was in Twin Forks." He looked into the adjoining rooms. "Doesn't look this big on the outside."

"I'd say it's about as big as Lord Talanvar's house."

Darstan stared at him. "How is it you know so much about Lord Talanvar? And why did he help us back in Sykor?"

"Just an old friend," Wisp said, and smiled.

Darstan looked at the paintings on the wall, the fancy vases, plush furniture. "I don't know how Aenaila lived in that small house in Khatara after being used to this."

Wisp sighed. "I don't know how she'd ever live anywhere else."

Laughter almost took hold of Darstan but then he realized that Wisp was serious. "Don't worry. You two will figure it out."

A WALK IN THE FOREST

*D*arstan decided to enjoy himself while he waited. *I'll not let her tug me around on a leash,* he vowed. "Adju, come with me tomorrow. We'll explore the city, perhaps the forest as well."

"I would be honored, Master Darstan," he said, then caught a glare from Aenaila. "Do not worry, Mistress Aenaila. My hands will not stray."

"Thank you, Adju," Aenaila said. "If you are to go with Darstan, you had better rest well tonight."

"But, Mistress Aenaila, in Khatara I stay up late. I—"

"To bed now!"

He nodded his head. "Yes, of course."

DARSTAN WAS SURPRISED to see a servant awake and preparing meals in the early morning sun. He and Adju ate, then departed.

"Where are we going, Master Darstan? What are we going to do?"

"Anything, Adju. As long as we get away from Aenaila and her father." And this blasted Prophecy.

"I want to go to the forest. I have never been in a forest."

They moved off the road and across the field toward the woods. The sun gave way to the trees, shade beckoning them into their embrace. As their footsteps left the grass, Adju reached for Darstan's hand.

"What do you think we will see in here?"

Darstan suppressed a grin. He remembered being young, and afraid. "Probably nothing. Some birds, squirrels, deer. A snake if we're lucky."

It was a beautiful forest, heavily populated with all the hardwoods: oaks, elms, maples, hickory, even some emeralds. Large pines took their place among the others also, a steady influence and a stabilizer of the forest. I miss the forest, Darstan thought, remembering times from Kamnor. What I wouldn't give to be back there with Rahg and Magmar.

The hills flowed in the forest, pushing trees up and letting them down. A creek cut a sharp edge through the softest soil, ripping roots, sometimes even trees from their firmly entrenched positions.

"Look, Master Darstan, that tree made a bridge over the creek. Can we cross it?"

"Sure we can. Rahg and I used to do that all the time."

Darstan marveled at Adju's balance. He nearly danced his way across the log, lightly stepping over branches as if they were nothing. The creek bed waited at the bottom of a one-span drop if he should slip, yet he paid it no mind. Darstan wondered if it was thieves or young people that held such balance. Rahg had been good too, Darstan recalled, and he was no thief.

Adju jumped the remaining distance to the bank, landing with a gleeful shout. Darstan jumped too, but as much out of necessity as anything. His balance was not what it once was, ever since he lost his hand. Darstan watched Adju run through the trees like a puppy on the loose. It felt good to see someone have fun. "Adju, come here." Darstan spoke just above a whisper.

Adju hurried over, fear quickening his steps. "What is it?" He searched the area as he asked.

"Sh. Look toward the top of the hill. Just past that cluster of big rocks."

Adju grew very excited. "I see them. I have never seen deer before."

Darstan knelt by his side. "You must be quiet. They hear well and can smell you too. See how the little ones keep close to the doe. She'll signal them if anything startles her."

deer in woods

Adju's eyes sparkled with excitement; it was enough to last all day. Darstan rubbed his head and stood when the deer darted off. "Something spooked them. Could have been anything."

They stopped to eat far into the woods. Some berries complemented the bread they brought, and the creek was clean enough to drink from. "I like this, Master Darstan. This is fun." Adju ate some more berries as he looked around. "Can you find your way back from here?"

"Don't worry. Just like you know the city, Rahg and I grew up near the woods." Darstan laughed a little. "Besides, all we have to do is follow the creek back to the city."

"We are deep in the forest. It is quiet here."

Darstan stood to stretch. "You wouldn't think it quiet if you spent the night. When Rahg and I were your age, we went to the woods with some friends. We planned on staying the night, but before the wolves howled their first song, we went home."

"You were afraid?"

"Indeed I was. Though I never let Rahg know."

"Perhaps we should get back. We have come a long way."

"All right. Let's go."

They walked a quarter league south with the creek, then followed it west, toward Cartena. "The crossing isn't far from here," Darstan said.

Adju walked ahead of him spotting for animals. He desperately wanted to see a snake. Suddenly he stopped. "Master Darstan."

Darstan heard fear in Adju's voice and hurried to his side. "What is it? Did you find a snake?" Darstan put his hand on Adju's shoulder. He fe;t him trembling.

Adju whispered. "No snake, but look on the other side of the creek." He pointed north.

black wolf

Darstan chilled when he saw it, a wolf bigger than any he had ever seen. "Don't move, Adju," he said, but the command was unnecessary. Adju had frozen to the spot. Darstan too remained still. No sense provoking it by moving. The wolf stood amid a grove of emerald trees, a majestic figure even among these ancient giants. Darstan couldn't help but stare, though fear told him not to.

It was a black wolf—huge, with fur that would keep it warm even in the Whites. Its ears stood fully stretched and turned slightly toward Darstan and Adju. A long snout curled to reveal the bottom of bared teeth. The tail was alert, and worst of all was the fierce yellow eyes burning into him. Not Adju, him.

The wolf stared for what seemed like days, then as suddenly as it appeared, it was gone. Darstan waited until his sight failed him before speaking. "I think this is the first breath I've taken, Adju."

"Master Darstan, can we go home?"

Darstan hugged him. "We're going now. We'll be there before long."

Adju trembled. "I mean home. I want to go back to Khatara."

Darstan squeezed tighter. "So do I, Adju."

Adju finally breathed easy as they emerged from the woods. "Mistress Aenaila will not believe we saw that wolf."

Darstan snapped at him. "Don't tell her, Adju. Don't you dare!"

Darstan shook violently, like the time in Khatara when he burned the guards. "If you tell anyone about this wolf..." He was beginning to calm, though it proved difficult. The Fire had already begun to warm him, and he felt the effect throughout his body. He sat for a moment on the grass. "Let's rest," he said, then stared at Adju.

Gods, I've scared him to death.

"Come here. I'm sorry."

The little one hesitated.

"I'm all right. I won't hurt you."

Darstan held him for a long time. "I don't want Aenaila and the king to hear about the wolf. With what he said about the Prophecy... I just don't want him to hear about it."

Adju smiled and rubbed his hand through Darstan's hair. "I understand, Master Darstan. I can keep secrets. Everyone in Khatara knows how to keep a secret."

"Let's go, then. I'm hungry."

SUK WON—OLD GHOSTS

Suk Won stood at the rim of the ancient village, its shattered ruins a reminder of glory past, the paradise Sethia once was.

His forefathers had walked among lush trees laden with fruits, and marble statues had decorated the village square. Birds had huddled on rooftops capped with Khataran tile—a song for each new day—and flowers blossomed from every windowsill. Silk garments were the order of the day, and houses were filled with laughter and wisdom.

Long ago, this had been a thriving town with a lot of activity, but that was before Mikkellana had erected her shield and sealed off Sethia from the rest of the world. Technically, Sethia was not restrictive to normal people, but normal people were so afraid of who was said to be trapped in Sethia, that they dare not venture inside. The result was trade died and so did the cities that had been built on trade.

deserted village

He stared at the crumbled rock, beautiful faces of once–proud buildings torn and shredded by the relentless beating of the wind and sands. He prayed for those who had lived here, spirits of an empty past. But once again, if only for a short while, this village would be blessed with the gift of blood, an honor that only battle can bestow.

Three of the prisoners had been released inside, armed with sword and knife and kunai. Suk Won only had a knife and staff, but danger and death lurked at each end of Suk-Won's staff—a tiger's claw, a wagger's bite.

Only one other Ligarn equaled his prowess with the staff, though not many chose it as a primary bedmate. Suk Won's staff was a shade shorter than him—a full two lengths of emerald that had been soaked in the juices of the mejana fruit, then baked in the searing Sethian sun. Afterward, it was treated with more special oils then baked again until it was as hard as stone, but not as brittle, maintaining a suppleness that a master could maneuver like the wind. A Ligarn's staff could sustain blows from the hardest metal blades with barely a nick, and it could strike like an iron fist.

Suk Won walked toward the center of the village, careful not to stray too far from the middle of what used to be the primary street.

They will strike soon if they are smart. And if not they will die sooner.

The Ligarn danced lightly down the street, feet never rooted to the ground. He kept a vigilant watch to the sides and to the back as he spiraled and twisted and turned his way down an old avenue of the ancient village, never staying in one position for more than the blink of an eye. His dance held no pattern, leastwise none a frail one could detect.

His challenge consisted of two Khataran hillmen and a caravan guard. He played through in his mind the weapons of each. The guard, the least dangerous, held a sword and a knife. He would be less than an expert with the sword and even less threat than that with the knife, but he must be vigilant, even a carelessly thrown blade can find a home in flesh that is not alert.

Suk Won did a continuous spin and caught a glimpse of a shadow that had ducked behind a wall a little too slowly. He pressed forward and around again, then back to the opposite side—all, as if he had seen nothing. There would be no wisdom in rushing in to slay that one when he didn't yet know where the other two were. If his guess proved correct, this one was the guard. He would wait for them to make a mistake, then he would slay them.

Just as he thought it, both feet left the ground in a double kick, a maneuver meant to draw them to attack while they thought he was disadvantaged. Frail ones had little patience and the tension building inside of them would force one of them to attempt a hasty attack soon enough.

The Khataran hillmen would likely have kept their short, curved swords and their kunai. The hillmen would have been allowed only one kunai each, but one kunai in the hands of Khataran hillmen made dangerous foes. Those round steel balls could knock him out with little more than a grazing along the head and with a full strike, could kill. At worst, they could break a bone if hit squarely. Yes, he would have to be careful of the hillmen; they would miss no opportunities to strike.

A lizard scurried from a low section of ruins where the wall stood only a half a man high. The lizard had not run due to his approach, that much he knew. He could dance in the shadow of a lizard and grab its tail before it knew he was there—so it must have been from the hillmen. And knowing the hillmen, they would never separate. From the first time they leave the tribe, they hunt and fight in pairs. Living or dying together. Now he knew where they were: the Sykoran whose shadow he had seen first and the two hillmen he had just discovered.

It would be to his advantage to draw the hillmen out first, as the guard would likely wait and see if they were successful before risking injury. Only when the hillmen lay dead would the guard realize he had erred.

Suk Won spun his leg quickly to the right, letting his waist and head follow the natural movement. Whether from luck or intuition, he stopped before the move was completed. Just as he stopped, he dove for the ground, but the kunai struck on the right side of his head. It was not a full strike—it only grazed him—but it was hard enough, and he felt himself going dizzy.

Even as he cursed himself, his hand rose instinctively to guard his head. He knew the second kunai would be following closely behind the first one. Just as his fingertips stretched in a race to guard himself, he felt the kunai hit the palm of his hand. Fortunately, he had the sense to be falling backward and let his hand absorb the blow. He must now fight for consciousness. If he could survive and remain conscious and alert, he could still win the contest.

They would be coming fast, so he forced himself to roll off to the left shoulder then back up, springing to his feet. Spinning twice, his staff was whirling as soon as he hit the ground. The hillmen met him, swords drawn and in attack formation, one at his right front and the other opposite him at the left front.

He did a double-whirl with the staff spinning furiously to parry them. He feigned to the left then right as he spun to see where the caravan guard might be. Suk Won had put himself in a position where he faced the two hillmen and the place where the guard still hid. At least he knew his backside was safe.

The hillmen attacked. Only the swiftness of his staff saved him, ringing with repeated blows. Perhaps Suk Won had been hasty in dismissing these foes. The caravan guard rushed from behind the building where Suk Won had seen the shadow move.

The Ligarn's hopes diminished; he had prayed the caravan guard stayed hidden until he had the chance to dispatch the others. The guard had his sword drawn, but Suk Won could see by the way he brandished his sword that he was no expert. Perhaps he would hinder the hillmen more than help.

Just as the caravan guard charged, Suk Won feigned an attack at him from the left, causing him to veer off and almost stumble into the hillman on his right. As soon as Suk Won confirmed the mishap, he lunged, delivering a blow to the hillman on his left. The hillman parried it with his sword, but Suk Won immediately spun his staff overhead and struck him in the jaw, a blow that sent him reeling backward.

He then shifted his weight to the right foot, his return jab a follow through to the confused caravan guard. It took the guard in the crux of the throat and pierced the shallow skin. The caravan guard gurgled blood but Suk Won had no time to savor the victory, or he would find himself as dead as the Sykoran.

He immediately shifted the weight back to the left and rolled sideways letting his movement yank the staff from the man's throat. If he had waited to pull it out first, the hillman's sword would have caught him. As it was, the sword swished through close to his ear, too close, as it caught a piece of his ear and took it off. If the hillman had been left-handed, Suk Won would have been dead.

His roll brought him right next to the other hillman, now recovering his balance from the blow to the jaw. As Suk Won came up, his right hand came in an overhead hook as he was rising to hit the man in the groin. Some races thought of this as a dishonorable blow, but to a Ligarn any attack during battle was honorable. The hillman would not stay disoriented for long; hillmen knew pain, and that blow would not hold him for more than a few heartbeats.

The hillman made the involuntary grasp toward the groin, but true to his tribe, he resisted the pain and stopped in mid-stream, bringing his sword arm back for the attack. Suk Won, however, had regained his balance and with his left hand, he seized the hillman's right ankle and pulled him inward while pushing on the hillman's left ankle with his left hand. The effect toppled the tribesman.

Suk Won spun his staff to intercept the blow from the remaining hillman. It caught it square in the middle. Suk Won thought the ferocious blow might break his staff, but it resisted.

He parried it twice, then another blow came, but now Suk Won was standing, and as he stood he jabbed the staff into the gut of the hillman lying on the ground as he attempted to rise. This time there was more than just the pain.

He rushed his staff back to a front-forward position. He was hoping to let the blow slide the sword away, and as the hillman delivered the blow, Suk Won pushed with his right, rising as he did and stepped with his right foot to press the attack.

The hillman was pushed off-balance as the weight of the sword, its momentum, combined with the retaliatory attack by Suk Won made him stumble. Suk Won followed through with a crack to the side of the hillman's head. Immediately, he tucked the lower-left part of his staff behind the back of the man's right foot and yanked forward, toppling him.

Now that he had both men on the ground, it was over with. Suk Won quickly struck a blow to the side of the one hillman's head, a direct blow to the temple that brought instant death.

The other hillman was already rising, but still holding his stomach. Three blows later, he too, lay dead. Suk Won checked to ensure that all had breathed the last. He wanted quick deaths for the hillmen; they had been valiant warriors. Even the caravan guard had been valiant.

The Ligarn was not seriously hurt. His hand would carry a deep bruise from the kunai, and he had lost a part of his ear, but other than that, and a lump on his head, he remained unhurt. He only hoped that he had performed well enough to be selected for the karn.

After checking again to make sure all lay dead, he made a slight nod of his head to their spirits then turned and walked out of the city of ruins. Jen Pal and Ghruehne were waiting at the edge, and from the expressions on their faces and the set of their eyes, he could tell nothing. Suk Won faced them both and bowed, once to Jen Pal and once to Ghruehne.

It probably irked Ghruehne that the bow to him was barely a discernible level lower than that to Jen Pal. Ghruehne was always upset that they didn't honor him more, but the Ligarns were favorites of Lukaan, so he was forced to let them live. For now.

"I surrender my honor to you," Suk Won said. "I cede my life to be chosen."

JEN PAL LET the slightest hint of a smile mark the left side of his lips, the side hidden from Ghruehne's view. Suk Won must have seen the glimmer, tiny as it was, in Jen Pal's cherry-black eyes, because he smiled also. Jen Pal had grown up with Suk Won—he had grown up with all the Ligarns—but he and Suk Won had been best of friends, had hunted together.

Suk Won stood silently for a moment before Ghruehne spoke. "You are chosen, Suk Won. You will make the fourth of the karn."

Suk Won let a smile crack his face, and Jen Pal smiled also. "We shall hunt together again," Jen Pal said, "as we did when we were young."

"Who are the chosen?" Suk Won asked.

Jen Pal's eyes shone more brightly. "You, me, Triala, and Shatir."

"Shatir!" Suk Won said. "I pray for the soul of the village boy. No one can track like Shatir."

Ghruehne interrupted their festivities. "Let us hope so. The Master will tolerate no excuses. No failures. You will not return without the boy."

WOLVES AND WAR

dju ran to hug Kender, squeezing him tightly. "We went to the forest today. And we saw deer and squirrels. Many things."

Wisp smiled. "Darstan knows a lot about the forest. You had a good guide." He tousled Adju's hair as they walked into the other room. "He and his brother, Rahg, used to spend a lot of time in the forest when they were young."

Aenaila had her probing tone at work. "What else did you see?"

His brown face paled. "Ravens, a hawk, even a chipmunk. I have never seen these animals before, Mistress Aenaila."

She stared at Darstan then Adju. "Nothing else?"

A suspicious glint formed in Darstan's eyes. He didn't like Aenaila's probing. "We came back because we were hungry. Adju had seen more than he hoped to."

"Yes, I imagine he did," she said. "No matter, supper will be served soon. Wash yourself, Adju."

Wisp watched Aenaila make her way about the house. She walked like a queen, spoke like a queen, and certainly looked like his picture of a queen. "Do you need help with anything?"

"No, Kender. Rest, and converse with Darstan and Adju. We will not allow you to go without supper."

Darstan watched her too. It was difficult not to. Her hair shined in the light from the window. "You're the one who needs the rest. You have to travel back to Khatara soon."

Her gaze unconsciously shifted to Darstan—hard, penetrating. "Yes, I suppose I must."

Mirana could not hide her disgust. "You cannot be BlackWolf. Black-Wolf is no coward."

THE SUPPER TABLE offered many of the same items Darstan had seen in Sykor, Pomanda, even Khatara. Beans, corn, potatoes, and beef filled platters in the center of the table while ample loaves of bread sat on small serving tables at each end. While they took seats, Darstan noted the red meat soaking in the blood.

Adju fidgeted nervously while waiting for everyone to be seated. Aenaila had taught him manners, at least some of them. But no sooner had Wisp pulled in his chair then Adju reached for a tray.

"Adju!" Aenaila's sharp rebuke stung like a slap.

He retracted his arm. "What did I do done wrong?"

"In Cartena, we say a prayer of thanks for all that we have been blessed with."

Adju didn't understand until Wisp leaned over and whispered. "It's like thanking the Lady for a successful venture," he said, and Adju nodded vigorously.

"Aenaila, would you pleasure us with the sound of your voice? We have missed it these many long years." King Marro sat at the end of the table in a large chair with armrests and cushions.

Genea looked across the length of the table at her husband, a frown twisting her otherwise beautiful face. "Perhaps our daughter has forgotten the words, husband. I would be honored to voice the blessing. " She knew her husband and daughter too well. There would be more than a prayer said, much more.

Aenaila bowed her head, shooting Adju a warning glare as she did. He quickly followed her lead. "The Makers have blessed us with the sun to grow green fields so that our crops will thrive. They have nourished our forests to keep the game safe and plentiful. They have shed their tears to feed our rivers with the source of life. And they—"

Genea shifted uncomfortably, moving her chair noisily to create the interruption. "My dear, I believe you have forgotten your words. That concludes the prayer of thanks."

Genea's glare was met by those emerald green gems of Aenaila's, and her look was as hard as the toughest of them. "There is more, Mother. Father taught me."

Genea nodded. "Then by all means continue."

"And they have blessed us with the promise of a savior, the One who will bring peace to our fruitful lands, the One who will protect our forests from the fire of our enemy, the One who will stop these centuries of war."

Her voice turned harsh now, demanding. "But where is this One, Makers? We have searched according to the Prophecy. We have done as the Prophecy demanded, and yet, the One is not here. Pray, send him to us, as I have nowhere else to search."

No sooner had she finished than Genea began the serving. "Adju, please help yourself. I see that hunger has taken a hold on you."

Adju laughed. "Thank you, Queen Genea. I am always hungry with such good food."

Darstan's face reddened. "If you thought to embarrass me, Aenaila, you did well. But I've been embarrassed before, and it won't change anything. I still want you to take me back to Khatara." Darstan put a large portion of corn on his plate, then a small slice of beef.

"You had better take more of that, One-hand. And take the reddest pieces. You need the courage."

Darstan noted that the blood ran freely on Mirana's plate. He took a few extra slices.

Perhaps she's right.

He looked again to Aenaila, sitting stiff-backed and as stern looking like one of Ludar's questioners. She could be relentless when she wanted to.

"People reported a large wolf near the forest today." She spoke between bites and as casual as if discussing a dress in a shop window. "Did you see anything, Darstan? Adju?"

Adju lost his grip on the fork, and the clank on his plate rang loudly among the silence that followed Aenaila's question.

"It must have kept to itself," Darstan said.

Her eyes darted between Adju's guilt and Darstan's lies. "You should be careful in the forest. If you return, I mean. With people reporting the wolf so close, it might prove dangerous. Our people revere the wolf, though I have never been comfortable with them around." She shivered. "When I was but a young girl I saw one. It frightened me."

"What did it look like, Mistress Aenaila? What color was it?"

Aenaila forced a pause. "If I recall, it was a large wolf, and it was black, as black as the night, with bright yellow suns for eyes."

Darstan finished eating and sat back in his chair. "Wolves seldom bother people. They take sheep and calves, even cows if food is scarce, but I've never heard of one killing anyone. Not in Kamnor."

Aenaila would not let go of the wolf. "Odd that it came so near the city. And on the day that you ventured into the forest."

Darstan ignored her barbs. "I think I'll walk some. Take some fresh air."

DARSTAN WALKED WELL into the night, anger and fear battling for dominance of his emotions.

What should I do? *These people need me for something, or at least they think they do. And if nothing else, Aenaila had been fair, true to her word at every turn.*

On the one hand, he could return to Khatara and be done with it—perhaps. Or, he could stay here and do whatever it was she required, then return.

What harm to stay? I owe her that much. And besides, there is Mirana.

Despite her disposition, Darstan felt a strong attraction to her. He walked up and down the strange streets, looking into shops and staring at stars. He realized no one was up and about, probably due to the late hour. When he finally returned to the house, only Wisp and Adju were awake.

"Did Adju tell you about our experience today?"

Wisp shook his head. "He did, but there was no need. Everyone at the table knew you had seen the wolf. Adju nearly fell from his chair when Aenaila asked about it."

"Master Darstan, I—"

"Don't worry. She just wanted a reaction from me. Wanted to try to tie me to this Prophecy."

"You look tired, Darstan."

"I am. I think I'll go to bed."

~

DARSTAN SAT at the table with only Genea and Mirana breaking fast. "Is everyone else sleeping?"

"Your friend Kender is awake," Mirana said. "He is outside."

Darstan nearly laughed despite his dour mood. He wondered if Wisp ever slept a full night. "Kender sleeps very little. I'm surprised to find Aenaila still sleeping though. When I traveled with her, the morning seldom got a start on her."

"My Queen is tired."

Darstan shivered when he sipped the khaffe. Perhaps the khaffe is what made their personalities so strong. "I'm going for a walk."

"I will go with you, One-hand. You will get lost without me."

Darstan bristled. *If she calls me that one more time...*

"Don't try to say no. I am going with you."

"Good, you can teach me more of your customs."

Queen Genea leaned toward her husband. "Do you think it wise to allow Mirana to accompany him? She wears her temper like most women wear a necklace."

The king nodded. "Let her go. It may do him good."

"Keep him from danger," the queen said. "Aenaila will want him back safely."

Mirana grabbed her staff from a rack beside the door. "Come, One-hand. Cartena awaits us." She set off at a pace that would challenge a soldier's forced march.

438

"I would like to see some different things, Mirana, not just race through the city."

Wisp would have trouble keeping up with her, Darstan thought and quickened his pace.

"Walk with your eyes open. I will stop when you need to see something."

Darstan liked Cartena, even though he tried not to. The city was as beautiful as Aenaila had boasted, and the structures were unparalleled. The people seemed happier than most, more friendly too. Except for Mirana.

He had been greeted by nearly every stranger he passed, though a few whispered more than greetings. "Wolf..." he had heard from some. "BlackWolf..." from others. Some said it proudly, pointing him out to companions, but a few held fear in their eyes when they said it. But of all the talk, it was the whispers from the children that hurt him most. Their fear he could not abide. He got upset at first, but soon he stopped listening.

In a way, he should have been thankful. These people knew he had powers, and the worst they did was fear him. In Kamnor, he would have been exiled, thrown out like a thief caught stealing. In Sykor it would have been worse; they would have killed him. Khatara too. Darstan frowned.

"Don't let them bother you," Mirana said. "They don't know you as I do. They think you will be a hero."

Darstan laughed. "Thank you, Mirana. Thank you for reminding me just how unimportant I truly am."

As they turned a corner, Mirana said, "You might be important to King Marro and Aenaila, but until I see a reason, you hold no special meaning to me."

"I understand."

"There are fountains that you should see..."

Darstan felt a smile forming. "You can call me by my name. I don't hold to your customs. I'll even give you my last name if you want."

"No!"

He laughed. "Don't worry. I won't tell it to you. It was enough to see the look on your face."

Mirana stopped walking and turned to him with her head bowed low. "I should not have called you One–Hand. I'm sorry."

"Just show me the fountains. We can still have a good time today."

The streets twisted through the city on tortuous paths. Few were flat; most climbed steep inclines or fell from towering heights. Cobblestones formed the base for them—even the alleys were paved.

As they passed by a bakery, Darstan paused, thinking of going in. He had not eaten much for breakfast, but the only coin he had was from Khatara. He was still pondering whether to ask Mirana to buy something when shouts from down the street roused everyone's attention.

"Fire! Fire!" A young lad no older than Adju ran up the hill with the alert on his lips.

"Where?" someone asked.

"By the old jeweler's shop. Two houses next to it."

Everyone ran toward the scene, and as Darstan wondered what they would do, Mirana grabbed his arm. "Come, Darstan. Hurry!"

A crowd had gathered before they arrived. The houses roared with flames and smoke. Darstan moved through the people to get nearer the house. Three men held a woman at the front; she was screaming and wailing.

"My baby! My baby is still in there!"

Mirana seized one of the men holding her. "Is her child in there?"

"If a child is in there, may the Makers bless it. That house is too far gone."

Darstan grimaced when he heard the noise—a child's cry! "We need to get in there."

～

MIRANA JABBED her staff on the ground, all the while staring at the flames growing taller and stronger with each breath. Her other arm rested lightly on the woman's shoulder. "He is under the care of the Makers now."

"No! He's still alive. I can hear him crying," the woman said and tried yanking away from Mirana's grip.

Within heartbeats, everyone within range fell silent, even the wailing mother, but no one dared do a thing—the fire raged.

Darstan shook his head vigorously. The call of the child would not go away. "I'm going in," he said, and removed his shirt and tucked it under his arm as he bolted for the house.

"No!" Mirana screamed. "Darstan, no! You'll be killed." She shouted as loud as she could, running after him all the while, but the roar of the flames and the crackling of wood devoured her warning. She stopped when he disappeared into the house, yellow and red flames engulfing him.

Only murmurs could be heard through the mass of people. A few spoke out of respect for the loss of the grieving mother, but mostly in respect for the bravery of the man who attempted the rescue, foolish as it was.

Soon the murmurs and whispers stopped. They heard the silence from the house. Silly to say silence when the building roared with fire, and wood snapped and popped, but it seemed like utter silence with no sounds of life to give them hope.

"He's gone," the mother said, and, as if in answer, the roof collapsed. Flames shot up, rejoicing in the new fuel.

Mirana lowered her head. "I should not have called him One-Hand. He was brave after all."

～

AENAILA AND WISP ventured out soon after Darstan and Mirana had gone. Adju had accompanied Jago, who went to visit his son. When Aenaila heard of the fire, she and Wisp ran to the scene, arriving just as the roof gave way.

"Mirana! Where's Darstan?" Her voice held a tinge of concern. *Had he started the fire in a fit of temper?*

A tear worked its way to the corner of Mirana's eye. "You will not have to take him home, My Queen. Even if he is the One, he could not have survived that." She pointed to the house.

"What do you mean?" Aenaila screamed, anger and fear together in her voice.

"He tried to rescue a child. I tried to stop him," she said, just before Aenaila exploded.

Wisp stared into the blazing inferno. "Don't dig a grave yet," he said.

As they watched the flames devour the house, Darstan emerged with a bundle under his arm. Flames covered his body; his pants were afire, and his chest burned like a field of dried wheat. Fire even danced on his face and hair. Screams of the child came from the bundle wrapped in the remains of Darstan's shirt, rolled up like a bedroll.

"I don't know how he's even walking," Wisp said as he rushed to his side.

"That beautiful face!" Aenaila said.

Mirana ran toward him, ripping off her blouse. She arrived topless, save a wrap that Cergalan women wore to support their breasts.

Before Darstan could say or do anything, Mirana smothered him with her shirt, trying to dampen the flames. He fell to the ground, choking but careful to keep the child from harm.

"Take him!" Darstan shouted, then collapsed.

Aenaila grabbed the child, hugging him to her chest. "Take care of Darstan!" She said to Mirana. As Aenaila turned, the child's mother was there to greet her, arms outstretched in anticipation and tears of joy mingling with those she shed only moments ago at her loss.

"Is he...?

"Yes," Aenaila said. "He's alive. He may need some healing, but it will have to wait until I see to my friend."

Mirana and Wisp smothered the flames that had covered Darstan, but smoke still rose from his body like a campfire that had just been doused. "He's breathing, My Queen. He's alive."

Aenaila sighed. "The Makers kept their eyes on him. I know of no one who could have survived this."

The mother of the child sobbed and thanked the Makers for the miraculous return of her child, but hers was the only voice in the crowd. The rest of them stared in silence at Darstan.

Wisp scanned the men close to him and found two who appeared composed. "Lend some aid, friends. We need to carry him to the house. Carefully!"

As they moved in and bent to help, Darstan opened his eyes and lifted his head. "I can stand."

The men stepped back in shock. "He was afire! I saw him!"

"Flames licked his hair and face," another swore. "There can be no denying that. No man should have lived through that."

Darstan raised himself on his elbow, and then Wisp helped him up. "Are you certain you can walk?"

"I think I can."

Mirana was struck mute. "How..."

"Wait until we get home," Aenaila said. "Help him."

Mirana grabbed her staff and cleared a path through the crowd. "Make way!" Her voice carried the tone of authority.

Aenaila singled out a soldier on the front line. "Go to my father and tell him to prepare for us. We will need clean water and bandages. Tell him what happened; he will know what else."

Aenaila faced the crowd. "He is the One," she said, nothing more. The news raced through the crowd like a blusterous wind. "The One" was whispered and muttered and, at times, shouted in awe. By the time those in the rear had heard, people in the front had fallen to their knees, bowing to Darstan.

Wisp and Mirana supported him, but he shook them off. "I'm all right. I can walk."

Aenaila gently touched his skin. It was covered in soot, but she could find no burns, no marks of any kind. "Do you hurt anywhere?"

"When I first came out, I had trouble breathing, but I feel fine now." Darstan looked at the people on their knees. "Tell them to stop, Aenaila. That bothers me. Besides, I only did what anyone would have. The boy needed saving."

Aenaila laughed, a scoff in her voice. "No one else went in, though the gathering has no shortage of brave men. And look at you, Darstan, you are not even burned, not a hair singed."

"Just lucky," he said. "I danced around those flames. I was running fast; I can tell you that."

Again that annoying chuckle from Aenaila. "Perhaps you don't realize it, but when you came out of the house, you were on fire. Look at your pants. They are all but gone."

"Blast it!" he howled. "Give me something to put on. I'm nearly naked." He grabbed one of the many articles of clothing flying from his worshipers, and he vowed not to ask for anything else.

"It was not just your pants, Darstan, your chest, your hair, even your face was covered in flames, and yet you show no marks. They are paying homage to you—not for saving the child, though no one else could have—but for being 'the One.'"

MARRO HAD PREPARED for an injured man to show up, but when he saw Darstan he motioned the servants away; he had no wounds to tend.

"Do you still deny your destiny, Darstan? It has been written for you," he said. "Nothing can change that. Nothing you do will alter what must be done."

Darstan ignored the king, though in his heart he knew Marro must be right. Still, something inside told him no.

Marro left the room but returned shortly with another piece of old parchment. It looked as if it had been dug from the ground a thousand years past.

"This is yet another part of the Prophecy. It is only a piece of what was once a larger example and as such, the Prophecy is only partially visible, but I believe you will find this part of particular interest." He moved toward the center of the room, then read:

He walks with fire his closest friend.

No man or beast will have him

War calls him to its deadly end

His fate, once bright, is ever grim.

— CERGALAN PROPHECY

Aenaila saw the look on Darstan's face; he was not ready to hear this. Not yet. "Father, I believe that Darstan would like to rest, perhaps eat. As you are aware, he has had a difficult experience."

Marro gave a slight nod as he left the room.

Darstan rested in a chair by the rear window. It offered him a view of something besides curious onlookers jamming the walks out front. Wisp sat on the floor close by with Aenaila next to him. Mirana paced.

"I hope Adju doesn't hear about this. I would like to tell him myself."

"Little promise of that. News seems to have traveled on the wind. Have you looked at the street? I doubt if a cart could get through without running over someone."

Darstan went to the front window. "Can't you do something about them, Aenaila? You're the queen."

Aenaila rose and walked to Darstan. Her arm rested comfortably on his shoulder. "You forget that my people sent their queen across the Endless Sea to search for you. It would be strange if I asked them to contain their excitement. Cergala has waited a long time for you."

They sat in near silence for a long time—until Darstan could stand it no longer. "Aenaila, why didn't the fire hurt me? You haven't asked, so you must know."

Aenaila motioned for Mirana and the rest of them to sit. "I have not told you all of my journey, Mirana. Darstan has the power of Fire, though he does not yet have full command of it."

Mirana glued her eyes to Darstan, as if her initial opinions of him were being shattered in just a day.

Aenaila continued. "Darstan, you might not be able to call the Fire at will, but it is within you. I expect that flames so small as a burning house will stand little chance of harming you."

Darstan thought about what she said and suspected she had the right of it. Just like water won't hurt a fish, he thought, and for the first time, he felt a degree of comfort with his power. He knew Aenaila was not bothered by his power, nor Wisp, but he was as sure that Adju was still bothered by what had happened in Khatara.

As Darstan pondered on this, Jago returned with Adju. The little beggar raced across the room to embrace Darstan. "Master Darstan! I heard about the fire. Are you all right?"

Darstan hugged him tightly. "Yes, Adju. Thank you. As you can see I'm fine." He felt relieved when he saw no fear in Adju's eyes and felt no hesitation in his embrace.

Jago shook Darstan's hand. "I could not keep him a moment longer. Once he heard what happened, he was at the door." Jago looked him up and down. "I see you are fine. Thank the Makers for that. People on the streets are talking about it. The stories claim you were afire when you came from the house. Is it true?"

Darstan nodded. "So they say. I don't remember."

Conversation filled the remainder of the day. Adju told stories of his visit with Jago's family and of the sights he had seen in Cartena. He talked more when he was excited, and by the time supper was ready he had worked his tongue dry.

"You should rest, Adju. I would think your jaws would ache by now." Wisp grinned as he spoke.

Jago let a grin widen his cheeks too. "Adju told so many tales of Khatara that Jodd had little time to talk, but he thoroughly enjoyed hearing of such a wonderful land. Adju made my stories of Khatara look dull by comparison."

Aenaila stood. "I think we should eat. Everyone must be hungry."

Adju reached the table before anyone. "I am hungry, Mistress Aenaila." He reached for a platter stacked with meat when he caught himself, recalling the slap he received for forgotten manners the last time.

Aenaila smiled when she saw him standing stiff, waiting patiently. "You may start tonight, Adju."

Darstan ate little at supper and spoke even less afterward. Then, when the night was still young, he announced he would retire. "Thank you," he said as he left the room. "Thanks to all of you."

DARSTAN LAY IN BED, unable to sleep. The bed was comfortable but the day had not been.

Why did all those people have to see me rescue that boy?

His mind wandered, jumping from one thought to another when he sensed someone in the room with him. He gazed to the left where a shadow hovered. Darstan shot up, ready to fight, but a voice forestalled him.

"It is Mirana."

Darstan was now sitting up. "Mirana? What are you doing here? How?"

Blasted people with their creeping around. Everyone around me seems to move in silence. Rhaven, Wisp, and now Mirana.

"Foltelli," she whispered.

"What?"

"My last name is Foltelli. I wanted to give it to you."

He didn't know what to say. This was an honor, but he had no clue how to respond. *I might get killed for a wrong answer.*

"You do not need to accept it. I do not expect so much. I just... I wanted you to have my name."

Darstan smiled, and when he stood the cover slid off him. Somehow it mattered little. "Fal–Thera," he said. "My last name is Fal–Thera."

Mirana's brown eyes caught the moonlight from the window.

She is beautiful!

"Darstan Fal–Thera, know that while a breath remains in my body that your name and your heart will ever be protected. As long as my blood is warm, so too, shall yours be warm. And as long as my soul is free, so too, shall your soul be free."

Somehow a knife had made its way to her hand, but Darstan felt no threat, not even when she pierced his skin to draw blood. She held the blade to her lips and tasted it.

"Let the blood of Darstan Fal–Thera fill my soul with life." She pierced her skin mixing his blood with hers, then offered him the blade.

Before he took it, he stared into her eyes, holding her hand with his. "Mirana Foltelli, know that while a breath remains in my body that your name and your heart will ever be protected. As long as my blood is warm, so too, shall yours be warm. And as long as my soul is free, so too, shall your soul be free."

Then he pierced her skin and raised the blade to his lips, letting it slide gently over his tongue. "Let the blood of Mirana Foltelli fill my soul with life." He completed the ritual as she had, by piercing his skin again and mixing her blood with his.

Darstan returned the blade to her then held her hand. "Now you have two people to guard. Aenaila and me."

"You embarrass me, to remind me. No one should be so honored in one life."

Gods, but she shined in this light. "Do you like to walk, Mirana?"

"It is late."

"The best time," he said, and led her toward the door.

"First you had better put pants on," Mirana said with a smile. "Even the One must wear pants."

Darstan's heart felt warm as he dressed. *Perhaps things were not so bad after all.*

～

THEY WALKED under the light of Ranal and Ranalla. It was good to see that was the same here. Darstan told her stories of Twin Forks, and of he and Rahg growing up. She told him of Cartena and how she became the queen's protector. They talked about everything except the wars.

"People here are nice, Mirana, a lot nicer than they would be back home to someone like me. No one seems to care that I only have one hand and few even worry about the Fire." He stopped, staring into the night, listening to the quiet. "If this had happened in Twin Forks I would have been cursed as a Banished One and exiled. And if it were in Sykor I would be dead, or worse."

Thoughts from Magmar kept popping into his head, more so of late than at any time since he died. "A man's got to do what he thinks is best, son" and "If you've got to go to town don't let a muddy road stop you." The remembrance brought a smile with it. Magmar had always taught them to do right. "Perhaps Aenaila and Marro are right," he said. "I'll have to think about this some more."

Mirana stayed close to him but didn't interrupt his thoughts. She waited until he appeared composed again. "I should not have called you One-hand. It was not meant to hurt you."

Mirana's statement eased Darstan's tension. Even a laugh wiggled out. "Of all the things that burden my mind right now, that's not one of them." Darstan reached over and brushed her hair lightly with his finger. "But with all the things that worry me, what you said has lightened my heart more than anything else could."

"The sun will be chasing Ranalla soon. The house of my king will be worried if we are not there to break fast."

Darstan worried about seeing Marro again, ever since he had recited that part of the Prophecy about walking with Fire. Darstan knew why he had not been burnt, and the others did too. He wondered if any of them had reservations about him, any fears.

Further deliberations got pushed aside as he saw king Marro's house atop the hill. It was almost morning, and he knew someone would be up, the servants at least.

I feel like Wisp coming in at this time, he thought.

At least the time he had spent walking and talking with Mirana had helped him arrive at a decision. Right or wrong, he had decided.

HALL OF ECHOES

Centarra opened the doors leading to the Hall of Echoes. She wove her shield and let the sounds of eternity assault her ears. A conversation between Mikkellana and Xanthes caught her attention; she remembered it from years past when the two had first become lovers. Other conversations, or bits and pieces of them, floated by. Some she recognized, others not.

The slapping of her boots on the floor ricocheted off the ancient walls of polished stone, ringing loud. A slight chuckle escaped, a chuckle that would prove to be never-ending, a chorus soon to mingle with the conversations and words of all the ages. She maneuvered her way to the center of the room—exactly the center—to a spot she had discovered long ago, a spot where every conversation, every word, every sound ever whispered in Vallah was recorded for all time.

Hall of Echoes

Aentarra didn't know how, or why, the Hall worked, but she no longer questioned what it did. She had discovered this by accident one day while walking through the Hall as a means to another part of the palace. She had been practicing with weaving new shields when voices had come to her, conversations she recognized. After several experiments, she was able to weave shields that allowed her to filter the noise and hear the voices.

Over many years she continued to experiment with the shields, refining them until it required little, if any, thought. The early thrill of her discovery soon waned, the novelty of this unique eavesdropping fading. It was then she discovered the real secret of the Hall of Echoes.

While examining a design in the floor she heard new voices, but they vanished, and it took several attempts to repeat the event. She discovered she must stand in the exact center of the Hall, and she must remain motionless for several long breaths. It was more than an accident that she had found this secret, it was destiny, and this was but another tool for her to use.

She struggled to concentrate, to screen out the loud voices; they disturbed her. Concentrate! She told herself. Focus on the others. Aentarra focused on the ones that could only be heard as whispers, and once she found them, she used the same process to hear the faintest of all whispers. Now I must decipher their hidden messages.

Several more sessions had her delving deep into the history of this strange place, but it wasn't until recently that she recognized some words from the "unrecognizable ones."

She thought they might have belonged to some of the Banished Ones, prior to the war that put them in exile, but comparisons to other conversations proved to be noticeably different, markedly different in both tone and accent. If there was one thing that Aentarra was certain of, it was that she had never heard these voices before. The other certainty was that whoever they were, they knew of the Forbidden Lands. She had heard them mention the Portals.

Who are they? she wondered, and what do they know of the Paaren?

Just as Aentarra exited the Hall, the pain hit her; her knees buckled, hands pressing the sides of her head before she hit the floor, a futile attempt to control the pain. Her knees slammed against the marble, jarring bones all the way to her hips. She managed to roll right to keep her head from direct impact against the floor, but when she landed, she found herself stuck, unable to move, her right side paralyzed.

She ground teeth together, only to bite her own tongue, the right side not responding. Blood oozed from the corner of her mouth, trickled down her chin. The throbbing grew worse, her head pulsing, about to explode.

Something ran from her forehead, down her nose, across the left side of her mouth. The coppery smell and the familiar taste told her it was blood. Hers. Something had to be done. The Others were gaining control. With her left hand, she let go of her head and reached for a tapestry on the wall. The pain was like a knife piercing her temple. Gritting her teeth, she pulled on the tapestry, creeping up a bit at a time. Once she attained a sitting position, she placed her left hand on her head, squeezed, and focused.

She remembered being a little girl, perhaps only six, and breaking the neighbor boy's leg because he had embarrassed her. Recalled the son of another nobleman who had been indiscreet, and how they never found him again. An image of ten dead guards flashed in her memory —guards who had dared to try and hold her capture. But most of all, she recalled the day her father had issued the Slicers to Nagasha. Millions dead, to avenge his wife.

She pictured the carnage, imagined the agony. Soon the pain subsided, replaced by a smile though it was still a crooked smile, her right side still numb.

It took a full day to recover this time. Sitting in a corridor, clinging to a tapestry with blood dripping down her face, her mouth a twisted mess.

Soon this will be over, she thought. *Soon, I'll kill them all.*

HOPE FORSAKEN

Sama finished her prayers, stood, then donned her heaviest coat. The bitter cold continued, and the wind accompanied it. "Stay here, daughter."

"Do you think it will do any good? They are all hard headed."

"Perhaps. But I must try." Sama opened the door to exit the hut, a blast of cold striking her.

"Stay warm, mother."

"Stay safe, daughter."

She walked alone, hands tucked into pockets in the lining of the coat, and a fur hood pulled snugly around her head. She nodded to one of the few villagers who happened to be out. A nod was not the Chun way, but it was too cold to talk.

Sama sighed. During better times, children frolicked in the square playing games or walking with parents or pets. Dogs claimed shade in summer and warmth in winter, but even the hardest of hearts let their dogs inside this winter, though some of the animals had faced a worse fate. Far worse.

The drought affected everyone. Spirits trampled. Hope crushed. Only the jagged Norkaan peaks remained tall and proud, piercing the sky like a warrior's spear. And now, with Korg and Kavi gone, Sama had to do something drastic.

Her brisk pace belied a depressed mood, but she had only moments to make it to the war council. They must not have a chance to decide without her input. Two guards held the flap aside as Sama approached. Although everyone assumed Korg to be dead, Sama still received the treatment due a war chief's wife and, among the Chun, that was as close as a woman could get to being a queen.

Sama entered the communal hut wearing a stern face. She meant to convey a message to the members of the council, and she wished no confusion as to her meaning.

They stared as she sat in the circle around the ceremonial fire, purposefully taking the seat reserved for Korg had he been there. For a moment, she almost lost control of her thoughts, important thoughts regarding the future of the Chun. Thinking of Kavi made her mind wander. Not that she neglected to worry of Korg, but Kavi was her son. He had yet to taste the joys and sorrows of life.

Mostly sorrows, she reminded herself. *At least of late.*

The fire flared; someone else had entered, the breeze stirring the flames. Sama did not turn to look. It would show weakness for her to worry about who approached her back.

The council had already opened the discussion regarding food and the problem with Cergala—the enemy to the north. Most of the council favored abandoning the Norkaan Mountains and going to live in the cities of Arangar. For as long as Sama could remember the Chun and Cergalans had fought. Every year the Chun turned them back, yet every year the Cergalans tried again. If Cergala was ever going to succeed, this was the year it would happen.

Sama did not wait to be recognized to speak. At the first sign of a pause, she began. "I just arrived from Chingua." Sama looked around to make sure everyone was listening. If anything, she had learned how to address a war council from Korg. His teachings would not go to waste.

"Chingua! Home to our king. There is no fruit in the market. There are no greens; no baked goods; and no meat worth eating. What meat there was smelled of rot. The flies that feasted on it told the rest. I saw a basket of fish brought in by two guards, and while I watched, they were mobbed and beaten by a starving crowd. The fish were stolen, the guards left for dead."

Again she paused, this time under the pretense of needing water to drink. "I saw a man follow a dog into an alley. They both appeared starved. Three steps into the passage the dog turned and attacked the man, who had already drawn his blade. Both, it seems were hunting for meat. Their skin was stretched taut, and bones struggled to break free."

She paused to let her words reach their hearts. "At long last, we made our way to the palace. Desperation showed on every face. Even the servants of the king go hungry, and I noticed a suspicious absence of the king's good hounds." Sama took another sip of water. A long sip.

"The king gave us our rations." Sama paused, this time for real as she wiped tears away, embarrassed. "Rations! To the Chun!" The pride of the Chun began to take hold in some of the warriors. "They had to escort us out of the city, so we weren't attacked by our own people. In Chingua they will kill anyone for food." Sama stood. "Are we to let this go on? Are the Chun to eat their pride with supper? Shall the Chun grovel in the dirt like Cergalan worms?"

She scanned the room for reactions, able to tell who was most moved, and she directed her next statements at them. And at the mothers. "What will happen next? What will happen when we run out of food?

Do we begin to eat each other? I have heard that is taking place in Solind, only a three-day ride from here."

Silence filled the room. Sama moved closer to the crowd of people stopping next to a young wife of one of the council, one who pushed hard to leave Chun and go to the city. Sama picked up the woman's baby and held it in her arms. "In Chingua I was told that the babies in Solind are dying first as the mothers have no milk. They also told of people who eat the babies after they are dead." Gasps could be heard from everyone. "Most while their bodies are still warm."

The young warrior's wife grabbed her baby as if Sama herself might eat it. There were tears in her eyes. Sama felt ashamed, but it had to be done. "The snows are deep in the mountains. The drought will be broken... but it won't do us any good now. The Shuthvin Valley won't have water until the snows melt. That's another year to wait for food. We will be dead by then. We need food now!"

People shouted questions. "What can we do?"

"What can be done?"

"Tell us."

Suddenly, a big man from the rear pushed himself forward. His bulk was threatening enough without his bellowing voice, but he had that also. People moved aside as he bulled his way to the front. Those that didn't, he shoved. "You shout harsh words, Sama, wife of Korg."

Sama stared coldly at Breng. She knew he had added that last to remind everyone that she was Korg's wife and not a warrior herself. She feared it might take some of the effect away from her words.

Breng spoke again. "Didn't Korg go out to find food. Maybe he found some and is keeping it secret. You don't look so hungry. Has Korg been feeding you?"

Sama remained silent, but anger burned inside as Breng raised his voice. "Has anyone ever heard of Korg losing his way? We have searched everywhere and found no trace of him or Kavi." He smiled. "Where is he, Sama? Tell us. I think he went to Chingua. That's where we should go. Chingua has food for the taking."

Sama stepped toward Breng. He was still talking, motioning with his hands and jeering. The crowd had begun to get into it, some of them anyway. When Breng turned back to face her, Sama struck! Her knife went into his belly. She shoved it harder, up under his ribs.

He gasped! Mouth agape, and stared down at his blood, hands clutching at the gaping hole in his gut. He tried to stop the bleeding, but it was no use. Sama had cut well as Korg had taught her, and she knew, as did anyone close enough to see, that Breng had thrown his last insult at Korg 'en Terdra. As the big man fell, Sama calmly strode back toward the center of council.

Several in the crowd had now taken up Breng's cry. "Tell us, Sama. Where is Korg?"

"Have we looked everywhere?" she asked casually.

"I have." It was Breng's friend who answered. "We crossed every path and looked in all the chasms. Even the dogs found no scent."

Sama waited for the noise to die. "And where does the scent end?" she asked with the confidence of someone who knew the answer and knew it would bode well for them.

Breng's friend responded again. "At the bottom of the Miska Trail, by the stand of the long-needled trees."

Sama walked slowly to the man, her eyes locked to his gaze. "And did the dogs lose the scent?" She paused, then raised her voice. "Or did they try to climb the Forbidden Trail, only to be held back by you?" The silence was stifling. Even the fire seemed to stop crackling.

Breng's friend held his head low. Shame covered his face and tainted his voice as he tried to offer an excuse. "No one can enter the Forbidden Trail. No one can go to..."

"The Paaren!" Sama finished for him. "Korg 'en Terdra did, and he took Kavi with him." Sama let her glance fill the crowd, let it touch every single one of them. She wanted them to know her sacrifice, feel her pain. "They went into the Paaren in search of food—for you!" She waved her pointed finger at them.

"And you." She pointed directly at Breng's friend. "You would have allowed their names to be covered with shame because you were afraid."

He bowed low, very low, and left the hut. Sama looked out over the now silenced crowd that only moments ago had harbored more than a few dissidents. All eyes now were filled with tears or fear.

To make an impact, she slid the bloody blade back into her sheath without cleaning off the sticky red stains. She knew she had to incite them. Now, she thought. Now, is the time to do it.

"We need food!" Sama said. "The Chun need food! Arangar needs food!" The people were responding, becoming more boisterous with each statement. They wanted to be incited. She could sense it. "Who has food?" Sama screamed. When no one answered. Sama screamed again, louder this time. "Who has food?"

Finally, someone from the front whispered, it sounded like a whisper compared to the level of Sama's tones.

Sama smiled a victorious smile. "Busla here has the right of it." She said. "Cergala has food!" She screamed it louder. "Cergala has food! And they try to claim our lands. Every day they press our borders. They only wait for us to grow so weak from hunger that we can no longer defend ourselves. Why wait?" Sama yelled at the top of her lungs. "Why wait when we can go and take that food now."

Rumblings began, and some of the warriors stirred. "How?" someone asked.

Sama spun her head in the direction of the voice. "How?" She asked with disdain. "We are Chun! Mightiest warriors in Arangar! We will show Cergala what that means."

"Who will lead us?"

Sama stared at them like a wolf eyeing a flock of sheep. "I am Korg's wife. I will lead the Chun into battle." She felt the resentment immediately. She knew they would resent her; she had expected it, but what to do about it. Something had to be done to sway them to her way of thinking. Quickly, she responded pointing a finger at the still bleeding body of Breng.

"Take the body of Breng. Cut it up and feed it to the dogs." No one moved. She had shocked them. To deny someone a decent burial meant to deny them access to the gates of the gods. "It is time we recognized our situation. The warriors must have food. If we are to defeat the Cergalans we must be strong! We must sacrifice the dogs if we are to go into battle healthy."

To a man and woman, they all stared at her. Some with defiance, some with hatred, most with fear. Sama realized her predicament. She gambled. With the boldness of the mightiest warrior, she strode over to the body of Breng. Kneeling, she withdrew her knife and severed his finger, holding it up for all to see. A warrior stood next to her with a war ax in hand. Without asking, Sama grabbed the ax and swung a mighty blow. Breng's arm separated from his torso. Two more blows and the other arm was detached.

The crowd screamed! Someone from the back shouted. "Bring the dogs. We will eat tonight!"

Sama sighed with relief. She was exhausted. Her stomach ached from the hunger, and she cried, eager to retch from the disgusting acts she had performed. It burned! It gnawed at what was left on her insides, which she suspected was not much. She struggled to maintain a stiff back and a steady stride. She could not let them see her weak, not after she embarrassed them into accepting her as the leader. Now she must perform. It would be easy to lead them to war. Easy, compared to the next task at hand. Once they had conquered the Cergalans, then would come the difficult part. They would have food; they would be tired, weary of the fighting, and after all that she must convince them to go down the mountain to the Forbidden Trail, and then to take that foreboding walk up the mountain of mystery and into the Paaren!

I will get my son back, she vowed. I will get them both back if I have to drive them into the Paaren myself.

SCALING THE NORKAANS

ahg's hunger grew when he saw the food Tobias brought back. "I can't believe we finally have food."

"Would have had a lot more if Rhaven hadn't given half of it away." Tobias laughed at the expression on Rahg's face.

"Ran across two families on the road. Hunger had bitten them hard, so we gave them enough to hold them over a while. Was worth it though, just to see the look on their faces."

Camissa's smile came quickly. She knew that underneath Rhaven's rough exterior lay a good-hearted man. "I am proud of your generosity, gentlemen. I have no qualms about giving up a meal or two to help those who need it more."

"I don't mind either, Camissa, as long as I have enough for supper."

Tobias nearly choked. "Lad, you cry like a piglet if a meal is late, let alone missing. Never saw anyone who put so much stock in food."

Tobias managed to embarrass Rahg, but he laughed it off. "I'll go get some more firewood. This might be a long night."

~

A FESTIVE MOOD prevailed at the campsite during supper. Troubles and danger seemed distant. "Eat your fill tonight," Rhaven said. "We will be rationing tomorrow."

Rahg waited until he swallowed his food before speaking. "Why ration? We have plenty of food."

"If we let you eat your fill, lad, it will be gone in a fortnight. I know you don't think much past supper, but you need to worry a little more about what you'll do tomorrow and the next day."

Rhaven filled his second mug of khaffe. "Concern yourself with practicing that shield. I'll handle matters of food." Before the evening ended, Rhaven gave orders for the morning. "We will be leaving early so be prepared. And don't worry, we won't go until after breakfast."

"Where are we going?" It was the first that Katsu had spoken all night.

"Into the mountains, toward the Chun."

Tomkins shook his head. "Not good business going to the Chun. They've been fighting the barbarians so long they're almost like 'em."

"All indications point to the Norkaan Mountains as the only way to enter the Paaren. Even Mulka confirms it from his people. You don't need to come with us, Tomkins, but your company is appreciated, and your knowledge of the land has been a great help."

Mulka offered his support. "Our people found the Paaren before, and they found it in the land of the Chun. I don't have a map, but from what I learned the portal to the Paaren lay near the highest peaks."

"By the great gods!" Tomkins hollered. "You'll have us climbing the Chugarran Path before long. I hope you've got it right."

Mulka bowed his head. "We will find out soon enough."

Camissa yawned, covering her mouth, and Rahg soon found himself doing the same. "I've got a full belly for once, and I'm tired," Rahg said. "Guess I'm going to bed."

"Wait for me." Camissa got up and followed him. They talked long into the night, revisiting shared times in Pomanda and more recently, Entiria. "It's hard to believe we met less than one year ago," Rahg said.

"Sharing so much danger makes it seem longer. We have been through more than most people experience in a lifetime." Camissa smiled. "Though there have been many good times as well. Times I will never forget."

Rahg wrapped a shield around them to forestall the wind and cold. Soon afterward, they both fell asleep.

RAHG WOKE TO SHIVERING, bitter cold. The secret to maintaining a shield during sleep yet eluded him, but he quickly wove one to block the wind. "It's freezing," he said, but to no one.

Camissa was at the fire with Tobias, already drinking khaffe. A bitter day to travel, thought Rahg, dreading the journey about to begin. He walked to the fire, rubbing cold hands to warm them. "Any biscuits yet?"

"If you put up one of those shields of yours and block this wind, I might give you a biscuit or two."

"Better be two. I'm hungry." Rahg ate quickly then helped pack the camp. Everyone showed the bite of the wind except Rhaven. Rahg sometimes wondered if he had a shield around him the way he ignored the elements.

Rhaven seldom wasted time on idle chatter, and this morning proved no different. "Tomkins, take the lead. Katsu, right flank; Jarrell, left. Rahg and Camissa, inside. Tobias, take the wagon and the rear. Mulka can ride with you. I'll scout with Kella. Mulka, have the welgar to stay with you."

"I'll ride with Mulka, but I don't want that welgar anywhere near me." Tobias clamped down firmly on his pipe.

Mulka frowned. "Garnock abides by his oath. He won't harm anyone unless they attack me."

Two puffs of smoke blew from Tobias's mouth. "Oaths from a welgar. This blasted world has gone half crazy."

Tomkins led the party through the forest toward the mountains, but as the altitude increased so did his fear. The Chun, legendary warriors of Arangar, could be ruthless to outsiders. Some said mercy had never found its way so far into the Norkaans.

A coat with fur wrapping the collar fit snugly against his neck. Cold as it was now, Tomkins knew that it would get much worse. The Norkaan range boasted the highest peaks and suffered the most severe weather.

He fought urges to go home, but these new friends had grown close to him, and he felt a tug of loyalty to continue. For the time being, he moved on. If he could muster the courage, he would stay for the duration.

Rahg practiced with his shield as they rode. The wind battering his weaves tested his strength and his stamina, and he knew that was the key to growing strong. "Stretch yourself every day," Aentarra advised, "and you will grow strong."

A shield to block the wind was one of the crudest and easiest designs, but because it struggled against an element it proved to be taxing. To incorporate an insulating factor and keep out wind and cold required a more complex weave, and while Rahg had learned the weave, he found it more than difficult to sustain at any useful size.

Camissa noticed the strain on his face. "Rahg, rest for a while."

"I have to keep practicing."

"I know," she said, "but if you exhaust yourself, and then we need you, what good would that do? Learn to keep a reserve, even while stretching your limits."

"All right." Rahg let the shield drop.

A gust of wind hit Tobias from behind. "Lad, I wish you would warn me when you do that. It's colder than a Victa's heart." Tobias pulled his cloak tighter. "Mulka, I'd like to have some of your fur right now."

Camissa laughed.

TOMKINS FACED a fork of the two trails. One broke quickly north and at a steep incline, while the other continued almost due east. "Which way, Rhaven?"

Rhaven stared down the paths as if he could see something the others had missed. "I should scout the trails first. Perhaps this is a good time to rest."

"No need," Mulka said. "My people told of this juncture before we departed. We head north into the mountains. This is the last direction we have from them. After this, we are on our own, though I believe we will find it easy to locate the Chun."

"More likely they'll locate us," Tomkins said.

Rhaven nodded. "You heard Mulka. Let's go."

After riding for half the day, Rahg grew anxious again. "Are you sure this is the way to go?" He asked the same question three times, and the response had been as consistent.

Mulka possessed infinite patience. "Nothing has changed since you first asked. The stars have not shifted, and the mountains have not moved. Trust me. This is the way, though we might all regret it when we meet the Chun."

"The Chun are the ones you spoke of—the protectors of these lands?"

Mulka nodded. "They have guarded the mountains for many lifetimes, defending against the hordes of Cergala. If not for the Chun, Arangar would have surely fallen."

Tomkins kept them moving at a strong pace, and though the wind had faded, it remained cold. The trail continued to narrow until they could no longer progress with the wagon. "We'll have to leave the wagon," Rhaven said.

Tobias began unhitching the horse. "Lend a hand, lad. We'll pack what we can on this one, and whatever's left over we'll split among the rest."

Rhaven spotted a nice clearing close to the trail. "We'll make camp there," he said, pointing to it. "Darkness comes quickly in the mountains."

AFTER SUPPER they sat around the fire telling stories; mostly listening to Tobias, but occasionally someone else got a stray word in. Rhaven walked off into the woods. He sat against a large maple tree, Kella by his side.

Mulka cast a glance to Rhaven. "Doesn't he have friends? Who does he share his thoughts with?"

"Rhaven?" Camissa asked. "The only companion he has is his shadow and perhaps that vargel. But he's not the kind to confide in another man."

TWO MORE DAYS of travel had them scaling heights that cast shadows on the lesser mountains. The cold grew colder, and the air grew thinner. Fortune had smiled on them though, as the wind had subsided, save the occasional flare-up, and even those proved not too unbearable. Late afternoon brought sight of a village tucked into the side of one of the mountains on a gentle slope.

Tomkins halted. Cautious fear forced the stop. No one knew what this encounter would bring. "Should we go in there tonight?"

Rhaven sat high astride Argus, keen eyes scanning the area. "They've already seen us. Probably knew we were coming since early in the day. Stay alert, but keep your hands away from your weapons."

"What about Kella?" Rahg asked. "And Mulka and the welgar? Mulka can't stay in these mountains by himself."

Mulka warmed at Rahg's concern. "It will not discomfort me to stay by myself; besides, I have Garnock. He has been with me since birth."

"We go in together," Rhaven said. "I'd bet the people in these mountains are less concerned about Mulka."

"I don't know about walking in there with a welgar," Tomkins said. "People don't like welgars."

Rhaven's face cracked the thinnest of smiles. "They don't like welgars because they fear them. It will help us to be seen as a friend of the vargel and the welgar."

THE VILLAGE WAS SMALL, forty or fifty huts, no more. Rhaven estimated that half of the people met them at the edge of town, though the sight of Kella and Garnock forced most to step back. He searched the crowd looking for the ones who didn't retreat. They would be the leaders, the people he needed to speak with.

Two large men caught his gaze. Rhaven dismounted, advancing with his palms facing upward. Some of their tension faded, but when their eyes found Kella and Garnock, the fear returned.

"You are strangers to our lands, yet I see you come with peace in your heart."

Rhaven nodded, slowly lowering his hands, but careful to keep them away from weapons. Two men facing him had lessened their grip on the swords. "We have more than peace in our heart; we have food to share."

The men tried to contain their smiles but failed. Other villagers moved closer, probably eager to confirm what they thought they heard. Mountain tribes, no matter the lands they are from, lean toward suspicion.

"Why share food with us? Has the drought passed and the Valley bloomed?" And what spirits do you dance with to walk with those who eat our flesh?"

Camissa caught their thoughts and immediately used her power to converse with Rhaven. This is Camissa. They fear Garnock, and that makes them distrust us.

Rhaven almost responded aloud, but caught himself and simply nodded. Can you hear me, Camissa? He noted her nod, so continued. Ask Mulka to show that Garnock means no harm. Then Rhaven turned to Rahg. "Bring me some cheese and meat. Jarrell, you help. Bring wine also."

The mens' eyes shifted to his side, and they tensed again, firmly gripping sword hilts.

Garnock advanced to stand beside Rhaven, rubbing against his leg. Camissa's thoughts came to him again. Garnock said he will let you pick him up.

Rhaven nearly growled himself.

Tell Mulka I will get even with him for this.

Rhaven bent down and gently lifted the welgar. Garnock only weighed about as much as a large dog, but he looked larger with the thick fur. Garnock acted his part though, letting Rhaven hold him without showing any threatening signs.

The villagers stared wide-eyed, and Camissa let Rhaven know that they felt more at ease. Once the villagers got past the shock of seeing a welgar and the vargel, the thought of the food overwhelmed them.

A mother of four young children embraced Rhaven, even while he still held Garnock. His face reddened, a rare sight, and he gently unwrapped the woman's arms, then placed the welgar on the ground. "Go back to Mulka."

After animated greetings, Rhaven assumed control of dividing the food. It was obvious these people had not eaten good meals in a long time. He gave a full one fourth of their supplies to the villagers.

They feasted well that night, celebrating with full plates and full stomachs. Sated appetites made friendly conversation, and the villagers all wore smiles while they listened to news of other parts of Arangar, told mostly by Tomkins.

Rhaven partook of the idle chatting, but his interests lay more with information gathering. He had been speaking with Nolar, the village chief, who seemed to know everything about the mountains.

"Where do you want to go?" Nolar asked. "I can help with directions or a guide."

Rhaven hesitated, not knowing how much to say. "To the Chun village."

Nolar stared at him. "Which Chun village? There are a thousand Chun towns in these mountains."

"So many?"

Nolar looked at him as if he knew nothing. "The Norkaan Mountains stretch for hundreds of leagues, and the Chun own the Norkaans."

Rhaven sat silent while Nolar continued. "Why do you seek the Chun? They don't like strangers. The Chun like no one."

Rhaven again wondered how much he should say. "We seek a place called the Paaren. Do you know of it?"

Nolar's face lost its color and its warmth. "Everyone in the mountains knows of the Paaren, but if anyone knows where it is, it would be at the village of Korg, chief of all Chun. But..."

"What?" Rhaven asked.

"It is a forbidden place. A place of death."

Rhaven sighed. "So I have heard. Do you know where to find Korg's village?"

"On the mountain with the highest peak. They say the Chugarran Path is on that mountain also."

"Will you show me which way to go?"

"I will go with you," Nolar said.

"Do you have a family?"

"A wife," Nolar said. "My child died."

"Stay with your wife. I suspect that few of us, if any, will return." Nolar began to protest, but Rhaven forestalled him. "No! You owe us nothing. Certainly not your life. We gave you the food because your people had a need. Just tell me where to go and we'll manage."

Nolar argued no more. "Enjoy the night, my friend Rhaven. We will speak again tomorrow."

IT WAS ALMOST mid morning before they were ready to leave. Nolar gave Rhaven instructions on how to get close to Korg's village, or at least to the mountain where the village was. "You will not need to know more than that, as the Chun will surely greet you long before you are lost. It is their greeting I would worry about. Remember what I said, many of the Chun tribes are as bad as the barbarians themselves."

"I remember, Nolar. Now we must leave. Farewell."

Nolar extended his hand. "My good friend, Rhaven, may your journey be as safe as the gods allow."

AENTARRA APPEARED in a shadow in the darkest part of the forest. It was still a long way from the Paaren, but she was beginning to get excited. Soon, the journey would begin, at least the first phase of the journey, and after that... "Ah!" Aentarra forced herself to remain calm. This phase must be completed before the next could begin. Many would die. The numbers held no meaning, no importance. Only the result mattered.

As RAHG DRIFTED off to sleep, his head seemed to be swimming, swirling in a violent sea. He felt dizzy, but when he tried to get up, he fell back down. Not the dragon again, he thought, but soon it became apparent it would not be the same dream.

A mist swirled inside his head, blurred his vision. Then the pain began, pain like he had never felt before. Throbbing started deep in his brain then worked its way outward, increasing as it moved. He rolled on the ground, grasping his head with both hands, but nothing would stop the pain, and when he tried to cry out, he was mute.

Rahg felt like quitting, giving up, letting whoever or whatever caused the torture to have what they want, but somehow he knew that if he did, he'd die. Something inside told him that if he stopped resisting, they would take his mind and never let go.

Rahg reached deep inside himself, deeper than he'd ever been before until he found the strength to go on, strength to fight back. He gritted his teeth, put one hand on the ground and pushed himself to his knees. Soon the fog cleared though the pain remained. Then a light shone, a huge column filled with millions of pulsing lights, and the pulsing seemed to keep time with the throbbing in his head.

"Stop it!" he managed to scream. "Why are you doing this?"

The column grew closer, bigger. The pulsations remained the same, except as he drew nearer the pain grew worse. He thought he heard a voice, distant, perhaps an echo, then it faded, and the incessant, pulsing vibrations returned. Torturing him. Tearing at his head from deep within.

Just when Rahg thought he could take no more, as he was about to give up, the voice returned, louder this time, more insistent.

"Kill them," the voice said. "Kill them all!"

ANCIENT ECHOES

Centarra quickened her pace. Around the next bend lay the entrance to the Hall of Echoes and the mysteries of the ages that it contained. The memory of whispered voices from aeons ago rang in her head, taunted her with riddles of the Paaren. *I must know who they are,* she thought and increased her pace even more.

She continued down the Great Path, the noise from her heels slapping the floors echoing as she walked. It didn't seem like so long ago that someone would have come to investigate the noise. Now it went unnoticed.

Great Path

Two slabs of huge marble barred the entrance, but they opened as she approached. Aentarra's excitement grew, for she knew that as soon as she crossed the threshold a thousand times a thousand conversations would assault the senses, crowd the air.

All that remained was for her to find the spot and decipher the meanings of the true voices, determine who they belonged to. She recognized her voice from only moons ago. It rang loud and true, each syllable distinct, each sound discernible. Another familiar tone caught her ear—Xanthes. His too was crisp and clear. And that was Sonella. Aentarra smiled.

She listened, filtering the familiar sounds and allowing only the unrecognizable ones to sift through. She heard the bellow of Lukaan and the treacherous whispering plots of the other Banished Ones. Ghruehne's grating voice brought a sneer, and thoughts of how she would kill him filled her mind as she worked her way toward the center of the hall. Once she was in the center she would not have to listen to all this banter, only the sounds she sought rang true there.

The Hall of Echoes rode high on Aentarra's list of favorite places to spend time. Listening to the carefully chosen words and phrases, and being able to identify the speakers of those voices would help her piece together the puzzle that hid behind the cacophony. There were voices in there that she could not recognize, could not put a face to. And there shouldn't be.

Those mysterious voices belonged to someone other than those she came with, and if that were true then it meant that they were from before, and if they were from before her time, from the race of whoever had built Vallah and many of the other places she had seen, then perhaps they knew the secrets to the portals.

Now she had proof, at least some proof, that whoever was here before them knew of the portals, otherwise how would the Entirians have known; how would their legends have spoken of them. Certainly, none of the immortals had ever talked of the portals, not with any outside of themselves.

Most were too afraid. They all remembered the horrors and the dread of the portals, even if they tried to banish it from their memories. And all had felt the touch of fear. Even Lukaan

But that was before he had grown so strong. From everything she could discern from her spies planted in Sethia, he had continued to grow stronger since the banishment. How strong he was now was only a guess, but if even a small part, if even the tiniest part of a small part were true, then he indeed was strong. Stronger than the rest of them combined.

Good. I will need that power to plan my revenge. When the time is right, the Seven Lights of Council will be no more than a memory.

Aentarra focused again, concentrated, cleared her head of all unwanted sounds, all unwanted thoughts. Even the faintest, most-remote thought would distract her, and even the hint of a sound would void what she might hear as a clue.

Trying to hear the voices of the ones she sought was like trying to hear the splash of a pebble in the endless sea as the waves hammered their fury on the rocks. But there was always that lull, that brief intermission no matter how minute, like when all the waves were receding, and the others had not yet crested.

There was the tiniest lull when there was no noise, the briefest hint of silence. If she could pick up those sounds during that period, she might gain clues. It would take time, but she had that, and she had patience. It took that too. The clever person, the dutiful one, the one who meticulously recorded the words of each conversation, could eventually piece together thoughts and conclude who said what to whom and when. It would be invaluable information.

Thoughts were always able to be distinguished from spoken voices, even though they might have sometimes sounded similar, there was a difference.

She listened to the banter of useless conversations—petty arguments, whispers of love and lies, and so many half-spoken truths. She listened carefully to the slightest intonations, the way a word was formed, the mouthing of it, the syllabic emphasis. And the cadence of the speech itself. Kiris had a melodic voice, an almost sing/song, up and down pattern that was as reliable as the sun's position at dawn.

Aentarra smiled at Mikkellana's whispers of love to Xanthes. She did not need to piece the thoughts together with this. She knew that they would be identical, they would mark the same. Not a hint or a whisper or an intonation that differed from her spoken words. She had doted on that fool Xanthes.

A chuckle escaped, one that would stay forever in the Hall. The thought that accompanied it soon followed.

But that is fine that she doted on him, it distracted him enough to allow me to accomplish what I needed. Allowed me to weave my web, and he fell into it. As did all the others, though I needed no distraction to snare them. Someday, someone might stand here and try to piece together my own words and thoughts, and if they are clever enough, they will see just how clever I was. Though I doubt they'd be able to unweave what I have woven.

She waited. Patience was not a virtue she had inherited, but for this, she forced it upon herself. More than half the day had gone by; she had already heard one of Sonella's nauseating songs. The poor woman thought she had a voice, but the frogs that crept the ponds at nights sung better than her. And she had heard Tirzinitzia's discourse on battle strategies twice already, but nothing of any importance. Nothing of what she sought.

She knew from experimenting that she had to stand in the right spot. It wasn't good enough to be in the center where she could hear the normal echoes; she had to find the precise center of the center. Even the weight of her feet had to be placed just right, and as she shifted here and there, she began to feel that it was growing right.

She felt a small tingling as if it were about to happen again. Instantly, Aentarra wove the shield, one she had practiced so many times. It was a special shield, but to her knowledge, no one else had ever investigated before, and if they had, they had never spoken of it. Though, that would not be unusual. She'd never reveal any secret that she discovered. A new way to use a weapon was not something to share with an enemy. Aentarra couldn't help but laugh as she recalled how she had discovered the new use of the shield, how to screen out sounds.

SHE HAD BEEN CLOAKED and watching Rahg practice with his shield shortly after he had discovered his powers. The boy was frantic with fear when she had told him Iazzo was coming for him, so when she had given him instructions on how to practice and grow stronger, he had taken it to heart. While practicing and having people shoot arrows and strike at him with swords, he made the delighted observation that even though the shield blocked everything out and nothing could hurt him, he could hear everything they said, and could hear the noise as the arrows and blades hit the shield. It was a sound unlike any he thought of. It was not a sound like steel meeting steel, but more like a crackling of fire when fresh pine was used.

Aentarra realized it was not a new observation, recalling the thousands upon thousands of times that she had woven a shield and heard noises seep through, but she just so happened to be thinking about the library and the Hall of Echoes when she heard Rahg's observation uttered aloud, and it struck a chord with her. A brilliant idea emerged, though she didn't know how brilliant at the time. Aentarra left immediately to go and experiment, where she shortly discovered without too many tests, that sound struck the shield in ways different than an object, or even light.

With enough practice, Aentarra mastered ways of filtering the sound. "By the blood!" She cursed herself for not having discovered this long ago. Especially her. She was the one with the powers of stealth, the only one with that long-lost power.

As she thought about it, she realized that it used some of the same principles. When fully Cloaked, no one could hear any noise she made, so it was simply working in reverse. And even while using the power of stealth, when no one could hear her, she could still hear them, that was the key, it was not simply a sound-proof shield, but a specially constructed one that filtered sound in some manner.

This was a new aspect, and it wasn't just a sword, but a double-edged sword.

As she experimented with filters, it proved easy to go from having all sound come in to having no sound come in, almost like building a "block shield" as it was called, the ones made only to stop large objects, not fire, or arrows. The tightest shield, the most dense would stop all attacks, including fire.

Then she experimented with letting in only a little bit of sound, or letting in certain sounds and not others. During a storm, she discovered she could block out the harsh, explosive sounds of the thunder and let the patter of the raindrops remain. She experimented in the forest, where she blocked the wind bending the boughs of the trees and snapping the leaves and small twigs, but she let the gentle chirping of the birds remain.

Aentarra went further to block all except the faintest of sounds and was amazed at what she could truly hear. When she blocked the wind, the birds could be heard plainly, clearly, each song a melody to be savored. Then when she blocked the birds she could hear other things that had been silent: the rustling of the squirrels as they jumped from branch to branch; the chipmunk as its claws dug into the bark of a tree to scurry to safety; a mother raccoon pushing her babies back into the nest; and a fox that ducked into the hollow of a log when it sensed her presence.

Her curiosity became greatly aroused. This was much more than she had hoped for. It could have far greater applications than even the Hall of Echoes, but it might prove to work wonders in the Hall itself.

As she blocked other sounds, she was amazed at the clarity of what she heard next. Among the duff of the forest floor, a whip snake nervously rustled a leaf or two and slithered under some bramble. And nearby a bee in its hive danced directions to fellow hive members on where to find food, the humming sounds reaching her ears as if they hovered beside her head.

At first, the experiments in the hall amounted to nothing—if anything she had blocked all sound, with no chance of her hearing the faintest of whispers. She grew exasperated, but she knew patience would pay.

She wondered anew how to use this knowledge to her advantage because, as difficult as it was to find the exact spot where she could hear them, the ones she wanted, how many times had she passed over them when other voices had been talking and she couldn't hear. How many countless precious moments had she already wasted because of that. If she could only find some way to curtail the noise, to filter that out and listen only to them—then, she could make progress.

She was relaxing one day, enjoying one of her greatest pleasures in life —listening to the birds sing. She filtered out all sound but the birds so that she could enjoy them undisturbed. Her heart swayed at the sound of the giant woodpeckers as one big male drummed a love song to his mate. Laughter came at the sound of the mocking bird, the great mimicker, and its rendition of a blue jay. She reveled in the deep-throated croak of a raven, but then stopped. Something was amiss. Not far from where she stood a dozen or more crows, the great alarmists of the forest were cawing raucously, but she couldn't hear them. She dropped her filters and, sure enough, she could hear the crows cawing loudly.

It didn't take many more experiments to determine that she could filter out certain birds and leave others to pleasure her. Aentarra didn't know how this was going to help her, but she knew it was important. Then one day, while watching Rahg, someone's voice reminded her of a crow, and that's when it struck her.

A crow!

Memory forced her thoughts to new areas. She listened to the remainder of their conversation as if it meant life and death. It very well could mean that, but for whom, she could only guess. When she was done, she went to listen to more people speak. A tavern provided a host of conversations to open ears, and if most were male it didn't matter, the voices were as different as if an equal mix of women and men had been there. Each one rode on a different wind. Next, Aentarra listened by the windows of peoples' homes to hear wives and children speak. She listened to old men and women, to babies' cries, and to young boys, before their voices cracked for the first time. She listened to them in all scenarios, and she cataloged the sounds in her mind, a mind that could hold so much information. Once she gathered enough, she shifted to the Hall of Echoes. It was time to note her observations.

All night she recorded her observations with meticulous detail and barely a moment's rest. Her blood raced too fast to rest. She could not afford rest now, not with what she knew. She had discovered that people were just like the birds, each had a separate sound, and though this was nothing new to add to a knowledge base in itself, everyone knew that they could discern most people's voice from another, most could even hear a whisper, even a disguised voice and recognize it if it was one they had heard often enough, but Aentarra discovered that voices were not just different, they were unique. Unique in such a way that once she heard them and thought of them in the way that they rode the waves in the wind, then, she would forever be able to recognize that voice, and she would be able to create a filter for that voice, and once done, whenever she heard that voice again, whether it was a whisper or a shout, it would be filtered.

In this manner, she could soon arrive at the point where she could recognize everyone she knew in the Hall of Echoes and create filters for them one at a time. Ultimately, she would be left with only the voices of those she didn't know, and that is what she needed. To be able to listen to "them."

TRIBAL OATHS

The paths grew narrower, the inclines steeper, the weather colder, and still Rhaven pressed on relentlessly. There had been no encounters with the Chun yet, but Rhaven said he had seen them watching. "They know we're here. It's only a matter of time before they confront us. Remember, give them no cause to attack."

Anxiety sunk to the depths of Rahg's bones, that he could conceal it from the rest of them gave him some pride. Practice with his shielding had almost ceased. Use of his powers required focus, and anxiety was the enemy of focus. He evaded questions about his practice with half-truths and near-lies. Shame spread its blanket over him, diffused every attempt to lift his spirits, to spark his will.

CAMISSA NOTICED the change in Rahg, but she kept it to herself. She sensed his fear, but she too had experienced fear, and the memory was far too recent for her to condemn him for the same. She had been working on new aspects of her powers, aspects she had tried to improve of late.

Suggestion could be a powerful weapon if she learned how to wield it like Rahg did his shield. She foresaw a time when she could instill the will to live in a sick person or infuse a strong man with fear. Camissa sighed. She would try to lend a little confidence to Rahg.

Camissa thought of all the times she felt so full, so charged with life, of all the times when confidence walked with her side by side. Then she recalled the air that ever-rode with Wisp, a man born with an excess of confidence, a never–ending, inexhaustible supply. She felt the experience, smelled it, tasted it, and saw it. She had come to realize that all feelings and emotions looked different and felt different.

With her recall of Wisp and her own experiences, she had the mark of confidence. Only one step remained. She went back into her mind and relived the times that Rahg had felt the power of confidence: when he protected her in Pomanda; when he worked his shield for the first time in Entiria; and when he had held against the ferocious attack of Iazzo, even if it was a momentary event.

There! She had it. The unique imprint of his confidence, with its twists and peculiarities. She pushed the thought out of her mind, slowly, ever so slowly she moved it toward Rahg. The first step was to let it touch him, then pull back. The next touch lingered longer, then retreated. Finally, after much massaging, she let it hover in a cloud above his head, like a morning fog over a wintry lake.

Soon she saw Rahg smile as he remembered the scene in Pomanda. He sat straighter in the saddle when he recalled his first shield. Camissa knew he was on his way. Soon his confidence would be restored. Camissa smiled. She had been successful in her first test of Suggestion, and there was much more to learn, so much more.

∼

MIDWAY ACROSS THE EXPANSE, Rhaven alerted them.

"Riders coming." Rhaven scanned the surroundings but saw no way to reach shelter before they arrived.

There were thirty to forty men, riding fast. As they drew closer the count seemed to grow; there were at least forty, perhaps as many as fifty or sixty. Being in the middle of a flat open plain there was no safe retreat, no trees or rocks, not even a hill to use for defense.

"Hold still," Rhaven ordered. "Katsu, with me. Jarrell, you and Tobias, and Tomkins take a second line, spread thin. Camissa, behind them in line with me. Rahg, keep to the rear and form a shield when necessary. Mulka, tell Garnock and Kella to flank you and only come up if trouble starts."

Rhaven sat still, awaiting their arrival.

RHAVEN MADE DECISIONS FAST. And he always seems to be right.

As the riders drew closer, fear crept in on Camissa. Rhaven had not drawn his weapons, but he never did until the last moment. Tobias and Jarrell had bows ready, arrows nocked. Katsu had his sword across his lap.

She watched, knowing that soon another battle would begin, more blood would be shed. When the attackers were almost upon them, Rahg initiated his plan, weaving a shield to throw between the two groups. He had almost completed the weave when Rhaven charged ahead to meet them.

"No, Rhaven, no!" Rahg shouted as he put the shield in place, but Rhaven passed through. The enemy crashed into the invisible barrier, stunning the first line and sending the others into confusion. Meanwhile, Rhaven swept through their left flank cutting down warriors at an alarming rate.

Tobias and Jarrell fired their first shots, only to see the arrows bounce off the shield. "Protect Rhaven," Tobias shouted.

Rahg wove another shield to separate the others from Rhaven, but five of them had gotten inside the shield and fought with him fiercely. Before Rahg could do anything else, Garnock got inside the shield also. He was merciless in his slaughter, between him and Rhaven the enemy stood no chance.

Soon those five lay dead, and Rhaven and Garnock were back within the protection of the shield. The Chun had retreated about twenty to thirty paces and sat astride their mounts staring.

One of them continued a maddening assault on the shield. His face was painted green and brown, and his hair had been shorn. Howls of rage emerged from him, and wild thrashing with his sword continued, though he could obviously see it did no good.

"Let him through the shield, Rahg."

"There's no sense in killing him. I can keep him out."

"Let him through."

Rahg let the shield down, and the man charged through, his attack aimed directly at Rhaven.

Camissa grimaced, sure she would witness yet more bloodshed, but to her surprise, Rhaven dismounted and used his sai to disarm the man.

The warrior drew a knife from a sheath at his side and renewed the attack as ferociously as before. He managed to surprise Rhaven and cut him badly on the leg, just above the knee. Rhaven pummeled him with the pommel of his sai, knocking the man to the ground.

He lay there, dead to all appearances, but then slowly pushed himself up and again attacked, this time barehanded. Rhaven casually knocked him cold, then checked the man for other weapons. "Tie him up. I want to question him."

Tobias worked on binding the man while Camissa tried tending to Rhaven's leg, though he pushed her aside.

"It has to be healed, Rhaven."

"Later. I need to speak to these people. Rahg, protect me with a shield." Rhaven approached with palms facing upward. The warriors wore cautious looks, and all hands gripped weapons. "We have not come seeking blood," Rhaven said. "We have come to visit the Chun in peace."

One man moved forward, his horse stepping lightly. "You face death like one who has lost his wife. I grieve for your sorrow and your loss."

Rhaven felt confused. "I have no wife and never have. I have no sorrow save the loss of your people. They didn't need to die."

The leader looked back to his brethren, bewildered. "If you have not lost your wife then we bow to your honor." The tribesmen bowed low.

There was a gaunt look to the men, a look Rhaven had seen in most everyone since coming to this land. Hunger. He bowed low himself. "I wish to honor your dead. And to share a meal with our new friends."

The leader snapped attentively. "You offer your food to us; I am ashamed. You have our honor in your hands."

Rhaven smiled at them. "I share my food to those I would call friend, not to claim their honor."

The tribesmen smiled. "Then let us go eat, new friend. My warriors call me Brun." He extended his hand in a closed fist.

Rhaven didn't know what to do but guessed. He extended his fist to touch Brun's, knuckle to knuckle. "I'm called Rhaven."

Another smile lit Brun's face. "Another good omen. Our tribe has long honored the raven. Let us eat."

They walked to where Rahg and Camissa were, but stopped short at the sight of Garnock; they had seen him kill. When they saw Mulka, all of them fell to their knees. "You didn't tell us you travel with the favorites of the gods. We had thought the Pathfinders to be gone long ago."

Mulka bowed in return. "As you now see, we are still with you."

The painted warrior awoke and came to kneel before Rhaven, his head hung low. Rhaven tried pulling him to his feet, but the man refused to stand.

"He is waiting for you to take his head," Brun explained.

Camissa gasped. "Take his head! Why?"

It is his right to request it since you defeated him in battle. His name is Jorn, and he has waited ten battles to be killed. Now it is time to visit his wife."

Jorn smiled. "My wife left me long ago. She went to the Chugarran Path alone. I promised her I would come soon, but no one has killed me." Jorn looked to Rhaven, eyes pleading with him to get it over with quickly. His wife waited.

Rhaven stared for a long time, lost in thoughts of his own. He knew the feeling, the desire to meet death with honor. How many times had he rushed to greet death only to be spared again and again. He would not let this one free so easily. "Get up, Jorn. I won't take your life."

"It is your right," Jorn said, then with more conviction. "It is my right. I demand it for honor."

Rhaven knelt to stare at Jorn face–to–face, his voice the softest whisper. "I'll give you your chance, friend. But you will have to earn it, just like I have to earn mine. I've been waiting for death for much longer than you. But I promise this, come with us, and before long, I will present you with many opportunities to join your mate. In one of them, you will be sure to meet her, as we all will. If you truly wish to die honorably and go to see your loved one, then join us."

Jorn laughed. "I accept," he said, and with that, he stood. Rhaven handed him back his weapons, and Jorn immediately put the knife blade to his heart, the hilt facing Rhaven. "As deep as your honor allows," he said proudly.

Rhaven looked to Brun for explanation. "It is a custom. You are allowing him to face death with you so you must take his honor to keep until each battle begins. You are to puncture as deep as you dare with the blade. If you go too deep it is dishonor to you; not deep enough and you shame Jorn."

Rhaven understood. Some tribes had customs that demanded that honor be proven over and over again. He grasped the hilt of the blade and pushed, swiftly but sure as a healer's touch. Jorn clenched his teeth tightly. He couldn't cry out, but this was not an easy touch; Rhaven had much honor.

Rhaven pushed a little more, runnels of blood trickled down Jorn's bared chest. If he had to ask Rhaven to stop, he would feel the shame of cowardice. Before the bleeding grew too bad, Rhaven withdrew the blade and handed it back to him.

"I now have your honor, Jorn, but you will have many causes to use it soon. Very soon."

*J*orn proved to be a valuable asset almost as soon as he agreed to join them. The location of the Chun village belonging to Korg was no longer a mystery; Jorn had been there before.

His presence also forestalled attacks by other Chun tribes. If Jorn was not known to them personally, his painted face and shorn hair told them what tribe he claimed allegiance to, and it let them know a fight would be to the death.

Rhaven asked questions continually, drawing information from Jorn like water from a well. Jarrell and Rahg walked together, climbing a steep part of the trail where they had to dismount. They had been walking almost all morning, and Jarrell found himself short of breath.

"Fast pace he's setting for this treacherous path. Would have thought that he'd slow down a bit with a wound like that in his leg."

Tobias had been close behind them, and his laughter made Jarrell turn. "Rhaven tolerates pain no more than he does foolishness; he'll not let a wound like that slow him down. I believe he'd have to lose a leg to get to a pace a normal man would set."

The trail finally opened up where the terrain softened. The horses had plenty of room, and large trees offered some respite from the wind that had battered them during the earlier phase of the journey. It was still a rugged trail, but one that was more comfortable than before.

Jorn saw an appropriate site for camp and suggested they stay there. "Korg's village is a half a day's ride from here. This would be a good place to spend the night."

Jorn stuck to Rhaven like Garnock did to Mulka. They talked most of the night until Rhaven suggested everyone retire. "Tomorrow will be another long day."

By late morning, they had reached the trail to Korg's village. Jorn took the lead to let the Chun see him. Halfway up the trail, Jorn called back to Rhaven. "They see us. We will soon be met."

At a juncture of several paths, a group of warriors waited with grim faces. "Hold, painted man. What business does the Pango tribe have in Korg's village?"

Jorn sat straight in the saddle, his back rigid as an oak. "My companions have business with Korg. We would speak to him."

Several of the tribe cast sidelong glances, then the leader spoke. "You will follow us," he said, and turned about, climbing yet again. The sun had just passed midday when they reached the village, larger than most Rahg had seen in these mountains, but nothing to rival even a small city. Warriors gathered to gawk, even women and children lined the way.

A large building dominated an open space near the center of the village. Standing before it was a line of people Rahg presumed to be the leaders. Some were obviously the elders, a few looked to be war chiefs, but obvious in her difference stood a small woman, frail of body, but her fierceness held her tall. She had eyes that matched the sky and wore an expression as hard as ice.

"Who comes to the village of Korg, Pango man?"

Jorn's feet hit the ground firmly, and he bowed his head. "Jorn of the Pango, husband to a wife who waits at the top of the Chugarran Path."

Sama wore an understanding smile. "May her wait be short, Jorn of the Pango." Her finger under his chin lifted him. "You address Sama, wife to Korg. I have wept for many, but I have tears left for you."

Jorn looked at her soft features, where before he only saw hardness. "I am honor–bound to Rhaven, who has come across many lands to see Korg. His honor is my honor."

Rhaven slid from Argus's back and somehow insinuated himself next to Jorn, in front of Sama. He motioned for Kella to stay behind, then bowed low to Sama. "I am called Rhaven. I have traveled far to speak with Korg, Chief of the Chun and Warlord of Arangar. These others travel as my companions with peace in our hearts."

Sama lifted Rhaven's chin as she had Jorn's, all the while she eyed Argus and the other horses—they could feed many. "Your companions include a welgar and a Pathfinder, and a beast I do not know.

Who are you to claim friendship to people who abandoned us so long ago? Who are you to walk with a welgar, whose teeth have tasted our flesh? Who are you to command the obedience of a beast that the Chun have never seen? And what do you wish from Korg?"

There was suspicion in her questions, doubt in her words. "What I have to say must be for Korg's ears alone."

Sama's face held scorn. "You will have to travel far to catch Korg's ear. He has not been back in several moons."

"I have come far already. I can go a little more."

She shook her head as if to dismiss Rhaven. "You will never find him."

Rhaven detected a note of sorrow in Sama's words. "I will try," Rhaven said, "If you tell me where to look."

Sama had heard enough and had wasted enough of her time. "He is gone!" she shouted. "Where he has gone you cannot follow. Where he has gone, he cannot return."

"The Paaren." Rhaven barely whispered, but Sama must have heard.

"What did you say?" Her voice showed renewed interest in the conversation.

"So I'm right," Rhaven said. "He has gone to the Paaren, the Forbidden Lands."

Sama nodded perfunctorily. "How did you know?"

Rhaven stared at her, and for the first time, Sama must have seen the ice in his eyes.

"I told you we came to see Korg, but the reason we came was to find a way to enter the Paaren. We are on a mission that takes us there. Can you show the way?"

Hope showed in Sama's expression. "Those who enter the Paaren never return."

Rhaven nodded. "Those who have entered before us have never had a Pathfinder."

Sama had learned to make quick decisions from Korg. She held no fear of being wrong. "Pau, gather thirty men. We will need no supplies; there will be food aplenty where we go."

Pau looked at Sama as if she asked him to walk through the Gates of Death, but he bowed stiffly, then hurried to complete his orders.

"If we truly don't need supplies, Sama, then I have plenty we could leave with your people. They look hungry." Rhaven grabbed her arm. "But if we go to the Paaren, I'll need to leave our horses here, and I expect them to be here when we return."

Sama's eyes teared. "The Ancient Ones have not abandoned us," she said. "They only test our resolve." She looked to Rhaven. "It is a long march to where we go. We need food for seven or eight days."

Rhaven nodded. "With as many men as you have, we'll have little left to share with your people."

"We need to find my husband first. Then we can worry about food."

CHUN PREPARATIONS

Sama and Pau had been gone seven days when Chande called a meeting of chiefs from all the Norkaans. More than three hundred came, with little else to do other than scavenge for food. Clan chiefs knew to bring food and tents, but still, the crowd taxed Korg's village. By the end of the second day, all of them had arrived. The air bristled with energy.

Torne stood taller than most men, sturdy too—an old oak among elms and maples. Famine had stripped the meat from his bones, but what remained a chisel could not cut.

"We crossed two peaks to get here, Chande. We have come, but we don't know why. Where is Korg? Where is Pau? The last time these fires warmed my blood, they stood above you."

Chande wore a thin frame, all Chun did now, but his was thin before the famine, thin even as a child. Ambition had been infused into his bones at birth, and he had lost none of that.

Fear had never grown on Chande's frame, though others said nothing grew on a frame so thin, not wisdom, not knowledge, and certainly not intelligence.

"Korg is gone." He shouted loud enough for all to hear. The winds were quiet this night, and with his first words, the crowd quieted, too. "Pau follows Sama. They would have us walk on the forbidden path." Murmurs raced among them, jumping from ear to ear. "When Korg is away, rule falls to Pau and then to rest on my shoulders."

A wave of heads nodded, bounced on necks as frail as half-year saplings. "Cergala has food!" he screamed. "Food for the taking. On the other side of the Norkaans, they fatten their bellies while our young starve."

Torne stepped forward. "Chande, war is not the answer to all problems."

"Have they shared their food? Will they weep when our children die?" Chande climbed atop a rock so all could see him. "No! Cergala rejoices each time a Chun dies. One less warrior to guard the passes."

Chande spread his hands wide. "Torne is right. War doesn't solve all problems, but it will bring us food. When we push them from the passes, we will find a land of plenty. A new land to call our own. And when we are done, there will be no need to enter the Forbidden Lands."

The rumblings grew louder. Some clan chiefs drew swords to wave in the air, mingle with their shouts.

A few chiefs would go home and continue as they had, others might meet resistance at their own village councils, but many of them, far too many, had been infected with the rage of war. They would go home and incite their people, and then the Cergalans would die.

Torne took his son's arm and pulled him aside. "It is time we left, son. We can do no more here." He lowered his head as he left. It was a long walk back to the village, long and cold and hungry.

"A bad day, father."

"It will only get worse, my son. Much worse. War is now inevitable. The only question that remains is who they will follow—Sama or Chande."

CHANDE'S RISE

More than half of the chiefs sided with Chande, and almost all of them had returned with their warriors, whose idle blades thirsted for blood. Chande had taken note of who had not come; he would remember them. "Torne has stayed to tend the fire," Chande said, and several other chiefs laughed, but not Dronl, and five thousand warriors followed him.

"Torne decides for his own, as we each did." He gave each of them a glare as a rebuke. "Even in Chingua the old women talk to your face. Have the Chun chiefs resorted to whispering in each others' ears?"

Chande could ill afford in-fighting. If he was to rise to power, he must have the support of the strong ones. And he would rise. Had not his vision predicted it? Had not he been promised the rewards?

"Dronl is right. Torne has decided. We cannot fault him for doing what he believes is right, just as he cannot fault us for doing what we know is right." Chande laid a hand on the shoulder of each of the strongest chiefs. "Come, sit in my tent and be warm. We shall look at these passes and decide how the Cergalans shall fall." The chiefs laughed heartily as they moved inside and sat around the fire. Victory stood only a few leagues away.

The Norkaan Mountains formed the highest peaks in the world, summits that pierced the clouds like spires of the temples in Chingua. Impenetrable in any season, winter's cold reinforced their security. Only six locations allowed passage, but four of those proved so narrow that warriors could not march through more than two abreast.

Dronl addressed the group of chiefs. He was the most celebrated of those present, and if not for the traditions of succession that put Chande at the head of this meeting, he might be leading them to war. As it was, his strategy was respected.

"We leave Birn to guard the eastern passes. Send Tam and Woat with the men from their villages. Morva should guard the western passes. Her village has enough warriors to hold against any force."

Chande looked to Dronl. "Morva?"

Dronl knew he questioned his suggestion of a woman leader. "Morva has proven herself. Do not forget that the last man to question her is now in Chugarra." No one else objected. "The Cergalan Pass and the Forest Pass will pillar our attacks."

"They always guard those passes, Dronl."

Dronl nodded. "Birn will stand in the east. With the few thousand he has, he can hold against an army of thirty thousand or more. We know their army at the pass cannot stand against a large force. They do not expect an attack of this size. We will crush their army, then Vennala will fall."

"What good Vennala? They will come with all their might once word reaches the lowlands. Vennala will do us no good then."

Chande looked to the chief who had just spoken. Ulur was not known for his tactics, only his bravery. "Ulur, Vennala will not benefit us as a fortress, but it does hold food and supplies. We can also make sure that it does not serve Cergala any longer."

Dronl patted Ulur's back. "We will make them suffer if they wish to retaliate."

The other chiefs had listened to the discussion without input, but they all agreed with Dronl. Chande's smile cracked both his cheeks. "It is settled then. We leave tomorrow."

"So soon?" Ulur asked.

"Men must eat," Chande said. "We have no food."

THE CHUN GATHERED, and they followed Chande. Almost twenty thousand of them had massed for the attack, providing no warning to the Cergalans. The few who guarded the pass and the others posted as guards to alert Vennala in the event of an attack fell quickly. Soon Vennala's gates were down, then the slaughter began. "Kill them all," Chande ordered. "Every man, woman, and child. Take all the food, all the animals."

The Chun did as Chande ordered, slaughtering the men, doing worse to the women, even slaying the children while their mothers watched. And when they had finished with the butchery, and when they had claimed the food, then they put the city aflame.

On the march back to Arangar, men ate heartily and drank, and some did worse with the women they brought with them, the few who had not been killed.

ANOTHER CONVERSATION

The courier came to Melissara's dwelling. His rap on the door was tentative. Fear coursed his veins and, though the sun was not yet hot in Sethia, perspiration ran freely from his brow and onto his cheeks. The door cracked open to reveal a servant in white robes with the fiery red sun emblem directly over the heart. "For what purpose do you call on my mistress?"

Servants tended to take on the attitude of their master, the Wolfen messenger had heard, and he saw that this one was haughty and terse. "I bring a message, for your mistress' eyes only."

"I shall deliver it to her," the servant said.

"For her eyes only," the Wolfen snapped back but wished he hadn't as soon as the words escaped his lips. "I cannot shirk my duty," he offered in explanation, an attempt to assuage the slight to the servant, who was likely to tell her mistress. He only hoped that the one who had given it to him had been correct, for if the Lady Melissara didn't deem this message important enough, she might look with no favor upon him, and he had heard horrors of what happened to those she didn't smile upon.

Few trees in Sethia were granted enough water to grow large, but the nut trees in Melissara's courtyard were shared the exceptions with the ones surrounding Lukaan's palace and resting spot. The shade it provided, however, did nothing to stem the fever he felt in his body right at this moment.

"Come inside," the servant said. "I must wake my mistress."

The last she said with a twisted grin and a sadistic snarl, knowing that Melissara would be upset at being awakened. The Wolfen tried to control his shivering, but the chill from the tiles seemed to have stolen the warmth from his body, at least he hoped that is what it was.

A set of footfalls caught his attention, and he cast his gaze down the same corridor that the servant had vanished into. "Did you tell—" he had been about to question the servant, but to his shock and displeasure, he saw that Melissara had come down the hall with the servant, her footsteps silent.

He fell to his knees and let the beads of sweat from his head brush the cold tiles on the floor. He shivered upon hearing her words, the tone was cold, yet full of fire.

"Who sent you with this message that was for my eyes only? If it was not the Master, perhaps you should pray."

He shuddered at the thought of what he must do next, but he didn't know who was the more frightening. He bit his tongue as he tried to find the courage to speak the words. He could sense the impatience in the air, so he knew he better say something before she spoke again, or worse before she acted.

"Mistress, I beg the deepest apologies, but the one who sent me instructed me to say it was not only for your eyes only but for your ears only too."

He felt sure she glared at the top of his head, as he had not lifted it to speak. "Do you mean my servant?"

"Yes, Mistress. It was for your ears only."

A smile crossed Melissara's face; it appeared she would have someone to torture today. "Leave me, Paka," she said. "I want to be alone with this fool."

The servant's footsteps faded, and the Wolfen breathed a sigh of relief, but he dared not look up until Melissara allowed.

"Speak. The servant is gone."

"Mistress, with your blessing—"

"Look up, you fool, and address me. Hand me your message and tell me who has sent you."

The Wolfen reached into the sleeve of his robe and extracted a thin roll of parchment tied with a band of blue silk knotted into a fine bow. He stayed on his knees even though the hard floor hurt. He stretched his hand out to her, and she snatched the parchment away.

"Well, who sent you? And be quick about answering, my patience is thin."

"Mistress, I'm sorry, it was your sister, she—"

"Mikkellana? The fool."

"No, Mistress. Your other sister." He heard the pause and had braced himself for punishment, but when nothing came, he listened, even though he dared not look at her. He thought he could almost sense a smile on her lips, but he'd not look to confirm.

"Aentarra?" Melissara's voice rung with curiosity, not anger. "How did you come to receive this message. Are you certain it was from her?"

He didn't wish to be premature, but he felt a sigh of relief was in order. "Mistress, I was in the desert, outside of the Shield—"

"Of course it was outside of the Shield, you fool. Now get on with your story and do not belabor me with less than important details."

"Mistress, we...we were going to the caravan route, and she appeared. From nowhere."

"Who is we?"

"Sorry, Mistress. There were five of us. We were going to scout the caravan routes for raiding. When she appeared, we drew blades. Mistress, I'm sorry..." tears ran down his cheeks from eyes full with them. Real tears not ones of perspiration. "One of them was my brother, Mistress. My twin brother."

"What happened to them?"

"Mistress, she...she killed them all. I'm the only one left. After she killed them, she stripped me of my weapons and held me with power. I thought for a moment she was going to kill me, but she handed me this, and instructed me to deliver it to you, Mistress Melissara.

She said it was to be for your eyes only and your ears only. That I was not to tell anyone upon pain of death. She said if I did she would know and she would reach inside of Sethia and strike me. She said she would kill my family too. I have children, Mistress, I—"

"Do not fear. You will suffer no punishment from me as long as you hold your tongue. Now be off with you. Or does this require a reply?"

"She said it did, Mistress. I'm to wait for her at the same spot."

"For how long?" Melissara asked.

"She said until she came. I was to wait until she came, no matter how long it took."

Melissara laughed. "That sounds like Aentarra. Very well. Stay put while I read."

> Dear loved one. Wipe that smile from your face, sister. There was a time when we were loved ones, do you remember? When we were young, before the Wars of Light or War of the Lights (as it should be).

Back then we were fond of each other. Remember when we played hide-and-seek and no one could ever find me? Ever wonder why?

Well, enough of that. Time is growing short, Melissara, and I feel it is appropriate that we speak now.

Aentarra

Melissara put the letter down, staring at nothing. The Wolfen stood rigid, awaiting a response. "Tell my sister that I will meet her in exactly two days, in the early afternoon, at the pond."

"That's all, Mistress. Just tell her that?"

"That's all she needs to know."

"I don't want to be wrong... if she—"

Melissara laughed but patted the Wolfen on the shoulder. "Don't worry. I know my sister. This will suffice." She walked the Wolfen to the front door, then went to the kitchen for food.

It will be good to see her again, she thought, a smile coming to her face for the first time in weeks.

That brought to light another issue, smiling. She wasn't happy in Sethia. How could she be? It was a horrid place with horrid people. And the worst of them was Lukaan. He had changed since Nelstar. Many things had changed since then. Melissara used a slim column of Fire to heat her khaffe. "But what to do about it?"

"About what?" Tirzinitzia asked as she entered the kitchen.

Melissara spun, startled. She smiled again. "Nothing. Just thinking about a problem I had."

"May I help?"

She dripped honey into her cup, then grabbed another mug from the shelf. "Pure or with honey?"

"I need it raw today."

Melissara poured a second cup of khaffe, then carried both to the table. "You just might be able to help, Tirzinitzia. I'll have to think more on it."

A NEW DIRECTION

*R*haven, Rahg and the others waited for Sama, secluded while she said her prayers. Rhaven had been in a dismal mood since leaving the village, as he had to leave Argus behind. Rahg thought he would have to fight the entire village before they left, as Rhaven made them take an oath to protect the horse, no matter what happened. Sama had reassured him that the Chun would safeguard Argus.

Pau and thirty others awaited Sama. They had all eaten well last night, and though the journey they were about to undertake seemed daunting, they felt some hope.

Camissa looked on from the side of the gathering. She had sensed their fear of Kella and Garnock, and though not as great as their concern over the Paaren, it remained a nagging bit of anxiety. She brewed a fog of trust about the vargel and welgar and dispersed it among the Chun while they waited. It would not eliminate their concerns about them entirely, but it should assuage their primal fear.

Sama strode confidently down the path to join the party. She looked every bit the warrior, and when she spoke her voice was bold. "I am ready."

Chun mountains

They walked for three days, traversing mountain trails that goats would find inhospitable and cold that could snap a piece of good steel. Rahg kept the coat wrapped around his head while they traveled, and at night, he maintained a shield as long as he could. By the end of the sixth day, they had reached a point where Sama said they would need to climb higher, take a different path.

Pau knelt, folding his hands in prayer; other Chun followed him.

Rahg watched as they prayed. "What are they doing, Rhaven?"

"Appear to be saying their words to the gods. This must be the path."

Sama stood beside him. "This is the path. The Forbidden Path. They don't think we will return, which is why they are offering themselves to the gods."

"But you?" Rhaven asked.

"I know we will return. If not, I will be with my husband and son on the Chugarran Path."

Jorn smiled. "And I with my wife. She waits for me."

"How much longer?" Rhaven asked.

"A day. No more."

Somewhere near midday, Rahg tripped, slipping off the path. As he tumbled down a steep incline, a tree branch gouged him, piercing the coat he wore and ripping a hole in his shoulder.

As he made his way back to the trail, Camissa noted the blood on his coat. "Rahg, you're hurt!"

"It's nothing."

"It's bleeding. Let me heal it."

Sama came over to inspect. "Take off your coat. A wound should be healed right away."

When Rahg removed his coat, Sama stepped back, mouth agape. "BlackHeart!"

"What?" Rahg asked.

"Pau! Come quickly."

Pau raced to Sama's side, not knowing what to expect. Seldom did she panic.

"You know the Book of Truth, Pau."

He nodded.

She pointed at Rahg, specifically at the amulet dangling from his neck. "Look at that."

Pau stared, then fell to his knees. "BlackHeart," he said. Nothing more.

"What is all this nonsense about BlackHeart?" Rahg asked.

Sama pulled Pau to his feet. "In the House of Our Fathers, there is a sacred book, the Book of Truth. It tells of the prophecies and of our role in them and what must be done. This changes everything."

Rahg and Rhaven looked at each other, questions in their minds, but the Chun were attentive. "Something about Rahg seemed familiar to me, though I could not understand why. I had never seen him before that night you came."

Rahg shivered with anxiety over the next announcement. It seemed as if everyone was telling things about him that he didn't know.

Sama walked to Rahg and held his amulet in her hand. "When I saw this it scratched my memory." Sama looked to everyone. "Remember the Prophecy written in the Book of Truth. If you do not recall it, I will recite. This is the time spoken of, the time no one thought would ever come.

> The day will come amid strife and death
>
> When south will come a warrior.
>
> One not born with Light's sweet breath
>
> But born amidst a furor.
>
> Though Darkness comes and Darkness goes
>
> The real Dark lies not shaken
>
> Till battles rage, when death flows
>
> Then Dark will start to waken.
>
> Then comes a warrior true and bold
>
> Through endless seas of yore.
>
> A warrior with the might of old

To thwart Evil evermore.

But do not trust words said so cold

Do not dare stay the attack.

The heart will be no heart of gold

It will be a heart of black.

— CHUN PROPHECY

Sama cast her eyes to all. The Chun stood as rocks; even news such as this could not break a Chun.

Rahg panicked. "I don't know what all that is supposed to mean, but I've got nothing to do with it. I'm just here to find someone. I'll not be fighting any gods or whatever your prophecy says."

Sama smiled and patted his cheek. He was not much older than her Kavi, and her heart filled with pity. "It is of no matter. We are with you. The Chun will be your army and not just the village of Korg, but all Chun."

Rahg stood dumbfounded, but Rhaven's interest piqued. "How many Chun are there?"

Sama looked at Rhaven. "The Chun number more than the wolves and deer and squirrel. There are more than forty thousand Chun warriors."

The number surprised even Rhaven. "A formidable army."

Sama's pride grew. "Warriors of Chun. We go to our destiny. The Prophecy of our Fathers has foretold our time. Now we must go to Cergala!" Rousing cheers of approbation rose from those gathered together.

Camissa reached out to sense their feelings and was amazed. The fear was gone. All of it. All that remained was a bloodlust, an over-whelming desire to engage in battle.

"Cergala!" Rhaven grabbed her arm. "I thought we were to go to the Paaren."

Sama's eyes hardened even more. "This changes everything. Now that we know he is BlackHeart, we must follow our destiny. Long have we waited for the signs. Long have we waited for BlackHeart to lead us to victory. We must return to the village, call a war council and gather all the Chun." She turned toward her people and raised her hands. "Where do we go, Chun?"

"To Cergala!" they screamed.

"Who will lead us?"

"BlackHeart! BlackHeart!" the chanting continued as Rahg shook with fear.

THE TRUTH

*P*au led the march back to the Chun village, his heart now lightened, the burden of going into the Paaren lifted. He would rather face a thousand Cergalans than go to the Forbidden Lands. Fighting men was something he knew how to do.

"Up ahead," a soldier called. "It looks like Chande."

Chande stood at the juncture of the pass near the top of the next hill, a contingent of soldiers next to him. Sama had moved to the front upon hearing this news and approached at a run. "What is it, Chande? Is the village safe?"

"Safe and well-fed," Chande said. "We have just returned from Vennala. With food!"

"Vennala!" Sama's surprise was evident. "Who gave orders to attack?"

"I did." Chande stood proud, and he appeared to have the backing of his men. And his men numbered in the thousands.

"Who holds the pass?" Sama asked.

"No one for now. I will send some later."

"No one! They will take the pass again. You can't let it go after we have worked so hard to get it."

Chande's laughter echoed in the mountains. "There is no one to take the pass. We killed them all. All of Vennala."

Sama's face went blank. "All? The women? The children?"

"All of them!" Chande leaned forward when he shouted, his face flush with anger. "Why spare a Cergalan woman? So she can have more barbarian babies? And why spare a child, so they can grow up to wield a spear against us? No, let them all die. Besides, that means more food for us." He waved a piece of meat in front of Sama. "Food, Sama. We have enough food for all of the villages now."

Sama nodded, her heart saddened. "But at what price? Who are the barbarians now?"

Rhaven brought the discussion back to the immediate need. "What do we do now, Sama? Do we go to the Paaren?"

"We must protect the pass, my friend. Chande thinks he has defeated the Cergalans but he has only served to stir their nest. They will be coming for us now, thousands of them. Many thousands."

Darstan was surprised to see that everyone was awake and breaking fast. Embarrassment painted his face. "Good morning," he said.

"Come and eat. The food is still warm."

His stomach craved food but Darstan wanted to get this with you."

Wisp began to rise so that they could be alone, but Darstan stopped him. "No, stay. I want you to hear this. I did a lot of thinking last night, mostly about the problem you face here in Cergala and about how it affects me. I'm willing to help you, but to help you find peace, not war.

I'm no general, and I'm certainly no diplomat. I'm not capable of waging war and have no skills or experience at negotiating peace, but I'll try. I just don't know how I can stop these wars when you haven't been able to do it for five hundred years?"

Aenaila rose to speak, but Marro stopped her.

"What, Aenaila? What were you going to say?" Impatience showed on Darstan. That he had not slept, aggravated the situation.

Aenaila and Marro exchanged looks again, then Marro motioned for Aenaila to speak. "I told you many of the reasons why I thought it was you, Darstan, and they are compelling arguments by themselves. The Cergalan Sword caught my attention that first night you stepped into my house. Then when I learned of your power with Fire, the evidence grew stronger, though I was still not prepared to say that it was you beyond doubt." Aenaila sipped some water and let her eyes roam the table, finally settling back on Darstan, now standing nearest her. "It was not until after the battle in Entiria that I became convinced, and there were two things that did that."

Aenaila emptied her glass of water, though Genea took it to refill as quickly as any servant. "The first was when I saw the bloodstains on the wolves, the stains that would not wash off your sword." She let her eyes catch Darstan's and linger. "But the real proof was when I heard the Shulan tell Rahg of his destination."

"What does that have to do with me?"

"The Shulan told Rahg he had to go to Arangar," Aenaila said. "Arangar is our enemy—the one we have been fighting for five hundred years."

"Mother of Rats!" Wisp said and stared at Darstan.

Darstan remained mute, even under the intense scrutiny of Aenaila and Marro.

"You must see, Darstan. If it is Rahg's destiny to go to Arangar, he will be their leader. This is the only way to make peace. You and Ragh can work out peace between our lands."

"And if we can't?"

"But you must, the Prophecy—"

Darstan slammed his hand on the table. "Burn the Prophecy, Aenaila! This is real. My life is not written on parchment. Suppose we can't make peace? What then?"

Aenaila sighed, almost as if the peace had been lost. "I should think we will. But if not the wars will continue. Only this time it will be to the end. We will spend the life of every last man in Cergala if we must. But we will stop these wars. One way or another."

Darstan nodded. He knew now that they were right. He was this One they mentioned.

But how am I to make peace? I hope Rahg gets the support of Arangar. He better. He must! I can't fight Rahg.

"I won't fight him, Aenaila. If we can't make peace, I'll not lift a hand against him."

Darstan had resigned himself to being the One spoken of in the Prophecy, but he still didn't like to discuss it, so the conversation touched on everything but the Prophecy. Darstan laughed suddenly. "I'll likely be in bed asleep before supper. I'm not accustomed to these all-night outings like Wisp."

THE SUN HAD HEATED the air to a comfortable level when a ruckus from the street closed on the house. An officer, Baldo, pushed through a few bystanders and hurried up the walk, his rough knuckles rapping harshly on the oaken door.

The servant had barely shown a crack of sunlight when he burst through and rushed into the sitting room, his rapid breathing a panicked man's symptom.

"They attacked!" he screamed. "The Chun crossed the mountains and took Vennala. It's war!" he cried. "Destroy the Chun!" Baldo gulped some water Genea gave him; then he collapsed into a chair.

Marro was out of his chair and standing before Baldo in a flash. "What happened? Be calm, and tell me everything."

Baldo gulped more water and took a few long breaths. "Reports came from the border this morning. Chun came over the mountains by the thousands."

Genea sat on the arm of the chair next to Baldo, her hand resting on his, providing comfort. "And Vennala?"

Baldo looked to both Marro and Genea, despair in his eyes. "Vennala's gone! No one alive, not even the children." He stopped, tears building in his eyes. "The women... they..."

Genea stayed him. "You need say no more. Go, see to your needs. Eat, rest."

Marro took time to digest the news. War! It was inevitable now.

Perhaps Darstan can reason with them. Or perhaps we have to have war first to achieve peace.

"Baldo, have the Chun left our lands, or do they still hold Vennala?"

"Vennala is ashes, My King. Nothing but ashes."

Darstan waited until they were alone at King Marro's house. "Now what? Am I to believe that Rahg is the one leading these people?" He didn't wait for the response. "No, it's not him doing this. And if Rahg isn't leading them, then how am I to help?" Darstan shook his head, already regretting his decision.

What do I do now?

Wɪsᴘ ᴡᴀᴛᴄʜᴇᴅ the seemingly endless line of people waiting to enter the house. The Trader's Inn on its busiest day didn't see as many people as Marro's house did this day. Guards, soldiers, and citizens of every rank filed in and out in a continual stream. Some sought news to take back to their families and neighbors; others sought comfort.

Delegates from all over the city came, and from cities throughout the land.

"I have never heard of a king who would let people come to his house, Master Kender. Not even a rich merchant would do that in Khatara."

"There are few people anywhere who would open their doors like this, Adju. King Marro is a unique man."

Darstan sat on the floor across from Wisp. "Look at them. All eager for war, ready to go kill at the first provocation."

Mirana stood against the wall not far from Darstan, shaking her head. "No one is eager for war, but the barbarians leave us no choice. They killed our people. You heard Baldo. They even killed the children. What kind of people kill children?"

Darstan nodded. "I know, Mirana. I don't know why I said that. I hope your soldiers can put a stop to this quickly."

The concern remained on her face, but her eyes had softened. "We will drive them through the mountains like the goats they are. They belong in the mountains, not in our sweet lands."

It took a moment to register but when it did, Darstan filled with fear. He stood and went to Mirana. "What do you mean? *You're* not going! You can't fight a war."

Her look was so fierce, Darstan stepped back. He felt certain that a growl had preceded the snarl on her face. "No one but my queen commands me."

Darstan held his tongue.

Perhaps Aenaila will talk some sense into her, he thought, and went out the rear door to be alone.

Wisp followed him. "Are you going through with this? You're not obligated. Your oath to Aenaila never included leading an army into war."

Wisp shook his head as he pulled out his favorite blade to pick at his nails. "Mother of Rats, Darstan. You just got through fighting a Banished One. No one would blame you for going home."

A long, contemplative pause followed Wisp's statement. Only the sounds of conversation from the house filled the air.

"There's nothing I would like more than to do that. Just go home, find a farm or anyplace to settle down to. I'd even live in Khatara, as bad as my memories of that place are." Darstan sighed heavily. "But I can't. Rahg is in Arangar, and he's probably feeling worse than me. Who knows what problems he's facing. From the sounds of it, these people are worse than barbarians. How can Rahg deal with them?" Darstan picked up a rock and scratched it against the wall. "I've got to help him. I can't leave Rahg to face the Cergalan army alone. If there's some way I can help..."

"Don't worry, Darstan, we'll make sure this war won't escalate. Somehow."

Darstan's eyes gleamed. "You'd do that for me? Come with me?"

Wisp laughed. "What else would I do? You have me trapped halfway around the world." After Darstan's laughter, Wisp went on.

"I can't leave you to do this on your own. The rats would have all the cheese with you in control." He finished with his nails and put the knife away. "Besides, you don't think I'd let Aenaila get that far away from me, do you?"

Darstan laughed for the first time in days. "I should have known," he said. "But I don't care why you come; I'm just glad you'll be with us."

Darstan reached out and grabbed Wisp's shoulder. "What about Adju? We can't take him to war."

"No, he'll scream and kick and connive, but he'll stay. I think we should ask Jago to keep him with his family. In fact, I think Adju will like it being with a real family."

PEACE OR WAR

*W*aves of people parted to make a path as Mirana returned to King Marro's house. Darstan's jaw dropped when she entered—leather top wrapped tightly about her body and a sheath across her shoulder supporting a sword. A bronze belt held two knives and sat atop a pair of brown leather breeches tucked into calf-high boots. Her figure was so perfect and her skin so golden it took his breath away. The thought of women wearing weapons didn't sit well with him, but the sight of steel against her skin excited him.

"You're not going dressed like that."

"What would you have me wear, my grandmother's dress?"

"Mirana..."

"There is nothing to be said. The army will soon be marching, and I will assume my place."

King Marro placed a hand on Darstan's shoulder. "Some currents are too strong to swim against, Darstan."

Darstan stared into the implacable expression of Mirana, then laughed. "All right. I know when I'm beaten. But you'll do as I say on this journey. I am—"

A smile came too quickly to Mirana's face. "Yes, Commander. Of course." She bowed then left the room.

Aenaila, concealing a laugh, whispered to Wisp. "If Mattu leads us as well as Mirana does Darstan, we will be all right."

Adju tugged on Wisp's shirt. "I am worried for you, Master Kender. I think that stubbornness has found a strong home with these Cergalan women."

Wisp nodded but didn't smile.

AFTER SUPPER, the king's advisors met to discuss strategy. It was no longer a question of whether they would go to war, the attack by Arangar had settled that. Now they only needed to determine how many troops to send and how far to push it.

"They are weak!" Baldo said. "Why else risk an attack on Vennala?"

"From what I've heard they're starving," Darstan said.

"Starving, weak. What difference does it make? They attacked Vennala! They need to pay."

Darstan started to speak then stopped.

"Continue, Darstan," Marro said. "We want to hear what you have to say."

"There is a difference between weak and starving. A dangerous difference. I would rather fight a fat wolf than a hungry one."

Marro looked as if he couldn't contain the pride that showed on his face. "And what would you suggest, my son? How would you have us deal with our enemy?"

The question caught Darstan by surprise. He wasn't expecting to be listened to, much less asked for his opinion.

He took two sips of the dark red wine then stood, pacing the floor. "Where we grew up—my brother and I—wolves often attacked the sheep, and usually they took good ewes. Every time it happened the farmers would get riled up and go out and try to kill the wolves, but it never stopped them. One old man, though, Ned Barker, he would take his sickest sheep and stake it out whenever there were signs of wolves in the area. The wolves would come in at night and take that sheep and leave his others alone.

"People said Ned was crazy, that he shouldn't be encouraging them to eat sheep, but old Ned said that wolves had been eating sheep for thousands of years and he reckoned they weren't going to stop. And people had been hunting wolves for thousands of years, and they hadn't killed them all yet. He said he had an understanding with the wolves, and he lived by his part of it.

"Most folks still ranted and raved at him, but the crazy thing was that Ned never lost a good sheep, only the ones he staked out."

"What do hungry wolves and sheep have to do with this? We're no sheep to be staked out for Arangar." Baldo gulped down the last of his wine.

The room erupted with angry shouts. Darstan tried calming them down several times, but everyone was speaking at once. It wasn't until Marro stood that silence came.

"Let Darstan finish."

Darstan caught the looks, angry glares, jealousy, rage, but he continued. "I'm not saying that we accept the role of sheep, but the fact is that no matter what we do if Arangar is still hungry, they will attack again. And again. And again. We need to feed them and make–"

"Feed them! They killed our people. They massacred our children! They–"

"Enough!" Marro's angry eyes found every one of his advisors.

"Let me finish," Darstan said. He waited for the silence then continued.

"Arangar murdered and slaughtered good Cergalan men. They defiled Cergalan women, and they butchered Cergalan children." All of the advisors nodded, some sat back in their chairs.

"There is no excuse for what they did, and there can be no pardon."

"They must die!" Baldo shouted.

Darstan held up his hand. "Yes, Baldo, they must die. They must pay a terrible price. But not all of Arangar, and not their women and children. Let's show them that we can be both strong and merciful.

We'll attack Arangar and exact a terrifying penalty from them. We'll wipe out several of their villages. Kill the soldiers that took part in the Vennalan raid. Take their weapons. But—we won't harm their women. Or their children. Or their animals."

Men cheered and clapped. Smiles formed on the previously rigid faces.

Darstan waited. "And when we're done with our butchery... when we've killed enough of them... then we'll feed them."

"What!"

"Why give strength to our enemy?"

"King Marro, we–"

"Listen!" Darstan slapped the table.

"I've listened to the tales since I came to Cergala. Five hundred years of war! Think of that. Do you want it to continue? Do you want your children and their children dying in Arangar, or defending a pass through the mountains?"

He stared at each one of them as he paced the room. "Do you want to keep spending money on weapons and building fortresses for the sake of war?

"I say take some of that money and some of that energy and try to make peace. One... last... time. Try peace instead of war. I'm not saying we give up or let them go unpunished—just that we show them there are benefits to peace. Believe me—when you give food to women so that they can feed their children, you then have a new ally in Arangar. No woman wants to see their child go hungry, and no woman wants to see her child go to war." Darstan allowed a long silence. "If we give food to Arangar, the women of Arangar will give us our peace."

King Marro nodded. *This young man my daughter found has wisdom.*

The room stayed quiet for a few long moments until Mirana interrupted the silence. "I didn't agree with Darstan when he started this, but I do now. I want to fight, but I want peace even more."

Two other advisors rose and consented. It took a while, but eventually, all agreed that Darstan's plan was a good one. One to pursue.

King Marro stood. "Everyone rest. Tomorrow we will meet and plan our strategy. I will have others work on a plan to feed them."

Darstan leaned back in his chair with a deep breath. He never dreamed they would accept his idea, but they had, and it made him feel good.

He felt fingertips massaging his shoulders and leaned his head back to see Mirana, a warm smile on her face.

"I am proud of you, One-hand."

He smiled back at her. Nothing felt as good as this.

NIGHT DREAMS

*D*arstan had lain awake all night, thoughts of war and plans to carry it out racing through his mind. He wouldn't participate in the killing but if he could help with strategy—anything to keep Mirana safe—he had to do it.

Mirana. He could feel her fingers on him now. Feel her warmth, her hot breath. Smell her, taste her.

Gods blood! Darstan jumped from the bed. I've got to stop this. I can't get her out of my head.

He lay back down, tried to focus on war but could only think of her. At last, he succumbed, dreaming the sweetest dreams. Her lips. Her hands rubbing him. Silky hair...

"Are you going to just moan all night, or are you ever going to kiss me?"

Darstan felt the smile in his sleep. Felt the reaction it brought, too. Soft lips closed on his. A wet tongue tasted them. "By God, she's beautiful," he whispered.

"Thank you."

Darstan sprang from the bed trying to find images in the dark. There, on the bed, he saw her. She was lithe, muscular, beautiful, and naked. "Mirana!"

"Shh."

He crept back into the bed. "What are you doing here?"

She pulled him to her and wrapped her legs around his. Her body seemed to be everywhere at once: her feet tickled his legs, the silkiness of her thighs caressed his own, and her gentle hands probed tenderly. Her sweet breath set him on fire, and when her tongue touched his, he lost all control.

They were still entwined at dawn, spent, yet bursting with life. Darstan opened his eyes and stared at the dark brown pools that captured him. "I love you, Mirana."

She smiled and kissed his lips, igniting a spark or two with so little. "I know you do, One-hand."

Darstan laughed, then laughed some more. He hadn't laughed so hard since before he and Rahg left Twin Forks.

"What's so funny?"

He grabbed her and kissed her again, stroking her hair. "You. You're the only person who could say that to me and make me laugh."

She laughed along with him for a while, then rose to dress. "It will be a long day. We must be prepared for the meeting tonight. Everyone will be there: Mattu and Baldo, all of Marro's strategists." She turned and stared at him. "I want you to have a say in what happens, so don't be shy."

Darstan sat on the bed, still unclothed with a smile painted on his face. "Marry me."

Mirana spun. "What!"

"Marry me. I want you to be my wife."

Her eyes lit like a cherry moon, and a smile crossed her face. "Darstan, I..." The spark left her eyes, and a frown replaced her smile. Soon tears came. She quickly finished dressing, then reached for her staff, ready to leave.

Darstan jumped from the bed, grabbed her by the arm. "What's the matter?"

"I am the protector of the queen. It is forbidden to marry."

Darstan shook his head, bewildered. All of these strange customs baffled him. "But I'm sure Aenaila will—"

"No! Aenaila is to be queen. She cannot make exceptions for friends."

He thought for a moment, then stared into her eyes. "I don't care who she is, and I don't care who you are. If they can't make an exception, we'll live with it." He pulled her to him, removed her clothes, then flopped on the bed. He pulled a sheet over them and kissed her breasts.

"If she won't let you marry me, I'll have to be satisfied with you as a mistress." As he continued kissing lower, she pulled him up, stared into his eyes.

"You mean it, One-Hand?"

"I'll never marry anyone but you."

She laughed. "In that case, finish what you started."

They surrounded Darstan after dinner, strangers interrogating him about everything they could think to ask. It reminded him of Ludar's guards back in Sykor.

A merchant he had met earlier posed a series of rapid-fire questions. "Now that Arangar has attacked, what will you do? Have you planned a response? Will the trade route to Solero be affected?"

Darstan didn't like the man. He had greedy eyes, and his interests were driven by that same lust for gold. "I have no idea what I'll do. I'm no general, and I won't be doing any military planning. As far as trade routes, I don't even know where Solero is, so how I am to know if trade will be affected?"

Queen Genea was making her way through the crowd. Darstan prayed she had come to rescue him. She seemed to float through the room without touching anyone, using only her smile, while others had to push and shove their way through. She arrived as Darstan was being peppered with more queries.

"I believe our honored guest has endured enough for tonight," she said. "Besides, my husband would seek his counsel on matters more pressing."

She grabbed Darstan's hand and led him back across the room. "Come with me, Darstan, but don't be so elated. I"m certain that Marro and that horrible daughter you have befriended will have you cursing before long."

"Is Mirana with them?"

Queen Genea smiled. "You know, Darstan, that the prophecy states that you will marry Aenaila."

Darstan flushed red but didn't hold back. "I've said it before, Queen Genea, prophecies can be wrong. I intend no insult. I think Aenaila is beautiful. When I first met her, I thought she was the most beautiful woman I had ever seen."

"But..." the queen said.

Darstan smiled. "But Mirana is who I love."

"People do not always marry who they love, Darstan. Especially people in positions of power."

"Some people might not do that, and for those people, I feel pity. But I'm not one of them. I'll follow my heart, not words written in a prophecy."

Queen Genea's smile was broad, and for a moment it surprised Darstan. "I happen to agree with you. Others might not, but I do. And I know my daughter much better than she thinks. I also happen to know she has pledged her heart to another, despite the fact that she might not have admitted it to herself yet."

"Wisp?" Darstan asked.

"I am quite certain," the queen said, and laughed. "And though your friend might heartily deny it, he would fall into the abyss after her if fate sent her there."

Darstan laughed for all he was worth. "You are full of surprises."

"It is good to see you laugh, Darstan. Laughter is the healing secret of the gods. As long as you can laugh, there is hope." The queen's expression turned somber.

"Remember that in the council room. Things can become quite agitated in there, especially during times like these."

They went through two more small rooms, then across a patio and into a large room with open-air windows. The house was much larger than Darstan imagined when he had first seen it.

"I'll leave you to the wolves now," Queen Genea said. "Good luck, and remember what I said."

The room rang with arguments and heated discussions about war. King Marro sat in a chair near the far end of the room, a window behind him open to a garden bursting with tranquility. Aenaila stood with her back to Darstan, arguing a point of strategy with one of the generals. Darstan found it odd that someone so beautifully disarming could discuss military strategy.

His emotions raced, though, when he saw Mirana pacing the room like a hungry wolf. She was the "First One" to Aenaila, the protector of the future queen, and even though that afforded her much respect, it gave her no say in the council of war. Mirana, though, was never without an opinion, or the will to voice it.

"We have been prepared for a long time now. It will take little to have an army ready to march."

General Cunio, a short, stocky man with hair as black as a wolf's mouth and as thick as its mane, politely waited his turn. He had been the leader of Marro's army since before Mirana was walking.

Darstan smiled to himself as he looked at the man. If ever anyone looked the soldier it was Cunio. Beneath his wolf-mane hair, a high forehead boasted the creases of worry over so many men's lives, and it rested on pillars of graying, burly eyebrows. A broad nose kept his eyes wide apart, but their intensity, peeking out of a deep recess, revealed his intelligence. His eyes were as gray as a winter sky before the snow, and they seemed to watch the whole room at once. His nose stopped suddenly short of where it should have, hovering above thin lips that were quick to turn into a smile. Cunio's chin was as square as his head, and if he were turned upside down, he could have rested a mug of khaffe on it.

Those steely gray eyes caught Marro, then Mirana. A voice with a hint of gravel rumbling in his throat demanded attention. "I never argue your right to speak, Mirana, as you often have wisdom in your words. Today you speak with the wise ones on your shoulder."

Darstan beamed with pride for her, as Cunio continued.

"When Darstan first came we began preparations. Our soldiers are almost ready to go; in fact, I could leave in two days with a force of six columns if need be."

Six columns! Darstan thought. From what Mirana had told him that would be about twelve thousand men.

Cunio paused to take a sip of wine. "But give me another week, and I could increase that to seven columns, and within three weeks we could have ten columns."

"With ten columns we could surely take back the pass," Mirana said.

"Probably so," Cunio said, "but it would cost dearly. I hesitate to say this, but BlackWolf has the right of it, and if a few wagons of food will suffice, there's no sense in losing good men."

Mirana stepped away from the wall. "We'll see," she said, "but one way or another, Arangar will pay for what they did. I'll be there to make sure of that."

A NEW ARM

irana cleaned the last scraps of food from her plate, then sipped on her khaffe as she stared at Darstan. "Since you are going with us to Arangar, you'll need a new shield."

"I told you, Mirana, I'm not fighting. I'll talk with Rahg, but that's all. This isn't my war."

"You still need a shield."

"What am I going to carry it with?"

"The king's metalsmith is a master at his craft. He can make you a plate for your arm that would serve as a shield."

"I can protect myself."

"Let me worry about that, One-Hand; besides, you never know what a battle brings. It is better to be prepared." The scowl on her face seemed to appear from nowhere. "Sometimes, those who seem to be friends are enemies. You would be wise to have all the protection you can."

Puzzled, Darstan queried her. "Are you talking about Cergalans? You think a Cergalan might try to hurt me?"

"You are not adored by everyone, One-Hand. Some believe you to be our savior, others..."

"Others what? Say it."

She looked to the king when she spoke. "Others believe the king has made a wrong decision by putting you in command. The people trust you, but many in the soldier's camp do not."

Darstan paced. "If somebody wants to kill me, a piece of metal on my arm won't stop them."

"No, it won't. But it might help, and if you wear mail—"

"No!" Darstan turned to her. "No more. I'll get the plate on my arm, but nothing else." He smiled as he pulled her closer to him. "You'll just have to protect me yourself, Mirana Foltelli."

She tried to hide the embarrassment but ended up laughing. "That is a big job, One-Hand." She pushed him away, then headed for the kitchen. "Help me clean these dishes. We owe the servants a rest."

Genea was busy scraping food from her plate. "Don't be silly, Mirana. Nina will wash them."

"Nina has enough to do," Mirana said, "besides, I want to see if One-Hand can do honest work."

Queen Genea smiled and set her plate down. "Then, by all means, continue. I am not one to stop a man from working, especially if that involves doing dishes."

MIRANA AND DARSTAN walked out the door and down the street.

"Where is this metalsmith?"

"Very close to the blacksmith's shop."

They walked along for a ways, Darstan growing suspicious about her lack of conversation. "How close to the blacksmith's shop?"

"Very close, One-Hand. It is not far now."

Darstan stopped, staring at her. "Are you taking me to the blacksmith? Is he the king's wonderful metalsmith?"

Mirana laughed. "Sometimes you do remind me of a horse, One-Hand. Don't worry; he's a master at his trade."

"Rats Blood! I knew this was a bad idea. I don't know why I listened to you."

"Because you are growing wise." She smiled. "Follow me, and we'll soon have you a new shield."

THE PUNGENT ODOR of molten metal caught Darstan's nose at the same time the clanging of steel grabbed his ears. The unmistakable sound of a smith's hammer pounding steel against an anvil. No matter what village a person found themselves in, that, at least, seemed the same.

Darstan presumed the smith would be an old codger, someone like Tobias or Fen back in Twin Forks, but this man was fairly young; looked barely more than thirty.

Like most smiths he was a burly man, arms bulging with muscles, and his face carried as much soot as the floor. The smith stopped his work when Mirana entered and stared at Darstan's arm.

"I'll need to look closely at that arm. Need to take measurements."

"I see you've already told him why we're here." Darstan saw a new sword on a table by the door. He picked it up, admiring the crafts-manship. "A fine job."

The smith nodded. "Good steel went into that one. The best."

"Is it for someone special?"

The smitty smiled. "A well-paying patron."

Darstan laughed. Things were more the same than he might have guessed. "Mirana suggested that you might make a guard for my arm since I can't carry a shield or a second weapon."

He walked over to Darstan, who lifted his arm for the man to examine. The smith studied him closely, then seemed to get lost in thought.

"Take off your shirt," he said, then strode to the side of the shop and returned with some different sized metal rings, which he slid onto Darstan's arm. He found the one that fit snugly on the upper forearm, close to the elbow, then trial and error had three more that marked the tapering of his arm all the way to the wrist. A smile crossed the smith's face. "A good arm you've got there. Solid and well-formed."

Darstan scowled. "I'd argue the good part of that statement. It used to be a good arm. Not now."

The smith simply nodded. "Come back in a few days. I'll have something for you to try by then."

"That's all you need?"

"That's all. Give me three days. Then come back."

Darstan thanked him, then left feeling pleased with the prospect of something to improve his arm.

IN THREE DAYS they returned to the shop, Darstan havingset a quick pace the entire way.

"Slow down, One-Hand. He won't close his doors."

"I'm anxious about this."

"Don't worry. It will be fine."

The clanging of metal quickened Darstan's pace even more, and as he turned the final corner toward the shop, he saw the smith busy laboring. Darstan waited while he completed the shaping, then cooled the metal in the bucket of water.

"Good to see you again, Darstan. I've been expecting you." The man's voice filled the room. He wiped his hands on a big apron then grabbed something from a shelf near his forge. "Take off your shirt again."

Darstan doffed the shirt and held out his arm. The smith pulled out a tapered, tubular shaped piece of metal and slid it onto Darstan's arm until it rested snugly just below his elbow, then he stepped back and looked to Darstan. "Well, how does it feel? Fit tightly?"

Darstan stared at it for a long time, lifting his arm, twisting it, turning it, even yanking on the metal. "Fits tight, but not tight enough. It'll come off with pressure."

The smith's smile turned to a frown. "Worried about that. I've been trying to figure out how to get it to stay. Can't shoe you like a horse."

"Burn it on, One-Hand."

The smith had a look on his face like Mirana had gone crazy, but Darstan smiled. "You might have something there, Foltelli." He turned to the smith. "You have anything you need heated up, real fast?"

The smith wore a puzzled expression. "I don't know what kind of jokes you two are playing, but you can't burn metal onto a man's arm."

"If I heat it enough to start melting it from the inside, will it form around my arm?"

"Can't be done."

"Will it?" Darstan persisted.

The smith nodded, but warily.

"Good. I'll do the heating; you tell me when to stop and how to cool it for the best fit." With that, Darstan focused on his power, reaching inside himself, digging deep into the mind, searching for the energy.

It came easily when he got angry or pressured, or when danger threatened himself or those he loved, but to just call it when he wanted was something that still required focus. Soon he felt that strange, eerie feeling, a tingling throughout his body. It normally started in his arms and moved slowly into other areas, but sometimes it just stayed in his arms, fire bursting out.

Today he had to control it, so he focused his thoughts on channeling the energy into that one arm, and containing it to the arm itself, not letting the fire out.

The smith gasped. Darstan's arm turned red; then small flames danced on the surface. The metal plate on his arm glowed, growing hotter and hotter until the underside began to break down, melt.

"By all that's holy!" he said, making a religious sign used mostly by older people to ward off evil. "Doesn't that hurt you?"

"You must be one of only three people in Cergala who hasn't heard. I'm the man who burns, the one who controls fire."

The smith stared at his face for a long time, then remembered his charter and focused on the plate again. "Okay, stop." He came closer, examining. "Give it time to cool on its own. It appears to be perfectly formed now. It is one with your arm."

"That's how I want it," Darstan said.

After the smith cooled it more, he did a final examination. He prodded with his tack hammer and pulled and tugged on it. "It's going nowhere now. It will sustain a blow from a sword or ax. It will hurt, but it won't cut your arm off."

Darstan laughed. "Someone already took care of that."

The smith smiled. "Another thing too. Watch this." He swung a small sword onto the top of the plate as if he were striking, and when the blade hit the metal two blades, like knives, sprung from under the guard, protruding straight out from where Darstan's hand would have been.

"I like that," Darstan said. "Really like that."

"Now you not only have a shield but a weapon as well. They'll trigger if struck hard enough, or, you can do it yourself by hitting the latch underneath."

"Beautiful!" Darstan whispered, and pushed the blades back in, then released them again. "This is far more than I expected. How can I pay you?"

The smith's face grew solemn. "Win our war, BlackWolf. My father died at Vennala. My older brother, too."

Darstan nodded. "I'll do my best."

STRATEGY

$\mathcal{M}$arro's house bustled with activity yet again. All of his advisors were there, as were the key leaders from the army, including Mattu, Baldo, and Leto. The thing that surprised Darstan the most was the fact that no one had reservations about speaking their mind in front of the king, and even more surprising was that Marro took no offense when people disagreed with him. Clearly, this was not a ruler like they had at home. Even in Pomanda, which had the most liberal government, the king and nobles ruled firmly.

Darstan felt out of place; he not only didn't know this land, but he had no idea of the issues at hand—taxes, roads to build and maintain, keeping supply lines and communication lines open. He sunk further into the comfortable chair, content to listen.

"How many men do we have in Cartena, Baldo?"

Baldo stood, scratching a bearded chin. "I have ten columns that could be ready to travel in a few weeks. That would leave us two to guard the city."

"How many in a column?" Darstan asked.

"Two thousand," someone answered.

"The Selian border can give us eight columns," Leto said.

Mattu shook his head. "We can't leave the eastern borders unguarded, My King. If the Selians suspect we're weak from being engaged in a war with the Chun, we risk an attack from the East. If that happens, we'd be in trouble."

Mattu whispered to his aide, then turned to face Marro again. "I think we could send four Selian columns. No more. They could join the march to Vennala."

Another aide whispered to Mattu, who then turned to face the king. "Our spies say that the Selians plan to attack us once we are engaged with Arangar. If that's true, we can't risk sending even four columns. We'll need to leave all eight there."

Leto stepped forward. "If they attack, eight won't be enough. They could muster thirty thousand men from the Solero region alone."

Marro nodded. "Ten columns is a start, but we will need more. We need to overwhelm the Chun this time." The king paced. "And what to do about Selia. I'm not surprised that they would plan this. Vostich is leading the garrison at Solero, and he has ever been the voice for expanding their borders."

"They would never try—"

"No, Leto, they would not try under ordinary circumstances, but once we commit ourselves to war with Arangar, we leave our eastern borders all but unguarded."

"We'll still have eight columns on the Selian border," Leto said.

"As I said, Leto, all but unguarded. Eight columns wouldn't hold back their women."

"As far as the Chun go, we can raise another two columns from the villages along the way to Vennala," Mattu said. "And we already have five thousand men at the pass."

"Where did they come from?" Darstan asked.

"When news of the attack spread, volunteers came in from all over. Went to guard the pass."

Baldo seemed worried. "We're going to have to raise another army. Get men from all the cities."

Marro nodded. "It will have to be done."

Solero was forgotten for a moment while talk continued about supply lines, raising food, and other logistics. Darstan made his way to King Marro's side. "May I speak with you?"

Marro nodded and slipped away. "They won't even know I have gone, Darstan." He walked with Darstan to a small room with a sofa and a few chairs. "I sometimes come here just to think and be alone." Marro took a seat and motioned for Darstan to do the same. "What is it?"

Some fidgeting preceded a long pause. "I've been listening to this talk going on. Raising armies, requesting food, keeping supply lines open... And then there is the talk of strategy and how they'll manage forty thousand men..." Darstan stood and paced. "It's not me. I can't lead an army! I wouldn't know the first thing to do." He turned to face the king. "For god's sake, I'm liable to get them all killed—if they don't kill me first." A long sigh escaped. "Why would they follow me anyway. I wouldn't follow some boy I didn't know."

Marro seemed at ease. "All of your arguments are valid, but you don't know my people—for good or bad. All you have seen is Aenaila and Mirana, though that does give you opposite ends of the spectrum." Marro motioned toward Darstan's chair. "Sit, please."

Darstan sat, leaning forward with his arms resting on his legs.

"Remember that they are not following you, Darstan—they are

following BlackWolf, and they have known him for one thousand years."

"Yes, but—"

"Wait, Darstan. Listen. I don't ask you to lead in fact, only as a figure-head and as a safeguard. I would never put the burden of war on your shoulders. That I'll leave to Mattu. Leto can handle logistics, and Aenaila will ultimately be responsible for everything. But I want a man who thinks in terms of peace leading my soldiers. I liked what you said about arranging peace. I liked what you said about fighting a hungry wolf and feeding the people of Arangar."

Marro took a sip from a jar of water.

"There is much wisdom in so young a man, and that, more than anything else, is why I want you as the leader. Mattu will plan the strategy. He will lead the soldiers, but if you disagree with him on any major point, seek out my daughter and let her decide. That way the soldiers will have no recourse. They will not disobey their queen."

Darstan's head drooped as he nodded. "I'll do my best."

Marro walked to him and patted his back. "That is all anyone can ask for. Now let's rejoin the others. They might even be wondering where I've been."

THE DISCUSSION WENT LONG into the night with the consumption of food and wine taking only moments away from the continuum. Inevitably, the discussion regarding Selia arose again.

"And what about Solero?" an officer named Mario asked.

"We're leaving all eight columns there," Leto said.

Mario scoffed. "Eight columns for the entire Selian border! As the king said, they'll pick the men apart."

"Perhaps they won't attack," Leto said.

"Our spies think they will," Mattu said. "Mario is right. Something must be done."

"How big is Solero?" Darstan asked.

Mattu seemed irritated, answering Darstan's question only as a courtesy. "Solero is the largest city in Selia. It's surrounded by large stone walls and sits atop a rise. The city has never fallen."

"Would a siege work?"

"They have probably twenty thousand fighting men, and that's just inside the city. And a siege isn't the answer. They have deep wells for water and ample supplies of food."

"Is it on the way to Vennala?" Darstan asked.

Mario nodded.

"Perhaps we can stop by. Talk with them," Darstan suggested.

Mattu laughed. "Is that all you do is talk? You want peace with Arangar; now you want to talk to the Selians."

Many of those in the room chuckled, though some hid their face while they did.

"Is there something wrong with peace, Mattu?" Darstan moved to stand in front of him. "Or do you just like to see men die?"

"I think we should focus on our strategy instead of arguing with each other." Marro's glare found both Darstan and Mattu.

Darstan nodded. "I'll leave that to the rest of you. I'm getting some sleep."

SEND WAGONS of food to Vennala in order to feed the soldiers, and if it came to that, to help feed the people of Arangar.

The rest of the food for the march to Vennala would come from the villages along the way. They would leave all eight columns to guard the eastern edge of Cergala, while sending messengers to raise more men from far reaching villages. Everyone seemed happy with this, even Mattu.

Marro brought his advisors together. "I have placed control with BlackWolf, and though many of you disagree with this, it is what I have decided. He will consult with Aenaila before making major decisions, and he will respect the wisdom of you as counsels, but do not forget, if it comes to it, BlackWolf is in charge. His word is my word." He looked at each of them, waiting for an acknowledgement, his gaze lingering longest on Mattu.

Finally, Mattu nodded. "Your will, My King."

"Good," Marro said. "Now let's all get some sleep. We have a long road ahead of us."

MARCH TO WAR

*D*arstan and Mirana took full advantage of the next few weeks, spending every moment together. She showed him everything Cartena had to offer: the waterfront; the river, with all of its attractions; the beaches, where children shouted with joy and played in the waves; the merchants' district, which put Khatara's to shame; and the magnificent plazas, dotted with statues and fountains that seemed to spring to life the closer he got to them.

She even took him to the poor sections of the city, and while they were bad, they weren't as horrible as the Dongrel or the River's Edge districts in Sykor.

Perhaps it all seemed so nice because he was with her, laughing, enjoying each day as if it were Wish Day.

People stopped and chatted with them as they walked, and never once did he detect any fear of his powers, nor did he catch any sideways glances to his arm. They were a friendly people, with an inquisitive nature. And Mirana! If she had been a statue, she would have been a goddess.

She's perfect! If you don't mind a growl now and then.

Mirana stared at him as they climbed a steep street. "What are you thinking about?"

"Nothing at all. Just enjoying the day." He turned and kissed her. "And you."

Her cheeks flushed, but she returned the kiss. "Save some of those thoughts for tonight." Her smile grew broader.

Darstan laughed, then began back up the hill. "I'm going to be sorry to leave Cartena."

"We'll have a tent."

He laughed some more, then more again. "Is that all you think about?"

Mirana reached over and pinched his back side. "You have something better to think about?"

"That hurt!" He grabbed her hand, squeezing it affectionately. "I was trying to think of someone better to dream about, but I couldn't."

"You better not, either."

Soon, they reached Marro's house, ate supper, and before too long were off to bed again.

The next few days were more of the same, and by the end of it, Darstan had seen everything of note in Cartena.

"We leave tomorrow," Aenaila said when they returned that night.

"I'm ready," Darstan said.

"I better help you pack," Mirana added, as Darstan just shook his head.

IT HAD TAKEN them twenty days to finalize strategy and make preparations, but they were finally off to war, leaving Cartena early, just as the sun showered the city with life.

Adju, tears in his eyes, was there to see them off. For a moment Darstan didn't think he would let go of Wisp, nor Wisp him, but Jago had promised to care for Adju like his own, and that relieved the worry. Darstan had never seen so many people gathered in one place, and this was just the beginning; they would be picking up more soldiers along the way, and more animals and supplies and workers to tend for them.

What had he gotten himself into?

After the king and queen said their goodbyes to Aenaila and the men, Darstan gave the order to move.

Within two days the terrain began changing, the steep hills of Cartena giving way to gentle slopes peppered with long-armed oaks and lush green valleys rich with black soil. The farms seemed much larger than the ones Darstan was accustomed to, each one boasting scores of farm animals and a variety of crops.

A paradise, Darstan thought, if only we weren't going to war.

The scenery reminded him of Kamnor near the border with Sykor, and the memory brought a strong desire to go home. He wanted to hear Magmar's voice calling him to dinner—even chiding him, and he longed to sit at Havril's Inn with a mug of ale and listen to the laughter. Laughter! It had been a while since he had felt real laughter like he used to back home. With the exception of Mirana, most of the people he had shared his joy with were gone: Magmar, Eru, Tomas... and Rahg was somewhere in Arangar with an army that Darstan had to make peace with—or fight.

"What's the matter, BlackWolf? You look lost." Mirana had moved beside him.

"Nothing. Just thinking," he said and increased the pace. "Let's move it, men. We have to make the pass before Arangar takes the rest of Cergala."

~

AFTER SEVEN DAYS OF MARCHING, they reached the edge of the Selian border. Darstan led the army through the forest south of Solero, insisting on walking himself, not riding as most of the officers did. They were still in Cergala, and it would be a while yet until they reached the Selian border. Trade caravans had worn the path from centuries of use, but worn as it was, the sheer numbers moving through here would beat it down more.

Black and green uniforms stretched for leagues, ancient marching songs drowning out the sounds of songbirds, even the alarming caws of the secretive crows.

A patrol leader under Mattu rode up and saluted. "Where will we stop, BlackWolf? The men are tired."

"The next person to call me BlackWolf will go without eating tonight."

Mirana frowned. "Accept what you are. BlackWolf is an honored name, one we have waited a thousand years for."

Darstan sighed and shook his head, tired of arguing with her, with all of them. "We'll march until I say stop. If that takes us into the morning, so be it."

When he quickened his pace, the bodyguards alongside him struggled to keep up. If they thought they had a weak leader, he would show them otherwise. The time he had spent with Rhaven had taught him many things, but how to set a fast pace stood out above all others. That was the one thing Rhaven always insisted on, a very fast pace.

"You look good in that uniform, BlackWolf. Perhaps tonight I will take it off you."

Darstan smiled. If one person could make him happy in this strange land, it was Mirana. "You look better in yours, and I will take it off you tonight."

~

THEY MARCHED until long after dark. Finally, Darstan ordered a stop. "Sleep quick," he said, "We leave again at dawn."

Even though they wouldn't be staying long, they set up tents for Aenaila and Mirana and some of the officers.

Mirana snuggled next to Darstan, her long legs entwining with his. "You must be tired, BlackWolf, after such a long day."

"Stop calling me that."

"It's your name. What else should I call you?"

"Darstan Fal-Thera is my name. I don't like this whole business of BlackWolf or fighting with Arangar." He stood and paced inside the tent. "If it weren't for Rahg being in Arangar... and for you, I wouldn't be here."

Laughter circled the tent. "Fate brought you here, not your precious honor or your brother in Arangar." She spat when she said the name. "And fate will lead us to victory over our ancient enemy... and your brother."

As Darstan lay down again, he pulled the blanket over him, his back turned to Mirana. "We'll deal with Arangar when the time comes. Remember though, I'm going to settle this peacefully."

"And what about my uniform? I thought someone was going to remove it. Should I ask one of the guards?"

"Get some sleep. Tomorrow will be a long day."

She slipped out of her clothes, slid in close to him and once again wrapped around him, her foot caressing his leg.

Darstan turned over, ran his fingertips up her side, traced around her breasts. She was so warm, so inviting.

"I thought you said to get some sleep," she said, then kissed him, lips locking, her tongue tasting his. She slid lower, down his neck, his chest.

It felt as if he slept a full night in just a short while, then awoke to whispers in his ear. Hot breath sent shivers down his body, coming to rest at his loins. "It's time to get up, BlackWolf."

A smile covered her face. She is more beautiful than life, Darstan thought and pulled her to him.

Mirana laughed as their bodies met. "Save your energy for the march."

"I have lots of energy," he said and pulled her closer.

OBELISK

*M*elissara and Tirzinitzia descended the steps to the caverns below the Sethian desert. A hive of activity kept lamps lit at every juncture, and the clang and thud of picks and shovels resounded throughout the spacious cavern. "Have you any new ideas, Tirzinitzia?

"I presume you mean about the obelisk. No, but not for lack of thought. I have labored on this and examined what we know every possible way, but it defies all logic."

The slaves working the mine-like tunnels, mostly Gnakas and Victas, bowed low as Melissara and Tirzinitzia passed, only rising after they were out of earshot. Melissara stopped, then walked back a few paces. Her gaze swept the line of cowed slaves until she found the leader. "You may bow in respect, or not, as you wish, but do not linger so long. I prefer that you return to work."

The Victa leader threw a clawed fist to his chest as he stood and hissed an apologetic response. "Your will, Lady Melissara," he said, then cracked his whip on the back of a lizard next to him. "Back to work, sloths. Hurry! Lady Melissara commands it. Hurry, and dig, or you will feel the lash of my whip."

"What did you mean by *logic*, Tirzinitzia? What logic does it defy?"

Tirzinitzia gathered her thoughts before speaking. "It does not react like anything we know. It appears to be some type of stone, and yet it does not absorb the heat of our fire. The Gnakas have tried to mark it with their hammers and chisels but failed to even make a scratch." Tirzinitzia's eyes grew starry like she thought of a long-lost love. "And the tower exudes an energy all its own. It is like nothing I have seen."

Tirzinitzia was right, Melissara had tested it with Fire herself, and to no avail. The strange stone was as cool as before she had started it. Perhaps answers lie at the base, she thought and wondered anew about that.

The tunnels already reached seven levels below the desert floor, and there was no sign that the base of the obelisk would be uncovered anytime soon. It might be with the next shovel of dirt, or it might go on countless more levels. There was no way to tell, at least, not now. "We cannot quit trying, Tirzinitzia. We must uncover the mystery. The stone is a source of power, a source we know nothing of. Perhaps the ones who built Vallah erected it. But, whatever the source, I intend to discover it."

Tirzinitzia nodded in agreement. "You are right about the power. And it is a power of some magnitude, yet I have detected no one nearby. No one who could be generating power such as this. And the frightful thought is, if that person is outside the range of our detection, they are outside of Sethia. If that's the case, then how powerful are they?" A tinge of curious fear showed in both of their eyes.

"We must keep digging," Melissara said. "I am convinced the secret is veiled at the base or inside. And there must be an entrance. There must be." Her voice held a sense of urgency.

They stood within reach of the mysterious black obelisk, almost basking in the aura that clung to the stone and the very air surrounding it. "We could use Lightning," Melissara suggested. "We have not tried that."

Tirzinitzia's pause was lengthy, and when she spoke, her voice was tentative. "If my lady will forgive me for contradicting—"

"Stop the nonsense, Tirzinitzia. I have no need of your obeisance here, or anywhere, except in the presence of the others, and only then for the sake of continuing the ruse. I have no love for you, Tirzinitzia, but then, I lost the ability to love when I lost Tarmon and Canno.

Melissara forced a false smile, one to cover sorrow, not to deceive. "And if I do not love you, Tirzinitzia, I harbor no hate either or envy you your many gifts. In fact, I favor you above all that are here."

Tirzinitzia let the silence grow until only the distant sparks of the metal picks striking rock could be heard. "A question has been burning in my mind for some time, and you have provided a fitting conversation with which to raise the issue."

"Go on," Melissara said.

Tirzinitzia's voice turned from meek to calculating. "Then if I may speak so openly, why did you spare me that day in Lukaan's chamber? Especially when it might have cost you dearly. If Lukaan had been in a foul humor—"

Melissara turned slowly to face Tirzinitzia, her eyes lifting to meet the taller woman's gaze. "I could say that it was because I like you more than the others, which I have already stated as true. Or I could say that it was because I truly believe we will escape one day, and when that day comes, I believe we will need every one of us, with all of our powers, to defeat Mikkellana and her allies. And I could say that I spared you to stand at my side should a rift develop between those of us who remain, even though it would be unwise for me to even think such things." Melissara never let loose her gaze. "But the truth, Tirzinitzia, is I did it for all of those reasons and more. In addition to everything I stated, and perhaps above all of those reasons, I wanted your assistance in solving this dilemma. The mystery of this obelisk." Melissara's stare seemed to go right through Tirzinitzia. "Yes, Tirzinitzia, perhaps that above all."

For the first time since the day in Lukaan's chamber, Tirzinitzia relaxed, and the smile that brushed her face was genuine. "Thank you, Melissara, for your honesty. And so that you will know, you have my support in whatever might arise. And not from my pledge of obeisance but my respect for your friendship."

Melissara suddenly felt nervous, emotions that sometimes surfaced didn't suit her well, and she blushed. "It would seem that we have strayed from our path of conversation, Tirzinitzia, and my interest lies there. What do you suggest as a course of action?"

Tirzinitzia didn't have to give it any thought. "As you have already perceived, Melissara, I feel that we must get to the root. When we uncover the base of this, I feel certain we will uncover its secrets as well. We must get to the root to solve the problem."

Melissara laughed at Tirzinitzia's imitation of an old instructor of military strategy. "He spoke of getting to the root with such passion like it was some glorious destination."

Tirzinitzia wore the smile of a girl on Betrothal Day. Melissara had blessed her with a new life—a chance to work her mind again. And with such a vexing problem, she thought.

"Very well," Melissara said. "I shall instruct them to concentrate all efforts on reaching its base. We shall soon see what mysteries this strange tower holds."

SIEGE

*D*arstan crawled across the floor of Mirana's tent, gathering clothes as he went. "If you don't stop this I'm not going to be able to walk, let alone fight." He slipped on his pants, then the socks and boots. As he struggled with the shirt, she came to him.

"Let me help with that."

"I'll do it myself. Can't rely on you to dress me." He finished buttoning his shirt, tucked it in, then walked out.

"Bring me khaffe, One-Hand."

He laughed. "Maybe."

As Darstan made his way to get khaffe, he saw the general was already having his meal. "Good morning, Mattu. How goes the day?"

Mattu saluted Darstan although it looked as if it pained him. "The day has yet to start, BlackWolf."

"I want a messenger sent to Solero. Tell them we are coming."

"Is it wise to announce ourselves to the enemy?"

"I'm sure they know we're here. I would be surprised if they didn't have spies scattered throughout the area, even in our own midst."

Mattu bristled at the hint of treason from a Cergalan, but Darstan continued. "It doesn't matter, they would know in a day or two anyway. And besides, this fits my plans."

"And what plans are they?"

"You will find out the moment their spies do, my trusted friend. Now leave me, I have much to decide."

Mattu lingered, his gaze focused on Darstan. "The warning gives them more time to prepare."

"And more time to worry over one so arrogant and confident as to announce his coming."

"And just what are your plans?"

"As I said, my plans are best kept mine until the time comes."

Mattu's face contorted under the tension from the implication, but he controlled his feelings. Darstan noted the anger in them, and while he didn't want their enmity, he also knew that they would follow him. It was their law, their tradition, and if he had learned anything about Cergalans by now, it was that they were strong on tradition. "When you send that messenger to Solero. Tell them we that we just want to talk."

Mattu stood perfectly rigid awaiting the rest of the order.

"That's all, Mattu. Tell them that and nothing more."

"I don't understand what you are doing, BlackWolf. If we're going to war with Solero, this isn't the right tactic. I believe—"

"I know it doesn't sound right, but let me worry over this."

For the next two days, Darstan stayed in camp, forcing the men to train twice daily to keep them sharp and to keep them from growing restless. Finally, news came from the scouts Darstan had placed along all the roads. Soldiers were moving into the city from every village within leagues, and not just soldiers, but farmers and merchants, and anyone else who could wield a sword or bow. The frustration showed on each scout, and as Darstan cast his gaze about he saw the advisors felt the same—their leader had erred, and now it was going to cost them.

Mattu was the only one bold enough to speak. "Now we face many times the number we could have if we had only acted sooner and caught them by surprise."

"Who said we were going to war?" Darstan turned to the scouts. "And their families? Are they going into the city also?"

"No, they remain at home."

Darstan dismissed them, but his smile was too pleasant, too cunning, for him to have been disappointed at the news.

Now we'll see if Wisp's plan works.

"Mattu, select four patrols to come with us. We go to the villages."

"Why?"

"To talk," Darstan said, then turned to Wisp. "Get some money from Aenaila and find someone who knows the local markets and prices."

Mattu and Wisp returned soon afterward, and they rode off toward the closest village. Darstan issued orders for no fighting unless he gave orders. The men grumbled, but he trusted them. As they approached the village, an elderly woman came to greet them with two older men at her side.

Darstan dismounted and bowed in respect. "I come in peace."

The woman stood no taller than his shoulders and was old enough to be his grandmother, but her eyes fixed him with a steely glare. "With armed men and an army camped across the river?"

Darstan smiled, an instinctive reaction of his, especially around women. It had worked all of his life, and he hoped it would here. "We are on our way to Arangar. They attacked one of our cities, and we seek justice. I want no trouble with Selia."

"I'm not the queen," she said, and the older men with her smiled.

Another smile, then. "I prefer to talk with the people, not the queen. We are not familiar with all of the villages of Selia, nor do we want to offend you by marching over your lands, so I'm here to ask you to deliver a message to the other villages."

"We listen."

"I offer peace and my vow of honor that no harm will come to any Selian unless they begin a war. In addition, I offer fair value for any food or horses that you can sell as we have a long journey."

One of the old men spat on the ground, close enough to Darstan that it could have been taken for insult. The woman stayed him with her hand, then stared at Darstan again. "I will discuss this. It will only take moments."

Darstan nodded and stepped back while she and the men walked toward the village.

"What are you doing, BlackWolf? This is not the way to deal with Selians. We should take captives, parade them in front of the city gates then kill them. Teach them a lesson."

"How many times have you captured Solero?" Darstan didn't bother to wait for an answer. "Never!" He glared at Mattu, Mario, and the other patrol leaders. "We will fight this war my way. I'm in command, and unless you kill me, it stays that way." He stared each one of them down. "If any of you cannot, or will not, obey my commands then leave! Go back to Cergala. Tell Marro that you wouldn't follow me, that you betrayed the prophecy." He waited but never let any of them doubt who was in control.

"We'll follow you," Mattu said. "All of us."

"I want to hear it from each one of them," Darstan said. "And then I want each of you to go to your men and extract the same vow. If any man cannot follow my orders completely, he is to be sent back. Is this understood?"

All of them nodded. "I will follow you," Barg said.

"I will follow you," Mario said.

Each chimed in his pledge until all the leaders had spoken and vowed to follow him.

"Good," Darstan said. "Now, get the same vows from your men."

The woman returned but this time with many others. Women with children in tow and young boys too small to fight. One of the village elders glared at Darstan. "What is it that you want from us?"

Another mother covetously guarded her three young. "What will happen to my boys?"

Darstan's warm smile disarmed at least some of them. "I want little, and none of it is bad. I do not want you to betray your husbands or your people. I do not want to use you as a shield or a bargaining tool. I simply want you to spread my word to the other villages, and I want some food for my men and their mounts. We could use extra horses if you have them. For this, we will pay you a fair market price—no less."

The village elder held disbelief in her eyes. "No Cergalan had ever shown mercy before, though your voice rings true." The elder paced. "Do we have your word, on your mother's eyes?"

Darstan frowned, but only for a moment. "I never saw my mother's eyes, that I remember. She died when I was but a babe. But I'll give you my word of honor, and I'll swear on the eyes of the man who raised me. His eyes I remember well; they were warm and kind."

The woman nodded her head in acceptance.

~

THE WALLED CITY OF SOLERO. Most of the women had insisted on accompanying Darstan to the city, eager to tell their husbands and the leaders of Solero that war was not necessary. It was a good city for defense, one that had all that was necessary to sustain a long and costly siege, so Darstan embraced the assistance.

They approached the city across an open field then began up a small rise. "I need a banner of truce," Darstan said. "Wisp, come with me. Mattu, stay with the army. If my ploy fails, you're in charge."

Wisp stood out from the rest of them as he wore no uniform or armor, but he rode up to be with Darstan.

"You can't carry the message yourself," Mattu shouted. "Let me take it. They might shoot you, regardless of the flag."

"I'll be the one to take risks. It was my idea." Darstan turned his head as he took the banner from a soldier and handed it to Wisp. "You carry this, Wisp. They're not supposed to shoot the one carrying the flag, are they?"

"Not on our side of the world, but who knows what they do here. They might do the opposite?" Wisp thought for only a moment on this. "Is that why I'm carrying the flag?"

Darstan laughed, despite the tension of the moment, and spurred his horse forward. "Well, Wisp, it was your plan."

The village elder that Darstan first spoke to led the way, followed by Darstan and Wisp and the rest of the Selians, mostly women and children. When they reached the top of the hill, the gates opened revealing armed soldiers at the ready. They quickly seized Darstan and Wisp, but when they reached for Darstan's sword, he yanked himself away.

"Are you so afraid of a one-handed man that you must take his sword?" He then nodded to Wisp, "And he doesn't even carry a sword." Darstan let his voice soften. "We're just two messengers of peace, here to speak to Lord Vostich."

"Let them be!" a voice from the crowd shouted and people parted to reveal the general approaching. He bowed in greeting. "I am General Nardo. Welcome to Solero."

Darstan and Wisp both returned the bow. "My name is Darstan, special envoy to King Marro, and this is Kender. We come in peace."

Nardo offered his hand in friendship. "Come, please. We must share a meal and some wine. Then we'll talk."

They walked through the city to a palatial house surrounded by columns and statues that rivaled one of the temples in Pomanda. "This is Lord Vostich's estate," Nardo said. "He will be eager to meet you."

ONCE THE SERVANTS had cleared away the food, Vostich motioned for the door to be closed. He picked up his glass of wine, sipped on it, then stared at Darstan. "Why do you bring so many men to the borders of Solero?"

Darstan laughed. "Please give our spies the respect we grant to your own."

Vostich frowned, but Nardo hid a smile.

"You are well aware, Lord Vostich, that we march to Arangar. They have attacked Vennala, razed it and killed our people. It's time Arangar was paid a lesson."

Vostich and Nardo both nodded.

"You are also aware that once we engage in this war with Arangar, it will take most of our resources, and that our border with Selia will be left unprotected." Darstan noted the surprise on Vostich's face, though he could detect nothing on Nardo's. "Perhaps you thought we would leave eight or ten columns here? I'm certain that is what your spies reported."

Darstan stood, paced while he sipped his wine. "This is excellent wine, My Lord. Compliments to your vineyard." When no one spoke, Darstan continued. "The fact is, Lord Vostich, I don't plan to leave any soldiers at the border. I'm here to ask you to guard our border for us. And to help us with food and supplies."

Vostich rose quickly from the table, his face twisted in anger.

"Of course we will pay you fairly for everything, and will even compensate you for your protection of our lands while we are otherwise engaged."

The nobleman's face turned to sweetness. "But of course, we want nothing but peace with Cergala. It was a horrible thing that Arangar did at Vennala, one we find reprehensible. I had even thought of sending a messenger offering consolation and aid to your people when we heard you were coming."

Darstan nodded. "Our thanks for that."

"Then I think the only thing left is to discuss what you need and terms of payment."

Darstan smiled. "I'll leave that to my negotiators. As you can imagine, I must be off. Arangar awaits."

Vostich grasped Darstan's hand and shook it. "I'm glad we had this meeting. May your journey be safe and your mission prosperous."

"Thank you," Darstan said, then he stared at Vostich and Nardo, a hard-eyed glare that held them paralyzed. "Just a warning, gentlemen.

If you betray me, I will know. If you even think of betraying me, I will find out. Punishment will be swift."

Vostich's mouth turned down. "Why you—"

Nardo put a hand on Vostich's arm before he responded. "There is no need for threats. We will abide by our word."

Darstan smiled again. "Good, then all is settled. Now I truly must be going."

He and Wisp exited the city with a guard of ten Selians, who turned about when they reached the bottom of the rise leading to the city. They rode quickly into the camp and straight to Aenaila's tent. "Hurry, Aenaila, Wisp will give you the location," Darstan said.

Aenaila grabbed hands with Wisp then Shifted to in a dark corridor inside of Vostich's palace.

"Remember," Wisp said, his voice barely audible. "They won't be able to see us, but they can hear us, smell us, feel us, anything else."

"I know. Just go."

Wisp moved silently toward the room where they had met with Lord Vostich and General Nardo. When he heard footsteps in the hall, he used his powers to cloak them, hugging the wall. Soon a servant came with more food and wine. When she opened the door, Wisp and Aenaila sneaked in with her, making their way to a safe corner.

Vostich sat at the head of the table with Nardo and what looked to be two generals occupying other chairs. Two men who Wisp had not seen before sat at the far end. It was Nardo who spoke first.

"Lord Vostich, I understand your reasoning, but we gave them our word."

"Our word? Did you hear how he threatened us? How long have we waited for an opportunity to take Cergalan lands? Even if Arangar doesn't defeat them, Cergala will be so weak that they'll take years to recover. We can take their central lands with few losses." He sipped more wine, paused... "We might even take Cartena."

Nardo smashed his fist on the table. "We are Selians, My Lord. We gave our word, and we should honor it. Besides, what's wrong with peace? They offered peace and payment for goods as well. It's an offer we should take."

"Peace? Payment for goods?" Vostich sneered. "What they offered were bribes to save their lands. They know we can take them over once they start this war. Arangar doesn't know it, but they have granted us the best present we could have asked for."

The other generals at the table nodded. "It is difficult to turn this down."

Vostich looked to his advisors at the end of the table. "And you?"

A short whisper among them, then the eldest stood. "We agree with you, My Lord. We should wait until they are engaged with Arangar, then attack."

"So be it," Vostich said. "Prepare the men, General Nardo. And have the servants bring more wine. This calls for a celebration."

Wisp squeezed Aenaila's hand, a signal for her to Shift. An instant later they were inside of her tent in the camp.

"Well?" Darstan asked.

"As you suspected. Nardo wanted peace and Vostich plans to attack."

"Can we trust Nardo?"

Wisp smiled. "I think we can. Especially after our next visit."

"When do we go?" Aenaila asked.

"Now," Darstan said. "I want the repercussions to be instantaneous." He looked to Aenaila. "Are you ready? Do you know what to do?"

She nodded, holding her hand out for them to grab onto. An instant later they appeared in the hallway just outside the room where Vostich and his men were meeting. Darstan flung the doors open, then marched in, slamming the doors shut behind him. Wisp and Aenaila stayed cloaked, invisible to the men in the room.

Vostich jumped up. "What are you doing here? Guards!"

"Don't be so frightened, Vostich. I'm alone, and I only have one hand."

The two generals seated to Vostich's right drew their swords, although Nardo kept his sheathed. The advisors remained seated, a shock to Darstan as he thought they would hide behind their master.

"I thought we had an agreement, Lord Vostich."

Vostich's face changed from anger to fear, his head darting about as if someone were watching him. Nardo, too, looked around. "What do you mean? I agreed to your terms."

"You planned on betraying me, Vostich. You were going to attack."

The nobleman's face turned gray. Fear had a firm grip now. "How do you know... What do you mean?"

"Don't try to deny it. I told you I would know if you even thought about it. Well, you did more than think." Darstan's glare found the other two generals and the advisors as well. "And your minions too. Not brave enough to think for themselves."

Nardo began to speak, and for a moment Darstan thought he was going to defend himself. "I'm certain that a peace can still be arranged. If we but—"

"I believe you're right, General, but not with Lord Vostich. He must die."

One of the generals moved closer to Darstan while he spoke and upon hearing this proclamation, he attacked bringing his sword down to strike at Darstan's left side. Darstan raised his arm, and when the sword struck his metal plate, it jarred the general. The knives sprung from the end of his stump and Darstan rammed them into his throat, under his chin. The man dropped to the floor, gurgling blood. Darstan drew his sword and started toward the other general, keeping an eye on Nardo.

"Stop!" Nardo called, and he was staring at his own general. "This is enough killing." He looked to Darstan. "What do you want?"

"You coward!" Vostich started toward him, but Nardo's stare kept him still.

Darstan sheathed the sword. "Vostich must die. And the others here as well." Darstan heard a door open very quietly behind him. He felt positive that a guard or two approached, but he also knew Wisp was back there.

Nardo gave nothing away. "And why should we sacrifice ourselves when we could wait for you to battle Arangar then attack as Lord Vostich wanted to." Nardo looked around the room. "I don't know how you got in here, that is a puzzle, and while I wouldn't want you killed, perhaps a night in our prison cells would soften your stance."

Darstan heard the soft footsteps as they approached him. "You couldn't understand how I got in here any more than you could understand how that guard behind me died." As Darstan spoke, Wisp stabbed the man in the neck, blood gushing out as he fell to the floor.

Nardo gasped, stepping back. Vostich drew his sword and screamed. "Guards! Someone call the guards."

"You better stop them," Darstan said. "I don't want to kill anyone I don't have to, but if guards come through that door, they'll die."

Nardo raced to the door, getting there just in time to stop the first guards from entering. "It's nothing," he said. "Lord Vostich just wanted more wine. Please have someone bring it."

"Now here's what I want you to do," Darstan said and detailed his plan to Nardo. "And, General, I would like to stay here alone while you arrange this. You have my word I won't stray from this room."

"It won't take long," Nardo said, then departed.

THEY GATHERED in the large courtyard in front of Vostich's palace, surrounded by guards under Nardo's command. Vostich, his advisors, and the other general were bound with rope, hands behind their backs. Darstan and Nardo stood on a platform overlooking the huge crowd that had assembled. General Mattu had been called in too. Wisp and Aenaila were situated near the front wall.

Nardo waited until the square had filled, then he spoke. "Many of you know of the envoy from Cergala who came to our city yesterday. He is a man of his word, who treated our villagers with respect and fairness." A lot of women in the crowd nodded and turned their heads to speak to others. "He came to Solero seeking peace and offering fair payment for food to help them in their struggle against Arangar. But Lord Vostich betrayed him."

Murmurs arose from the crowd, especially among the soldiers. "Listen! I was in the room, as was Lord Vostich and his advisors, and General Tuma. We gave our word to him; then when he had gone, we made plans to betray that word and attack Cergala after they were engaged with Arangar." Most of the women seemed offended by this, but the soldiers were not. Few of them seemed to be bothered by what Nardo said.

"Who betrayed Lord Vostich?" someone from the crowd hollered.

"If the Cergalans were gone how did they find out?" another person yelled.

Nardo started to speak, but Darstan forestalled him. "I'll answer that." He stepped in front of Nardo, turned slowly to let his gaze fall on as many people as possible. "Many of you have heard of the Cergalan prophecy, the one predicting that a savior will come to lead them to victory over Arangar." He saw the nods of acknowledgment. "Black-Wolf is his name, and he is said to carry a legendary sword and wield powers. Be blessed by the gods."

Soldiers in the square snickered, while others laughed outright. Darstan made sure he was standing straight and tall, then he held his left arm straight up. "I am BlackWolf," he said and unleashed a column of BlackFire that roared into the sky. People screamed, falling back, tripping over each other in an attempt to escape. Even Nardo moved quickly to get away. "Wait!" Darstan screamed. "Stop!"

His shout stopped them. He suddenly realized that he had used some power that affected his voice and it seemed to have commanded the crowd. He would have to explore that at a later time, for now, he had to gain control of the crowd. "I am here in peace. No one will be harmed."

The people showed signs of relaxing, though they stood as tense as a prisoner waiting on the ax to fall.

"Lord Vostich and his advisors will be put to death, as will General Tuma." Angry shouts arose from the crowd, from the braver ones. "They betrayed your people," Darstan shouted. "That is the punishment. As for General Nardo, he will be put in charge of the city until your leaders decide on a different course of action. All I want is peace. Arangar has attacked Vennala, killed everyone in the city and shamed our women." He noted the men shaking their heads, and he saw the empathy in the women's eyes. "We march to Arangar seeking revenge. We want no trouble with Solero. Not now. Not ever."

Darstan sensed that there was still dissension amongst the ranks of the soldiers, so the next phase of the plan went into effect. He raised his voice to a high level and addressed them again. "Listen well, people of Solero. If you betray me, the punishment will be swift and merciless." He gestured with his arms to the walls surrounding the city. "These walls that have protected you for so long will crumble, and I will come back to exact payment."

He waited for the soldiers to begin their shouts of disbelief, then he acted. "Do not believe me? Then watch." He held his left arm out, pointing it at the wall where Wisp and Aenaila had concealed themselves, and at this pre-arranged signal, Aenaila used her Illusion.

The people gasped as a large section of the wall fell, stones tumbling down like a landslide until a huge breach lay open. Many in the crowd ran, as if escaping the inevitable, others simply stared. Darstan quickly resumed his speech. "If I want, these walls would all come down." He let that sink in. "But I can also rebuild them." He raised his arm into the air, signaling Aenaila to drop the Illusion and let the people see the walls intact once again. Most of the women in the square fell to their knees, hands folded in prayer. Many of the men did, too, even soldiers.

"No," Darstan shouted. "I don't want your worship. I don't even need your respect. I just want peace."

Nardo had come beside him again, and this time he grasped Darstan's hand and shook it. "You have my respect and my friendship. And you can be assured you have our peace. I will let no one break it."

Darstan stared at him. "I trust you, Nardo, and I respect your word, but hear me well. I am leaving no soldiers here to guard our border. I leave that to you. If you break this peace, I will return, and I will kill every living thing in this city. Bar none. Don't think that Arangar will have me so preoccupied that I can't spare time to do this. It won't take long."

Nardo nodded. "You have my word. I'm not one to break it."

Darstan smiled. "Good. And now I must go." He nodded to Vostich and the others. "I presume you will take care of the punishment of these."

"It will be done today," Nardo said. "And may fortune smile on you in your struggles with Arangar."

"Thank you, General."

As Darstan and Mattu left, Nardo stared at their backs. And may god help the people of Arangar.

SECRETS

The flap on Aenaila's tent cracked open, moonlight sneaking in.

"What is it, Mirana?"

She stepped in, soft as a breeze. "How did you know it was me, My Queen?"

"Only you and Kender are so quiet, and he wouldn't dare come to my tent at night."

Mirana smiled. "Perhaps he needs encouragement. If you—"

"Enough!" Aenaila lit a candle and motioned for Mirana to sit. "Tell me what brings the First One to my tent so late. Trouble with Darstan?"

"Just a visit." Mirana paced, and all the while rubbed the hilt of her sword.

"Just a visit? And last night, when I heard you outside the tent? And two nights before that, when you were on your way here and Flavia stopped you?" Aenaila fixed a hard, discerning gaze on her. "Were those just visits as well?"

Mirana picked up a pillow from the bed, ruffling the edges of the casing. "It has been a hard march, and I have been with Darstan every night. Sometimes I just want someone else to talk to."

"Then talk."

She sat on the bed, fumbled with another pillow, then stood and paced some more. "What do you think we'll face when we get there? To the pass, I mean."

Aenaila's brow wrinkled. "You know better than I do what we'll face. Stop the nonsense, Mirana, and tell me why you came. I'm tired."

"It's nothing, My Queen. We will talk another time." She started to leave but never got as far as the center of the tent.

"Your queen orders you to stay. And I order you to tell me why you came here. I won't be kept awake any more nights wondering what is bothering my protector. You are still my protector, aren't you?"

Mirana spun toward her, fist pounding chest in salute. "Always, My Queen. Until my last breath."

Aenaila's eyes softened. "Then sit. And talk."

Mirana sat on the edge of the bed, head hung low, hands fidgeting. Silence filled a long gap. "I'm carrying a baby."

"What!"

"I am carrying BlackWolf's baby."

"You fool! How could you? What did..." Aenaila stood in front of Mirana. Tears filled her eyes. She lifted Mirana's head and pulled her toward her in a warm embrace. "I'm sorry. I should never have spoken so." She squeezed her tightly. "This is not good timing, but mother always said babies never were."

Mirana tried to restrain her tears, but they broke loose. "I'm sorry, Aenaila. I failed you."

Aenaila stroked her hair and sat her down. "You didn't fail anyone. You just got pregnant." She dried Mirana's tears. "Now we have to determine what to do. Does Darstan know?"

"No!" She leaped from the bed. "Don't tell him. You can't."

"Calm down." Aenaila held her hand. "Why can't I tell Darstan? Do you love him?"

Mirana smiled. "I love him more than life, but if I told him, he would keep me in that tent. He would never let me fight."

Aenaila laughed. "And he would be right. You can't go to war with a baby."

Mirana stomped her feet and kicked. "I came here to get help," she said. "You sound just like him."

"You want no help. You want my protection in case Darstan finds out. He will find out, you know. You can't hide a baby for long."

"I made my clothes looser. I can hide it for a while."

Aenaila nodded her head, moved to face Mirana. She stared into her eyes and wagged a finger at her face. "If I catch you not eating, I promise Darstan will find out with my next breath. And with the one after that, I'll issue an order to take you back to Cartena."

"My Queen—"

"Heed me, girl. I might put up with some of your nonsense, but I will not sit by while you harm a child."

"How dare you speak to me that way! This is—" Mirana's eyes went wide, then she fell to her knees, hands in supplication. "Forgive me, Aenaila. I only—"

Aenaila knelt beside her. "Enough of this. We are both upset. Now get up on this bed while I pour some wine. A little wine will make this baby strong."

Mirana laughed. "You are right, My Queen. They say red wine will make a strong son. White wine a beautiful girl."

Aenaila hesitated. "Which should I pour?"

"Red. BlackWolf needs a strong son."

They laughed and talked and told old tales for long into the night, only stopping when dawn threatened to rouse the morning watch. "You had better sneak back into that tent as quietly as you left," Aenaila said. "Darstan will be setting another grueling pace today, even if it's to march around the camp."

Mirana stopped before she opened the tent, turned to Aenaila and smiled. "Thank you, My Queen. I could march all day now, with this burden relieved."

Aenaila nodded, but as Mirana left, she whispered. "I'm afraid your burden is only just starting, my friend."

MESSENGER OF TRUCE

They marched for nineteen more days, a blistering pace that had the men complaining every night. Darstan had fore-gone the normal policy of building a camp each night, knowing that no one would attack an army that size, and besides, as tired as the men were, they would have been hard pressed to do anything other than sleep at the end of the day.

Mattu went to Darstan's tent, two goblets of wine in his hand. He offered one to Darstan, then sat on the ground next to him. "I haven't told you what a brilliant game you played in Solero, BlackWolf. Perhaps it has taken me this long to swallow my pride, but..."

"No apologies necessary, Mattu. We needed the extra soldiers, and I saw a way to get them with little or no bloodshed."

Mattu nodded. "Yes, and you earned the men's respect. Especially with that show of knocking down the walls and rebuilding them. How did you do that?"

Darstan laughed. "That's a secret best kept with me."

Mattu sipped on his wine, looking as if he wanted to say something.

"What is it, General? You came here to say something, not just to compliment me on Solero."

Mattu smiled. "We'll reach Vennala tomorrow. I wanted to know what plans you had."

Darstan stood, patting Mattu's back. "I have no plans, General. This is your responsibility. I know enough to know I'm not a general, so I'll leave that to you. I just want to make sure I speak to Rahg first, try to arrange peace or some orderly war that could lead to peace. I don't know what that is yet, but I'm thinking on it."

Mattu seemed relieved. "Good. I will keep you informed of everything we plan."

IT WAS NEARLY DUSK when they caught sight of the encampment, just across an open field, beyond the edge of the forest. Darstan smelled the stench before he even saw the tents. Cergalans had a good system for getting rid of their waste but no matter how good, that much waste left an odor. "We need to get upwind of that," he said.

"Don't worry, BlackWolf, I'll fix your tent nicely."

"Mirana, how can I ask the men not to call me BlackWolf when you keep doing it?"

"Then don't ask," she said and smiled.

Mattu rode up beside Darstan. "Who's in charge here?" Darstan asked.

"Refugio. A good man."

Darstan frowned. He didn't like Mattu, but he couldn't blame the man for being upset. Marro had undermined Mattu when he put Darstan in charge, and Darstan knew it grated on the man.

"He is a good man and a good soldier," Aenaila said. "He has served my father for many years."

As they neared the camp, Refugio rode out to greet them. "My Queen," he said, and pounded his chest with his fist. "We didn't expect to see you here, but you are a welcome sight. The men will be inspired."

Refugio turned to Mattu and once again hammered out his salute. "General Mattu, an honor to have you. Your wisdom is sorely needed."

"I'm not in charge. BlackWolf is," Mattu said and pointed to Darstan.

Refugio's face went blank, but he recovered with a smile as he turned to Darstan. "We are blessed to have your presence, BlackWolf. I have heard of your coming."

Refugio sat low in the saddle; Darstan put him at no taller than his chin, and he had a balding head, gray painting what brown was left. His skin looked rough though, rough as a rock. His left ear was caked in blood, and his right arm and hand were splattered with a lot more.

Darstan bristled at the name of BlackWolf, but decided not to fight it. It seemed like no matter what he did, the name was sticking. "Thank you, Refugio, but I'm here more to watch. Mattu will be leading the men. He's the one who knows the soldiers, and he's the one who knows the Chun."

A look of relief seemed to cross Refugio's face, but he nodded and saluted Darstan. "Your will, BlackWolf." He then turned to Mattu again. "You came none too early, General. We have barely held on these past few days."

"What's happened?" Mattu asked, leaning forward in his saddle. "Do we control the pass? How many men do they have?"

"Far as we can tell they've got twenty columns, eighteen at least. But the—"

"How many men have we lost?"

Aenaila touched Mattu's arm. "Let him finish speaking, General."

Refugio nodded to Aenaila. "The problem isn't the number of men.

Only so many men can fit in that pass at once, but they've got magic. Every time we try to advance there's something stopping us, yet there's nothing there. The men are terrified. A lot of them are talking about going home."

Darstan and Aenaila nodded at once. "Rahg's shield," Darstan said. "That's good."

"Good!" Mattu looked as if someone had struck him. "How can that be good?"

"If Rahg is here, we can arrange a peace."

"We don't want peace! Not after what they did to Vennala."

"We all want an end to the wars," Aenaila said. "But we must have some justice first." She stared into Mattu's eyes. "What we don't want, General, is a slaughter. We won't become the barbarians that the Chun are."

"I'm going to see Rahg."

"No! They'll kill you," Aenaila said.

"I'll go under a flag of truce."

"We can't risk that the Chun will acknowledge a flag. Send someone else with your message."

"Then I'll send a message asking Rahg to meet me. That way—"

"No, Darstan. Emotions are too strong in both camps. I wouldn't trust our people any more than I trust the Chun. Either you or Rahg could end up with an arrow in your back. Just send a message."

Darstan nodded. "All right. That should do okay. But I sure would like to see Rahg."

"When this is over," Aenaila said. "Now let's get settled in." She turned to Mattu. "General, go with Refugio to learn what you need about the situation and have some men set up the command tent. After supper, I want reports from you."

~

DARSTAN SAT at a makeshift table in Aenaila's tent, writing aletter to Rahg.

Rahg: It's been a long time, brother. I hope you haven't had any difficulties in Arangar, though I imagine a new land brings plenty of new challenges. Fate seems to find us at opposite ends of a burning rope this time. Me in Cergala, and you in Arangar. Who would have thought that we would end up so far from home?

This seems like a hopeless situation, but there is a solution, and thankfully, we're the ones who can provide it. Maybe that's the way fate works. Maybe it was fate for us to come to these lands—one on each side—so we could bring peace to people that haven't known it for so long. Anyway, I propose to let them fight—one more time, without us interfering. Not you. Not me. Let the Cergalans and the Chun have this battle.

I'm sure you had no part in it, and I don't know how much you know, but the Chun destroyed a whole city here—killed the men, raped the women, even killed the children. I know you and Rhaven wouldn't have done this, but the Cergalans don't know that. They want peace, but they want justice first. I got them to agree—to promise even—that if we let them fight this one time, then we can have peace. I even have food for the Chun, and from what I've heard they need food.

I'm staying out of this fight, so I hope you will too. Say hi to Rhaven, and Tobias, and Camissa.

See you soon,

Darstan

By the way, Rahg, these people think I'm part of their prophecy. They call me BlackWolf. Can you believe that?

Darstan finished the letter and took it to Aenaila. "If you can send a messenger right away, Aenaila, that would help. I want to get this over with."

"Let me seal it first, then I'll send someone." Aenaila opened her chest and removed the seal, a large wolf head surrounded by a forest. "Flavia, call a messenger and get a flag of truce rigged. Make it a large one. I don't want that messenger shot for lack of a sign."

The messenger soon arrived, a veteran soldier, though Aenaila didn't recognize him. "What is your name, soldier?"

"Mosca, My Queen. I served with Baldo many years ago under your father's command."

"Mosca, I shall tell my father that you have served me as well. I have an important mission for you. Take this to the enemy camp and tell them it is for Rahgnar Fal-Thera. Await his response then return to me."

"Yes, My Queen. Your will." The soldier pounded his chest in salute then departed, making his way through the camp.

As he neared the front of the line, Mattu stopped him. "Dangerous journey you're going on, Mosca."

Mosca spun, surprised to see the General. "Mattu, you old bear. Good to see you." The soldier then looked around to see if anyone was in earshot. "I thought that you were in charge."

Mattu kept a false smile on his face. "I am in charge. They just don't know it. I still don't understand why they give such weight to what a young boy says; he doesn't even know what being a soldier is. And he sure didn't lose anyone at Vennala."

Mosca frowned, nodding his head. "Lost a cousin myself. A few friends too."

Mattu placed his arm around Mosca's shoulder. "We all lost someone, my friend." Mattu started toward his tent. "Walk with me. We'll talk."

"I can't, General. I've got to get this message to the Chun. Very important."

"Before we do that, Mosca, let's look at the message. I don't know if I like the idea of that young one determining our fate."

Mosca looked around again, his eyes darting in all directions. "All right, but let's be quick."

ONCE INSIDE THE TENT, Mattu took the letter from Mosca and grabbed a knife to cut the seal.

"That's the queen's seal!" Mosca shouted as he reached for the letter.

"Let me worry about the seal. We have to see what's in here." Mattu read the letter then tucked it inside his shirt. "Have a taste of wine, Mosca. We have to think."

After a while, Mattu shared a plan with Mosca. He cracked the opening of his tent and looked around. "It's dark enough now. Work your way through the camp and then back again when enough time has passed." As Mosca started to leave, Mattu grabbed him by the shoulders. "We're doing the right thing; you know that. Besides, you know the Chun would kill you as soon as they saw you. They're not about to honor a flag of truce. Not after what they did in Vennala."

Mosca nodded, but he appeared to be a reluctant ally.

Mattu shook him, then stared into his eyes. "Mosca, you're in this now. Do you remember the message, word for word."

Mosca repeated it for the third time, then when Mattu appeared satisfied, he departed.

A MESSAGE FROM THE CHUN

*I*t was early morning when news of Mosca's return roused Darstan.

"He's here, BlackWolf," Flavia announced.

Darstan jumped from the bedroll, throwing the covers off Mirana as he did.

"Let Mosca wait," Mirana said, tugging on him to bring him back down.

"Mirana!" Darstan's face reddened. "That's all, Flavia. Tell Aenaila I'll be right there."

"Tell our queen he might be a little late," Mirana said.

Darstan's face reddened even more. "I'll be right there!" he called to Flavia, then he turned to Mirana as he slipped his pants on. "I swear, Mirana, you embarrassed me in front of Flavia."

"What, you don't think Flavia does this?"

"You know what I mean," he said and reached for his shirt.

Mirana pulled the covers off her lower body, sliding her legs up and down the sheet. "Can't Aenaila wait a little while?"

Darstan stared, but he stopped buttoning his shirt. When she stretched, arching her back, he began to undo his pants. "You're going to get me in trouble." He smiled as the pants fell. "But it should be well worth it," he said as he slipped in beside her.

AENAILA HID the smile on her face as Darstan and Mirana entered. "Trouble waking, Darstan?"

"Sorry, didn't mean to be so long."

"I'm certain," Aenaila said, "but Mosca has been patient."

Darstan turned to the messenger, his face taut with anxiety. "Did you get it to him? Did you see Rahg?"

"He sent me back with a message, sir. He—"

"Give it to me. Let me read it."

"Wasn't a written message, sir. Said they had nothing to write with, and from what I saw that was true. Just rough camps and men sleeping on the ground."

"Then tell me what he said, all of it."

Mosca stood, appearing nervous. "Said that he wished you were there on that side of the mountain with him. Said he understands, and he didn't know about Vennala. He said he would not interfere. And he said to hurry and get done."

Darstan nearly jumped out of his skin. "I told you, Aenaila! I knew we could count on Rahg. This war will be over with soon; then we can arrange a peace."

Aenaila smiled, but a small smile. "It appears promising, but I wouldn't count the war as over yet. The Chun still have many thousand warriors guarding the pass. I can't see us getting through them anytime soon. Perhaps never with that many."

"That's fine," Darstan said. "We'll let them fight a few days, then when enough of the Chun have been killed, when the men have tasted some vengeance, they should be ready for peace. After all, Aenaila, no one wants war." Darstan stood, nodding as if he agreed with himself. "Yes, that's it. After a few days, I'll send another message to Rahg, and we'll stop this. He'll be able to stop them, even if he has to put a shield around the camp so they can't get out."

"He could do that?" Mirana asked.

Darstan laughed. "He's strong. And he's stubborn. If Rahg sets his mind to it, he'll do it."

Mosca wiped sweat from his forehead. "Will that be all, My Queen? I must report for duty."

"Yes, that will be all, Mosca. Thank you. This was important. I will tell my father how you served his daughter."

Wisp had been sitting on the ground, cleaning his nails. As Mosca turned to leave, Wisp called to him. "Is that all Rahg said? What you told us?"

Mosca looked to Wisp, then back to Aenaila. He addressed her. "I told you everything, My Queen."

Wisp put himself between Mosca and Aenaila. "I know what you told her, but I'm asking you, is that all Rahg said?"

"He doesn't answer to you!" Mattu jumped between Mosca and Wisp, then addressed Aenaila. "My Queen, it was enough for you to put Darstan in charge, but I'll not have my men be questioned by this... this man who can't even be a soldier. If you want Mosca questioned, I'll do it myself."

Wisp started to speak, but Aenaila stopped him. "Enough! Mattu is right." She glared at Wisp, then turned to Mosca. "Go back to your camp, soldier, but do not go to the front lines. Mattu will find a safer position for you."

"Before you question him, Mattu, there are things I'd like to know." Wisp risked Aenaila's ire again.

"Kender Darnell! You have no business interfering in any of this. You do not command my soldiers, and you definitely do not question them." Aenaila's hands were firmly placed on her hips.

Wisp nodded, grabbed Darstan's arm and left.

Mattu watched them leave, then turned to Aenaila. "I should have killed him for such insubordination."

Aenaila narrowed her eyes. "My dear General, that insubordinate man would have killed you three times before you ever drew your sword. He is the fastest man I have ever seen wielding a knife, and the most deadly."

Mattu began to respond, but Mirana's touch restrained him. "We have enough to worry about with the Chun. We don't need to fight amongst ourselves." When Mattu nodded, she continued.

"I have been working on a strategy to take the pass. If we can take the pass we will have them," Mirana said.

Aenaila scoffed. "It will cost us too many men to take that pass, Mirana. Since we have no plans on taking over Arangar, there is no need to take the pass."

"But, My Queen—"

"No, Mirana. Save it for tonight. Mattu, bring your officers to dinner, and we will decide how to proceed."

Mattu nodded. "All right, My Queen, but we need to do something. Every day the Chun raid our outer guards. Last night we lost ten more men."

"Now that we have our truce, we will act. We will decide tonight."

CHUN ARCHERS ATTACKED during the middle of the day, finding a vantage point behind an enclave of rocks above the northeastern line. Several volleys of arrows were fired, and three hit their mark, two of the men dying, one wounded. Mosca delivered the report to General Mattu.

"Bring the wounded one here. Have them bury the others. And, Mosca, you come back here also. We need to speak."

When they were alone inside of Mattu's tent, the general stooped to examine the man's wound, an arrow to the gut. "Soldier, I'm going to have to remove this arrow. Be still."

Mosca cringed. "Shouldn't we get a healer, General?"

"I've taken care of plenty of battlefield wounds. This one's not too deep, and it's a straight-tipped arrow. Just get me some wine to cleanse it and some bandages."

Mattu yanked the arrow out with a swift jerk while pouring wine over the open sore. "Put pressure on that with these bandages," he said to Mosca.

The soldier moaned but stifled his screams. After a few moments, Mattu knelt and wrapped the man with new bandages. "Now pour us some wine," Mattu said as they stood.

Mosca went to the table, grabbed two glasses and poured from a half-full bottle. As he turned, Mattu plunged the arrow he had removed into Mosca's heart. He dropped the wine, reaching for his chest with both hands, but it was too late.

Mattu shoved it in further, twisting it as he did. "I'm sorry, my friend. But I couldn't have them question you anymore. I'll ask the gods to clear a path for your coming."

Mosca gasped as he fell to the floor.

Mattu placed a pillow over the other soldier's face and pressed until the man drew no more breaths. He cleaned the wine and moved Mosca to a spot beside the other soldier, then he leaned outside and called for a healer.

"Nothing to be done with either of them," the healer said. "Next time call me first, general. This one with the stomach wound should have lived."

Mattu wiped false tears. "Let's pray there is no more next time," he said, then ordered a detail of men to take them for burial.

"MOSCA IS DEAD. SHOT DURING A RAID."

Aenaila's face turned crimson. "What was he doing on the lines? I told him not to join the ranks."

Mattu nodded along with her rantings. "He was a soldier, My Queen. Soldiers fight."

"Strong coincidence," Wisp muttered.

Mattu spun toward him. "If you have something to say, speak it clearly."

Aenaila's glare was firmly fixed on Wisp, and he didn't need Camissa's abilities to read her mind. "Nothing, General."

Aenaila nodded. "Flavia, serve the meal. We'll talk as we eat."

Wisp remained silent during supper, and even Darstan was unusually quiet. Refugio and Tesla detailed their suggestions for an attack on the pass, while Mattu countered with rebuttals when he saw a flaw.

Mattu took a long sip of wine. "They send a raiding party almost every day, and we never know when it will come. If we have everyone ready to strike, we could counterattack as soon as they come in, and we do it with full force. Once we start, we keep going, drive them all the way into their lines, confuse them. Push them back up the pass."

Mirana paced as she listened. "They will have to open their ranks to let the others in, and if we are on their heels, we can breach their lines."

"You're not going, Mirana. Quit saying we."

"We are all one people, BlackWolf."

"Sit and eat," Aenaila said. "You surely must be hungry." Aenaila's glare succeeded in forcing Mirana to sit and eat.

"I'll be leading the right flank," Tesla said. "I know that area best."

"That leaves Refugio for the left," Mattu said. "I'll take the center."

Aenaila looked at each of the officers. "We are all in agreement though, that the pass cannot be taken. Not without losing too many men?" She waited for each of them to acknowledge her. "We will strike as planned, do as much damage as we can, then retreat and sue for peace with Darstan's brother."

Tesla mumbled something about a chance to do it all, and Refugio seemed to be steaming, but General Mattu nodded. "We agree, My Queen."

Aenaila sipped on khaffe, listening. "Then it is settled. How long will it take you to prepare, General Mattu?"

"Two days, My Queen. We need to execute perfectly if we are to have a chance. And remember, Tesla and Refugio, we don't want our archers to take out their horses. We need those horses to be charging into their ranks. The wider the gaps they have to make, the more disturbance it will cause."

Aenaila smiled. "Good, now let's all join Mirana in enjoying the meal. She looks to be starving."

MIRANA

Darstan came out of his tent scratching tired eyes. "It's a cool morning, Mirana. Feels good."

Her face was rigid. "Death is better on cool mornings."

"Don't talk like that. After today, Rahg and I will work out a peace."

"It is too late for peace. Before Vennala perhaps.... but not now. Not after what they did."

"We'll see," he said. "Have you seen Wisp?"

"I saw him going to get khaffe. Which reminds me, I have to see Aenaila. I will be back later."

Darstan walked off to get khaffe and find Wisp. Mirana waited until he was out of sight, then quickly changed into her fighting garb.

TWO THOUSAND MEN followed their leaders up each of the trails, the rest held in reserve. Mirana and Mattu led the main group, with

Refugio on the left flank and Tesla on the right; walls of rock separated each unit.

Mirana held up a hand, stopping the advance, then sniffed the air. She couldn't see them yet, but she could smell them. Smell their fear. This would be her time, and after Arangar's defeat she and BlackWolf would raise their children in a land of peace. Already she could feel him growing inside her. It would be a boy, a strong boy.

Three short whistles sent the signal to Refugio: the attack is soon. Two more shrill blasts to the right told Tesla the same.

Mirana led them into the pass, eyes alert. They had been fighting Arangar for five hundred years, but this time would be different. This time she would break their lines. Breach the pass. Avenge Vennala. Soon, Mirana Foltelli's name would go down in the books for all to remember, for all to sing about. Mirana Foltelli, the one who conquered Arangar.

More than thirty thousand soldiers at her command. Brave souls willing to die at her orders. A hundred times Cergala had tried to breach the pass and a hundred times they had been pushed back. But today would be different; they had BlackWolf.

BlackWolf swore he wouldn't fight, but Mirana had seen it in her dreams, his Fire destroying the ranks of Arangar's soldiers as if they were dry timber. "Move slowly. They're up there, waiting."

There was one main pass at the top of the mountain and on the Cergalan side three trails that led to it. "Wolf Guard, go up the center behind Mattu and me. Tesla has the right flank; Refugio, the left. When we meet at the top, we attack."

"We've done this before, Mirana. We've done this for five hundred years, and nothing has worked. Why should it be any different today?"

Mirana let her gaze find each of her generals. "I know you are brave, but your words drip fear. Cergalans don't show fear. Besides, today we have BlackWolf."

"He won't fight."

She smiled. "We don't need him. Their leader with the shield will not fight, so we can do this on our own. "But if necessary, BlackWolf will fight. Believe me, he will."

The general shook his head. "If we don't have him—"

Mirana glared this time. "I said he will fight. Now move, General."

IN THE PASS looming above the Cergalans, Rahg waited with the army of Arangar. "They're almost here, Rhaven. What should I do?"

"Let them fight Sama's men for a while, then have them fall back. When we get them in the narrowest part of the pass, do your part."

MIRANA'S LONG, shrill signal sent Refugio and Tesla's men headlong into the pass. She raised her fist high in the air. "Soldiers of Cergala, it is time to claim our victory. It is time to claim our vengeance!" A roar from the men behind her followed her into the waiting Chun. Her sword found two of the enemy before her soldiers caught up with her, dashing to protect her sides.

"Form a guard around the First One," one soldier hollered, and a dozen men rushed to obey. Despite their protection, they gave her room to wield her blade, already covered in blood. A tall Chun warrior bearing an ax charged her, but she dove on the ground in front of him and came up with a blade to his groin followed by a jab to his throat. A backhanded slash caught another Chun's arm, though his sword drew blood on her thigh. This one was quick, and he spun then slashed at her again, and again he found blood, this time on her sword arm. She almost dropped the blade, faltering, stepping back. He moved in for the kill. Mirana blocked his strike, then drew the blade from behind her and drove it into his side, shoving with all of her weight until it punctured the lung.

RAHG NODDED, then watched as the armies clashed. Metal clanged, men wailed, and blood flowed. The Cergalans fought like demons, especially the woman leading the center, her sword cutting down men twice her size.

The fighting raged for half the morning, Chun and Cergalans alike suffering great casualties, though the Chun were taking the brunt of it. At Rhaven's command, Sama's men pulled back, a controlled retreat that ceded the pass to the Cergalans. Soon they were approaching the top of the mountain, the pass filled with soldiers in green and black uniforms.

Rhaven grabbed Rahg's arm. "A few more moments. Wait for my signal."

When the pass was full, Rhaven squeezed his arm. "Now."

Ragh sought the energy that danced beyond the reach of others, beyond their sight and feel. He closed his eyes, felt for it, then brought it to him. His hands tingled, then his arms, until soon his whole body felt charged. Rahg shaped the energy into wedges of shield that he jammed into the crevices along the pass. When he had them just where he wanted them, he expanded the shields, splintering columns of rock, collapsing the rock into the pass, onto the Cergalans. The entire mountain was falling on them, crushing them.

DARSTAN WATCHED THE ADVANCE, watched them push the Chun back up the mountain. Wisp and Aenaila stood next to him.

"God's blood! That's Mirana up there." Darstan started moving toward the front lines. "What's she doing there? I told her not to go."

Aenaila grabbed hold of Wisp. "Go get her, Kender. Get her out of there now!"

"How am I going to even get to her, let alone convince her to come back with me. If anyone can do it, it's you or Darstan. But if you want me to, I'll—"

"No!" Darstan's scream tore through the camp. "Mirana!"

The walls of the canyon collapsed. Wisp reached to grab Darstan, but he tore free, running for the pass. Wisp followed.

Aenaila buried her face in her hands, sobbing.

"Now," Rahg ordered, and two thousand reserves steamed over the rocks, slaughtering what remained of the Cergalan troops. The ground they had ceded was regained, and before long they were charging down the three trails leading into the heartland of Cergala.

THE SOLDIERS RAN PAST DARSTAN, retreating from the onslaught of the Chun. He grabbed hold of Refugio, and dragged him to the ground. "Mirana! Where is she?"

Refugio pulled himself to his feet, head hung low. "Gone, BlackWolf. She went down when the rocks fell. And now the battle's lost. Hurry, we need to get out of here." He tugged on Darstan's sleeve, but Darstan stood still as a rock, staring into the canyon.

He shivered, felt chilled. The heat started in his gut, a feeling like he had drunk wine too fast. Soon his chest felt as if it burned, then his skin.

Refugio grabbed Darstan's arm again to pull him away and screamed. His hand turned red, burned as if he had thrust it into a fire. "Black-Wolf, you're burning!" He held his wrist with the other hand and shook it as if it would relieve the pain.

Flames danced on Darstan's skin, up his arms and onto his face. He was a man afire. Three soldiers stopped to smother the flames, but couldn't get close enough even to try. When Darstan started walking into the pass, they ran.

The burning gathered strength inside of him, raced down his arm and erupted from his hand in a fiery inferno. BlackFire raged up the pass, charring the walls, splintering rock. The screams of the Chun warriors seemed to separate the flames, almost drown them. Black-Fire burned through them, eating skin, then bones, leaving nothing but ash.

The Chun advance turned abruptly amidst the wailing of men and women. The stench of burning flesh filled the pass, clung to the walls of the stone.

"Put up a shield, Rahg. Hurry!"

Rahg wove a shield and bridged the gap in the pass, cutting off the flames. "Who is that? Darstan? How did he get here?" Rahg shivered, then moved toward the edge of the cliff waving his hands. "Darstan! By the gods, it's me. Stop!"

Darstan felt a jolt as the fire met resistance, staggering back. It took him a moment to realize what had happened. A shield. I've hit a shield. He stared at the mountain, saw Rahg waving at him.

"Rahg! You killed her!" Rage burned in him, ate at his soul. He funneled his power and shot a column of BlackFire into the pass. "No shield is going to stop me!"

AENTARRA GOT the message and Shifted at once, appearing in the pass next to Captain Katsu, fully cloaked. She quickly assessed the situation: a battle raged in the pass below. Rahg had a shield wedged in the pass, and someone—Darstan, it appeared—assaulted them with fire. Chun warriors scrambled to get out of the narrow pass, trampling the weak and injured in an attempt to get to safety.

An interesting struggle, she thought, a smirk on her face. I wonder who is the stronger.

The column of fire struck the shield, jarring Rahg. He fell back, bracing himself against a boulder, then focused on holding the shield.

Aentarra saw him faltering, sensed the weakening. She reinforced the shield, a test if nothing more, curious to know how strong Darstan was.

Another column of BlackFire roared up the canyon. The collision knocked Rahg down, and he lost consciousness. It even jarred Aentarra.

God's blood! He is strong. She let go of the shield, releasing the fire into the pass once again. The Chun retreat was now a massacre.

"Fall back," Rhaven ordered, pulling Rahg to his feet. "Hurry. We can't stay here against this."

Rahg stumbled, kept looking back. "Why is Darstan doing this? Is it him? Is it him?"

Tobias grabbed hold of his other arm. "It's him all right, lad. Don't know why he's doin' it or how he got here, but now's not the time to be askin'. He's killin' soldiers faster than a wolf can kill a lamb."

Chun were dying in droves, cries of death echoing in Rahg's head. "I can't leave them. I've got to help."

"You'll be doin' well to stay alive, lad. Just keep movin'."

Sama grabbed hold of Rhaven. "Only one place we can be sure to be safe," she said. "We need to go into the Paaren."

DARSTAN FELT THE SHIELD COLLAPSE, heard the cries of death as his fire swallowed the Chun. "Refugio! Get the men ready. We're going to Arangar."

Aenaila had come alongside him, worry painted on a pretty face. "You can stop, Darstan. They retreated. We'll claim the pass later."

Darstan pushed her aside, a glare accompanying the shove. "Refugio, get your men here now! If any of them try to stay behind, I'll kill them myself." He knelt and turned over a body of a woman, but it wasn't her.

"We'll find her, Darstan," Aenaila said. "I'll have a dozen men searching until we do."

Refugio rushed ahead of Darstan, his men close behind.

Darstan stood like a statue in the middle of the narrow entrance, glaring at the men as they ran past him. "Fill the pass, soldiers. Come back with blood on your swords or a blade in your heart. Today the Chun die. Today Arangar falls!"

Steel scraped leather as Cergalan swords were drawn, thousands of warriors charging ahead." Darstan began to move with them, at first a fast march, then as the fervor increased he ran. All the while the men chanted his name: BlackWolf! BlackWolf!

"Let us go first, BlackWolf. You are too valuable to risk."

Darstan pushed him aside as he had Aenaila, stepping over dead bodies and ashes, scanning the remains for Mirana. "Let them try and kill me," he said. "Let them try."

THE CHUN HEARD the war cries, and some in the rear turned to see death chasing them. "Faster!" a soldier from the rear called. "He's coming."

Rahg yanked away from Rhaven's grip. "Got to stop him. I can't let them all die."

Tobias grabbed hold of Rahg and spun him around. "We need to move, lad. And we need to do it now. Darstan will kill you."

"I can stop him. He'll listen."

"You tried stopping him already and couldn't. And he will kill you. Don't know what's happened to him, but he's killed near two thousand men already, and it looks like he's not done with it."

Rahg lowered his head, shaking, mumbling. "Darstan, what happened?"

An explosion sounded behind him, and splintered rock flew like spears, one shard taking Rahg in the arm. "By the gods!" he screamed and grabbed his arm.

"Move it, lad!" Tobias yelled and pushed him forward.

"This way," Sama said. "The path lies ahead."

Sama wasted no time getting to the Forbidden Path. "It is up this trail. I will not ask anyone to follow me into the Paaren, but you must choose now. Once we head up this trail, there will be no turning back."

The trail was like any other in the mountains, if less worn. The legends of the path and the fear it inspired kept most Chun away. Sama led the men upward, ever–upward until the morning passed and midday showered sun through cold thin air. She didn't know exactly where the entrance to the Paaren lay, but legend claimed it to be the top of the trail. Soon, they came to a narrow ledge, the only way over a great ravine.

Only the bravest dared look down and those only once. Halfway to the opposite side, Pau screamed, then fell backward into the mountain. Two Chun following him also fell. The rest of them stopped. Sama called from a spot near the rear, still on the trail before the ledge. "What is it? Where is Pau?"

It was Chengal who answered. "He fell, Sama. He fell through the mountain! I believe we have found the Paaren, right here on this ledge."

Sama grew excited. "Then go, Chengal. Go into the mountain after him. We seek the glory of the Prophecy, and we seek Korg."

Chengal said a prayer to the Ancient Ones, then he stepped into the mountain pass, through the portal. Each warrior in turn followed, some reluctantly, some with the fervor of those who believed. Finally, it came to Rahg, first among the party he traveled with. Rahg felt more fear than he had ever experienced in his life, more than when he faced the Victas, even more than when he fought Iazzo.

Camissa stood close behind him. "Everyone fears death, Rahg. With all that we have yet to face, I sometimes think death would be welcome."

Rahg nodded, but he was afraid to turn around. This was like walking the ledge above Rainbow Bridge in Kamnor, only worse. Camissa had the right of it though. If falling through this mountain killed him it would be a merciful end.

Forgive me, Magmar, if I die. With that, Rahg plunged into the sheer rock of the mountain.

Camissa and the rest soon followed until only Rhaven and Kella remained. "Go on, girl," Rhaven said. "I'll be with you. We'll face destiny together."

It took Kella a long time to go, but she finally did, with Rhaven right behind her.

DARSTAN HURRIED through the top of the pass, spraying fire in all directions. The few remaining Chun fell to his flames amid screams of agony. A short distance ahead, he saw Rahg and the others turning up a trail. "I've got them now," he said and increased the pace.

Refugio moved ahead of him with a full patrol. "We take the lead, BlackWolf. This is a Cergalan fight." Soon Refugio met a contingent of Chun who had stayed behind to guard the trail. Metal clanged, then swords tasted flesh as the Cergalans took them. "Death to the Chun." The chants began anew.

When Darstan arrived, Refugio and his men were hammering away at what appeared to be nothing in the middle of the trail. "There's nothing here, BlackWolf, yet we can't get through."

"Move aside," Darstan said, and focused on finding his fire. It came quickly to him, almost instantly, and he broke the barrier on the first strike. "Now move up that pass."

RAHG GASPED as if the wind had been knocked out of him. "By the gods, he took my shield out that quick."

"Go," Camissa shouted.

"Let's go," Rahg said. "It can't be worse than what we face here."

FINALLY! Aentarra thought when she saw the portal. One more phase of her plan had fallen into place. She realized that Darstan would get to them before they all got into the portal, so she erected a wall of shield along the trail to keep them at bay.

REFUGIO and his men ran up the trail, swords drawn. Darstan was just behind them, fire flickering at the tip of his hand and dancing in his eyes. A soldier hit the shield first and immediately fell back. "Black-Wolf, another one."

Darstan saw them disappearing into the rocks above and wondered what was happening. Panic set in. He blasted the shield, but nothing happened. Again and again, he struck, but it held firm. "Argh!" he screamed, and funneled his energy into a focused strike, like a spear jabbing a warrior's heart.

THE STRIKE JOLTED AENTARRA, making her misstep, almost fall from the ledge. She instinctively garnered Lightning to retaliate, then restrained herself. This one was strong, but no need to kill him. Not yet anyway.

The last three Chun entered the portal, followed by Aentarra, still cloaked. Her shield vanished as soon as she entered.

DARSTAN RACED up the trail firing salvos of BlackFire as he ran. Refugio followed close behind, caught him just as he neared the ledge, and yanked him back. Darstan spun, almost struck, but stopped.

"No, BlackWolf. Death waits in there."

Two more of the men grabbed him, holding him back. Finally, Darstan relented, sagging against the wall of the mountain. His knees buckled, and his eyes teared. "She's gone, Refugio. Mirana's gone."

FORBIDDEN ENTRY

ahg stood upon lush, green grass in a valley that rivaled any in Kamnor for its beauty. The Chun all wore smiles, even Sama.

"Didn't I tell you?" she said. "Look at the grass! Look at the stream that brings life to this valley. I have not seen its like since the Shuthvin Valley last bloomed."

She gave him her full attention. "What is it?"

"Our path is written by whatever it is that calls a man to his fate. We might find ourselves traveling different trails before long. I can't stray from our path to search for Korg."

Sama nodded. "When I thought to go with you, it was only to find Korg and Kavi, but when I opened the Book of Truth and read the Prophecy, everything changed. I am Korg's wife, but I am a Chun first. I must obey the Prophecy. We go where you go. Lead us."

Rhaven understood. These were good people, people with honor. "Rahg, does your amulet tell us where to go? Did the Shulan explain how it would work?"

Rahg shook his head. "I don't know. There's nothing I can say as certain, but..."

"Just wait a while. We'll rest a bit, drink. Perhaps you'll know soon."

Pau had his men fill casks with water before they began the journey, though as yet no one had said where they would go. Rhaven told them to rest until he called, but to be prepared.

Soon enough, Rahg came to Rhaven. "I don't know if it's anything. It could be nothing at all, but..."

"Just tell me."

"I have an urge to go that way," Rahg said, pointing toward a mountain range that appeared distant.

"That must be it. Let's move." It felt odd to be moving without Argus, but at least he would be safe. The Chun had sworn an oath not to harm him, and he knew them as honorable men. "Pau, station men as scouts—forward, rear, and both flanks. We can't assume it will be safe just because we see no danger."

RAHG LED them for seven days through rolling terrain and plains, until they stood within a day's walk of the foothills. Food supplies seemed like a gift from the gods to the Chun—game in abundance, nuts and berries to spare, and more than enough water for all. Along with that, Pau's scouts had seen no sign of danger; in fact, they had not seen signs of anything—no towns, no people, not even a road.

On the first day in the foothills, one of Pau's scouts returned, panting from shortened breaths. "We spotted four animals, but they walked on two legs and were fast."

"They showed no signs of attack?" Pau asked.

"No, they ran when we saw them."

Pau looked for his second–in–command. "Chengal, send two men to the forward and flank positions. I want no surprises."

They spent most of the following day climbing the foothills with no further sign of the mysterious animals. By mid morning the foothills gave way to more precipitous mountains and canyons that flared behind almost hidden crevices.

Four deer entered the shallow mouth of a canyon, and Chengal opted to give pursuit. Several of the beasts were stalking the deer. He turned to Kevl. "Tell Pau to come. We'll guard the entrance."

Pau arrived quickly, six Chun and Rhaven and Rahg were with him. The beasts had seen them and advanced slowly toward their only exit. There were three of them, and they showed no fear.

They had long claws, and they walked with confidence, straight toward them.

Rhaven stared, never letting his gaze fall. "Be prepared but don't draw weapons. They might simply want to get away. There's no sense in—"

Two of Pau's men drew their swords before Rhaven finished. Pau turned to issue the reprimand, but Rhaven's shout alerted him. "They attack!"

The beasts moved the instant they saw the swords clear the sheath, their speed astonishing. The talons of one raked the man to Pau's right while the other Chun who had drawn steel had his neck ripped apart. Blood spewed, death instantaneous.

Rhaven flew into battle, the Sword of Mikkellana found its first victim fast. One of the enemy had been about to get Pau, but Rhaven's sword cut it down. He severed an arm, then finished with a stab to the chest. He whirled to catch one of the others in the back, the sword cutting almost through to the stomach. Pau recovered and joined with Chengal striking down the last of them.

Rhaven scanned the area before sheathing his sword. "I never saw anything so quick. Only the welgar could equal it."

Pau nodded. "We have two dead to show for it."

Rhaven paused. He didn't like to speak ill of the dead, but this had to be said. "The next time one of your men disobeys an order, I'll kill him myself." He looked to the bloody mess on the ground. "They might have truly died for nothing."

THE JOURNEY CONTINUED with an added state of alert. Scouts were brought in closer so that aid could come quickly if needed, and Garnock and Kella filled in gaps on the left and right forward flanks. Rhaven and Jorn assumed the lead positions, with Rahg, Camissa, Sama, and Mulka shortly behind them.

Just before darkness, a man leaped from a rock overhead, landing just in front of Rhaven, his sword drawn.

Rhaven reacted immediately, but he couldn't elude the blade; it sliced thinly on his stomach, but deep. He stumbled back, his sword now drawn. The warrior's sword aimed for Jorn, knocking the painted man's blade aside. Rhaven interceded before Jorn fell to the onslaught.

Rhaven struck, his sword on a path for the warrior's back, but the man spun, fending the blow with a buckler on his forearm. His spin continued with his blade going for Rhaven's legs. Rhaven didn't have time to avoid the attack, though he did jump up and backward to try.

Rahg appeared just as the blow was about to strike Rhaven. His weave came instantly, and he threw it between the two combatants. The warrior's blade struck the invisible shield, and the force stunned Rahg.

Rhaven had not regained his footing, the stance not firm, and he knew the warrior's blade would be on its way. The stranger didn't waste a movement, preparing to strike Rhaven yet again. Tobias and no less than six Chun rushed into the fray with swords drawn, but before they reached them a shout like the bellow of a demon shocked them all.

"Arton!" Aentarra's scream took everyone by surprise, even the warrior.

Something in the sound of the name struck him, halted his attack. And that voice.

He recognized the voice. Her beauty didn't lend itself to forgetfulness, yet it was her scent that struck a chord. It brought back memories of long, long ago. Of a young girl trapped under her horse, of a battlefield tent sweet with the aroma of love, and of gray smoke and stale blood...

"Aentarra!" he whispered, almost daring not to, afraid to believe it. "I thought you dead." His memory played a scene from a thousand years or more, a scene that had been trapped along with so many other memories in his mind—all but the horrors.

A hundred had been there that night, under siege for days. Or was it more? And the beasts would not relent... "Dorgans!" he said aloud. He remembered now. He remembered.

Aentarra stared back at him. "We escaped, Arton, though we presumed you dead as well. I saw you being carried off... how?"

Rahg gasped. "Aentarra! How did you get here?"

She smiled. "You can't escape me so easily. We have business yet to do."

Rhaven wanted to strike the warrior, but his interest was drawn even more by his sword. It was the other one that Mikkellana made. This was the man she spoke of.

Everyone circled the group, even Garnock and Kella had returned. Kella growled, teeth bared and eyes fixed on Arton. The man almost growled.

Gods be dead, he's fierce, thought Rahg.

Aentarra focused her attention once again on Arton. "How did you escape?"

"I woke and killed it before we got to its lair." The words came to him as the memory returned. "I came back for you, but no one was alive. I presumed they had carried you off as well. Where did you go? How?"

"A portal," Aentarra replied and noticed the shock on his face.

"Who escaped? How many? How did you get back here?" Anxiety filled Arton's eyes. "Take me out, Aentarra. It has been so long."

She felt pity for him. There was a time when she had loved him. What must it have been like to be trapped in here this long? "Lukaan is alive, Arton. And he is much stronger."

Rahg shrank from the primeval scream that emerged from his lips. Was the man part beast? The Chun stepped back, gripping swords, prepared to fight. There was hatred in Arton's eyes. Malice in his expression. He panted like a rabid dog. Once he calmed, he queried Aentarra again.

"Who sides with him?

Aentarra smiled sardonically. "Melissara, Ghruehne, Tirzinitzia, Sendra, Zorn. I killed Iazzo."

It was now Arton's turn to smile. "Lukaan is not the only one to have grown stronger."

Aentarra's arm swept wide to encompass Rhaven and the Chun. "These are... friends," she said to Arton. "We have a common goal—to defeat Lukaan."

Arton bowed to them all. "Forgive my attack, but I will make amends. I will kill Lukaan."

By the gods, thought Rahg, by the great gods, what kind of madman has joined us now?

STRANGE ALLIES

The early morning sang news of rain and, for once, rain lifted Rahg's spirits. Just like back home, Rahg thought, recalling spring days in Kamnor, happy days. Problems and worries were all that filled his mind these days, and with Arton around it only got worse; every conversation dwelled on battle.

"You attacked my allies," Arton said to Rhaven, explaining why he had attacked.

Rahg had labeled Arton a madman already when he attacked their entire force by himself, but to hear him call those beasts allies left little doubt.

Arton looked to Rhaven, whose wound yet bled at the slightest provocation. "I'm glad your reflexes were so good. Now that we share an enemy your sword will prove valuable." He paused, his gaze lingering on Rhaven's sword. "Mikkellana made that?"

Rhaven nodded. "She told me of yours, though she thought you dead."

"I don't remember you from before, were you with us when we fought the dorgans? Did we fight together in the Wars of Light?" Arton shook his head in frustration. "My memory has not worked in a long time. Until today I didn't even know my name. It is this place, it...does things to you."

Rhaven smiled. "One hundred years ago, my mother wasn't born."

Arton appeared confused. "Then you and your sword have much to learn, though I can see already that Mikkellana didn't put her talents to waste."

Sama pushed her way to stand beside Rhaven, waiting for a break in the conversation. "Are there others like us here? Have you seen other men?"

"Some," Arton said.

Sama's head drooped. "My husband and son came here moons ago. My heart longs for them."

Arton's eyes showed no sympathy. "I knew of two such men who pined for their family—Korg and Kavi."

The shock sent her reeling, only Pau's quick action caught her. When she recovered, she had to ask again to be certain she had heard it right. "You saw them? Korg and Kavi? Do you know where they are? Where we could find them?"

"They rest safely in my home." *I was right not to kill them. They might yet get me out of this place. It has been so long. So long.*

"Take me there!" Sama shouted.

Arton didn't acknowledge her demand but turned to Aentarra. "When do we fight Lukaan?"

Rhaven stood. "Before we talk about Lukaan, tell me about Korg and Kavi."

"Like most in this strange land, they found themselves fighting someone stronger until I saved them."

Sama wept while Rhaven continued.

"As to Lukaan, we have a mission to complete before we do anything else." He pointed to Rahg. "He is foretold in the Prophecy as the one to stop Lukaan from being freed."

"Lukaan is imprisoned?"

Aentarra chimed in. "Mikkellana, dear sister that she is, designed a shield that trapped him. All the others as well. He has been inside that shield for a thousand years."

Rahg had never heard such maniacal laughter. He held no doubt now about Arton's madness.

"Which direction do you head, Rhaven?"

"The mountains east of here."

"I will return in two day's time, though it could take longer. Sometimes things are not... the same in this place." Arton turned to Sama. "Korg and Kavi will be with me. And I'll bring something to heal that wound. Unless Aentarra has changed her nature, she won't be able to help you."

Arton started, then turned. "If any krengs come, they are my allies, tell them that you claim me as a friend... and tell them that the Nameless One now has a name. They understand your language." Long, powerful strides carried Arton up the mountain and soon out of sight.

CAMISSA WORRIED MORE than she had since before entering the Paaren. She had used her senses to probe Arton's mind and what she found disturbed her. The inner workings were a vortex of unimaginable horror. An eddy of madness, blood, and battle whirling uncontrollably around a core of vengeance.

Camissa gave a wide berth to Aentarra, unsure what her feelings might be regarding her since their last encounter in Entiria. She seemed to treat Rahg all right, but Camissa held no special place in Aentarra's heart.

~

SAMA PACED the campsite for the hundredth time.

"Will you sit, Sama? You will soon wear a path on this ground."

Pau tried to comfort her, but her excitement could not be contained. She had always held out hope, but in her heart, she thought them dead. Now, after all this time, to know they lived. Kavi, her only son, and Korg, the love of her heart. Only two more days, the warrior said. Sama could not wait.

Rhaven sat close to the fire, dizziness striking him yet again. Camissa had tried three times to heal his wound, but it resisted all her attempts. The bleeding had to stop. He must do something. "Tobias, help me sear this wound."

Tobias shook his head. "Too much for searing, Rhaven. I'd be burning half your gut."

Rhaven insisted. "I've got to stop the bleeding, or I won't be able to go on."

"I can help."

Rhaven looked to see Aentarra standing above him. He would sooner trust a Victa, but he had little choice. "I thought you couldn't heal."

"I can't. I can barely mend a broken finger, but I can stop your bleeding, and I can do it without damaging you." She stopped to stare at him. "There will be pain. A lot of pain."

"How would you do it?"

"I can sear it with Fire. But I can make the seal no wider than the wound itself. My Fire can be as thin as a ray of light."

Rhaven nodded. "Do it."

Aentarra turned to Camissa. "Spread some blankets on the ground. Rahg, come and learn something." She looked at the others with scorn. "The rest of you leave. Don't disturb me."

Camissa spread the blankets neatly and removed Rhaven's shirt. "Call me, My Lady, if you need anything else."

Aentarra knelt by Rhaven. "It's just as well you stay, girl. I know you can't make Fire, but you might learn something anyway. You too, Rahg," she snapped.

AENTARRA FOCUSED HER POWER, delved deep into her mind and sought the Fire. She thought of thin things—a strand of hair, a grain of sand, a blade of the finest grass, a ray of light. Then she formed the Fire and wielded it into a fine-pointed tool. Rhaven winced when it touched him, natural reflexes pulling the muscles of his stomach taut. "Steel yourself," Aentarra said, and moved along the open wound.

RHAVEN BIT and ground his teeth, clenched his fist. The farther she went, the more he tensed. The muscles of his feet, legs, even his eyes hurt from squeezing them tight. Finally, the pain subsided. He opened his eyes to see Aentarra, still above him, staring at him. He never realized until now how beautiful she was. Even her voice was warm.

"We're done. Lie still for a short while. When the pain subsides, you can move about. The pain will be with you for a few days, but the bleeding is stopped."

"Thank you, Lady Aentarra. I'm in your debt."

Aentarra smiled the infamous thin smile that had irked so many over the centuries. "Yes, I believe you are."

~

KORG AND KAVI walked behind Arton as they rounded a bend in the mountain trail. When they saw the campsite excitement grew. "Father, they are Chun. Look! There's Pau."

Korg could barely believe his eyes, but then he saw Sama. He raced for her and they almost collided into an embrace. "Sama! How did you get here? Why?"

Sama put her finger to his lips. "Shush, husband, don't talk. Just hold me." She broke the embrace to bring Kavi in, enfolding him in her arms. "Kavi! You are all right. I prayed every day to the Ancient Ones for your safety."

The tears flowed freely now. "We were wrong, Korg. They didn't abandon us."

"What are you doing here, Sama? Why did you come? Now we're all trapped."

Sama pointed to Mulka, sitting with Garnock by the fire. "We travel with a Pathfinder," she said.

The look on Korg's face told his surprise, but Sama continued. "The Prophecy of the Book of Truth is here, my husband. Rahg is his name, and he wears the Stone of BlackHeart." She pointed out Rahg as she spoke.

Korg shook his head in disbelief. "The Prophecy... Why did it come on our watch? Our people have suffered enough." Korg stared at Rahg. "Look at him. He's just a boy. He can't bear the burden of the Prophecy."

Sama never lost patience with Korg. "The Ancient Ones honor you, husband. They waited until the Chun bred a Chief strong enough to complete their mission. They chose you for your strength—a wise decision. Don't question their choice of this man. Whether he looks a boy to you matters not, he has accepted the responsibility of a man.

All that remains is for us to support him. He has already attracted great warriors to his cause."

Kavi nodded in agreement, even if Korg would not as yet. He walked to Rahg, hand extended. "I'm Kavi, son of Korg and Sama. May your days be bright with sun, and your hut keep you warm."

Rahg eagerly took his hand. "I'm Rahg," he said. "I know that your mother is overjoyed. She's been worried." Rahg bade him sit. "How long have you been here? In the Paaren, I mean."

"A few moons, if you can trust the moons here. I've seen strange things happen, and I'm not always certain these are the same moons that we had in Arangar."

Rahg broke off a piece of cheese and handed it to Kavi. "I haven't been here so long as that, but we saw some beasts that I never saw before."

"The krengs! They're fierce, but..." Kavi looked around. "The Nameless One frightens me more."

"You mean Arton?"

Kavi nodded. "He told us he found his name. Arton, that's him."

Guilt weighed heavy on Rahg. Once again he was dragging an innocent person to death. The gods only knew, there would be deaths, many deaths. "Kavi, this is a dangerous mission. I fear—"

Kavi laid a hand on Rahg's arm. "Your concern is understood, but the Chun have waited for more moons than there have been snowfalls— waited for the One that has been Prophesied. And now you are here. I see the BlackHeart Stone." Kavi smiled. "You can't keep a Chun from helping you. You are BlackHeart."

AENTARRA WATCHED as Rahg practiced his shield. If nothing else, he worked himself diligently. "You work hard, Rahg, but you must work harder. Strength comes from strength."

Rahg smiled, but inside he seethed. Aentarra unsettled him, even when she was nice. "Tell me what to do, My Lady. I will do my best."

Aentarra's lips barely parted, but her eyes sparkled. "Call four of the Chun here and have them attack you. You must protect yourself with short shields. No shields larger than a sword."

"A sword! I'm no blade master. How can I fight four Chun with a sword made of shield?"

Aentarra's weave created a staff made of shield, which she wielded like a bounty-man. She spun it quickly, and Rahg didn't have time to move before it struck him in the gut. He doubled over, but recovered quickly, jumping back from the reach of the staff.

"Leave me alone!" he shouted, but he had the presence of mind to weave a sword and shield of his own. He blocked her next blow with his shield, carried on his left arm, then attacked with the sword. Let her feel the brunt of this.

She easily warded Rahg's blow, then assaulted him with vigor. The staff struck Rahg five times without him countering a blow. Knees buckled from successive strikes, then his back, side, and head. The final strike knocked him down.

She stood above Rahg, the leer on her face a taunt. "You would have fared better with the Chun."

Rahg rubbed his head as he got to his feet. "The Chun wouldn't have struck so hard."

Aentarra laughed. "A Wolfen would have killed you. You will likely be outnumbered in most battles, or, at the very least, be facing enemies with superior powers, so you had better be prepared. A mistake against an enemy and you won't have a head to hurt."

"I'm just learning—"

"The Banished Ones won't wait until you learn your craft. If they wait for you to draw your sword count yourself fortunate." He looked as if he was beginning to believe her. "Are you ready to practice?"

Rahg began to object but thought better of it. "What do you want me to do, My Lady?"

"The strongest shields are concentrated ones. I'll show you. Form a large shield, like a blanket spread before you, and watch what happens when I attack with a pointed blade." Aentarra's weave—in the shape of a sword—pierced his shield with little resistance.

"How did you do that? I held off Rhaven and Tobias both with that weave."

"Neither Rhaven nor Tobias can weave a shield. I concentrated the power at the point of it; the result, you experienced. Now weave a small shield. Focus the energy, feel the strength."

Aentarra attacked as soon as he finished the weave, but this time his shield held, though the impact jarred him. He smiled, despite the discomfort.

"Did you feel the difference? I struck with even more force this time, and yet your weave sustained the blow."

"But that was small. Suppose I—"

"You want the security of a large shield, I know. But once you realize how weak a large shield is, you will think differently. There are improvements you can make to the larger shields. Practice, you will discover them."

Aentarra drilled Rahg for more than half the day, driving him further than he thought possible. She switched sessions too, forcing him to learn new weaves as well as hone his skills on ones he already knew.

The worst experience Rahg had was with Fire. Aentarra made him weave two shields no thicker than the broad side of a blade, and then she initiated the attacks. At first, balls of Flame came at him two or three at a time, but slowly.

He fended them off easily. Soon, however, the Fire not only grew in strength, but the rapidity and frequency of the attacks increased, and every time that Rahg failed to intercept one, he body felt the mistake. When Aentarra mercifully ended the training session, Rahg had no less than nine or ten burns to show for his errors. The last one knocked him to the ground.

Aentarra offered him a hand to get up. "Can you walk?"

"I don't know. My leg is bad." He accepted her extended hand and pulled himself to his feet. "That was enough practice for a lifetime but thank you for teaching me."

"I'm glad you harbor no ill will. We'll continue our sessions in the morning." With that, Aentarra left.

Rahg was too dumbfounded to speak. *She means to kill me. By the gods, I can barely walk. How can I practice with her?*

Camissa had kept her distance while Aentarra trained him, though her jaw ached from grinding her teeth at the torture Aentarra had put him through. "Rahg, are you all right? I saw what she did," Camissa said, the last a cautious whisper. "Come sit by the fire. I will try to heal you."

"Not the fire," Rahg said. "I've had enough of fire today." His eyes held warmth for Camissa. "But if you can do anything to ease the pain, I would be forever in your debt."

"You already owe me more than you can repay. I might someday ask for payment on these debts."

"And you shall have them as soon as we kill the Banished Ones and Lukaan. After that, I'll repay you."

She laughed. "Sit here while I get a blanket." Camissa spent a long time nursing his wounds. Burns were difficult for her; she had little experience with them, and Healing proved to be a complicated process. She had plans to heal his burns, but after the first two, she realized that she would not have the strength to do them all, so she elected to focus on the worst ones.

After a grueling trial, she had healed the worst one, the one on his leg, and two of the other more serious wounds, but now, no matter how she tried, nothing worked. Exhaustion affects the powers first. "That is all I can do. I have tried, but I cannot do more. I'm sorry."

Rahg grabbed Camissa and pulled her to him. "You helped me tremendously. My leg feels much better. Some soreness, that's all. The others aren't so bad."

Camissa sighed. "Thank you."

From a concealed state shortly behind them, Aentarra sighed. Camissa had learned more healing—some practice for her—and Rahg had grown greatly today. She could feel him growing stronger.

You will need it. You might need it a lot sooner than you think. Before this is over Camissa will have many wounds to heal. Many burns. The Banished Ones all have Fire.

DESERT SANDS

It took four more days to get through the mountains. Rahg had new wounds to show for each of those days. Aentarra had been relentless in her pursuit of Rahg's training and even more relentless in the ferocity of her attacks. Much as he hated to admit it though, Rahg felt the growth in his powers. Every weave he made proved to be stronger than the previous one, and old weaves came with the speed of a thought. He now practiced with five Chun warriors and, where he would have struggled with three before, he withstood the attack of the five without a bruise to show for it.

Camissa had also grown in her healing powers. The burns no longer caused her the trouble they did before, and the healing didn't drain her like it used to.

Rahg's confidence increased daily, as did his comfort level with Aentarra. She no longer loomed as a dreaded immortal waiting to kill him.

"Have you come to receive your daily burns, Rahg?"

"I think, today, Lady Aentarra, that I shall receive no burns."

"Ah, it does my heart good to see such overconfidence. I once saw a kitten chase a pup away, but then she thought she could do the same with a wolf. It proved to be fatal."

Nothing dampened Rahg's spirits today. "So what will it be, My Lady? Will I battle with a pup or a wolf?"

Time to teach that kitten a lesson, I see. "Prepare yourself."

Rahg wove two shields in preparation for the assault. He countered the first salvo easily, then the second and third with little more effort. Two more Fireballs came, which Rahg met with a shield, but then a spinning disk of sharpened shield, no thicker than an oak leaf came straight for him. Gods be dead! he thought, and raised both swords to block it. The spinning layer of shield struck Rahg's shields and cut right through them—severing them at impact. Rahg gasped, awaiting death, but it stopped spinning just in front of him.

Rahg took several long, heavy breaths in an attempt to calm his panicked breathing. "You almost killed me!"

"If I had wanted you dead, I wouldn't have stopped the shield."

"Why?"

"To teach you to be prepared for anything, from anyone."

"That's not fair. We were practicing with Fire."

"And will you tell that to Tirzinitzia when she gets free? Or Sendra? They don't have the power of shielding, but they have more tricks than you can dream of. You better pray to those gods you always invoke the name of that you never face Ghruehne. He enjoys killing almost as much as Iazzo, but he is far more experienced. Far more."

Rahg shook his head. "I'm done for today. And tomorrow and the next. I don't know when I want to practice again, but it won't be for a while."

"Enjoy yourself while you can. You'll return soon enough."

"WE KEEP GOING STRAIGHT, Rhaven. It's the next mountain range, that one peak."

mountain of the gods

Rhaven knew the one Rahg meant, no clarification was needed. The range stretched in a north/south direction and ran consistent with one exception—a towering peak embraced by dark clouds that didn't move, and with a blanket of snow on its shoulders and a blazing sunset. "We could have guessed this without the amulet. It is foreboding enough."

Rahg smiled; the mere mention of something being foreboding from Rhaven seemed ridiculous.

Rhaven called Pau, Tobias, Korg, and Arton to the front. "Arton, we head for that mountain. Do you know the terrain? What we will face?"

Arton's voice held a rough accent, unlike any Rahg had heard before, but it did nothing to diminish his confident tone. "All the land between us is desert. The journey will be a difficult one, one a thirsty man would not survive."

"What about the mountains? What will we find there?"

"The mountain kills all those who try to scale it."

"What do you mean it kills them? What does it do?" Rahg's head darted between Arton and Rhaven.

"The krengs say a god lives in the mountain. I have seen no god, but I have stood close enough. Something fierce lives there and the ones I traveled with didn't return. Legends say no one returns."

"You haven't tried?" Rhaven asked.

"I'm no fool. The mountain is nothing worth risking life for." Arton considered something, then continued. "The krengs will be here soon; perhaps they know more."

"Krengs! The beasts we saw in that canyon?" Rahg's worry grew, but as he looked at Arton, he thought the man would growl.

"Krengs are allies. They have honor. If they give their word, it won't be broken."

Impatience showed on Rhaven's face. Arton had explained why they should let krengs travel with them, but Rhaven didn't like waiting. "How long until they arrive?"

"We share too much," Arton said to Rhaven. "I too, wait for no one. Leave when you're ready, the krengs will find us. They can track anyone, even in this place."

Rhaven nodded. "You lead. I'll keep right flank, Korg—left, Tobias and Tomkins will take the rear. Rahg, do you still train? If so, take a spot behind me, if not, stay in the center."

Rahg looked around, seeking Aentarra. "Not now. I'll practice on my own for a while."

"Fill the water casks," Rhaven ordered.

Almost before the Chun had finished, Arton led the way. It would not be a long journey across the sands, not in terms of days, but it would be a grueling one.

MOONLIGHT CAST broad beams in the desert sky, a deep red light that appeared almost white against such a dark canopy. The night had ridden in with currents of cold air, and it chilled through the light layer of clothing most of them wore.

moon in red sky

Arton prowled the camp like a wolf searching the flock for weakness. One of Korg's Chun warriors had taken two swigs of water and now lifted the cask for a third. Arton snatched it from his grip, a scowl serving as reprimand. He capped it and laid it on the ground. The Chun knew better than to pick it up again. Soon, the men had the message.

Rahg practiced little that nights. The day had been a tough one, and he felt the pangs of exhaustion. He moved over to sit beside Camissa, who looked more tired than he felt. Cold too. "No fire tonight," Rahg said. "Makes it seem a lot colder."

Camissa shivered, legs tucked up to her chest with her arms wrapped around them. "It is colder, Rahg. And I doubt if we will see fire anytime soon. There are no trees here. Nothing but sand and rock."

Rahg moved closer, his arm across her shoulder. He comforted her, but he got more comfort for himself in return. Camissa was one of the only people who calmed him, soothed his nerves.

Rahg focused his power and created a weave he had practiced for several days on his own. A shield wrapped around them in an arc, protecting them from the wind. A second weave, much thinner, completed the circle leaving only a small opening in front.

Camissa felt the difference immediately; the wind stopped, and the cold abated. "Thank you, Rahg. This will help for a while, though I'm not eager to lose that shield when we sleep."

"Tonight you won't have to Camissa. At least for a while."

"You learned how to keep the shield up while you sleep?"

"Last night was the first time. It wasn't there when I woke, so I don't know how long it lasted, but I think it held for a while after I fell asleep."

"We will see how long it lasts tonight."

BY THE FIFTH DAY, the water supply was low and most everyone complained about how little Arton and Rhaven allowed them to drink. The sun burned fiercely during the day, and at night the wind and cold continued. Rahg's shield had proved effective but for only a short time after they fell asleep. Rahg was practicing again but by himself.

"Where is Aentarra? I haven't seen her since you last trained."

"I don't know, Camissa, but I hope she stays there. She is—"

"Hush!" Camissa checked the area, relieved when she saw no sign of Aentarra. "Watch your tongue, Rahg. You might think differently, but I still believe she's dangerous, even to you. Just because she's helping you train means nothing."

Rahg had his protest ready when Tobias came up behind him. "Camissa is right, lad. You can't trust her any more than you can a wagger. And another thing, just because you don't see her around doesn't mean she can't hear you. I don't claim to know much about these powers, but I wouldn't be lettin' my tongue wag so much if I were you. She might come and put a knot or two in it." Tobias's chuckle could be as irritating as it sometimes was funny, and today Rahg found it anything but funny.

"Looks like we've got more than a few days till we get there, lad. I'm concerned about some of Korg's men. They look to be on their last legs, and trouble is we don't know if we'll even find water when we get there."

"There's bound to be water there somewhere, Tobias. The mountain has snow, and that snow has to melt before it hits the desert."

"That it does, lad. But that water could be two or three days from where we meet the mountains."

"I hope you're wrong, but we'll have to wait until we get there."

By mid afternoon the scorching sun had sparked the thirst in all of them, save Arton and Rhaven. Mulka never complained, and the welgar and Kella had not slowed their pace, continuing to scout with relentless fervor.

Korg and Kavi fared better than the other Chun, perhaps because a good number of them had been frail from hunger before the journey had even begun.

The camp at nights was quiet; few of the Chun warriors talked at all. Korg and Sama spoke a little, but mostly to each other, and even Tobias had quit entertaining them with his tales—a parched throat to blame.

The only ones healthy enough to sustain a normal conversation were Arton and Rhaven, but by nature, the two of them spoke sparsely. Getting words out of Rhaven was like prying a bone from a dog's mouth, and Arton was even worse. Rahg had even quit weaving shields at night, as he couldn't muster the energy.

Rahg woke early the next morning and watched as Rhaven practiced his ritual with the weapons. He always worked the sai and the sword, and at times, incorporated other weapons into his practice. Then there was the stretching and meditative exercises—these formed the bulk of his work—and Rahg had learned early on that he tolerated no disturbance.

When Rhaven finally finished, Rahg approached. "We'll get there today, won't we?"

"To the foothills, yes. I'll send Kella ahead to find water. Camp will be better tonight."

"Will we have to come back this way?"

"We'll deal with that after you finish. Perhaps the amulet will tell you. Or Mulka, he might know." Rhaven put his sai and sword away. "But if we have to come back this way we'll be better prepared."

During the late part of the day, Tobias reported that they were being followed. Rhaven and Arton stopped to check. Arton raised his head in the air, sniffing for a scent. "It is the krengs," he said. "Kyra, with several packs."

Rhaven stared at him, but Rahg nearly choked. He sniffed the air! Gods be dead, the man is half beast himself.

Camissa agreed, sending a message to Rahg through her senses. She and he had been practicing that at night, among other things. He frightens me, Rahg. I do not trust him; not even as much as Aentarra.

Rahg simply nodded.

"We can continue," Arton said. "They move much faster than us."

In short time, they reached the foothills where they made camp. "Kella is searching for water," Rhaven said. "We'll camp here and wait for her and the krengs."

"Kyra will find us water. She can find water in the middle of the sands."

Kyra arrived shortly with three packs trailing her, thirty-five in all. Kyra bowed to Arton, wary eyes scanning the rest of his pack. "We heard that your pack had returned, Nameless One."

Arton bowed also, but he held the position, his head hung low. He would finally complete the ritual initiated in his cave. "I am Arton. I give you my name. All that is mine is now yours to protect."

Kyra smiled, though to Rahg, whose eyes had fastened to this odd ceremony, it looked more like a snarl. She now assumed the position Arton had used, head hung low. "While I live your young will live. If they die, then I shall die."

Arton had no young, but it mattered not. He might someday, and Kyra would be honor-bound to protect them as if they were her own.

Rahg could barely believe that these beasts could speak, especially the same language as him, but he learned later that only Kyra and her young had learned the language, and they learned it from Arton. They apparently learned quickly. Rahg heard some guttural sounds emanate from her lips, then three of the kreng ran off into the foothills.

"They will find water," Kyra said.

Two of the kreng scouts returned with news of a fresh creek that flowed with cold water from the mountains, and it was only a short distance away. Soon after that, Kella made her way back into camp also. Rhaven had sent several men with one of the krengs to fill casks with water while the others rested.

Rahg's curiosity was stronger than his fear, and so he and Camissa had taken a seat close to the kreng leader, Kyra, while she discussed things with Arton and Rhaven. Korg and Sama sat next to Arton, and Kavi had joined Rahg and Camissa. It somehow eased the tension with Kavi there, since he had spent time with both the kreng and Arton. It made them seem less frightful. Rahg was telling Kavi some stories about growing up in Twin Forks when there came horrible growling sounds from the north trail that led into the mountains.

Kyra jumped to her feet quickly, faster than a cat.

Rahg heard the grunts and growls of the kreng, but then through all of it, he heard Arton scream, a sound that pierced the night with its chill. "Dorgans!"

All the kreng massed, wasting no time. Kyra darted up the same path that the scout had used, and her packs followed.

Arton had a sword drawn and issued orders to Rhaven. "Get everyone! Dorgans are here!"

Rhaven looked as puzzled as Rahg, but Arton's boots were already kicking up dirt as he climbed. Just then, Aentarra appeared in the midst of them.

"Rhaven, everyone arm yourselves. We have a battle on our hands. And keep that Pathfinder safe. We can't afford to lose him."

Rhaven managed to get a few questions out. "Who are they? How many?"

Rahg had never seen Aentarra so upset. She had nearly laughed at the

Battle of Sunnara, as they called it now, when he had fought Iazzo. Who were these dorgans?

"It doesn't matter how many. They are here."

Rhaven issued orders as if he had been planning them all day and they lay memorized in his mind. "Tobias, you and Tomkins stay with Mulka and Camissa. Korg, keep ten of your Chun with them as well. The rest of you follow me. You too, Rahg." With that, he was off.

Rahg heard the screams before they rounded the bend, and as horrific as the sounds were, he wasn't prepared for what he saw. In a small valley stood six of the most monstrous things he had ever seen. Each one had four arms that reached out like tentacles, but with claws bigger than a bear's. Their flesh was red and blue and black, and he could see during flashes of light from Aentarra's Fire that they bled white blood.

Rahg ran to catch Rhaven, who had already joined the fray, his sword singing its dance of death, but even though he drew blood with each strike, he couldn't bring them down. The krengs had circled the beasts, coordinating their attacks with feints and rushes that drew the beasts off guard. Rahg grimaced at the blood-curdling howl of a kreng. One of the dorgans had seized it and ripped its body in half. Gods be dead!

"Down, Rahg!" Rhaven shouted.

Instinct forced Rahg to duck and dive to his side, just barely in time to miss the sweep of a monstrous arm. Fear turned to a rush of vengeance and Rahg joined the attack in full. He had his sword in hand and had a shield to protect his other arm from attack, though he didn't know if it would hold against these beasts.

Arton proved himself the madman Rahg had labeled him as he met each attempted strike by the dorgans with a cackle that any madman would envy, followed by his drive to carve another piece of flesh from the dorgan's legs.

The dorgan directly in front of Rahg had turned to attack krengs slicing at its hamstrings by leaping in the air. Rahg took the opportunity to strike his sword deep into the calf of the beast. He had used two hands to thrust the sword, but it only sank one-third the way in, their muscle a strong resistance to the blade. Two more howls from behind brought two more deaths from the krengs, and for the first time, Rahg didn't fear the krengs. He felt sorry for them. Respected them.

Kyra and one of her packs concentrated on one dorgan and had herded it away from the rest of them until they had it alone. It was obvious she had experience fighting these beasts, and for that reason alone he felt great pity for her.

Aentarra used a shield to separate two of the dorgans from the rest of the pack. The invisible shield panicked them, distracted their attention long enough for her to strike with Fire. She began with Yellow and Red Fire, an attempt to conserve energy while maintaining the shield, but it did too little damage to the dorgans. The flames caught quick enough, but one sweep with their giant paws and they smothered the flames. "Move aside!" Everyone but two krengs moved quickly, keenly aware of her powers, but the krengs had never seen her, didn't know what she was capable of.

Aentarra let the shield drop and focused her power. A rolling wall of BlackFire descended from the slight rise she stood upon, destroying everything it touched. Rocks melted, the ground steamed and smoked, and worst of all, the two krengs disappeared into the darkness it brought, leaving only ash in its wake.

The dorgans charged Aentarra when the shield dropped, not knowing the power they rushed to meet. Soon, though, the ground shook with their agony as the Fire consumed them. They tried to swat the flames out, but it only spread to their paws then arms. It went from the legs to the chest, until soon the two beasts were completely afire. With their final screams, Aentarra's knees buckled. It had taken much to maintain the BlackFire so long.

Three dorgans faced about twenty krengs, Rhaven, Arton and the rest of the Chun. It would have been over quickly if not for the combination of Rhaven and Arton with Kella and the welgar.

Rhaven carved a large piece of flesh from a dorgan's leg, large and painful enough that it drew the full attention of the beast. Two, giant arms swung to capture him, and he saw no escape. Just then, Kella leaped from a ledge behind them, landing on the dorgans neck. Three powerful snaps from her jaws ripped the neck enough to cause profuse bleeding. It proved enough to stave off the attack against Rhaven as the dorgan focused its attention on Kella. She leaped again, back to the ledge, then down to be with Rhaven.

"Another one I owe you," Rhaven said, then called to Korg's men. "Rush it from all sides." The beast yet had life in it and swept down to grab two of the Chun. Another of its paws seized Chengal. He would soon meet the Makers on the Chugarran Path.

Rahg found himself fighting alongside Arton, how he didn't know. He didn't even like to sit next to the man let alone fight these beasts with him. But it was comforting to see him in action. He had never seen someone move so swiftly.

Aentarra had recovered enough to join the battle again with about six krengs against the dorgan farthest east, close to the one Kyra fought. This time, she used a small shield to separate the krengs and then focused on the dorgan. She didn't have enough power left to use BlackFire on this one, and as she knew too well, the other Fire would not likely kill it. It would have to be Lightning. She called on the powers of Storm and reached to the towering peak where the dark clouds hid an ever-present storm. She delved into the dark mass until she found what she sought, then struck. YellowLightning flashed its brilliance across the sky then down to the dorgan, striking it like an arrow shot from an archer's bow.

The dorgan's mouth opened like a cavern, and a howl emerged that rivaled the thunder emanating from the dark masses at the peak of the mountain. Another dorgan lay dead. Aentarra again felt the weakness and knew she had to renew herself if this battle was to be won.

Rahg leaped from the clutching paws of a dorgan, and when the beast reached for him, Arton jumped on its arm and scaled it as if he were running up a hill. The dorgan reacted quickly but not quickly enough as Arton had gotten close enough to jump to its shoulders, his deadly blade now digging flesh from the dorgan's face.

Arton howled in the language of the krengs, and the ones who had been fighting with Aentarra came running. They swarmed the legs of the dorgan in a relentless assault with no regard for their own lives, barely dodging the claws as it tried to thwart their attack. Rahg recalled the way Aentarra had made that spinning shield and how dangerous it looked, so he created a weave as best he could, sending it spinning toward the dorgan's chest, but when it reached the target, it didn't have force enough to penetrate.

Arton hung on desperately as the dorgan tried to shake and pry him loose, but he somehow stayed attached to the dorgan like a leech. When the dorgan dropped an arm to reach for Rahg, Arton positioned himself and struck with a two–handed thrust into the dorgan's ear, his blade sinking all the way to the hilt. One more fell.

Only two remained: the one that Kyra fought and the one Rhaven and the others fought. Kyra's pack had been reduced to her and five others, but the dorgan was far from dead, while Rhaven, Korg, Kavi, and what remained of the krengs and Chun struggled with the other. Rahg rushed to help Kyra, hopelessly outmatched with the few warriors still with her.

"Use your shield to protect them," Aentarra shouted as he ran past her. "You can't hurt them by yourself, but you might buy protection for the krengs." The dorgan's roar sounded victorious, but as it stooped to attack, Rahg threw a shield to cover Kyra and three of hers.

Just then, from out of the darkness, Jorn came running, wielding his sword and shouting like a madman. He attacked the dorgan from the back of the legs, stabbing and slicing for all he was worth. The dorgan kicked back, nicked Jorn and sent him reeling, but he recovered and charged again.

"Stop!" Rahg shouted, but Jorn went straight for the leg again, now wielding both sword and knife. This time the dorgan turned around and reached down with one of its massive arms. It seized Jorn in its hand and crushed him, then tore his limbs from his body.

Rahg nearly puked but managed to strengthen the shield he had put around Kyra and none too soon, for the dorgan turned back around and focused on them. The dorgan's first reaction was surprise, but then it pummeled the invisible shield with three huge fists. Rahg had been running to join them, but the force of the assault astounded him. It felt like Iazzo's Fire had, even the Lightning. Twice, Rahg fell trying to get closer, hoping his protection would be stronger if he could only get closer.

Inside the shield, Kyra wore a puzzled look on her face. She had said her last words, told her mate that she would be coming. But something had stopped the dorgan's attack. Something she could not see. It must be them, she thought.

She had already seen the Fire that the one female had called forth. And then Lightning had struck a dorgan, saving several of her pack. She doubted that Lightning had been an accident. The Nameless One who calls himself Arton had powerful allies.

"Retreat!" she ordered her pack members. Retreat was not an option for krengs, not a permanent one, but she would not wait for death's touch while something she could not see prevented her from striking.

The next two blows from the dorgan proved too much for Rahg to handle and he collapsed. Kyra saw him fall and realized that the dorgan had diverted from the focus on them to going after Rahg. Kyra ran to Rahg.

He must have called the invisible shield, she thought.

Kella had sustained a huge gash on her side, severely hampering her movement, and several more Chun and kreng had fallen.

Korg fought furiously alongside Kavi and five of the Chun, one of whom was Kyra's son Pharr. The dorgan couldn't last much longer: milky white blood ran from its neck; it had lost the use of two of its arms; and one leg had been hacked so badly it looked as if it might fall like a tree to a woodsman's ax. But it still had the strength to attack, and it did so with vigor. Four more Chun and two krengs fell. Korg and Kavi looked to be next as the dorgan was almost upon them.

Garnock had refrained from joining the fight until now. He had never promised to protect the race of man; he hated the race of man, but this was enough. These creatures were different. They only wanted to kill.

The welgar sprang from his crouched position on the hill and rushed headlong into the battle, teeth eager for blood and flesh. Perhaps it would taste like human flesh. The day might not prove a failure after all.

Kavi dodged the claw by a thin margin and rushed to his feet. His only hope to get out from under the dorgan, but Korg lay on his back, hurt. "Come, father!" he screamed as he ran to Korg's aid.

Garnock scaled the dorgan, running up its fur as if it were a tree to climb. The dorgan never even knew it was on it until the welgar reached its face. Teeth as sharp as knives dug deep into the dorgan's facial structure. The welgar attacked the lip first, then he sought the eyes. If anything, welgars knew how to kill. Garnock's blade-like claws dug into the right eye, then without a pause to relish the assault, he jumped to the left eye and struck harder. Now blinded and in a fury, the dorgan screamed and raged, but mostly it panicked.

Garnock's descent to the right side of the neck proved easier than dropping down a vine, and he soon found himself at the wound that Kella had initiated, a gaping gash, but one that had not reached lethal depth. The welgar burrowed into the wound and used its teeth to dig yet deeper, then deeper still until it found the main river of blood. A final attack severed the channel, and the white milky substance erupted with force enough to eject the welgar from the wound. He caught hold of fur at the shoulder, then scampered to reach the ground. The dorgan fell with a crash.

The final dorgan reached for Rahg, but Kyra had scooped him in her arms and was moving away rapidly, though perhaps not rapidly enough. Aentarra saw the danger but wondered if she could act in time. Aentarra formed the image in her mind, called on every reserve she had, then used her power to create an immense spear of Black-Fire. When the dorgan was just about to reach Kyra and Rahg, she unleashed it, sending the spear straight to its heart. She only hoped it had a heart.

The spear proved to be as deadly as its creator; the dorgan stopped dead, BlackFire burning it from the inside out until it melted to the ground like so much ash.

Arton rushed to Aentarra's side. She lay on the rocks at the crest of the rise where she had stood. "I am fine, Arton, just a little weakened. Rest and food will heal me." Aentarra stood on her own, shaking off Arton's assistance. "You know we must hurry. Dorgans seldom travel in groups so few; these must have been scouts."

BURY THE DEAD

*P*au bristled at the order to depart immediately. "We have wounded to care for, and the dead must be buried."

"The wounded come with us," Arton said. "The dead we can bury later, but for now we need a strong defensive position to rest the night."

Rhaven arrived, carrying a kreng warrior over his shoulder. "Do you expect more trouble?"

Arton picked up a wounded Chun to carry back to camp. "These were but scouts."

Rhaven nodded, then looked for Rahg, and saw him tossed over Kyra's shoulder. Rhaven turned back to Arton. "We passed a spot not far from here that would be suitable. Large rocks for defense and a narrow entrance."

"Lead us."

"Korg, take who you need to help you and bring the wounded. Leave the dead." Rhaven looked around until he spotted the vargel. "Kella, stay with Korg and bring him to us." He was going to send someone back to camp, but he noticed Garnock already running in that direction.

Somehow the welgar knows, Rhaven thought and continued.

THEY SETTLED INTO CAMP, though no one could rest. Camissa was shocked at the severity of the wounds, and she struggled with the healing, asking everyone who was healthy enough to give a hand. Even Mulka joined in, cleaning wounds and bandaging the wounded —people and krengs alike. The few Chun who remained had gathered wood for fires, everyone longing for warmth and light—two things sorely needed this night. It was cold, and no one trusted the dark, but before they could put a striker to the kindling, Arton stopped them.

His fierce expression would have been deterrent enough, but what he said had more effect. "The dorgans hunt for fires at night; lighting a fire would be a beacon to them."

Rahg seemed to have recovered, and with Aentarra no one could tell, but at least she acted normal.

Rhaven walked the camp checking on everything. "Have you posted the guards?"

"We have them on the rocks above, plus two at each flank and the rear, though I can't believe anything could reach us there." Korg paused. "The guards are mostly krengs; they see better at night, and their smell is the best."

Korg remained nervous, uncomfortable being around Aentarra. He had seen the Fire and Lightning she wielded. By the heart of the Ancients, he thought. No one should be able to do such things.

He walked back to Sama, busy helping Camissa with her healing. "We lost many men tonight. Good men. Chengal fell, though I believe he went quickly. I hope he did."

"How many, husband?"

Korg paused to count. "Nine Chun dead, eleven krengs. Almost as many wounded."

Rahg overheard the conversation, bringing more sad news on his shoulders. More dead because of me. He waited for Rhaven and the others to leave before he addressed Aentarra. "What were they, My Lady?"

Aentarra thought about how to answer. "They only live to kill. And they do that savagely, as you saw."

Rahg's chin rested on his chest. "I couldn't stop them. I couldn't save them. All those people, dead."

"You did well. No one can stand up to a dorgan onslaught."

"I should have done more."

Aentarra grabbed his head and pulled him to her. He shivered at her touch, yet it was so soft, so caring. Her eyes too were warm. "You couldn't have done any more than you did. I used all my powers and couldn't stop them. Not with Shield, Fire, or even Lightning."

"But..."

Aentarra stared at Rahg. "You must realize, no one can stop them when they decide to assault. And be thankful this was a small group. Even Lukaan couldn't stop a large assault."

Rahg's eyes almost popped out of his head. "Lukaan! Did he fight them? When? How do you know?"

"It was a long time ago, a very long time. I know because I was with him. He used powers that dwarf mine but to no avail. No matter how many he killed, more came. It was only good fortune that allowed some of us to escape."

Rahg was more alert now than before the attack. More afraid, too. "How many were there? Much more than this?"

Aentarra rested folded hands on her lap. She even allowed a brief smile. "Lukaan killed more than this with every two strikes. And one hundred more of us struck every time we had energy enough, to do so. But that was so very long ago."

She stood and turned away. "I must see to the others. I need to know what we have left to battle with in the event we meet more of them. Also, I might help the girl. I'm not a healer, but I might offer advice."

Rahg didn't want her to go. He wanted to learn more, and yet, he was afraid to. "What happened after that, Aentarra?" He suddenly realized he had called her by name and hurried to correct the grievous error. "I mean, My Lady. I'm sorry, I..."

Aentarra faced him and smiled. Another warm smile. "No need to apologize. It is, after all, my name. And now that we are on better terms you should know my last name as well. Du Savarra. Aentarra du Savarra. One day I will tell you more about my family."

Rahg stood as she departed; excitement bursting from him. "Aentarra du Savarra," he muttered.

RAHG WOKE to find Camissa's head resting on his shoulder. She had stayed up most of the night. Each time he had awakened she was still working, trying to heal the wounds of men and krengs alike. She must be exhausted, Rahg thought, and gently slipped her head onto his bedroll. He covered her, then walked to join Tobias at the fire. "No sign of more is there?"

Tobias shook his head. "Not a one, lad. And I suspect Rhaven's got those scouts out several leagues by now."

Rahg sipped the hot khaffe and devoured two biscuits before Tobias could scold him. "Better save some for Camissa. She sat up nearly till dawn mending wounds like old woman Parton darned socks. Two of the Chun and one kreng I'd not be cooking for this morning if not for her."

"She's a good woman, Tobias. Pretty too."

"Told you that first time I saw her, lad. I know a good heart when I see one."

Rahg held a mouthful of khaffe and nearly spit it out. "You treated her like she was a wagger. Darstan and I were the ones who liked her, but you reminded us two or three times a day not to trust her."

Tobias laughed but denied it. "Lad, I'd challenge your memory on that, but I don't wish to tire you out. You might need your strength today."

Rahg sipped another cup of khaffe as he made his way back to Camissa. As he stared at the mountain with snow brushing the high altitudes and the ominous dark clouds hovering above, it suddenly struck him. "By the gods! No! It can't be. I won't do it."

Camissa jumped from her bed, startled. "What's wrong?"

"I can't do it!"

Camissa stood right in front of him, face to face. "Can't do what? What are you talking about?"

"It's the dream." He pointed frantically to the towering peak. "That's the mountain in my dream!"

The shiver traveled the length of her body. What if the rest of his dreams proved true? Worse, what if hers did? She hugged him, held him. "We will help, Rahg."

THE CAVE

"Kella and I will come with you," Rhaven said.

"I need to go alone. I can't explain it, but I know it's something I must do alone." Fear oozed through Rahg even as he said it, swirling in his chest, then sinking to his gut. It lay there churning in him, almost taunting him.

Rhaven remained silent. He looked at the mountain then back to Rahg. "Whoever it is that controls our fates wouldn't have let us come this far to have it end here. You will come back. And I will be waiting."

Rhaven seldom said so much at one time. "Thanks, Rhaven," Rahg said. "I plan on returning, but..."

"There's no alternative. Never make plans for death, that way it won't come to greet you. I believe death only comes for those who invite it."

"Then may you live forever, Rhaven."

Rhaven watched as Rahg climbed ever-higher. A brave lad, he thought proudly. He shook to clear his head. It looked as if the dark clouds descended as Rahg rose. He put a mark on the mountain with his eye and soon knew that the ominous clouds did fall. Don't let this be death, Rhaven prayed, but to whom he didn't know.

~

"WHERE'S RAHG?" Camissa asked.

"Went to the mountain," Tobias said.

Camissa's tears came instantly. "You don't understand. He is terrified! He cannot make it alone. Get him. Send someone. Please?"

"He needs to do this alone," Tobias said.

Tobias did everything he could to keep Camissa busy, as it helped him too. He was as worried as she was. When nothing seemed to work, he prayed. For the first time since Shia died, he prayed.

Take care of him. Don't fail me now like you did with Shia and Whisper. If you care at all about the good people, take care of that lad. He's a good one.

~

AENTARRA WATCHED from a point partway up the mountain. She had planned to follow him, but as she climbed, a strange sensation warned her against it. She had an innate sense of danger, and it usually proved to be true. This was as far as she dared go. The itch of curiosity burned her, like someone scratching from inside her skin, desperate to get out.

May you fare well, Rahg. I need to know what you find in there.

~

RAHG'S EYES fixed on the path before him, never seeing more than a few paces ahead of where he was. Somehow, though, he knew where to go, and he knew what to do. An eerie sensation crept into his mind as the cloud descended upon him.

What will it do?

He also wondered of the dream. In his dream, he always went through a great sea with the whirlpool and the waves that threatened to bash him against the rocks, but there was surely no—"Gods be dead!"

His head began to swim in circles, dizziness set in. It was the eddy. "There's no sea here!" he screamed. But no matter what his mind said, he heard the swells, and he felt them, and he was wet, soaking wet. Fear settled deeper into his body, sinking as deep as the waist.

He struggled to keep his head above the water, gasping for air as he swallowed a mouthful. No sooner had be started choking then he was back again, still climbing the mountain.

The next breath brought the wind in gusts. The waves roared, and rose from the sea with white foamy caps, then smashed him against the rocks, bashed him until he thought he would lose his grip. A precarious grip on wet rocks kept him from death, but his grip was slipping, skin peeling off with the effort.

He suddenly was higher up the mountain, grabbing dry rocks as he pulled himself even higher.

Up toward the top he went, hands working feverishly to ascend faster, while his legs and feet scraped craggy edges, leaving blood stains on the chiseled points and knife–sharp ridges. He climbed until he found himself at the top, as he always did in his dreams. The wind howled, snow blew, cold settled in like nightfall, and below it all the sharp-pointed rocks waited eagerly to taste his blood. The storm painted the sky a misty gray that brought snow with such force that he found it difficult to see. Finally, he found himself crawling over a jagged-edged spire of stone, his bloodied hands leaving their mark.

Rahg sat on a rock to rest, but mostly to think. How can this be? There's no sea here. The mountain had no cliffs that I could see. By the gods, what is this place? His eyes were drawn to the top of the mountain as if someone had pulled a string attached to them. Looming above him was the peak, calling him, summoning him.

He trudged on for what seemed like days. Perhaps it was. How was he to know in such a place? But soon enough he found himself where he knew this would lead—the cave! It was even more foreboding than in the dream.

A perfect circular entrance suspended in the air with an unnatural fog that filled the opening and its surrounding area. The mist had an aura of evil. Rahg breathed deeply and stepped into the darkness, his body shaking like a wagger's tail.

The mist was damp, steamy. Cold, then hot. Soon the blackness enveloped him. Rahg closed his eyes; it felt better to pretend that his closed eyes caused the darkness. He dared not open them for he knew what awaited him.

Unwilling feet took each step carefully, fear holding him back, strong fear, bone–deep fear.

And so, you have come, Young One. As I said, you would.

Rahg locked his knees to prevent their collapse. He felt the voice more than heard it, and it chased the fear lurking in his bones deeper, down to the marrow itself. He tried to speak, but he found his tongue immobile. "I..."

You do not need to voice your words. Just think them.

I have come.

And what do you wish, Young One?

Rahg thought. He had no idea what he wanted or why he was here. He only wished he could be home, in Twin Forks. Home, with Magmar and Darstan. Home, and safe.

Home is gone. Safe is gone.

Rahg shook his head. Now he didn't even have his thoughts. Even his mind wasn't safe anymore. Somehow he found the courage to speak. "I don't know why I'm here. You do. You must. And if you won't tell me, I'll leave."

The laughter shook stones loose from the walls. ***Go then. Leave.***

Rahg's hopes shot skyward. "I can leave? Just like that?" He didn't wait for the response but turned to flee. All he wanted was to get back to camp, to Camissa.

He rushed as fast as he could through the darkness until his hands touched stone walls. When he found no egress, he panicked, searching hand over hand to find the exit. "Where is it?" he screamed. "How do I get out?"

Again the ominous, taunting laughter. ***This way, Young One. The only way out is through me.***

So, it was to be games it played. Well, he had endured enough of this. When once again facing the dragon, he demanded answers. "Where is the way out? What do I have to do to get out of here?"

The dragon pointed a claw nearly the size of Rahg's arm to the tunnels beyond it. ***Remember, Young One. All you need do is to choose a path. It is as easy as that.***

"And you won't try to stop me? I can just go?"

I am here to help. Not hinder. Remember this. I might be your only friend.

Rahg scoffed. Only friend! Curse that day when I need a friend like you. "Stand aside. I'll pass now."

Rahg stood facing three tunnels of darkness, each a path he could take. But to what? Suppose I take the wrong one? Suppose they're all the wrong ones? He suddenly realized that in his dreams there had been four paths. He felt certain of that. Why only three now, when everything else in this place mirrored the dream?

For the longest time, he contemplated the decision. If he knew what the outcome would be, could be, then his decision might be easier. Time meant nothing in this cavern, and Rahg had no idea how long he had been standing here undecided. It was time to choose. As he made his way toward the first pathway, inspiration struck him. The amulet!

Rahg wrapped both hands around the black stone and focused all thoughts on it. It only took a brief moment, before he felt it. The third path. Ah. Yes, I see. He wiped perspiration from his brow, sighing in relief. He didn't know what would have transpired if he had taken the wrong path, but he now knew how to decide. The amulet had led him here; it wouldn't steer him wrong.

Rahg used his sword as a walking stick, feeling his way through darkness that resisted all attempts to peer through it. Even the tip of his sword was bathed in blackness. The trail led him up steep tunnels and down stairs carved into the stone. It curved left and right, more twists than Briar's Creek back in Twin Forks. A grueling journey came suddenly to an end. Rahg felt the way ahead blocked, but when he turned left or right it remained blocked. After poking around with his sword for more than a few moments, he decided that this must be a dead-end, and he turned to go back.

Blinding light flared in the pathway ahead of him. He shielded his eyes, letting out a scream as he did. "By the gods, what is this?"

The light was so bright Rahg thought he could see it through his arm. The stone wall pressed against his back and the fear of a trap overwhelmed him. The light faded, and he lowered his arms. He gasped as he saw what lay ahead of him. He was in a great room with a ceiling as high as the palace towers in Sykor. The walls glowed and sparkled like gems, and before him—By the gods! By the gods! Rahg fell to his knees, his head bowed to the floor.

Sitting upon a throne of gold sat what could only be a God. He glowed! There was an aura that surrounded him, radiated from him.

Everything it touched seemed to glow too, even the columns of marble, the floor of the cavern.

Rahg waited. He had never favored any gods above others, never knew much about gods at all. And now, here he sat, completely unprepared, not even knowing what to call him.

You may raise your head, Rahgnar Fal–Thera. As to what you may call me—I am Zuchar, God of Protection.

The voice touched Rahg; he felt it roll through him. The warmth traversed his body, soothed his soul. The pain of losing Magmar finally left him. Then Eru and Tomas left, then Kanella and all the others: Gregor, the people of Entiria; Katsu's men; and more recently Chengal.

Rahg shivered so fiercely that he thought he might break. He cried, tears flowing with no shame. Each tear took sorrow with it until his heart was free—free for the first time in so long. Free like it was in Twin Forks. Rahg lifted his head slowly, no longer fearing that which sat before him. "Thank you, Zuchar."

It is called a cleansing. Those whose work matters the most need it often.

"I'm yours to command, Zuchar, but... I'm confused. I don't know what you expect of me."

You will know. Soon you will know. I will tell you some of what you need.

Rahg stood to receive the message, but before his knees left the stone floor, his mind was assaulted.

Kneel! In my presence, you shall kneel. Do not think yourself raised to such a level, that you might stand in my presence.

Pain filled the inside of his head, like a dam about to burst. "Stop it! Please, stop it?"

The pain subsided, but Rahg had no time to savor the respite. His head now pressed firmly to the floor, he awaited the next communique with great anxiety, not knowing what to expect.

We have chosen you. You are to be our champion.

"What do you mean, "chosen me"? Champion for what?"

There is much for you to learn. Too much. But I will tell you some of it.

Rahg grew more anxious with every breath. He had come this far to learn, let it begin.

A great danger is upon your world. A great evil that must not be allowed to escape.

"But how can I kill Lukaan? He's too strong."

The "voice" was so loud it knocked Rahg to the floor, pain reverberating throughout his body.

Once again you have assumed too much. Heed my words. I did not say to kill Lukaan. If you try, you will fail. Your mission, your only mission, is to prevent the Awakening. Whether you kill one or one million matters not. The sacrifice will save millions more. Understand me, Rahgnar Fal–Thera, you must never go to Sethia. Never! Death waits in Sethia.

Silence settled on Rahg. Fear kept it there. He dared not speak again, and yet he felt he must. "How will I find him, this Messenger?"

You will know when you know.

More riddles, Rahg thought. "What about the Prophecy? It—"

Men use Prophecies to wield power. There is more for you to worry over than that. Words on a scroll cannot harm you.

Rahg was pleased, the Prophecy had worried him. Perhaps needlessly.

Zuchar was also answering his questions, and that brought another thing to mind. Should I ask? he wondered. Should—

Ask.

Rahg jumped, his knees aching from the stone floor. He should have been used to guarding his thoughts with Camissa, but he wasn't. He feared to ask the question but felt he had to.

Rahg slowly pulled his cloak open, his hand reaching even slower to the pocket inside. When his fingers felt the cold crystal shard, he halted, afraid suddenly to show it to Zuchar. But he must. He must know. It shimmered and shook as he removed it, or perhaps it was him that shook. "I found this after the battle in Sunnara," Rahg said. "I wondered if you could tell me what it is?"

Rahg waited. He thought he had seen his eyes glow, but that might have been the crystal. The rumbling began on the floor. His knees vibrated, then the walls trembled, jarring loose rocks firmly entrenched for centuries. Rahg prayed, but he didn't know who to pray to anymore—this was no merciful god. His body rattled, teeth chattered, and his head shook so that he could no longer think.

She gave you that?

Fear spat his words out. "Yes, but—well, not really."

Put it away! Put it away and never touch it again. Never!

Rahg didn't want to know why. It mattered not. He just wanted out of there.

Stand before me, Rahgnar Fal–Thera.

Rahg cautiously rose, expecting a jolt of pain at any moment. He walked slowly toward Zuchar, then stopped when commanded to. The stone floor held a marking just like the one in Entiria in the Shera's hall. It was too much coincidence for Rahg.

Look at me, but first, shield your eyes. Do not close your eyes.

Rahg wove a shield, a strong one, to cover his eyes, then he raised his head to gaze upon Zuchar. Eyelids blinked rapidly in response to the light, so bright, even with the shield. Behind the aura, Rahg thought he could see the image of a figure more clearly defined.

You will need much help on this journey. I will provide you the first of your gifts.

Rahg felt the disturbance in the air. It reminded him of how the heat looked rising in the distance on hot summer days. The air swirled around him, but he felt no breeze, no stirring.

Do not move.

Rahg felt the command and knew he must be still. The chamber grew cold, very cold, and Rahg shivered. He hoped that didn't count as moving and again willed his body to a rigid stance. The cold grew worse, worse than when he and Darstan got lost in the snow storm on Mount Balgria. He focused on warmth. Summer days in Kamnor, sitting by the fire with Camissa, anything to remind him that there was warmth in the world. The cold soon stabilized. He was still cold, but it grew no colder.

A light shot from the marking on the floor where he stood, surrounded him, engulfed him. The cold dissipated, but when it had gone the light remained. A beam of light no wider than he stretched from floor to the ceiling of the cavern. The light danced with a rhythmic pattern weaving a thread about his chest, a thread so fine he couldn't see it, but he felt it. When his chest had been wrapped top to bottom, the light increased. It was now so strong Rahg felt as though he could touch it, feel it. A powerful sensation overcame him: hairs stood on end, skin prickled, and muscles quavered. The pulsation grew more powerful, then it penetrated deeper, sunk to the marrow of his bones, to his very soul.

Rahg didn't know how long he stood there—a moment or a year. He would have believed either one. When the assault finally ended, he stood as before, staring at Zuchar and his ever-present ambiance.

"What did you do to me?" Rahg asked though terror waited in suspense for the reply.

A shield has been fused to your body. Every part of you now bears shield. It will not protect you from powerful enemies, but it will guard you against those who would get close to you. A knife, even a sword, will do little harm.

Rahg was dumbfounded by the gift. He was nearly invincible, save the Banished Ones.

This is meant to steel you for battle, and to protect against those who get close.

There it was again, another warning about people close to him. Even the dragon had said that in one of his dreams. "Who can I trust? Will you tell me that?"

No one.

"No one? Not even Camissa or Tobias, or—"

Not even yourself.

Not even myself? By all that's holy, what is that supposed to mean? "What must I do next?"

You must leave this place, for you have been here too long as it is. The Forbidden Lands are not kind to those who linger.

"Where do I go? Will the amulet lead me?"

BlackHeart only leads you here. And you must be in the Forbidden Lands for it to work.

"Do I have to come back here?"

Rahg felt the rumble, though it was only a slight one.

I have told you. You have been here too long. Now, go! Leave this place. Seek the true Prince of Arangar, then return to the dragon once again.

"Who is this Prince of Arangar? And what do I have to do?"

Kill him!

"Kill him! But who—"

Kill him, or he will kill you.

Rahg bowed low. "Thank you, Zuchar, for your kindness and aid. I will do my best to serve."

You had better, Rahgnar Fal–Thera. More than a few lives are resting on your shoulders. Now, go. But heed me. Use the Mordi to find your steps. Go back the way you came. Only the way you came.

EXIT WOUNDS

A flashing light forced Rahg to shut his eyes, but when he opened them, he was no longer in the cave. The towering peak stood high above him, and his feet rested on the firm ground of a small plateau. A breeze carried the smoke from the camp to him, and riding on the same currents, the sweet smell of biscuits and khaffe. Is it still morning, or did I stay an entire day, wondered Rahg.

Camissa had waited for Rahg like a faithful hound. She shrieked when she saw him.

"Camissa!" He ran the entire distance between them. Rahg wrapped strong arms around her and squeezed. "I'm so glad to be back. So happy to see you."

For a moment Camissa didn't speak, just relished the embrace. "I was so worried," she said. "We all were. When you didn't return that first night, I... we..."

Rahg pushed back from the embrace. "First night? How long was I gone?"

Camissa looked at him as if his brain had been addled. "You've been gone for six days. We were all worried, most thought... well, most thought you dead. We nearly had to tie Rhaven down. He insisted on going after you, and it was only Aentarra wrapping him in a shield that stopped him."

Six days! Rahg couldn't get over the time.

Camissa grabbed his arm and tugged. "Come along. Everyone will be glad to see you. And we have to get some food in you. You must be starved."

Food! That was something he could go for right now.

Kavi greeted him first, with a firm handshake and a strong slap on the back. "We thought you lost, at best," he said. "It's good to see you have not walked the Chugarran Path just yet."

Rahg acknowledged the congratulations as he made his way through camp. He saw the light in Tobias's eyes as the worry left them, and in a way, it reminded Rahg of how Magmar would have felt.

"Lad, I've had two extra biscuits here every morning since you've been gone. Was just about to eat the two in this pan when I saw you coming. Guess you're a little hungry."

Rahg laughed and greeted him with a hug. "It's good to see you, Tobias."

Tobias brushed off the show of affection, busying himself once again with his cooking. "Rhaven fretted over you lad. Thought for a while he was going to draw steel on that witch when she kept him from going after you, but she stopped him."

Camissa scanned the campsite, with worry showing in her eyes. "You should watch what you say. Remember, you were the one who gave Rahg that same advice."

Tobias nodded before she finished. "I know I did, lass, but it's different. I don't think she'd bother herself over an old man like me."

Tobias chuckled a little, but about what Rahg had no clue.

"Anyway, I was telling you about Rhaven. After she held him back with a shield, he started pacing like a mother waiting for a lost child. He sent that vargel out five or six times, though I think she just went 'round the bend in the trail and hid for a while. It was..."

Tobias continued talking while Rahg ate and drank his khaffe. Soon Rhaven approached with Kella. The vargel bounded over to Rahg planting a few sloppy kisses on his face, and Rahg enjoyed the reunion more than he imagined. Rhaven offered an extended hand, and a stoic face, though Rahg had gotten used to him by now, and he could see a smile lurked underneath his solemn expression.

"I knew you would return," he said. "Fate hasn't finished with you yet." Rhaven sat on a rock next to Rahg. Tobias and Camissa were there, and Korg and Sama had just arrived. "Tell us what happened. What did you learn?"

Rahg paused. He should have known to expect the questions. They will all want to know. After all, they are in on this too. The problem was, he didn't know what he should say. Perhaps Zuchar didn't want too much revealed. Rahg saw the impatience spreading in Rhaven. He seldom waited for anything.

"I learned a lot, Rhaven." Rahg turned to look at him. "Some of what I learned I could tell. Some... some I cannot. I think though that everyone will want to hear what I have to say. We're in this together."

Rhaven jumped up like a spring beetle. "I'll gather everyone. Stay and eat. We'll rejoin you shortly."

RAHG HAD NEVER FACED SUCH an audience, though he discovered, to his surprise that his nerves had not gone edgy. He stood. "I learned a lot from... from my visit to the mount." He scanned the campsite. Rhaven, Camissa, and Tobias were sitting close, Katsu, Tomkins, and

Jarrell right behind them, and Korg and his Chun off to the right. The kreng and Arton remained to the rear, but there was no sign of Aentarra. He looked again, trying to find Mulka and Garnock, only to realize at the last moment that they were just beside him, along with Kella.

"What was there? Did you see anyone? What can you tell us of what we face?" It was Katsu who shouted.

Everyone else waited patiently. "I know that you wait to hear the news, and all of you deserve to hear it, but there are some things I cannot say." Rahg lowered his head. "On that, you must grant me your trust."

Everyone nodded, but there was doubt in some of their faces.

"There are only a few things that must be told. We must leave this place, the Paaren, and we must do it quickly."

I'll not tell them we have to come back. No need right now.

"We must leave the same way we came, and with Mulka's help, we will. Lastly, and best of all, I learned that we don't have to battle Lukaan—all we need to do is prevent him from getting out." Rahg smiled broadly. "I'm happiest of all about that."

Rhaven noticed the confidence surge in Rahg as he spoke. He leaned toward Tobias, who had moved to sit close to him. "Something happened on that mountain. Much more than he's saying."

AENTARRA SAT SILENT, and concealed, on a bare spot of ground behind Rahg, her thin smile only a twitch today. So the boy believes he doesn't have to battle Lukaan. What fool has planted such ideas in his head? Aentarra seethed, burning inside. There is one truth he learned though, the Forbidden Lands are no place to linger.

"When will we leave?" Pau asked. "I long for the cold, hungry lands of Arangar."

Rhaven stood to answer, but Rahg made the decision on his own. "I'd like to rest today. Perhaps sleep a night. We will leave tomorrow morning."

A smile crossed Rhaven's face, the first to visit it in a while. The lad had grown on his short journey. Rhaven had Pau and several of the krengs get fresh supplies of water for the trip. With the extra casks that the dead had carried, they would have more water for the journey back across the desert.

AFTER SIX DAYS in the desert, spirits still ran high. The desert had not proved any more accommodating, the burning sun scorched them during the day, and the nights ran cold, but they were on their way home, and that eased tensions.

Mulka proved to be as true as the legends of the Pathfinders, finding their old trail without even looking for signs. Rhaven insisted on scouts at all times, and he doubled the watch at night, but no one complained as the memory of the dorgans remained fresh.

Rhaven kept a keen eye to the ground, and every so often he fell further back, searching both flanks as well.

"What are you looking for?" Tobias asked as Rhaven came alongside him.

"She has been with us ever since we entered here, Tobias, and I have yet to see a track even though the boots she wears are unique. I have seen the marks when she is around; they were there after the battle with the dorgans, but at those times when she seems to come from nowhere there are no signs. I have checked."

Tobias thought for some time as they walked in silence. "I knew a man who raised chickens, and he had a problem with a weasel. No matter what he did that weasel would take a chicken every six or seven days. After a while he got a dog to guard the hen house, but it did no good. Then he got another dog, then another yet. But still, the weasel got what he wanted. Finally, he got rid of all the dogs and quit trying, and you know that weasel still took only one hen every six or seven days."

"I'm not concerned with chickens. I'm worried about Rahg, and though she has shown new faces since we first met, I'm quite certain she has not discarded the ones she wore before."

"I'll keep my eyes sharp, Rhaven, but I would spend my time on other things if I were you."

One of Pau's men came forward from the rear watch. "A storm coming from behind, Rhaven."

"Bring the scouts in. We'll increase our pace to gain ground." The Chun acknowledged the order, then departed. "Tobias, have Tomkins and Katsu bring the other scouts in, all except the forward position."

Shortly before nightfall, the forward scouts brought disturbing news. "Pau had trouble catching his breath. "Ahead, and to the right, something in the air. It..."

Arton and Kyra stood in the front ranks, along with Rahg and Mulka. "What is it, Pau?" Rahg asked. When Pau stumbled with the explanation, Rahg interrupted. "How far?"

"Not half a league."

"Then we all move," Rahg said.

The pace had increased yet again, amid reports that the storm behind them gained ground.

"Look!" Korg shouted. Several hundred paces ahead of them, near the crest of a small hill, a mass of fog filled the evening sky. The fog seemed isolated though restricted to that small patch of sky.

"What is it?" Rahg asked.

The scene looked eerie, unnatural. As they drew nearer, the mist glowed against a sky quickly losing its light. A faint, but distinct, low reverberation emanated from the mist.

"What is it, Rahg?" Camissa had kept the pace remarkably well, maintaining a spot near the front line.

Another hundred paces would place them directly in the mist, but Rahg halted their advance. "Rhaven, Arton."

It was Aentarra who answered, advancing from the left flank, hair perfectly in place. She wasn't even winded, though she had not been there a moment ago. "A portal," she said, simply that.

Mulka spoke for the first time. "This is not the one we entered through."

"Then we go around it," Rahg said, not waiting to consult with the others. He knew what he must do, and, what he must not do. He started moving them east, left of the eerie mist. They only walked ten paces before they felt it, a rumbling like thunder, but it was on the ground. Rahg thought to ignore it, but the tremors increased. He felt the vibrations in the soles of his feet.

Kyra called the alert. "Dorgans!" Her warning more a howl than a shout.

Aentarra spun and stared as if she could see something. Rahg tried but saw only darkness behind them. Aentarra focused on the sound; she had heard it before. All other sounds were filtered out except the rumbling, thunderous pounding.

Rahg saw the look in her eyes. Was it fear?

Aentarra turned to him, a tinge of urgency touched her voice. "We must use the portal, Rahg. The dorgans come."

"No!" Rahg's response was instinctive, though he had no alternative in mind.

Aentarra's voice reached everyone in the group and far beyond. "The dorgans are coming, and there are far too many!" All eyes were drawn to her finger pointing behind them, and all could now tell that the ground shook from more than tremors. "We take the portal," Aentarra said.

Rahg looked back at what seemed like a moving wall of darkness, then forward to the eerie mist. "We must go back through the same one," he said, desperate to explain his position.

Aentarra seized his face and spun him to the rear. "Look! They're coming fast, and there are far more than the last time. They're on the hunt, and they have our scent. We have no choice. If we don't go through that portal, we all die. And if we delay much longer, the portal will disappear. These Portals only remain open so long."

Rahg made the decision. "Through the portal!" he shouted, and they all ran. With less than thirty paces to go the portal began moving.

"Hurry!" Aentarra shouted. "It will be gone in a moment."

The ground shook so much that Rahg risked a glance back. The dorgans were almost upon them, at least a few, and the rest followed closely. "Run, Camissa!"

Korg and Kavi reached it first, along with Arton, Kyra, and several other krengs. The Chun chief helped Camissa make the step into the portal, as it now had lifted from the ground and stood as a floating window in the night sky. He pushed Sama through next.

"Come, husband," she called, hand outstretched to help him, but he refused, and reached for Pau to shove him through. "Keep her there, Pau. And, Pau, help Kavi."

Pau understood, grabbing Kavi's arm as he made his way to the other side. Kavi screamed his objections, but no sooner had he passed through than his words were lost.

Rahg stood by the gateway, focusing on something to the rear. "Go!" Rhaven ordered.

Rahg ignored him. "I need to keep them back. I've got a shield up, but I can't hold them long."

"You're the one who must get through," Rhaven said. "Without you, all is lost."

Silence greeted Rhaven's statement. Rahg was expending his energy to maintain the shield, and the pounding of the dorgans was taking a heavy toll on him.

Arton moved like lightning to Rahg. "If you are needed to defeat Lukaan, you must go." He picked Rahg up as if he were a child and threw him into the gateway.

"It moves faster," Aentarra said. "Hurry!"

Aentarra dropped her shield. Five of the dorgans now waited to get at them only thirty paces away. When she let go the shield, she sent bolts of Lightning at three of them, then leaped into the mist.

THE PORTAL HAD NOT ONLY BEEN MOVING but narrowing too. Now only two could fit through the opening at one time. Katsu and Jarrell made it, then Tobias and Tomkins. Two krengs jumped in, and at the same time, a horrible roar as the dorgans came upon them, finding three Chun their first victims. A group of krengs engaged one of the dorgans—Phay was with them.

Arton raced back to help them. Phay battled with the dorgan, already delivering numerous gashes to the back of its legs. Arton grabbed the kreng just as he struck again, and threw him over his shoulder. The portal was closing.

Arton moved faster, pushing harder with all his strength. Only Rhaven and Kyra remained, then Rhaven went through. Kyra would never go while her pack was here, Arton knew, so as he made his final leap, he latched onto Kyra's arm with his free hand and dragged her through with him. A blood–curdling howl emerged, then faded as the portal closed.

From the other side of the portal, they witnessed the devastation just when Arton came through. The dorgans feasted on flesh this night.

Rahg looked about nervously but saw no dorgans. He sighed. "Thank the Gods," he said, but inside he hurt. How many lost? More Chun, all those brave krengs... and Korg! He looked around for Kavi and saw him holding Sama, trying to comfort her as she wept. A brave woman. A strong woman. Kyra's howls only deepened his sadness. How many will die for me? he wondered anew.

Rhaven stood with Kella and Garnock, ever-present at Mulka's side. He had not even seen Kella go through and wondered when she had.

Everyone felt some degree of relief, even if it was dampened by the losses. Everyone but Aentarra. Camissa must have noticed. "What is it, My Lady? We made it."

Aentarra continued her scan of the surroundings. Rahg and Rhaven came to join her. After several silent moments of focused sensing, Aentarra looked into each set of eyes, stopping at Camissa, then shifting her attention to Rahg. "Rahg, Camissa. Do not dare use any powers. We have escaped the dorgans, but we have not quite made it safely home."

"Why? What do you mean?"

Aentarra remained stoic. "Pay attention! Whatever you do, do not Shield! Use no powers. Camissa, no sensing, not even to touch a thought. Tell everyone to be alert and to speak in whispers and only then when necessary."

The scowl on Rhaven's face would have cowed a patrol leader. "Why?"

Aentarra stared at Rhaven, and for perhaps the first time, his icy eyes had met a match. "Because we have come through the portal into Sethia!"

"What!" Rahg shouted.

Aentarra glared at him, but she fought the urge to teach him a lesson. "I told you to whisper. Yes, Rahg, this is Sethia. And lurking somewhere in these lands are the Banished Ones—and Lukaan."

"Gods be dead!" Rahg said. "Gods be dead!" And all he could think about was what Zuchar had said to him—"Death waits in Sethia."

"For all that they can help you now, they might as well be dead," Aentarra said. "I believe even the gods abandoned Sethia."

SETHIA

They had been walking for almost a full day, searching for supplies and food but especially water. If they were to have any chance of survival in Sethia, water was mandatory. Aentarra darted her head from side to side, checking for signs of life. They could not afford for anyone to see them. If Lukaan finds out—She felt the surge of power, spun to see Rahg weaving a shield.

"Stop! You stup—"

She focused, then screamed. "Everyone grab hold of me. Hurry!" At the same time, she wove a wedge-shaped shield to protect them. Just as she finished, a rift opened, and Lukaan appeared, BlackFire shooting from his hands. The shield collapsed as they shifted, but not before the fire struck Camissa on the arm.

They appeared at the spot near the portal where they first entered the Sethian desert. "Nobody move. Nobody say anything." Aentarra spun to face Rahg. "You stupid, stupid, boy. How could you? Now he knows we're here, and he won't stop until he kills us all."

Camissa moaned from the pain, the fire burning deeper into her arm. "I can't stop it," she shouted.

"Shut up, girl, or I'll kill you myself."

Arton rushed over and applied a healing leaf from a pouch at his side. "This will stop the pain."

Rahg shook, fear overcoming him. "Was that him? Lukaan?"

"Who do you think it was?" She shook her head, as if in denial. "He just crushed my shield with one strike. Lights Blood! If I hadn't put it up..."

Rahg stood by Camissa's side, shaking his head. "Why can't we just leave?"

Aentarra grabbed him. "You are an ignorant boy. Not worthy of your power. Your friends can leave, some of them. Tobias, Rhaven, even Arton. But not you, and possibly not even her." Aentarra scowled. "Don't worry, though. He'll kill you last."

"I won't go without Rahg," Rhaven said.

Tobias shook his head. "I'm here till the end."

Arton looked at Kyra, her fangs bared, and then he nodded. "We stay to kill Lukaan. I have waited an eternity for this."

"It's more likely he'll kill you," Aentarra said.

"I have waited an eternity for that too," Arton said.

"All right. Now that we have cast our votes to die, we should determine how best to do it."

Aentarra thought for a moment, though she kept a sharp lookout for trouble. "There are only a few places in Sethia I can shift to. Only three right now." A long silence filled the air. "Lukaan will know there aren't many. He'll be scouring these lands to find us, and once he does —" Aentarra looked around, worry on her face. "I sense something...almost as if someone used power, but different."

"Why are there only three places you can shift to?" Rhaven asked.

"Because I have to have been there before to be able to shift again.

There is the spot we are in, and there are two other places close to the border that I know well enough. He'll know that I'll need spots close to the border and he will start searching. The place we just came from is close by, so we must leave now to one of the border spots. It will buy us time; besides, we can't let him find this spot. We need to return. Grab hold." Everyone locked hands, and Rhaven grabbed hold of Kella, then Aentarra shifted.

LUKAAN SNIFFED THE AIR, tasting her scent. *Aentarra! Come to play with me, have you?* The air shivered, and Melissara and Tirzinitzia stepped through the rift. Within moments, the rest of them arrived.

Aentarra is here. In Sethia!

Melissara's eyes went wide with disbelief. "Aentarra!"

I almost had them. There are others with her, including the boy.

Lukaan stared at the others. *She can't have gone many places. A few border spots at most. If we find them, she'll shift again, so we will leave someone behind to guard the spot they left.* Lukaan smiled. *Soon she will run out of shift points. Then she will be mine.*

AENTARRA STEPPED THROUGH THE RIFT, followed by the rest of them. They emerged on top of a large formation of rocks, within an enclave of rocks. She peeked out from a narrow opening then signaled the others to follow.

formation of rocks

They were about three span above the desert floor, and the terrain was rolling desert with a lot of shrub brush. A short distance away lay a steep hill riddled with crevices and large boulders. "I have a plan," Aentarra said.

"Arton, you and Rhaven will be an integral part of this, so listen well." She described her plan as they walked toward the next hill, the only place nearby that offered shelter. The boulders were large and close enough together so that they could sit in a group and not be seen.

"Arton and Rhaven are coming with me. The rest of you had better be still. No movement. No noise. If they discover you, you have no options." She turned to leave, then stopped. "And remember, be ready. When I come back, we may have only a heartbeat to get out of here, so be joined and ready to link to me." With that, she headed back toward the shift point they had recently left. They walked quickly, Arton setting the pace, with Rhaven and Aentarra on each side.

"Are you sure they won't be able to see us?" Rhaven asked.

"They won't be able to see us, or hear us, or sense us. Once I have us Cloaked, we will be invisible."

"How long have you been able to Cloak?" Arton asked.

"A long time, but it has developed into something stronger. At first, I could only hide, as if camouflaged. Then to be not seen at all. Later came other degrees of the power."

Arton nodded. "If I had this, I would kill Lukaan."

"Let's worry about surviving a few more days. We have time to plot Lukaan's death when we are out of Sethia."

As they neared the spot, Aentarra went through everything again. "We will draw them here by using a touch of power. When Lukaan and the rest of them arrive, we will be Cloaked."

"If he can sense such a small amount of power, why can't he sense you when you shift?"

"Something about the way Shifting works, the way it disturbs the air. He can sense that a small amount of power was used somewhere, but he cannot know where. It would be like hearing a sound in the forest at night."

"Then why didn't we just shift to where the others are hiding and shift back again," Rhaven asked.

"It was too far for me to Sight Shift, and even though I know he can't pinpoint a single shift, perhaps several from the same place he could. No need in taking chances. Besides, Shifting takes power, and I might need it all."

Rhaven nodded.

Aentarra looked around one more time, then pointed a scolding finger at both of them. "Remember! You can't break the connection between us. If you do, you will be seen."

When they nodded, she continued. "Lukaan will likely scan the area then leave someone here to guard this spot so we can't return. After he leaves is when we strike, but it has to be swift, and it has to be simultaneous. We must kill whoever he leaves in one attack." She looked at each of them. "Are you ready?"

Aentarra wove the tiniest piece of shield then darted away, holding tightly to Arton and Rhaven. Within half a moment, a rift opened, Lukaan and the others stepping through, along with several patrols of Sethian Guards.

"Remember, they can't hear us, but if anyone bumps into us, we will be felt. So if someone comes near, we need to move."

LUKAAN SCANNED THE SURROUNDINGS, searching for a sign. "I felt her," he said. "I know she was here."

"She must have Shifted," Sendra said, though she, too, cast a discerning gaze all about.

"Check those rocks," Melissara said, and a patrol of guards rushed over, swords drawn.

For the next few moments, they stared in all directions. "No sign anywhere," Ghruehne said.

Tirzinitzia had been busy wandering about the area. "Over here."

The others immediately joined her.

"There are tracks here," Tirzinitzia said. "Coming from that direction, but they end here."

Lukaan looked toward the other hill, where Rahg and they lay in hiding. "She must have Shifted there, then walked here, Shifted again somewhere else." Lukaan shook his head. "But why?"

"To gather more shift points," Melissara said. "She knows we will track her down, so she is getting as many shift points as possible."

Tirzinitzia nodded. "That means she's leaving the rest of them hidden somewhere, taking only two as guards for when she shifts. Risky, but bold."

Lukaan laughed. "Aentarra has ever been bold, but she made a mistake and used power." He spun toward Zorn. "Stay here to guard. I will leave two of the Sethians with you." He then turned toward the commander of the guard. "Take six men with you and scout that hill, then post a watch until you are relieved." The guard commander saluted and left.

"Sendra, Ghruehne, go back to Sethia and get four patrols each. Take them to likely spots on the border by the Caravan Trail. Have the patrols split up, going north and south and space them several leagues apart. Keep doing that until we find her." Lukaan's eyes seemed to glow, and the air about him grew dark. "I want Aentarra, but I want the boy even more."

The first patrol returned from the enclave of rocks that Melissara had them inspect. "Nothing, My Lady."

Lukaan took a last look around, scouring the area. "Come with me, Melissara, Tirzinitzia, and bring that patrol. We go to hunt."

"LET ME KILL HIM," Arton whispered.

"Just keep quiet," Aentarra said. "Remember, when I let the Cloak go we are instantly visible and able to be sensed. Lukaan would kill you before you took a breath."

ZORN STOOD ALONE on the side of the hill, leaning against a large boulder. Ten paces away, in the open, the two guards paced, alert for danger. To the south, the commander and his six men were almost half way to the next hill.

"We need to be quick," Aentarra whispered. "I will get us right next to Zorn, behind his back, to give you every advantage, but it will be up to you. Remember, I cannot use powers. The moment I release the Cloak, you must strike. And no misses or second chances. Cut off his head. One of you needs to get Zorn, while the other gets the guards."

"I'll take the guards," Rhaven said, drawing the dart tube from his back. "I can get both of them from here before they even know it."

Arton smiled. "Then Zorn is mine."

Aentarra walked them on a wide swath behind Zorn, up onto the rocks, then descended slowly until they stood one step above him and only a pace away. "Now," she said and released the Cloak.

ZORN SENSED SOMETHING, movement, energy, and spun to look behind him.

Arton's sword was drawn. He planted his foot before him and stepped forward, striking with all his power. The sword made a whistling sound, and it seemed to glow as it struck Zorn's neck, then sliced cleanly through, severing his head. He barely had time to register the shock before his head fell to the ground.

Meanwhile, Rhaven had pumped two darts into the guards, each of them succumbing to seizures almost immediately, but their screams caught the ear of the commander and the other guards.

"Hurry," Aentarra said. "We need to get out of here."

"What about the other guards?" Arton asked.

"Forget them! He'll be here any moment. Grab hold!"

Arton and Rhaven grabbed hold of her, and she Shifted to the next hill where Rahg and the rest of them waited. "Hurry! Link to me."

LUKAAN FELT the sensation and knew that Zorn had died. "Melissara, Tirzinitzia, back to the shift point. Zorn is dead."

The rift opened, and Lukaan stepped through, assessing the situation with a glance. He looked south and saw them standing just above some rocks on the hill. BlackLightning streaked the air, a furious barrage that blasted boulders all around them.

AENTARRA CONNECTED with everyone then focused on her Shift. She was tired but had no time to worry or to rest. Just then the Lightning struck, and a boulder behind her exploded. A shard of stone, the size of a knife blade, splintered off, burrowing into her back. Another struck her left leg. She started to collapse but managed to stay focused long enough to shift, falling to the ground once they stepped through the rift.

"Get her help," Camissa shouted.

Arton picked her up, looked around and carried her to a level area by some rocks. "She's bleeding badly, and I have no leaves left."

Camissa knelt beside her, inspecting the wounds. "Her leg is bad, but not deadly. The one in her back is the problem."

Aentarra groaned. "Don't try any of your healing on me, little witch. I don't trust what you'll do."

"This needs to come out," Rhaven said. "We can remove it and clean the wound, but the rest will be up to you."

"Do that. And make sure you clean it well. I don't intend to die in this forsaken place."

LUKAAN STARED at the head of Zorn, then the bodies of the Sethian Guards.

"She must have Shifted back here after we left," Tirzinitzia said.

"Yes, she did. But she did it from those rocks right over there," Lukaan said. "Otherwise she would not have known when we were gone." His face grew tense, and his blood began to boil, then without warning, he started to laugh. "She is Antar's daughter, this one is. It was all a trap—her using that smattering of power. A trap, when I thought it a mistake."

"What do you mean?" Tirzinitzia asked.

"She shifted here on purpose, used power on purpose, just enough to make me think it was a mistake. Then she hid in those rocks, shifted back and attacked." Lukaan looked lost in thought. "The only question is how did she do it without Zorn having enough time to alert us."

As Melissara and Tirzinitzia thought, Lukaan issued new orders. "I want every water hole guarded. Send a message that six patrols, armed with bows, will stand guard at every water hole in Sethia. She must have water to survive. That is the one truth in Sethia."

"Don't worry, Lukaan, we'll find her."

"You are right about that, Tirzinitzia. We will find her."

RHAVEN CLEANED the wound on Aentarra's leg and bandaged it using a piece of his shirt. The wound in her back was another matter. It needed stitches and plenty of them.

"I can do stitches, but I'm not very good," Camissa said.

Arton moved to her side. "Let Kyra do it. She has sewn me up when I was much worse than that."

Kyra growled, but knelt and went to work on Aentarra, despite protests and threats. Her smallest claw was as good as a needle, and they used fiber from a nearby shrub brush to sew her shut. Throughout it all, Aentarra remained conscious, but barely. She had lost a lot of blood.

"I need to rest," she said, "but if they come, wake me immediately and be prepared to shift. Right now we only have one place to go, but I don't want to go there unless we have to."

As she drifted off to sleep, Aentarra thought of what options they had. Not many. Lukaan would slowly cover the entire border, which meant her only real hope lay in shifting back to where they exited the portal, then walking from there to find new shift points. But a lot of that was open territory, and they would be easily spotted. Any useful shift point would have to be far apart, and worst of all, water would be non-existent.

Regardless of what else he did, Lukaan would soon realize he must guard the water. That meant they only had two real options: go back through the portal—assuming it would re-appear—and take their chances with the dorgans—or kill Lukaan.

I'm through with fighting dorgans.

TO FULFILL AN OATH

"What will we do, Aentarra? Lukaan will find us soon."

"Be patient, boy. I'm thinking. This is no easy matter."

"Can we go back through the portal?" Rhaven asked.

"If the portal opens. And if we want to face the dorgans again."

"The dorgans are better than Lukaan," Rahg said.

Aentarra nodded. "You might be right, but before I go back to those lands, there is one thing I need to try." Aentarra paced the area, deep in thought. "You need to stay hidden, all of you. I will be gone for a while."

"Where are you going?" Rhaven asked.

A long pause followed. "To kill Lukaan."

"I'm going with you," Arton said, jumping up from a spot on the ground. "Besides, you're not healed enough."

"Not this time. This is something I must do myself."

"But you're not healed yet. You—"

"That's no more than a pesky little wound. It won't make the difference in what I have to do." Aentarra packed a flask of water and a few bites to eat, then started off. She turned to address them before leaving. "If he comes, everyone charge him at once. At least that way, he'll kill you quickly. Don't dare let him capture you. Fight until you're dead."

~

SHE WALKED through the desert toward Sethia, eyes scanning the surroundings for any sign of life. It would not do for one of Lukaan's spies to see her. She had to get to the Sethian Palace undetected.

Two days of walking brought her to the edge of the city, close enough so that guards on patrol could be seen on daily rounds. Aentarra waited for a lone guard then dispatched a Slicer.

The guard didn't feel it enter—she had put a numbing agent on it—and the instant it struck he turned and came to her. She waited until nightfall, then issued instructions. "Take me to the palace," she said and pulled a cloak over her head. No one would suspect a guard taking a peasant woman to the palace.

He nodded then turned and headed east. They made their way through the city, then up the steps and into the enormous structure. Once inside they were stopped by a Palace Guard, white-robed, and with a symbol of the Red Sun emblazoned on his chest.

"Halt."

Aentarra had been prepared. A Slicer slid from her pouch and whisked into his mind. She dismissed the first guard then instructed the other on what she wanted him to do.

As they walked down the long corridor, she took note of everything.

At one deep alcove with a large pillar in the center, she stopped to imprint a shift point in case it was needed. The corridor was dark, unlike the Great Path in Vallah, and she suspected that was at Lukaan's instructions. He always liked things dark.

They passed two more guards, who eyed them suspiciously but never questioned their purpose. Good thing, as she could not use powers in here and had no desire to use all of her Slicers; she might need them.

The guard turned right and headed down a new hallway. "Not far now."

"There is no need to talk. Just follow your instructions." A tinge of anxiety crept into her chest, threatened to turn to fear. She breathed deeply then silently repeated her mantra, a reminder of what had to be done. What must be done.

> An oath of life I swear by Blood, to be an oath of death,
>
> and each page of the Sacred Book I whisper with each breath.
>
> To the Seven Lights of Nelstar—this day I swear your death.
>
> — AENTARRA'S MANTRA

A smile replaced the fear, her mind now at ease. This was a dangerous task she faced, but her Stealth combined with her previous knowledge gave her an edge, perhaps enough of an edge.

When she had sent Kardel and Vennel to kill Lukaan long ago, she learned from the Slicers that Lukaan used Illusion while he slept, a false image of him in his bed. Valuable information to have. Now, this pitiful guard would serve as her decoy. While he attacked Lukaan's image, Aentarra would be Cloaked. When Lukaan did appear, she would sneak behind him and stab him through the ear—right into the brain. It had to be quick though. A normal knife might not suffice; Lukaan could have infused himself with power. If so, she would have to shape Shield into a weapon and use that, and that required she become visible.

They walked past a door with an insignia of a great bird of prey. Ghruehne's room, then past another with a symbol of a creature recognized from the Forbidden Lands—Melissara's room. They passed an open section with a sitting area underneath a canopy.

We must be close.

The next room boasted huge double doors and an eerie mist that hovered above the floor. This is it, she thought, and fear crept up her spine.

The guard slowed, then headed for the door, knife drawn. Aentarra drew her knife, then Cloaked. It was time. The doors opened silently, and the guard crept toward the bed where Lukaan lay sleeping.

Aentarra moved to the side of the room, anxious. Silent steps carried the guard to Lukaan's bed, where he raised the blade and plunged it into Lukaan's heart. As Aentarra surmised, the image was an illusion, and Lukaan appeared in the room only a few steps from where she stood, his eyes focused on the guard.

"Not a wise decision. I think you shall suffer dearly for this."

Taken by surprise, the guard did the only thing he could, and charged Lukaan, wielding the knife like a madman.

Lukaan laughed, mustering Fire to destroy him.

The time to act was now, and as Lukaan threw Fire at the guard, Aentarra advanced to a spot behind him. She focused then unveiled herself, while simultaneously weaving Shield into a long, pointed knife, almost like an ice pick. She drove it straight for the center of his ear, smiling as the blade raced toward Lukaan, about to puncture his brain.

WHEN SHE BECAME VISIBLE, Lukaan sensed her presence, realized a trap, and ducked, turning his head at the same time. The blade struck him just behind the ear, in the back of the head, a deep wound that spewed blood like the gutting of a deer, but she had missed the mark, had not gotten into the brain. Aentarra must have realized immediately that the blow was not deadly and ran for the door.

Lukaan exploded, fire blasting out from every pore in his body. The shock made Aentarra stumble to the ground, though she quickly recovered and raced for the corridor. Lukaan had slain the guard, now he focused on Aentarra, spinning toward her in a rage.

She got out the door and turned right, running down the corridor for all she was worth.

corridor in Palace of the Sun

Blood pouring from his head, Lukaan raced after her. "Aentarra!" he screamed and entered the corridor, Fire already shooting from his hands.

Aentarra composed herself, Cloaking just as Lukaan exited his chambers. She dove to the floor, invisible now, and crawled to the side of the corridor, then she headed back toward Lukaan. It would be what he would least likely suspect.

Lukaan stopped when he didn't see her, looked back the other way. *Where did she go? She had no time to shift.* Then realization hit him. *She has Stealth!*

He had seen her turn right, so he blanketed the corridor with fire and lightning.

Aentarra made her way back down the corridor, fortune keeping her under Lukaan's assaults. As she got to within a few paces of him, she stood, slowly, then knowing she was undetectable, raced past him, down the corridor behind him as fast as she could go.

Lukaan stopped firing, sniffing the air. He focused, using his senses to try to find her.

What in Her sweet name ... how has she learned that? No one has had the full power of stealth for ten thousand years. Not even Antar could hide from a Sensing. She is strong! Dangerously strong.

He seethed. *And she's so unpredictable, who would have thought she'd dare an assassination in Sethia? Suddenly it struck him. Unpredictable! She turned and went the other way.*

Lukaan spun, realizing now she went the other way. He filled the corridor with BlackFire, wall to wall, floor to ceiling. ColdFire roared from his hands. Marble cracked and splintered. Columns buckled.

Aentarra pumped her legs harder, running for all she was worth, but a quick glance to the rear told her she didn't have time. The fire would catch her before she got to the end of the corridor. *Going to have to Shift,* she thought and made plans. She thought of the enclave of rocks just inside the Sethian border, near where she met Melissara. The Coldfire raced toward her. She could feel the heat of its coldness—a strange sensation, like burning ice.

The air rippled, and Aentarra slowly materialized, wobbling into a recognizable figure of a woman. The back of her legs felt on fire. She pushed harder. She had to be fully visible, out of the cloak before she could shift. Around her, the air grew intensely hot—and cold—both at once. Suddenly it coalesced, rippling into a rift.

Aentarra jumped through, rolling on the ground until she hit one of the rocks of the enclave. She leaped over the rock, hid behind it, shaking, trembling. What if he saw where she was going. What if he could sense where she was.

She tried to cloak again, but it was too soon. She had nothing left. Curling into a ball, she hugged her arms around herself and waited.

Help me, father. Don't let me die without my vengeance.

FINAL STRIKE

*R*haven and Arton jumped to alert when a rift appeared in the middle of the night.

"Sheathe the swords but stay alert. I wounded him, but he's still alive."

Arton sheathed his sword, hurrying toward Aentarra. "You hurt him?"

"I stabbed him in the head, but it wasn't enough. He has the gods' luck, and he's now out for vengeance." Aentarra laughed. "I thought he would tear the palace down trying to get me."

"What do we do now?" Rahg asked.

"Nothing has changed. We have two options: wait here for a portal to appear, or let the shield down. The trouble with the latter is I don't know how to let the shield down."

"The portal is the better option, especially with Mulka, but we have no water," Rhaven said.

"With no water, the portal may not be our best option. Remember that desert we were in? There was no water to be had. Regardless, I need to rest, then we make a plan."

"What happened with Lukaan?" Rhaven asked.

"I got behind him, but he sensed me at the last moment and moved before I could pierce his brain. I got him in the back of the head though. Got him good."

~

FOR MOST OF THE NIGHT, until early morn, Aentarra told stories of Nelstar and her father. On occasion, Arton added stories of his own, his memory now returned to him. He smiled broadly, like a little boy, when Aentarra recounted the tale of his heroics at the Battle of Syrnia, when he led them to victory.

"And he was the only one without powers," Aentarra said. "For the next ten years, it seemed as if half the babies born were named Arton."

"Those were the days of glory, Aentarra. Days I have longed for these many years." His smile disappeared, a frown taking its place. "In the Forbidden Lands, there was no glory. No one to challenge. Nothing to die for."

He shook his head, slowly, and it seemed as if a tear might form. "I didn't even know my name until you came."

"Don't worry, my friend, there will be time to fix that. When we get back to Nelstar—"

Arton jumped up. "Nelstar! You can go back?"

"I have plans, yes."

"But the Lights will kill you."

Rahg leaned forward. He had heard her mention that her father was one of these Lights. The Light of Lights she had called him. And Lukaan was one.

"I intend to kill them first."

Arton shook his head. "They have the Book, Aentarra. No one can kill them. Not even Antar—"

She leaped from the ground and grabbed him by the neck. Flames already danced on her fingers, burning his neck. "They had him trapped in a shield! He would have killed them if they had not deceived him. You saw him kill Boledar. You know how he destroyed Nagasha. He would have—" Aentarra collapsed, though she remained conscious.

Arton knelt beside her, his neck still red and burnt on one part where she had gripped him. "You know I meant nothing by it. I loved your father. I would have died for him."

She nodded. "Help me up. I'm bleeding again from that wound in the back."

Camissa rushed to her side. "I can help. I'm not much of a healer, but I can do some. I watched Aenaila and Mikkellana enough to learn small things."

Aentarra stared at her, but with soft eyes. "I would tell you to do it, girl, but we can't risk using powers even for something as simple as this." She looked to Arton, held his hand. "I'm sorry about your neck, Arton. I... forgot myself it seems." Aentarra grimaced. "I need to rest for a while. We will decide what to do when I awaken."

THE PORTAL still had not appeared, and the water was now a serious problem. The Sethian sun was already scorching them, and it was only mid morning. Depleted of water, throats parched, they decided their only option was to lower the shield and try to escape.

"Can you do it?" Rhaven asked.

"I don't know if I can, but it's worth a try. The problem is, there is only one spot left I can shift to," Aentarra said. "From there most of you can leave—the rest of us need to wait for the shield to drop. If we have any luck, I can weaken the shield enough for us to get out. I'm certain you can, Rahg, and you Camissa. I'm just not sure about me."

"What if you can't get out?" Arton asked.

"Then I stay. I'll try to finish the job I started."

"I stay with you," Arton said.

"I won't leave without you," Rahg said. "You helped us, so I'll help you. No matter what happens."

Aentarra laughed. "If you stay here, boy, you die. And there is much more I have for you to do."

Rahg shook his head. "If he gets out, I die anyway. I'm staying."

Aentarra smiled. "It might be moot. If he senses the shield weakening and gets out before I can fix it, then we're all doomed." Aentarra seemed lost in thought. "If only Mikkellana were here."

THEY SHIFTED TO THE BORDER, and as they stepped through the rift, a patrol of Sethian guards saw them and began firing arrows.

Aentarra realized the only option was to shield, but at the same time, she knew if she shielded, Lukaan would sense it and find them. The arrows hurtled toward them, about to strike. She had no recourse. Weaving the weakest shield she could, hoping it would be too small to notice, she simultaneously issued orders for everyone to stay linked.

LUKAAN SENSED THE SHIELD, recognized the location and recalled a shift point not far from there. He sent for Melissara and Tirzinitzia, then they shifted to a spot within striking distance from where Aentarra stood. He formed a bolt of Lightning as soon as he stepped through the rift, hurling it at them. It struck the shield with a thunderous roar, staggering Aentarra.

"No time to shift now," Aentarra screamed. "Rahg, a shield. Quick!"

Rahg wove a shield, the strongest one he could, a convex one that surrounded them, protecting them from the arrows and Lukaan.

Lukaan's second strike hit Rahg like a sledgehammer. The inside of his head shook, throbbed. "I can't hold it!"

Another bolt hit. Rahg fell, blood trickling from his nose. "Aentarra!"

"If you don't hold it, we die. Focus! I've got to get this shield down so we can get out." Aentarra reinforced Rahg's shield with her weave, but she couldn't risk too much. She needed her energy to lower the shield. "The rest of you get out of here while you can. He'll kill you if you don't. Rhaven, Arton, be prepared to use those swords Mikkellana gave you. They'll withstand a few blows even from Lukaan."

"I'm staying," Tobias said, "even if it's just to drag Rahg's body out of here." The others joined him in his decision.

Suddenly Aentarra heard a voice in her head.

Protect us. I will worry about the shield.

"Mikkellana!" she said, looking about.

No time for pleasantries, sister. Do it!

Aentarra formed one of the strongest shields she could, but all the while she looked around, trying to see where Mikkellana was.

Can she cloak?

RHAVEN AND ARTON STOOD READY, swords drawn.

Rhaven, protect me.

Rhaven didn't know where the voice came from, or who said it. He looked around, seeing no one. "Camissa?"

From the rear, Kella moved apart from the others. Suddenly she began to change, to morph into something else. Her back feet grew longer, forming toes, heels, ankles, then her legs added length. Girth as well. Her body became a torso, and her front legs grew into arms, hands, fingers. Fur turned to white, milky skin, and her head shrank, the large snout becoming an Asoran nose.

"Mikkellana!" Rhaven screamed, and at the same time, Aentarra saw her.

"All this time! You've been here all this time and offered no help."

"Until now you did fine, but no time to bicker. I'll lower the shield while you hold them off."

A huge explosion rocked the air, then BlackLightning pummeled them. Rahg fell again, writhing on the ground. Camissa ran to him, but he pushed her aside. "Got to get up. Got to help." Once again he focused on a shield, but the force was too much, the shield was being battered by all three of them: Lukaan, Melissara, and Tirzinitzia. He prayed, certain he would die.

"You can't lower the shield now, Mikkellana. He'll see it and shift out of here."

"Better than dying."

"No! Put a shield in front of us, while I do something."

"What?"

"Just hold them off, and while you do that, I'm going to create a sand storm, blind them temporarily. While they can't see us, we will shift again, back to the portal."

Mikkellana wove a shield while Aentarra brewed up a desert storm. Sand ripped through the air, becoming miniature projectiles and forcing Lukaan and the others to create a shield of fire around themselves, though with that in place and the storm raging, they could see nothing.

Aentarra joined hands with the others, then shifted. As they reappeared and stepped through the rift, they all looked toward the spot where the portal was.

"Nothing," Arton said.

"What now?" Rahg asked.

"We have no more options than before," Aentarra said. "We need to shift near the border, lower the shield, get out, then repair it before Lukaan detects it."

"And if he finds us again?" Camissa asked.

"Next time we might not make it." Aentarra shook her head. "I'm exhausted already."

"I can lower the shield easily," Mikkellana said, "but fixing it takes longer."

"Do you know anywhere we can shift?" Aentarra asked.

Mikkellana shook her head. "None he wouldn't have thought of—the watering hole in the northeast, and the oases in the west... No, wait. I do know a spot." She straightened, smiling. "The place where Darstan lost his hand. I marked it as a shift point. It's perfect! Desolate. No water. No reason for anyone to be there."

Aentarra nodded. "Let's go, then," she said, and extended her hands to join with Mikkellana.

LUKAAN EXPANDED his ring of fire until a large circle had been cleared around them, then he let go a massive explosion of fire that cleaned the area.

"They've gone!" Tirzinitzia said.

Lukaan seethed. "She may be cloaking. Attack everywhere. Leave nothing to chance." And with that, he began a methodical assault on their former position and every area around there. After several moments, they stopped.

"She has shifted again. But where?"

"We'll find her," Melissara said.

Lukaan nodded. Soon.

Suddenly Tirzinitzia perked up. "I know where. The spot where the boy used his powers. We know Mikkellana was there with the boy. Maybe Aentarra was too. If she was, that would be another shift point."

"Let's go," Lukaan said.

THEY CAUTIOUSLY STEPPED through the rift onto ground charred black, ground that looked primordial.

"What happened here?" Rahg asked.

"Darstan did that," Mikkellana said. "When Takar cut his hand off he went berserk."

Rahg looked about him. "He did this?" he asked, then thought about his shield buckling in Arangar when Darstan's fire struck, and how it had knocked him out. God's blood!

Aentarra's hawk eyes scanned the surroundings, though it was easy to tell that nothing or no one was around. "Stay alert."

Mikkellana went to work, her hands deftly working what to most of them was an invisible shield. Aentarra watched, and although she could see the shield, she could not see Mikkellana's weavings. Curse that woman.

Tense moments passed until Mikkellana stood, whispering. "It's done. Go. Hurry!"

Aentarra nearly jumped to get through, followed closely by the others. As soon as they were on the other side, Mikkellana resumed work, now trying to mend it.

GHRUEHNE AND SENDRA had dispatched four of the patrols already, only two remained. Sendra had the patrols link, then addressed Ghruehne. "There is a spot by the narrow pass in the Empty Lands. A good place to let these last ones go."

They linked and shifted, coming through the rift onto a small plateau overlooking the Caravan Trail. "Patrol Leader Marg, send half your men south; you and the others go north."

He saluted, issued the orders then departed.

Sendra strolled about the plateau, staring at the road below them. A Khataran merchant with a small detachment of mercenaries had just come through the pass. As she watched them a flash of light caught her eye—then another. She knew they were at the shield. Perhaps this was a sign. Hope filled her heart as she pushed her hand forward. When she met no resistance, she stepped through. "Ghruehne! Hurry, the shield!"

Ghruehne spun around, and when he saw her through the shield, he ran for it, going through with no trouble. "We're out!" he said. "What happened?"

"I don't know, but I'm not going back in."

"Do you think Lukaan got out?"

Sendra looked around, checked her surroundings. Her mood suddenly turned somber. "We need to be careful, Ghruehne. We don't know if Lukaan and the others are out, or even if Aentarra is out, but Mikkellana is still out here. As well as Xanthes, Mesan, and the others."

Ghruehne's eyes glazed over, the veins in his forehead bulging. "I have waited a thousand years to kill her."

MIKKELLANA WORKED FURIOUSLY on strengthening the shield, anxious that Lukaan or the others might detect it being down, then from the periphery, she caught a glimpse of a rift opening. "Aentarra! They're here! Weave a shield."

"I can't from out here. Not while you're fixing it."

"Then get inside!"

Aentarra hesitated for only a heartbeat, then stepped back inside the shield. "Don't you dare leave me in here. Let me out before you're done." She wove a shield, double-layered and tight, just large enough to protect herself and Mikkellana.

The assault began immediately. Lukaan's blacklightning was so strong the air exploded around it, a thunderous roar that shook the earth. Aentarra fell with the first strike, shouting as Melissara's and Tirzinitzia's strikes followed. Blackfire surrounded her shield, clawing to get in, while lightning continued to hammer away at her.

"Almost there, Aentarra," Mikkellana hollered. "Hold on."

Aentarra stood, refocused, strengthened her defense.

Lukaan hurled two more barrages of lightning. She fell again, and as she tried to get up the ColdFire hit, shattering the shield.

"Mikkellana!"

"I've got to finish this," Mikkellana said.

ARTON JUMPED THROUGH THE SHIELD, his sword drawn, fire in his eyes. "Get her, Kyra."

Kyra screamed her objections, but Arton kept running straight toward Lukaan. "It is time for me to die, friend."

Arton's powerful legs pumped harder than ever, driving him closer to Lukaan with every breath. A bolt of lightning raced toward him, but he dodged it and continued on his mission. He blocked the next bolt with his sword. The sword absorbed the lightning, but it burnt the blade and seared his hand.

The warrior grimaced, but focused his will and pressed on, determined to kill Lukaan. He fended off an attack from Melissara and several from Tirzinitzia, but the assaults were wearing on him, and he didn't know how much more the sword could take. Only twenty paces away now, he pushed harder. He could almost taste the blood he would spill.

Lukaan smiled as Arton advanced, and at the last moment, he released the ColdFire, sending a column of it directly toward the charging warrior.

Arton raised the sword to fend off the ColdFire, praying it would withstand the blow. The sword splintered upon impact, and with it went Arton's hopes. His skin felt on fire, then as if it froze. His heart seized up and stopped, then his body shattered.

KYRA DRAGGED Aentarra's body outside the shield, all the while saying a blessing for Arton, wishing him a place in the Big Hunt with her sons.

"I hope you're finished," Rhaven said to Mikkellana.

"Almost," Mikkellana said, daring to glance in Lukaan's direction.

LUKAAN SUSPECTED the shield was down and tried shifting to Vallah, but he was instantly knocked back. He fumed, firing lightning and fire at the shield, all to no avail. "She got it up again!"

Aentarra lay unconscious on the ground, blood oozing from her nose and ears.

Mikkellana looked about, nervous, then touched the shield, judging its strength. "Some of them may have gotten out," she said. "We need to shift out of here."

"Heal her first," Rahg said. "She looks like she's going to die."

"There's no time. Everyone lock hands to shift. We must leave here now. Rhaven, get Aentarra."

When the link was complete, Mikkellana shifted them to a spot in the Blackthorn Forest, just outside of Skyethorn. The forest was dark but safe. None of the Banished Ones could know about this spot.

"Lay her in that clearing," Mikkellana said as they stepped through the rift. "I must get her healed right away." She knelt beside her sister and started to work. "There should be no trouble here, but keep an eye out. I don't want any surprises." Mikkellana struggled, trying to hold her sister as Aentarra kept moving, uncontrolled spasms. "I need two men to hold her still."

Katsu and Jarrell came over, knelt next to Aentarra and kept her legs and arms still.

"No need for pressure. Just make sure she doesn't jump."

Kᴀᴛsᴜ sᴀᴡ the light emanating from the pouch at Aentarra's side, pulsing, throbbing light that beckoned him. Mesmerized, he stared until the temptation grew too great. His hand slid up her leg in a slow, silent fashion, coming closer with each heartbeat—heartbeats which seemed in rhythm with the pulsating light. A tremulous finger pried open the lid of the pouch, and two slender slivers of crystal peeked out, like serpents peering out of their den.

He withdrew, hesitating, then once again crept forward until he was within reach. Katsu closed his hand around them, yanking them from the pouch, eager to secrete them within his cloak.

Katsu screamed, falling backward. The Slicers entered his body through his hand, then up his arm. He could feel them inside of him, shivers that raced through his body.

"Get them out!" He rolled on the ground, writhing, scratching at his body, tearing his flesh. "Get them out!"

Rᴀʜɢ ʀᴀɴ over to his side, along with Camissa.

"Don't touch him," Mikkellana shouted. "Stay far away."

Rahg looked at Mikkellana then back to Katsu. The flesh on his face bubbled like a cauldron of boiling soup, and his eyes appeared to be reaching out, trying to get out of his body. "We've got to do something."

Mikkellana looked to Rhaven. "Kill him There's nothing we can do. But you have to use my sword, nothing else."

Rhaven drew the sword, brought it down on Katsu amidst cries of protest from Rahg. The strike sliced cleanly through his neck.

"By the gods!" Rahg screamed. "By the great gods! You just killed him."

Mikkellana knelt beside Aentarra. "It had to be done."

Just like Darstan, Rahg thought. That's what Dar said she did to him. Just told Takar to cut his hand off.

Rahg moved toward Katsu's body. His head was severed, but his legs still twitched. "We'll have to bury him. Say some words." He wiped a tear from his eye. "He had a family, wife, and kids. He didn't want to come on this trip. Told me that before we left. I think he knew he was going to die." Rahg shook his head slowly. More dead people because of me.

"He should never have touched the Slicers," Mikkellana said.

Rahg spun toward her, wild eyed. "Why did he die? What happened?"

For a moment, Mikkellana stared in silence, deciding what, if anything, to tell him. "They belong to Aentarra," she said and began the healing.

A crowd began to gather around her, watching her work. Camissa crept closest.

Rahg pushed one of the Chun aside. "That's all! They belong to Aentarra." He grabbed at Mikkellana, but Camissa restrained him. "I just saw a man cooked in less time than I could strike a spark—cooked by things that glow on their own—and you tell me they belong to Aentarra."

Mikkellana once again stopped what she was doing to stare at Rahg. "Even if I could explain the rest, you would not understand. Could not." She shook her head again. "Now get down here and hold Aentarra. If I don't get her healed, we'll have a lot more to trouble us than some foolish fisherman dying."

Rahg continued to stare, eyes agape.

"Get down here!" she screamed, her face as taut as cold steel. "Do you think I'm playing games, boy?"

Rahg dropped to the ground beside Aentarra and held her leg and arm still.

"And don't dare touch that pouch or anything that comes out of it."

As she moved to lay her hands one more time, before she could reach her, a dozen Slicers slid out of the pouch, taking up positions, hovering about Aentarra's body, their shining, coruscating, pulsing light daring anyone to come near. Four surrounded her head, and the rest held post near her heart, stomach, and legs.

Mikkellana moved back, alert. "No one move. Rahg, Jarrell, slowly remove your hands from Aentarra, but do not stand or attempt to leave. No one else come near."

Rahg gulped. "What are they doing? Who is doing this?"

Mikkellana shook her head. "She must have...I don't know. I was never skilled with Slicers like Aentarra."

"What do we do now?" Rhaven asked.

"What we had better do is figure a way to get my sister healed. If she stays unconscious for too long, the shield will weaken enough for them to get out. Perhaps not Lukaan, but probably Melissara and Ghruehne—if he's not out already."

"And you can't move the Slicers?"

"No one can," Mikkellana said, then cocked her head in thought. "Though I might try...yes."

She wove a shield like a dense, flat piece of upright steel, then moved it between several of the Slicers, just above her stomach. As Mikkellana moved the shield, attempting to nudge them aside, she gulped, astonished. The Slicers stayed in place, passing right through the shield as it moved.

"How's that possible?" Rahg asked. "I can see that shield, and they are going right through it."

Mikkellana dropped the shield at once. "Pray to your gods that she comes to," Mikkellana said, "because they won't let me heal her."

"What do you mean they won't let you? What are these things?" He made a motion toward Aentarra, and two of the Slicers darted forward, stopping a hair's width away from his eyes.

"Back up slowly," Mikkellana said. "Very slowly."

Rahg felt as if he had met the end. He stared at the Slicers, transfixed by them, but moved ever so slowly away from Aentarra.

"She's breathing harder," Camissa said.

Mikkellana looked, and indeed, Aentarra was breathing better, chest rising and falling in a healthy way. "Come back, dear sister. If I ever needed you, now is the time."

Before long, Aentarra opened her eyes. "Where are we?"

"Near the Lorns," Mikkellana said. "But before you do anything, put these Slicers away and let me heal you."

Aentarra looked about them and nodded. Without a word, the Slicers disappeared into the pouch.

Rahg breathed a heavy sigh, then leaned toward Aentarra. "Are you all right? We thought you were going to die."

"It will take a lot more than that to kill me." She started to sit up then fell back down. "All right, Mikkellana. Heal me."

Mikkellana worked on her and told her about Arton and how he had provided enough time for her to strengthen the shield so Lukaan couldn't escape.

"Are they all in there?"

Mikkellana cast concerned glances all about her, then whispered. "I think someone got out. Perhaps Ghruehne or Sendra. Melissara and Tirzinitzia were with Lukaan, so it's not them."

Aentarra's eyes narrowed. "But someone got out?"

Mikkellana nodded.

Rahg was close enough to hear. "Who got out?"

Aentarra sat up, arms wrapped around her knees. "One of the Banished Ones. Perhaps two."

Rahg wore a look of fear.

"Whoever it is has likely fled. But don't let any false hopes lighten your heart, Rahg. No matter who it is they will be after you before long. Lukaan will kill them if they fail. From now on you had better sleep with one eye open."

"You're right," Mikkellana said. "We will need to find a safe place. Somewhere they cannot find us."

"There's only two of them," Rahg said. "We can handle two of them. I even held a shield against Lukaan for a while."

"Foolish boy. My shield supported yours the whole time; otherwise, you'd have been dead." She laughed. "You couldn't even hold a shield against Darstan."

"I did!"

Aentarra stood, drew close to him, eye to eye. "No. You didn't. I reinforced that shield in the pass. If I hadn't, he would have killed you." She shook her head. "Trust me, he almost broke my shield, though I wasn't quite prepared for that degree of strength."

Rahg shrunk under the criticism. "Then where do we go?"

"Entiria," Mikkellana said, "Or Arangar."

"Not Arangar. Darstan wants to kill me, and I can't fight him."

"Then Entiria it is."

"What if some of them did get out? What will they do?"

"Whatever they want," Mikkellana said. "And if it is Ghruehne, that could be a horrible proposition." She walked toward where Tobias was starting a fire and collapsed.

Rhaven grabbed her, lifted her up and lay her on a soft bed of leaves. "Are you all right, My Lady?"

A smile came to her face, though it hurt even to move. She had exhausted herself. "My lady? Am I no longer your warrior?"

At first, Rhaven was embarrassed, recalling the nights he had spent talking to Kella and now realizing it was Mikkellana. His face reddened, then he broke into laughter. "More a warrior now than ever. Though I find it difficult to refer to a beautiful lady as a warrior."

Mikkellana's smile broadened despite the pain. It was the first time in her long life that anyone except her father had called her beautiful and meant it. "I would rather have the title of warrior than any other," she said and closed her eyes.

Aentarra was now up walking about. "Keep a wary eye," she warned. "Even Sendra, if it is her, could kill you with little exertion."

AFTERMATH

*D*arstan's screams echoed in the canyon, rolling through the pass on columns of fire, searching for enemies to strike. Refugio and his men hid behind trees, though if he had struck in that direction, it would have done no good. Finally, he stopped, fell back against the wall again.

Refugio ran up to him, eager to forestall more madness. "BlackWolf, please, we must leave here. Get back to camp."

Darstan nodded and accepted Refugio's hand to help him stand. "We need to find her body."

"We will, BlackWolf. Just come with me."

When they reached the top of the pass at the Arangar side, Refugio ordered a guard of one thousand men to hold the pass while he took Darstan to the camp. "At the first sign of Chun, send a messenger, and we will reinforce you."

As they descended, Darstan searched every body, tears mixing with prayers to help him locate her. Halfway down the pass, a soldier arrived with a message from Aenaila—they had found her body and brought it back to camp.

Darstan ran the rest of the way, followed closely by the men in Refugio's command. Aenaila and Wisp awaited him at her tent.

"Where?" Darstan asked.

"In the tent," Aenaila said. "She is—"

Darstan didn't wait. He entered the tent, expecting the worst, but her body was intact. He had worried all the way here that his Fire had desecrated her body. He fell to the floor, cradling her in his arms, pressing her to his chest. Tears rolled down her stomach. "My fault," he cried. "I should have been there for you. Should have fought like you wanted me to."

Wisp opened the tent to enter, but Darstan spun around shooting fire. "Get out! I don't want anyone in here."

An entire day passed, and still, Darstan wouldn't come out. Aenaila could hear him from outside, mourning, talking to her, then shouting at the gods, cursing them.

"Darstan, you should come out now. We need to—"

"I'll kill the first one to come in here."

Aenaila paced outside the tent with Wisp. "He doesn't know yet. I don't even know if I should tell him. He'll—"

"You have to tell him, but when is the question. Maybe I can reason with him."

"He almost killed you last time. Don't go in."

"I can go in Cloaked."

Aenaila thought for a while, then nodded. "Be careful. He is not himself."

Wisp cloaked himself then sneaked into the tent. Darstan raised his head, looked about. "I can feel you, Wisp. No need to stay hidden."

He released the concealment. "How did you do that?"

"Something changed," Darstan said. "I feel stronger. Much stronger. As soon as you came into the tent, I could sense the powers. At first, I thought it was Aenaila, but then I was able to sense your specific presence."

Wisp nodded. "I noticed when we were in Solero that your voice affected the people. It didn't bother me, but it did them."

"I noticed too."

"Aenaila said she had heard of it before."

Darstan pulled her closer to him. "She's gone, Wisp. I killed her."

Wisp moved very slow, approaching Darstan at a crawl until his hand rested on Darstan's shoulder. He knelt next to him. "It wasn't you, Darstan. It's this war. I don't—"

"No, it's my fault. I killed her, and there's no going back." He let go of Mirana and turned to Wisp, wrapping his arms around him. Tears fell freely on Wisp's shoulder. "Why did we ever come here? Why did we ever leave Khatara?"

Wisp let him go on for a while, then he asked if Aenaila could come in.

"Of course. I'm sorry." Darstan got up and walked outside. "Come in, Aenaila. Please."

She mourned alongside Darstan for a few moments, hugged him and then sat. "Darstan, I can't imagine how you feel, but duty commands me to tell you something. Something you won't like to hear."

"Say what you will, Aenaila. There's nothing that could hurt me more than this."

Aenaila went to him, embraced him. There was no way to say it but straight out. "Mirana was with child. She was carrying your son."

Darstan slowly pushed her away, shaking his head. His eyes glazed, skin glowed.

"Darstan, listen. You must—"

Wisp grabbed her and dragged her from the tent. "We need to leave, now!"

Inside, Darstan's clothes smoldered then burst into flames. Fire shot from his eyes and his arm, engulfing the tent, destroying everything in it. A column of Fire shot up through the roof of the tent, high into the air.

ColdFire roared from within him, smothering the flames, but taking out an entire patrol of guards nearby. Soldiers panicked, ran, sought shelter, while the animals broke their restraints and raced off. All the while, Wisp and Aenaila screamed to him from behind a large boulder, tried to stop him. After a while, he settled down, falling to the ground in a heap, his powers exhausted.

Wisp ran to him, as did Aenaila. "I'll get water," she said and rushed off.

"Don't let anyone near here," Wisp called to her.

Long into the night, they talked, Darstan's grief seemed to know no bounds. "We need to take her back to Cartena, Aenaila. Give her a proper burial."

Aenaila shook her head. "She always knew she would die in battle. She said she wanted her ashes spread over the battlefield where she died."

Darstan nodded. "So be it, then. Have the men build a pyre."

THEY BUILT a pyre suitable for a king, and lay Mirana atop it. Aenaila said the customary Cergalan words, then kissed her friend to send her off.

Darstan stayed with her for a long time, speaking softly to her and holding her hand. At last, he knelt beside her, kissed her lips and stood.

"Tell everyone to move away," he said, and when they did, he unleashed his Fire, engulfing the pyre under both of them. He stood with her, flames soaring above his head, dancing around him, seeming to swallow him.

Murmurs from the crowd caught his ear; soldiers struck with fear of the one they had sworn to follow. He stayed with her until the flames had consumed her body, then he reached for a handful of ashes, flung them into the air, letting the flames carry them away. He walked to where the others waited. The flames seemed to have done more than consume Mirana, they hardened his heart and mind as well, forged them into steel.

"What now?" Refugio asked. "I have men guarding the pass, but—"

"Prepare the men to march," Darstan ordered.

"March where?" Aenaila asked.

Darstan ignored her. "Refugio, select five thousand men, the rest will stay here. Tell them to pack for a long journey."

Refugio pounded his chest in salute. "Yes, BlackWolf. Your will." He turned to leave, but Aenaila grabbed him.

"Wait, Refugio," she said, then addressed Darstan. "We are done here. Enough have died. With us in control of the pass, we can ensure that Arangar never invades us again."

"I don't care about the pass. We're marching into Arangar."

"For what reason?" Aenaila demanded.

"To kill them," Darstan said. "I'm going to kill their farmers, their merchants, even their women, and children. They killed mine."

"What good will that do?"

"It will do no good, Aenaila. But I'm going to kill them all..." He stared off into the distance. "And then I'm going to kill Rahg."

Wisp stood to the side, shaking his head. "This isn't any way to win a war, Darstan. This is no way to treat any person, not even the enemy. Instead of sending more soldiers, bring wagons of food. Show them mercy and trade food for goods. If you do this, you will conquer them without a drop of blood being shed." Wisp reached for his sleeve. "And I'm sure Rahg had nothing to do with this. There must be some explanation."

Darstan spun toward Wisp, fire again dancing in his eyes. "I want to shed blood. I want all of their blood. But most of all I want his blood."

Darstan shook, his fist clenching. "You were right, Wisp. I didn't kill her. He did. Rahg is the one who killed her, and he's going to pay." He grabbed Refugio and shook him. "Get the men ready. We march on Arangar. It is time for Cergala to have its vengeance."

Aenaila's hand caught his arm. "No, Darstan. We have been shedding blood for five hundred years. It's time to put a stop to this madness. It is time for peace." Her other hand found Darstan's face and turned him to her, those magical green eyes seeking his soul. "Don't let this ruin you. Don't let Mirana's death be tainted with more blood. Let her be remembered for bringing peace to two lands so troubled by war."

Darstan pulled away from her, heading toward the soldiers gathering at the foot of the pass. He climbed atop a rock overlooking them and shouted, using his newfound powers of Voice. "Fellow Cergalans. For five hundred years you have lived with these barbarians to your south. For so many years you have tolerated their intrusions and invasions. But this time, they have committed sacrilege, raping our women, killing our children." He let them digest his words. "Five hundred years," he repeated. "But tonight we avenge our brethren. Tonight we march into Arangar."

They began a chant as he said this, but he held up his arm to stop them. "Yes, tonight we march, and that is good. But tomorrow... we draw blood." And with that he shot a column of fire into the air, rousing them into a furor.

As one they banged their swords and staffs on the ground, stomping their feet and chanting his name. "BlackWolf! BlackWolf!" A few of the brave men climbed the rock and dragged Darstan down, hoisting him upon their shoulders then racing into the pass, shouting all the way. "BlackWolf! BlackWolf!"

Aenaila and Wisp stood alone by the remains of the pyre. "I don't know how to stop him," Aenaila said.

"I'm afraid there is no stopping him. May the gods be merciful on Arangar."

Aenaila shook her head. "A prophecy foretold this."

"I'm tired of prophecies. They've done nothing but cause trouble as far as I can tell."

"Listen to the words, Wisp. Then tell me it's wrong."

From darkness, from light, where day can be night,

Comes a warrior, comes a savior, comes one who will fight.

One hand wields a sword, BlackFire the other.

A man alone, without friend, none to call brother.

Cergalan Prophecy

"There is more to the saying, but these are the words that matter. There can be no denying who he is now. He is the One."

<<<<>>>>

ACKNOWLEDGMENTS

It is with great honor that I give eternal gratitude to my wife and all four of my grandkids: Joey (Giuseppe), Dante, Adalina, and Carmine. They give me the inspiration to keep going.

ABOUT THE AUTHOR

Giacomo Giammatteo is the author of gritty crime dramas about murder, mystery, and family. He also writes non-fiction books including the No Mistakes Careers series, No Mistakes Publishing, No Mistakes Grammar, and No Mistakes Writing.

When Giacomo isn't writing, he's helping his wife take care of the animals on their sanctuary. At last count they had forty-five animals—eleven dogs, a horse, six cats, and twenty-six pigs.

Oh, and one crazy—and very large—wild boar, who takes walks with Giacomo every day and happens to also be his best buddy.

nomistakespublishing.com
gg@giacomog.com

You can see all of my books here.
And you can buy them on the platform of your choice here.

Nonfiction :

No Mistakes Resumes, Book I of No Mistakes Careers

No Mistakes Interviews, Book II of No Mistakes Careers

Misused Words, No Mistakes Grammar, Volume I

Misused Words for Business, No Mistakes Grammar, Volume II

More Misused Words, No Mistakes Grammar, Volume III

No Mistakes Writing, Volume I—Writing Shortcuts

How to Publish an eBook, No Mistakes Publishing, Volume I

How to Format an eBook, No Mistakes Publishing, Volume II

eBook Distribution, No Mistakes Publishing, Volume III

Uneducated

Whiskers and Bear—Volume I of the Life on the Farm Series (sent to editor)

Fiction:

Friendship & Honor Series:

Murder Takes Time

Murder Has Consequences

Murder Takes Patience

Murder Is Invisible

Blood Flows South Series:

A Bullet For Carlos: A Connie Gianelli Mystery

Finding Family, a Novella

A Bullet From Dominic

A Promise of Vengeance (Fantasy)

Redemption Series:

Necessary Decisions: A Gino Cataldi Mystery

Old Wounds

Promises Kept, the Story of Number Two

Premeditated

OTHER BOOKS COMING SOON:

You can always see the current and coming-soon books on my website.

Fiction:

My first fantasy, and the first book in a four-book series—the Rules of Vengeance. (Three are already written and the fourth is being outlined.)

Memories for Sale (mystery/sf)

The Joshua Citadel (SF novella)

Nonfiction:

No Mistakes Writing, How to Write a Bestseller

Children's Books:

No Mistakes Grammar for Kids, Volume I—Much and Many (sent to editor)

No Mistakes Grammar for Kids, Volume II—Lie and Lay (sent to editor)

No Mistakes Grammar for Kids, Volume III—Then and Than (sent to editor)

Shinobi Goes to School—Life on the Farm for kids. (working on illustrations)

Get on the mailing list and you'll be sure to be notified of release dates and sales.

Mailing list

And don't forget to leave a review!

By the way, if you're an author and you liked the formatting in this book, you might consider us for your next book. Information can be obtained here.